Julia

will "make your flesh creep.... Is Julia Lofting's husband coldly plotting to drive her insane? Is she unbalanced by the death of her child? Or is she truly being haunted by the ghost of a quite obscenely nasty little girl whose spirit appears to infest the Loftings' fashionable London house? You'll have to find out for yourself...."
—*Cosmopolitan*

"GENUINELY FRIGHTENING ... a taste for the depraved." —*Chicago Tribune*

"I haven't read anything that so terrifyingly evoked the presence of evil and supernatural threat since *The Exorcist*. *Julia* may be better." —*Buffalo Evening News*

"A CRAZY QUILT OF HORROR." —*Milwaukee Journal*

"Definitely spooky . . . Julia is haunted and haunting in this clever, frightening, well-told tale." —*Publishers Weekly*

Books by Peter Straub

Ghost Story
If You Could See Me Now
Julia

Published by POCKET BOOKS

Julia

Peter Straub

PUBLISHED BY POCKET BOOKS NEW YORK

POCKET BOOKS, a division of Simon & Schuster, Inc.
1230 Avenue of the Americas, New York, N.Y. 10020

Copyright © 1975 by Peter Straub

Published by arrangement with Coward, McCann & Geoghegan, Inc.
Library of Congress Catalog Card Number: 75-10464

ISBN: 0-671-49564-X

First Pocket Books printing October, 1976

20 19 18 17 16 15

POCKET and colophon are registered trademarks
of Simon & Schuster, Inc.

Printed in the U.S.A.

*For Thomas
and Alice Tessier*

Contents

So a war begins. Into a peace-time life, comes an announcement, a threat. A bomb drops somewhere, potential traitors are whisked off quietly to prison. And for some time, days, months, a year perhaps, life has a peace-time quality. But when a war has been going on for a long time, life is all war, every event has the quality of war, nothing of peace remains. Events and the life in which they are embedded have the same quality. But since it is not possible that events are not part of the life they occur in——it is not possible that a bomb should explode into a texture of life foreign to it——all that means is that one has not understood, one has not been watching.

—DORIS LESSING, *The Four-Gated City*

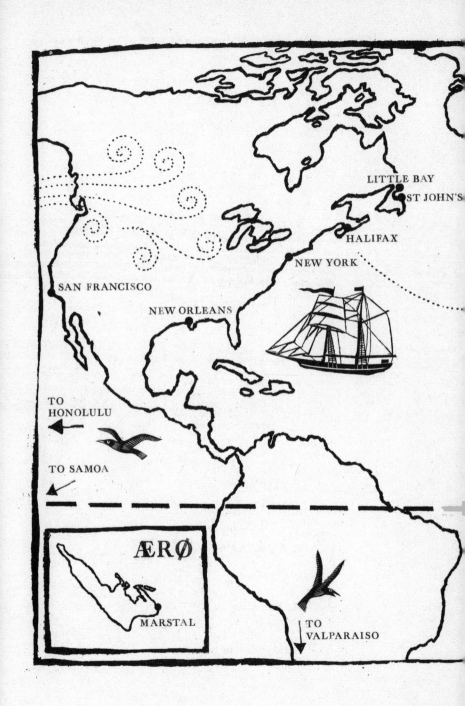

LITTLE BAY
ST JOHN'S

HALIFAX

NEW YORK

SAN FRANCISCO

NEW ORLEANS

TO
HONOLULU

TO SAMOA

ÆRØ

MARSTAL

TO
VALPARAISO

CONTENTS

For Lizzie, the love of my life

First Mariner Books edition 2012
Copyright © 2006 by Carsten Jensen og Gyldendal
Translation copyright © 2010 by Charlotte Barslund

For information about permission to reproduce selections from this book,
write to Permissions, Houghton Mifflin Harcourt Publishing Company,
215 Park Avenue South, New York, New York 10003.

www.hmhco.com

Library of Congress Cataloging-in-Publication Data
Jensen, Carsten, date.
[Vi, de druknede. English]
We, the drowned / Carsten Jensen ; translated from the Danish
by Charlotte Barslund with Emma Ryder.
p. cm.
"Translation of: Vi, de druknede"—T.p. verso.
ISBN 978-0-15-101377-7   ISBN 978-0-547-73736-2 (pbk.)
I. Barslund, Charlotte. II. Ryder, Emma. III. Title.
PT8176.2.E44V513 2010
839.8'1374—dc22   2009046568

Translation of *Vi, de druknede*

STATENS
KUNSTRÅD
DANISH ARTS COUNCIL

This translation has been sponsored by
the Danish Arts Council Committee for Literature.

Book design by Lisa Diercks
Map by Joe McClaren

Printed in the United States of America
DOC 10 9 8 7 6 5

The author is grateful for financial assistance from the following:
Statens Kunstfond
Litteraturrådet
Autorkontoen
Statens Kunstråds Litteraturudvalg
Politikens Fond
J. C. Hempels Fond
Konsul Georg Jorck og hustru Emma Jorcks Fond
Fonden Erik Hoffmeyers Rejselegat

We, the Drowned

CARSTEN JENSEN

Translated from the Danish by Charlotte Barslund with Emma Ryder

MARINER BOOKS
HOUGHTON MIFFLIN HARCOURT
Boston   New York

"Expertly told . . . . Jensen is a sympathetic storyteller with an eye for the absurd, with the result that if this novel descends from *Moby-Dick*, it also looks to *The Tin Drum* for inspiration."

—*Kirkus Reviews*

"A novel of immense authority and ambition and beauty, by a master storyteller at the height of his powers. This is a book to sail into, to explore, to get lost in, but it is also a book that brings the reader, dazzled by wonders, home to the heart from which great stories come."

—Joseph O'Connor

"The canon of great seafaring literature just got bigger by a book . . . [Jensen] has taken onboard the landmark achievements of his predecessors, absorbed all their salty wit and wisdom and produced something that tips its hat to their brilliance while being a completely new departure."

—*The Scotsman* (UK)

"[A] rich, powerful, and rewarding novel."   —*Financial Times* (UK)

"Spellbinding . . . A magnificent addition to the canon of seafaring writing, a brilliant new reworking of the ancient theme."

—*The Times* (UK)

"Extraordinary . . . A huge achievement."   —*Globe & Mail* (Canada)

"Epic . . . Carsten's focus on the larger-than-life sailor Laurids Madsen and his heirs . . . will hold a sustained fascination for readers." —*Los Angeles Times*

"A tour de force, a colossus, that gives Americans an opportunity to witness the gears of a great writer at work, turning the ordinary into the extraordinary . . . Sentence after sentence is strung together like bright bulbs of light . . . This novel may be big and heavy, but it's worth every single page." —Three Percent

"A huge saga, poignant, bitterly compassionate, cruel and occasionally humorous, told in a powerful compelling voice. Barslund and Ryder's translation renders the writing as an elegant blend of everyday detail, a potent, almost myth-like quality, and vivid description of northern lights and rough seas." —*Historical Novels Review*

"Brilliant, funny, and heartwarming, told through fabulous writing which begs to be savored." —Blogcritics

"For all the brutality and suspense in the manner of Conrad, Melville, and Stevenson, Jensen's oceanic novel . . . is tenderly human . . . [His] resplendent saga, an epic voyage of the imagination, is mesmerizing in its unsparing drama, fascinating in its knowledge of the sea, wryly humorous, and profound in its embrace of compassion, reason, and justice." —*Booklist*, starred review

"An odyssey taut with action and drama and suffused with enough heart to satisfy readers who want more than the breakneck thrills of ships battling the elements." —*Publishers Weekly*, starred review

Wall Street Journal Best Fiction 2011

"Precisely what the long contemporary novel ought to be. Epic in length and scope, it wanders to exceptional depth and breadth ... [A] eulogy for a bygone way of life and a timeless account of human suffering and pleasure ... In its large, miraculous gestures, Jensen's quiet and tight braiding of the mysterious and the mundane opens an entirely new conversation about what magical realism can do. Like García Márquez, he crafts occurrences of seemingly impossible proportions ... Haunting."   —*The New Republic*

"An epic of grand design ... a thumping success."

—*San Francisco Chronicle*

"Grand ... [Jensen] has written a visceral chronicle of the murderous modern era and animated it with a zest for yarn-spinning that derives from the oral traditions of the Middle Ages ... The novel is most memorable for the sheer gusto of its narrative. The author ennobles the old-fashioned art of storytelling."

—*Wall Street Journal*

subtle contempt for her, Julia yet felt it possible that the estate agent attributed some of this behavior to her being merely another comically "rich American"; and so she felt, with a little flare of independence, only the smallest qualm about obeying her second response to the sight of the running blond girl, a feeling that she must follow her. The impulse was overwhelmingly strong. The man from Markham and Reeves was holding her by the elbow, very delicately, and beginning to produce the third key from his waistcoat pocket—he had tied a bright yellow ribbon through the hole at the top of the key.

"Yellow for remembrance, Mrs. Lofting," he was saying, the edge of condescension clear in his voice. "Confess I pinched the idea from a pop song. May you—"

"Excuse me," Julia said, and went quickly down the steps to the pavement.

She did not want to run until she was out of the man's sight, and restrained herself until she too had rounded the corner to the park and was shielded by the wall. The girl looked remarkably like Kate. Of course she could not be Kate. Kate was dead. But people sometimes caught sight of friends in a crowd or riding past in a bus when those friends were in reality thousands of miles away—but didn't that mean that the friends were in danger or about to die? Julia ran a few awkward steps into the children's play area and, already panting, began to walk. Children were everywhere, in the sandboxes, racing around on the patchy grass, climbing the trees she could see from her bedroom window. The blond girl could be far into the park by now, Julia realized, either on the long sward of green to the right or on one of the paths up ahead, or over toward the Orangery. The child might not even have taken the

path into the play area but run straight up the long
lane to Holland House. Surely Holland House *was*
that way? Up there past the peacocks? Julia did not
feel sure enough of the park's geography to pursue
her phantom—who in any case was just an ordinary
little girl on her way to meet friends in Holland Park.
Julia, who was still unthinkingly walking up the path
past the sandboxes, stopped. Chasing after the child
had been unreasonable, perhaps hysterical: typical
of her. I really am losing my grip, she thought, and
said "Damn" so loudly that a stout man with a
brushy gingery mustache stared at her.

She turned about, embarrassed, and looked up
across the back walls of gardens to the upper row of
windows in her new house. The house was monstrously expensive: she could not allow Magnus to
know that she had purchased it, that she had signed
every paper put in front of her. For a moment the
thought of Magnus—the idea of Magnus, enormous
with rage—drove everything else from her head, and
she felt a second of terror. She might have been
unreasonable, even unbalanced—he would be quick
to say it—but about Magnus, reason was not possible. The long, restrained lines of the house, which
she had thought beautiful the moment she had seen
it, helped her to quiet her feelings.

Holding one hand to her chest, Julia walked back
down the path to the corner of Ilchester Place. She
remembered the man from Markham and Reeves
only when she saw him leaning against the front
door, his expression one between confusion and
boredom. *He* had written her off when, telephoning
her bank from his office, he had learned how much
money she kept in a checking account.

She expected the man to say something, but he

appeared to be past courteous formulas. He merely straightened his shoulders and offered the key, holding it by the flagrant yellow ribbon. Now he did not look so much bored as weary. And in any case, what could Julia say? She could not explain her sudden action by telling him that she had wanted to look again at a girl who reminded her of her dead daughter: he did not know anything about Kate or about Julia. She did the best she could.

"I'm so sorry," she said, looking up into his gray, rather compressed-looking face. "I wanted to check on something around the back before you left."

He looked at her oddly: to examine the back, of course, she would have gone through the house rather than around the corner.

"Not a lot of children on this street, Mrs. Lofting," the man said. "They play in the park of course but you'll find that Ilchester Place is a quiet sort of neighborhood, as I've told you." Was this, too, more tired sarcasm? But the man had noticed the girl, and was making an effort to be courteous. He had looked straight through her weak excuse.

"Thank you," she said, taking the key and putting it in one of the short pockets of her dress. "You've been very patient with me."

"Not at all." The man looked at his wristwatch, then for a moment at his car, and then at the Rover, where suitcases were piled up on the backseat, crowded in with some potted plants, two short stacks of books tied with string, and a box of floppy dolls she had had since childhood. These were the only things she had taken besides her clothing, and they were all from the room she had been using since leaving the hospital. The books were an indulgence, but they were hers, not Magnus'.

"No, you needn't, please," Julia quickly said. "I couldn't dream of asking you, after . . . everything."

"In that case," he said, palpably relieved, and began to go down the steps, "I have some things to attend to at the office, so if you'll excuse me, I'll be leaving you to your new house." He glanced up at the long, warm brick exterior. "It *is* a beautiful house. You should be quite happy here. And of course you have our number, should anything arise. Am I correct in thinking that you do not know Kensington thoroughly?"

She nodded.

"Then you have before you all the pleasures of investigation. Where was it you were living before? Before today? Hampstead, wasn't it?"

"Yes."

"You should find this part of Kensington very sympathetic."

He turned away to walk toward his car. When he had opened the door he faced her again and called across the pavement and lawn. "Do ring us if you have any problems, Mrs. Lofting. By the by, I think you might have some spare keys made for you at one of the shops in the High Street. Well, good day then, Mrs. Lofting."

"Bye." She waved from the steps of the house as the man drove away. When his car was out of sight, Julia went down to the Rover and looked back up at her house—now truly her house. Like all the other houses on the short, elegant length of Ilchester Place, it was neo-Georgian, brick, secure. There she would be safe from Magnus. The house had spoken to her need for quiet and for restful seclusion the moment she had seen it: almost as if it had in fact spoken to her. Buying it had been as much a

compulsion as following the little Kate-like girl had been. She *could* live in it, apart from Magnus: in time she could telephone him or write a note, after he had got used to the idea of her bolting. She had spent the previous night in a Knightsbridge hotel, afraid that every step meant the approach of Magnus, his face red with false sympathy, with the effort of trying to contain his violence. Magnus could be terrifying: it was the other side of his impressiveness, that huge male authority. No, she would let Magnus be for a while. Her note had explained all that could be explained.

Now the suitcases and the rest of her things had to be got into the house somehow. She pushed the button beside the door handle and, when it resisted her, pushed it again harder. The car was locked. Julia pulled a key from her pocket, but it was the house key on its taunting yellow ribbon. She bent over to look through the window and saw the rest of her keys dangling from the car's ignition. *Helpless.* She felt the oncoming of tears. For a moment she experienced an intense gratitude that Magnus was not beside her. "Julia, you are completely incapable." "I wonder if you ever do anything right." Or a short, brutal condemnation: "Typical." A barrister, Magnus had an arsenal of techniques for suggesting that other people, especially his wife, were weak in the head.

"Oh, thank God," she said aloud; she had noticed that the window on the passenger side of the Rover was rolled down, although that door too was locked. "Typical" as that might be, Julia took it as a good omen for the first day she was to live in her new house. Perhaps Magnus really might be kept from finding her—for a week or two, at least.

As if the two were related, the thought of Magnus

recalled the girl again, and Julia, opening the other door by reaching in through the window and pressing down on the inner handle, thought of trying to find her inside Holland Park. She fought down the image of herself and the girl, sitting together on a bench, talking. Beneath this lay another image, an image of horror and despair, and Julia, sensing it coming to her consciousness as it had during the weeks in hospital, deliberately made her mind empty. She would think about the luggage and the plants; one of the pots had broken, shearing away a section of clay nearly seven inches long and exposing granular black soil webbed with thin white roots. Julia had, she realized, bought the house on Ilchester Place the same way she had taken Magnus for her husband, in a rush.

But she had spent *her* money on *her* house: it was the first utterly free thing she had done since she had married Magnus eleven years before. Then, in 1963, she had been twenty-five, a rather more than pretty young woman with striking reddish hair and a soft, unlined, contented face: "the face of a girl at an Impressionists' picnic," her father had said. She had gone through her private school and Smith College, it seemed to her now, in a sort of trance, at a great distance from herself. Little but her courses and a few professors had moved or touched her. She had lost her virginity to a boy from Columbia, a tall, intense Jewish student of English. Most of his courtship had consisted of anecdotes about Lionel Trilling and the sex lives of famous poets; they had seen a great many French movies together.

Afterward there were other boys, but none of them came any closer to the inner Julia than the Columbia student; she slept with none of them.

When she graduated from Smith, she took a job with Time-Life, in the clipping library at *Sports Illustrated,* but quit a year later when she overheard another young woman, one she had thought of as a friend, describe her as a "fucking heiress." Quitting was a relief: she knew that she was incompetent at the job, and had lasted a year because the head of her department, a married man named Robert Tillinghast, was fond of her. She liked him, but not enough to remove her clothes in his company, which was clearly what he had in mind. For six months, then, she lived in her parents' home, reading novels and watching television, feeling more and more afraid of any world beyond the front door or the Smith campus; then she ran into a Smith friend in a restaurant and heard that the publishing company she worked for was looking for a young woman to do editorial work; in a week she had another job. Here, she enjoyed an almost mechanical, rootless pleasure in the work, editing academic books in the firm's college department; she was fond of saying that she learned things from each new book. She took an apartment in the West Seventies. She seemed to be settling into a dazed, busy, thoughtless life: taking the bus to work (on principle, she rarely rode in taxis), doing her correspondence, working with manuscripts, eating with one man or another, she often thought that she was merely watching herself perform, as though life had not yet truly begun. Then one morning she woke up in her bed beside Robert Tillinghast, and decided, panicked, to leave New York and go to England. "I'm moving horizontally since I'm not able to move vertically," she told her friends. Robert Tillinghast drove her to the airport and said, Good God, he wondered what would become of her. "I guess I do too."

In London, she first took a room on Drury Lane, and six months later, after she had found a job with a publisher of art books, moved to a two-room flat in Camden Town. "You're living in a kennel," her father had blustered when he flew across to inspect her new life. "Where the hell are the want ads?" He found her a self-contained, large-windowed flat with two bedrooms ("You need a room to work in!") in Hampstead, three times the cost of her place in Camden Town. One night several months after she had moved in, she met Magnus Lofting at a party given by a married couple who both worked for the art-book publishers.

They were Hugh and Sonia Mitchell-Mitchie, both Julia's age; Hugh, who wore denims and T-shirts and the golden curl of an earring in one ear, was the head of the art department. Sonia, like Julia, did editorial work. In manner, both were bright and inconsequential; Julia, who liked them while she was a little unsettled by them—both seemed to spend an abnormal amount of time discussing their love affairs—had not known that their idea of a party was to spend two hours drinking as rapidly as possible and the rest of the night playing parlor games.

When the others began to play, Julia faded backward in the room, hoping to go unnoticed: she was made insecure by all games. Sonia began to taunt her; in a moment, twenty people were staring at her. Julia felt cruelly exposed.

"Don't be a bully, Sonia," a man said. "I'll talk to your friend."

Julia turned to the source of this authoritative voice, and saw a big rocky-faced man in a pinstriped suit; he was years older than anyone else at the party. The hair above his ears was already going gray. "Sit down next to me," the man ordered.

"You saved my life," she said.

"Just sit down," Magnus ordered.

She gladly sat.

Ten years later, she could not remember the conversation they had had, but she knew that, immediately, there had been something impressive about him: he was purely male, with a suggestion in every gesture that he could take her as easily as he could light a cigarette. With the instincts of someone who had grown up surrounded by prosperous people, she recognized that he was successful at whatever it was he did; he seemed to understand her utterly, or to be utterly indifferent to anything he did not understand. In a chilling way, he was fascinating. They spent the rest of the evening talking to one another, and while Hugh and Sonia and the rest of the party were beginning another game, one in which a "murderer" assassinated his "victims" by winking at them, Magnus said quietly to her, "I think I'll be going. Shall I give you a lift? How did you get here?"

"I took a bus," she confessed.

"Too late for a bus now." He stood up. He was a head taller than she and too big to be merely burly. When he raised a hand, she flinched; but he carried it to the back of his head and smoothed down his hair. "I'll take you home unless you live somewhere unreasonable. Blackheath or Guildford are out of my range."

"I live in Hampstead," she said.

"Grace abounds. So do I."

They walked to his car, a black Mercedes, parked on the Fulham Road; she learned that he was a barrister, and that he had once lived next door to Sonia Mitchell-Mitchie, who had become a kind of adopted niece. He asked few questions of her, but

Julia found herself talking compulsively. For some reason—a reason she was not to understand for years—she even mentioned Robert Tillinghast when describing why she had left New York.

It was only when she knew that she was going to leave Magnus that she recognized that she had married him—had fallen in love with him—in large measure because he reminded her of her father. And they were both prodigal, casaul adulterers. Julia saw very early that Magnus had other women: he was brutally offhand about them. On the ride back to Hampstead, he had said that he wanted a drink, and drove to a club behind Shepherd's Market, where he signed her name in a guestbook and led her into a dark, half-filled room in which elegance was still a few paces in advance of shabbiness. The waitresses wore long pastel gowns revealing out-size, separated breasts. A third of the men were drunk; only two women, besides Julia and the hostesses, were in the club. One of the drunks put his arm about Julia as soon as she entered the room. Magnus pushed the man away without looking at him. He ordered drinks and began to look aggressively about the room as if he were looking for another man to knock down. Both of the other women, Julia saw, were looking at him. She felt pleasantly excited, stimulated, sipping at her drink.

"Do you gamble?" Magnus asked her.

She shook her head.

"You won't mind if I do?"

"No," she said. "I suddenly feel very awake."

Julia followed him through a door at the end of the lounge and continued, following his broad back, to a grilled-in counter where Magnus took money from his wallet and bought chips. She watched as he placed five fifty-pound notes on the counter, and,

after hesitating a second, a sixth. He seemed to get a surprisingly small amount of chips for all this money.

Together, they skirted various gaming tables and went up to a roulette wheel. Magnus placed four of his chips on the red. Breathless, Julia watched the ball spinning across the ratchets. It landed, clattering, on red. Magnus left his chips where they were, and the ball landed again on red. Then he moved everything he had won to black; again he won. How much money did those chips represent? Five hundred pounds? More? As she watched Magnus glowering down at the stack of chips, she felt exhilarated, slightly disoriented: he must have loathed the party, she realized. The next time the wheel spun, he lost some of his chips, but his face remained immobile.

"Your turn, Charmaine," he ordered. He shoved a stack of chips toward her. With desperation, Julia realized that they were worth at least two hundred pounds.

"I can't," she said. "I'd lose your money."

"Don't be cowardly," he said. "Bet any way you please."

She pushed the chips onto the red, since that was what Magnus had first won with. This time the ball clattered down onto the black. She looked up at him, stricken.

"Doesn't matter," he said. "Put more on it." He slid chips toward her.

She did as he said, and lost again. She stepped away from the table.

Magnus continued to gamble, seemingly indifferent to her. She stood beside him, watching chips pile up before him. Winning seemed not to affect him in any way; he simply stolidly stood there, scowling at the table, moving piles of red and white chips back and forth. Several times men approached and spoke

to him, but Magnus replied with short, curt sentences and turned away from them.

After half an hour, a thin black-haired woman Julia remembered seeing in the lounge came up and kissed Magnus. "Darling," she said, "you haven't been here in ages. You might lose all your old friends." Saying the last two words, she looked tauntingly at Julia. Julia felt at once undressed.

Magnus whispered a few words to the black-haired woman, and then turned back to the table. When he cashed in his chips, Julia saw that he had won nearly a thousand pounds.

In the car she said, "Was that woman your mistress?"

It was the first time she had heard him laugh.

When he left her at her door he asked for her telephone number and, after she had given it, brought two fifty-pound notes from his jacket pocket and put them in her hand. "I'll ring you Wednesday," he said, and moved out the door before she could protest. Julia put the money in a drawer, intending to give it back when she next saw him; two months later, when she found the two notes again, it was too late to return it. Evenutally, she gave one note to Oxfam and the other to Amnesty International.

At work the next Monday, she learned two things about Magnus: he had been Sonia Mitchell-Mitchie's first lover, and Julia had been expected to sleep with him. "Magnus always does that, picking up some girl at a party and then taking her home and ravishing her," Sonia said to Julia. "Weren't you ravished?"

"He barely touched me," Julia protested.

"He must have been off his feed," Sonia said.

In the following weeks, Magnus came to occupy more and more of her time; but he made love to her

only when she had begun to wonder if he ever
would. He was certainly the biggest man she had
ever gone to bed with. By that time, two months
after the Mitchell-Mitchie party, he had become a
reference point in her life. She tended to judge other
men by Magnus' standard, or by trying to guess if
Magnus would like them. Certainly no other man
was as exciting as Magnus Lofting: he had an
absolute assurance a younger man could not possess,
still trying to consolidate both his manhood and his
career.

Yet it was only after he had described his childhood to her that Julia, already in love, knew that she
must marry him. He and his sister—"poor Lily," a
year older than he—had been raised by monumen-
tally distant parents. Entirely absorbed into themselves, entirely indifferent to the opinions or sensi-
bilities of others, the Loftings had traveled much,
leaving the children at home with a succession of
tutors: before she drew Magnus out on the subject of
his childhood—he was seemingly callous about it
now—Julia had not known how far off, therefore
cruel, it was possible for parents to be. Except for
the tutors and "poor Lily" Magnus had grown up in
near silence, abandoned in the glassy marble tomb
of a house in Hampshire. His childhood was heartbreaking for Julia, whose own father, unlike Sir
Greville Lofting, had been intrusive, verbal, and
commanding. Magnus' childhood, that early isolation, she thought, went a long way toward explaining
Magnus' compulsions; as a young man, he had
apparently been ruthless about his professional life,
and even now he invested it with enough psychic
energy to power a steam engine. Magnus' childhood
not only helped to explain Magnus to Julia, and
thereby make him more accessible, but it also helped

to humanize him. At first, that Magnus had once *had* parents seemed impossible, slightly shocking; that he had "poor Lily" and a much younger adopted brother, Mark, seemed a revelation.

She was further surprised by the depth of his attachment to "poor Lily." But again, their childhood made it accessible. Magnus and Lily had grown up a society of two, intensely devoted to one another, each other's only company. They had invented a language ("Durm") in which at playful moments they could still converse. They were "Magnim" and "Lilim." They had constructed elaborate games using every portion of the house and grounds, games in which Magnus apparently from the age of five or six had taken the commanding role—king, general, prime minister, Coriolanus, Odysseus, Priam. This had endured up to the time Magnus entered Cambridge. Lily had never married, and Julia learned that Magnus spent at least one afternoon or evening a week with his sister. In fact, she thought that the inevitable usage of "poor Lily" had been adopted less from any intrinsic absurdity of Lily's than from a wish to counter any jealousy Julia might be expected to feel. Despite her oddities, her spiritualism, her general appearance of genteel dissipation, Lily did not deserve the epithet. She proved, when Julia finally met her, gray haired, undoubtedly lovely, and so finely made that separate facial muscles were visible beneath her skin. Lily made Julia feel awkward and hot, probably smudged in some conspicuous place. And it was only two years later, after the birth of Kate, that Lily became friendly.

Mark, the son of a young friend of Sir Greville's, a consular official in Africa who had killed himself,

was another matter. The Loftings had adopted the child, then two years old, out of an uncharacteristic generosity, having promised his mother, dying in a tropical hospital, that they would care for him. Their notion of care was to send the child and nurse to England, with only a telegram and a breezy following letter to warn fifteen-year-old Magnus and sixteen-year-old Lily that a new brother was to be dumped in among them. They hated him. Their world had been a sacred alliance of two for too long to admit a third. Magnus invariably referred to Mark as a "waster" and a "troublemaker"; Lily too remained suspicious of Mark. Sometimes he was "bad, very bad," which Julia supposed was a reference to his having impregnated a girl in the Hampshire village when he was fifteen. It might also have referred to the first action of his adult life, having his name altered by deed poll from Lofting back to Berkeley—a mute comment on the Lofting methods of childrearing. Mark was a disappointment: he had never learned their secret language, never having been given much chance to learn it; he had obtained a third-class degree at Cambridge; he was now lecturing at a polytechnic in sociology, a field Magnus claimed did not exist. Mark had flirted with fringe political groups all his life, he had marched and passed out leaflets, and he was now supposed to be a Maoist—Magnus had once scornfully seen him carrying a copy of *Red Star Over China*.

—Well, I don't see what's wrong with reading any book. And neither do you.

—I didn't say he was reading it. He was carrying it. For effect. In his circle, it's the equivalent of a Rolling Stones record.

—Now, honestly, I'm not defending Mark, but you are being malicious and unfair. You condemn him whether he's reading the book or not.

—Does it matter what I say about some Notting Hill Maoist?

Mark generally dressed in blue jeans and a chambray work shirt; he lived in the same rooms in Notting Hill Gate he had taken after leaving Cambridge, sleeping there, in a fabulous mess, on a mattress on the floor. Julia had heard most of this from Lily, with Magnus grunting disapproving asides, over a period of three or four months. She herself did not meet Mark until the day he appeared at Magnus' house on Gayton Road, three weeks before Julia's wedding, saying that he wanted to meet the victim. She heard his light, wry voice—a very un-Lofting voice—from the front steps, and then heard Magnus say, "The what? I take it you mean my fiancée."

"Your victim, Magnus."

She heard Magnus sigh. "Well, you might as well come in then, since you're here."

"You are typically generous, Magnus."

Julia had thought of Mark as a potential ally since she had heard Lily and Magnus first disparage him; he was at least flawed and might be expected to be sympathetic to her. Her heart beating a little quickly, she thrust the *Guardian* behind her chair and stood to meet him.

Magnus came scowling into the room, leading a tall young man with long, shining black hair. Julia saw Magnus' grimace at the sight of the wrinkled newspaper, wadded up behind the chair; then she saw that Mark Berkeley was the kind of man women might turn around to stare at in the street. He was beautiful—sexually beautiful. The long dark hair

framed a face a few shades lighter than olive, with high Mongol cheekbones and a full, curving mouth. Beneath black eyebrows, in the dark amused face, his eyes were unbelievably blue. When he held out his hand, she noticed that his fingernails were filthy.

"You're almost as pretty as Lily said you were," he said. "I wish I'd seen you first. Be nice to have another beautiful woman in the family, won't it, Magnus? Now that Lily is getting a bit past it."

Holding his rather grubby hand, Julia felt, as an undercurrent to Mark's remarks, that he was looking straight through her; he might be an ally, but not of the sort she had anticipated. Mark too was formidable. Yet he seemed far from unsympathetic. As Julia felt herself warming to her fiancé's younger brother, a number of impressions went rapidly through her mind. Mark seemed more like Magnus' son than his brother: he had an air of irresponsibility which seemed nearly cultivated. It was impossible to imagine Mark holding a job—any job but lecturing. And she considered, still holding his hand, that perhaps she was being conned by an expert. It was certainly all too easy to find oneself instantly liking someone so attractive. She disengaged her hand. She was not sure that she approved of men as beautiful as this.

"Really, Magnus," Mark said, "doesn't she look like a vision Lily might see in one of her crystal balls? What an extraordinary person she must be to want to marry you."

"Oh," she said, trying to save the situation, "sometimes I think half the women in London want to marry Magnus."

But Magnus had turned impatiently away from her. The rest of the afternoon had staggered painfully along, Mark taunting Magnus, Magnus becoming

increasingly blustery. Julia had not known at all how to read Mark.

A year later, when Julia realized, sickened, that Magnus had not ceased to see his other women for as much as a month, she had angrily, furiously proposed to him that she could begin taking up with his brother. "Why should you have all the fun?" she had demanded, raging.

Magnus had gripped her hard enough to raise bruises on her arm: she saw, trembling with both fear and anger, that he was barely restraining himself from clubbing her. Then the pressure lessened, his jaw unclamped, and he moved a step backward. "I'd happily kill you if you ever slept with Mark," he said. His tone was so cold that she believed him at once: despite all that talk about "unbalanced" Mark, she had never before seen that he hated his brother. At least, that was what she thought she had seen.

It was not long after this explosion that they began to discuss having a child.

Kate was born the following summer. For the next nine years, the Loftings lived conventionally in Hampstead, traveling abroad—Magnus bought a farmhouse a mile from the Dordogne River, and they spent three summers doing it up—seeing Lily at intervals, seeing Mark two or three times a year when he dropped in unannounced. Clearly, he was kept informed of events in the Lofting house by Lily: he sent a beautiful dollhouse on Kate's first birthday, he frequently telephoned when Magnus was out of town, and conducted cool, flirtatious conversations with Julia. Magnus undoubtedly carried on his affairs, but they had lost much of their power to wound Julia. They seemed entirely peripheral, taking little away from Julia and Kate. Still unpredicta-

ble, still sometimes frightening, Magnus loved Kate
absolutely. Julia spent the nine years of Kate's life in
a homebound trance, superficially content. Once, at
a party, she had heard herself say, "Can't live for
another person? Of course you can live for another
person, I live for my . . ." She was on the verge of
saying "daughter," but saw Magnus staring at her,
and substituted "family."

Now she thought: I'm going to start being myself,
freely myself, and discover what that means. And if I
go crazy that's okay too.

Julia stood at her bedroom window, the shades
parted, looking out at the play area, filled with
desultory children, and the green of the park
beyond. She pushed up the window and leaned out,
thinking *a woman on the verge of a new life leaned
from her window. . . .* The room was unbearably
stuffy. The air drifting across Holland Park seemed
cooler, more invigorating despite the warmth of the
day. Unpacking her clothing, untying the books,
Julia had felt damp, sticky, and oddly ruthless—the
clothing could go anywhere, since the bedroom, like
the entire house, was solely hers. When she put the
box of dolls for the moment in one of the bedroom
closets, she sat on the edge of the bed for a moment,
feeling heat rise from her in layers like steam. Julia
felt the presence of the house about her, for a
moment almost oppressive in its size. Yet she had
wanted it, and she had it. The McClintocks' furniture was old-fashioned and a bit worn, but comfortable, tending toward plush and cushions. In time,
she would get rid of it and buy new furniture, but for
the moment she was as pleased with the old furniture
as with the house, since it had the same settled,
familial look of prosperous comfort.

It was odd, the way this house had claimed her. At first, she had thought of moving to a service flat, probably somewhere in Knightsbridge; the temporariness of such a home depressed her, however, even in imagination, and she had gone to a real-estate agent's office, thinking vaguely of buying a lease on a flat. But having seen the house on Ilchester Place—"Quite unsuitable, of course," the man had said—she had known that she had to have it. It was nearly the first time in her life that Julia had used her money in a high-handed, reckless fashion. With Kate dead, did it matter how much she spent? The image of Kate's last minutes threatened to rise up again, and to put it off Julia moved quickly away from the window. She had been half-consciously looking for the girl she had seen that morning, the blond girl. How lovely it would be if buying the house brought her into contact, friendship, with another child, a girl like Kate, with whom she could have an easy, relaxed companionship.

But that was impossible: she could not make a stranger's daughter her own. She really was getting less realistic, less responsible to the world of ordinary truths. Was it possible that instead of beginning a new life, she had merely further confused and muddled the old one?

She could not afford to think that way. If she had been garrulous, disorganized, sloppy, everything that Magnus had accused her of being, perhaps these qualities were wrong only to Magnus: she had a right to her own foibles. And even now, free from him for only two days, Julia could simply feel how oppressive Magnus—Magnus' values—had been. She said to herself, I think it means my marriage is over, and surprised herself with the thought. Leaving Magnus had everything to do with Kate's death, of course,

that horrific scene on the kitchen floor, Kate's blood everywhere, boiling out of her panicked body—but leaving him, Julia now thought, might also come from a deep knowledge that marriage to Magnus was no longer possible. Really, Kate had kept them together. Kate had been their focus.

Interesting, she thought, and then realized that she had spoken the word aloud. "I'm going to be the kind of woman who talks to herself," she said. "Well, why shouldn't I?" She turned to the McClintocks' mirror and began to arrange her long hair, which now glowed a little in the light pouring in the bedroom window.

When she had put everything away, scrubbed the already spotless kitchen and vacuumed the living room carpet, Julia took a shower and afterward left the house. She had been making up her mind that she would see Lily after all—Lily now lived in Plane Tree House, just across Holland Park. Surely she could persuade Lily not to betray her to Magnus. "Poor Lily" had become, during the past nine years, a good friend: one of the attractions of Ilchester Place was that it was so close to Plane Tree House. In fact, Julia had moved near to both of the other members of the Lofting family. Mark's flat in Notting Hill was so close that she could walk to it.

Julia made sure she had her key in her pocket, and then turned up into the park. Almost immediately, she saw the blond girl again. The child was sitting on the ground at some distance from a group of other children, boys and girls, who were carefully watching her. Julia stopped walking, almost fearing that she would interrupt whatever performance was going on if the child should notice her. The blond girl was working intently at something with her hands,

wholly concentrated on it. Her face was sweetly
serious. Julia could not see what it was that required
such concentration, but the other children were as
grave as the little girl, indeed scarcely breathing.
This was what gave the scene the aspect of a
performance. Thinking of Kate, who could keep a
dozen other children still while she loosed some
fantastic story from her imagination, Julia, smiling,
stepped off the path on the side opposite to the play
area, so that she was perhaps twenty yards from the
girl and her audience, and sat on the grass. The girl
was seated, her legs straight out before her, in the
sandy overspill from one of the sandboxes: a sort of
pit like a golfer's sand trap. She was speaking softly
now to her audience, ranged on the scrubby grass
before her in groups of three and four. The other
children playing in the sand took no notice of them.
They were certainly unnaturally quiet, completely
taken up by the girl's theatrics.

Julia forgot that she was going to see Lily: she
forgot all about Lily. It was five thirty and still very
hot; Julia felt the sun's great weight on her forehead
and arms. Like most London women, she was as
white as if she lived under permanent clouds, and for
a second considered that for the first time in years,
she might get some color. Watching the child
continue her intricate movements and brief,
admonitory-looking bursts of speech, Julia felt
peaceful, slowed by the sun, her tension for the
moment gone. She *had* been right to buy the house;
she had turned a corner, and could begin to live
differently. For a second she thought the blond girl
had darted a quick glance at her, but it was far more
likely that she had merely looked sideways, aimlessly. There could be no doubt that she was the same
blond girl Julia had seen before, floating along up

the street: she did not really look like Kate, except for the accident of that silky, innocent, nearly white shade of hair, but she somehow suggested Kate. Oddly, watching her was not painful for Julia: Instead, there was a rootless exhilaration in it. Julia felt disconnected from everything, watching the girl, a pure, happy, sun-struck disengagement. The girl's face, at Julia's distance, looked aristocratically fine featured: her profile was heartbreakingly clear. She seemed to be not so much storytelling as lecturing— holding the others by force of personality.

Her hands were moving; something was held in her right hand. That was where the other children were looking. The girl laughed excitedly, and Julia saw some object flash in her left hand. She applied it to the thing in her right hand, apparently a square of green. The green square flipped in the air; it was like a rag. A little girl in the audience bent her head, and Julia saw her shoulders shake, as if she were overcome with giggles. The blonde girl spoke a few sharp words, and the other girl raised her head. Now the group of children had a huddled look; they were creeping forward, fascinated . . . but fascination, Julia saw, was not quite the correct word. It was as though, almost, they felt trepidation about getting nearer the girl: she was undoubtedly their leader.

Now the girl spoke quickly to the others, pointing an index finger. It was extraordinarily like a class-room. She gestured with the limp green thing. One of the other girls flinched. Then the blond girl continued working with her hands, the other children slowly gathering about her. Julia strained her neck to see what they were doing, but could see only the crown of the girl's head. One of the smaller children began to cry.

In another second the performance had ended.

The other children drifted away, some of them running, excited, shouting. Others moved slowly, going toward the first sandbox, where they aimlessly milled about, scattering sand. These continued to glance at the blond girl, who remained sitting where she had been, her back to them. She was smoothing the sand with the palm of her hand, seemingly filling in a hollow she had made. It was clear from her posture that she knew she was being looked at, and that she expected it; she was at once self-conscious and unconcerned. When she had patted and smoothed the sand, she stood up in one motion and briskly wiped her hands. She seemed regal, lifting her head, and Julia's heart contracted for her. The girl walked out of the little sand trap toward the path, moving directly toward Julia. Her face still bore an expression of watchful self-awareness. What complicated roles and rituals children have, Julia thought. She knew the girl would not look at her, and she did not. Once on the path, the girl turned deeper into the park, and after walking a few determined steps, broke into a run. In a moment she was traveling at top speed, racing up the path; in another moment, she had vanished before a knot of teenage girls whose long straight hair flipped like the tails of horses.

Julia stood—less gracefully than the blond girl had done—and went across the path into the play area. She still felt a little disoriented, as if she had just awakened after deep sleep. The sun felt unusually strong on her face. She wanted to see where the blond girl had been playing.

A small black girl, two or three, with a curly ruff of hair and huge mournful eyes appeared directly in front of Julia. She clasped her hands before the bib

of her overalls and tilted back her head, staring up at
Julia with her mouth open.

"What's your name?" she asked.

"Julia."

The girl's mouth opened a fraction wider.

"Doolya?"

Julia raised her hand for a moment to the child's
springy ruff of hair. "What's your name?"

"Mona."

"Do you know the girl who was just playing in
here? The girl with blond hair who was sitting and
talking?"

Mona nodded.

"Do you know her name?"

Mona nodded again. "Doolya."

"Julia?"

"Mona. Take me with you."

"Mona, what was that girl doing? Was she telling a
story?"

"She does. Things." The girl blinked. "Take me
with you. Pick me up."

Julia bent down. "She does what? What does she
do?"

Mona expressionlessly backed away a few steps,
continuing to stare at Julia. "Poo," she said. She
giggled, revealing small perfect teeth. "Poo." She
turned away too quickly, fell on her bottom, and
then struggled up on her feet and staggered off.

Julia looked after Mona for a moment, wobbling
in the direction of the next sandbox, and went to
where she thought the blond girl had been sitting.
Julia knelt down above the spot. For a second she
hesitated, wondering if she were trespassing on a
secret or a code, and then she drew her hand along
the sand as the girl had done. Her hand met no

resistance. She repeated the action. Then she delicately scooped a little of the sand out of the hollow she had made. Very slowly, she continued to drag her fingertips through the little hollow. When the depression was three or four inches deep, her fingers touched something hard and metallic, and she dug cautiously around it, still using only one hand. Gradually she uncovered a small knife. Gummy sand was sticking to its blade. Julia looked at the knife in puzzlement and then scraped more sand from the hollow. Her fingers caught an edge of something hard, and almost without any pressure, she levered up from the sand the corpse of a small turtle of the size that had been sold to children for a quarter in Julia's own childhood. It took her a moment to see that it had been mutilated.

Vomit rushed up from the floor of Julia's stomach, and dropping the mutilated turtle and the small knife back into the hollow, she swallowed the bitter stuff back down again. With her foot she scattered sand over the turtle and the knife. Julia left the sand trap quickly, fearing she might faint, and moved toward a shaded bench on the main path through the center of the park. I'll just sit here and catch my breath, she thought, before I see Lily. She unthinkingly rubbed her hands on her dress, and after a few minutes noticed that she had left a small smear of blood along one seam. Sweat had broken out over her face; Julia blotted it on her sleeve, which instantly showed a series of dark crescents and ragged blotches. She made her mind empty: she concentrated on the sun, on the prickling she felt along her forearms and on her forehead. She was unable to look at the children.

After some minutes had passed, Julia raised her head and closed her eyes against the strong sunlight.

She needed sunglasses. Somewhere, she had sunglasses. They were back at Gayton Road. She could visualize them, their bows crossed, lying on a formica counter in the kitchen. She'd buy another pair. Yes, she thought, I jumped into reacting, I did not think. There was no proof the girl had killed the turtle or cut it up that way. Julia may even have been probing the wrong spot in the sand. Little girls so pretty did not do things like that: it was an unfair psychological rule that handsome children were healthier and more stable than ugly ones. In fact— Julia allowed the idea to seep cautiously into articulation—she had been upset because the sight of the turtle reminded her of what had happened to Kate.

She could speak of none of this to Lily. Making that resolution, Julia stood up from the bench and cut across the long stretch of grass, going toward Plane Tree House. She really did feel peculiar.

2

The two women sat on Lily's terrace in the sun, now milder than it had been an hour before. "Poor Lily's" hair, prematurely gray like Magnus', had been cropped since Julia had last seen her sister-in-law, and it lay flat and short as a boy's, emphasizing the fragile lines of her face and making her look more than ever at an oblique relationship to the rest of the world. Yet Lily had remained unruffled by Julia's news and Julia's highpitched, taut mood. For half an hour, Julia had considered that Lily might be pleased that she would have Magnus to herself again, but she knew that this was grossly uncharitable: Lily simply did not respond as other people did. In the end, her news given, Julia had allowed herself to relax, cosseted by Lily's hospitality—she was now drinking her third gin and bitter lemon, served in a tall glass chiming with ice—and Lily's unpredictability.

"You *are* extraordinary, though," Lily was saying. "Extraordinary and precipitous. You're a regular heroine. I can't imagine myself ever doing anything so reckless and brave."

"God knows I'm not brave," Julia said, laughing.

"Oh, but you are. You have a brave soul."

"Then I'm a coward with a brave soul."

"You mustn't think it is cowardly to fear Magnus.

Magnus is not like anyone else. He has always been a terribly apart sort of person. He has *command*. Sometimes I think that Magnus is not from this world at all, or that he is thousands of years old, preserved by some black magic. I've had a reservoir of fear of Magnus since he was three years old. Even then, Magnus had an ancient, powerful soul. Of course, I think you were wrong to leave him, and I hope with all my strength that you will return to him." Lily was drinking tea, and she followed these words by taking a birdlike sip at it, making it clear that she had at least one more thing to say. Julia, listening to this description of her husband, wondered how many times Lily had pondered in just this way on Magnus' "ancient, powerful soul." It was typical of her romanticizing of her brother. "But as my advice is universally ignored, I don't suppose that you will immediately follow it."

"You heard from him, Lily? What was he like?"

"Desperate, simply desperate. Of course, I couldn't give him a crumb of solace. And his solace, you know, would be mine—I'd be desolate for him if I thought you were never going back to him."

"I can't."

"He loves you. Since the only other person, apart from Kate, that Magnus has ever loved is myself, I am able to be quite certain."

"Lily," Julia insisted, "please don't. I can't take that now."

After a moment while both women looked away from one another toward the park, Julia asked, "Was he angry?"

"I wouldn't call it anger," Lily said. "He was distressed."

"Lily," Julia said, "you have to promise me that you won't tell him where I am. Never mind what you

think is in my best interest or Magnus', please don't
tell him. Promise me. Please."

"I'll promise you anything you like. But I'd be
happier about it if you made me a promise too. I'd
like you to tell me that you will consider going back
to your husband."

"Lily, I've bought a house," said Julia, almost
laughing. "I've bought *furniture*. It's just . . . just
impossible for me to face Magnus. I can't make a
promise like that to you. I can't even think about
Magnus."

"On the contrary, it is my impression that you
think of him all the time." She looked interrogative-
ly at Julia.

When Julia said nothing Lily went on. "It was no
one's fault about Kate, darling. You both very
bravely did what you had to do. Magnus and you
were both commended at the inquest, you know."

"I can't help that."

"But it's a pity that you were unable to hear it."
Conscious that she was too crudely leading Julia into
an area she would be unable to enter for perhaps
months, Lily resisted the impulse to be Magnus'
advocate in the matter of Kate's death. The facts of
her niece's death were at least as clear in Lily's mind
as in Julia's, and Lily knew, and could fully understand, that Julia had broken down afterward. In fact,
Lily realized, she must have begun looking at houses
only a day or two after she had come out of the
hospital where she had been kept under sedation.
Julia had left the hospital only to attend Kate's
funeral; even that had been a mistake. That pale,
confused, drugged creature stalked through the rain
by photographers—it was unlikely Julia had any
memory of that morning. Apparently she had begun
to make arrangements for bolting on her first day

back at Gayton Road: Lily supposed that she had been unable even to look at Magnus straight. Of course, Kate's death had been horrible. She had choked on a piece of meat, and Magnus and Julia, after dialing 999 and waiting minutes for an ambulance while their daughter fought uselessly for breath, had frantically decided to attempt an emergency tracheotomy. Kate had bled to death by the time the ambulance arrived. By Magnus' report, Julia had been very calm, very controlled throughout: only the next day did she get funny. Even now she looked flushed and breathless; and was drinking far too much gin.

"Well, tell me about this house of yours," Lily said. "What number in Ilchester Place is it?"

"Twenty-five."

"How odd that you should move to that street. Perhaps it is not odd at all, given that London is the sort of place in which all sorts of recurrences and coincidences occur."

"Lily, what are you trying to say?"

"My brother used to visit a house in Ilchester Place, a long time ago. It was while he was at Cambridge. I believe he had a friend there."

This comment fed a familiar stream of bitterness in Julia, who said, "Magnus and his friends. How boring all of that is. Maybe it comes from his having such an old, powerful soul."

"Yes, it does," said Lily, who seemed to be a little hurt.

"Lily, I'm sorry," Julia quickly said. "Can't we two be friends, without any relationship to Magnus? I want to begin a new life, I have to live on my own, I can't stand to think of Magnus and I'm afraid to see him, so that's done, but I want your friendship very much."

"Why, my dear," said Lily, "of course you have it. I want what is best for you. We *are* friends."

Julia felt close to tears. "I'm going to have a new life," she said, almost defiantly. "I want your help."

"Of course," Lily said, reaching out and taking Julia's hand. It was cold from her icy glass, and some grains of sand still clung to it. She allowed Julia to weep for a few moments in silence.

"You need something to do, you know," she said after Julia's noiseless crying had ended. "Only bores suggest their interests to other people, but how would you like to attend our next gathering? Mrs. Fludd is our new interpreter. She was a real find, the most *sensitive* sensitive I've met since poor dear Mr. Carmen died. Not personally, of course. She is a real old cockney, tough as a boot. But she has the gift to an astounding degree. I am very enthusiastic about her—but if you scoff at these old-fashioned performances, my feelings won't be bruised. It would be something for you to do, however."

Ordinarily Julia would have made some excuse, but she was touched by Lily's kindness, and this made her feel guilty for her earlier deliberate rudeness. "Just tell me where and when," she said. "It might be fun." Then a troubling thought occurred to her. "They won't . . . she won't . . . do anything about getting in touch with . . . I mean . . ."

"There's no question of it," Lily said firmly. "Really, people have the most obsolete idea about what we do. I suppose you expect ectoplasm leaking from shadowy cabinets."

"Okay," Julia said, smiling. "Just call me whenever your gang has its next meeting."

"Fine," Lily said, clearly pleased. "Now I think I want to give you a present. In return, I hope you will

allow me to snoop enviously through your house as soon as possible. Now excuse me."

Lily left the terrace, and Julia closed her eyes for a moment. We make a wonderful pair, Lily and I, Julia thought, we're both out of our tiny minds. She thought of going round to see Mark, and then she ceased to think of anything at all.

Lily awakened her by stroking her shoulder. She was carrying a large yellow book under her arm, and had a pair of scissors in her other hand. "My dear, you've been asleep for half an hour," she said.

"I've just been thinking about Mark," Julia said. "I'd like to see Mark." She felt once more full of energy.

"That might not be very clever, dear," Lily immediately said. "You'd be far wiser to leave Mark alone."

Lily, having lost one brother to Julia, did not wish to lose the other; she had come closer to her adoptive brother over the past ten years, as Magnus had not; "poor Lily's" defensive psychology seemed quite clear to her sister-in-law.

"Mark is so interesting," Julia said, "and I hardly feel that I know him. Magnus scarcely let him in the house. He used to telephone me sometimes and we'd have these long, sweet conversations. He's probably the only man I've flirted with since I married Magnus."

"He would be," said Lily. "Let me give you these presents. I'm sorry I haven't more to welcome you into your new house, but it's on such short notice. First, here's a lovely big book full of pictures, and it's all about your new neighborhood." She held the big volume before Julia's eyes: *The Royal Borough of Kensington,* by Eda Rolph. "Full of astonishing tales. Haven't read the book in years. The other

present is some of these flowers." She waved her hand at the small, vibrant garden growing in boxes at the end of her terrace.

"Oh, I can't let you cut these beautiful flowers," said Julia, who disliked all cut flowers. "That would be a terrible crime. You can't cut them for me."

"But I can," said Lily, bending down and beginning to snip off nearly a dozen flowers. "Some tulips, some of these beautiful begonias, some of my favorites here, these monstrous pinks, and a few more of everything else. Now. Take these home and put them in water," she said, giving Julia the double handful of bright flowers, "and they'll stay fresh for as long as you like."

Julia looked apprehensively at the flower boxes, but was relieved to see that the loss of her dozen scarcely affected their appearance at all: the flowers grew there in such abundance that only a few small gaps were now visible. The massed scent of the flowers in her hands made her light-headed. They were overwhelmingly sensual. One of the fleshy tulips brushed her face.

"I don't mean to look as though I'm sending you away," Lily said. "These flowers can always be put in water here until you leave. Why don't you have dinner with me tonight? I've got . . . let's see, some nice little chops. Or was this one of my vegetarian nights? There is enough food, anyhow. Afterwards we could watch a delicious new series on the television. One of those wonderful costume dramas. I've never read much Trollope, you know, but it means so much more all acted out. And the language is so beautiful, none of the vulgarity the younger playwrights go in for now. Will you watch it with me? It's fascinating, and I could tell you what's happened in the earlier five hundred episodes."

"I'm out of the television habit," Julia said, smiling. "Your brother wouldn't allow one in the house. I do think I'll go home. Thank you for everything, Lily."

"Have you a telephone?"

"I'm not supposed to, but I do," said Julia. "It's still in the name of William McClintock. But I could practically shout across the park to you."

Lily nodded, apparently satisfied.

Julia slipped the book under her arm and, still holding the flowers with both hands, turned to leave the terrace.

"Now remember your promise!" she called over her shoulder to Lily.

Later, Julia regretted that she had not accepted Lily's offer of nut cutlets and *The Pallisers*. She had fallen asleep on the McClintocks' enormous gray velvet couch just after lying down on it to rest her feet; she had been trying to read a novel she had bought and begun in the Knightsbridge hotel the night previous, a Penguin edition of *Herzog*, but had fallen asleep after two pages. When she awakened, the smell of Lily's flowers pervading the large room, her mouth felt unpleasantly thick. She was very hungry, despite a dull pain just behind the frontal bone of her forehead. She marked her place in the book with a wrinkled tissue from the pocket of her dress and went through the long room to the kitchen.

The light bounced, harshly white, from the gleaming surfaces of the oven and refrigerator. Julia looked in the cupboard for a glass, but realized despairingly that the McClintocks had taken all of the kitchen and dining things with them, as well as all the linen. The kitchen held no food, no drink.

And now it was hours past closing time for shops. Julia turned on the cold water from the taps over the sink and applied some of it to her face; then she cupped her hands and tried to drink from them, but she could not hold enough water in her palms. Eventually she reduced the flow of water from the tap and bent her head so that she could drink directly from it. The water tasted metallic and brackish: she let it run for a minute, and tried it again. Now it was slightly better, but it still tasted as though it were full of metal particles. She supposed she would have to buy bottled water; but maybe she would get used to the taste.

Julia dried her hands and mouth on the long reddish drapes over the outsize hall window. While doing this, she remembered the bloodstain from the morning and looked down at the side seam of her dress. The light-blue seersucker showed a stiff brownish crescent an inch long. The stain seemed larger than it had that afternoon. What an odd scene that was, reflected Julia; surely she had found those things in the sand by some bizarre accident, she had probably been nowhere near the place where the girl had been playing. No child would do a thing like that—well, a boy might. She could imagine Magnus cutting up live turtles as a boy.

Did hot or cold water remove bloodstains? She had been told a hundred times, but could never remember. It was the one you didn't think it was, so she decided to try cold water. Julia went back through the hall to the big ground-floor bathroom, the one the McClintocks had lined with rose-tinted mirrors. (The McClintocks, in most ways utterly conventional and even a shade stuffy in their tastes, had revealed a secret decadence in their bathrooms. The tubs and sinks were marble, the upstairs tub

shaped like a huge sunken shell; the taps were swans' necks, gold. Most surprising were the walls, lined with tinted mirrors. Julia's bathroom upstairs had black mirrors, against which the gold faucets dully gleamed.) Julia took off her dress and draped it over the edge of the sink, so the stained portion would soak, and then filled the sink with water. Cold was right, she thought.

She turned away from the sink and caught sight of herself in the wall mirrors. Funny to see yourself front and back, half nude. Julia wore only underpants and tights. *My shell,* she thought. She was beginning to get a little fat: she would have to be careful about pants. But, she told herself, you don't look so bad, considering: if no Playmate, no matron either. The rose tint made her skin look darker and healthier than it was; Julia decided to get more sun this summer. It was a vision of Magnus-free peace— to be able to sprawl in the sun in the park outside her home.

Leaving the bathroom, she sprinted up the stairs to the bedroom she had chosen that morning. Though it was still not dark, she turned on the lights in the hall and bedroom. This gave the house a cavernous, echoing aspect which made Julia realize how little she knew her new dwelling. She crossed to the windows of the bedroom, pulled the drapes together, and began to dress. In a few minutes, buttoning on a floppy blue blouse she had always liked, Julia realized that it had become very warm in her bedroom; she was perspiring as she had outside. The rest of the house had not seemed so warm. She drew apart the drapes and opened the window by pulling it up from the bottom. The air which streamed in seemed magically cooler than the air within the room. It could have been because the

house had been empty for a month; or could it have been something else?

Julia went to the storage heater set against the wall and touched it with the flat of her hand. She snatched it back in pain. The heater had been turned up to the full. The real-estate agent must have turned it on, Julia thought, so that he would not be showing customers a chilly house. Perhaps some of the downstairs heaters were on as well. She switched off the bedroom heater at the wall and went into the black-mirrored bathroom to comb her hair. The small heater in this room, she discovered, was also on. She flicked it off at the wall, and straightened up to look at herself. In these bathrooms it was impossible *not* to look at oneself. Julia wondered what sybaritic tricks the McClintocks had got up to before these sinister black mirrors. Yet her hair shone in them: and she supposed that she looked good enough for a restaurant. There was a decent-looking French restaurant, she remembered, just off Kensington High Street on Abingdon Road. And hadn't she seen a Chinese restaurant too? Now, she was embarrassed that she had cried, however briefly, before Lily; Lily had, though, demonstrated an almost otherworldly kindness. It seemed to Julia that she had very little to weep about—the sensation of debating between restaurants was one she had not had since her wedding, and it was charged with a nostalgic, delicious liberty. Still drowsy, hungry as she had not been in years, Julia felt for the moment young and capable of anything.

She decided, once on Kensington High Street, to try the French restaurant, remembering that it had been awarded a Michelin rosette some months before. On this first night, she could afford to be lavish with herself. She had, in the past, argued

bitterly with Magnus about restaurants; spending twenty pounds on a meal for two at Keats was obscene; but surely tonight she had something to celebrate. Julia drifted down the busy street, looking in the shop windows, conscious of the multitude of cars surging past on her right, noting where she might buy things she needed for the house. She saw a bank: she would transfer her own account here and leave Magnus what she had put into their joint account. Up ahead was a W. H. Smith for buying books. She noticed a surprising number of package stores. At length she reached Abingdon Road and crossed the High Street to walk up toward the restaurant. The night air moved languorously about her, slipping past her skin. As she opened the door of the restaurant, a beautiful black-haired girl wearing large tinted glasses coming down Abingdon Road smiled at her, and Julia smiled back, feeling as though the girl had given her the liberty of the neighborhood. She too was a capable young woman, living alone in Kensington.

After dining luxuriously and slowly, relishing every mouthful of her snails, then half a seafood pancake, and finally a *suprême de volaille,* Julia paid for her meal with a check and walked back along the crowded street. Traffic seemed perpetual here, gnashing and snarling past as if it too were on its way to a meal. Only when she reached the quiet corner of Ilchester Place did she remember she had left the house key in the pocket of the dress now soaking in the sink.

"Christ," she moaned. She went up the steps and tried the front door. It was locked. Julia looked up at the windows and saw that she had left lights burning in the bathroom and bedroom. At the rear of the

house, she had left the bedroom window open, but it was far out reach. Perhaps a window in the kitchen or dining room might be unlatched. Julia walked around the side of the house, pushing randomly at the windows she could reach. After she had walked down the entire length of the right side of her house, she looked down in frustration and saw that she had trampled many of the little flowers the McClintocks had grown in a border around the house—small, brilliant flowers with thoughtless, optimistic faces. They lay crushed and broken in a weaving line down the side of the house, just visible in the darkness. Julia felt as though the massive dark bulk of the house were rebuking her—it was a strong but momentary impression: she did not deserve this house and the house knew it now. "Oh, please," she breathed, and pushed at another window. It resisted her.

Julia rounded the corner at the back of the house and found herself in her moonlit back garden. The grass looked spectral, some color between green and black. Indeed, the entire garden looked unearthly in the dark light, the flower banks at the far end massive and colorless, like stationary clouds. Behind them reared the brick wall at the end of her property. Julia had a momentary tremor of fear that someone besides herself was concealed in the garden, but pushed this from her mind by the decisive action of vigorously trying each of the windows in turn. At the far end she discovered that the small window in the bathroom was opened out at the bottom, unlocked and with its ratchet set so that the window protruded two or three inches beyond the frame.

She reached in and released the ratchet, freeing

the window so that it swung freely, opening a space about a foot high and fifteen or sixteen inches long, set in the wall at the height of her head. When she threw up the window and poked her head beneath it, she could see, in the rose mirror opposite, the light space of the window filled with the black orb of her head. Ordinarily, she would not think it possible that she could lift and squeeze her body through this small space, but now she had no other choice. The air in the bathroom felt silkily warm to her facial skin; she had to crawl in this way. The only alternative was to break a window, and she shrank before doing violence to the house.

On the verge of pulling her trunk up to force her shoulders through the window, Julia again sensed that another person was somewhere in the back garden: her stomach frozen with fear, she whirled about. No one was visible. The grass, tinted that expressionless color, lay unbroken to the mass of the flowers. Nothing moved. Julia narrowed her eyes and tried to see into the McClintocks' flowers. She braced her legs and felt some of the zinnias of the border crush beneath her feet. "I know you're there," she said. "Come on out. Now." She felt both foolish and courageous, uttering these words in as commanding a voice as she could summon. Still there was no movement from the featureless dark bank of the flowers. After another long scrutiny, she felt safe enough to turn her back to the garden.

Again she felt the heavy warmth emanating from her house. She braced her elbows, bowed her head, and scrabbled up the wall with her feet while pushing her shoulders through the window frame. The window, let loose, dug her painfully in the back of the neck. Hitching up on one arm, she banged the

aluminum border of the window with her other hand; this gave her enough leverage to push herself through the window nearly to her waist.

She wriggled, dropping her upper body so that her weight might drag her bottom through. Instead, she stuck in the window like a swollen fruit. She jerked forward twice, abrading the skin at her hips: from sudden though tolerable pain, she knew she had begun to bleed. Julia pushed with all her strength at the wall, bending with as much torque as she could muster, and felt her hips slide through another half inch. With one further push and bend, she came through, banging her heels on the protruding window, and fell to the bathroom carpet on her right shoulder. She had lost both shoes.

She lay for several minutes on the bathroom floor, breathing heavily. Her fingers found the cool marble of the tub. Her hips ached; her stomach fluttered. For some minutes Julia was unable to move, fearing she might be sick. The skin of her face and hands felt very hot. Eventually she sat upright and rested her back against the bathtub. Through the material of the blue blouse, the marble felt very cool. Modern urban people, peaceful and sedentary, are crippled by shock when they receive otherwise ordinary physical distress; Julia had read this theory in a magazine recently, and she now ruefully reflected that it seemed true in her case. She could nearly feel the blood beating in her facial skin.

Supporting herself with one hand on the rim of the tub, she unsteadily stood up. The wall mirrors reflected a tangle-headed, stooping female figure in pale, ripped trousers. Everything glowed darkly, pinkly, as if through a haze. What she could see of her face looked black. Julia moved slowly to the sink. She tugged at the seersucker dress and let it

drop wetly to the carpet; then she pulled the plug, not moving until the standing water had been sucked away, and ran fresh water, which she splashed on her face. The water smelled like greasy coins. When she peeled off her trousers, she saw that she had scraped skin from both hips; the trousers, bloodied, were ruined. By morning, she would have the beginnings of spectacular bruises on both hips. Julia bent down to the sodden dress, extracted her key from the pocket, and turned on trembling legs to the door. Then she had a second thought, and patted the heater by the door. It nearly burned her fingers, and she flipped up the wall switch to turn it off. Before leaving the bathroom, she remembered to place the blue dress back in a sinkful of fresh water.

The entire house seemed sluggishly hot; Julia thought it might take her an entire morning to find all of the heaters. Yet the warmth spread seductively throughout the living room, and she sat on the gray couch to relax for a second before attempting the stairs. Her hips ached. One of the downstairs heaters was set into the wall beside the big windows; yet another smaller heater was in the kitchen. Julia leaned back in the couch, stretching her legs out before her. She closed her eyes. Her hips smarted, but at least had stopped bleeding from the abrasions. Then she blinked, imagining that she had heard a series of sharp clicking noises from the dining room. Perhaps they had come from the kitchen: refrigerators made all sorts of noises. She heard one sudden, definite clicking noise, and her eyes opened involuntarily. It had come from the dining room—the noise had sounded like someone tapping at the window. Julia looked across the width of the living room into the dining room, directly off it. Its large French windows were set in line with the living room

windows, so that a passerby could look through the house into the garden. The dining room drapes hung a foot apart. Through the gap, Julia could see nothing but black. She felt an extreme disquiet; she wore only the blue blouse and underpants, and sat in view of the window. Perhaps someone had been hiding in the garden after all.

Her heart accelerated. Julia bounded up from the couch and ran through the hall to the bathroom and latched the window through which she had crawled. Then she crept back through the warm house to the dining room and peered out, concealing her body behind the drapes. A second later, she thought she had distinguished a standing figure—it was a darker shape posed before the mass of the flower beds. It moved slightly. She had no impression of height or sex; she needed none. Julia knew that it must be Magnus. She fell to the floor as if by instinct. Julia lay there for some minutes in a panic before she recognized that she must have been wrong. Magnus did not know where she lived.

If it were Magnus, and he wanted to hurt her, he would have assaulted her in the garden. He could scarcely have missed her scramble through the bathroom window. And it was possible that no one was in the garden. The motion might have been a bush, moved by some breeze.

Julia opened her eyes and peered out to the garden, her face at ground level. The garden held nothing untoward. Her heart had begun to beat normally once again, and Julia sat up, blotting her face with the heavy drape. The grass still had that spectral, shining blackness, and she could see the brick wall quite clearly. Nothing between the house and the wall was moving. Julia stood up and, holding one hand to her chest, went back into the living

room, moving slowly in the darkness. *Heaters*, she thought, and glided across the room to the big storage heater set into the wall. It too had been turned on, and she flipped up the switch set into the wall.

Julia woke with a start several hours later: she had been dreaming, and the dream eluded her from the second of her waking. She could hear noises from below; at the same moment she was aware of the noises, she became conscious of the heat in her bedroom. The window remained open, but the bedroom had not cooled since Julia had left for the restaurant. Her entire body was perspiring; this connected in some way to her dream, which had been frightful. She went taut with attention, listening, but heard nothing more. But there had been noises. She had not imagined them—rustling, soft, hushed noises, as of some person moving about in the dark. Her first thought was *Kate's up*, but this was only a half-conscious formulation on the surface of her mind when she thrust it away, aware that Kate had been in her dream, somehow threatened. Spurred by the image of Kate in peril, Julia sat up in bed, listening. She could hear no further noises. She rose from her bed and moved to the doorway. Standing halfway out into the hall, she loudly said, "I'm going to telephone the police. Did you hear me, Magnus? I'm telephoning the police."

Not knowing if she were to be attacked in the next instant, she hung in her doorway, listening with her entire soul. Sweat ran in a distinct line down her back to her buttocks. The hall seemed a shade cooler than her bedroom, less concentrated and dense. Julia remained poised in the doorway a long moment; hearing nothing, her mind empty of all but

physical sensations. She began to count silently to one hundred, forcing herself to pause between numbers; when she reached one hundred, she went on to two hundred. Still she heard nothing. She must have been mistaken; yet she was too frightened to go downstairs to check. In the end, she went back inside the bedroom and locked the door. Then she thrust up the window and let the cooler night air pour over her. In her garden, in the visible areas of the park, all was still. Eventually she returned to her bed and lay down on the damp mattress.

The next morning, while Julia was writing a provisional shopping list on the back of her checkbook, the only paper she could find in her bag apart from a few wrinkled tissues, the telephone shrilled in the living room. Her first thought was that Markham and Reeves were ringing with some question about the house; but realizing that Markham and Reeves were likely to ignore her until she annoyed them with yet another request, Julia thought that Lily must be telephoning her. She put down her checkbook and went from the kitchen into the living room. Light streamed slantwise through the big south windows and the front of the house. The terrors of the previous night had seemed unreal and slightly hysterical to her, waking uncovered in the sunny house and moving through it during the morning, deciding what she needed to buy—food, dishes, glasses, pots and pans, sheets, towels, blankets, eating utensils. For the time being, bottled water. Books and whiskey.

"Hello?" she said, looking at the windows across the street. A man down the block washed his car, sluicing water across its top. Who were these people, who were her neighbors?

In the next instant all the optimism was battered out of her by the sound of Magnus' voice. "Julia, I expect you know who this is. I want you to leave that building and come back to Gayton Road. That's where we *live*. I've been on to the estate agents, and I made it clear to them that no contract you could sign would be considered binding, so we might just emerge from this ludicrous deal of yours with only a small loss. At the moment, Julia, I consider you incompetent to handle your own affairs, and certainly incompetent to make decisions about our future. In the meantime I want you here where you belong. You must leave that house. It is unthinkable—"

She hung up.

When the telephone rang again, she plucked the receiver from the hook and held it away from her ear. Magnus' voice went harshly on, but she could distinguish only isolated words. *Irresponsible* . . . *featherbrained* . . . *Kate* . . . marriage . . .

"I don't consider myself married to you any longer," she said into the receiver. "You frighten me. You're a bully. I can't think of you without seeing Kate. So I can't look at you, live with you, be married to you. Please leave me alone, please. Stay away, Magnus."

"Like hell I will," she heard him say. "You're disturbed—when you face up to certain things—"

She shouted, "If I catch you hanging around my house, in the garden or anywhere else, I call the police." Then she snapped the receiver down.

She stood over the telephone, waiting for him to ring again, threatening, bullying, lying to her. When a minute passed without his making a third call, she thought: he ripped the phone out of the wall.

Yet, a few seconds later, he did ring again.

"Julia, Magnus. Don't ring off. I was so angry I

couldn't telephone back immediately. Julia, I want you here. I want you with me. I fear for you. You're in danger down there, alone."

Julia felt herself stiffen. "Why am I in danger, Magnus?"

"Because you're alone. Because you need help."

"On the contrary, Magnus," she said. "I feel safe for the first time in two months. Lily promised me she wouldn't call you, and now that she has, the only danger I can imagine is from you. Maybe I'll move again. I know you were here last night. You were watching me. When we have something to talk about, I'll invite you to my house. Until then, stay away. Or you will be in embarrassing trouble."

She could visualize her response to this: his hands tightening into fists, his face reddening, his mouth compressing.

"Damn you," he said. To Julia, it was as though the weight of their ten years together was behind his curse. She made no reply; a second later, Magnus hung up. Now she felt as though in battle with Magnus—perhaps the chiefest effect of eleven years of marriage was that threats and curses were no longer suppressed by politeness. They knew each other too well for politeness.

Twenty minutes later when for the first time she heard the sound of her doorbell, Julia started violently, spilling the contents of her bag. It was just long enough since her telephone call for Magnus to have driven down from Hampstead, intent on forcing her back to the house—or back to the hospital. There was no question that Magnus was capable of clapping her back in a hospital bed, muddled by drugs: in the meantime he could find

some legal maneuver that would make her his prisoner. This was a new thought, and Julia, stuffing things back into her bag, resolved that she would fight him physically, violently, rather than submit to being dragged away.

She crept behind a large brown chair and peered around the drapes to the front steps. She could see only a squat, foreshortened shadow. Then the person took a backward step and came into view. It was Mark Berkeley. Julia jumped up from behind the chair and hurried to the door. She threw it open just as Mark, still walking backward and looking up at the house, had reached the steps to the pavement.

"Mark, you darling," she said. "What a wonderful surprise. I thought you were Magnus. Please come in."

Mark stood in the sunlight grinning at her. He really was incredibly handsome. His denim shirt and trousers were so faded they might have been the same ones he had been wearing when she first met him.

"Do you mind my knowing your secret?" he said. "Lily rang me yesterday evening. She's full of admiration for you, and I must say I am too. What a beautiful house.It's perfect."

"Lily has a terribly big mouth, but in your case, I don't mind." Julia held the door as Mark came into the hall beside her. For a moment she had a strong impression that he was about to embrace her, and she moved fractionally away from him. Mark put one warm hand on her back.

"She called Magnus too? So he knows where you are?" Julia nodded.

"He rang me up two nights ago, in an utter rage. He accused me of hiding you from him."

"Damn him." Julia was shocked, and then considered that such a suspicion was characteristic of Magnus. "Oh, I'm so sorry, Mark. I don't want you to be bothered by him. Well, come on in and sit down. Can I get you anything? Actually, I can't. I don't have a thing in the house and I was just about to go shopping. Oh, I'm so happy to see you, you're just like fresh air."

"Why do you keep this house at nursery temperature? It's warmer in here than outside." Mark flopped onto the couch. "Julia, you know you needn't be apologetic about Magnus with me—I've known him even longer than you have. In fact, I was never quite sure why you stayed with him all those years. I suppose I can say that now."

"You can say anything you like," said Julia, though she did not actually wish it, and disliked his remark. Almost against her will, she added, "We did have Kate," and then thought that her marriage really was over if she could make such a statement. Seeing handsome, banished Mark at rest in her home, his scuffed boots crossed on her carpet, Julia felt alarmingly free of Magnus. She said, "I can't bear to think of him right now, Mark. I'm still frightened of him. But I'm getting stronger. You do think I did the right thing?"

"Julia released from bondage," Mark said, laughing. "Of course you did the right thing. I'm just worried that he won't let you be. Do you think he won't bother you?"

"I don't know," Julia admitted. "I think he might have been sneaking around the house last night. It was just an impression, something I saw out in the garden, a figure. In fact, he as much as admitted it this morning on the telephone. He scared me out of my wits." Mark was regarding her very seriously,

which gave Julia's narrative some impetus: she would have hated Mark's easy dismissal of her fears.

"But that's terrible," he said. "That's just what I was afraid of. You have to keep him away. To be frank, I wouldn't trust anything he says. It would be just like Magnus to try to frighten you into returning to him."

"Oh, let's not talk about Magnus," Julia pleaded. "I want to show you my house. Do you really like it? I bought it in such a rush that I'm not sure myself. I've never done anything like this by myself before."

"It's perfect for you," he said. "But where did you get all this astounding furniture?"

"It belonged to the people who used to live here," she said. "I like it. I don't want to have to think about furniture."

"Then you're all right," he said, smiling.

Julia led him through the house, taking him into each room in turn until they came finally to her bedroom.

"But it's roasting in here," Mark said. "Even with the windows open. You must have the heaters on. Where are they?"

"No, I switched them off yesterday," Julia said, going across the green carpet to the big gray block of the heater. She looked at the wall outlet and saw that the switch was in the down position. "That's funny, I thought . . ." She paused. "Maybe I switched in on. No, I couldn't have, because it was so hot when I moved in. I must have been mistaken in some way." She bent down and flipped up the switch. "Up is off, isn't it? On these switches."

"Usually," Mark said. He went across the room and lightly touched the top of the heater. "Well, that's on, anyhow. It's turned up all the way. Maybe you have a poltergeist."

"Oh, I hope so," Julia said. "That's nice. You just smile when I say something drippy and girlish like that. Magnus would look disgusted."

"Magnus has Standards."

"And a powerful soul."

"Hah! Do you forgive her for letting me know your secret?"

"For telling you, but not for telling Magnus. He gave me a wretched night."

"Let me go shopping with you, and I'll help you put Magnus right out of your mind."

"You're a dear. I'll need lots of help carrying heavy things."

"Consider my back yours." These words, coming from Mark, had an almost explicit sexual overtone; Julia took his arm as answer. No one as irresponsible as Mark could ever be threatening.

"If you help me, maybe I'll return the favor by helping you clear up that legendary mess of yours in Notting Hill."

"Agreed," Mark said.

3

Even later, Julia could look back on that afternoon of shopping with nostalgic, regretful pleasure. It had been as though she really were free of all ties, unattached, spendthrift and carefree—the girl she might have become ten years ago if she had not been mesmerized by Magnus Lofting. She and Mark had taken the Rover first to Oxford Street, where Julia bought towels and sheets and some kitchen things she needed, and then to Harrod's. Mark had insisted on buying her an odd little green bracelet, not expensive by Harrod's standards. Finally they had gone to Fortnum and Mason's, where Julia spent a ridiculously happy, ridiculously costly hour buying exotic groceries. Julia several times caught other shoppers looking at her queerly and realized she was making a lot of noise but for once did not feel embarrassed or rebuked; Mark, for his part, seemed delighted by her effusiveness. His enjoyment of her high spirits fed them: Julia felt nearly intoxicated with pleasure, uncomplicated and cloudless. She and Mark had tea at Fortnum's; then they abandoned the laden Rover in a parking garage and went to a pub; in the evening he took her to a small restaurant in Notting Hill. Magnus had never entered a pub in all his adult life—Magnus would have fled The Ark (providing that he could have been coaxed into any

restaurant in Notting Hill) at first sight of the menu which was chalked on boards hung on the walls. After dinner, now in a second pub, Mark rather shyly invited Julia to his flat: "Room, actually. You've never been there."

"Some other time, dear Mark. I have all those things to put away. And I've had too much liquor to trust myself in your room."

That night her dreams were lurid. She was walking slowly, ploddingly, through Holland Park—a Holland Park full of statues and bronze monuments. She was alone; Magnus had vanished somewhere, and Julia knew that he was seeing another woman. Kate gamboled up ahead, her head bobbing, her white dress winking in the gray-green light. Julia tried to walk faster, in order to protect Kate, but each step took enormous effort, as though she was walking through a bog. Then, looking ahead, she saw that Kate had a companion, the blond girl she had seen on her first day in the park. The two girls danced ahead of her, unheeding. Their identical heads, each white gold, flew through the dense air. Far ahead of Julia, on a long hill, they sat down. Julia tried to run, but her legs were as if paralyzed. The second girl was speaking rapidly to Kate, uttering some vile business—Kate sat enthralled. When Julia came nearer, the girls turned their faces toward her, their identical eyes glowing. "Go away, Mother," Kate said.

Then she was carrying Kate's body through a city. The blond girl, as before, danced ahead of her, leading. Julia followed after, crossing busy streets in bright sunshine, until they had left the crowded downtown part of the city and were in a sinister, dilapidated area: grimy, sunless courts and filthy brick buildings with boarded windows. A hunch-

backed man scuttled past, grinning at her. The blond girl entered one of the buildings through an open arch. Julia, frightened, forced herself to follow. She found herself somehow on a rooftop, stared at by shabbily dressed, lounging men. Her arms were in great pain and Kate had got very heavy. The blond girl had vanished through another arch. Julia understood that she would have to stand on the rooftop, holding her daughter's corpse and gazed at by the shabby men—she would have to stand there for hours. The entire scene had a despairing, criminal atmosphere of moral failure; Julia wanted to leave, but she could not.

She awakened in the hot room. The despairing flavor of the dream still clung to her. Julia missed Kate terribly: at the moment, as she stared up into blackness, her life seemed empty of anything but loss and uncertainty. With a tiny shock of disapproval, she realized that she wanted Mark's company, not sexually, but for the fact of his sleeping near, his chest rising and falling. She turned over on her other side and buried her head deep into her pillow, which still smelled of the shop; the single blanket she had put on the bed had been kicked off during her sleep. She closed her eyes, trying to overcome the mood of the dream. Then she heard the noise which had awakened her the night before. It was a soft, rustling, rushing noise, coming from the hall or the stairway. Julia tightened, then relaxed. It must have been a breeze on the drapes in the hall.

A crash from downstairs made her sit bolt upright in bed—she immediately thought that Magnus had broken in and was now storming about, breaking things. At first she felt her familiar fear of him, but as she listened, her fear hardened into anger: she would not have Magnus in this house. She lifted her

wrist near to her face and squinted at her watch. It was past two in the morning. If Magnus were out at this hour, he was probably drunk. In the past years, he had begun to drink more heavily and often came home to Gayton Road smolderingly intoxicated, incensed by something that had happened in the night. She slid from bed, pulled a nightdress over her head, and then wrapped herself in her bathrobe. When she opened the door to the hall she listened intently, cautiously, but heard nothing.

Julia left her bedroom and crept into the hall, moving as quietly as possible. When she reached the head of the stairs, she heard the rustling noise again, and her heart nearly stopped. She flailed out with her right hand and banged the switch for the stairway light. No one was there. She could see the edge of the drapes over the downstairs hall window; they hung straight and still. The rustling noise had suggested rapid movement, a two-legged presence; yet it was a feminine noise, and it was impossible to imagine Magnus producing it. Julia went quietly and slowly down the stairs and paused in the hall. She heard nothing from any of the rooms. Still using the light emanating from the staircase, she pushed open the door to the living room. Moonlight lay over the couch and carpet, silvery and weightless. The yellow cover of Lily's book shone from the floor. "Magnus," she enunciated, taking a step into the room. "*Magnus.*" There was no answer. Julia became aware that her eyes hurt; her flanks, too, throbbed where she had abraded them the previous night. "Say something, Magnus," she said. It would be very unlike Magnus to crouch silently in a dark room. Much more in his style would be to seize her, shouting.

Julia glanced rapidly around the room, but saw

nothing amiss; the living room looked drugged, impersonal, not hers; the McClintocks' furniture lay like heavy beasts sleeping around a water hole. She walked through the moonlight to the dining room. These drapes too were open, and she could see out into the garden, eerie in the silvery light. There too nothing moved. Julia turned around to look into the corners of the room.

And then she saw what had made the noise. Lily's flowers lay in a puddle on the carpet, the vase she had put them in shattered into four or five large irregular pieces. Julia stifled a scream rising in her throat, and put one hand to her mouth: someone had smashed the vase against the mahogany table and then thrown the flowers to the carpet. She ran to the windows and tugged at the handle; it moved smoothly down, and the window swung out into the garden, admitting a wave of cool night air. It was unlocked. Last night, outside, she had pushed at the handle, and it had not budged. Now she turned the key, locking the window again. Magnus must have entered somehow—had found his way in here—and after smashing the vase, had fled through the garden. The scene, in her imagination, had the same stench of moral failure, the same hopelessness, as the moment on the rooftop in her dream—it was overwhelmingly despairing.

Julia bent to the soaking carpet and picked up the sections of the McClintocks' vase. These she took into the kitchen and set on the counter. Later she would try to glue them together. When she returned to the dining room she gathered the foolish broken flowers, took them into the kitchen and pitched them into the small bin beneath the sink. She thought of Magnus reeling home, furious, talking to himself, staggering bearlike up Kensington High

Street. She supposed that he would visit one of his women.

After she had blotted up some of the water with a dish towel, Julia went back upstairs to her bedroom. She felt flushed and restless and lay down in her bed to await morning. It would be impossible to sleep, she thought, but her eyes, heavy, began to close almost immediately. Just before she dozed, she imagined she heard far off laughter—an unfriendly, mocking noise. Heat settled on her in layers; in one of the broken dreams she had between intervals of wakefulness, she dreamed that she and Kate were birds, gliding birds, riding currents of warm air. Up there, they were free: no one would notice them. She desired anonymity, apartness, isolation. Perhaps, she thought, she really did want to go mad.

"Well, I told you I wanted to see your house," said Lily. They were speaking on the telephone, shortly before noon. "And it would be a heaven-sent answer to our problem. Normally we meet at Mr. Piggot's rooms in Shepherd's Bush, but he's been doing some painting and the flat simply reeks of it—extremely unsuitable, as you can imagine. Mrs. Fludd won't come to Plane Tree House because she insists on working in a ground-floor room, and I don't imagine we should occupy the lobby, do you? Miss Pinner and Miss Tooth live together in a bed-sitter in West Hampstead, but that too is on the second floor. Mr. Arkwright says his wife won't hear of having our session at his house. So, my dear, you see our position. Might we meet at your house? I know it's an intrusion, especially as it's your first experience, but I'm at my wit's end trying to invent a ground-floor room which simply does not exist."

"No, it's my pleasure, really," said Julia, who was

in fact dubious about having Mrs. Fludd and the rest
of Lily's circle in her house. Then she thought that if
Magnus were hanging about outside, watching the
house, it would serve him right to see a crowd of
people drive up. She saw the house from his point of
view, all its lights blazing, cars parked outside on
both sides of the street: it would be an emblem of
her independence from him. She said, "I'd be happy
to help out. What time do you usually meet?"

"You *angel,*" breathed Lily. "Nine o'clock. The
others will be so gratified."

"Should I have any refreshments? Anything to
eat?"

"Coffee or tea. Some biscuits. We're not a very
particular set."

For the rest of the morning Julia sat out in the sun
in her garden, alternately reading *Herzog* and
dozing; after lunch she went again into the garden,
taking with her an iced glass of gin and bitter lemon.
The drink, the hot sun, reminded her of summer
afternoons in America, at home or at Smith, afternoons of Nat Cole on the radio, boys appearing to
sprawl on the grass. In this mood of nostalgic,
sun-drugged leisure, Julia passed the afternoon,
reading steadily through *Herzog*.

At four, struck by an idea, she went into the house
through the dining room and telephoned Mark.

"It's probably totally crazy," she said, feeling a
little dishonest. "Lily practically insisted that I join
her gang of devil-worshipers or whatever they are,
and now that they're meeting here I feel sort of
swamped by them. Could you come over to hold my
hand?"

"Lily won't like that," said Mark.

"Bugger Lily. I haven't even mentioned to her
that she broke her promise to me by telephoning

Magnus. I know she couldn't help it. Besides, I don't
know that she wouldn't like it if you were here.
Aren't you two friends these days? I thought you
and Lily were getting on?"

"She's got some peculiar ideas about me," Mark
laughed. "I think Lily fancies herself my warden."

"As mine too," she said. "Please come. We're all
meeting at nine, but you could come over earlier."

"Done. Do you want me to bring anything?"

"Bring yourself," Julia said.

Lily and a squat, red-faced woman in a flowered
dress covered by a shapeless, ancient gray tweed
overcoat straining at one large button arrived at
eight fifty. As a pair they were unavoidably comic:
Lily like some aging, silky moth accompanied by this
little bulldog of a woman who needed only a
carthorse's straw hat to complete her ensemble. And
Julia could not keep from smiling at the two of them
when she had opened her door. Of all the women
who looked like Lily, she thought, only Lily would
appear in public with this person. They looked like a
vaudeville team—Lily would be the "aristocrat"
who is doused with water and slapped with cream
pies.

"Mrs. Fludd and I had a lovely walk through the
last of the sun," Lily said. "Julia Lofting, Mrs.
Fludd."

"How do you do?" Julia said. "Please come in.
Did you walk through the park?"

"Holland Park is locked at sunset," said Lily. "It's
tight as a drum. Mrs. Fludd wanted to see the
neighborhood."

"It ain't half hot," said Mrs. Fludd. "It's tropical,
I call it. Still, it's nearer than Shepherd's Bush. Not
exactly cool in here either, is it?"

Julia apologized, explaining about the heaters.

"You want to go to a nice air-conditioned bingo," said Mrs. Fludd.

She bumped to a halt following Lily into the living room. Mark rose from the couch, grinning. "Nice to see you again, Lily," he said. "And you must be the wonderful Mrs. Fludd I've heard so much about."

Lily glanced at him, and then at Julia; her disapproval clear, she turned to attend to Mrs. Fludd, who appeared to have become even redder and more squat in shock.

"There's two new ones," she complained. "You said one. You never said two new ones. I come all this way for nothing. Too much interference with two new ones."

"This is my brother, Mark Berkeley," Lily quickly said. "He's a friend of Mrs. Lofting's. Mrs. Fludd, please don't say it's impossible. All the others will be arriving soon. And I wanted Mrs. Lofting to witness our transcendences."

"No transcendences with two new ones," Mrs. Fludd said firmly. "No transformations, no interpenetrations, and no consummations neither. This one"—she pointed at Julia with a stubby finger—"is skeptic. All the vibrations will be muddled. Aren't you skeptic, dear?"

Julia looked at Lily, not sure what to say. Lily was no help. She was still upset by Mark's presence. "I suppose I am," she finally said.

"Of course you are. Your aura's dark—dark as pitch. Confusion and despair in the seventh plane. That's the plane of domesticity. Right, dear?"

"Well. . . ."

"Right, then. And there's another cloudy aura," nodding to Mark. "Dirty as an old pond. But that one's open to things. He's receptive. Maybe too

open. Pretty men are like that. He needs special care, he does."

"Does that mean you won't do it?" said Julia. She was charmed by Mrs. Fludd.

"Did I say I wouldn't? I said, no transcendences, no transformations, no interpenetrations and no consummations. You couldn't follow them proper anyhow, being skeptic. But *he* could—he's open. He wants to be filled, like a bottle."

Mark laughed delightedly and said, "Mrs. Fludd, you're a genius. You're worth twice your fee."

"Don't take money," said Mrs. Fludd, unbuttoning the single button and permitting the front of the tweed overcoat to spring apart. "Money soils the gift. I take tea, though. PG Tips is my drink." She moved unhesitatingly toward the couch. "Mr. Piggot makes a wonderful cup of tea." She sat, exposing thick white calves and a pair of tight, black policeman's boots, and looked expectantly at Julia.

"Oh, I'm sorry," Julia said, "but I don't have any tea. I bought coffee, thinking. . . ." She looked again at Lily, who merely shrugged, still distressed by Mark's presence. She had moved far across the room from him, and after her gesture to Julia, pretended to examine the garden through the long dining-room windows.

"Can't drink that muck," said Mrs. Fludd. "Sometimes I take a little Ribena. Smashing for the upper regions, Ribena is."

"I don't have any Ribena either," Julia said, nearly wailing.

"Humph."

"Sherry?"

Mrs. Fludd cocked her head and considered. "Well, as there's to be no special tricks tonight, I could accept a tiny amount of sherry, yes. Next time,

you want PG Tips, love. We all drink tea here. Miss Pinner and Miss Tooth dote on Mr. Piggot's tea. Here's my coat, love."

When Julia was going toward the kitchen for the sherry the doorbell rang, and she asked Lily to open it for her. When she returned to the living room, a tall spindly man in his sixties with a severe long face and a little Hitler mustache was regarding Mark with an expression of grave disquiet. "Two will never do, Miss Lofting," he was saying. The man had thrust his hands into the pockets of his long tan canvas coat—a coat like a park attendant's or a movie IRA man's—and showed no inclination to remove it or his large-brimmed hat of the same color. Mark, perfectly at ease, merely smiled back at the man.

"Now, Mr. Piggot," Lily coaxed, "Mrs. Fludd is willing to go ahead, and so. . . .And here is Mrs. Lofting, our hostess. Mr. Piggot, Julia."

Mr. Piggot glanced sharply at Julia, softened a bit, and removed his hat. His hair grew in a graying mousy fringe above his ears, leaving a high, mottled bald scalp which looked as fragile as an eggshell. "Well," he said. "Looks like she makes a good cup of tea."

"Have a nice glass of sherry, Mr. Piggot," Julia said, trying desperately to win over the old scarecrow.

"Sherry, is it? We generally imbibe tea at these gatherings. PG Tips, I use. Mrs. Fludd fancies it, don't you, Mrs. Fludd? But I won't say no to a nice sherry, not from your hands. British, is it?"

"Uh, Spanish," Julia said. "Manzanilla."

Mr. Piggot's face contracted. "Well, it'll wet the whistle. I feel a bit dry after cycling over here from Shepherd's Bush. We generally have these sessions at my place, you know. Expect your—aunt?—has

told you that. But Mrs. Fludd won't go into a place that's been painted too recently. Distorts the reverberations."

"Something horrible," Mrs. Fludd cheerfully agreed, accepting her sherry. "Throws me whole system off."

"There's Mr. Arkwright," said Mr. Piggot when the bell rang again. "Punctual as the Irish Guards is Mr. Arkwright."

Julia said, "Will you let him in, Lily?" She took a third glass of sherry to Mark, who said something sardonic about filling up his bottle and moved over to sit beside Mrs. Fludd. Mr. Piggot still gazed at him with affronted blue eyes, spaced rather too closely together.

"Hullo, all." A compact little gentleman in a frayed gray gabardine suit bounced into the room a few paces ahead of Lily. He too had a mustache and a bald head, but his mustache was larger than Mr. Piggot's, and his cranium seemed almost aggressively solid. Julia noticed a medal pinned to his jacket before she saw that one of his sleeves was pinned up. "Am I the last?" He looked around briskly, paused at Mark, and then made for Julia. "See the West Hampstead ladies aren't here yet. You must be Julia Lofting. Pleased to meet you. The name's Arkwright. Nigel Arkwright. And you have sherry, how thoughtful. Lovely house you have here, eh? My cousin Penny Grimes-Bragg took a house in this neighborhood many years ago, over in Allen Street. Not far from here, is it?"

"No, not at all," Julia said, wondering if Mr. Arkwright got out of the house much. But she had decided that he was an "ally" against the unpredictable Mrs. Fludd and the as yet unknown West Hampstead ladies.

"No more than a brisk walk," he was saying. "Driving my old bus down here, I was just thinking of the old days when Penny and I—"

"Do join me, Mr. Arkwright," Lily broke in. Her innate sociability had apparently overcome her resentment of her brother's presence, for she smiled at Julia once Mr. Arkwright turned his back.

"With pleasure, Miss L.," he chirped. "Ah, Mrs. Fludd, two new ones tonight. That'll limit the old bag of tricks, won't it?"

"Drink your sherry, Nigel," said Mrs. Fludd amicably. She had moved some inches away from Mark, who was now slumped far down on the couch so that his bottom seemed in danger of slipping to the floor. He looked profoundly bored, but Julia sensed some area of tension—unreleased, concealed—in him. Mrs. Fludd too appeared to have been accumulating psychic power, for she glanced toward the door a second before the bell rang again.

Julia went into the hall and opened the door. Two women, both thin and elderly and dressed in long, threadbare black coats, stood on the doorstep. Behind them Julia glimpsed an ancient black bicycle propped against the curb, and an even older-looking, rusty Morris Minor behind it which must have been Mr. Arkwright's "bus." The West Hampstead ladies had presumably taken a combination of buses. If Magnus were lurking outside, watching the various arrivals, the effect would not be what she had intended. In fact, she saw, the effect would be the reverse of her intention: Magnus would suppose her to have slipped over the edge into total incompetence. Still, she found a smile for the two women.

"I'm Julia Lofting. You must be Miss Pinner and Miss Tooth."

"Such a long way."

"But not as far as Shepherd's Bush."

Miss Pinner and Miss Tooth entered Julia's house, remarking upon its niceness. When they reached the living room, they darted in tandem across to Mrs. Fludd, spoke a few words to her, and then turned around to smile at the others of their group. When Miss Pinner finally saw Mark, her smile disappeared. Miss Tooth, however, cast him a glance full of vague benevolence.

"Who is this young man?" asked Miss Pinner.

"Now, Norah," said Miss Tooth.

"Who is he?"

"Mrs. Lofting's brother, Mark. Very dark in the aura, he is. *Your* aura's very strong tonight, Miss Pinner. Bright orange, the color of powerful movements in the fourth house. Perhaps we shall have luck tonight." Saying this, Mrs. Fludd looked about the room, her attention visibly distracted from Miss Pinner; she had grown, since Julia had last looked at her, slightly apprehensive.

"There will be no question of the higher states with two new ones," said Miss Pinner.

Lily said from Mr. Arkwright's side, "Mrs. Fludd has very graciously agreed to limit herself to the elementals."

As Julia looked at the two old women their faces, which had seemed so similar at the doorway, separated. Miss Pinner bore a certain resemblance to Mr. Piggot, at that moment engaged in describing to Lily and Mr. Arkwright how he caught fish in Hyde Park by fixing bread to his fishhooks: both of them had long narrow faces and small bright-blue eyes like chips of sky. Miss Tooth looked rather dusty and faded, with her small, deeply-lined face the image of a retired governess. Miss Pinner could have been an exheadmistress noted for her disciplinary acumen.

Julia took all the coats to the hall closet and returned
with sherry for the two women. Miss Tooth glanced
at Miss Pinner before accepting hers and, receiving a
nod, took the glass in her small, trembling hand.

Mark gave Julia a despairing look and rose from
the couch to join Lily, listening to Mr. Piggot
describe his illicit fishing experiences. For these old
people the spiritualist gatherings were social occasions; Mr. Arkwright kept punctuating Mr. Piggot's
adventures with loud bursts of soldierly laughter.
His rush of talk hadn't denoted any special sympathy
for Julia, but demonstrated instead pleasure at his
release from loneliness. Julia's house was filled with
people whose company she could not enjoy; even
Mark was sullen. Miss Pinner and Miss Tooth were
now examining Julia's furniture. They were in an
ecstasy of approval, everything being "so nice."
Julia wished she could leave and lock the door
behind her; but she took a sip of her sherry and sat
beside Mrs. Fludd on the couch.

"I shouldn't stay here," said Mrs. Fludd.

"No? Mrs. Fludd, I'd be so grateful if you could.
Lily has been looking forward so much. . . ."

"You needn't be false to me, Mrs. Lofting, you'd
be happy if the lot of us went home. But you don't
take my meaning. I shouldn't stay here if I were you.
Shouldn't stay in this house."

Julia looked at the woman's red puggish face in
surprise; she was further surprised to notice that
Mrs. Fludd's eyes were shrewd and perceptive, not
at all vague. It was as though she had seen that Mrs.
Fludd was actually a man, wearing that absurd
clothing; the shock was as great as that. She had
been seeing Mrs. Fludd as a "character," someone
not to be taken seriously, and this quick glance of
recognition made her blush for her assumptions. If

the others of Lily's gang were lonely eccentrics, Mrs. Fludd's cool, startling gaze revealed a person composed of flintier materials than the gibberish about transcendences and interpenetrations had suggested.

"Something's funny in this house," she said.

"You think I should leave?" said Julia, transfixed.

"Do you see anything? Hear any noises? Has anything unexplained occurred?" Even her diction had altered.

"I don't know," Julia confessed. "Sometimes I think I hear things—"

"Yes." Mrs. Fludd nodded sharply.

Remembering something Mark had said, Julia asked, "What are poltergeists, exactly? I feel sort of foolish, asking you, but is it possible that there might be one here?"

"Never any harm in a poltergeist," replied Mrs. Fludd. "They move things, sometimes break a mirror or a vase—mischievous creatures. You'd be in danger only if you were very receptive, like your pretty friend across the room. Or if you were dominated by some strong destructive emotion. Hate. Envy. Then, if the spirit wished revenge, it might influence you. That's rare, but it does happen, if the spirit is particularly malefic. Or if some coincidence links you to it. In Wapping, a thief dead for fifty years set fire to a house containing a burglar's family. Killed them all."

"But how do you know?" asked Julia.

"I felt it. I knew."

Such monolithic assurance always influenced Julia. In any case, it permitted no argument. "You feel something here?" she asked.

Mrs. Fludd nodded. "Something. Can't pin it down yet. But I don't like this house, Mrs. Lofting. Who lived here before you?"

"A couple named McClintock. He made carpets. I bought this furniture from them."

"Any deaths in their family? Any tragedies?"

"I don't know. They were childless people."

"But you've seen something. Things in this house."

"Well, I'm afraid it might be my husband," Julia said, and laughed.

Mrs. Fludd immediately closed up, separating herself from Julia; then, relenting, she took Julia's hand. "Ring me if you ever want advice," she said. From her bag she extracted a white card which read *Rosa Fludd, Interpreter and Parapsychologist*. Printed at the bottom was a telephone number.

Mr. Piggot approached the couch, followed by the perky Mr. Arkwright. "It *is* time?" said Mr. Piggot. I'm eager to investigate some theories I had at the shop since our last meeting."

"Of course, love," said Mrs. Fludd, firmly back in her former role. She clapped her hands together twice and conversation in the room ceased. Miss Pinner and Miss Tooth turned their white faces raptly to the couch.

"*Time,*" breathed Miss Tooth.

At opposite ends of the room, Lily and Mark also turned to face Mrs. Fludd; Lily with an expression combining eagerness with satisfaction, Mark wearily. Julia had time to wonder what was wrong with Mark before Lily asked her to turn off the lights.

She jumped up and went quickly to the light switch. Glowing gray light entered the room from the big windows; in this soft diffused semidarkness, Julia could see the fixed, rapt expressions on the faces of the "group." She and Mark were outsiders here, and she moved to his side.

"Have you a candle or small lamp, Mrs. Lofting?"

Julia went into the dining room and turned on a little ceramic lamp in the shape of a toby jug.

"Move it further away, please," commanded Mrs. Fludd. "I must ask you all to join hands at the beginning. Look at the light behind me. Cleanse your minds."

The little lamp cast only a feeble light into the living room. Julia, joining the group, found herself being gripped by Mark on her right; he was holding her hand tight enough to hurt her. On her left Mr. Piggot's hand was surprisingly soft and damp. His wafery skull shone palely in the twilight.

The group members, once they had joined hands, moved to sit on the floor, awkwardly, pulling Julia and Mark down with them. Only little Miss Tooth accomplished the move from standing to sitting with grace, seemingly floating to a cross-legged position; Miss Pinner moved with a machinelike efficiency. Julia, covertly watching her, thought she could smell oil and gears.

Once on the floor, the group members looked past Mrs. Fludd's head to the soft light emanating from the toby jug lamp. Mark, brooding, had set his face into a mask of weary tolerance. Both apprehensive and skeptical, Julia too looked at the lamp. After a bit her eyes began to burn. When she glanced at the others, she saw that the group members had closed their eyes; their faces hung in the air like death masks. Mrs. Fludd sat in a perfectly ordinary position on the couch before them, her hands folded in her lap. In the pane of the tall back window, her head and the lamp glowed against the darker glass. Whitish clouds scudded above the flamelike, dissolving orb of the lamp.

"Close your eyes," said Mrs. Fludd, her voice

very slow and quiet. Mr. Piggot, to Julia's left, sighed and slumped backward, tugging her hand. "You may open them later if you wish."

She closed her eyes. About her she heard breathing. Mark gripped her right hand harder, and she shook her hand in his, signaling him to loosen; he pinned her hand yet more tightly.

"One of us is having trouble," said Mrs. Fludd. "Who is it?"

Mark said, "I'm getting out of this." He broke contact with Julia and stood up.

"Close the group," said Mrs. Fludd. "Mr. Berkeley, you will sit quietly outside the group and observe."

Julia hitched sideways and grasped Lily's cool hand. It lay passively in hers. Lily had not opened her eyes when Mark had spoken, though all the others had. Mark now sat behind them, still facing Mrs. Fludd.

"I need your help, Mrs. Lofting," said Mrs. Fludd softly. "Make your mind empty, completely empty and white. Let nothing enter it." Her voice was slowing and becoming deeper in timbre. Julia opened one eye and saw, looking up toward the couch, Mrs. Fludd's heavy jowls outlined by the soft light behind her. Her hair was a white gauze. She seemed to have become heavier and older. Julia closed her eyes again and thought of a white saucer.

Miss Tooth, at the left end of the seated line, began to breathe stertorously. Lily's hand still lay utterly passively in Julia's. After a bit, Julia felt an ache in her thighs. Her eyes closed, she began to see flashes of scenes, people's faces or landscapes appearing momentarily before her and then melting into other scenes. Moses Herzog, his face that of an elderly English professor at Smith, metamorphosed

into Blake's flea. The hideous features of the flea in turn were transformed into Magnus' face. By an effort of will, Julia dismissed this last vision—she thought of clouds covering that big, powerful face, obscuring it. When the clouds blew off, they revealed one of the lounging, shabby men who had been in her dream. Now the man was her father, and he examined her with an expression of exhausted pity. She could see herself standing on the black tarpaper of the rooftop, Kate dead in her arms. Both of her thighs ached; the right was on the verge of cramp. Julia lurched to one side and twisted her legs out before her. Mr. Piggot twitched at her hand in rebuke.

Opening her eyes, Julia again saw Mrs. Fludd, who now sat slumped in the chair as if she had fallen asleep. Her mouth was open, black and toothless in the fleshy mass of her face surrounded by the penumbra of her hair. The woman's squat body was as if compressed—"slumped" was the wrong word, for she appeared to be under gathering tension.

"Close eyes," she said in a gravelly voice. Julia, startled, immediately pressed her eyes shut. She heard Mrs. Fludd's heavy boots scuffing on the carpet. She was again on the rooftop, now alone with the men. Her father, who had died one summer while she and Magnus were in Perigord, turned his face from her. Internally, she began to speak to him, as she frequently did when moved by guilt. *You were a decent man, but too forceful. I can see that now. I married Magnus because he had your power, he could dominate like you, and then I saw what a weapon your power was. But Daddy, I loved you. I would have gone to your funeral if I had known, I want you to forgive me for being away, I loved you always, please forgive me, grant me that. . . . As the*

words became rote, the vision dissolved. She was alone on the roof, oppressed by the comprehensive atmosphere of moral loss. All was grimy, all was inferior and flawed. She bent her head. The scene turned to opaque blackness through which she fell: Julia was dizzied, and seemed actually to be slowly falling. The room seemed to have turned about; surely she was now facing the front window instead of Mrs. Fludd? She resisted the temptation to open her eyes. Again, she imagined the white saucer—cool, without blemish, entirely surface—and filled her mind with it.

For a time the only noises in the room were Miss Tooth's strained breathing and the hushing noise of Mrs. Fludd's boot scuffing the carpet. Julia grew calmer and wondered what Mark, behind them, was doing and thinking in the darkness. He had begun to be uneasy after he had crossed the room to sit beside Mrs. Fludd. She must have said something to him—as she had to Julia. And now how did they look to him, seated on the carpet like fools before the massive image of Mrs. Fludd? She could scarcely restrain the impulse to turn her head to look for him. Mr. Piggot's boneless hand, stirring momentarily in hers, returned her to her context.

"*Agh. Agh.*" The soft choking noise came, Julia thought, from Miss Tooth. Then she heard a wail which was unmistakably Miss Tooth's and realized that the insistent choking noise was made in Mr. Arkwright's throat. Lily too was making a noise; the most mothlike, ladylike of noises, an exhalation of breath carrying the slightest coloration of voice. This was astonishingly sexual. Julia's hands were tugged forward and back, and soon she too began to rock. Her legs had once more begun to ache, but she could not think of interrupting the resistless rocking

motion to swivel them back under her. Daringly, she
slitted her eyes and saw, as in a haze, the dark heads
on either side bobbing forward and back. Each was
making some low noise, rhythmical and insistent.
Miss Pinner was growling like a cat. Before them sat
Mrs. Fludd, her feet now still, her face distorted.
Mr. Piggot's hand had grown very sweaty. Julia
closed her eyes and resumed rocking back and forth.
Not wishing to remember the image of Mrs. Fludd's
face, she made her mind utterly void of thought. She
thought of the thought of nothing. Soon she was a
rocking particle of nothing.

Then she saw Kate—Kate with her back turned to
her.

A deep croaking voice stopped them all. "*Aah,
stop.*" Jolted back to herself, shaken by the vision of
Kate, Julia withdrew her hand from Mr. Piggot's
while still clinging to Lily's. She opened her eyes.
Mrs. Fludd was pressed back against the cushions of
the couch, her face nearly purple. She had none of
the repose Julia associated with the notion of
mediumistic trance: her eyes bulged, her mouth
worked. "*Stop. Stop.*"

"Something's wrong," whispered Mr. Piggot.

Together they watched Mrs. Fludd struggling, not
knowing what should be done. Lily tugged at Julia's
hand, indicating that she was not to rise. Gradually
Mrs. Fludd's face cleared of purple and her eyes
closed; she lay back drained and apparently powerless, her face heavy and dead. As Julia watched, the
old woman's face became chalky. "It's over," she
uttered, her voice low as it had been earlier in the
evening. Yet it seemed to shake. Her hands, too,
trembled as she placed them on her chest, forcing
herself to breathe regularly.

"Over?" inquired Miss Pinner. "Why, we were just—"

"This must stop," said Mrs. Fludd in her trembling voice. "I'm sorry. I can't do more. I can't finish." The woman, Julia saw, was terrified. "Get my coat," she ordered. She was trying to struggle up from the sofa. "No more tonight. My coat. Please." She fell back exhausted, and Julia saw with horror that the old woman had begun to blink back tears.

The group members stood about in the darkness, uncertain and disturbed. Only Miss Pinner seemed indignant. While she hissed something to Miss Tooth, Lily approached Mrs. Fludd. "Get my coat," said Mrs. Fludd. Now she was openly weeping.

"Somebody get some water, please," Lily said, and Miss Pinner looked up from her intense talk with her companion. Julia stood by, frozen, incapable of movement.

"What happened?" she asked. "Mrs. Fludd, what happened to you?"

"Get out of this house," Mrs. Fludd whispered. She lolled back on the cushions, her mouth dryly opening and closing. Tears continued to roll down her meaty cheeks. "Some water." She began to whimper.

Miss Pinner exasperatedly went from the room. Julia noticed that she was going not to the kitchen, but in the direction of the hall bathroom.

"She's frightened," Lily whispered to Julia. "What was that she said to you?"

Julia shook her head. Mrs. Fludd was again trying to speak. She bent near. Foul breath assaulted her. "Danger. I'm in danger. You too." The woman was trembling violently. A sharp, acetic odor floated up to Julia, and she recognized it only when Mrs. Fludd

gasped and made a violent, thrashing attempt to get up from the couch. Now she was both humiliated and terrified, and Julia, the sour odor swirling about her like ammonia, could not hold her to the couch. She looked into the dark recesses of the living room, over the heads of Miss Tooth, Mr. Piggot and Mr. Arkwright, but Mark was nowhere in the room. He had left the house unseen.

Miss Pinner's shriek stopped her speculation and froze her as she stood, her arms on Mrs. Fludd's shoulders. Miss Tooth rushed from the room. Mrs. Fludd too had heard the scream, and sank back into the couch, closing her eyes. Julia ran after Miss Tooth. When she reached the bathroom, she saw Miss Pinner supine just inside the door; Miss Tooth was cradling her friend's head. Julia stepped over Miss Pinner's body and entered the bathroom. The mirrors reflected her startled, wide-eyed round face, making her look unnaturally healthy and beautiful. Then, momentarily, flickeringly, she saw someone behind her move out of her field of vision: she whirled around, but no one else was in the room. And if anyone had been there, Miss Tooth would have seen him. Julia turned back to the mirror; and there the figure was again just slipping from sight. Yet Julia, like everyone, had seen this happen before: it was a common experience brought on by nerves. It was no more unusual than hearing one's name called in the street. Surely, this or something similar had startled Miss Pinner. Julia approached the sink for a glass of water and saw that her blue seersucker dress, forgotten, still soaked; the water in the basin had turned the color of rust, but the dress still bore its stain.

4

When Julia finally returned home that night, shortly after eleven, she went early to her bed. She felt as though she would be apprehensive all the rest of her life—and half of the disquiet lay in the inability to be definite about what was its source. She and Lily had taken the quaking Mrs. Fludd to her flat in a taxi; driven through the grim, hopeless streets which were so much like the streets of her dream, they had come to Mrs. Fludd's block of flats, in a cul-de-sac off the Mile End Road. The street-lamps had all been broken, and whitish shards of glass shone up from the dirty pavements; the road too was littered with broken glass, the pebbled green spray of shattered windshields. A lighted plaque on Mrs. Fludd's building announced that the gray, prisonlike structure, one of a series of similar buildings forming a compound, bore the name Baston; before Baston, roving gangs of boys in rolled-up Levi's passed back and forth, shouting in raucous voices. Several of them stopped to gape at the taxi. When they saw Mrs. Fludd they began to hoot. "Bloody ol' witch! Bloody ol' witch!" Mrs. Fludd had not spoken a word during the long ride from Kensington, though Julia had twice asked her what had happened to her, what had she seen. The

old woman's mouth had tightened wth such pressure her upper lip went white. The gang of boys terrorized her even further, and she initially refused to leave the cab. Lily, on the street side, got out and at first disconcerted the boys. When they began again to hoot, it was at Lily. She ignored them and, together, she and Julia coaxed Mrs. Fludd from the taxi. "Wait for us," Lily said to the driver, and the two women helped Mrs. Fludd into the open court. Several of the boys trailed along behind, calling out obscenities. "Here," said Mrs. Fludd, flipping up a hand at an entrance: she lived on the building's ground floor, as Julia had expected.

Julia supported her through the small, antiseptic flat to the tiny bedroom where a dusty budgerigar slept in its cage. The bedroom, no larger than a big closet, contained a single bed and a dwarfish chest of drawers. On the white walls hung crosses, star charts, a dozen odd paintings which Julia scarcely noticed. Lily had gone into the kitchen to see if anything could be found for Mrs. Fludd, and Julia helped the old woman down onto the cramped bed and bent to unlace her boots.

Bending and struggling with the tight knots, Julia felt a pudgy hand settle on the nape of her neck. "Get out of here," Mrs. Fludd croaked.

"I just thought I could help," Julia said, looking up into the old woman's flaring face—she wondered if Mrs. Fludd's heart was all right.

"No. I mean, get out of this country," muttered Mrs. Fludd. Her breath was like a buzzard's. "Go back to America. Where. You belong. There's danger here. Don't stay."

"Danger here in England?"

Mrs. Fludd nodded as if to a backward child, and rolled onto her bed.

"Does it have to do with what we were talking about? What did you see?"

"A child and a man," Mrs. Fludd said. "Be careful. Things could happen to you." She closed her eyes and began to breathe heavily through her mouth. Julia, looking up at the wall, found herself looking at a Keane print.

"Is the man my husband?" she asked.

"The house is yours," Mrs. Fludd said. "You must leave."

Then she turned her heavy face again directly to Julia and gripped both of her hands. "Listen. I do. Fake things. Frauds. For the others. Mr. Piggot and Miss Pinner. Expect it. Not all. All that about transcendence—it's fraud. But I do see. Things. Auras. I *do*. But I hypnotize them, like. Now I'm scared. They were a man and a girl. They put you in danger. Me. In danger. They're evil. Just evil."

"Is the man my husband?"

"Get out," Mrs. Fludd groaned. "Please."

"Please, Mrs. Fludd, who is the girl? You must tell me."

The old woman rolled on her side, groaning. A wave of corrupt air rose from her body. "Go."

On the ride home Lily demanded to know what had happened. "She was frightened out of her wits. What did she say to you?"

"I'm not sure I understand it," Julia defensively said. Soon after this the cabdriver confessed that he was lost, and they switched back and forth on dark, oppressive streets before finding their way again. Julia got out of the taxi at Plane Tree House and paid the fare over Lily's protests: it took most of the money in her purse. Then she walked home, skirting the park, where voices and laughter came to her from the dark regions beyond the locked gates.

Once in her house, she went into every room, looking for she knew not what and finding nothing: most of the lights had been left burning, and the house had a blank, emptied, waiting air, as if no one lived in it. Half-filled sherry glasses adhered to the tables. One had tipped over, and poured an irregular dark stain onto the carpet. Probably because of what Mrs. Fludd had said to her, the house seemed malevolent: "malefic"—that extraordinary word the old woman had used.

In the unused bedrooms, where the furniture had been covered with dust sheets and vacancy lived like a guest, Julia felt insubstantial, drifting without purpose, looking for what she knew she would not find. Dusty and untouched, these rooms seemed chilled by their emptiness. When she checked, she saw that the heaters here had been left in the "off" position. Yet the house was a giant structure, a huge form, which hedged her out and kept her at bay: it would resist her impositions, it would not yield to her. Her sense of the house's obduracy was immense. She felt, more than ever, that she was living inside a comprehensive error, the mistake that her life had become: bigger forces lay without, waiting. A child and a man.

This hopelessness drove her finally to her hot, claustrophobic bedroom. She undressed quickly and threw her clothing over a chair; before she got into bed, she looked at the heater's wall switch. The switch was down. Julia remembered having flicked it up yesterday morning when Mark was in the room; certainly she had not turned it on since. She touched the metal surface of the heater, and found that it was as hot as if it had never been turned off. That meant that it had been on last night, since these heaters did not function during the day; yet hadn't she looked,

last night? She cursed her memory. But last night Magnus had been *in the house*. Could he be so childish as to go about turning on the heaters?—but if he could stoop to smashing things up, terrorizing her as bluntly as the boys had Mrs. Fludd, it was impossible to say what he might not do. Angry, Magnus was capable of anything. She turned the heater off once again; then, on an afterthought, took a roll of tape from her closet and taped the switch to the fixture.

Though she shrank from the very idea, Magnus had to be faced: as did her feelings about him. What *were* those feelings? Julia felt at once as though she were on the crumbling lip of a precipice; her control, her hold on things sound and normal, was fragile; she knew that much of her seeming calm and placidity was a performance. Horror lay beneath the surface—horror was what inhabited the abyss below the precipice. The image of Magnus murdering Kate, that sight of him plunging the knife into Kate's throat while she thrashed on the floor, could rise in her at any time, as it had before she had been taken to the hospital and drugged into insensibility. Even then she had been tortured by waking dreams. Over and over, her wrists strapped to the side of the bed, she had imagined grasping Magnus' arm and turning the knife to her own throat. That image too had haunted her. Dying for Kate—she would gladly die for Kate. Instead, she had passively watched the clumsiest of murders. Magnus was inextricably tied to this horror, the horror of inanition, of drift which meant loss, of lying, of emptiness without end or meaning: that was death indeed, and it seemed to crawl forth from the walls of this house.

A child and a man. Kate and Magnus. Mrs. Fludd had seen them. And what had she said, before the

trance? It had been something about hate or envy—
they were what made a spirit "malefic." Kate was
present; Kate lay behind Magnus' mad forays into
Ilchester Place. She was unforgiving. Logic took her
relentlessly to this illogical conclusion. Julia began to
rock from side to side on her bed, moaning. She was
breaking down. It was an image, again, of the
precipice where she had so carefully walked, of clods
and pebbles shredding away, breaking up on the
long fall down. It was Kate. Mrs. Fludd had seen
Kate. In some vivid, dreamlike way, Magnus was
dominated by Kate; he was an unthinkable danger to
her mind.

Unable to sleep, unable to control her thoughts,
Julia snapped on the reading lamp at the head of the
bed. She forced herself to extend her arms alongside
her body. Flatten the fingers so the palms touch the
sheet, extend the thumbs. Relax. She breathed
deeply, twice. She would talk to Mrs. Fludd. If she
had to leave the house to escape the danger Magnus
posed, she was capable of leaving. For now, sleep
was impossible: but she would not leave this bedroom. This room was hers. If she were to be driven
from the room, she would leave the house.

Julia turned her head to see the books on the little
stand beside the bed. She had finished the Bellow
novel, and now had *The Millstone*, *The White House
Transcripts*, *The Golden Notebook* and *The Unicorn*
on the table; she needed something less stimulating
than any of these. Kate and Magnus: Mrs. Fludd's
hints and warnings outlined a dread possibility.
Kate's spirit still living, hating her and using Magnus' anger, feeding that anger, Kate's spirit seething
through this house. . . . All of this was real, happening to her.

Julia had to call Miss Pinner as well as Mrs. Fludd;

before the departure of the West Hampstead ladies, Miss Pinner had been too shaky and distraught to describe what she had seen in the bathroom.

Then she saw another book which she had recently placed on the bedside table, hidden behind the little stack of paperbacks. It was *The Royal Borough of Kensington,* Lily's present to her. A sober, judicious list of facts, a few anecdotes, color plates—it was just what she needed, a book about as tangy as a suet pudding, a sleeping pill of a book. She lifted the heavy volume into her lap and began to flip the pages, reading paragraphs at random.

Prominent inhabitants of Kensington in the eighteenth century . . . Kensington as a village . . . political history of the royal borough . . . the planning of Kensington Gardens . . . merchant princes included . . . a notorious Mr. Price, hanged for the theft of a whippet. . . . Flipping a page after reading about the fate of Mr. Price, Julia saw a heading which read "Crime, Ghosts and Hauntings." At first she turned over several pages, not trusting herself to read such a chapter, but her curiosity was too great, and she went back to the heading and began to read.

At first she found nothing more exciting than had been the lists of prominent Kensington aldermen and merchants; the author had tracked down a number of conventional haunted-house anecdotes and set them down in colorless straightforward style. The ghost of a headless nun in a "manorial" building on Lexham Gardens; two sisters who had killed themselves in adjoining houses on Pembroke Place and had been seen crossing the gardens, hand in hand, by moonlight; the Edwardes Square "paterfamilias" of 1912 who had been possessed by the spirit of his mad great-grandfather and taken to dressing in

the extravagant style of a century before and had
finally murdered his children; Julia read all of these
stories with a dulled interest.

Then a sentence and a street name burst from the
text.

One of the most vexed and troubling of all
Kensington murders [Julia read] was that of the
case of Heather and Olivia Rudge, of 25
Ilchester Place. One of the last women to be
sentenced to death in England, Heather Rudge,
an American, had purchased the house on
Ilchester Place from the architect, who had built
it for himself in 1927 but in two years wished to
move, due to family troubles; at the time, Mrs.
Rudge, who was separated from her husband,
had a reputation as a brilliant, rather reckless
hostess, and was considered by many inhabitants of her social world as "fast." [Eda Rolph
implied a fondness for handsome younger men
and wealthy businessmen from the City.] One
contemporary, the author of several mild books
of verse and a once-popular series of theological
novels, described her as possessing "a small,
vivid, distinctly alarming face in which beauty
and avidity fatally conjoined. *Vanitas* indeed: yet
we found in her a helter-skelter charm." The
birth of a daughter, Olivia, twelve years after
the purchase of the Ilchester Place house,
occurred in wartime, and so did little to affect
her already damaged career as a hostess—the
morals of a rich, aging playgirl whose greatest
notoriety had passed six or seven years before
interested only a few.

The parties continued, at intervals and with
considerably less splendor than previously, and

then ceased altogether; little was heard of the Rudges until 1950. In that year, the nine-year-old Olivia Rudge was mentioned in connection with the death by suffocation in Holland Park of a four-year-old child, Geoffrey Braden of Abbotsbury Close. Olivia Rudge and what the popular press briefly referred to as the "Holland Park Child Terror Mob"—a group of ten or twelve children apparently led by Olivia—had been seen tormenting young Braden on the day before his death. The following morning, Olivia and several others, according to a park attendant, had again pursued young Braden and abused him. The attendant had chased away the gang of older children and advised young Braden to go home; when he had returned to that area of the park, he had found the boy's body lying in a shadowed place beside a wall. Public and police interest shifted from the gang of children when it was learned that young Braden had been sexually injured before his death; and subsequently a vagrant was hanged for his murder.

Two months following the execution of the vagrant, Heather Rudge telephoned the Kensington police station to confess to the murder of her daughter. Police arriving at the house found Olivia stabbed to death in her bed; the coroner later reported more than fifty stab wounds to the body. Mrs. Rudge was immediately taken into custody and hence was protected from the crowd of journalists who wished to harry her—the murder of Olivia Rudge had quickly become a front-page speciality of the scandal press which had soon unearthed the past of Olivia's mother. ("Society Sex Queen Mur-

ders Daughter.'') In time, Heather was convicted of murder and sentenced to death. Later her
sentence was commuted to life in prison.

Certain questions remain. Why did Heather
Rudge kill her daughter? Why was her sentence
commuted? Was there a connection with the
murder, a year previous, of Geoffrey Braden?
Certainly the press had implied such a connection. Newspapers had seized on the case, claiming that Heather Rudge had been driven mad by
her daughter; the more sensational papers as-
serted that Olivia had taunted her mother with
her knowledge of the Braden murder, and that
Heather had decided that her daughter could
not be permitted to live. In time, Heather, now
represented as a victim herself, was found to be
insane by a special examining board. She is at
present an old woman living in the permanent
seclusion of a private mental hospital in Surrey.
The questions remain unanswered. Heather
Rudge will take the secrets of her daughter's
involvement in the Braden case to her grave.
Forgotten by the public, her mind shadowed and
confused, Heather Rudge is a living ghost.

Julia's first thought, after reading this, was an
irrelevance: so that's where those mirrors came
from—Heather Rudge, with her wild parties staffed
with young men, not the proper McClintocks. Then
in the next half second, she knew that she would find
out, that she was compelled to find out, everything
there was to know about Heather and Olivia Rudge.
She read the two pages over again quickly, then
flipped back and read them once more, slowly and
carefully. Eda Rolph nowhere stated directly that
Olivia Rudge had murdered or had helped to

murder the Braden boy: what grounds were there for
the implication? Julia immediately began to think of
how she could discover information about the Rudge
case. Newspapers: surely the British Museum, if not
a branch library, had newspaper files on microfilm.
Could Heather Rudge be living still? She turned to
the first pages of the book to look at the publishing
information. *The Royal Borough of Kensington* had
been published by the Lompoc Press in 1969, five
years ago. She might easily be still alive. ". . . a
private mental hospital in Surrey." How could she
find the name of the hospital? Heather Rudge had
lived in this house, she had slept in this bedroom; in
sleep, her body had occupied the very space Julia's
body now did. Julia seemed to be spinning through
time; time seemed plastic, distorted, unsafe: the past
seemed to rise up all about her, like a foul gas.

Then she sat upright, her heart speeding. Perhaps
Heather Rudge had stabbed Olivia in this very
bedroom. Olivia dying as Kate had died, bleeding as
though blood willed to depart the living body, her
blood foaming out over this spot around a hidden
corner in time. . . . Julia nearly bolted from her
bed.

But it could not be true. This must have been
Heather's bedroom, she thought; her daughter
would have had one of the smaller bedrooms down
the hall. And that was where the murder would have
been done.

Why am I so interested in this, in these people?
Julia thought. Because it will be an explanation.

Julia felt wide-awake, as stimulated as if she'd just
had three cups of strong coffee. She wanted to
telephone Mark, to see Lily—she wanted to telephone Eda Rolph, to ask her the name of the
hospital where Heather Rudge had been kept for the

past twenty-four years. But she is here too, Julia
thought, she is part of the character of this house,
and she lives here still, moving up and down the
stairs, her skirt rustling, turning down a bed,
running to the door to greet a lover or a friend,
locked in the bubble of her time. Every moment
lives parallel with every other moment. What *had*
Miss Pinner seen, to make her faint?

As if in answer, a clicking noise came to her from
downstairs. It was the same noise she had heard
before when, crouching beside the drapes, she had
seen Magnus standing motionless in her garden. It
was the noise of something outside wishing to come
in. Julia realized that, paradoxically, she was now
less afraid of Magnus than she had been before
reading about Heather and Olivia Rudge—Magnus
was flesh, Magnus was blood. All about her moved
intimations of the past of the house, those echoes of
her own past. She lay in bed listening to the soft
rapping at the downstairs windows. Some minutes
later she picked up *The White House Transcripts;* she
read doggedly for two hours, getting through very
nearly half of the book, before she finally fell asleep,
her light still burning. The rapping, patient and
insistent, continued to sound through the house.

Sweating, she dreamed of Kate.

Julia came drowsily awake two hours later feeling
that she had just been touched: no, caressed. Her
light still burned. She reached up to switch it off. The
bedroom was even hotter than it had been when she
had first come in; her entire body seemed filmed
with sweat. The bedroom curtains hung straight and
unmoving; in this room, air refused to circulate, but
piled atop itself, densely. The sky shone through the
window, lighter than the dark of the bedroom. Julia

could still feel, along her bruised left side, the afterimage of a hand, stroking lightly. The caress was gentle, seductively soothing. Of course there was no one else in the room; she had conjured up the caress herself, summoned it up out of her needs.

Julia settled down into the sheets again, deliberately relaxing. The rapping from below had ceased: Magnus had gone home, unable to bring her wandering and calling through the house, having failed at least this once. She closed her eyes and crossed her hands on her midriff. Perhaps Heather Rudge had nursed Olivia in this room, talking to her daughter in baby talk . . . perhaps Mrs. Fludd had seen Heather doing violence to her daughter. Surely such an event still lingers in its physical setting, still reverberating there. . . . Julia's mind began to drift. She heard a snatch of music playing: it was big band music, tinny, as if on a radio, and then it dissolved, along with everything else. She fell immediately into dreams which were indistinguishable from semi-wakefulness. Once again she was being caressed. She was being touched by lingering, stroking hands beside her own hands. Small hands moved lightly down her body. They paused, and began again, stroking. Julia saw Kate beside her: they clasped one another. Kate was with her. The caresses were like music—soft, moving, layered. Julia felt infinitely quietened, infinitely soothed; the small, moving hands were like tongues, lapping at her. She gave herself to this comfort. Broken dreams, fed by these long caresses, filtered through her mind. She and Mark sat side by side on the gray couch, speaking words she could not hear. Mark's hand surrounded hers. She was swimming in warm water, a pool of water as warm as a bath. She wore no bathing suit, and the water slipped about her like oil. Her skin

was opening. She was beneath strong sun. The
flickering touches ran insinuatingly over her opening
body. Mark and Kate: then, shockingly, only Kate.
"*No*," she said, groaning, and her voice brought her
up through sleep. "No." She could still feel the last
touch of the hand, stroking between her thighs: she
felt sickened and frightened, roused. Now she was
absolutely awake.

She had been dreaming of Kate. What horrible
thing had she dreamed? She listened for the sound of
Heather Rudge slipping down the stairs. Now, the
thought of Kate was fearful: Kate, she realized, must
hate her. She was caught in a terrific dislocation, her
body moving toward its resolution, her consciousness stunned by what was logically inexplicable.
Slowly, feeling as though soiled for life, Julia slipped
her hand to the part of her body which needed its
touch, and with hard circular movements of two
fingers brought herself over the edge. She felt like
the unappeased ghost of the living Heather Rudge.
Her body smelled of loss and failure, of airless
exertions.

The next morning, with trembling hands, she
dialed the number Rosa Fludd had left with her. For
the first time in her life, she had taken a drink in the
morning—a smoky, unwatered slug of malt whiskey,
choked down while she was still in her robe. She had
immediately wanted another. The quick explosion of
warmth, intimating relaxation and pointing to an
eventual extinguishing of consciousness, was uncan-
nily like being back in the hospital, seconds after her
morning injection. Now, she thought, I know why
people drink in the morning. It's better than breakfast. She had quickly screwed the top back on the

bottle and gone to the telephone. Beside it was the white card Mrs. Fludd had given her.

She heard the telephone going *brrr brrr* in Mrs. Fludd's white antiseptic flat. It trilled six, then seven times without answer. Was she still there, watched over by her budgerigar and the huge sentimental eyes of the girl in the Keane print? It was imperative that Julia speak to her: what would the old woman have said to her—admitted to her—if Julia had known about Heather and Olivia Rudge last night? On the tenth ring the telephone was answered.

"Yes," said a young woman.

"I'd like to speak to Mrs. Fludd, Rosa Fludd. My name is Julia Lofting."

"Wait a minute." Julia heard muffled voices; the young woman had covered the receiver while turning to speak to someone else in the room.

"My aunt says she can't talk to you."

"Is anything wrong?" Julia asked.

"Anything wrong? You should know. You were one of them brought her home." The girl's accent was so strong that Julia had difficulty distinguishing the words. "You're one of them put her in a state."

"A stite? Oh."

"A *state*. You and them others. You bunch of airyfairies near drove her out of her mind, didn't you? That's not proper, is it? Poor woman don't even take money to jolly you lot along, and. . . ."

Another voice was raised in the background and the hand again clamped over the receiver.

"Tell her I have more information," Julia said. "This is terribly important."

". . . she says she has more information. You sure? You want to?"

In a moment Mrs. Fludd had taken the telephone.

"I'm here," she said. Her voice sounded tightly contained.

"Mrs. Fludd, this is Julia Lofting. Are you all right? I've been worried about you."

"You can't waste your worry," said Mrs. Fludd. "What did you want to tell me?"

"Well, I read, just by accident, a story about my house in a book on Kensington, and I had to tell you what it said. Mrs. Fludd? This house used to be owned by a woman named Heather Rudge, an American, who had a daughter named Olivia. Mrs. Fludd, she stabbed her daughter to death. My own daughter was stabbed to death—my husband wanted to save her life, she was choking to death, and he killed her. The other little girl was killed right in this house more than twenty years ago. Is that what you saw? Is that what Miss Pinner saw in the bathroom?"

"Don't know about Miss Pinner," said Mrs. Fludd.

"Mrs. Fludd, could—could my own daughter be haunting me? Could she try to harm me? Is that what you meant the other night? Did she try to harm *you?* Is my daughter behind this?" Hysteria and tears mounted in her, and she stopped talking to force calm into her voice. "Can't you help me, Mrs. Fludd?"

"Go back to your own country."

"Can't you tell me what you saw?"

"I didn't see anything."

"But you said—a child and a man. Kate and Magnus."

"I saw *nothing*. Miss Pinner is a old fool, and she saw nothing either. Get out of that house, get out of this country. That's all I can tell you."

"Mrs. Fludd, please don't hang up. I've been doing so much thinking—I have so many things to

ask you. How . . . how do people in the past work through people in the present? How do dead people control living people? Is that possible?"

"I told you that," said Mrs. Fludd. "You're wasting my time. Good-bye."

"You said hate or envy," Julia quickly said.

"You remember, then. Sometimes they might want to take something of yours, and to give you something. It helps the malefic spirit. But strong spirits don't need help, Mrs. Lofting. They does what they want to do. I can't talk, Mrs. Lofting. Please leave me alone."

She hung up and Julia kept the telephone pressed to her ear until she heard the dial tone.

She pressed the button, wanting to dial again, but in that instant her instrument shrilly rang. Julia released the button.

"Yes," she said softly.

"I'm going to get you back," came Magnus' deep voice. "You can't get away from me. Do you hear me? Do you hear me, Julia?"

Julia clapped the receiver down. Some figure behind and beside her seemed to move quickly away, just out of the line of her vision, and she whirled around, her breath caught in her throat. No one else was in the room. "Kate," she whispered, "Kate, don't."

When Julia went into the kitchen for a glass of water, she recoiled as soon as she turned on the tap. What gushed from the faucet was a foul brown stream, stinking like ordure. Julia clapped one hand to her mouth, then twisted the knob and shut off the flow. Now it smelled like metal, like coins. After a moment, testingly, she turned it on again: the greasy stuff foamed from the taps. Frantic, Julia again

twisted the knob to make the flow cease. Malvern water from the Safeway, a dozen bottles, ranked beneath the sink, and she took one, pried off the cap, and poured a glassful. It tasted incredibly sweet: drinking it, Julia realized how close she had come to being sick. Even now from the sink rose the stench of that rushing brown fluid, making her stomach contract.

Then she remembered something, brought back by her physical discomfort. The night she had climbed through the bathroom window, she had lost her shoes; they had fallen outside when she had finally pushed herself through the little frame. And out there they had lain, to be found by Magnus: something taken, something given, Mrs. Fludd had said. Nearly everything she owned had been given her by Magnus. She wore his ring; he had bought earrings, pendants, beads, clothing for her. Julia would nearly have to walk naked to divest herself of everything given her by Magnus.

But how long had those shoes lain outside? Three nights and two days. They might still be below the bathroom window. Julia ran out of the kitchen into the hall and down the hall to the bathroom. Reflected in the rose mirrors, she threw the rod off its ratchet and lifted the window out. On tiptoe, she leaned forward, holding the window with her left hand, and put her head out. She looked down at broken white and yellow flowers, some snapped off at their stalks, others trodden into the soft dirt. She could not see her shoes. Julia leaned farther out of the window—she leaned forward as far as she could go. Still she could not see the shoes. They were gone: someone had taken them. It seemed like a proof. A girl and a man. They wished to do her harm.

For some moments Julia thrashed back and forth in the bathroom, out of control. She knew she was making some low, dreadful noise; the noise could not be stopped, and it echoed within the mirrored room, bouncing back and forth like her body. *I have to stop this,* she told herself, and forced herself to sit on the floor. The noise came out in hiccoughs and then concentrated itself in her throat, where she could stop it. When she became aware that she had been drooling, she wiped her mouth.

She looked dumbly around the bathroom. She was sitting, glassy-eyed, her mouth open, near the tub: her face in the rose mirrors looked slack, exotic. Magnus had taken the shoes.

Julia unsteadily rose, gripping the sink with both hands. Within it, the seersucker dress still lay in an orangey-brown pool. She could still see the blood-stain; it seemed to have got larger. Now it appeared to be several inches long. Julia tore the dress out of the sink, pulled the plug, and squeezed the soaked material while the discolored, odorous water was sucked away.

She was not really thinking. She knew that she had to destroy the blue dress, and the knowledge instantly became action, bypassing thought. She had to burn the dress.

Julia carried the dress through to the kitchen where she picked up matches and then continued on to the fireplace in the living room. She dropped the dress onto the grate and applied a lighted match to a dry corner of fabric. The dress did not light. Julia lit a second match and held it to the same point; this time, the thin material flared up, crumpling and darkening beneath the spreading corner of flame. An acrid odor spread into the living room, followed by smoke. About half the dress burned before the

flames guttered out on sodden material. The room
stank of charred fabric—it was the smell of burning
fur. Julia scarcely noticed this stench. She tried
holding matches beneath the wet remaining half of
the dress, but the fabric merely blackened, still wet.

Then she saw the morning's *Guardian* on a table
near the couch and moved across the room to get it.
She shook four pages loose, and stuffed them
beneath the dress in the grate. When she picked up
the sodden lump of dress, ashes and soot clinging to
it, she saw the large, rust-colored bloodstain leading
out from the seam. She thrust papers over the dress
and tossed matches into them. Greasy yellowish
smoke boiled out from beneath the papers. Julia
threw match after match onto the smouldering
newspaper, but the damp fabric would not burn. Her
hands were black with ash.

Abandoning the effort to burn the dress, Julia
went into the kitchen for one of the big black plastic
garbage bags, which she flipped open and carried
back to the fireplace. Using the small ornamental
shovel, she scooped the mess of ashes and charred
spongy fabric into the mouth of the bag. She then
twisted it shut and carried it outside into the path
beside the house.

Sunlight and warmth surprised her. The past half
hour—hour?—seemed to have been visited upon
her. She had been dominated by an urgent, thoughtless revulsion she had been unable to resist. Julia felt
her pulse slow; she became aware of sensation again,
the light defining a million blades of grass, the sun's
warmth penetrating her hair. Julia began to breathe
more regularly, suddenly conscious that she had
been panting. That *thing* in the black bag: she had
had to destroy it as though it were alive. Now,
grasping the neck of the bag, she felt all of her

revulsion once more and thrust it into the bin and clapped the lid over it. Big smudges of ash dirtied her quilted robe. Other smears of ash covered her legs. Julia felt as though she had just run a race.

Magnus: she had lost all reasoning consciousness when he had appeared, as if by evil magic, on the telephone. Now she could not even remember his words, but she remembered their import. They had been threatening. He had her shoes. She flew back into the warm confines of her house.

Twenty minutes later, another visitation: this young woman standing before her, a neighbor, living in Number 23, the house next door. Smaller than Julia, her hair nearly as short as Lily's, a creamy, shy, smiling face only just beginning to show wrinkles. Her name, Hazel Mullineaux. From the woman's first words ("I don't know if I should bother you now"), Julia suffered from an acute awareness of her smudged robe and blackened hands. Her face too— from Mrs. Mullineaux's glances at her cheeks and forehead, Julia knew she was a patchwork of filth. She hid her hands behind her back.

"You seem so busy that I don't know if I should take up your time like this." A smile.

Julia, bent on appearing normal, did not think to invite this hesitant young woman inside. "Oh, I have all the time in the world," she said, and then cursed herself for overstatement.

"It's just that we thought we should ask. We thought you should know," she amended, and then gave a further amendment. "And of course we wanted to meet our new neighbor."

"Thank you."

"I didn't really catch your name, I'm sorry."

She had not given it. "I'm Julia Lofting."

Hazel Mullineaux peered past Julia to see the interior. "You are a Canadian? I'm trying to catch the accent. . . ."

"I'm American," Julia said. "But I've lived here a long time."

"That explains why it isn't so broad."

"Oh," Julia said, "I never think about it at all, it's changing all the time, I guess. My husband used to say that I sounded like an Iowa farmhand, and I've never been in Iowa in my life, but then neither was he." She babbled, smelling the reek the burning dress had made: for ten minutes, she had fanned a newspaper in the living room, but the smell hung on, as though she had burned a cat.

Mrs. Mullineaux seemed disconcerted by this chatter about Iowa. "Well, as I said, we thought you should know about it. Last night my husband saw a man standing outside your house."

Julia froze. "What time was that?"

"At ten, when he came home from his office. Like all publishers, he works too late. Then at ten thirty he happened to look out the window, and he saw you going into your house and the man was still there. Perry said he didn't look like a criminal, but he had moved further down the block and was beside the tree in front of number seventeen, the Armbrusters' house. Perry was curious, so he kept watching the man, and after you'd gone in, he began to come up the block toward your house again. Then he just stood across the street and watched the house. Perry said he stood there for at least an hour. Of course, there's no law against looking at a person's house, but it did seem odd. He asked me if I thought he should have telephoned the police. I said I would speak to you about it. In case he returns. I

hope you don't think we have been prying into your—circumstances."

"No, oh, no," Julia said. Now she could smell the burned-cat odor all too definitely, and she saw that Hazel Mullineaux also had caught it: the creamy little woman looked at her oddly, and moved a step backward. "I've been doing some cleaning," Julia said. "I know I'm a mess."

"Yes. I mean, no, of course not. But *as* this man seemed to hang about so long, I did want to tell you. I hope you don't think we did wrong not to ring the police."

"It was my husband," said Julia. "I think he's watching me. I know he is."

"Watching . . . ?" Hazel Mullineaux's face expressed a perfect incomprehension.

"He doesn't live here," Julia supplied, feeling herself slip into a bog of explanations and not knowing how to avoid it. "You see, I bought this house for myself. I can't see him—he's been bothering me, making telephone calls. I think he broke in here one night. . . ."

Mrs. Mullineaux now radiated shock and disapproval.

"Oh, please, I want us to be friends," Julia said. "Neighbors should be friends, don't you think? I haven't even invited you in. Would you like a cup of coffee? You were so kind to tell me what you saw. I don't know if the police should be called or not. I don't know if there's any danger. . . . Everything's gotten so confused in the past couple of days, it's because of Kate, our daughter, I mean late daughter. . . . Really, I'm terrified of him, but I don't think I should call the police, it's not a story they'd understand. But thank your husband for me,

for worrying about me, that was a friendly act. . . ."
She looked at Hazel Mullineaux's rather dazed
expression. "Won't you come in for a cup of coffee?
I'll have to air out the living room to get rid of that
terrible smell, but we could sit in the kitchen, or
even in the back garden."

"I can't right now, thanks," said the other woman.
She was already moving down the steps. "Some
other time."

"Oh, I have to ask you," Julia said before the
other woman could get away. "Did you know the
people who used to live here?"

"Of course we knew the McClintocks," said Mrs.
Mullineaux. "They were older, and a bit remote, but
quite nice, really."

"No, not the McClintocks," Julia broke in. "I
mean the ones before them. Mrs. Rudge. Heather
Rudge. She had a daughter."

"Before the McClintocks? We moved here in
1967, and the McClintocks had been here for twenty
years, we thought."

"Yes, of course. Of course. You couldn't possibly
have known her."

Mrs. Mullineaux turned away, went down the
steps, and before walking down the pavement to her
house, looked back at Julia. Her face twitched into a
grimace approximating a smile.

That woman thinks I'm crazy, Julia thought. And
then she thought of Magnus, patrolling the street.
He had rapped at the dining room window for hours
last night—Magnus was trying to push her over the
precipice. She wanted Mark's easy presence, Mark's
careless masculinity: he was a talisman against
Magnus. Even Lily could not be trusted to save her
from Magnus. She heard Hazel Mullineaux slam her

front door. Against that, too, Mark would stand as protection.

"I think you need help, darling. You're under so much pressure, and I can't blame you for being apprehensive, even suspicious."

"Apprehensive, Lily? Of course I'm apprehensive. That performance the other night put me right at ease. . . ."

"That's *just* what I mean. I rang poor dear Mrs. Fludd this noon, and the telephone just kept ringing. She never goes out, never, except for her sessions. Something terrible has happened, I'm sure. I can't help it, I'm worried for the old dear."

"Well, I'm worried for myself. Magnus was seen loitering outside the house last night. I'm sure he broke in here two nights ago. He's trying to drive me back to him. He's out of his mind, and I think I might be too. Do you want to know what I think? I think Kate is punishing me. It's what Mrs. Fludd said—a man and a girl. Kate is in Magnus' mind. Sometimes she's in this house too, and she hates me. She believes Magnus' lies."

"Oh, darling. . . ."

"You want him for yourself, don't you? You want Mark for yourself too. You'd like Magnus to think I'm going crazy. I suppose you'll call him right now and tell him what I said, but you won't get him because he's probably hanging around here, watching the house."

"Julia, you can't think that of me. . . ."

"You called him. You broke your word."

"Because I wanted you to be back with him."

"But you do want him for yourself, don't you? And Mark."

"Julia, this does us no good. That is terribly unfair. Please listen, Julia. Kate has no reason to hate you, nothing you did was meant to injure her. You were brave."

"Magnus killed Kate. Magnus hates me for leaving him, and now Kate hates me. Mrs. Fludd saw them."

"Julia, why don't you come over here so we can talk about that day? Please come over. That's at the bottom of everything. . . ."

"What do you mean by that? What are you trying to get me to say?"

"Nothing, Julia, nothing. I just thought that talking about it would do you good—if not to Magnus then at least to me—but if you're not ready yet, that's fine. I still think you should come over and stay with me for a few days so. . . ."

Julia had a sudden, clear vision of a man in a white jacket jabbing a hypodermic into her arm.

"Good-bye, Lily. Sorry."

She hung up, trembling so severely the receiver rattled out of the cradle and fell to the floor. She had to get out of the house.

Julia ran upstairs to her bedroom and threw off the filthy robe; in her bathroom, she hurriedly showered, avoiding looking at herself as much as she could avoid it, afraid that a glance into the mirrors would show a slight figure just flickering from her sight. The telephone began to ring as she was toweling herself, and Julia let the bell shrill, counting the number of rings. After twenty, it stopped. She continued dressing, deliberately not thinking of what Lily had said to her. She thought, instead, with longing of more books—of buying books—of slipping into a narrative of other people's lives. *That* was release.

It led her, as she went rapidly along Kensington High Street twenty minutes later, her damp hair adhering to her neck, to sudden, vivid memories of her girlhood: of summers at their home in New Hampshire, where it had been as warm as this every day. Her great-grandfather had bought the estate after he had retired from the board of his railroad company, having made several hundred million dollars in the boom; the soil itself, the texture of the air had seemed different there, wholly, innocently absorbed into her family's life. For an instant, Julia ached to be back in America. She stood on Kensington High Street, between a package store and W. H. Smith's, the sound of car horns dividing the air, and was transfixed by the particular memory of a New Hampshire valley. And beyond the valley, the endless innocent unrolling of the continent: but it was not like that any more, she knew. It was her own past for which she had ached. Yet there lay in her an undigested yearning for the visionary and fruitful continent; her childhood, it seemed to her, had been spent there. She turned into W. H. Smith's and bought a fat paperback of *Gravity's Rainbow*.

Toting the book, Julia passed through the crowds on the High Street. It really was as hot as New Hampshire in August. She debated walking up Kensington Church Street to Notting Hill Gate, to see if Mark were home. She remembered his address, and thought she knew where the flat was; it was on one of the long curved streets, Pembridge something, intercepting Notting Hill Gate, one of the streets lined with large houses now broken up into bed-sitting-rooms and two-room flats. Mark's was a "garden flat": it was in the basement. She imagined a flight of steep steps down from the pavement into a dank lightless room—the vision was

enough to turn her back to Holland Park, where she could lie in the sun. She did not feel ready, yet, to visit Mark's flat. To go there unbidden would entail a chain of consequences of which she was a little apprehensive.

As she walked along past the row of shops, Julia scanned the crowds for a glimpse of Magnus. He could easily be facing a window, unseen, tailing after her; certainly she had to assume that Magnus had taken to such tactics. Or, even more unsettling, perhaps he was now forcing his way into her house. But she could not rush back to inspect the house, she would never catch him there, she was sure of that. Still, Julia could not rid herself of the image of Magnus hovering behind her. In front of the long piazza of the Commonwealth Institute, she whirled around quickly, and caught a priest in the stomach with her elbow. While they each apologized, they recognized one another as Americans; the priest, a neat dark man with a witty face, looked at her oddly as they swapped pleasantries. She could only surmise that he was responding to something in her own manner or regard. What was wrong with her, that even a pleasant stranger found her peculiar? Julia brought one hand up to wipe her forehead and saw the hand tremble. Her forehead dripped sweat. "It's nothing," she said to the priest. "Just anxiety. I'm a normal person. I don't usually punch men in the stomach."

She turned up into Holland Park. The paths were crowded, and every five feet of ground supported a new body. A pack of children ran squealing on the long sward, breaking apart into pinwheeling clusters and then, clamoring, reforming. Boys in jeans, girls in long filmy dresses, girls in jeans, Germans strapped into cameras and expensive clothes. She

skirted a party of twenty Japanese, singing to one
another. A young couple directly before her exchanged a long kiss while the boy rubbed and
kneaded the girl's buttocks, uncaring of the crowds.
Julia felt a hot, direct physical pang until she saw the
American priest, walking quickly up ahead without
looking back. She deliberately thrust down the
memory of her last night's dream and its aftermath.
Without purpose, she began to drift after the
American priest. The book felt very heavy in her
hand.

The priest turned off the main path to enter the
smaller walk which, Julia recalled, passed the area
where peacocks and other birds strutted beneath
dark trees. Julia followed, watching the black suit as
if it held a meaning. The priest paused to look at the
peacocks for a second and then continued walking
toward the woods which circled the top half of the
park. He strode along briskly, and soon was disappearing around a corner into the sparse woods.
Three women pushing baby carriages, accompanied
by a single man carrying an open winebottle, crossed
before Julia, and the priest was gone from sight.
Then she saw Magnus.

He was sitting on a bench, not looking at her. He
looked very tired. Julia froze; she took two cautious
steps backward, and then turned around, the vision
of Magnus in a light-gray suit, bending forward, his
face rumpled, burning into her: if he turned his
head, he would see her. At first she took light quick
steps, gliding up the path; when she passed around
the bend, she moved more slowly until she dared to
look over her shoulder. He had not followed her.
Julia looked across the park—an exit lay ahead to
her right, just before Plane Tree House. She would
circle the park to get home. Julia trotted down the

path, ignoring the stares of men she met, setting her face.

There was no longer any question of staying in the park to read her book: she had to get home and lock the door. But just before she reached the final stage of the path to the side gate, she saw the tiny black girl who had been in the park that first day. The girl was staring up at her just as she had that day.

"Hello, Mona," Julia said. "Do you remember me?"

"Poo," said Mona, smiling open-mouthed at Julia. Her eyes shone.

"That's not a nice word."

"Poo. Shit." Mona giggled and turned away. "Fuck you."

Julia stared at the tiny girl.

"Fuck you. Shit. Fuck."

"What. . . ." Julia turned and found herself looking into the face of the little blond girl. She was touching a bicycle which was leaning against the fence bordering the park, and she was looking straight into Julia's face. No other children were near; the closest people were a man and a woman twenty yards away, asleep on the grass with their faces to the sun. About Julia and the blond girl a charged timeless vacuum seemed to exist. The child wore curiously old-fashioned denim trousers, with a high elastic waist and floppy legs. The resemblance to Kate made Julia's heart pulse with fear. They stood looking at each other, not speaking; Julia had nearly the sense that the girl had been waiting for her in this secluded place.

Then the girl smiled, and her resemblance to Kate vanished. One of her front teeth had been broken in half, chipped away in a rising arc which left her smile uncentered and asymmetrical.

"Who are you?" Julia said.

The girl's smile tightened in a curiously adult, challenging way. Her joined hands moved, or something in them moved. When Julia looked at her hands, she saw that the girl was not actually touching the bicycle, but holding her hands near the rear wheel. It took her a moment to see what the girl held captured between her cupped palms. Only when the small brown creature quivered did Julia see that it was a bird.

"Is that bird injured?" Julia asked.

The child made no response, but continued to stare at Julia, smiling her adult, unbalanced smile. The whole being of the child seemed hurtled together, compacted.

In one quick sure movement the girl thrust the bird into the wheel of the bicycle, jamming it securely between the spokes and the metal rods which held the mudguards to the wheel. The scene printed itself with utter clarity on Julia's mind: as in the second before some foreknown disaster, time seemed as fixed as the girl's smile. Julia stared at the bird, the instant before the girl jerked the bicycle forward—it was held between the two metal rods, not in the wheel as she had first supposed. Its body projected through the spokes.

"Don't . . . no . . ." she stammered.

The girl jerked the bicycle and the bird instantly became a pulp of bloody feathers. Its head fell softly to the ground.

Julia snapped her head up to look at the girl, who was now mounting her bicycle. She did not immediately ride away but straddled the bike, intently staring at Julia.

Julia opened her mouth to speak, but caught sight of the bird's head lying with open eyes beside the

rear wheel, and felt her stomach irresistibly begin to draw itself upward. She turned away and vomited into the dust.

When she had finished, the girl was no longer beside her. The bicycle was rolling away through the gate, the girl pedaling slowly and unconcernedly; soon she had slipped into crowds and traffic.

Julia took a step and found that her knees shook: she forced herself to run. Heedless of Magnus, she raced directly toward her home, her mouth open, her body jouncing, her breath straining at her ribs. She flew across the green, narrowly missing the curious who parted to let her pass, and into the path which curved around past the children's play area. By then her mouth had turned to cotton and her side felt pierced by swords.

She came racing around the corner of Ilchester Place and stumbled to a walk. Her breath dragging in her, face pumping with blood, she went up the three steps to her walk. The house seemed impassive, unwelcoming; she wanted no more than to fall into her bed and close out the whole world in sleep. The book in her hand seemed to have tripled in weight.

When Julia reached her front door she felt in her pocket and touched a used paper tissue, an earring with the pin broken, a loose mint, two small coins. The key, she remembered, lay at the bottom of her bag, on a counter in the kitchen. Her knees seemed to disappear altogether. Her body pitched into the springy grass. Before her eyes went shut, she saw the creamy startled face of Hazel Mullineaux staring at her through a side window of Number 23.

The old woman sat up in her narrow bed; a long, white page of moonlight lay folded at the juncture of

wall and floor. Pulling her gently from sleep, a low voice had uttered her name repeatedly, lightly, as if teasing her. It came again, this time from a greater distance, somewhere else in the house. The woman did not want to follow the voice; she clung to the sheets, resisting. But she knew that she could not resist long. The voice was cool water, long blue slices of water she needed. The weak muscles in her arms began to tremble. And she knew who it was. Her tongue dryly scraped her teeth. Her name issued teasingly from the hallway. At last her body ceased to strain. Without her guidance, the woman's arms parted the upper sheet from her body and folded it back. Her legs swung over the edge of the bed.

She rose on unsteady legs which knew where to take her. The voice seemed the only thing in her mind. Her feet found her low shoes and slipped within them. She moved out of the hallway and saw the open door. Just outside, luminous in yellow light, stood her visitor, calling.

The woman moved down the hall. Knowledge lay ahead, knowledge and peace. Her hand moved to grasp the heavy tweed coat as she passed the coat hooks. Silly hand; silly coat; not needed. It was only to cover her nightdress. She pulled it across the bulge of her belly and fastened the single button.

Teasing, gentle, the visitor waited. Seductive— extraordinarily seductive. The woman padded toward the door, then passed through it into a wide familiar space.

The visitor moved quickly, walking backward, beckoning. White light on hair, on the beckoning backs of hands. All about the visitor was indistinct and hazy. Other voices filtered to her, but she did not turn her head.

The teasing voice was the last thing she heard.

Part Two

The Search: Heather

5

"I almost understood everything," Julia said. "I was lying in bed, reading that book you gave me, and when I came to the bit about Heather and Olivia Rudge, I knew that I was getting close to understanding what's been happening to me—because I *haven't* just been making it up, Lily. It was all mixed up with Kate and a little girl I saw before I fainted—I was so close, I had this amazing rush of energy and I almost called you, I had so many ideas. There's something about the house that Mrs. Fludd saw, and it's important because of what Magnus did to Kate. Somehow, the energy in this house is focused on me because of that. Mrs. Fludd *knew* she was in danger, and she said I was too. Doesn't that convince you I'm not just making it all up?"

There was a long pause on the line while Lily balanced the effects of several statements. Finally she said, "Darling, Mrs. Fludd was killed in an accident. It was a hit and run, very near her house. Apparently she just wandered out into the traffic on the Mile End Road, and the car was gone before anybody knew what had happened. It's always best to look for a reasonable, rational explanation before . . . before deciding on the other."

"I know. But some things don't have rational explanations."

"Darling, there is nothing supernatural about a hit and run. As tragic as it is."

"Evil isn't rational. Lily, I know that something hates me—something in this house. Mrs. Fludd felt it too—it's what she kept saying to me. I was so close to understanding everything that night I read about the Rudges. I almost broke through—I had all of these thoughts and ideas—I could feel the past all around me. The past is *in this house*. Don't you see that I'm connected to that story? Because of Kate? It's the key to everything."

"Well, as to the key to everything," Lily began, and then stopped. She had promised Magnus (they had worked it out together, with some strong advice from Julia's doctor) that she would not lead Julia into that territory; if Julia were ever to admit the truth about Kate's death, she would have to come to it herself. So she finished her sentence by saying, "I think it is in your state of mind." Immediately she regretted her choice of words.

"My state of mind? That's nice of you, Lily. Thanks."

"I didn't mean that the way it sounded. That's the truth, my dear."

"I can't believe that you of all people won't even discuss the possibility that something out of the ordinary is happening. Lily, if Mrs. Fludd saw something or felt something, as she did, isn't that just in your line? Isn't that just the sort of thing you *do* accept?"

"Only under the proper circumstances, Julia. You know I have a firm belief in the supernatural, but. . . ."

"And how about Heather and Olivia Rudge? Lily, there are no accidents. *There are no accidents*. These things have been happening to me for a reason.

Maybe it takes a coincidence to set it off, maybe
there's some kind of plan, I don't know, but I've
been doing a lot of looking into the Rudge case for
the past few days, and I'm sure that's the direction I
have to go. I found out the name of the clinic where
Heather Rudge has been kept, the Breadlands
Clinic, and I wrote to her, asking if I could see her."

"How did you find it?"

"It was in an old copy of the *Times*. My neighbor,
Perry Mullineaux, got me a reader's ticket for the
British Museum's periodical collection, and I've
spent the past three days going through old newspapers. Remember telling me that I needed some
interest? Well, I've sure got it. I tell you, sometimes
I almost see the two of them, I can feel them all
around me in this house—I hear the music they
listened to, sometimes I think they've just left a
room the moment before I entered it—did you know
about the heaters? I kept turning them off without
ever turning them on, someone else was doing that, I
thought Magnus, but eventually the only room
where it happened was my bedroom and I taped the
switch to the wall and the heater still wouldn't go off.
So I cut the wires, and the thing still stays hot. That's
just a small thing I know, but then there was that
bloodstain on my blue seersucker that wouldn't go
away and kept getting bigger, there are the flashes of
someone I keep seeing in the mirrors and the way
the water has been getting so foul, it simply reeks,
it's like shit, like diarrhea but full of *money,* sometimes it smells like greasy old American pennies, I
haven't taken a real bath in a week. Then there are
the noises and the whole general feel of the house—
it wants me here, but it doesn't like me. Lily, why
did I buy this house? *This* house? Don't you think I
have a right to find out? That's why Mrs. Fludd was

killed, it's horrible, it's awful, that intelligent old woman was killed to keep me from knowing too soon. I'm going to see Heather Rudge, and I'm going to find everyone I can who knew Olivia—I keep seeing signs of evil in children, not just malevolence but real evil, Lily. Kate's behind all this, she's evil now she's dead and I have to work at it, I have to see what I can do, it's so unfair. . . ."

"Julia," Lily said when Julia's voice had broken down into a series of excited hiccoughs, "I want you to move over here with me. I don't think you should be on your own."

"I can't leave. Everything I'm interested in is here."

"Julia, have you been drinking?"

"Not much. Why? It doesn't matter. Magnus drinks."

"I want you to come to stay with me, Julia."

"That's funny, everybody wants me to live with them. I'm very popular with the entire Lofting family. I can't tell you how wanted that makes me feel."

"Are you sleeping?"

"I don't need sleep anymore. I'm too excited to sleep. Well, I suppose I get a couple of hours a night. I've been having the most amazing dreams—I keep dreaming about that girl I saw in Holland Park. She's a sort of metaphor for Kate, I guess. She seems totally without any redeeming virtues."

"Julia, guilt shouldn't. . . ."

"I have no guilt. I leave that to your brother."

Julia hung up.

Worried, Lily took her watering can into her efficient little kitchen and filled it at the tap. She carried the can out onto the terrace and began to sprinkle water over the flowers, which had lately

showed the effects of the past month of hot dry
days—particularly intense weather for a London
summer. Eventually the weather would break, she
supposed. Lily's clearest memory of such a long spell
of hot weather was a summer more than twenty
years before; she remembered it because that had
been the year Magnus bought the house on Gayton
Road. He had not been so fat then, and he had told
her that he liked to go on Hampstead Heath and
take off his shirt. One day she had met him in
Gayton Road and walked over the Heath with him;
in a green sloping vale Magnus had removed his shirt
and fallen asleep in the sun. He had looked enormous, hieratic to her, his big pink trunk and
massive, handsome head against the brilliant green
of the grass. Lily had watched him for an hour,
admiring how even in sleep Magnus seemed more
powerful, more authoritative than other men. Of
course, he was cruel, though not to her. "Magnim,"
she had said, stroking one of his bristling
eyebrows—it was his name in their private language.
She had been happy that he had women, but equally
happy that he seemed incapable of marriage. Lily, in
those days, had thought that most women would
know better than to desire marriage with Magnus.

Julia had been a shock: at that time, an innocent,
radiant girl with beautiful hair and a modest manner
absurdly at variance with her general air of healthi-
ness, she had been eminently the type of girl Magnus
seduced (physically, she was rather an American
Sonia Mitchell-Mitchie, then Hoxton), but far from
the kind of woman he might reasonably have
married. Lily had for some reason always thought
that were Magnus to marry he would take a woman
older than himself. "It's her Burne-Jones eyes,"
Mark had suggested—poor envious Mark would

have wanted any woman Magnus claimed as his own, even if she had looked like Mrs. Pankhurst. Later she had discovered the extent of Julia's wealth, and Magnus' marriage had become far more comprehensible.

But not for years did it become less painful. Really, Kate had helped with that reconciliation, had perhaps effected it, since Magnus, while altering little in other ways, had revealed a surprising capacity for fatherhood. He had loved Kate so deeply that Lily could not herself do otherwise; and eventually she and Julia had become friends. That Julia from the beginning had wished for that friendship encouraged it; but perhaps the change had begun when Lily arrived one morning to find a nursing Julia reading not a baby manual but *Middlemarch*. Julia might have been absurdly young, almost too wealthy, but at least she had good taste in fiction. Eventually, Lily had given her some volumes on the occult—books recommended by Mr. Carmen and Miss Pinner—and had been pleased that Julia had read them carefully. (Though she had thought more of Mr. Carmen's Roheim and Mircea Eliade than Miss Pinner's books on astral projection.) Later, she had more reason to be grateful for Julia, though Julia was unaware of it, for she had purchased the flat in Plane Tree House largely with money allotted to her by Magnus from his joint account. And she knew without asking that it was Julia's money which paid for most of Magnus' expensive presents to her.

The main thing, Lily thought, was to get Julia back with Magnus—never mind how much money was lost on the house and its contents. Both of them needed healing. Lily knew perfectly well that she was at times jealous of Magnus simply because he

was a man, and jealous of Julia because she had
come between herself and her brother as even Mark
had never done, but it was in everyone's interest that
they begin to knit themselves together again. Magnus, this past week, had been worse than Lily had
ever seen him. Sometimes he did seem almost to
hate Julia—though, proud as he was, he needed no
supernatural assistance in that—while he desperately wanted her cured, wanted her back.

And Julia needed Magnus far more than he
needed her. She had begun to look shockingly weak
and ill. Her marvelous hair had gone dull and limp,
and her face soft and pouchy. Sometimes she
seemed hardly to be listening to what you said to
her. Julia was running on sheer nervous energy. It
was no surprise that she saw evil children everywhere or that she had built up a sick fantasy about
Kate.

And now this obsession with the Rudge case,
which was perfectly explicable in the light of what
Julia was determinedly repressing. Lily imagined
Julia in a reading room, flipping crazily through old
newspapers, making mad notes—she must look like
Ophelia floating downstream on a sea of newsprint.

I have a duty to Julia and to myself, Lily thought.
When she had finished watering the plants she put
the can down on her terrace and went inside to
telephone Magnus.

Most importantly, she had to keep Julia from
Mark. There was something missing in Mark, a
moral space filled by his resentment of Magnus. Lily
knew that Mark would miss no opportunity to
humiliate Magnus. Julia, now weakened and perhaps hysterical, would be more open to Mark's
entreaties than she had ever been. That must be
blocked.

She first dialed Gayton Road. When there was no answer, she tried his chambers, where a secretary had not seen him all day and had been told not to expect him. She knew what that meant. Lily went down a list of his drinking clubs, and finally reached him at the Marie Lloyd, a certain sign of trouble. Once at the Marie Lloyd, the least prepossessing of all the little clubs he patronized all over the city, he began looking for a fight—he had once knocked down a truck driver outside the club who had sneered at him. She had to carefully judge the state of his intoxication, and calibrate her statements to it. Magnus' spy, she also saw herself as Magnus' protector. From his first words, she knew that it would be dangerous to irritate him, and so Lily omitted from her account of her conversation with Julia most of the material about the Rudges.

"Yes, she's much better," she said. "I think she fainted from exhaustion, and she's been getting some rest. She has a project she wants to begin working on, and that will help her fill her time. It seems harmless enough. Magnus, you must not go to that house anymore. That is absolutely the wrong tactic."

"Were you there when she fainted? Did you see her?" This meant, Lily knew, that Magnus wished to ignore her advice.

"A neighbor saw her faint," Lily said. Now was not the time to inform Magnus that Mark had come along moments later. "Someone got word to me, and we helped her get inside. She'd locked herself out, but the French windows at the back were unlatched and we helped her in that way."

"Those damned windows are always open," Magnus grumbled. "I'm going to go down and see her. Take her home."

"I wouldn't," Lily hastily said. "In her frame of mind that would only hurt things."

"Bugger that."

"I think you should go home. I think you should let things go their own way for a few days, my love, until she has settled down a bit more. She's a terribly confused girl."

"She looks like hell," Magnus said. "I saw her. But who isn't confused?"

"Magnus, before long she will have to face what really happened to Kate. I know it is dreadfully unfair to you that she blames you for what happened, and my dear, I feel your pain, but I do think now that the best thing for you would be to go straight home and perhaps telephone her later and try to speak calmly to her. I'm certain that is the best tactic, in the long run."

"I have the feeling you're hiding something from me, Lily."

"No. I am not."

"What's this project?" Magnus belched loudly. "Christ, I have to pee. What's this project she's working on?"

"I gather it has something to do with that house she's taken."

"Christ," Magnus said and brutally rang off.

Julia, hanging up the telephone, still kept her mood of excited elation. This had little to do with liquor, despite Lily's implication, for she had only sipped at a watered whiskey during the afternoon after her return from the periodical collection in Colindale. Yet the feeling was akin to that of one stage of drunkenness—an optimistic, impulsive sense that wheels had begun to move, that a resolution was near. She had no doubt that this

would have a connection with the Rudges: the Rudges were to help her exorcise Kate, help her finally lay Kate to rest. How this was to happen she did not know, but she felt a certainty that it would happen. In any case, she no longer had any choice—she was driven to discover the truth about Olivia Rudge.

The old copies of the *Times* and the *Evening Standard* she had read had convinced her of at least one thing. Olivia Rudge had been psychotic. One member of her group, the gang of children in Holland Park, had been anonymously quoted as saying that Olivia was "bent"; even a detached reporter had called her "disturbing." If Julia could determine the truth about the murder of young Geoffrey Braden, perhaps that would appease Kate. Wasn't proof of that the extraordinary change in her mood since she had read those pages in *The Royal Borough of Kensington*? She still had trouble focusing her mind on remembering what she was supposed to do from one moment to the next, but she felt as though she were riding a great wave, borne along on it resistlessly. She burned her dinners, left half-filled cups of coffee all over the house, but since she had thought to ask Perry Mullineaux to help her get a reader's card, she had one great sustaining purpose—even Magnus had receded in importance. Let him skulk about the neighborhood; he was merely in the present; he had no connection with what mattered.

Turning, still pleased with herself for her parting shot at Lily, vaguely toward the dining room and the doors to the garden, Julia reminded herself of an idea she'd had at the end of her day's stint at the library. Before she talked to Heather Rudge—she had no doubt that she would hear from her—she

would look through old copies of *The Tatler*. Surely, in the hostessy period of her life, she had been photographed for that magazine; there might even be pictures of her parties.

Then she remembered something Mark had said when he had appeared, as if by sympathetic magic, at her side when she had fainted. She had come conscious to find herself cradled by Hazel Mullineaux, Mark holding her hand. Even then, groggy and confused, she had been aware that Mrs. Mullineaux was not blind to Mark's appearance, and she had tried to fight her way upright into parity. Mark had taken her hand more firmly and said to Hazel Mullineaux, "I don't know who you are, but as you're being so kind, do you think you could go across the park to fetch Julia's sister-in-law, Lily Lofting?" He gave her Lily's address and said he'd "stay on" to watch over Julia—a little bemused, but glad to be of use, Hazel had left them.

"That was neat, don't you think?" asked Mark.

"Do women always do what you tell them?"

"Nearly always. They're usually thoughtful enough not to terrify me, too. I thought you were about to live up to your mortuary eyes. Like that Burne-Jones girl at the Tate you've always reminded me of."

"Mortuary eyes? Burne-Jones? What are you going on about? I feel better already." Julia straightened up, her grogginess nearly gone.

"The girl in *King Cophetua and the Beggar Maid*. Same eyes. I noticed it years ago, when I first met you. What brought on this fit?"

Then she had told him about the blond girl in the park, rushing to finish the story before Lily's arrival. The incident was so private that, at least then, it could be shared only with Mark.

Julia threw some things in her bag and rushed out of the house just as a taxi appeared at the far corner of Ilchester Place. When it came near she hailed it and told the driver, "The Tate Gallery, please." Better than driving: she felt too excited to trust herself to the Rover.

When the taxi pulled up before the Tate she gave the driver a pound note and went quickly up the gray stone steps, passing the usual crowds of tourists, and went through the entrance and turnstiles. She said to a guard, "Could you tell me where to find the Pre-Raphaelites? I'm looking for a specific painting. A Burne-Jones."

The man gave her detailed directions, and she went down the stairs and eventually turned into the room the man had indicated. She saw the painting immediately. The girl sat, backed by a cushion, on a long shelf, shyly holding some flowers; the King, seated on gold beneath her, gazed up. She did look like the girl Burne-Jones had painted. Mortuary eyes. Were hers so round? But the King: the King, but for his short sharp beard, was Mark. She gasped with pleasure. Julia stood before the painting for ten minutes, and then, still looking at it, moved to a bench where she could sit and keep looking at it. The little room endured several waves of spectators, swelling in, circling, and then draining out again. Julia shifted her place on the bench whenever her view of the painting was blocked. Eventually, alone in the room once again, she silently began to cry.

She had Mark—at least she had Mark. Both of them were Magnus' victims. Mark's phrase encapsulated the futile history of her marriage; she did not know if she were crying for her nine wasted years or for relief that Mark, however slightly, had shown her a way out of them.

Mark, Mark.

When the next dribbling of strangers entered the room, Julia dabbed at her eyes and went up the stairs back through galleries to the entrance. She walked outside into warmth and light and the noises of automobiles, went down the stone steps, crossed the street to the embankment and began to walk along the river. After a time she ceased to walk and leaned on the railing to stare at the gray and sluggish water. Low tide had left some scraps of weed, a bicycle tire, a battered doll and a child's cloth cap stranded on the mud and gravel of the riverbed. Julia was certain that she would soon hear from Heather Rudge; she felt oddly disembodied, as though she were floating above the river muck. She found herself adopting the expression of the girl in the Burne-Jones painting.

That girl is going to pieces, Lily thought, and if she does, she'll ruin everything for all of us. Drying her hands, Lily tried to think if any explanation had been given for Mark's appearance by Julia's side. Had he been invited? Was he in the habit of calling on Julia? The first possibility was less dreadful than the second, but only marginally. In any case, she had to talk sense to Julia, she had to try to break her out of her wild and irrational mood. Julia had almost certainly come out of the hospital too soon. Magnus would be able to correct that. The girl had become fixated on the sordid Rudge case, of which Lily had a dim memory. It had been in the newspapers for several weeks a long time ago—now that she thought of it, all of that had happened the same summer Magnus had purchased his house. But it was merely one of those newspaper sensations, having no con-

nection with herself. Surely it was a reflection of Julia's loss of control that she had focused on that ancient story.

No connection. Unless . . . no, that could not be. Despite Julia's frantic assertions, accidents and coincidences occurred all the time. You had only to think of Rosa Fludd to see that. Poor dear Rosa Fludd. Poor Rosa. The horrid niece had been very rude to Lily on the telephone.

Lily went through her living room to her bedroom, stopping on the way to regard the Stubbs drawing which had been Magnus' last birthday present to her. Perhaps she could still persuade Julia to sleep in the spare bedroom. She had to make some sort of assault on Julia—all of them had been too easy, too lenient with her brother's wife. The image in Lily's mind was of a butterfly battering itself against a window: to keep its colors safe, the butterfly had to be pressed between glass. Once Julia was safely in the extra bedroom at Plane Tree House, Magnus could be brought in to make her see good sense. Thinking of this, Lily thought of asking Magnus about the coincidence she'd had in mind a moment before, just to see if it could possibly be true—and if it were, might Julia discover it? Lily cursed herself mildly for her lack of knowledge of the details of Magnus' life. Where exactly had he gone when he had visited Ilchester Place? But surely it was stretching things to suppose . . . ? Lily shrugged the idea away and turned to her wardrobe closet. She had already decided to change her clothes.

The more soberly she were dressed, the more convincing she would be. Flipping through her clothes, Lily pulled a dark blue linen suit from the

closet. She'd owned it eight years, and it still looked elegantly crisp. Then she opened her scarf drawer, sighed, and began to change.

Wearing the blue linen suit and an off-white blouse Julia had given her the year before, Lily returned to her scarf drawer. She tried on three before settling on a long rectangular Hermès scarf in a red and white pattern; then she regarded the effect in her long mirror. She looked slightly more practical than usual—like a retired lady lawyer, or the wife of a prosperous professional man. Now she had to rehearse what she would say to Julia. She glanced at her watch and saw that it had been half an hour since she had spoken to Julia on the telephone. Surely she would still be at home.

Use the Rosa Fludd story, Lily advised herself. Remind her that Mrs. Fludd told her to leave the house; now was the time to take hold of herself, very firmly, before things got utterly out of hand. She must not mention Kate unless Julia did so first. It was monstrously unfair to Magnus, but, as Lily reminded herself, Magnus had taken up the doctor's suggestion more quickly than she had herself—Lily would have to put an end to Julia's fantasy.

Now Lily supposed that she'd have to use the plural. One fantasy had burgeoned into half a dozen. "Wants a little cold water thrown over her," Lily muttered, and checked the angle of her skirt in the mirror. She was ready.

Outside in the warm sun, she strode into the park. It was Friday afternoon, and Holland Park seemed always to be more crowded then than at any other time save the weekends. Lily's neat figure moved, her bag swinging in time with her heels, through crowds of young people. Layabouts, most of them. Students. Though what they found time to study she

couldn't say. Of course there's one famous subject, she thought, seeing a couple kissing on the grass. Magnus should really have married someone his own age: a man like Magnus needed a respectable woman for a wife. And certainly not an American. Americans failed to understand so much, for all their automobiles and electric toothbrushes. Magnus should have been Queen's Counsel by now, but any chance of that had disappeared when Julia became Mrs. Lofting. She *was* a dear girl, of course, and no one could say that all that money hadn't been helpful. But even that had its shady side. The old rogue who'd made it was a sort of pirate, from what Lily could gather. Julia's great-grandfather had been one of those ruthless railroad barons of the end of the last century—he had blood on his hands up to the elbows, Magnus had said. The grandfather was cut from the same cloth, apparently: whole forests had been felled for him, rivers spoiled, wars fought and companies stripped and men killed to increase his holdings. There was a taint, an historical stain, to Julia's money. Lily lifted her head and turned, her heels making a neat staccato sound on the asphalt, deeper into the park.

Descending a short flight of steps beside the little gardens, Lily noticed a small blond girl leap up from one of the benches where old people sunned themselves and run in the direction she was now walking. After a few yards, the girl began to walk. What a sweet old-fashioned-looking child, Lily thought: she even looked a little like Kate, at least from the back. After a moment she recognized that it was the girl's trousers which gave her the old-fashioned aspect: they were high-waisted and elasticized around the top, like children's trousers of twenty-five years before. The girl seemed almost to be leading Lily to

Julia's house. She began to skip ahead of her, slowing to a walk whenever she got more than fifteen or twenty yards away, and then, Lily approaching, skipped and ran once more—just as if, Lily thought, she were on a leash.

When they reached the children's play area, within sight of Julia's house, the girl vanished. Lily checked her stride for a moment, puzzled. She looked over the children playing in the sandboxes and sporting beside the trees, but saw no flash of that astonishing hair—that hair like Kate's. To her left, on the long stretch of grass, she saw only three small wailing children, none of them the girl.

Lily glanced from side to side once more, then shrugged and was about to resume walking when she felt a quick chill over her entire body. She had seen, she was now looking at, a stout elderly woman seated on a green bench, her profile to Lily. It was Rosa Fludd. She was far off to Lily's right, staring straight ahead of her, unmoving. She wore the hideous tweed coat she had worn the night of the last gathering. Lily slowly turned in the woman's direction; her stomach felt frozen, and the ends of her fingers were tingling. She realized that she was unable to speak.

By a violent effort of will, Lily turned her head away from Mrs. Fludd and looked back at the children. They played on, scrabbling in the sand. Their voices came clear and sweet to her. She snapped her head back to look at the park bench. It was now empty. Like the girl, Rosa Fludd had disappeared.

Lily's breath gradually returned to her body, as if it had been suspended for some minutes in the air before her. She self-consciously straightened her back and patted the back of her head. She looked

once again at the bench. No one sat there. No sad gray fat lady. Of course. No one had ever been there. What an extraordinary thing, Lily thought. And to have an hallucination just at the time when she was preparing herself to drum sense into Julia! A less stable person than herself might immediately join Julia's fantasies and condemn himself forever to unreality. Lily permitted herself a smile at the thought of the response of Miss Pinner or Miss Tooth to the resurrection of Mrs. Fludd. Then she wondered just what Miss Pinner had seen in the bathroom on that awkward night; and then reminded herself on no account to bring up the subject with Julia. She found herself, she reflected, in the position of a priest taking a hard line on miracles with an overenthusiastic new convert.

By now Lily felt recovered; well, nearly recovered. The experience had been decidedly *dégoûtant*. She glanced once more at the bench—empty—and firmly marched on her way down the path.

On the corner of Ilchester Place Lily paused, trying to marshal her arguments. She had nothing in mind as to her exact words, but she knew she must have a lever—Julia in effect had to be pried from that house. Perhaps she could use Magnus. Some subtle threat was needed. If she could drop the word "hospital" in the proper way. . . . Lily stood for a moment, enjoying the unaccustomed flavors of power and connivance.

She glanced up at Julia's bedroom windows. Or were those for the unused rooms? The house did have an empty look: more romancing, Lily thought. That damnable hallucination had upset her. Yet she could look obliquely through the side windows and see that at least half the living room was empty. From directly across the street she'd be able to look

straight through the house: and if the drapes were
drawn, wouldn't that mean that Julia was probably
at home? Lily felt an inexplicable reluctance to begin
her crusade immediately.

She took the ten paces across the street and
looked through the double set of windows to the
garden which glowed greenly, as if reduced in scale,
through its frame. She'd have to ring the bell. Why
this odd reluctance? Some memory pulsed below the
level of consciousness and then opened to her: Mrs.
Weatherwax at a postwar cocktail party (in the
Albany, she remembered). A giant hulk of a
woman, the wife of a Minister, the queen of her set,
Mrs. Weatherwax had been in particularly foul
mood, and had occupied a settee, her face frozen
into disapproval—she had nearly dared anyone to
approach her. Absurdly, the house had reminded
her of Mrs. Weatherwax, exuding hostility from a
flowered settee in the Albany. Those crushed flowers along the side of the house: had it been some sort
of visual pun? Yet pun or not, the impression had
been clear and strong.

What nonsense, Lily thought, and took a step off
the pavement. Then she saw Magnus' face appear in
the light square of green at the back of the house,
and she froze in the attitude of taking her second
step. She quickly retreated backward. After a
second, she moved as far to one side as she would go
while still watching the windows at the rear of the
house. Magnus was jerking on the handle, his mouth
working. As Lily watched aghast, he took some sort
of card from his wallet and slipped it into the frame
where the two halves of the window joined. His arm
pumped rapidly; the windows parted, and Magnus
climbed into the house. Lily could watch no more.

6

Magnus stood in the sunny dining room, listening carefully. Somewhere in the empty house a switch moved, inspiring a hum from machinery hidden behind the walls. Magnus fumblingly replaced his Access card in his wallet. He lurched forward a step, then paused again and listened like an animal. Perhaps the buzzing noise came from inside his head. He'd had no more than seven or eight hours' sleep all week, fueling himself with whiskey, keeping his adrenalin flowing by imagining scenes with Julia—sleep was caught in his office between clients, on park benches; once he'd fallen asleep in the flowerbed in the garden, keeping watch on Julia's window. He could imagine beating Julia, making love to her, waking her up an hour before dawn and talking to her urgently, cogently. Like many gregarious men, Magnus hated to be alone, and at times this week, locked into his house, patrolling from room to room with a bottle in his hand, he had talked to Julia so earnestly that he seemed to see her before him, her own ghost. Twice he had heard her calling his name in distress or pain and sped drunkenly across town to park before the dark house on Ilchester Place. He didn't know what he expected to see—unless it was Julia pinned by Mark, fighting him off a final desperate second before yielding.

That scene came into his dreams and sent him
rocketing awake, his heart thudding. He had begun
to masturbate again, as he had not done since
adolescence. There was a woman five minutes from
this house, a former client who lived in Hammersmith, another woman nearly as close, the wife of a
man in prison, but Magnus knew that he went to
them largely because he frightened them; and they
made sense only as temporary alternatives to Julia.
Without her, they were useless to him. So he had
come to lurk outside this house at night, his anger
and frustration undimmed by whiskey, with no plan
other than to speak to Julia the words he could
always find when alone. On the telephone he could
not control himself: she sounded snippy and pert,
dismissive. It infuriated him.

Now the memory of that anger, and the tone of
Julia's feigned coolness which inspired it, momentarily helped Magnus to quiet his apprehensions. That,
of all the houses in London, Julia had chosen this
one was nearly enough to encourage belief in all of
Lily's mystical claptrap. Twenty-five Ilchester Place
contained too many frustrating memories for him to
feel comfortable with Julia's living there. Even after
all these years, it was the past stirring again,
wretchedly.

Now, Magnus thought, I should burn this place to
its miserable roots. This idea gave him a shade more
courage, and he moved around in the dining room,
picking up things and putting them down. He would
not be spooked by the place. And now it was bright
day, unlike the other times when he had crouched
outside, tapping at the windows before trying to
force his way in. Then he had felt the house beating
at him, almost—it was the only way he could
describe it.

Magnus pulled the little bottle of brandy from his pocket and took a long swallow before entering the living room. Noticing that he had begun to perspire, he loosened his tie and swabbed at his forehead with his handkerchief. In the old days, the house had never been so hot—if anything, it had been rather cold. Someone had installed these damnably ugly storage heaters. This warmth was unpleasant, oppressive. Magnus tore the tie from his neck and balled it up in his trouser pocket.

He called Julia's name. When no answer came, he staggered toward the couch and leaned on its cushiony back. He bellowed her name again, then swore when he heard only the soft, buzzing noises of the house. Looking toward the staircase, he saw double for a moment and forced himself to stand straight upright. He focused his eyes. Of course all the furniture was different. Years ago the room had been brighter, with satin wallpaper—could that be right? It had looked like satin. Her sheets had been satin too, and silk. Down here had been small couches, bright paintings: the room had looked much larger. Everything gets smaller as we age, Magnus thought. This isn't a bit like the room where I came years ago—that room had been cheerful, frivolous, a bit silly. And we silly young men had thronged here. As an alternative to Cambridge, the house had attracted him by its carelessness, its perpetual atmosphere of carnival, the license he had thought of at the time as American. That was not to neglect the attractions of his hostess. He could visualize Heather Rudge slipping through the arch of the doorway with a cocktail shaker in her hand, a Sobranie cigarette wobbling in her charming mouth.

But all of that was what he wished to keep Julia from discovering. And what he must not think of.

Magnus pushed himself away from the couch and went toward the kitchen.

There too everything had changed. Now all was white—white as a hospital. Magnus threw open several cupboards. Bottles of Malvern water, plates, glasses. A drawer of new silverware. To one side beneath the sink he found a clutch of whiskey bottles. The malt he'd taught her to like. He touched one of the bottles. They were somehow reassuring.

She must be dead by now, he thought. Then his mind blurred, and he thought he had meant Julia. The fear he had felt on the night he had broken the vase began to leak back into him. No, it was the other one who was dead, not Julia. She must have died in that place where she'd been put. That weak, foolish woman. He'd sent her money for years. Presumably other men sent her money too. She kept the same claim on all of them. Magnus slammed the door to the liquor shelf, hoping to chip away some of the white paint or damage the catch.

From the kitchen he stalked into the downstairs bathroom. He hovered just within the door, sensing that someone was near. Cunningly, he glanced into the rose mirrors. Something was just flickering out of sight. He was drunk. There was nothing to be afraid of. His head seemed to hum in sympathy with some deeper vibration. Watching himself in the mirrors, he took another pull at the brandy. And there it was again, just vanishing from sight. "Damn you," Magnus uttered. His thick gray hair lay across his forehead; his suit was spattered and wrinkled. He combed his hair with his fingers. "You're not there," he said aloud. "Bugger yourself."

What was it that had frightened him that first night he had come in from the garden? He had been slightly more sober that night: he'd half wanted to

pound sense into Julia's fuzzy mind, half simply to sit in her house and relish her atmosphere. He had lifted the vase of flowers to smell them. The house was a particularly *taut* web of noises, none of which he could identify. But he'd thought he could hear Julia moving about upstairs, talking to herself. Then, at first quietly, almost modestly, a feeling had grown in him that he was being watched, as if by some little animal. A feeling of eyes on him. Irrationally, this had grown: the mouse had become a tiger, something baleful and immense and savage. He had never felt such sudden terror. And it was as much despair as fear—an utter and complete hopelessness. Gripping the vase, he'd been afraid to turn around, knowing that something loathsome crouched behind him. Kate's death. That very second seemed to hang behind him, about to engulf him. His head had hurt intolerably. Something rushed toward him, and he threw down the vase, making an awful clatter, and raced outside into the little garden without looking around.

Now he repeated "Bugger yourself," and left the bathroom to stand at the foot of the stairs.

If Mark were up there he'd . . . he'd strangle him.

Magnus put a foot on the lowest stair.

Something was up there. His skin seemed hot.

He stepped back down to the carpet and felt an immediate release of pressure. Even the buzzing in his head diminished. The upstairs of the house was full of noises. A running, rushing noise: for reasons Magnus could not begin to define, this meant an appalling danger to him. He put his foot back on the stair and felt the atmosphere thicken about him. An iron band clamped about his forehead and tightened; his chest pulled for air.

He backed away further into the hall. Now the

house almost palpably lay about him—to stay there would kill him. He felt it with utter certainty. He tried to pull his handkerchief from his pocket and found that his fingers were unable to close properly. His hand shook. The fingers could not coordinate. He was afraid to turn his back to the staircase. Eventually he made his way to the door.

When he stood outside on the front doorstep in the sun, Magnus wobbled a little and touched the bottle in his pocket, stroking it as a man pets a dog. Out of the side of his eye he saw a face peering through a window at him and he wheeled to face it. The woman's face, as pretty and mild as a saucer of cream, hung there by the drapes for a second and then jerked back. Magnus contracted his face at the spot where she had been. If he saw Julia, he'd beat the life out of her. Someone had to pay for this— humiliation. He'd batter anyone who got in his way.

The day after these events Julia drove her car south along the motorway, following the directions given her by the director of the clinic. She felt bright and illuminated with sleeplessness, her consciousness high and clear. She was driving very fast, and became aware of her speed only when she accidentally glanced at the dashboard. It seemed to her that she had never driven so well, with such confidence. Below the bright center of her consciousness, her body piloted the little car like an extension of her nerves.

In Guildford, the sight of a restaurant made Julia suddenly aware that she was hungry. She had not eaten since receiving the letter; two letters, actually, the short scrawled note from Mrs. Rudge folded within a typed sheet from the director. The first of these had read:

Julia Lofting,

Is that your real name and do you live in my old house? You remember my case. Visit me if you wish.

HR

In her excitement she had been able only to skim the covering letter, which claimed for its writer a great pleasure that Mrs. Rudge was to be visited after so many years and that no official impediment would block such a visit. There had once been a problem with the press, who had treated "the patient" badly. It would be a further pleasure to the director if he could meet Mrs. Lofting after her talk with "the patient." This had the whiff of a laden desk and busy secretary, behind them the stronger odor of hospitals and ammonia, and Julia had thrust it away after memorizing the directions to the Breadlands Clinic. She had reread Heather Rudge's scrawl a dozen times, looking for whatever she might find in her cramped, spidery letters. It was, most noticeably, an American handwriting, without the copperplate flourishes and separations of that generation's hand in England.

Julia had spent that morning and afternoon foreseeing her meeting with Mrs. Rudge—she was like a greyhound pulling at its leash, blind to everything but what had just scrambled out of the bush. She had let the telephone ring unanswered, had finally left her home and walked until dark, through dingy sections of Hammersmith and Chiswick; past eleven, she realized that she was wandering near Gunnersbury Park, and took the underground back to Kensington. Not even the increasing noises and furies in the house had frightened her: they were a

sign that she was indeed getting closer to whatever was directing her life. She was at last able to act.

And the poltergeist, the spirit, was pleased. It was almost showing itself. Of course if it were Kate's spirit, it could not reveal itself until the very end—she was certain of that. But the heat in her bedroom had doubled in intensity and the noises at night—the rushing and rustling—were almost frantic. At times Julia heard voices, a woman's and a girl's, muttering from the hall. Snatches of music. Magnus had dwindled in her imagination. He was merely an outside force—baleful but not central to her. Magnus was a tool. Julia felt as though she were approaching the center of a blinding light too burning and intense to permit fear; she had to stand in the full clarity of that light, she had to understand all. Otherwise, Mrs. Fludd had died in vain. Perhaps even Kate's death would be for nothing. She felt the full weight of the past impelling her toward this hot center of light.

Just out of the center of Guildford Julia saw a Jolyon restaurant and her stomach again cramped savagely. She pulled up to the curb and went inside. Going down past the ranks of cafeteria food, she grabbed at whatever fell beneath her hand, at the cash desk finally paying for yogurt, chips, two sausages, an egg, toast and coffee. She carried her tray to one of the room's few clean tables and, scarcely bothering to look around her, began to bolt the food. After a few bites her hunger ceased as abruptly as it had begun, but she continued to eat until the sausages and egg had been consumed. The rest lay untouched on the table as she hurried out.

Half an hour later Julia saw the brass plate identifying the Breadlands Clinic and turned into the

long narrow drive, which circled through a small wood before ending at a gray manor house. Julia's mouth was very dry: her heart seemed to be skipping beats, skittering. To calm herself she called up the photographs she had seen of Heather Rudge. Finally she was able to open the door of the Rover and walk across the crunching gravel to the steps of the manor.

An elderly woman in white greeted her. "You are Mrs. Lofting? Mrs. Rudge is *so* pleased that you wrote. And you know that Dr. Phillips-Smith wishes to see you afterward? Good. It's rather a long way away, so please follow me—of course, the poor old dear's not so difficult, not any more, but we have to obey all the regulations, don't we? Of course. And she does have her rough spots. Keeps going on about her daughter, as I expect you'll know. You look as though you could use a rest, dear. Do you want to take a minute before you see her?" Small, bright squirrel's eyes.

"No, please, no," Julia got out.

She received a professional smile which seemed to conceal a good deal of metal. "Then please come this way, Mrs. Lofting."

They went briskly down a featureless corridor, past numbered doors. All eggshell-white. "We *were* able to move her into E wing," the elderly woman said.

"Oh? How—how does she look?"

"Much better."

"Better. . . ."

As the nurse inserted a key into a locked metal door, Julia turned her head and looked into a small white room where a motionless form lay beneath a sheet. Beside the bed stood a steel table crowded

with ampules and hypodermics. Julia nearly stumbled. The food bounced in her stomach like an angry cat.

"Just through here." At the end of the corridor, another heavy metal door. A large bald man in dirty white hoisted himself from a stool. His stomach wobbled as he came forward.

"Will you fetch Mrs. Rudge, Robert? I'll take Mrs. Lofting to the visitor's room."

Robert nodded and moved slowly off. The nurse led Julia through a small room bright with watercolors—a few old men working about a scarred table gaped at them. The men looked frightened, their faces oddly smooth and unmarked. One wore dark glasses which froze his face into granite.

Why am I here? Julia thought. I can't stand this place.

The feeling grew as the nurse brought her through two more chambers, each with the unsettling contradiction of bright, haphazard walls and pale, stunned-looking inhabitants. Faces which fled from experience. . . . Julia felt trapped by their hunger.

"Here we are, dear." The nurse had turned another corner and was holding open a door to an anonymous little room where two chairs stood on either side of a green metal table. Gesturing at a tattered pile of magazines, the nurse said, "She will be right with you."

Julia took the far chair as the nurse pivoted from the room.

A second later footsteps came. The door opened on Robert, who then stood aside to allow a woman to pass by him. Julia at first thought he'd brought the wrong woman. The flabby creature in the faded housedress bore no resemblance to the photographs of Heather Rudge, who had been trim and oval-

faced in her forties, clearly sensual. Julia glanced at Robert, but he had moved to the stool in the corner of the room and now sat with his hands locked across his belly. He stared at the floor.

The woman still stood just inside the door. She was the sister of the faded, hopeless women Julia had seen in the other rooms.

"What is your name?" the woman asked. Her words scattered Julia's first impressions.

"I'm sorry . . ." said Julia, rising from her chair. "I've wanted so badly to meet you. You are Heather Rudge?"

"Mrs. Lofting?"

They've tricked me, they've given me someone else, thought Julia.

"Mrs. Lofting?"

"Yes," Julia said. "I'm sorry, it's just such a moment, meeting you—I bought your house, you know. I think about you. I think about you a lot."

The old woman shuffled across the floor and sat facing Julia. Her jowly face sprouted a few white whiskers.

"Why were you interested in my name?"

The woman looked slyly at Julia. "Nothing."

Julia leaned forward. "I don't know quite where to start. . . . Do you like having visitors? Do they treat you well here?"

"It's bad here. But better than prison. I was in prison, you know." Julia could hear in her voice the flat vowels of the Midwest. "You don't have to tell me about outside. They let us read—things."

"Oh, I should have brought you something, a book, something, or magazines, a stack of Penguins—I didn't think."

The blunt-faced woman stared impassively at her.

"I came to talk about you."

"I'm nothing. I'm safe here. Nothing happens to you here."

Julia could not speak. Finally she blurted, "My daughter is dead too. We have things we share, things in common, important things."

"You think mine is dead?" The old woman shot a quick sly glance across the table. "That's what they all think. But they didn't know her. Olivia isn't dead. And why should I care about your daughter, Mrs. Lofting?"

"Not dead? What. . . ."

"It isn't 'what.' It's what I said. Why are you interested in Olivia? Didn't you come here to talk to me, Mrs. Lofting?" Unexpectedly, the old woman chuckled. "You poor cunt. You don't know where you are."

The heavy food churned in Julia's stomach. "I have to begin at the beginning. . . ."

"First you have to know where it is."

"Something's been happening to me and I have to tell you about it. I've been reading about your case in the old newspapers, I've been reading them for days, I believe there is some connection between us. . . ."

"Look at me, Mrs. Lofting," said the other woman. "I'm the one who is dead, not Olivia. Mrs. Lofting. Nice Mrs. Lofting visiting the crazy woman. Eat your own shit, Mrs. Lofting. Rub yourself with your shit. Then you'll know what I am."

Julia threw herself into it again. "I think I can help you too—part of you is caught in my house, I can hear you there sometimes. Does that make me crazy? Why did you talk about being safe?"

Now Mrs. Rudge's attention was wholly fixed on Julia. "I can't do anything for you, Mrs. High-and-

Mighty Lofting. I scorn you." Her face grew distorted; she nearly spat her words. "Live in your house. I'll tell you about Olivia, Mrs. High-and-Mighty, Mrs. Nice. Do you want to know? Olivia was evil. She was an evil person. Evil isn't like ordinary people. It can't be got rid of. It gets revenge. Revenge is what it wants, and it gets it."

"What—what was her revenge?"

The silence was better than scorn.

"Do you mean that she made you do what you did?"

"She's laughing at me. She's laughing at you too. You hear her, don't you? You don't know anything." The flabby white face, contracted about a writhing mouth and narrowed eyes, loomed before Julia. "*I* did what I did, Mrs. Shit, because I saw what she was like. Do you have to ask me what her revenge was?"

"Mrs. Rudge," Julia pressed, "did she do what people thought she did?"

"What she was was worse than what she did. Ordinary people can't touch it. I'm happy to be in here, Mrs. Lofting. Do you want to know a secret?" Malevolence gleamed from her distorted face.

"I want to know," said Julia. She was leaning across the table, straining to hear the thick words.

"You'd be lucky to be me."

Robert snorted from the corner.

"You're stupid, Mrs. Shit. As stupid as us in here."

Julia bowed her head. Spittle shone on the table's battered surface. The room seemed horribly small. A rank odor floated about her and for a moment she felt dizzy, assailed.

"Who else can I talk to?" she brought out. "Who else knew you?"

"The Braden bitch," snarled Mrs. Rudge. "Talk to that sauerkraut eater. Talk to my daughter's friends. They'll have found out."

"What are their names?" Julia softly asked.

"Names. Minnie Leibrook. Francesca Temple. Paul Winter. Johnny Aycroft. Do you want more? David Swift. Freddy Reilly. Hah! Go ask them about your problems, Mrs. Shit."

"Thank you," Julia said.

"You're just what I thought," said Mrs. Rudge. "You belong in here. Stupid cunt. Now get out."

"You have eight minutes," said Robert from the corner.

"No, I'd better. . . ." Julia began. She stood up.

"Stupid cunt bitch. Stupid murdering cunt bitch."

Julia bolted around the body of the old woman and threw open the door. Robert looked up startled and held out a pudgy hand. Julia ran down the corridor and turned blindly at a corner. When she saw a large door with a light over it, she rushed through; impelled by a vision of Mrs. Rudge's sullen, working face and Robert chasing heavily after her, Julia fled the hallways and spun into a long hall filled with men and women.

Their faces were sagging and gray, or drawn and gray. They had all swiveled to stare at her entrance. Julia at first stopped, and then moved quietly among them toward the far end of the hall. The men were bent; their faces mooning and unconscious, they shuffled aside to let her pass, some of then fumbling toward her with unsteady hands. One cadaverous man grinned slackly from beneath wild hair. Julia only half saw the Ping-Pong table, the metal chairs pushed together to form rows. The odors of clean linen and sour flesh and disinfectant swam about her, as if Heather Rudge had leaped on her back.

These faces—they looked as though they would leak sawdust. A hand with enormous knuckles brushed at her wrist, snatching at her. Julia flinched, and the elephantine man at her left hissed at her. A squashed-looking woman with terrible bright hair joined his hissing. A man whose face was all drawn to one side, as if snagged by a hook, scuttled before Julia and grabbed for her elbows as she twisted to pass him. She felt as if drowning in grotesque, stinking flesh . . . She pushed at the man in blind revulsion and ran to the end of the hall just as Robert appeared at the far corner.

She was in a long dim corridor. Behind her she could hear lurching bodies, heavy footfalls. She ran. At the corridor's end there was a flight of steps down to a narrower, darker hallway with a rough stone floor. Here she ran in darkness for half its length; then, holding her side and gasping for breath, Julia walked quickly to a large barred wooden door. She pushed aside the bolts and swung the door open, grunting with the effort. Three broad stone steps led upward to a grassy lawn. At the far end of the lawn, the wood began. The names Heather Rudge had spat at her came thrillingly into her mind. *Braden. Minnie Liebrook. Francesca Temple. Paul Winter. Johnny Aycroft. David Swift. Freddy Reilly.* She looked into the dark tangled wood and moved up over the steps toward the wood's darkness, repeating the names.

Magnus stood in shock beside the sandboxes, children all about him. He was staring up at the window of Julia's bedroom. It was impossible, what he had seen there for a moment. He touched the bottle in his jacket pocket. A little boy brushed against his legs and Magnus stepped backward,

feeling sand grind beneath his heel. His pulse
seemed to have stopped. Gradually, into the silent
vacuum which had dropped over him like a bell jar,
sounds began to come. He heard children's piping
voices and the far-off booming wash of a jet. One of
the children pressed against his left leg. He had
walked through the park from Plane Tree House,
irritated. Lily had been more than usually coy with
him, as if she were keeping a secret. She'd assumed
her you're-such-a-naughty-boy manner, as she
sometimes did when she had learned something
upsetting about him, but she had refused to speak
directly about his supposed transgression. Instead,
she had babbled about Julia's "privacy," about her
need for "an honest meeting" with Magnus, about
"the needs of all concerned," all the while her eyes
shining with bright, needling admonition. He had
supposed that all this had to do with his drinking.

Then she had got onto his not being a Queen's
Counsel again.

"For God's sake, Lily," he had said. "I've explained this to you a hundred times. If I wanted to be
a QC I could be one. But all I would do would be to
double my prices and drop my cases down to a
fourth of what they are now. You don't understand
what a Queen's Counsel is. For a man in my position
it would be a ludicrous mistake."

"I wany my distinguished brother to be a QC."

"You mean you want to be the sister of a QC
without first understanding what it means. Absurd.
And it has nothing to do with Julia. Can you get that
into your head?"

"Magnim. . . ."

"And don't start to stroke me with Durm."

She had brightly pulled back. "You should have

your clothes looked after. That suit looks as though you've slept in·it."

"I probably did, damn it."

By the time he had left Lily's flat, he had a headache and the sour beginnings of indigestion. He had walked gloomily through the park, irritated with the sunshine and the loafers sprawling on the grass. The newspapers predicted a change in the weather in the next few days, which suited him. He wanted rain. He longed for clouds and cold blustery weather. Eventually he reached the play area and stepped off the path onto the springy grass. Then he looked angrily up at Julia's window and saw Kate—the back of her head shining through the glass. In the next second she had disappeared. But it was Kate. He knew the color of that hair better than he knew the color of his own. For a long moment Magnus forgot to breathe.

He extracted a grinning black girl of two or three from his leg and, gulping air, stepped forward on the grass. His stomach burned. His tongue was a wooden oar lodged in his mouth. He could not have seen Kate. Yet he *had* seen her—that hair shining like the hair of a princess in a fairy story. For a moment Magnus felt one of the strongest and most unselfish emotions of his lifetime, an overriding fear for Julia's safety.

His legs took him over the lawn, racing, to the road out of the park. He ran a few laborious steps into Ilchester Place and then, puffing, began to walk quickly. He scanned the expressionless facade of the house. Impossible to tell what was going on inside. The great moment of the fear had receded, but it lay close enough to bring Magnus up the walk, leaping the three steps, to the door. He pushed the bell.

From far within the house Magnus heard the bell's chime, falling away: the house was empty.

He jumped off the doorstep and half circled the house, peering in the windows. The interiors he saw looked motionless, tomblike, immaculately dead. He pounded on the window of the kitchen until its whiteness and sterility repelled him; then he continued around to the back of the house where he tried the handle of the French windows. They were locked. He leaned forward and looked past the parting of the drapes, cupping his hands about his eyes. The stolid furniture bulked on the floor as if it had come from a taxidermist's show window. Before taking out his Access card he glanced at the house next door and saw Julia's kittenish little neighbor staring down at him in horror from an upstairs window.

He shook his fist at her before noticing the tall, weedy man cutting around the corner of Julia's house to come toward him. The expression on his face, that of a policeman about to dress down a tramp, infuriated Magnus, as did everything about the man, his modishly long blond hair and his velvet jacket and glinting ascot. When the man glanced suspiciously at Magnus' rumpled and stained, tieless exterior, Magnus whirled to face him, balling his fists.

"Just a minute," the blond man began. "Just a minute there, you."

Glowering into his face, Magnus saw, with the sureness of years of sounding witnesses and juries, an essential weakness beneath the bluster. "Piss off," he growled.

The man stopped, as if hesitating, and then approached to within two feet of Magnus. "I don't know what your game is, mister, but you shall be in

trouble with the law if you don't leave this house alone. I've seen you here before and I don't like the look of you."

"You utter twit," Magnus said. "Piss off and leave me alone. My name is Lofting. My wife lives here. I don't know who the bloody hell you are and I don't care. Now get going."

Amazement came into the well-cared-for face. "My name is Mullineaux," he blurted. The admission caused him anger and Magnus, seeing it, braced himself. "I live next door to this house you were about to break into. Now I must ask you to leave."

Magnus leaned his forehead against the window-pane, grinning ferociously. "You have a lot of guts for a Golden Wonder," he said. "I'm going inside. I think my wife is in danger." He straightened up and smiled at the man, knowing despairingly that he would have to fight him.

"Your wife isn't here," said Mullineaux. "And I doubt if you could do anything for her, in your condition." He lifted an admonitory finger. "If you go away this instant, I promise you that against my better judgment I will not speak of this to the police. Now please go."

"'Now please go,'" Magnus mimicked. "Now *you* will please go, twit, because I'm going inside. You can stand here and watch or you can help me."

"I must say . . ." the man said, advancing and placing a hand on Magnus' arm.

An absolute conviction of his size flashed through Magnus, and he punched the man on the side of his head, knocking him aside. Because Magnus had used his left hand, the blow was weak, but Mullineaux crumpled to the ground. At that instant Mark's face floated into Magnus' mind. He ground his teeth, enraged, and took a step toward the pale

figure now groveling on the grass. He lifted his right
boot back, intending to kick Mullineaux on the point
of his jaw, but looked upward at the neighboring
house and saw the pretty little woman inside shrieking through the glass. "Come and get this idiot
inside," he muttered, his fury dissipating, and
stalked off back around to the front of the house. He
had left his car at Plane Tree House.

Kate? Kate? As he stormed through the park, the
slightly hazy, glowing summer air seemed to darken
about him.

7

Mark came awake in darkness, the dirty sheet twisted about his hips. He had been dreaming about Julia, a variation on a dream he had been having regularly for the past three or four years. Usually the dream began with his entering a classroom, perching on the desk, and suddenly realizing that he was totally unprepared. Not only had he no lecture or plan for this particular class, he could not even recall which course he was supposed to be teaching. Students from various years and classes regarded him quizzically, already bored: if he could not think of something to say, soon the whole hour, an hour he hadn't the barest idea of how to fill, would be lost. Was this *Working Class Movements in England*, Monday, Wednesday and Friday, 9:30-10:20? *New Trends in Socialist Thought*, Tuesday, Thursday and Friday, 1:30-2:20? *Crowd Theory*, Monday and Wednesday, 4:00-5:25? He would realize with growing desperation that he did not know what day it was. Last night, the dream had progressed to this point, and then Julia had risen from one of the chairs and, pulling a sheaf of notes from her bag, began to lecture brilliantly on the London Corresponding Society and its Secretary, Thomas Hardy. He had resented her usurping his class at the same time as he

had listened dazzled to her initial summary of information and the cascade of her ideas, which defined exactly what he had been struggling to express to this class over the past year. He had been certain he would remember everything she said so that he could use it in the first chapter of the book he wanted to write, but all of it had vanished in the first second of wakefulness. Instead of her ideas, he would remember how she had looked—dressed in a white blouse and yellow skirt, her hair hanging softly about her shoulders, she was the Julia he had seen that first morning at Magnus' house. She looked enchanted, like a woman who conversed with fairies: a woman to whom clung the last bewitching traces of childhood. Mark stared up at the low ceiling of his room, realizing that the dream had caused in him a terrific sexual arousal. He wanted Julia very badly. She could not consider herself married to Magnus after his brutal appearance at her home yesterday afternoon; the thought gave him energy to roll over and punch the light switch beside the mattress. Magnus seemed to have at last exploded. Both Julia and Lily had described the incident to him, each of them advising him to stay away from Magnus for the time being. Well, when *hadn't* he avoided Magnus? One of the first utterly clear impressions of Mark's life was that his adoptive brother detested him.

Maybe loathing was more the word for it, he considered, and giggled.

Still grinning, Mark untangled his legs from the sheet and stood up beside the mattress, carefully avoiding the stacks of plates and half-empty tins strewn over the floor. He had begun eating in bed the previous winter, when his bed was the warmest place in the flat, and had not yet got out of the habit. A pile of clothing lay atop a chair near the mattress,

and Mark extracted from it a shirt and trousers, which he pulled on over his body, taking great care with the zip of the trousers. From the pocket of the shirt he took a pack of Gauloises and a lighter and applied the flame to the tip of the cigarette, relishing the smoke's occupation of his mouth and lungs. Then he felt beside the mattress and found his watch. It was eleven o'clock. He glanced for a moment at his desk, set below the window at the opposite end of the room, and immediately felt the loss of all sexual desire. There lay his typewriter, some pencils in a small bottle, a stack of paper, a few sheets of notes and a dozen books in two piles—all the material for beginning work on his book. They had lain there since the previous summer, when he had deliberately not taken any teaching work so that he could write. But that summer had passed in a series of casual meetings with women, daydreams, grandiose plans which had never come to anything. He had spent an alarming amount of time asleep, as if exhausted by inactivity. After another three terms of teaching, Mark had thought that he could at last get down to the book, but now he could not look at his desk without feeling a panicky fluttering of guilt. He was less sure of his ideas now than when he'd first thought of writing his interpretation of working class social movements. When he could bring himself now to think about the book, he chiefly visualized the reviews it would earn. "The breakthrough in socialist thought achieved by this brilliant young lecturer. . . ." "This classic of Marxist praxis. . . ." He snubbed out the Gauloise on a plate and went down the hallway to the bathroom.

When he returned Mark separated the curtains above his desk and let a drained, weak version of the sunlight enter the room. Well below street level, the

little flat required electric lighting at all times of day.
Forever gloomy, on overcast days it held large areas
of brownish obscurity. The windows, like the smaller
window in the kitchen—the flat's second room—
looked out onto a wall of concrete which had once
been white. Soon his headache would return. It had
first come nearly a month ago, just after he had
awakened. Ever since, he had been haunted by it, an
insistent throbbing behind his temples and a feeling
of constriction over the entire top of his head. On
mornings when he had dreamed of Julia, it seemed
worse. These sensations, never actually painful, had
affected his concentration. Even if he were able to sit
at his desk and begin work, he thought, he would be
unable to construct a decent paragraph: he found
himself losing the thread of conversations, of suddenly being aware, as in his classroom dream, that
he was uncertain of what he had planned to do next.
Several times on the street, he had been unable to
remember where he had been going. He often found
himself brooding about Julia and Magnus. A dis-
placed, lost child himself, Mark had lately begun to
see Julia—whom he had for years thought of as no
more than a sweet, moderately pretty housewife—as
his counterpart. Magnus' possession of her seemed a
cruel and blatant injustice. No man as bastardly and
arrogant as Magnus deserved any sort of wife,
certainly not one as sensitive as Julia. And Julia's
money, which he could use to further a thousand
worthwhile purposes—the writing of his book only
the most immediate of these—had been squandered
on drinks and bourgeois dinners, and almost certainly funneled off to Lily. At times, Mark nearly hated
Julia for tolerating so long her brutish parody of a
marriage. And the money had come from that old
crook, Charles Windsor Freeman, Julia's great-

grandfather, one of the classic American plunderers and exploiters: Mark could turn it against that very class and cleanse the money of its stain.

It was time for his exercises. Mark extended himself on the carpet, which showed strands of thread beneath its scuffy greenish tufts, and deliberately emptying his mind, first lifted one arm and then the other straight upward. He tightened his muscles and pushed upward with all his strength. He repeated this with his legs. Loosened, he sat in the lotus position and attempted to touch his forehead to the ground. He extended his tongue until its roots ached. Then he sat blankly, expectantly. He closed his eyes to a furry darkness.

He stared deeply into the opaque darkness, letting it take shape around him. No movement, no thought. He was a vessel to be filled.

Within ten minutes the chaos of the flat had spun away, leaving him in a vibrant, circling universe. He was a dancing point of light in darkness, a slit of entry for spirit. Stars and worlds moved about him like spheres. The single burning lamp was a glorious golden wheel of consciousness toward which he flew, circling. It breathed and pulsed, trembling with life and knowledge.

His body, no longer tiny, became immense. His whirling encompassed worlds, galaxies. Mark-body became Mark-self, breathing in gusts of spirit. Time cocooned him, light as dust. Everything was holy. He could blow time away and fracture the world, leaving only Mark, only holy light. His hands lay across continents, weightless as the buzzing of a fly. His arms lifted themselves, and extended through vast distances. Wordless chanting filled the glowing space about him. Disembodied peace indistinguishable from tension illuminated and lifted him. Mus-

cles, birds, flight. He was up. Now he was traveling toward a swarm of bright particles which coalesced as he traversed the great distance separating himself from them. He ached for union. He saw first a golden city, then a face he knew to be Julia's even before it came fully into focus. He was creating her from spirit. Space began to hum with energy, to sing. He was dissolving into flames and candles, into sheer brightness. The face he saw was not Julia's, but that of a beautiful child. The brightness unbearably, gloriously intensified.

Outside, far away and to his left, a taxi blared. Mark began to spin downward, heaviness invading his body's vast molecular spaces. He collapsed forward onto the carpet, his thighs cramping. His tongue caught a dusty web of hair. Mrs. Fludd, sitting beside him on a couch in Julia's living room, said to him, "You are being blocked." With the repetition of the taxi's bright, horrid noise came his headache, settling like night over his scalp.

"I'm so grateful that you agreed to see me," said Julia to the pleasant, smiling middle-aged woman who had opened the door of the large white house at 4 Abbotsbury Close. "It's very important that we talk, important to me—I was so surprised to see your name in the directory, I thought you would have moved after your tragedy. Do you remember speaking to me on the telephone, Mrs. Braden? I'm Julia Lofting. You said I should come over this morning before lunch. . . ."

The woman opened the door further and admitted Julia to deep gloom. All of the house she could see appeared to be dark brown; a far wall held a cluster of old photographs layered with dust. "I am not the one you spoke to," the woman whispered to Julia.

"Mrs. Braden is upstairs in her room. She is waiting for you. It is about Geoffrey, yes?" Her German accent sounded like that of the voice Julia had heard over the telephone yesterday: but this woman's voice was higher in pitch, silvery. Julia immediately, irrelevantly thought of it as the voice of a hypnotist.

"You're not. . . ." Julia glanced up toward the staircase, which ended at a darkened arch.

"I'm Mrs. Braden's companion," said the woman, her voice insinuating, lulling. "I am called Mrs. Huff. I have known Mrs. Braden only since the tragedy. At first there were so many, those men from newspapers, the police, many wicked people coming to pry—the curious. I kept them away from her. Now no one comes for a long time. She wants to see you."

Mrs. Huff, moving with a stiff efficiency that recalled Miss Pinner, and which Julia only now recognized as arthritis, pulled open a door at Julia's left and revealed a musty parlor. Brown overstuffed chairs faced each other across a mottled carpet. Beside each rose a hairy plant. "Please to wait here until I return. It will not be long."

"Is there a Mr. Braden?" Julia stood uneasily beside one of the fuzzy chairs.

"He died in the war," Mrs. Huff said, and was gone. The door clicked behind her.

Julia did not want to sit in the chairs; they reminded her of some sticky plant that trapped insects and then digested them. She turned in the dark little room and began to pace, too excited to take in the room's furnishings, which seemed to hang in the dusty gloom. Her steps took her to a wooden bookcase; Julia looked at the titles, odd in some way, uniformly stamped in gilt on the thick spines. Then she saw that they were all in German. She ran

her hand along the books, and her fingers came away black. Wiping her fingers on a tissue from her bag, Julia walked in small circles on the dark carpet. Surely it was Turkish? Her grandfather had owned a carpet much like it. She became aware of a pressure in her bladder. Where was the bathroom? It was only the excitement, she knew, and it would soon pass away if she could take her mind off it. She began to pace more rapidly; if the pressure increased, she would have to sit cross-legged in one of the awful chairs. Then her steps took her immediately before a small canvas, and she stopped pacing, puzzled by its familiarity. It was not a painting she had seen before, but surely she knew that arrangement of uptilted table, pipe and gash of newsprint. Braque—it was a Braque. She peered at the little painting more closely. It had to be a reproduction; but when she read the signature she saw the buttery raised strokes of paint. Surprise dissipated the urgency in her bladder.

She turned about just as the door opened. Mrs. Huff beckoned stiffly with one hand, smiling. "Mrs. Braden will see you now. Please follow me."

"This painting—I can't believe it!" said Julia.

"Please to come. I know nothing about painting."

Julia hurried from the room, propelled by the silvery, lulling voice. Mrs. Huff gestured toward the staircase, smiling, and then began to ascend. Julia followed. When she had passed through the darkened archway, she saw Mrs. Huff opening a door halfway down a lightless hall. Julia had time to notice rows of paintings lining the walls, but the obscurity within the corridor effaced them. She went hurriedly through the door Mrs. Huff was holding open for her.

"Please sit down, Mrs. Lofting," said the large

gray-haired woman dressed entirely in shining black who had risen at Julia's entrance. "I am Greta Braden and it was I to whom you spoke on the telephone. Please take the chair to your left. I think you will find it comfortable. Thank you, Huff." The door closed softly behind Julia.

She found herself staring at a painting encased in a gold frame from which depended a sliding red velvet drape, now pulled to one side to reveal a fleshy naked woman whose skin seemed to absorb all the room's light. It was, unbelievably, a Rubens. The rest of the bedroom shared with its occupant the atmosphere of elegance gone down in neglect. The flocked wallpaper, once red-gold, had been darkened by grime to a mute shade of brown. Books and newspapers lay over the floor, many of the papers yellowing with age. On the worn black velvety expanse of material covering the massive bed lay a tray holding the ruins of breakfast. Mrs. Braden's large angular face seemed to have caught dust in every fold. The gray hair was stiff with grease. Looking at her, Julia was not sure that Greta Braden was quite sane.

"You wish to talk with me about my son. Why is that, Mrs. Lofting?"

Julia sat on the chair Mrs. Braden had indicated, and felt the cushions slither beneath her weight. Now she was looking at a photograph, hung on the wall above the huge bed, of a small frail-looking boy in spectacles. Beside it hung a second photograph, of a tall, gaunt man wearing pince-nez and a Norfolk jacket.

"That was Geoffrey," said Mrs. Braden. "My husband stands beside him. What is your interest in me, Mrs. Lofting?"

"I saw Heather Rudge two days ago," said Julia,

and saw the woman's body stiffen inside the shiny
black shell of her clothing. "She was abusive and
disturbed, but she did mention that I might speak to
you." Overriding a curt, dismissive gesture from
Mrs. Braden, Julia hastily added, "I am not working
for Heather Rudge, not in any way. You see, I
recently bought the Rudges' former house. I was—I
was recovering from a long illness. Something about
the house demanded that I buy it. Since then I've
been looking into the past of the Rudge family—the
past of the house. It's been something like a
compulsion—I want to know everything I can find
out about them. I don't think the truth ever came
out about your son's death, Mrs. Braden. There's a
lot more, but you might think I was crazy if I said it
all. The chief thing is, I have to find out about the
Rudges."

Mrs. Braden was looking at her very shrewdly.
"And then you will perhaps write about what you
find?"

"Well," said Julia, afraid to risk expulsion by
uttering the wrong answer, "I'm not sure about
that. . . ."

"Twenty-four years ago I would not have talked to
you," said Mrs. Braden. "Especially if you mentioned the name Rudge. Now much time has passed,
and I have waited for someone to speak the truth
about my son's death. Many have gone unpunished.
When my tragedy happened, the police would not
listen to me. I was a foreigner, a woman, and they
thought me suspicious, foolish. They ignored me,
Mrs. Lofting. My son's death has gone unavenged.
Now do you understand why I am speaking to you?"

"I . . . I think so," said Julia.

"My world is in this room. I have not left my
house since twenty years. I have become old in this

room. Huff is my eyes and ears. I care for nothing but my husband's collection of paintings, his memory, and my son's memory. Even Huff does not know everything about my son's murder—doesn't that word sound awesome and terrible to you, Mrs. Lofting? Do you know what murder is? That it is the greatest crime against the soul, even the souls of the living? It is an eternal crime."

"Yes . . . I feel that," Julia breathed. "But what I need is proof. Or knowledge more than proof."

"Proof." The older woman expelled the word from her mouth as if it were rotten meat. "I need no proof. That man the police executed was a harmless vagrant. He was a simple man, a child himself. He liked to talk to the children. What proof did the police have when they killed him?"

"So you *are* convinced he was innocent," Julia said.

"Of course, of course! Listen to what I am saying to you. There were no secrets between Geoffrey and myself, Mrs. Lofting. I know what they did to him in that park. Those others tortured him daily. They made his life a hell because he was sensitive and because he had asthma. And because he was partially German. They called my son the Kraut, the Jerry, the Hun. They were all bad children, those others."

"And you knew Mrs. Rudge?"

"That one. She laughed at me. She scorned me. I begged her to help me for Geoffrey's sake, but she was blind and foolish. She could not see what was happening within her own house. She could not see she was defending a monster. I have no doubt about what happened to my son, Mrs. Lofting. The Rudge girl mutilated him and then killed him. And the others helped. Now. Do you think that I am wrong?"

Julia gently touched the sheeny material of Mrs. Braden's sleeve. "What did Olivia look like, Mrs. Braden? Can you describe her?"

The reply destroyed her expectations. "She was just a girl. Her exterior was unimportant. She looked like one of a hundred girls. She has been dead as long as Geoffrey. You must be aware of that."

"I am aware of it, yes, but there are reasons—I have to know what she looked like. Did she have blond hair? How tall was she?"

"Those are foolish details. Blond, yes, she may have been blond. But you couldn't tell she was evil by looking at her, Mrs. Lofting."

"That's the same word her mother said."

Mrs. Braden smiled. "That stupid woman," she said. "That rude common little fool. No, Mrs. Lofting, you must not dwell on the wasted lives of the Rudges. You must find the others. You must make them confess."

"I have to find them," Julia agreed. "I know some of their names. Minnie Leibrook and Francesca Temple and Paul Winter. . . ."

"And John Aycroft and David Swift, yes. And the Reilly boy. You surprise me, Mrs. Lofting. Those were the children who helped Olivia Rudge kill my son. If you want your proof talk to them. And I can help you."

Julia waited tensely, unable to guess what would come.

"Some of them have died. None of them have prospered. As you can imagine, Mrs. Lofting, I have been interested in the lives of this group. I have 'kept up,' as you would say. I can tell you that the Reilly boy disappeared in America, your country, ten years ago—he is lost. John Aycroft killed himself when his business went bankrupt. Minnie Leibrook died in an

automobile accident while drunk. Francesca Temple was very wise and became a nun. She now lives in the Slaves of Mary convent in Edinburgh, under a vow of silence. Paul Winter became a professional soldier, as was his father, but was cashiered by his regiment. He lives in a flat in Chelsea. David Swift ruined his family wine business and lost his wife in a freak accident—she was electrocuted. He lives above a pub in Upper Street, Islington. Talk to those two men, Mrs. Lofting. If you can make them talk, you will have your proof."

Julia was stunned. "How did you find out all this?"

Mrs. Braden flexed her shoulders, making the cloth creak. "My eyes and my ears. Huff. I pay Huff very well. She has many talents. I will ask you to leave now, Mrs. Lofting. But first I will give you some advice. Be very thorough. And be careful."

"Well, careful is what you'd better be," Mark said that evening. "I never heard such a tacky idea. You mean you really intend to march up to those two people and grill them about a twenty-four-year-old death? For which a man has already been executed? Look here, have another drink instead and forget all about it. God knows what you'd be getting into."

"I'll have another if you let me pay for it. Please, Mark."

"If you insist, I reluctantly accept." Mark had counted his money a few minutes before in the men's room, and knew that the last round had left him with sixty-three pence. He owed twenty pounds to a colleague, and when he'd paid that, his next check from school would leave him just enough to pay his rent and buy a month's food and drink. Still, he supposed, he could always put off Samuels for

another month—maybe he could put him off until the second term. He watched hungrily while Julia withdrew a small purse from her bag and took from it a ten-pound note. With a start of anticipatory pleasure, Mark realized that he already thought of Julia's money as his own. "That's sweet of you, darling," he added. He took the note from her fingers.

When he came back from the bar with the two drinks he put the pile of bills and change on the table between them. He said, "Are you bothered about the change?"

She looked up at him, startled. "Why, do you need money?"

"Just something to tide me over. I've had a tight month."

She pushed the bills at him, her face beautifully focused on his. "Mark, please take it—please. Do you want any more? It's silly of me to have so much when you don't have enough. Really, do you need more?"

"We can talk about that later," he said. In the soft light which filtered through to the back corners of the pub, Julia looked much better, he thought. Her face still seemed milky from lack of sleep, but she was more confident, vibrant, like the Julia of old, before Magnus had sunk his claws into her.

"Are you feeling well, Mark?" she asked.

"Just a headache. It comes and goes." He adjusted his face to put on his most endearing expression, what an old girl friend had called his "sheep in wolf's clothing face." "I have to say," he went on, "that I think you should just drop the whole business right now. I don't think you should have upset yourself by visiting those two old grotesques. I don't understand your worry about Kate. You still have Kate, my

love. Kate is part of you. She can't hurt you. I blame Magnus for planting all that fear in you. I could kill him for what he's doing to you. You should have let Perry what's-his-name go to the coppers." His headache had tightened up a notch, but he kept his face steady, putting, if anything, more warmth into his eyes.

"You hate Magnus, don't you?" Julia sounded faintly startled.

"Magnus is a bastard."

"I do think of you as my protection against him. It was magic, how you appeared that time I fainted. And you and Lily are the only people I can talk to about what's been happening to me. If it weren't for poor Mrs. Fludd, I probably wouldn't be able to talk about it at all. Did you hear about her?"

Mark nodded, and his headache made the pub swirl. "Lily told me. Too bad. Funny old girl."

"*She* saw something, and she knew she was in danger. I think she was killed so she couldn't tell me what it was. Mark, I'd think I was going crazy if it weren't for her—I have to make her death mean something." Julia took a big swallow of her drink. "She was murdered. I'm sure of it."

"She walked in front of a car, didn't she? That's what, manslaughter, not murder."

"Why did it happen, though? And if it was a straightforward accident, how did she know she was in mortal danger? Mrs. Fludd said there was a man and a child—I've been thinking all along that they were Magnus and Kate, I thought Kate was haunting my house, but there's another possibility. Of course the man is Magnus, I know that much—he's completely irrational—but the girl might be someone else. That girl I saw. And that's why I have to see those people."

Mark rubbed his temples. "I think you're making a mistake. I think you should forget about the whole business." Julia had got an exalted, excited look which rasped on his nerves.

"What did Mrs. Fludd say to you that night? I have to know, Mark. It might help."

"Nothing. It was nothing. I can't even remember."

"Oh." She seemed chastened. "Really? Please try."

"I can't tell you how much my head hurts. Well, I think she said something like, 'You're being blocked,' and then she said that I should leave your house."

"It's what she told me! Oh, Mark, she wanted to save you too." She reached toward him and stroked his wooly hair. The pain seemed to ebb. He looked at her flushed face and her brimming eyes and saw that some of her exaltation was from the whiskey. "Dear Mark," she said. "Your poor head."

"Maybe she was trying to keep me away from you." That was in fact what he had felt.

"I went to the Tate this week," he heard her say. Her fingers continued to caress his hair. "I looked at that painting. The Burne-Jones. You're in it too. I am so grateful for you."

When he looked up from his cupped hands he saw that Julia was crying. "Finish your drink and let's go," he said. The headache had resumed its normal proportions.

Then they were standing in the squalor of his flat, holding one another. Carefully adjusting his stance to support Julia's weight while avoiding a crusty dish on the floor, Mark stroked her long, rather unkempt hair. He saw a profusion of split ends and wiry single

hairs thrust up in a fuzzy corona. "Mark, I don't know what is happening to me," she was saying. Each word floated out into his collar and burst in a haze of whiskey. "Sometimes I'm so frightened. Sometimes it's like I'm not in control of myself. Ever since I read about the Rudge case I've been kind of *dominated* by it—it's all I think about. Because it would mean that Kate. . . ." Her back shook with her sobbing.

"Don't talk about it," he said. He slipped his right hand between them and began to stroke her breast. Julia gasped, and then tightened her hold on him.

"Stay with me," he said. "I need you."

"I want to," she uttered into the side of his neck. His back was beginning to ache from supporting her. Julia was heavier than he had thought. "You're the only man I've ever wanted, except for Magnus. But . . ."

"I need you," he repeated. "You're beautiful, beautiful, Julia." He swung her body around, kicking a plate and knocking over an empty, clouded milk bottle, and, grunting a little, lowered her to the mattress. "Please, Julia. Stay with me." He bent and began to unbutton her blouse, brushed his lips on the mound of her belly. In the light from the single lamp beside the mattress, her face looked blotchy and flushed.

"I can't," she moaned.

"You can do anything you want." He peeled her blouse away from her breasts and put his mouth to one of her nipples. Then he leaned sideways, rolled one hip onto the mattress beside her, and kissed her mouth. It was warm and fleshy, with the feeling of crushed fruit.

"Mark. . . ."

"Shh."

"Mark, I can't." But still she did not move. "Just stay beside me," she said.

Mark pulled the blouse over her shoulders and slipped it down her arms, then tossed it aside. He rapidly stripped off his own shirt, and gave her another long kiss. Julia lay inert, her eyes glazed and bloodshot, out of focus, in the light of the lamp. After undoing his belt and pulling off his boots, Mark shed his trousers. "I will," he said. "I'll just stay beside you."

"Promise. Please."

"Yes."

He discarded his underwear as she distractedly, uneasily, removed the rest of her clothing. "Your house is a mess," she said, laying her skirt atop the blouse.

"Touch me." He guided her hand.

"You're soft." She smiled into his face. "Sweet. Big soft Mark."

"I still have my headache," he confessed. "This doesn't usually happen to me." Julia's hand warmly cradled his penis, holding it hesitantly. "No. Keep your hand there." Now he was beginning to feel a fractional urgency, and he stiffened a little. Her hand jerked him awake. He tongued her nipples, sliding his hand between her legs. Julia's body seemed an immense, fruitful meadow of warmth.

"My God," he said. "What happened to your thighs?" They bore enormous purple bruises.

"I hurt myself crawling in a window one night when I lost my key."

"Damn it," Mark said. He had lost the small erection he had just gained. His headache throbbed. He lowered his head to the place beside hers on the pillow and reached down to pull the sheet up over them. He touched a warm knee, the curve of a calf,

then looked down to see that the sheet lay tangled at their feet. He closed his eyes again and felt her hands pulsing warmth into his back. He slid one hand between her thighs and caressed a bush of long coarse hair.

"Don't," she said, suddenly gripping him tight. "Don't. Just stay with me."

But Mark was incapable of anything else. His head seemed to have grown to twice its size. There was a whirling vacuum between his legs. He punched the button on the lamp and held to Julia's warm body because it anchored him in the room. His head found the cushion of her breast. Everything spun about him. He tried to create an erection by willpower, but his brain could not retain the necessary images. His body felt as though it were traveling—traveling great distances toward a cluster of lights. Julia's voice brought him closer to his real size, but he could not focus upon that either.

". . . keep seeing grotesques. Did you see that man in the pub? He had a red stump instead of a hand—just scar tissue—and his mouth. . . ." He forced himself to think: he had not seen a man with one hand in the pub ". . . a roomful of blank, flabby people reaching for me . . . that old woman at Breadlands . . . swearing. . . ." Her voice slipped away altogether.

In the morning she was gone, and his body stretched uselessly, achingly, into air. Beside his head on the pillow he found a note which read *You're a darling. I'm off to do my detecting. Love.* Beneath it was a check for a hundred pounds.

8

The spirit did not like her leaving the house for an entire night. When Julia entered her home, wanting to wash and change clothes before looking for Paul Winter and David Swift, she saw with little surprise that some of the furniture had been tumbled about, chairs overturned and cushions flung to the corners of the living room. From upstairs came an angry knocking and banging that she knew would disappear when she set foot on the staircase. In the midst of the din, she could hear a radio playing some vapid forties dance tune, and that noise too would vanish. The odd, fumbling night with Mark—he had lain against her unmoving all night, as unconscious as if drugged—slipped away. As much as tenderness for Mark, she had felt all during the long hours after the alcohol had worn off an acute awareness that she was not in the *real* place, the place where the important things happened. Mark's inability to make love had been a relief; apart from her house, deflected from her quest, she wished only for comfort from the desolation. Back in her house and close again to the source of the mystery, she felt that desolation as her familiar element—it was the gray commanding sea in which she swam. What was happening to her was necessary; she was at home.

Julia went into the kitchen and experimentally

turned the tap. A pipe clamored in the wall like a trapped owl. A viscous brown jelly plopped at the mouth of the faucet, and she hurriedly twisted the knob of the tap. Into the air she softly said, "You're angry with me." The hullabaloo upstairs quieted for a moment. When she had poured three bottles of Malvern water into a pot for heating, she quickly went through the living room, uprighting chairs and replacing the cushions.

"You're not Kate," she said, tilting her head back. "You're Olivia. I'm going to prove it. I'm going to find out, I'm going to *find out*—it's what I'm here for, isn't it?"

The toby jug lamp crashed to the floor and shattered.

"I'm going to help you," Julia whispered. The house seemed to get warmer with each word. "You are very powerful, but you need my help. And when I find out, I'll find out everything. I'll know why you are torturing Magnus. And then I'll be free too."

She waited for another bang from upstairs, but the house seemed to hover about her, expectant.

"I'm going to free us," Julia repeated softly. "You want Magnus to hurt me, but I'm going to set you free. That's why I came, isn't it? You needed me. You had to have me live here."

A heavy painting thudded to the floor, cracking the glass with a sharp noise like a pistol shot.

"I'm not afraid," Julia said, and then added, "I don't have to be afraid until I know." She was lying—at any moment she expected something to fly at her head—but it was a lie which contained a glowing corner of the truth. Fear could not keep her from the hot center of the truth: fear was only personal.

After she had washed at the sink, scrubbing

herself in armpits and private parts with a sponge,
Julia ascended to the throbbing heat of the upstairs.
Her bedroom door gaped open. An elbow of noise
seemed to pulse from the walls. The heat from her
room gusted out in a breeze which lifted her hair and
dried her skin as she entered the bedroom. The paint
on the storage heater had blistered, leaving brown
ulcerlike disks on its surface, curling upward in
serrations. Julia heard rustling footsteps in the hall
where she had just been. The closet door hung open.
She went toward it, pulled it fully open and looked
inside, her throat clenched. Some of her clothes had
been pulled from their hangers and lay tumbled and
twisted on the closet floor, mixed up with her shoes.
Then she saw the box of dolls. It had been burst
open, and the dolls scattered all over the back of the
closet. Their floppy, uncomplicated bodies were torn
and slashed. Ancient gray wool foamed from their
chests. The terror poured back into her, and she fell
gasping to her knees. Her certainty blurred with her
vision. Kate had treasured the dolls; a malevolent
Kate would destroy them. For a moment she was
sick with yearning to be back in the hospital.

When she dashed into the bathroom, she first
noticed that the figure in the black mirror—*her?*—
looked haggard and old, her hair a mess and her eyes
big with shock. Then she saw that the large untinted
mirror over the marble sink had been heavily scored
with soap. She stared at the lines and slashes until
they coalesced into a list of obscenities. All the
details of lying next to Mark flamed in her mind,
dirtied by the words glaring at her from the mirror.
The spirit knew, and hated her for what she had
done. The last word jumped out at her: MURDER-
ESS. *"Liar,"* she snarled, bone-jolted, and seized
the nearest heavy object—a large ovoid rose-veined

stone, polished to glassy smoothness—and with it shattered the mirror. Her heart froze, contracted. Magnus seemed all about her, wrapping her in a chill, despairing blanket of deception. That accusing word still burned in her sight. After a few minutes she breathed deeply and began pushing together the long silvery shards of the mirror. Her mind skittered away from her as her hands mechanically brushed at the smaller pieces of glass. Had she written those words herself? Had she mutilated the dolls? For a moment she was certain that she had.

Winter, Capt. Paul S. 2B Stadium St. SW 10. Both of the men had been in the directory. Stadium Street occupied the seedy lower end of Chelsea, near the four wharves and World's End: Julia drove the Rover down the crowded carnival of King's Road from Sloan Square, and after inching through the packs of young people parading in costume from one boutique to another, crossed Beaufort Street and found herself in a different world. The brilliant, nervous crowds had vanished, the restaurants and boutiques replaced by factory walls and the peeling facades of bed-sitters. Here, the few clothing stores hung their wares from their awnings; bent old women with shopping carts trudged along the pavements, mumbling to themselves. When she turned the corner of Cremorne Road she fleetingly saw through the side window a grossly fat man in a ripped topcoat bunched at the waist by string struggling to force a terrified spaniel into a paper bag. He was gripping the dog by the throat, working the bag around the dog's frantically kicking legs . . . *murderess* in letters of crusty soap appeared in Julia's mind.

The bright red side panel of a bread van blocked

her windscreen, and she wrenched the wheel to avoid a collision. The letters MOTHER'S PRIDE wheeled off; the Rover fishtailed to the right, ticking a parked car, and then swung back in its lane. Car horns and shouts erupted about her. She sped away.

On desolate Stadium Street she left her car and immediately caught the smell of the Thames. Its sunless, oily odor seemed to settle on her fingers and hair. She felt as though she were inhaling damp cobwebs impregnated with the smell of fish. Julia peered at the door nearest her, and made out through encrustations of paint Number 15. She moved slowly down the block, hearing blinds rattle as she passed the row of mean, dwarfed houses. The rusted frame of a bicycle lay beside the curb like the corpse of a monstrous insect. 10, 8, 6. Number 5 had been painted in swarmy patches of red and blue and yellow across which had been written in large black letters REVOLUTION IS THE RIGHT OF ALL and HENDRIX; the front door was fixed by a big gray padlock. Julia crossed the street and pushed open the small stiff gate to Number 2. At the end of the line of cracked paving stones, the front door was festooned with a rank of bells beside nameplates. She went up the walk and read the names scrawled on the plates—Voynow, a blank, Mertz & Polo, Gandee, Moore, Gilette, Johnson. No Winter was listed, and she felt unable to ring any of the unidentified bells. Her confidence sinking, Julia stepped back and saw on the pitted concrete facing a glossy black letter *B* above an arrow. In relief, she looked upward and truly noticed for the first time that the weather had changed. The sky held a shifting mass of clouds, obscuring the sun and piling toward a top layer of hard, thin gray.

B was a narrow door set into the rear of the house.

Through it seeped a trace of some tinny music.
When Julia knocked the door almost immediately
opened upon a thin figure dressed in black turtle-
neck and black trousers. The music, swelling past
him, resolved into Ravi Shankar. Julia first took in
the man's prominent, bitter cheekbones and then
that he wore an obvious wig several shades lighter
than his hair.

"Captain Winter?" she asked, unsure.

"It's been ages since anyone called me that,
dear," the man said. "I suppose you're Roger's
outraged sister. Well, you'd better come in."

Julia stepped across the threshold into a heavy
musk of incense. "I'd better explain," she said. "I'm
not who you think I am. My name is Julia Lofting,
Captain Winter—"

The man groaned. "*Please* don't. Call me anything, but don't call me Captain."

"Mr. Winter."

"Paul."

"Paul. Thank you." Looking at Winter's alert,
essentially dishonest face, Julia was surprised to see
that the man was roughly her own age. She realized
that he must have been about thirty when he had
been forced to leave his regiment; though, looking at
his crowded, exotic little room crammed with paisley
cushions and African wall hangings interspersed
with reproductions of paintings and bright Druze
rugs, she could not see Paul Winter as a member of
any sort of army. But she permitted herself the
disloyal thought that Winter had solved the problem
of how to live in a single room better than had Mark.
Except, she saw, that this was the kind of room
which implied that it was forever night beyond its
door: it was a room which denied daylight.

"You can't be Roger's sister," he said behind her.

"She'd never take such a time appreciating my little collection of things. You like my chambers, don't you?"

"Yes, I do," she answered simply.

"When I close my door," he said, "I close out the world and exist here in a world I've created. It's my oasis, my haven. In fact, I rarely leave it. It contains all my needs—beauty, peace, art, refined sensation. And it does have a Chelsea address, which is important, don't you think? I wouldn't live anywhere else, and I've lived all around the world. The army, you know." He was preening himself before her, and Julia caught an odd mixture of failure and arrogance in the man; he saw himself as an Oscar Wilde, but the absurd vanity of the toupee made him pathetic. In a minute, she sensed, he'd begin inventing weak epigrams. "But of course you know," he said. "My distinguished military history," and his cheekbones seemed to sharpen into points. "All in the past. Would you care for a cigarette? They're Turkish."

"No thank you," Julia said. "I'm sorry to bother you like this, Capt—Paul, but for personal reasons I am interested in something in your past."

"Oh, God," he groaned theatrically. "The past doesn't exist." He considered that a moment, and revised it. "No intelligent man believes in the past." Finally he satisfied himself. "Those who believe in the past are condemned to live in it."

Julia seemed to catch a justified suspicion in the man's glance. "Well, the past has everything to do with my present," she said. "It's very difficult to explain." For a second, she saw before her the box of ripped dolls and the accusing words soaped across the mirror, and her blood swung heavily downward.

"Say, you look about to faint," Winter said,

alarmed, and pushed a chair toward her. When she sat, he moved to one of the cushions and perched on it. "What's the matter?" he asked.

"I'm being haunted," she blurted out.

"My *dear*," he cooed. "Turn yourself into a tourist attraction and charge admission."

She smiled at him.

"Am I to understand that this delicious condition has something to do with me?"

Julia nodded. "Yes. . . ."

"How fascinating. Ask away. I have no secrets any more, my dear. I simply *am*, and people must accept me or reject me, for it's not worth the trouble to conceal one's inner nature. One's truth always wins out in the end. I only joined the army because my father wouldn't hear of anything else, you know, and I found it simply rife with hypocrisy. That was why they got rid of me, I must tell you, because I could no longer tolerate their petty restrictions and poses. I had to be myself. It made it pretty awkward for them, I can tell you, my being a general's son. Like Rimbaud, was it? The French poet. I say, you're not taking some sort of survey, are you? I couldn't bear that. Or doing research for a book?"

"No, this is personal," repeated Julia. "I've become involved with something you can help me with, if you would be so kind."

"I've always been so interested in the spiritual side of things—I'm Virgo with Aries rising."

"I want to ask you about some people you might remember."

"Fascinating." He scrunched down further into the cushions. "Ask away. I'm *so* glad you're not Roger's sister."

"I don't know how to begin. Do you remember, um, Francesca Temple? Or Freddy Reilly?"

He blinked. "Good heavens, you are going back. I used to play with them."

"You do remember."

It was too intense for him, and he backed away from a definite statement. "Barely. Just faintly . . . one catches the outlines, as it were. One isn't oneself in childhood. Childhood is a lie adults tell themselves. The man fathers his own childhood, if you see what I mean. Now let me see. Francesca Temple. A very modest little girl, with the loveliest brown curls. Yes, I can"—he pivoted a hand in the air—"catch her now. She was a follower. *She* was a soldier, if you will. Do anything you told her to. Freddy Reilly was a bit butch, if you understand me. A great one for games. Don't tell me you're being haunted by Freddy Reilly!" He silently clapped his hands together and revealed an even row of small, slightly discolored teeth.

She took up all her courage. "Can you tell me anything about any of the others? For instance, do you remember Olivia Rudge?"

He gaped at her, then toyed with the fringe of the cushion. "Can't remember her very well, I'm afraid. Rather a strange little girl, I seem to recall." He suddenly stood up and straightened the crease of his trousers. "Would you like a cup of anything? Tea? I make an excellent cuppa—half China, half India. Exquisite."

"No, please," said Julia. "What can you tell me about her? Olivia?"

"I think," he said, "I think you're beginning to be just the tiniest bit boring." He radiated an emotion it took Julia a second to recognize as fear. "Childhood is our least interesting period, I've always thought. I don't think I wish to answer any more questions about mine."

"I have to plead with you," said Julia. "You won't be in any trouble—there are just some things I have to know."

He ostentatiously examined his watch. "I don't think I have time for any more of this fascinating reminiscence. That woman was supposed to be here at two, and I can't tell you what a bother she'll be—now *there's* trouble for you."

"Mr. Winter—Paul—how did Geoffrey Braden die?"

He went nearly white with shock. Or was it shame? "I'll have to retract my invitation to tea, darling. I must ask you to kindly push off before my visitor arrives. Can't say I really heard your last question. Did you have a jacket?" He was prodding her shoulder with the tips of his fingers. "Really, dear. It's a waste of time asking me about ancient history. That was always my worst subject." Julia reluctantly stood.

"Could you just describe Olivia . . ." she began.

"I know I'm an old fool for being in such a flap," he said, urging her toward the door, "but that is one subject on which I do not propose to expound. The book is closed, my dear."

She was standing outside the narrow door, looking at his painfully contracting face beneath the cheap blond wig. The Indian music built to a frantic climax behind him.

"She wants me," she said. "Olivia."

"I believe it," he said. "Don't come back, please. Leave me alone, whoever you are."

"Julia Lofting," she said, but the door was closed.

The two of them sat on the terrace at the beginning of the evening, watching the rain pelt down onto the park, bending the leaves and tor-

menting the small bushes outside the walls. When a gust scattered drops onto the floor of the terrace, she delicately hitched her chair back out of the rain's territory; he ignored the spattering of drops and allowed it to dampen his shoes. They were, Lily noticed, already caked with mud and webbed with cracks. Magnus' whole being seemed in disrepair, and she experienced a moment of sheer distaste for Julia, who had done this to him, and for her brother, who had allowed it to be done.

"So it was *that* house," she said. "This is a fine time to discover it."

"I didn't think it was any of your business."

"Magnus," she said in exasperation, "how do you expect me to help if you conceal things from me? Concealment amounts to a lie. Is there anything else you've been hiding from me which might affect Julia?"

"An impossible question," he grunted. He stared dully at the rain. "I like this weather. It's more English than all that sunshine."

"Oh, you're simply maddening. Don't you realize that she has been looking into that wretched old case? I don't think she even bothers to eat anymore. She's convinced it's got something to do with Kate. In fact, she told me she was being haunted. Haunted! In her condition, every detail becomes exaggerated and blown up and inflated—Magnus, you must tell me if there is anything else she is likely to discover."

"I don't know. What *has* she discovered?"

"I'm not sure she would tell me."

"She'd tell that bloody psychotic Mark."

Lily tactfully ignored this remark while silently agreeing with it. "If you want your wife back, and I

can only assume that is the motive behind your extraordinary performance this past week, you must tell me whatever you know so that I can use it for your benefit."

"You mean that you want to use Julia for *your* benefit."

"I will ignore that remark." She glanced at him before saying, "If you don't move out of the wet you'll catch pneumonia."

Sighing, Magnus shoved himself backward in his chair.

"Is there any way you can be connected to that house? That would push her right over the edge, you know. Well. At least then we could put her in hospital, where she belongs."

"Is that what you want?" Magnus stared at his sister in genuine surprise. "She's coming home with me, not back into hospital. But no, I don't think there's anything. All of that was so long ago."

"What about the daughter? Did you know her well?"

"Never met the little lady."

"You're sure."

Magnus winced. "Of course I'm sure. Now stop grilling me. Have you anything left to drink?"

"It was drink almost put you in jail, remember. That and your temper. But help yourself, if you want something."

He said, "I don't want it, I need it," and went across the terrace and into the kitchen. A few moments later he returned with a tumbler half filled with amber liquid.

Lily waited until he was settled again in his chair before saying, "Well, what did you do this last time? Leave notes about?"

"I threw some of the chairs around. That's all. She'll know it was me." He drank with visible satisfaction.

"And I suppose you think that will help. Magnus, there are two things that I regret. One is allowing her to keep her fantasy about Kate's death. She needs to be shocked out of it. I'd tell her now if she were here. The other thing is introducing her to poor Mrs. Fludd. Those two together got her started on this ghost business."

"Mrs. Fludd? Oh. Your guru."

"Before her death she stirred Julia up with all sorts of dark hints. Rosa had the gift, but she could never resist playing to her audience. And she died at the most unfortunate time."

Magnus was clearly not interested in the fate of Mrs. Fludd. "I think Julia needs a psychotherapist," he said. "Maybe I do too. I don't know what's been happening to me lately. I have funny blackouts. I see things. One day I saw Kate."

"Poor baby," said Lily. "So you agree with me that we must get her back into hospital?"

"Maybe I do," Magnus mused. He looked at Lily for a moment with perfect complicity.

"Tell me something," Lily said, now that was settled. "What did you feel when you went back inside that house again? Did you feel no shame?"

"No," he said. "It was simpler. I felt fear. I was scared out of my wits. It made me want to murder someone."

"You should have married someone your own age," said Lily.

"Someone like you, you mean."

"We do have a marriage of a kind," said Lily. "We understand each other."

Mark Berkeley stood beneath the awning of the package store, watching the rain spill down the gutters and gradually form a black slick pool which would cover all that part of the street. He still had in his pocket about seventy pounds, after cashing Julia's check and buying some tins of food, a pair of boots and a snakeskin belt—and just now, the two bottles of whiskey. He could remember deciding to put Samuels off until next term, for the sake of the boots; he could remember shopping and dialing Julia's number several times that afternoon; but he could not remember leaving his room in the rain to walk to the package store. He stared down at the blocked drain by the side of the curb—the street-lamp revealed on the surface of the water the shifting, mesmeric pattern of an oil slick—and tried to reconstruct the walk from his building. His shoulders and hair were soaked with rain. Maybe, he thought, these lapses were somehow derived from his exercises, lately far more successful than ever before. He was more than slightly fearful of where these long, otherworldly sessions might take him; but weren't they proof of what the old woman had said about his "receptivity"? This, he was certain, lay behind his headaches—proof of a power he hadn't known he possessed. He was Mark, he was special, he was the child of luck.

A tall girl whose name he could not remember stepped out of the rain and stood beside him. She shook her hair and smiled, and he knew the shape and taste of her mouth.

"Going to a party?" she asked. "Good night for it."

"What?"

"A party. The bottles, Mark. Are you going to a party?"

He looked at the bottles in the white bag. "I couldn't tell you what I was going to," he said. "I sort of don't remember."

She looked at him bristlingly. "I suppose you're on something."

"No. No. I've been meditating. I'm doing it a couple of hours a day."

"Well, it's too late to meditate now," she said firmly. What was her name? "Do you want to come back to my place? We could have our own party."

Then he remembered: Annis. Annis was one of last summer's girls. Looking at her wide, greedy black eyes and hair in which drops of rain sparkled, he felt a spasm of sexual interest, but then Julia's face superimposed on hers. His mind seemed to waver. "Annis, I can't tonight," he said. "There's someone I have to see."

"Well, do me a favor and fuck yourself," Annis cheerfully said, and ran off through the rain.

Swift, David N 337 Upper Street N1. Julia stirred restlessly on the passenger side of the Rover's front seat, trying to find a comfortable position while still looking directly at the inconspicuous door immediately beside The Beautiful and Damned. She had already tried to fill in the time by trying to remember how many other pubs in London were named after novels, but could only recall The Cruel Sea in Hampstead, which Lily had entered once and decreed "puerile, like its namesake." Julia had come to Swift's address at eight, driven aimlessly around Islington before returning at nine, had again found him not at home and driven on impulse over to Gayton Road, where all the lights burned and open drapes revealed empty rooms, and then returned to wait for Swift's return. Now it was just past eleven,

and her back was beginning to hurt. From time to time she thumped her feet on the floor of the car to keep her legs from falling asleep. When a man in a shabby overcoat and tweed cap loitered before the door beside the pub, Julia switched on the wind-shield wipers and leaned forward, tense. The man turned his back to the street. Not daring to breathe, Julia waited for him to open the door. But the man merely hunched his back against the rain and stood spread-legged beside the door. Finally Julia under-stood what he was doing, and she looked away in exasperation.

More people slouched past the pub, and Julia idly watched them until they had gone into the Wimpy bar down the block. At eleven fifteen the pub disgorged a group of young men who hung, half in and half out of the rain, beneath the small canopy, wrangling and stuffing their hands into the pockets of their jackets. They obscured Swift's door, and Julia groaned, silently praying for them to break up and go home. More young men left the pub. They formed a desultory, nearly unmoving mass all along the side of the building. If Swift were to come home now, she could easily miss him. "Please," Julia whispered. David Swift was her last chance.

As she watched, one of the men began to shout. A friend gripped his arm, but the man violently pushed him away, sending him sprawling off the street. In a second, half of the crowd had vanished; a third man circled the first, who still shouted, and then they were brawling. Julia watched them slipping on the wet pavement, clutching at each other's wrists and shoulders before separating to begin punching again. The street had become wholly quiet around them, except for the rain's spatter. One of the men—Julia was not sure which—gave a solid, thunking blow to

the face of the other, who went down in the heap of his clothes. His attacker kicked him savagely once, then again. Julia, terrified, put her hand to her mouth. The attacker picked the man up from the pavement and began to strike him again and again in the face. *He's a Magnus,* Julia thought, and in desperation stabbed at the switch for her headlights. The attacker turned his head into the glare of the lights—Julia saw a bearded chin and a prominent nose—and then pushed the bleeding face away. He turned and ran slap-slapping along Upper Street. His victim lay alone on the pavement, his clothing soaking in the rain. All the others had scattered. As Julia watched, the man's body trembled, and then inched across the pavement like the hulk of a wounded boar. The man rolled against the side of the pub and sat up. His face was a gash of red.

Julia pushed down the lever in the door and leaned out. She had to call for an ambulance—she looked frantically about for a phone booth, but rain, flying directly into her face, blurred her vision. She wiped her eyes and saw, far up the block, a red booth outside a darkened cinema. She crossed the empty road and began to run toward the booth. A burly coatless man cradling a dark clanking bag passed her, but she scarcely noticed the man until she was within the kiosk. Then, looking through the streaked glass, she saw the man set down his bag before Swift's entrance and dig out a key from his pocket. She hung in the booth for a moment, deliberating, and then slammed down the receiver just as the man disappeared from the street.

She pounded down Upper Street to the pub. The beaten man now crouched over the pavement, his elbows planted in his own blood. He was moaning incoherently, perhaps drunkenly. She pressed

Swift's bell rapidly several times, then held it down. The man against the pub rolled over on his side and clamped his hands to his face.

Heavy footsteps thumped down a staircase. When the door jerked open, Julia saw a man's bulky frame in the shadow of the tiny hallway. Far above, a single light burned, illuminating the top of the dingy staircase. "Mr. Swift?" she asked.

"That's me," the man said. Julia caught a pungent whiff of whiskey. "What is it?"

His upper-middle-class accent both surprised and comforted her. It was the accent of Magnus and his friends—the accent Mark had consciously discarded.

"I have to talk to you. And there's been a fight. This man's been hurt. We must telephone for an ambulance."

"I don't clean up after drunks," Swift said. He thrust his head out the door, revealing in the reddish light from the pub a broad, pinkish face and close, rather curly black hair. His jacket looked oily and frayed. "Let him rot. You said you wanted to talk to me?" He looked at her appraisingly, and Julia nodded. "I'm willing. Come on into the fleapit."

As Julia stepped into the hallway, again catching the clear, biting odor of whiskey, she promised herself to telephone for an ambulance no matter what Swift said. He was already moving a bit unsteadily up the stairs. "Come on and talk, if that's what you want," he called down.

At the top of the stairs he was holding open the door to a shabby sitting room. Blotchy yellow wallpaper, a stained green carpet as threadbare as Mark's, battered furniture she recognized as coming from a discount warehouse—it was like the furniture in her Camden Town flat, years before. Swift was standing at a low table, pulling bottles out of the

paper bag. Grunting, he broke the seal of one of them. "Drink?"

"May I?"

"I asked you."

"Then yes, please."

Swift removed two glasses from a wall shelf and poured several inches of whiskey into each. He gave Julia her glass, and she saw above the line of the whiskey fingerprints, water spots, smears, She set it down on the table.

"Can I telephone first? That man downstairs. . . ."

"No," Swift said. In the electric light, his pink face was scrubbed with hot reddish spots, as if scoured. "Fuck him. What did you want? Who are you, anyhow? A solicitor?"

Julia moved to one of the unsafe-looking chairs and sat. She wiped some of the rain off her face. "My name is Julia Lofting, Mr. Swift."

"You must be a solicitor."

"No, I'm not, I promise you. I'm interested in—involved in something you can help me with, if you would."

"Don't tell me it's a business deal." Swift snorted. He was still standing, holding his glass in one hand and the bottle in the other. "I'm afraid Swift and Company is no longer. Three generations of sharp practice end in the wreck you see before you. Do you want some sort of towel?" He gulped down whiskey as she shook her head. "Well, don't just sit there looking all confused and sexy and helpless."

"It's about your childhood," Julia quickly said. "I have to know about something that happened then. I promise you that I won't divulge anything you say to me to anyone else—that I'm interested for purely personal reasons." I won't tell this man I think I'm

haunted, she vowed, he'd throw me out. She had to avoid the mistakes she had made with Winter. "I'm not a writer or anything like that," she said. "Or the police."

He rolled his eyes up toward the ceiling. "I'd better sit down." He moved heavily to the couch and fell into it facing her, still holding the glass and bottle. "My childhood. I suppose I had one. Now what the devil do you want to know about my childhood?"

Julia knitted her hands together, stared at the filthy carpet, and then looked directly at Swift. He had a froggish, unlined, well-brought-up face. She could easily see him in an expensive suit, ordering secretaries about. That she disliked him on sight somehow made it easier to talk to him.

"I live at Twenty-five Ilchester Place," she said. "Olivia Rudge's old house. I want to find out all about her."

Swift was momentarily shaken. His head bobbed toward his drink; but he made no move to throw her out. "God," he said. "That wicked little bitch. She's been dead over twenty years." He gazed at the liquid in his glass, clearly not intending to offer more information.

"This afternoon I spoke to Paul Winter."

Swift brightened. "That poof. I bet *he* wouldn't say anything."

"You're the only one left," Julia said. "The Aycroft boy killed himself and Minnie Leibrook died in an accident. One of you disappeared in America. Another girl is in a convent. And Paul Winter made me leave his house."

The man facing her snorted. "I don't suppose he liked the idea of having a woman in his room. I relish it, I can tell you. He was probably expecting one of

his chums. That's why they pitched him out of his regiment, you know. He fell in love with his driver, but the driver wouldn't reciprocate. Paulie got a little too passionate, the driver kicked up a fuss, and they rubbed Paulie out as if he were a little foul spot on the rug. Bang. Finish." He took another swallow and repeated, "Finish. General's son in disgrace. As for Aycroft, he put paid to himself when he was found embezzling money from his firm. Excuse me, bank. His bank. Good-bye, Aycroft. And Minnie Liebrook. . . ." He caught himself short. "What do you want to know about all this for, anyway? So you live in the old Rudge house. Congratulations. What's that got to do with me?"

"It's personal," said Julia. "I just want to know about Olivia."

"You're fascinated." He poured more whiskey into his glass. "You've been looking into her short and nasty life and now you're keen on her. How do I know that you won't use whatever I say against me?"

"I promise," said Julia, and inspiration came to her. She dug in her bag and withdrew two ten-pound notes and put them on the table. Swift's eyes gleamed at her. She put down another note. Her heart fluttered. "I want to buy information from you."

He snaffled up the notes. "I guess you do. A woman like you doesn't come up here every day and offer me money." He leered at her. "I'll talk to you if you come over here and sit beside me."

Julia hesitated, and then went around the little table to the couch. Cautiously she sat beside him. "Now you have a drink," he said. "You're behind." Julia sipped from the bleary glass. "More." She did as he commanded.

"Tell me about Olivia," she said. "Please." She allowed his hand to rest negligently on her knee.

"You'd never forget her if you ever met her. She was really wicked. It was the most impressive thing about her. It was the reason all of us, the kids you know about, followed after her. We had a club. Do you want to know the rules?" He squeezed her knee, and Julia nodded. "Have another drink." He poured more whiskey into her glass, and she sipped at it. "The first rule was you had to kill an animal. Aycroft killed his dog. He brought it to her and she ripped it open with her knife and made him drink some of its blood. Proper little ceremony. We all did it. I brought a neighbor's cat. Same folderol. I was clever—just touched my tongue in the blood. Then we had to light fires. We had to burn a house or a shed, something in that line. We did that together. She watched us and told us what to do."

"You did it?" Julia asked.

"We tried. She stole a can of petrol from somewhere and we soaked the porch of a wooden house behind the High Street. The bugger wouldn't burn. Olivia was madder than a hen—she looked just like a witch. Maybe she was a witch. We all thought she was. Anyhow we burned most of the porch, but the firemen came before the rest of the building went. Then we had to do lots of thieving and give it all over to her. You see, we had to see her every day—we had to spend all day with her in the holidays. We all had a crush on her, I suppose, even the girls, and she had us scared out of our wits. We knew there wasn't anything she was afraid to do. We learned all about sex from her, in her bent little games. If you didn't do what she wanted, she'd tell your parents about everything else. She had ways. If you told anyone in authority, she'd kill you."

"Yes," said Julia.

"She would, too. She would have. She was evil. She made the Temple girl—who did everything Olivia wanted—lick her. You know what I mean, lick her?" He stroked Julia's knee. "She could beat up any of us."

"And she killed Geoffrey Braden," Julia softly said.

The hand tightened and released on her knee. "A man was found guilty of that and executed."

"A harmless vagrant," said Julia. "He liked the children. He used to talk to them. You know he didn't do it."

Swift turned his pink face toward Julia and drained his glass. "You were a fool to give me that money," he said. "You were a fool. Nobody's thought about Geoffrey Braden in twenty-five years. Nobody's going to do anything about it now."

"That's not why I have to know."

"I don't care," he said, and her heart sank. Then he added, "I was going to tell you anyhow. You were stupid to give me that money. I was innocent. I didn't do anything."

"You just watched," Julia guessed. She could feel her pulse thrumming in her neck.

He grinned at her. "I watched."

"So she *did* do it," Julia whispered.

"Of course." He looked at her with an expression like triumph. "She covered his head with a pillow. She tried it twice before, but an attendant heard his yelping and ran over. She hid the pillow just in time. Then one afternoon she did do it. Three of the bigger kids held him down and stuffed things in his mouth. Then she put the pillow on his head and sat on it. It was what she always wanted to do. To kill

someone. You could see that. It was what she was all about. I'll bet the little bitch had an orgasm."

"What did she look like? Was she blond?"

"Sure. Blond. A color anyone else would have to get out of a bottle. It was the most beautiful hair I ever saw. And a sweet little face. Oh, she was charming. Sometimes I think about the way she'd look if she were still alive—Christ, that bitch would have changed the world." His hand slid over her leg. "I like talking about this, you know. If I weren't drunk, I'd probably chuck you out, but I like telling you about it. It was funny. She made us feel that we were all in a war. Soldiers."

"Her tooth," Julia said. "Didn't she . . . ?"

"How did you know about that? The first day she tried to do little Braden, he hit her mouth with the top of his head—broke one of her front teeth. He didn't have a chance after that. She had to have him. But he never really did have a chance, the little bugger. Do you know what happened afterward? With Paulie? Your poof friend?"

He was gripping the underside of her thigh, and she put a hand on his wrist. It was feverishly hot. She shook her head.

"Paulie was bent even then. She liked that. She made him bite him after he was dead."

"Bite him?"

"Bite him. Bite his cock. She made him bite his cock."

He leaned over and snared her wrist. His mouth slurred on her cheek. "She said if he didn't do it, she'd do it to him."

Julia twisted away and stood up. She broke her hand away from his grip and tottered backward toward the door.

"You're not leaving," Swift growled. "You're going to stay with me." He struggled to stand.

"I have to talk to Olivia," she said, facing him.

It stopped him long enough for her to seize the doorknob and pull it open.

"You're crazy," he shouted, half-crouching before the table. His trousers bulged at the fly.

When she fled down the stairs she heard him yelling above her. "Cock-teaser! Remember—nobody cares anymore, you bitch. You can't do anything."

She slammed the street door. The beaten man no longer lay beside the pub, but still some blood remained, tinting the puddles of rain. Julia ran toward her car. She knew, she knew. It had been Olivia Rudge all along: Kate was safe. Once in the car she began to sob, whether from horror or relief she could not tell.

You know. The words had been smeared in soap on the black mirror above the bathtub. From the atmosphere of tense quiet within the house—for the first time in two weeks, Julia had not heard the rustling noises from upstairs—she had expected some atrocity, and had been fearful of leaving the ground floor of her house. She had no idea of what Olivia intended to do with her now that she had discovered the truth. Julia mounted the stairs, looking for signs of triumph or outrage. In her throbbingly hot bedroom, all lay undisturbed from the morning: the burst dolls sprawled at the back of the closet, sprouting gray curls of wool, their power to frighten her gone. Every time she looked over her shoulder, she expected to see Olivia Rudge. That adult, challenging smile. Or she feared to see Magnus, controlled by her. But all she found were

the two words of confirmation. YOU KNOW. She scraped them off with a table knife, and wiped the remaining flecks and smears with a towel until the black mirror held only a foot-long blur which translated her reflection into cloud. There would be more, much more. This lull, this truce, and the two words were more frightening than Olivia's displays of power.

Julia gazed out of her bedroom window into night and rain. Out there, everything had disappeared into darkness. Reality lay within.

She snapped off the light, undressed in the dark and felt her way to the bed. Then she lay beneath the burning sheet and watched the darkness move. A black plane composed of millions of particles sifted down toward her, withdrew, and sifted down again. Perspiration trickled into the hair above her ears.

She stabbed the reading light on in sudden fear and the plane of darkness disappeared. There was nothing. There was no giant pillow of dark. She switched off the light, and saw it return.

When the first touch of small hands came, she went rigid, aware that she had somehow fallen asleep. A cool hand slid up her inner thigh, and she rolled over, twisting in the sheet. The hand returned on her buttocks, caressing, probing. Julia gasped at the violation and spun around, rolling to the other side of the bed. Arms braced her shoulders to the bed. They held her immobilized; her legs, trapped in the twisted sheet, were as if pinned to the mattress. The cool small hand found her pubic hair, then her cleft. It began, delicately, to rub. Her body felt naked to the dark air, though the sheet bound her. Julia groaned as the hand pressed toward her clitoris and stroked. Feathery: feathers, tongues. She was a fly caught in a sticky cocoon, ministered to by the

spider. Against her will, with horror, she felt her
body build up a rhythmic tension. The relentless
hand stroked, rubbed, as if dipped in oil; it circled,
insinuated into her. Her back arched. She felt her
nipples harden. Sweat broke out on her chest. Julia
inhaled a gulp of burning air. She seemed to be
falling into a deep well. Her knees twitched. The
tight sheet, wrapping her like a shroud, was itself the
lightest of caresses, palms on her taut nipples. The
pressure, arching her back, subtly increased and
began to beat outward in circles. Suddenly she saw
Mark before her, his body taut with longing. The
oiled rubbing hands were the huge tip of his penis.
The embracing arms were his. Her legs moved wide
apart and his shaft slid deep within her. She bared
her teeth. Arms, legs, hands, deep velvet held her.
She saw, felt him stiffen and plunge and a sound died
in her throat as everything burst.

And the next morning when Julia tottered sick
with nausea into the bathroom, Olivia showed
herself within the house for the first time. She did
not jump out of sight at the last second; she did not
flicker away. She stood, a small blond smiling child,
behind Julia as Julia looked into the black mirror
opposite her. Julia placed a protective hand over her
abraded, sore cleft and whirled around. Again, the
child appeared behind her in the facing mirror.

As Julia watched, Olivia gave her asymmetric,
challenging smile and slowly drew an index finger
across her pale throat. Her other hand gripped the
pulped, still trembling body of a headless bird.

*A Thames gull slapped into the window late at
night, making a noise like a train wreck, and startling
into wakefulness the man who reclined on a fluffy
Indian cushion. Uneasy—he had been close to fear
for the past twenty-four hours—and not as yet quite*

certain where he was, the man extended one hand and knocked over the bottle of Calvados. His room, crowded with details of his life, reassuringly came together about him; the needle of the record player crackled and hissed in the final grooves. He righted the bottle, shaking his head. None had spilled, for he had consumed most of what was left during the night, after his guest had left. His mind seemed thickened, syrupy; the aftertaste of his heavy cigarettes coated his mouth.

From beyond the door, his name quietly sounded. He sat up straight, pulling his legs under him, and listened to the sound of the voice. It uttered his name over and over, beseechingly, in a voice neither male nor female. "Foolish little scut," the man muttered, and for several seconds considered his promise not to open the door again. But that too was foolish. Both had had far too much to drink. The man bent forward and stood in one motion, feeling the muscles in his thighs protesting. Upright, he patted his hairpiece and straightened his pullover. He moved to the door as slowly as he could, relishing the sound of his name, half whispered, urgent, full of need.

He opened the door to a stranger—a stranger? The voice was a voice he knew. The visitor smiled, and he knew the contours of that smile.

Too late, he saw the knife slide from beneath the coat. His mind fluttered with bright, hopeless panic and he stepped backward as the visitor moved through the doorway, still voicing his name.

Part Three

The Closing:
Olivia

9

Julia moved hesitantly up Kensington High Street at the end of day, buffeted by the crowds returning home late from work, unsure of where she was going. Confused, she had taken the wrong way, and was dimly aware of this. Her left wrist was still oozing blood, and she dabbed at the deep cut with a wrinkled yellow tissue, hoping it would stop; but the cuff of the blouse was stained and smeared with blood, as her sheet had been. Because of the pills, her mind had difficulty in retaining images, and she looked at the sky twice before being certain that it had stopped raining. All of the sky was a vast dark undifferentiated gray. *No holes,* she thought, *no air spaces,* and saw herself beating at the undersurface of gray cloud as if it were a thick layer of ice trapping her in arctic water; the pavements and street were still filmed with black rain. Ascent, escape, ascent, escape, revolved in her brain. But she could think of no escape. Olivia held her fast.

She thought of the beggar maid's king, Cophetua, his face immobilized by love. Mark. Was he safe? He had rung immediately after the grinning specter of the girl had vanished from the mirror.

Take some pills and go to sleep, he'd said. Do you have anything?

—Yes. Pills? Yes.

—You need rest. Take a couple of pills and get a really good rest.

—I have to see you. I'm in danger. Like Mrs. Fludd said. I am, Mark.

—Listen to me. Ghosts don't kill. Your danger is entirely from Magnus, and you're staying away from him. Julia, love, you're overtired. Lock your door and knock yourself out for the rest of the day.

—I need you, Mark. She wants me.

—Not half as much as I do, he had laughed. I'll see you this evening, sometime tonight.

—Save me.

Had she said that, *save me?* Perhaps she had imagined the entire conversation. All that was clear, besides gulping down two pills—memories of the hospital making her shudder—was running back upstairs and heaving the polished, rose-veined stone at the walls of the bathroom. Heaving it, again and again, until the black mirrors had showered down, leaping off the walls and shivering past her face. Then she had slipped on a large panel of glass and gone down into the mess, gashing her wrist. She had barely felt the pain. *Now she can't come in here,* Julia had thought, uncaring of the blood which welled out of the gash and down across the palm of her hand. The walls were unreflecting gray-white plaster marked like a graph with small black studs, to a few of which adhered an inch of mirror. Broken glass, some of it catching muted light from the ceiling, was strewn over the bathroom carpet, tumbled in long snaky shapes in the sink and tub. She felt warm blood falling onto her bare feet and snatched a towel from the rack and wound it about her wrist. Pebbles of glass snagged at her cut. Then she had swallowed the two pills. And staggered across twelve feet of broken glass to her bedroom.

(Thus she did not hear the bell seven hours later when Lily and Magnus came together to her front door.)

As in the hospital, she was visited by long fluent dreams. Those had been of turning the knife on herself, of sacrificing herself for Kate, that Kate's vibrant little life could be restored: her blood for her daughter's, a barter. She had felt Kate's forgiving approach at such times. But now her dreams all had the same flavor; they were as ashy as failure and loss. Even as she began to slip steeply into them, she resisted, sensing the approach of that hopeless territory. She was again walking through the gritty streets, carrying her daughter's corpse. The child she knew to be Olivia lurked ahead, unseen, and it was her duty to find her. The sky above the blackened roofs of tenements was lurid, red and orange shot with black streaks. Again, her long, burdened wandering took her to a mean courtyard. She moved across the filthy cobblestones and past abandoned, bricked-up warehouses and passed through the arch of the yard. A hunched leering man in a tattered coat winked at her, summoning from a doorway a small black girl with a curly ruff of hair. Julia ascended broken stairs and came out, as she knew she would, on a flat rooftop. A little woman in a large brown coat sat alone on the rooftop, her weight supported by a rickety chair. The woman was Mrs. Fludd. Seeing her, Julia felt tears welling in her eyes.

—I'm sorry, she said. I put you here. And I still need your help.

—I cannot help you.

Kate's body was taken from her; it had been needed to bring her here, and now it could vanish.

—You called her up.

—Yes, said Julia.

—You invoked her. She needed someone to call her back, you see, and you were chosen. This happened because of your daughter.

—What do I have to know?

—She won't like you knowing her secrets.

Mrs. Fludd turned sideways in her chair, refusing to speak further.

—Talk to me.

The old woman's face, heavy and washed of color, turned again toward Julia.

—She will have your friends.

Then she had been running into a long tunnel, noticing even as she ran that the tunnel led nowhere, that it narrowed the further and deeper she went. At the end was Mark, the New Hampshire valley, peace . . . but she knew that at the end of all her running would be only a black narrow hole. About her rang Heather Rudge's coarse, wheezing laughter.

She had awoken with this laughter still reverberating above her, joining the other noises of the house. The towel had been dragged off her arm, and the left side of the bed was stained by irregular red blots. For a moment she sensed that, as in her dream, Olivia Rudge hung nearby, just out of sight, waiting to appear. It would not be long. Mrs. Fludd's final words had then come back to her. Struggling to impose firmness and direction on her dream-tattered mind, Julia had wrapped her wrist in the top sheet and groggily sat up. She looked out the window across the room and saw rain drizzling down from a ghost-gray sky. A scarf of cool wind reached her from the open window and instantly vaporized in the

heat. For the first time, Julia was consciously aware of the hot, feral smell pervading the bedroom, the reek of a lion's cage.

Throwing aside the ruined sheet, Julia had risen and looked at her watch: now it was eight, and she had slept through the entire day. *Your friends.* Mark, her truest friend, was in danger. Her mouth filled with dust. When she had glanced into the closet and seen again the ripped, scattered dolls, she staggered away from the bed and felt blood begin to move sluggishly down her wrist. She tore several sheets of Kleenex from the box near her bed and clamped them over the slash, which had begun to pulse and complain. When she struggled into her robe, she buttoned the left sleeve to fasten the Kleenex to the wound and went down the echoing stairs to telephone Mark.

Olivia was abroad; Olivia would have anyone she wanted. *It can't be got rid of. It wants revenge,* Heather Rudge had said. *It wants revenge.*

Mark's telephone had shrilled a dozen times. She would have to go to his room.

So now she walked blearily along Kensington High Street, the wad of sodden Kleenex dropped somewhere behind her and blood seeping into the cuff of her shirt. Between the flat gray sky and the rain-blackened streets, the streetlamps had already switched on, and cast an acid yellow light over the crowds through which she pushed. From time to time, a wave of oblivious men carried her back a few paces, making her stagger as she was thrown, almost unseen, from one comfortless shoulder to the next. She looked in all their faces for Mark, and found instead—it seemed to her—only sneers and laughter. Julia realized that the men thought she was drunk. Sleeping pills had never affected her so

strongly before. Maybe it was due to lack of food.
But the image of food—a greasy pile of pinkish-gray
meat—made her stomach lurch and tighten.

A heavy curtain of dark appeared before her
vision, blotting out the bunched, jostling crowds and
the snarling jungle of traffic beyond them. Julia
tottered, blind, and fell sideways against the rough
facing of a building. For a moment, as the people
sweeping past brushed her elbows and knees and
trod on her feet, she lost all awareness of her identity
and surroundings. The wave of nausea and dizziness
was nearly a relief, sucking responsibility from her,
and she gave herself over to it, forgetting why she
was out on the street and where she was going. Her
mind fled back to the image of the drained Mrs.
Fludd, seated on a rickety chair alone on a rooftop.
Your friends. Then the long, long flight down a
narrowing tunnel. Kate had been her nearest friend.
Her thought bucked like a rearing horse.

She opened her eyes to a dark burned with acid
yellow. I'm in her world now, she thought. Soon I
will meet her again. I nearly know it all. The two
imprisoned women, the two ruined men had nearly
brought her to the full knowledge she sought, and
she had to make her way through Olivia Rudge's
world to find the rest. Men like beasts rutted past
her, each eyeing the stricken woman leaning against
the brick wall of a bank. A high thin red line—a
scream—traced the sky.

Men followed her with their eyes. Before her, as
she watched them quicken with lust or amusement
(*What in the world can I look like?* she wondered),
they drew their faces into the masks of beasts, boars,
bulls, wild dogs. Bristles jutted from their snouts,
their feet were hooves tearing the ground. Their skin
burned in the yellow light, unhealthy and sallow. In

the babble of voices, she thought she discerned Magnus' low growl, and started, her mind a fluttering rag.

Her hands brushed her thighs: cotton. She was wearing cotton trousers. She could not remember dressing. Looking down, she saw that she wore a pale shirt, a short tan jacket. She touched her hair and felt oil. The voice was not Magnus', merely that of a man shouting to another man in the street.

Four young men passed before her, their hair languorously curled; as they turned to stare, she saw their faces inflamed with pustules, death in the pouches of their cheeks, their eyes like razors cutting pieces from her body. In the high, curved, bald forehead of a man thrusting past she saw death, the skin tightening on his skull; and she saw in a woman's colorless lips death, as they parted over her teeth. And she saw they were all dead, sweeping past her in the noise of raised voices and automobiles. The dark gained on them all.

Bone-shining foreheads, skeletal umbrellas against the dark, now nearly invisible sky and the wash of yellow from the lamps and headlights. It was the world of her dream life.

Julia fought to right herself steadily on her feet. Simple movement would cure this dreadful trick of vision. The boys, now further down the block, were only boys; the men and women merely weary from work and the journey home. She felt a familiar pang—an echo from her old personality—as she realized that the little tan jacket would probably cost two weeks' wages for any of the men crowding past. Magnus had persuaded her to buy it: or had he bought it, using her money? After so many years, it made little difference, but she wanted him to have

bought it. Possessions were shameful. Then why had she bought the house?

She had been chosen. In that was the last mystery.

One step, another; she tugged at the hem of the jacket and straightened her back. No one was looking at her, in all the sweeping flood passing by. Julia began to walk more steadily, and recognized she had come over half the way to Kensington Church Street. It was one way of getting to Notting Hill, though roundabout. She hung unmoving on the crowded pavement for a second, debating whether to go back and take the walk along the side of the park which went directly north and ended at Holland Park Avenue, but then decided, in the cool gauzy air, to continue on the long way. The unaccustomed coolness would clear her head. She moved on again, passing W. H. Smith's, a package store, a clothing shop where mannequins flung out their arms as if wailing.

Then she caught sight of herself in a shop window and hurried past, unable to look away. Her face was a formless white puddle, with discolored blots beneath her eyes—it was the face of one of the women in the Breadlands Clinic, the face of a dazed animal fleeing experience. For a moment she saw how she would look when old, and she turned wildly away and rushed down the street, her bag bumping at her side.

A known face at a queue at a bus stop across the street from Biba's made her shorten her stride. The old woman in the long black dress hadn't yet seen her; Julia turned her back to the line of people at the edge of the pavement, feeling an instinctive desire to escape. . . . Still, she might have been mistaken. She edged sideways and back, and dared to turn

around. The long narrow face now in profile, the dogmatic chin, tendrils of white hair escaping from beneath a black hat: it was Miss Pinner.

Her first response had been panic: perhaps she did not want to know what the old woman had seen in the mirror that disastrous night. Perhaps she already did know.

But her curiosity about that evening was too great to be dismissed; she could not flee from Miss Pinner too. Julia's decision seemed to help her dispel Olivia's world, for the tired people at the bus stop all appeared reassuringly ordinary, and she waited until two or three men had walked between them and then crossed the blackly shining pavement to tap the old woman on the shoulder. She pronounced her name, and heard her voice emerging levelly, distinctly.

"Yes? Yes?" The old woman started out of her reverie and turned her headmistress' blue eyes on Julia.

She doesn't recognize me, Julia thought. "Excuse me," she began, and saw the old woman purse her mouth expectantly, as if she were about to be asked for directions. "I'm surprised to see you here, Miss Pinner," she said.

Fear jumped for a second in the woman's eyes, and she stepped out of the queue. "Mrs. Lofting?" she said. "I'm sorry, I didn't recognize you at first, you see . . . you look ill, my dear. Yes, you are quite right, I am not here often . . . and I am afraid that I shall have to be getting off home." She lifted a small brown parcel. "We used to enjoy shopping here, and since Miss Tooth's birthday is approaching soon, I wanted to see if I could find anything for her at Derry and Tom's—but I found that they had been

replaced by that very curious store across the street, and the little restaurant on the roof was shut, so I bought her something elsewhere." As she chattered, she glanced down the street obviously looking for her bus. "I'm late already. I must be home in time to prepare our dinner. Heavens, it's past eight."

"Do you have time to talk to me before your bus comes, Miss Pinner?"

"I can't say, I'm sure." Then the little flicker of fear was replaced by something like cunning. "I'm sorry that I was taken ill at your charming house, Mrs. Lofting. It was a very distressing evening for all of us, I'm sure . . . and then poor Mrs. Fludd's sudden demise . . . her niece forbade any of us to attend the funeral . . . but I was remiss in not writing to thank you for your hospitality. Miss Tooth and I were entertained in many grand houses years ago, when Miss Tooth could still follow her career, as you know, and we never sinned against hospitality in that way. I do hope you can forgive me."

"You were taken ill?" said Julia, focusing on the one sentence she had been able to follow.

"A spell of faintness," said Miss Pinner, showing the faint but detectable embarrassment honest people bring to their untruths. "I've been kept very busy these past months, going through all our old scrapbooks." She hitched up her shoulders painfully, in the movement of one adjusting to the twinges of a long-standing arthritis. "I can't do it in the mornings anymore, so my afternoons are very tiring. But Miss Tooth"—here the dogmatic face forgot all embarrassment—"Miss Tooth can still do her exercises."

"Can she?" said Julia, wondering if the drug were still clouding her perceptions.

"She can still work at the barre," said Miss Pinner with great satisfaction. "Miss Tooth is very supple yet."

"At the bar?" said Julia, trying to visualize little Miss Tooth serving up pints of bitter in a public house.

"Oh, yes. Of course she hasn't the stamina she had when she was younger, but she has all of her grace. We are preparing a book from the scrapbooks. Many people still remember her, as I see you do yourself. Of course, you would only have heard of her. You're too young to have seen her dance."

"Unfortunately, I was too young, yes," said Julia, seeing it at last. She remembered how, during the séance, Miss Tooth had seemingly floated to the floor in one effortless motion. "But she was very famous, wasn't she?" Julia guessed.

"How kind of you to remember," said Miss Pinner, and now her manner was entirely friendly. "Rosamund was a great artist. I was her dresser for twenty-five years and we retired together. After working for Rosamund Tooth it was impossible to work for anyone else. And I wouldn't touch any of the young lot. All technique and no poetry."

"Did Miss Tooth see anything in the mirror after you'd fainted that night?" Julia said brutally.

Miss Pinner's face trembled into an utter blankness of expression.

"I thought I saw something when I followed her in," Julia added. "And I know what it was."

Miss Pinner looked aghast, and Julia felt a twisting of guilt for making the old woman confront her lie. "Perhaps you saw it too."

"No—no—Mrs. Lofting, you should not be asking me about that night. I was tired from the long ride

down from our home and from putting the scrapbooks in order. I don't know what I saw." She
stepped nervously back into her place in the queue,
and Julia followed her.

"Was it a little girl? A blond child? She is, she
was, a wicked person, Miss Pinner. Please tell me,
Miss Pinner." But she was already confused by the
expression of mixed astonishment and relief on Miss
Pinner's angular face. "Wasn't it the blond girl?"

"I am afraid to tell you, Mrs. Lofting," said Miss
Pinner. "Oh. There's my bus down the road. Please
don't detain me. It'll soon be here."

Julia, afraid that she would never know, gently
touched the thick black stuff of Miss Pinner's coat
with her right hand. "Wasn't it the little girl? She
does horrible things. She once made me faint too."

Miss Pinner shook her head. "I don't think . . ."
she began. Down the block, the bus swerved into
traffic and came toward them, its headlamps beaming yellow through gathering dark.

Julia suddenly felt a sick certainty that her assumptions had been wrong; she was again at the
edge of the abyss, afraid to look down. The bus
swung heavily toward the curb, a wing of yellow light
flashing below the upper deck. In his cage behind
rain-streaked glass the driver looked totemic.

"I must get on now or wait another twenty
minutes," said Miss Pinner. The queue moved
forward slowly, a crippled insect laden with parcels
and umbrellas. "I would not have said so much
except that you knew about Rosamund." She was
nearly at the steps of the bus, kept from them by
only a fat woman struggling with two small dogs and
a little girl with the face of a pampered pig.

"I have to know," said Julia as the woman swung

the pig-child up onto the steps and gruntingly lifted herself and the dogs into the bus. "I have to know." She raised her hands, as if praying.

Miss Pinner looked in shock at Julia's left hand and shirt cuff, and then gazed straight into her face with a tense compassion. "I saw you," she blurted, and the conductor raised her up onto the platform and the bus was gone.

Earlier that day, brother and sister were sitting across from each other at Lily's table, two empty wine bottles and soup bowls and plates littered with bones between them. Magnus sat slumped in his chair, staring at the unappetizing remains of his lunch. He looked flushed and puffy, but he had changed into a clean suit and shirt, and wore immaculately polished shoes. He was impressive. Locked into his face, at a complicated level beneath the features but informing them, was a combination of authority and power and malice which she had seen in him all her life.

She said, "Magnus, you are a beautiful man."

"What!" His head jerked up and she saw his bloodshot eyes. "For God's sake, Lily. I am fifty-three years old, I'm nearly three stone overweight, and I have not been sleeping well. I am tired."

She wanted to reply, but he cut her off. "And I'm not sure about this. I think you're rushing it."

Enjoying this moment as she did each of those rare occasions when she was stronger than he, Lily said, "Yesterday you agreed with me. We both know that she must be put back into professional care as quickly as possible. Magnus, your wife is in danger—she may do permanent harm to herself. Not to mention the damage she is doing to you."

"Humph." Magnus shook his head.

"I trust you wish to keep her from Mark," she said slyly.

"Mark is a wretch. He is a failure. There has always been something wrong with him. You know that."

"You are what is wrong with him, and of course I know it. Does Julia? Magnus, she scarcely knows him at all."

"Yes, I do want to keep her from him."

"Have you ever told her about his breakdowns?" He shook his head. "They were a long time ago."

"Well, you see my point," she said, "she really only knows Mark's surface. And that is very seductive."

Magnus was not ignoring her now.

"You do take my point, and you needn't pretend that it hasn't been preying on you as it has on me. If we can get her back into the hospital, we shall have taken care of *that* problem. Now. As I see it, we must first persuade her to leave that house, by whatever means, and to move into my spare bedroom. It's possible to—I mean to say that the door locks from the outside."

"Yes," he said. "Are you certain—are you absolutely certain there couldn't be anything in that story of hers? I saw Kate in the window of her bedroom one afternoon. That afternoon I struck that ninny. I'm certain it was Kate. I couldn't be wrong about her. I know it was Kate. It knocked the breath out of me. And I have felt—things—in that miserable house. I don't know how to describe it. All I know is that I want her out of there. That place upsets me."

"You upset yourself," Lily said calmly. "You see your daughter, whom you miss terribly; Julia is

obsessed with a case a quarter of a century old in which a mother stabs her daughter to death. You haven't been eating or sleeping regularly, and Julia is burning herself up. Of course the two of you see things. But as far as Julia actually being in touch with spiritual manifestations, any such thought is absurd."

"How can you be so certain? I was certain too, until I saw Kate."

"Experience," she said dismissively. "Ghosts are seen all over this country by people who are upset, or have had too much to eat or drink. Magnus, this is my field as the law is yours. I assure you, if a spirit were to appear to anyone in this family, it would appear to me. An untrained, inexperienced person like Julia would simply not have the faintest idea of how to interpret an authentic sighting. Magnus, with respect, do let me tell you that when an untrained person gets it into her head that she is in contact with a spirit, a sort of hypnosis begins to take effect—the untrained person has all sorts of fancies—wild thoughts—and she can easily persuade others to share them. I'll confess that I had a small trace of this myself."

"Lately?" Magnus said with interest.

"Yes."

"So you saw Kate too." His big face was suffusing with blood.

"No, but if I listened long enough to you and Julia I very well might. I saw—I supposed myself to see—something far more mundane."

"*What?*" Magnus seemed to be increasing in size, and Lily felt a thrilled, appreciative trace of her fear of him.

"Actually, I imagined that I saw Mrs. Fludd," she said, and Magnus slumped back into his chair.

"Which simply proves how careful we must be not to be swayed by Julia's delusions."

"But what if she *is* right? What if I was right, and not merely overtired?" But even in his tone of voice, Lily heard that he did not want to believe it.

"Then I expect that we should *all* be endangered. Any truly vengeful, destructive spirit, once set free, draws strength from its own evil. It might even control any mind weak enough to be open to it. But such cases occur very infrequently. There isn't one in a century. Genuine evil is as rare as that. Most of what we call evil is merely lack of imagination."

"Most murderers are an unhappy lot," Magnus agreed. "I've defended several who didn't so much commit murder as fall over it."

"Precisely," Lily said. "So I think we can dismiss the possibility of this being a case of genuine manifestation."

"What did I see in the window, then? And what did I feel in that house?"

"You saw and felt your own fear. If that can happen to my commanding brother, then I think this has gone far enough. I should never have introduced Julia to Mrs. Fludd. Neither of us should have permitted Julia to indulge her ill fantasies about Kate's death."

"That's enough of that," Magnus said warningly, and pushed himself away from the table.

"Except for this," said Lily. "We—you and I—must accept the truth. We are going to institutionalize Julia. For her own good and for ours. Do you think that she might be suicidal?"

"I don't know," Magnus said.

"There you have it. We don't know. You can't afford to have her divorce you, and you don't want her to die. She must be put back into the hospital,

and kept there until she is docile. And I suggest that you take whatever steps are appropriate to ensure that her money is accessible. You must be able to control her money. You must be able to control *her*."

Magnus was leaning forward, his elbows on his knees, staring directly at her. "You are being very frank, Lily."

"It is too late to be anything else," she said straight to him. "In truth, Magnus, we all desire to own her. That is what we wish. You, I—and Mark. We wish to possess her."

"I wish to save her," he flatly said.

"Did I say differently?"

"Fine, then," Magnus said.

"I adore you when you're reasonable," Lily half sang, "and there'll never be a time when I don't. I think we should go over there now. We can walk across the park."

"I'll begin to look into things tomorrow," Magnus said, and shrugged; he stood up and dropped his napkin beside his plate.

When Julia had numbly watched the bus disappear around the corner and up Kensington Church Street, exhaustion seemed to invade her with every breath, weighting the marrow of her bones. Her body seemed very heavy; she no longer felt able to trudge up to Notting Hill; she wanted to lean on Mark's arm. She thought with longing of her bed, of long sleep, of reading a book propped against the blanket while a light kept her safe from the dark. She saw me dead, she thought. Or had Miss Pinner seen—an idea fragile as a moth's wing, but freighted with all of Olivia's darkness, flickered for a half second at the borders of her consciousness and was

then tamped down, forgotten, and her mind veered away, not recognizing what it had done.

And with it she veered, turning to her side, blinking, knowing only that she wished to be at home.

She got halfway back up the street before her burning feet could carry her no farther. A few steps away was a bench, and she limped toward it and collapsed onto it, sighing. A man in a black raincoat with the collar turned up sat beside her and brushed her legs with his. Very lightly, he brushed her leg again. Julia peeked at him, hoping he would leave, and saw—thought she saw—that the man had no lips. His face seemed to be chopped off below the nose, and to begin again at the chin. Between was a white scream of teeth, a permanent snarl of rigid teeth and blackened gums. She was afraid to look again and was too tired to move on, so sat hunched within herself, staring directly ahead of her, seeing nothing. He too hunched in his black raincoat, the collar turned up, and stared ahead. His leg hung against hers, with almost no pressure save that of the thin black cloth of his trousers. After what seemed an hour the man shifted, and she glanced quickly at him and saw that his face was, after all, utterly normal, rather pudgy and full-lipped. She realized that she had been holding her breath, and noisily inhaled. The man pressed his leg to Julia's but now he was just an ordinary man, and she moved down the bench, pretending to look for something on the wet sidewalk, so that she would not offend him. After a time he moved away, leaving behind a copy of the *Evening Standard*. Julia unthinkingly picked up the newspaper and numbly walked home. Noises and screams drifted across from Holland Park.

The house pulsed with heat and expectant, waiting

quiet, its lights flaming. Julia walked through rooms which seemed alien and dead, utterly apart from her. She heard none of the by now familiar noises of the trapped echoes and spirits of the Rudges. Julia thought, as she sat wearily on the McClintocks' ugly couch, that Olvia might have withdrawn, leaving Julia in her world forever: that was the strength of evil, she saw, its absence of hope, its stink of moral failure. For a moment she saw the tramp on Cremorne Road savagely stuffing a dog into a bag; from an accumulation of these sordid, hopeless moments evil was condensed.

She bent her neck backward and closed her eyes and suppressed a half-formed image which threatened to flood into her mind.

To distract herself, Julia took up the newspaper she had taken from the bench. In time she would have the energy to face the stairs and her bedroom. Then she remembered the carnage she had made of the upstairs bathroom—bare white-gray walls like dead skin and skeletal shards of black mirror over everything. That mess: Olivia seemed alive and present in its midst. She could not bear to look at it now.

Julia skimmed the news on the front page—it seemed remote and irrelevant. She read the names of politicians, looked at their photographs, and scarcely remembered who they were. They had nothing to do with her, nothing to do with Olivia Rudge. Why was she reading this? It was the first current newspaper she had looked at in weeks. She felt the atmosphere of the house intensify around her, and turned the page.

At the bottom of page four she saw the little headline. Paul Winter had not been judged worthy

of much space. The headline read GENERAL'S SON
FOUND DEAD IN CHELSEA FLAT.

> Captain Paul Winter, 36, son of General
> Martin Somill Winter, second in command to
> Montgomery at Alamein, was found dead this
> morning by a friend in his small flat in Stadium
> St. SW 10. Captain Winter, who had left the
> army several years ago, suffered multiple stab
> wounds. General Winter was informed of his
> son's death soon after discovery of the body.
> The General and his son are said to have not
> been on speaking terms for many years. Captain
> Winter was unmarried.

Julia's first thought was of David Swift: he had to
be warned. As she began to move dazedly across the
room to the telephone, she heard the sound of
chattering, high-pitched laughter—gleeful hiccuping
childish laughter. "Damn you, damn you, damn
you," Julia screamed, at the same time recognizing
with a part of her mind that Olivia Rudge could
never produce a sound so innocent. It was the
delighted laughter of a young child.

Where was it? For a moment it seemed to ring all
about her and pervade the house. She forced herself
to be still and quiet, and then heard that it came
from beyond the kitchen. She knew where. If she
had not shattered the black mirrors, it would come
from upstairs. Julia ran through the rooms, her
warning to David Swift forgotten, and rushed down
the hall to the bathroom.

Some figure lurked in the mirror, pouring out that
delighted laughter. When she banged open the door
she saw its shape crouched on the side of the tub,

darkly reflected in the rose mirrors. She stabbed on the light.

The little black girl, Mona, perched on the side of the mirrored tub, rocking with glee. From her upturned throat poured gasping high trills which bounched off the shining walls, redoubling. Mona saw her and raised a short pointing finger and continued to screech.

"What . . ." Julia uttered, and spun around. Olivia Rudge passed the bathroom door and was proceeding calmly, her back to Julia, into the kitchen.

"*Stop,*" Julia shouted. She sprinted out of the bathroom, Mona's screams of glee locked in her inner ear, and saw Olivia, in jeans and a red shirt, going out the side door of the kitchen into the dining room. As Julia reached the door Olivia twisted the handle of the French windows and disappeared out into the garden. Rage flashed through Julia's entire nervous system, and she followed.

She went around the side of the house and saw the blond child moving easily and swiftly, well ahead of her, down the street. You won't get away from me, Julia thought, not with that highly visible hair, and began to walk quickly down the street after her in the direction of Kensington High Street. Olivia's hair shimmered in the dark air like a beacon, drifting twenty or thirty yards ahead of Julia. The child turned left on the High Street and was lost from sight.

Alone in the darkness, Julia ran to the corner, hearing her shoes clapping on the pavement. At the corner she looked to the left and saw Olivia moving resolutely up the street, two blocks ahead. A cocoon of silence seemed to have descended over the two of

them. Julia was unconscious of the babble of voices and traffic sounds which had so penetrated her earlier; the other people on the street, now merely evening strollers, were insubstantial specters between herself and the girl's flickering hair. She crossed an intervening street and came up onto a long block, following Olivia. Anger and determination were joined presences, thin, high and sweet, thrumming in her blood.

The girl drifted ahead of her, slowing whenever Julia was detained by a knot of people or by traffic at an intersection. When Julia tried to gain on the girl and ran for the length of a block, Olivia effortlessly and without seeming to increase her pace quickened her movement and maintained the distance between them. Around Julia, the cool gauzy air, still smelling of recent rainfall, seemed to congeal into a glowing envelope which contained only herself and Olivia Rudge. Energy—Julia's energy—burned within this envelope, beating at the pulse of her blood.

After a time Julia ceased to be aware of the stream of traffic, to see the other people on the pavement. When her view of her quarry was blocked, she crossed to the other side of the walk and saw her moving easily and determinedly up the street, jeans and red shirt beneath the pale flame of her hair. There was no one else in the world; there was no other movement in the world.

At the long terrace of the Commonwealth Institute Olivia paused and turned. A block away, Julia saw her unsmiling, intent face and for the first time did not find in it a challenge. It was nervous and blank, waiting for her to come closer, almost fearful. Julia pushed off a curb to give leverage to her running and nearly went headlong into an oncoming car. "Look here," came a man's outraged voice, but

Julia barely recorded the protest. Olivia was leading her somewhere; Olivia seemed almost to be pleading to her.

From her right she heard the clang of gates and knew that the attendants were locking the park. It was nine o'clock. As if it were a signal for her, Olivia turned her face from Julia and scampered up the steps to the terrace, passed through a line of columns and began to move quickly up the lane running north alongside the park. A few stragglers emerged just as Julia reached the path and blocked her view of Olivia; and then they were alone again, walking rapidly up the long dark path. The girl's hair shone.

"Olivia!" she shouted as the girl slipped into the darkness between the rows of trees. Again she followed, trying to lessen the distance between them, and began to jog, feeling her muscles catch like gears. Olivia was now far ahead, lost in the dark.

Then she appeared in the flaring circle of a lamp, still moving effortlessly between the twin rows of trees. Julia passed the lower portion of the silent green length of park and reached the gate to the youth hostel just within the grounds. Olivia had vanished again. She shouted her name; silence. Making a frantic guess, Julia pushed through the wooden gate and ran up another smaller, twisting path: far ahead, confirmingly, she thought she heard the sound of Olivia's footsteps.

At the bar of the metal gate pulled across the path she hesitated for only a moment, and then swung her trunk over, awkwardly lifting her legs, and half tumbled into the locked park. Her body was a weapon, an arrow for Olivia. Before her, the path wound darkly past the side of Holland House and the wooded hostel. It went far up into the area of the park Julia did not know, a woods traced with many

small unpaved paths. Olivia was moving resolutely, unhesitatingly up the narrow way toward the woods.

"Olivia! Olivia!" Julia screamed, but the child did not turn. Julia went after her.

After a few minutes she had left the path and was running across soft grass. Olivia's shining hair appeared flickering between the trees, moving steadily forward. Julia's cuff snagged on a low branch, and then ripped away. Her shoes sank in loamy earth, and admitted chill moisture. In the sparse wood she lost her quarry, then saw a gleaming flash of white up to her right, cutting through bushes and across a barren dark space. They went deeper into the wood, Olivia floating over the low wooden fences and Julia tripping over them, staying on her feet by sheer momentum. In this way, Olivia seemed to lead her for nearly a mile, tricking her into loops to one side or the other, disappearing behind trees and surfacing in wide clearings, tracking back to the right.

Where the wood ended Julia saw the girl racing through low bushes to a wire fence, and ran after. When she reached the fence Olivia was already beyond it, going slowly down a pitted asphalt walk. In the darkness Julia saw only a shimmer of white, pale as breath, to mark her going.

She would have to get over the fence, which was chin-high. Pulling at the top bar with her hands, she lifted herself up to place a toe between the links of chain, then her other foot, and pushed on straining leg muscles so that her torso was above the top bar, where sharp twisted strands of wire prevented her from rolling over. She tremblingly balanced herself, leaned out across the bar, and raised her right leg over the top. Down the sloping path she would find Olivia: this conviction allowed her to swing her other leg over the top, catching the ripped cuff on one of

the strands of wire. She tore it impatiently away, and pushed herself off the fence onto the lightless path.

From ahead of her came the sound of running. With all of the breath left in her, Julia forced her body into a trot; the downward slope of the path carried her into a run she was unable to control. It was as if she were running down a mountain, her legs flying out to keep her body upright. Gravity brought her forward, falling like a boulder, toward the sound of Olivia's movement.

Light, noise, astonished faces met her as she tumbled out onto the street below the path. Still ahead of her, she heard Olivia's noise, and she bounced off and around a metal containing fence and raced out into the middle of Holland Park Avenue. Headlights fixed her like a pinned butterfly; her upper body, head, arms and shoulders were still traveling faster than her legs. When she fell, a car squealed to a stop, horn blaring, only inches from her body.

10

_____

Olivia had murdered Geoffrey Braden; she had murdered Paul Winter; she had murdered Mrs. Fludd; and she had tried now to kill Julia. She had been called up from whatever rank, resentful obscurity she had inhabited; Julia's appearance on Ilchester Place had clothed her in flesh, and now she was a bodily presence in the house. Or so Julia had felt: she could not enter a room without imagining that her tormentor had just quit it. When alone in her bedroom, she locked the door, knowing that Olivia could reach her at any time she wished. The long run through the park had been something like playfulness. Olivia had been toying with her, trying to reproduce Rosa Fludd's "accident."

They were in a new configuration: the screw had tightened, and Olivia wanted her blood. Julia stood on weak, aching legs in the kitchen, waiting for her coffee to boil. It was as dark beyond the windows as if it were still night; the sky, a patch of which Julia could see above the wet brown boards of a fence, hung motionless and woolly, looking as if it might snag in the trees. A few small drops dashed against the window.

Paul Winter. Someone had visited his room and butchered him. Someone under Olivia's control, some man driven by hate so that Olivia could enter

him; a man whom absurd, touching little Paul
Winter had trusted. Someone who was his Magnus.
Whoever it was would not know that he had killed a
man for talking to a woman named Julia Lofting.
Maybe he wouldn't even remember committing the
murder—maybe Olivia could sweep into a mind and
then flow out again, leaving no real memory of her
occupation. This thought weakened Julia's legs, and
she leaned against the counter on shaking knees,
perspiring.

The disturbed, reclusive woman in Abbotsbury
Close would read the newspaper item or hear of it
from Huff, and be savagely glad. She too was
Olivia's victim.

And David Swift would be the next, if she
understood what Olivia was doing. Julia immediately left the kitchen and went into the living room. She
had to check in the directory to find Swift's number.
Would her story convince him of his danger? He had
seen Olivia at work, but Swift was a stupid and
arrogant man. She had no choice, she had to
persuade him. She dialed the number and listened
intently as the telephone shrilled at the other end.
She prayed for him to answer it, but the telephone
continued to ring. He might be outside, she thought,
or in his bed, sleeping off a hangover.

Julia did not want to look at the third possibility,
but neither did she evade it. In the A-D directory
she found the listings for police departments, and
rang the Islington police. "A man may be dead," she
intoned. "Look at Three Thirty-seven Upper Street,
the flat just above a pub called The Beautiful and
Damned. His name is Swift. This is in connection
with the murder of Captain Paul Winter. Hurry."

"What is your relationship to Mr. Swift, madam?"
inquired the policeman's drawling voice.

"I'm afraid for him," Julia said, and hurriedly hung up. Relieved that she had at least done something, she went back into the kitchen, where the kettle full of Malvern water was emitting its high shriek. She promised herself to telephone Swift later.

She drank her coffee standing at the white counter, trying to decide how to act, what to do to meet Olivia's challenge. Olivia would try again to kill her. All the previous night, after she had been aided by the puzzled, half-solicitous, half-furious man who had nearly hit her, she had lain atop her sheet in the steaming bedroom, afraid to close her eyes. Then, she had vowed to leave Ilchester Place; Olivia's secret was known, there was nothing left to find; she had to defend herself. Yet in the morning she had realized that Olivia could reach her anywhere. No house was any safer than her own. She had cleaned up the bathroom, filling pails and bags with sections of black glass, with that certainty lodged in her mind.

She thought of it just as she finished her coffee: if freedom from Olivia were anywhere, it would be in America. It was time to return. Her marriage was finished. She did not want Magnus or need him. She was closer to Heather and Olivia Rudge than to anyone else in England—save Mark. But she and Mark had almost never had even so much as a serious conversation. Would he like to live in New Hampshire? She realized with dismay how little she knew about him.

But the thought of him gave her courage to answer her telephone when it began to ring in the living room. She braced herself, thinking that she might hear for the first time the voice of Olivia Rudge. But it was Lily's voice she heard.

"Julia, I hope you won't mind my asking you how you are?"

Julia found that she could speak to Lily only in the coolest, most detached manner. Lily seemed to have emerged from another era.

"Good morning, Lily. How am I? I don't know. I feel sort of suspended. I feel very odd. A lot's happened. I know how Mrs. Fludd was killed. Olivia almost did the same to me. I think it was her idea of a joke."

"My darling, if you are saying . . ."

"That Olivia tried to kill me. That's right. Next time, she won't be so playful. What would you do if your life were in danger?"

"I'd go to Magnus," Lily said simply.

"Well, so you would. But I can't. The next time, it might be Magnus trying to run me over. So I can't do that, Lily, can I? No."

She could almost hear Lily's patience snapping.

"I understand that you're overtired, darling," said Lily. "But you should realize that you're being almost absurdly unrealistic. Magnus loves you, Julia. Magnus wants you for his wife. He wants to begin rebuilding your marriage. We—Magnus and I—went to see you yesterday, just past lunchtime. I wish you had been at home, so you could have seen how pathetically distressed he is."

"I was at home, I was asleep. I'd taken two sleeping pills. Olivia had just given me a message. Do you believe me, Lily? And last night she tried to put it into effect—she lured me outside and ran me into traffic. I was almost killed. It was like being hypnotized. It's what she did to Mrs. Fludd. Would you have called it an accident, Lily?"

"Have you ever wondered why it is to you that all these things are happening? Why is it you?"

"You're clever, Lily. That's all I have left to find out."

"You have been very active and you have been through a great deal, my dear. How long has it been since you've been out of the hospital?"

"I don't know," said Julia, feeling her artificial detachment begin to recede. "What difference does it make? A month, maybe."

"Not as long as that, I shouldn't think. My dear, darling Julia. You've had such a rotten time of it. Don't you think you really deserve another rest? Don't say anything now, but I do want you to think about it. And I want you to consider moving in with me for the time being. All alone over there, you might be hurt, or injure yourself in some way, and no one would know anything about it. That's what Magnus and I wanted to talk about with you yesterday afternoon. We wanted to beg you to move in with me for the time being."

"You and Magnus," Julia said. "You and Magnus wanted, you and Magnus thought, you and Magnus this and that. So you're afraid I'll hurt myself. What do you mean by that, Lily?"

"Nothing, darling, we were simply . . ."

"I want you to know something, Lily. I was just thinking, this morning, right before you called, that I would like to go back to America. There's nothing here for me any more, unless it's Mark Berkeley. I want to divorce Magnus. He seems impossibly remote to me. If I live through this siege, I'm going to divorce him. There. What do you think of that, Lily?"

"I think it's calamitous," said Lily. "It's psychic disaster. You still blame Magnus for what happened, and you should not be permitted to do that."

"I see," said Julia coldly. "I think you'd like to have me back in the hospital, Lily."

"I just want you, darling, to *think*," wailed Lily. "How much sleep do you get? How well do you eat? Can you take care of yourself? Why, why, why do you think this Olivia person wants to kill you? You—out of all the people she might have chosen."

Julia listened, her mouth open, almost thinking that Lily would tell her.

"We're not making any progress," Lily said finally. "Please think about staying in my guest-room, darling. You don't truly want to return to your troubled country and leave dear old England and Magnus. You need Magnus. You need help. Julia, none of us shall be happy, none of us shall be what we were until you accept some basic truths. The truth about Kate—"

Julia shouted into the telephone, "You don't know the truth about Kate, you don't know the truth about Magnus!" Then she hung up.

Lily rang back several seconds later. "Julia, you are still heroic, I respect you in every way, darling, but you are also a bit erratic. Did you ring off on me?"

"Give up, Lily," said Julia. "Give up on me. I'm not in your world anymore. I'm in hers. Ask Miss Pinner."

"You'd better begin thinking very quickly and very well," Lily said five minutes later to Magnus, having roused him from sleep with her telephone call. "She wants to divorce you. And she mentioned that she is thinking of returning to America."

"Good God," Magnus managed to utter. "Is she mad? She can't divorce me."

"I should imagine, brother dear, that she has

grounds sufficient to divorce you fifty times, should that be necessary. But, yes, I think she is mad. This Rudge affair has utterly unhinged her. She has snapped, Magnus. There is surely some way that you can have her put away in the hospital. Put away for good, if necessary. Or at least until she is capable of listening to reason."

"Lily," Magnus wheezed, his voice foggy and menacing, "what the devil did you say to her? Did you wave Kate in front of her again?"

"No," Lily said, "at least not directly. She is much too full of this Rudge matter to consider Kate. Will you go to your chambers and look up in your musty old books whatever law you can invoke to get her safely put away? Because if you do not, you will not have a wife at this time next year. She could go to Reno, or wherever it is Americans go to be especially vulgar."

"I'll see what I can find," Magnus growled. "I'll look up what's needed for an involuntary commitment."

"You might have done that when she left you," Lily offered in her sweetest tone.

"I needed you to suggest it, Lily."

One question of Lily's stayed with Julia. *Why is it you?* She could have answered, because it was I who bought the house, but that merely pushed the question back a step. She was not satisfied with what she already knew; it seemed to her that the force which had taken her out to Breadlands and had led her to Olivia's group had not yet released her.

What she most wished to do was to take two more pills and sleep out the rest of the day. But there had been something, some idea she had not followed up. . . . Her mind traced the flicker of memory

back, almost catching it. A magazine. Then she had it: *The Tatler*. She had been going to look for pictures of Heather Rudge's parties in *The Tatler* on the day she saw the Burne-Jones painting.

Well, she thought, why not? Since making the discovery of Olivia's role in the Braden boy's death, she had felt occupationless. Now it seemed that she was only to wait—wait for Olivia to decide in what way she would move. Leafing through magazines in Colindale was far more attractive. Let Olivia appear in the reading room, let her wave her knife over bound stacks of *John O'London's* and *Punch*. The image was so bizarre that Julia, for the second time, caught at the fluttering tails of her sanity. Was it possible that she *had* ripped the dolls and written on the mirrors? Turned on the heaters? Perhaps she had imagined seeing Olivia. Her doubting mind bent back on itself.

Yet someone had killed Paul Winter. She had not invented that. Olivia was no delusion. Aware that she was on the verge of feeling grateful for Winter's horrible death, Julia dressed in her hot silent room, went out to her car, and drove through drizzle and glittering streets to Colindale and the periodical collection.

Her reader's card was inspected with almost insulting thoroughness by a uniformed guard; as she walked down the symmetrical rows of desks she obliquely saw two young men seated behind a large heap of Victorian magazines smirk at each other as she passed. Julia supposed that she looked more than ever like an actual beggar maid. Her shoes were mud-stained from the chase through Holland Park, her tights were ripped, and she hadn't washed her hair in a week.

The desk she was accustomed to using was occupied by a large black man wearing gold spectacles which seemed to emit fierce light. His long flat cheeks bore triple raised scars, purplish black. He glanced aggressively at Julia, a bear defending his territory, and she wandered to the other side of the room, looking for a vacant desk. Two or three men tracked her with their eyes, looking benignly amused.

At last she found a desk near the wall and dropped her spattered raincoat over the top of the chair. After filling in a request slip for all the copies of *The Tatler* from 1930 to 1941, she took it to the desk and gave it to a new librarian, a dark-haired young woman with large tinted glasses. Julia watched the young librarian take her card to one of the runners, and realized that, two weeks ago, she had seen her outside the French restaurant on Abingdon Road. It was the girl with whom she had felt a sympathy, the girl who had smiled at her. They had been members of the same species. Now she felt nothing of the kind. She had nothing in common with this pretty young librarian.

With her hair a reddish mass of tangles, in her ripped black tights and muddy shoes, dark circles beneath her eyes, Julia sat behind her blond desk, her mood lifting. She would not feel sorry for herself. A boy set half a dozen fat black volumes on the desk before her. "They'll send up the others when you have finished with these," he said, nearly apologizing, as if he expected this strange woman to shout at him.

She knew that she would find something. She felt morally renewed. Julia pulled the top volume off the stack and began to leaf through it, staring hungrily at

the pictures of men and women in evening dress,
remembering her childhood. Almost, she could hear
them speak.

The first hour she found nothing, nor the second;
it was slightly before noon when she had even a faint
success. She had flipped halfway through the volume
for 1933-34 when a picture, a face, on an earlier page
burned back to her, and she tore backward in the
book to November, 1933. There on the right-hand
side of the book, grinning up at her, was Heather
Rudge, holding a cigarette and a champagne glass,
her shoulders gleaming; the sexuality of the woman
scalded Julia's bowels. On both sides of her dangled
young men. Julia rushed to the caption. "The
well-known American hostess Mrs. Heather Rudge
at Lord Kilross' party, here seen with Mr. Maxwell
Davies, Mr. Jeremy Reynolds, Lord Panton, the
Hon. Frederick Mason, and Viscount Gregory."
That was all. None of the young men, who glittered
with an identical infatuation, were familiar to Julia,
and she saw no other photographs of Heather at the
party.

She went slowly through the remainder of the
volume, but Heather did not reappear. Nor did she
for another forty-five minutes, when Julia saw her
oval, challenging, vain, sensual face again rising up
from her dazzling shoulders on a fluted neck. More
young men surrounded her—Mr. Maxwell Davies,
Viscount Gregory and the Hon. Frederick Mason
among them. They looked unchanged. The occasion, Julia read, was a party given by Lord Panton,
who appeared beside a frilly little blonde, the Hon.
Someone-Someone, all teeth and curls. These were
her young men, undoubtedly: Julia wondered which
of them had owned the honor of siring Olivia.

Thrice more, in the volumes leading up to 1936,

Julia found photographs of Heather. She seemed to travel usually in the company of the same young men, with a slight mixture of mustached older gentlemen with straining bellies and popping eyes. Oliver Blankenship, Nigel Ramsay, David Addison. But every time one of these older men appeared, he was shadowed closely by several of Heather's younger set. Heather was always "the well-known (or popular, or famous) American hostess" in these photographs, but there were no pictures taken of her parties.

Julia signaled to the runner to take the six heavy volumes and return with the later set. Her face was warm and hectic, flushed, and she began to drum her fingers on her desk and look wildly around the quiet room, where men bent their heads over books as though drinking from them. Her watch said three thirty. She'd had nothing to eat or drink since morning coffee.

One wing of the library contained a small cafeteria. Julia wondered if she should get a sandwich before going on. The impulse grew out of her rising mood, the optimism she had begun to feel, and she decided to follow it, even though she felt no hunger. She scrawled a note for the boy and went quickly down the aisles and out of the reading room, giving a bright, unfocused smile to the guard at the door.

Julia flew down the long lightless hall to the cafeteria, selected a tray from beneath the gaze of a bored Indian woman wearing a hairnet, and looked over the available food. "Too late for hot lunch," the Indian woman announced from her stool. Julia nodded, examining the sandwiches. "No hot lunch now, only sameges," the woman insisted.

"Fine," Julia said. She took from the rack a cheese and tomato sandwich wrapped in thin cello-

phane; touching the whispery layer of cellophane, Julia instantly imagined it plastered across her face, adhering there, stuck to her nostrils and mouth. She dropped the sandwich on the tray.

"Coffee?" Julia said, standing before the shining coffee machine.

The woman shook her head. "No coffee. Too late, coffee again at half four."

"Fine," Julia said, and plucked a container of orange drink from a carton.

When she reached the cash desk, the Indian woman left her stool and moved slowly past the racks of food, audibly sighing. At last she reached the register and rang up Julia's purchases.

"Two pounds."

"That can't be right—one sandwich?"

The woman stared deeply into Julia's face, then looked with great boredom back at the tray. She punched more buttons on the register. "Thirty-two pence."

Julia took the tray to a clean table, and looked back at the waitress, half expecting to be ordered to one of the uncleaned side tables. The woman was shuffling back to her stool, conspicuously not taking notice of Julia.

The orange drink felt cool and sweet on her tongue, and it opened a channel all the way down into her stomach. She chewed experimentally at the dry sandwich; its bread seemed poreless, synthetic, and the cheese did not separate between her teeth. For a few moments she continued to chew distractedly at the stale sandwich, lubricating it with orange drink.

When her insides contracted, she quickly left the table and rushed across the room to the door marked LADIES. Inside one of the metal cubicles she vomited

neatly into the bowl, and tasted the heavy sweetness of orange drink; when her stomach contracted again, only a thin yellowish drool came up.

She went to a sink and wiped water across her mouth. The mirror showed a drugged-looking, raddled harridan of indeterminate age; gray showed clearly in the frizzy hair at the sides of her head. Her lips were cracked, and beside her right eye was a small bruise she'd got when she had fallen down in Holland Park Avenue. Julia tried to comb her hair with her hands, and managed to coax it back into mere disorder before she left the washroom and returned to the reading room.

The five fat volumes sat atop her desk. Within minutes, Julia was lost in the first, examining all the photographs on a page and then flipping it over. By four o'clock she had seen two more pictures of "the famous American hostess," once in company with Mr. Jeremy Reynolds and the other on the arm of Viscount Gregory. Heather was unchanged, but the young men, five years older, were visibly coarser and meatier, beginning to show double chins and jowls.

In the volume for 1937-38, Julia found a photograph of Heather standing beside a wheelchair. Strapped in the chair, incredibly shrunken and frail, was David Addison, one of the portly, pop-eyed older men who had customarily accompanied her; on the other side of the wheelchair stood Mr. Maxwell Davies, his earlier slender and dark handsomeness now softened and blurred by fat. Davies' face was opened in a thoughtless, greedy maw of a smile—it made Julia shudder. It seemed to her that she could smell his breath, taste the thin flavor of the man's mouth. Heather Rudge glinted, smiling a cool winner's smile, between the two ruined men.

There were no further pictures of Heather in that

volume, and none in the next. Some of the young men, Lord Panton and Viscount Gregory and others, appeared at balls and dances, grown fatter, gross of face, with the ruddy look of once-athletic alcoholics. She closed this volume at five o'clock. The library closed at five thirty, and Julia debated whether or not it was worthwhile to leaf through the remaining two big volumes.

She decided to skim through them in the half hour left to her, and then to telephone David Swift again. Julia hefted the volume for 1939-40 and turned to the first number and began to flip through the issues more quickly than she had before. When she reached the issue for May 19 she glanced down at a page of Cambridge photographs and gasped aloud. A young Magnus Lofting, standing erect in a dinner jacket, beamed out at the world from the page; beside him stood Mr. Maxwell Davies. "Two Cambridge men discuss the Blues," read the caption and gave their names.

From that moment Julia burrowed into the last two volumes, looking for the picture she knew she would eventually find. Even isolated shots of Heather, or of Heather with her familiar retinue, did not long delay her; Julia flipped through, scanning the pages for one inevitable photograph.

The photograph appeared at the end of the 1939-40 volume, in an issue for February, 1940: the year before Olivia's birth, Julia remembered. "Wartime Spirits Kept High in Kensington," the article was headed. One of the pictures showed, unmistakably, a corner of the living room at 25 Ilchester Place. The wallpaper looked gaudy, and instead of the McClintocks' heavy furniture, graceful small chairs and lounges stood against the walls. Men of various ages seemed to fill the room, many of them in

uniform. Heather, looking as young and sensual as
she had in 1930, appeared in over half of the
photographs. She danced with Lieutenant Frederick
Mason and Captain Maxwell Davies, and was seen
in ardent conversation with Colonel Nigel Ramsay;
but the photograph at which Julia stared until the
bell clamored throughout the reading room was on
the second page of the set, and showed an elderly
couple, wildly out of place at the party, smiling
somewhat tremulously into the camera. They were
identified as Lord and Lady Selhurst. Behind them,
in one of the corners of the room, twenty-one-year-
old Magnus Lofting had his right arm about Heather
Rudge's bare shoulder.

She looked up as the African at her old seat was
rising from his chair and gave his ferocious counte-
nance a glance of such peculiarity that he dropped a
sheaf of paper. She thrust the volumes to the back of
the desk and stood up—only she and the African
were in the reading room, apart from the pretty
librarian and the last two or three stragglers already
passing the guard. Her heart seemed to blaze. Now
she knew how to answer Lily's question, *Why is it
you?*

"Because," she thought, "Magnus is Olivia's
father. Because both of his children were stabbed to
death. Because Olivia wants revenge. Because the
patterns are clear."

Light-headed, she left the library and entered a
steady gray falling of rain. Chains of black clouds
printed the dark sky. Julia absently searched her bag
for her keys, unlocked the car door, and bent in
behind the wheel. Her face felt chilly and slick with
rain, and her hands were cold, wet. These sensations, like the bitterness at the base of her tongue,

skidded off the reflective surface of her mind; at that moment, if asked, she would have hesitated before answering in what country she was. All of the puzzle had finally been connected, it had clicked into place, and the answer to Lily's question had been found, as it must have been, in the past. Julia did not need Magnus to confirm or deny her knowledge: she knew that she was right. Magnus was Olivia's father; he'd had a youthful affair with Heather Rudge and then deserted her. It explained everything. And it clarified Heather Rudge's conduct when Julia had met her at the clinic. Now she knew why the old woman had thrice asked her, *Is that your real name?* Julia leaned back in the car seat and looked up at the black chain mail of the sky, seeing each of the pieces fall into place. What could make more sense than that Olivia Rudge would seek to kill her deserting father's second wife, Olivia being what she was? That she would make a deadly rhyme of her own murder?

There was a place she had to go. One area of her mind knew this with utter clarity, even while all the rest still floated, stunned by Olivia's symmetries. Ordinarily she would not have trusted herself to drive—she felt as though she'd had half a bottle of whiskey—but there was no other way of getting where she had to go. She pulled the key over in its slot and heard the Rover's engine kick into life. She slammed the car into gear and shot forward across the parking lot. Rain blurred across the windshield, and Julia flicked on the wipers at the same moment as she turned out into the street. The map in her head would lead her where she had to go, though she did not know how to get there.

Olivia, Magnus.

Olivia, Magnus. She had known from the night of

her meeting with Mrs. Fludd, but only now did she see how the connection worked, how she was a part of Olivia's web as she was of Magnus'. Olivia could have been Kate, she thought, and the Rover rocketed forward, just scraping past a yellow Volkswagen. She meant, Olivia could have been her daughter. She and Heather Rudge were interchangeable.

"*No*," she said aloud, and swerved her car out into the passing lane, stepping on the accelerator.

Sisterhood. They were sisters. Women of the same man. Mothers of murdered daughters.

Julia brought the car to a squealing stop when she finally saw the red light, and ignored the curious glances from beneath umbrellas on the sidewalk. She sat, her mouth slightly open and moistureless, behind the wheel, looking upward, waiting for the light to change. Magnus seemed more incalculable than ever, a sea of possibilities and surprises: she could never encompass him nor dismiss him. The poison which was Olivia came from a level deep within him, from some power stunted and sent awry in his childhood. (Like Mark, said a disloyal cell in her mind.)

Horns erupted behind her, and she threw the car into gear and shot across the intersection. She knew where she was going. The sky's darkness leaked down, staining her hands on the wheel.

Had she hit a dog? She could not remember: indeed, she could not remember most of the drive. There had been a dog, in the vicinity of Golders Green and the Finchley Road, a rust-colored dog bounding out into the road; Julia had cramped the wheel immediately, instinctively to the side, and had sent the Rover into the side of a parked car, crumpling one of its doors; but she thought that

when the Rover had ground its way out of the
parked car, a second thudding sensation had come
from the left front tire. Speeding away, she had been
afraid to look in the mirror.

Now she stood beside her car in Upper Street, a
steady rain dripping into her hair, thinking about
how terrible it was to kill a dog. She could not look
at the Rover. Magnus' present to her (bought with
her money), it had been importantly clean and sleek,
feline: an exemplar. It was like Magnus to buy
something for her with her own money and then use
it against her. From the side of her eye she caught an
impression of a wrinkled rear end and a back
bumper curled in like a ram's horn. She hunched her
shoulders against the rain. Where was her coat? Not
in the car. She had left it slung over her chair in the
periodical library. She hoped that she had not hit the
dog. It would leave no marks, but still be dead.

Across the street the lights of the pub burned
softly red through the windows; glasses hung upside
down, bat-fashion, gleamed like Christmas, points
and blurs of red. Rain jumped in the street and ran
in rivulets toward the drain. The streetlamps produced a shining streak along the pavement, a harsh
acid yellow, a color which eats the skin. Water
caught in Julia's eyebrows and lashes. She looked
above the pub and saw no lights in the windows.

She had to go up to the flat; she had to see.

There were no police, what did that mean, no
police?

Julia moved across the street, forgetting to turn
off the lights of her car or to remove the key, pausing
to let half-seen cars splash by before her. She came
up on the pavement before David Swift's door, and
knocked twice. Then, her head and neck streaming
with water, she found the bell and pushed it down.

When no one came, her insides seemed to freeze. What had happened to the police? Hadn't they understood her message? Julia pushed at the door. It held against her. Numbly, in baffled frustration, she turned her head and saw the Rover's headlights shining at her from across the street; she was pinned within them. They were all of the car she could see.

Frantic, she turned again to the door. Something Magnus had once described to her came back to her in miraculous detail: he'd been defending a house-breaker, and he had told her how the man had used a plastic card to slip the catches on locks. He had used her check card to demonstrate. She dug in her bag for her wallet and pulled the card out, spilling loose papers and bills into the bottom of her bag, and inserted the top edge of the card between the door and the jamb. She pushed it up and in. A hard sloping edge floated back: she heard a loud click. When she pushed at the doorknob, the peeling door swung in. She slipped inside, escaping the beams of her lights.

It was the dingy staircase where he had called to her, shouting. From the top she heard a muffled noise. Julia's heart clenched, and then released her, though fear poured through her like cold water, and she went up the filthy stairs. She had dreamed of doing this, though she could not remember when. Her fingers shook on the wood of the door at the top; muttering came from the other side, a meaning-less series of syllables. She pressed her trembling fingers to the wood, and pushed the door gently in. Her fingers left small dark stains on the wood.

She was conscious of Olivia: that tense, webbed atmosphere of waiting tension. Olivia's air seemed to fill the room. Her lion's smell. She was here, or had just left. Julia saw the knife first. Wonderingly,

she picked it up from the floor, feeling her palm
adhere to the handle. She remembered—as though
it too were dreamed—the penknife she had uncovered in the sand on her first day in the house.
Holding the knife, she could feel sand in her palms,
grinding at her skin. Olivia.

She whirled about, certain she had heard Olivia
calling. But it had been a noise from the couch, the
repetition of that whiffling noise she had heard on
the staircase. As if truly in a dream, Julia walked
smoothly across the bare carpet to the couch and saw
David Swift lying on his back, his eyes open and his
mouth working. Broken syllables came from him.
He was sleeping, Julia thought, talking in his sleep.

As she looked, his head snapped to one side and
his chest seemed to bloom. A red slot opened up
from his breastbone to his belt, and redness spurted
out, foaming over his shirt. It was as though a flower
had opened, revealing a sudden configuration of
great complexity and intricacy. More blood flowed
from beneath his chin and sheeted across his neck.
He stared up into Julia's eyes and tried to speak.
Blood filled his throat, and it welled from his mouth,
garbling his words.

"She . . ."

"She's just left," Julia finished for him. He had
already lost an appalling amount of blood; Julia took
up a cloth from the little table and pressed it over the
long wound on the man's midriff. She must have
seen it wrong, she thought, her mind surprisingly
calm; he had been dying when she had come in. As
Julia held the useless cloth over the long wound,
David Swift thrashed on the couch and sent a wave
of blood over her hand and then fell back. Julia
dropped the knife into the sticky fluid beside the
couch. She stood up, blinking. Olivia had got here

first and had killed him while he slept. Her stink was in the room.

She washed hands at the sink, her back to the dead Swift. When she was free of blood, she fled down the stairs and left the street door ajar, so that a policeman would look within. Through increasing rain she ran in the beam of the Rover's headlights toward her car. Laughter and music from the pub followed her.

The horror what she had seen broke over her when she sat again in the car, rain sliding down her collar from her hair, and she shook back and forth, slamming from the seat to the steering column, yanking and pushing back with her arms, her hands locked on the circle of wood. She had been too late; even the police had been powerless against Olivia. Julia slammed the Rover's door and cowered within, shaking and freezing. Her mind cleared long before she was able to control her body. Images of America, of valleys and green distances, invaded her.

11

She drove through dark, rain-slicked streets, her window wipers thumping, on what she knew was the wrong side of the road. She should have been on the right, because she was driving through the back reaches of a city like Boston, which was familiar to her in a surrealist, dreamlike fashion; yet all the other traffic was on the left, and that too was dreamily familiar. Julia went with it, driftingly, faintly pleased by her knowledge of this strange city, and faintly annoyed that she could not get her bearings properly. She saw a spot of blood on her thumbnail, and in reflex wiped it on the seam of her trousers.

Her turnoff, the access road to the expressway, lay somewhere nearby; from there it was only a couple of hours' drive to New Hampshire. She knew that because she had never in her life been more than a couple of hours' drive from her family's valley: Julia could visualize all the roads, the highways and expressways and turnpikes and seal-coated county roads and gravelly tracks used by farmers, which formed a lacy web of connections between where she was and the valley. And she could visualize with a perfect wholeness the last turning before the valley, the sweep of the exit ramp from the freeway down through dark hills, a few mysterious lights shining in

deep vales, far off the glow of a town. She could see every inch of that dark access to the valley, and she knew where the river was, though you couldn't see it. She wanted to see it now, before her.

She was driving through an American city, a city like Boston, bearing generally south. Nineteenth-century houses, built of red brick, now a grimy brown, stood on either side of narrow streets. Cold rain rattled on the top of the car.

Driving through an American city, driving through America. London was a furry patch in her memory; London did not exist. She was in Boston, and there was no London. Soon she would find the Berkshires, and that lovely long highway through banks of trees. Tanglewood. Julia pressed hard on the accelerator and her car slewed on wet Penton-ville Road, fishtailing in its lane. Except for all these cars, it looked like the outer edges of Boston. She knew that people drove on the wrong side of the road here. It was habit with her by now. Why should that be? She pushed the question down.

She was of no age, she was going home, nothing had happened to her. Her father waited, dressed in an elegant dark gray suit; her grandfather had just died, and that was why she was going home from Smith. Boston was a mistake, she should not be in Boston; but she knew the way to go.

Now she was near the Fens, she thought. It would look much different, for everything had changed, and she had not been at Smith for years. She wheeled the car around a corner, blindly, her mind fluttering. A vision of a man's chest gouting fluid. . . . It meant nothing, though her feet had slipped on red blood. Nothing. Julia forced herself to smile at a young man striding across the road, walking on broad white stripes, and he returned the smile. He

had an American face, round beneath floppy hair.
Wet with rain. A slippery face, a face which left no
traces.

The Rover jolted forward past the boy. Soon she
would find the way, and then she would be sailing,
with no mental effort at all, down the turnpike,
leaving the city behind, moving toward the sloping
bank of the exit, turning down between hills, passing
small ghostly lights deep in a vale where the winding
of the road shone under the trees.

At the same time, she knew where she was going,
though her mind seemed to detach itself at times and
go floating through Boston. As she drove down
Marylebone Road, she noticed on the back of her
left wrist another smear of blood, and hurriedly,
disgustedly, wiped her wrist on the car seat.

But she could not rid herself of the feeling of being
in Massachusetts until she had left her car parked
outside a house in Notting Hill, rushed up the path
in the rain, gone down six steps at the side of the
house. Her mind seemed to be flying apart, a wispy
cloth tugged by birds. She pounded at the bell. A
basement, a valley. Breath caught and tore, chug-
ging, in her throat. Her mouth open and cottony.
Finally the door opened, and she rushed against the
man who stood within, touching his wet face with
her hands. He held her tightly while he struggled to
remove his coat. Raindrops coursed down her face,
and she butted against his chest, shaken by what she
recognized as crying only after what seemed a long
time of it.

Mark stood just within his door, letting her sob.
His damp coat hung uncomfortably on his shoulders,
and while he cradled Julia he shrugged first one arm
out of its sleeve and then the other. He allowed the

coat to fall squashily to the floor and hugged Julia
tighter. She trembled against him like a trapped
bird, her elbows and forearms whipping at his chest.

"Oh, thank God you're home," she finally uttered. "I was so afraid I wouldn't find you and then
I'd have to . . ." Her voice became too damaged
and soft to continue.

"I just got home, just this minute," he said down
into the wet hair on the crown of her head, plastered
down on either side of a natural part. "Good Lord,"
he said, "I never thanked you for that money. I
really shouldn't have taken it, but it came just when I
was short, and—"

Julia's distorted face tilted back to look at him
confusedly. She had obviously forgotten all about
the check.

"Never mind," he quickly said, and hugged her to
him again. "What's happened to you?"

She rested her cheek on his shoulder, and
breathed heavily for a moment. "Everything's happened," she finally said. "She's going to kill me. I
saw—I saw—" Julia stared at him with blurred eyes,
her face looking directly into his without recording
it.

"You saw?" Mark stroked her cheek, but she
made no response.

"I thought I was in America all the way here. I
thought I was driving through Boston. I was looking
for the turnpike, so I could get to New Hampshire. I
was going to my grandfather's place, in the valley.
Isn't that funny?"

"You're under strain," Mark said.

"I'm going to be killed," she said again. "Nobody
can stop her. I don't want to die. Can I stay with you
tonight? You're all wet." She touched his face.
"Why are you wet?"

"I was out," Mark said. "I was having a chat with Lily. About you." He smiled at Julia. "I got in just before you came crashing in. Come in."

He led her into his room and helped her to sit on a cushion and removed her shoes. Then he dried her feet with a towel and wiped her hands. He finished by dabbing at her face.

"You have another bruise."

"I fell down. In the street. She was playing with me then."

"And what's this on your wrist?" He stared at the thick dirty bandage under the cuff of her blouse.

"I cut myself. Not on purpose. It was after I saw her. I called you." Julia was looking straight before her, as if now that she had come to him, he could offer no further help. "She wanted me to be hit by a car. Like Mrs. Fludd. She doesn't care about murder. She likes it. She makes other people like it too."

"Hold on," he said, taking her hands and chafing them. Mark was squatting down before her, looking at her unfocused eyes. "Who's this 'she'? That girl you were talking about earlier? Olivia Rudge?"

Her eyes snapped into clarity. "I didn't tell you her name," she said, staring at him and beginning to snatch back her hands.

"Lily did," he said. "Just now."

"Lily doesn't believe me. She can't. It's because of Magnus."

"Don't worry about Lily. What about this girl?"

Julia watched in fascination as an ant crawled out of Mark's shirt and traversed one of the wings of his collar. The ant, small, red and very quick, sped down the collar and across his chest and fled again into the interior of Mark's shirt.

"She wants to murder you."

"Yes."

"She knows that you found out about that child, whoever it was, twenty years ago."

"Geoffrey Braden." Julia thought of the ant struggling through the hair on Mark's chest. She felt astonishingly light-headed.

"And now she wants to kill you."

"She's killed two other men. Paul Winter and David Swift. I just came from Swift's flat." Julia spoke in a level voice, looking straight at his shirt front. "May I lie down on your mattress?"

"You'd better," he said, and lifted her up and helped her across the room to the mattress. Sheets and blankets lay rumpled at its foot, and Mark pulled them up over her legs. Then he sat on the floor beside her, shoving clothing and plates to one side.

"I'm going to find you some sleeping pills," he said. "They'll help you relax, Julia."

"I don't need sleep," she said.

"You need to rest," Mark said. He lifted her head and pulled the grimy pillow across the mattress to place beneath it. Then he left her staring up at the ceiling and went to his kitchen for a vial of pills and a glass of water. "It's just Valium," he said.

"Take too many pills," Julia mumbled, but swallowed one anyhow. Then she focused her gaze on his eyes—he could see her pupils contract—and said, "I found out that Magnus is her father. That's why it's me. That's why she wanted me from the start."

"Just close your eyes, Julia," he said, "and we'll talk about it all in the morning. We have a lot to talk about. You'll see."

She obediently closed her eyes. "I washed my hands because I had blood on them." She turned her head toward Mark and opened her eyes to look at

him. "I want you to protect me. Just tonight. Please."

Against his will, Mark was looking at the outline of Julia's thighs beneath her trousers. He noticed a smear of some dark, brownish substance along the seam of the wool, and felt everything within him leap as though touched by a live electrical wire.

"I think I might be sick," he heard Julia say. "I feel so funny. I don't want to die. I don't want to die, Mark."

After Mark had switched off the light, he threw off his clothes in the darkness, unsure of where to sleep. Julia lay unconscious and fully dressed across his mattress. He did not dare to move her—Julia's condition seemed dangerous to him, fully bearing out everything Lily had said. It was as though she could spin off into outright lunacy if she were as much as touched. And her suggestion about Magnus had upset him, reminding him again that she was his adoptive brother's wife, despite the events of the past week or two. Mark knew all too well that Magnus was stronger than he, and would not hesitate to beat him senseless if he suspected him of sleeping with Julia. Magnus had beaten him twice during his youth, and Mark shied away from the memory of these experiences. He pulled a patterned Indian rug, given him long ago by a girl whose name he could no longer remember, from the closet and arranged the stiff scratchy thing over his body as he lay back in a chair.

Magnus seemed to be everywhere, behind every rock and round every corner: Magnus' virility, according to Julia, had spawned Olivia Rudge, Julia's fantastic wraith. Though they were approximately the same height, Mark invariably thought of

Magnus as much taller than he, twice as massive, twice as serious a presence. Was it really possible that Lily could control him? Her offer had been a neat instance of payment for services rendered, but it would be a valid offer only if Magnus agreed that his efforts to persuade Julia were worthy of recompense. Mark knew that Magnus considered him an incapable, nearly insignificant man, but he did not think that Magnus would cheat him. Certainly none of them could permit Julia to leave England.

Mark lay back in the chair, his head lolling and the blanket scratching his skin as if it were sandpaper. Julia still lay motionless beneath the sheet. Magnus and Lily were right about her needing a long rest, under supervision. All he had been doing was humoring her along any direction that seemed to lead away from Magnus, but perhaps it was now time to be more thoughtful. His academic career, in truth, was at its nadir; Mark could not imagine enduring much longer the boredom of teaching. His book was a phantasm, a dead thing which had lived only in illusion. Teaching was his only income, apart from the beggarly amount Greville Lofting had bequeathed him. There had been no nonsense about equal division of wealth in that old bastard's head. Not that, in comparison to Julia, he'd had much anyhow.

She groaned from the mattress, and muttered something.

He had expected his headache, which had descended on him when he was leaving Plane Tree House and had not left for four hours, to return with Julia's arrival, but he was surprisingly free of it. It was, he thought, because of her condition: a Julia so weak, so dependent, could not pull whatever trigger it was that launched his headache. (For in these past

few days, it felt like that, as though a bullet, a red-hot foreign substance, had tumbled into his brain.)

He heard Julia's voice: "Mark?"

"Here," he grunted. "In the chair."

"Why aren't you with me?"

"I was thinking."

"Uh-huh," Julia offered, already half asleep again.

Had she used to talk in the night, half muttering, to Magnus? Wanting him to come to her bed? This thought stirred Mark, and he sat up in the chair and examined Julia's sprawl beneath his sheet. Her face was dug deep into the pillow, her hair bursting out around it. With her hair disarranged and uncombed, she looked far more like most of the other women whose heads had rested on that pillow.

She pronounced his name, very clearly, in her sleep.

Involuntarily, Mark suddenly imagined Magnus' heavy, serious body straddling hers, Magnus' belly pressing on Julia, Magnus opening her legs, Magnus' confidence taking her. She was his. Mark could see Magnus' arms circling her, her legs bent at his hips. His penis surged forward against the roughness of the cloth, and he threw the blanket off and crossed the room to climb onto the mattress beside Julia. A little later that night, after a quick struggle with buttons and elastic, he felt his mind traveling over enormous distances as he plunged atop his brother's wife. It was like making love on LSD, but even that had been a pedestrian experience beside this, for during all of the night remaining, hallucinations and visions lifted and inspired him: he was a gorgeously sexual bird, fertilizing the air. Innocence irradiated the air, canceling odors of sweat and old cooking.

In the morning Mark left the flat to shop for eggs, bacon and bread, and Julia, alone in the squalor of his room, began to weep. She felt abandoned and helpless, beached on a gray shore. Even Mark could not restore her to the ordinary human world or save her from the bleakness. She cried for a few minutes, and then arranged the sheets atop the mattress. They bore ridges of dirt and crusty stains, which Julia rather consciously overlooked. She was wondering if the police had discovered the body of David Swift; and if they had, if the papers would carry a story about the death. Swift was not a general's son. Someone had to be told what had happened. Mark had only pretended to believe her; and she had been too weary and shocked to fully explain the events of the night. She realized that she knew only one person she could telephone.

Lily picked up the receiver on the first ring, thinking that Magnus had discovered what had to be done to have his wife safely hospitalized.

"Yes," she said, and looked dartingly around the room at her Stubbs horse, her vases, the Persian screen. Julia's voice came to her, tired and faint, making each of her possessions seem locked in its place.

"Lily? Lily, I have to tell you some things. Listen to me."

"Where in the world are you?" Lily swiftly said. "Magnus and I tried to talk to you last night. You weren't at home."

"Well, now I am," Julia lied. "I was out last night."

"Do you think that's wise, darling? All of us feel that you should get as much rest as possible. I'd be

happy to help you move some of your things over here, so you wouldn't be alone. . . ."

"It's too late for that, Lily," came Julia's faint voice.

"Darling, speak more directly into the mouthpiece."

"You must believe me, Lily. No one else will. I can't talk to anyone else." She sounded far-off and desperate, and Lily for a moment visualized her sailing off westward, a figure in an airplane getting smaller and smaller in the sky.

"You've been fretting again," she said. "Why don't you come over and tell me about it?"

"Lily, Magnus is Olivia's father. I know it. He used to meet Heather Rudge—in my house. There's a picture of them together here. Taken less than a year before Olivia's birth. He's Olivia's father, Lily. That's why she picked me. I saw her kill someone last night. David Swift. He knew her, and he talked too much, like Paul Winter. She made someone kill them. I came in just after, and he was dying. I'm next, Lily, there's no one left but me. I'm next."

Lily scarcely heard the latter half of this announcement. When Julia had said that Magnus was the girl's father, Lily had immediately felt that she was speaking the truth. Rage at Magnus' deception and lies flashed through her like an electrical explosion. She felt completely betrayed. "You're certain about Magnus," she managed to say.

"I'm sure," came Julia's bruised voice. "That's why it was me she wanted. It's the pattern."

"My God," said Lily, immediately seeing another pattern. "Do you see what you are saying? Julia, if what you are saying is true, there *is* a reason why you were chosen by Olivia. Magnus . . ."

"Magnus and Kate," Julia whispered. "Magnus

and Olivia. The difference is that Olivia was evil. And she can work in people's minds."

"Julia, this is important," said Lily, her mind spinning among possibilities.

"Look for that man's name in the newspapers," Julia said, not listening to her. "Swift. He was one of her gang. He told me about Geoffrey Braden's murder. She had him kllled. I saw his body—I saw his blood, all over him."

"Ju—"

But Julia had hung up. Lily dialed her number and, her mind still whirling, listened to the phone ringing in Julia's house. "Pick it up," she urged, "pick it up, pick it up." Eventually she depressed the button with a finger and after hearing the dial tone again, tried Magnus' number at Gayton Road.

"Lily," he said. "I can't just flick a switch, you know. There are a couple of options. It'll all happen. I'll let you know tonight."

"That's not what I rang you about," she said angrily. "I want to ask you something, and I want you to tell me the truth, Magnus."

"What now?" The boredom in his voice made her furious.

"Were you the father of that wretched child? The Rudge girl? I've just spoken to Julia, and she says she has proof you were her father."

"Syntax, Lily," Magnus said. "Did you say proof?" His voice came through with an amused incredulity that was as good as a confession.

"She knows that you were—I think those were her words. I want you to tell me the truth, Magnus."

He said, "I don't know the truth."

"Meaning?"

"I don't know if I was her father. I could have been. So could two or three others. She bled us all

for money. Perhaps the child was a committee effort. Some weekends, one nearly had to punch a clock."

"You are a fool, Magnus. You could have told me that a week ago, and perhaps done a deal of good. Now I expect that you shall be lucky ever to see Julia again."

"Can't you do *anything* while I find out about the paperwork? I can't do it all myself."

"You petulant fool," she snarled at him. "At the moment, I am going to see if I can find anything in the morning papers about a fellow named Swift. Your wife says she saw him killed."

"For God's sake, now you're going mad too."

"Good-bye." Lily delicately put the phone back in its cradle and went to the couch, where the morning's *Times* and *Daily Telegraph* had been folded over one of the arms. She ripped the two papers off the couch and spread them on the carpet. She flipped through the *Times*, scanning the headlines on each page. When she had reached the sports news, she went through it backwards, making sure. No mention of a David Swift, no unexplained deaths at all.

With great relief, she turned to the *Daily Telegraph*. It was a hallucination of Julia's, another reason for locking her away. Nothing, of course, on the first page, and nothing on the second. Lily scanned the third page with a growing certainty that she had been rushed into a foolish panic; she would have to find a face-saving formula for apologizing to Magnus. A headline on the fifth page, two inches from the bottom, put an end to these thoughts. KNIFE DEATH, it read.

The body of David Swift, 37, was discovered by police in his Islington flat during the early hours of Thursday morning. Police were investi-

gating the open doorway to the flat when they found the body of Mr. Swift, who appeared to have died from multiple stab wounds. Witnesses located by Islington police say that an unidentified woman was seen leaving Mr. Swift's flat approximately one hour before discovery of the body.

Lily hastily read the short paragraph again, and then stood and dropped the paper to the floor. It was true: Julia had been seen running from that man's flat. Magnus was Olivia's father. The pattern she had seen while talking to Julia became clearer and clearer to her. Julia was unable to see it, and so had invented another pattern to suit the facts she could acknowledge. All along, Lily had dismissed Julia's stories because there had been no compelling reason for her to have been the object of a genuine manifestation. Now the reason seemed so obvious—so glaring—she could not think how she had failed to guess it. (But she shamefully knew how much her dismissal of Julia's story had to do with pride.) Blood rushed to her face. Lily walked to her window and looked down at the empty park. Rain leaked from a dark sky.

Now more than ever it was important to get Julia out of that house. Suppose Olivia Rudge were to appear there . . . Lily shuddered, and returned to the telephone. She was afraid, she recognized, for all of them. If Julia were right, none of them were safe. Suppose Rosa really *had* seen something, and had died for it? Lily groaned, and picked up the telephone to ring Mark.

Julia knew that Lily would call her back at the wrong number. Then what would she do? Look in

the paper, she hoped. Surely a man could not meet a violent death in London and not have a paragraph written about him. Someone has to believe me, Julia thought, and now there's only Lily. Mark's attitude, whenever he wasn't in bed, was distant, doctorly, calming; she had seen that he hadn't believed her, and had been surprised that, even in shock as she had been, she was not more wounded by his disbelief. It was confirmation of her isolation: what was Olivia's atmosphere if not that? The atmosphere of the rooftop dream.

She sat on the edge of the mattress, her mind vague, uncertain of what to do. Eggs and bacon had been Mark's idea. For Julia, the thought of food was almost anthropological in its remoteness. What she wanted, though her vagina throbbed, was to cling to Mark again, to put her arms about him and nest beside him without thought, in a deep blankness.

She allowed her eyes to rove over his incredible flat. The floor was crowded with articles of clothing and plates and cloudy milk bottles. Books were heaped in odd places. Underlying the general odor of Gaulois cigarettes was an odd grainy smell like that of an uncleaned birdcage.

She unsteadily stood up, having decided to do something about the floor. When she bent to pick up several plates stacked together, blood pounded into her head and she saw moving blots of red and black, and sat heavily on the mattress again until her vision cleared. The room seemed to wobble about her. She touched the plates. Brown stuff had hardened on the top surface, and glued all the plates into a single unit. Julia held them in her lap until the room ceased to vibrate and then carried them into the kitchen.

The sink was already jammed with china and glasses submerged in cold greasy water, so Julia set the plates on top of the little fridge and returned to the other room to pick up more things. When she came back to the kitchen with two glasses and two milk bottles, she found two dozen webby milk bottles ranked on a ledge behind the sink. Complex green spidery growths and furry tendrils linked the bottles. Julia rattled them backward and squeezed in her two bottles.

The telephone shrilled from the other room and Julia hesitated before she left the kitchen to stand over it. Perhaps Lily had guessed where she was: did she care to hide it any longer? Indifferent, she lifted the telephone. A rich breathy female voice floated into her ear. "Mark, what *have* you been up to lately? Annis said you were positively rude to her, and garbled something about meditation; well, *we* think you've got some Great Love taking up all your time, it's just not like you, why don't we all meet sometime at the Rising Sun to—"

"He's not home," Julia said and hung up on a whoop of startled laughter which caused her to drop the telephone. When it hit the floor, the plastic base cracked apart like the shell of a snail.

Julia wandered across the room to Mark's desk. She sat in his chair and pulled the drapes to one side. Rain fell into the gray well before the window, flattening the few spears of grass which had struggled up through the concrete. A wedge of gray sky hung in the upper corner of the window, seeming out of perspective, crazily tilted. Julia touched Mark's typewriter and then licked the dust off her finger. She could not make sense of the telephone call. Now, behind her, the broken phone began to buzz

periodically like an angry bee. Great Love? Annis? Was that a girl's name? Julia could not make her mind understand the words of the girl on the telephone. She felt as though she had been jeered at, made fun of, by the whoop of laugher. Even that had been in a Knightsbridge accent. She put her head down on the cool keys of the typewriter.

His desk, his books, his papers. He was working on something. She felt intense gratitude for his working, for his being part of that comfortable line of men who did things, who made bridges and books and decisions. She caressed the stack of paper beside the typewriter. Mark. His name seemed to heat in her chest. He could not be blamed for his inability to accept her mad story. Later in the day she could show him a newspaper and prove that she had not invented the death of David Swift.

The afternoon seemed an impossible distance away; even thinking seemed to require an unreasonable amount of effort. She was sure that the breathy woman on the telephone had laughed at her. Again, she thought of leaving for America.

She rolled down onto the mattress, hoping that Mark would soon return. The door of a wardrobe gaped open beside the mattress, and Julia idly looked at Mark's few clothes hanging on wire hangers. He seemed to possess only one necktie, nearly six inches wide, silvery in color, with a sunburst painted on it in orange. Julia thought of Magnus' neat rows of striped ties, hundreds of them, and managed to smile. Mark owned a green tweed suit which clearly derived from the late fifties and looked as though it had not been worn since then. Magnus had seemed not to care for clothes, but he had owned a lot of them. He had, for

instance, owned seven pairs of shoes, all exactly alike and made by the same bootmaker on Cork Street who had made his father's shoes. Mark appeared to own only boots, no shoes at all. Black and brown boots, one pair of each, with zips up the side. One pair of sandals. Something brown and partially hidden by a bag at the back of the wardrobe caught her eye, and she looked closely at it. The particular woody shade of brown was familiar, and even as she registered its familiarity, she felt the beginnings of alarm, as if a bell had begun to ring.

She reached from the edge of the mattress into the closet and twitched the bag aside with her fingers. She was looking at the backs of a pair of shoes with chunky low heels and a benchmark stamped discreetly into the leather just at the bottom of the back seam. It was a small letter *D*, and stood for David Day, who had made the shoes. She had purchased them four years ago, and even now she could remember how much they cost. They were the shoes she had lost climbing in her window on her first night in Ilchester Place.

Julia stared at the backs of the shoes for a moment, panting slightly, her mind unable to reckon with what she was seeing. She reached into the wardrobe as though it contained a rattlesnake and extracted the shoes. Their uppers were waterstained and scruffy from their two days outdoors. It was Mark, not Magnus, who had taken them.

"Wait," she told herself, touching the brown shoes. Her heart had begun to thrum. She looked at her right wrist where she wore the little green bracelet Mark had given her. Something taken, something given, Mrs. Fludd had said. Julia tugged off the bracelet and dropped it onto the dirty sheet.

Mark had appeared in Olivia's wake several times; sympathetic magic, she had once thought it was. But he had appeared every time, every time.

Could he have just found her shoes? Then why would he hide them in the wardrobe?

Receptive, Mrs. Fludd had said. *He wants to be filled, like a bottle.*

Julia became aware she was making a noise in her throat, but found she could not control or stop it. Her heart seemed to thunder, banging her rib cage like a noisy drum. She plucked at her bandage and tore it off her wrist. She could feel herself breaking, as though she were a thin bone. The long wound on her wrist pouted, a ragged weal along the skin, and she tore it apart with the fingers of her right hand, separating the lips of the wound. A bright surprising ribbon of blood appeared in the gash.

He'll know, her mind said. She tore at the wound and the ribbon of blood bannered out across her hand and onto Mark's bed. She rubbed the shoes in her blood and left them on the bed. Her arm began to throb. She realized that the noise in her throat had subsided to a choked gurgling noise, half a snarl. She printed the mark of her wound on Mark's sheets.

When she stood from the mess she had made, she wound the bandage around her wrist again, ignoring the fresh stains on her trousers, and then ran toward the door. She had to get out before Mark's return. Her vagina throbbed in the same rhythm as her wrist. Wounds. She gasped, realizing that five minutes before, she'd been thinking about safety. There was no safety, only its illusion.

Julia opened the door and looked fearfully up the steps, as if she expected to see Mark Berkeley smiling down at her. Rain filtered gauzily down onto

her face. Julia went up the six steps to the street. Within seconds, the thin material of her blouse had adhered coldly to her skin. She ran down the block, pursued by Olivia's taunting smile and the thought of Mark. Only one escape, only one safety, existed. Kate was there before her. In her haste and fright, she forgot the Rover until she had reached the end of the block.

Her house seemed as hot as Ecuador. Julia slammed the front door and bolted it, knowing that Hazel Mullineaux had seen her come limping up from the sidewalk, her hair streaming and her clothing soaked. Her neighbor had been standing at the side door of her home, her face white and gleaming beneath the cover of a wide black umbrella. She had looked like an advertisement for skin cream. Breathing hard, Julia waited behind the door for what she knew would happen. Before thirty seconds were out, the bell rang down the hall. "Go away," Julia whispered.

Hazel Mullineaux knocked on the door, then rang the bell again.

"I'm all right," Julia said, a little louder.

After knocking again, Hazel Mullineaux bent to lift the flap of the mail slot and called, "Mrs. Lofting? Do you need any help?"

"Go away," Julia said. "I don't need your help."

"Oh!" Julia could tell that Hazel was kneeling outside the door. She probably looks adorable doing that, Julia thought.

"I thought you looked . . . well, upset," came the low voice through the slot.

"Leave me alone," Julia said. "Get away from my house."

"I don't mean to intrude."

"I'm glad to hear it. Please go." Julia remained leaning against the door until she heard her neighbor's footsteps go reluctantly down to the pavement. Then she went into the dark living room and yanked the cord of the telephone out of the wall. Holding the severed telephone in her hands, Julia noticed that the weeks of abnormal heat had effected some chemical change in the walls of the house, for the wallpaper had buckled in places; one strip curled down from the ceiling like a dog's tongue. The whole room seeemed to have aged during the weeks of heat, to have become wrinkled and shabby. The McClintocks' furniture had lost its solid fat Victorian look, and now appeared to be peeling, like sunburned skin. The glue had cracked in one of the dining room chairs. The carpet lapped up at one end of the room.

Julia dropped the useless telephone to the floor. Her wounded wrist, the muscles in her calves, and her vagina all ached. The flesh on her face felt as though it were blubber, puffing out from the bones. She could trust no one.

Upstairs, she sat on the edge of her bed, waiting. The house hung emptily about her. No one could telephone now, and she would not answer the door. The others knew what they needed to know. It was Mark or Magnus, one of them. One of them had been used by Olivia Rudge, and Mrs. Fludd had seen it weeks before. She had been tricked by Mark. It was Mark. It could be Mark.

Julia got up and moved to her desk and pulled a sheet of paper and a pencil from a drawer. Somone would have to know, or Olivia would never be stopped, she would keep on filling people's minds, using them, going from one to another like a disease. *If I am found dead,* she wrote rapidly, *it will be no*

accident. *If I am found dead in this room or anywhere else, whatever the cause of death may appear to be, I shall have been murdered. The murderer will be either my husband or his brother, Mark Berkeley. One of these two is planning to kill me. This same person will have been the cause of the death of Rosa Fludd, and will probably have killed Captain Paul Winter and David Swift. (But maybe not.) This is because—This has to do with a dead child named Olivia Rudge, who died in the same way as my own child. My husband Magnus was also the father of Olivia Rudge. Look her up in the newspapers for the year 1950. But leaving the supernatural aside—since it may prejudice the opinion of whoever reads this, I beg you to know that I am not suicidal, and that my death will in no way be an accident. PLEASE KNOW THIS.*

Without rereading what she had written, Julia folded the paper and inserted it into the pages of her address book, and then slid the book between two sweaters in a drawer. Then she lay down on her bed and stared up into the heat and watched patterns move across the surface of the ceiling. She waited. Gleeful noises seemed to well up from other parts of the house. Hot air and a feral stink blew about her. Eventually she swallowed three of her sleeping pills.

12

Once, everything had been different. There had been a pretty, rather placid young woman named Julia Lofting, who had lived in North London with her successful husband and their beautiful daughter, and all three of them had unthinkingly led happy, contented lives, each devoted to the unity they made, each devoted to the other . . . once there had been a girl with a great deal of money named Julia Freeman, and she had married an older man, an Englishman named Magnus Lofting, and lived with him in London, tolerating his infidelities and his angers for the sake of their daughter (her daughter) . . . once a confused, uncertain American woman named Julia lived in a house with her daughter, seeing her husband late in the evenings when he came home from one of his drinking clubs . . . there had once been a beautiful and imaginative child named Kate Lofting . . . but she was dead . . . once there had been a couple, Magnus and Julia, with a nice house but not as nice a house as they could afford because they (she) hated extravagance, and with two cars and one daughter, and they'd had few friends outside the family because many people did not like Magnus and because Julia was a bit shy and their daughter was all they needed, really . . . once an American girl had thrown herself at a man named

Magnus and made a daughter with him, she used her money to make him sleep with her (marry her) . . . once there had been a girl everybody liked. Julia looked up at the cracked ceiling of her bedroom, thinking of the girl she had been, her father's darling (her hair was her best feature). She waited. Her best and truest self was in the past which had sent her Olivia Rudge. Whose father she had married. She was too tired to move from her bed, and her mind spun from version to version.

From downstairs came the noise of a rampage—she could hear glass breaking, a series of popping, hollow explosions, and ripping noises, fabric being torn. The noises had started in the kitchen and then moved into the dining room. It sounded now like chairs being thrown up against the wall. I wanted to set you free, Julia thought, meaning that I wanted to send you away in peace. But you don't want peace. You want control. You hate all of us, and you hate this house. I did set you free, but in the wrong way. Wood splintered somewhere in the house, and this sharp sound was immediately followed by another series of popping explosions. The cups in the dining room. Then the broader, flatter sound of the china plates being broken. A bottle of some kind smashed against a wall? Wine? Whiskey? Julia, half in a daze, sniffed at the air but caught only a faint odor of excrement.

"It's settled."

"In what way?"

"We need a certificate signed by her physician and one other. Two doctors at the hospital, Dr. Whatever and another one, will agree to sign it. Then she goes in for a period of examination. It's a temporary order, but it gives me time to look into ways of

keeping her there out of trouble. Does that satisfy you?"

"I don't know what would satisfy me now."

"Lily, don't go soft on me. This was really your idea, you know."

"My idea for your good, brother."

"For ours. And hers."

"Chiefly yours."

Magnus looked across the room to where Lily sat on her delicate little couch beside the Persian screen. She was staring at him oddly. Her eyes seemed slightly larger than usual, and the hazel irises appeared to swim in the surrounding white. Lily's whole face was pale. "For God's sake, Lily," he said, "are you still angry with me about that wretched child? You're making it all up, you know, I did not lie to you. I never did see the child. Anyone could have been her father."

"Anyone wasn't."

"It's a trifle late for a blood test, Lily."

"I wish you weren't so obtuse at times."

He looked at her in complete puzzlement. "Lily, let me explain our position. Julia can be put into the hospital as soon as I have the doctors' signatures. That should be no later than Tuesday. I have control over all monies, whether held jointly or separately, in case of Julia's hospitalization or death. I mention the latter only as the extreme case. The legal point in question is mental incapacity—which shall be proven by the doctors' authorization of our request that she be involuntarily hospitalized. It is very simple."

"Try to ring her," Lily ordered. "Right now."

"What? Do you want to bring her here? There's really no need for that now, since the doctors—"

"Try to ring her."

"Lily, what in the world is going on?"

"I'm terrified, you idiot," she said. "She has been telling us the truth all along, and I was too stupid and vain to recognize it. She is in mortal danger."

"What in the world . . ." Magnus stared at her in disbelief. "Are you telling me that you believe in that cod's wallop now? Didn't you just assure me, two days ago, that it was all fantasy? Didn't you say that?"

"Yes," she admitted. "But I was wrong. We have to try to save her life. Please ring her, Magnus. I want to know that she is still safe."

Magnus reluctantly lifted himself heavily from his chair and padded across the room to the telephone. He dailed Julia's number and listened silently for some time. "No answer," he said. "What's this all about, Lily?"

"Revenge," she answered. "Olivia Rudge's revenge."

That was it, Julia thought, listening to the savage noises from downstairs. It was revenge. She hated being thwarted, and Heather had cut off her career: so Heather was part of her revenge, Mrs. Braden immured in her bedroom was part of her revenge, and all of her gang had shared in it too, seeing their lives disintegrate or grind to powder, nothing accomplished except by the severest penance.

She had been meant to buy the house. Olivia had reached out and found her, the only woman who could release her into the world again.

If only Kate had not tried to swallow that piece of meat . . . if only she and Magnus had waited longer for the ambulance. Julia seemed not to be lying on her bed, but to be suspended above a thrashing seacoast, sharp upthrust rocks and seething water.

Her skin was boiling, as with fever. She imagined holding Kate in her arms. But Kate was in that small deep hole, in that small box in the deep, deep hole. In wretched Hampstead cemetery. She wanted to carry Kate away from here. To float with her, far above the sea and the rocks.

Then she saw Kate with her back turned to her. It was what she had seen before Mrs. Fludd stopped the séance. *I am responsible*, she thought, without knowing what she meant.

A black bird zipped past Mark's head and muttered some message to him, as it would to another bird. It was a single word. *Brief*, perhaps, or *free*. Or *be*. He watched the bird whirl off into the glowing area above the tops of the trees, where the sky was unnaturally pink. The cottony undersides of the thick clouds, which had just ceased to release their drizzle of rain, seemed to reveal some incandescent color laid across their upper surfaces. They looked as though they had been painted by Turner, and Mark, thinking this, was moved to the edge of tears. His scalp tingled. Birds spoke to him, he walked beneath Turner clouds. Since completing his last meditation, he had felt almost unbearably, uncomfortably happy—he had reached ecstasy. Colors of the grass and trees boomed out at him, as if they were shouted through loud-speakers; so many different greens! He felt that he had never truly seen any of these shades before, how they rippled next to each other, jumped forward or receded in space. Color was a stupendous bounty.

Julia had bled on his sheets. That too seemed a sign of grace. Blood after making love. He felt as though Julia were his other half, as though they shared the same limbs, or the same heart. She had

dug the shoes out of his closet, knowing in what love he had spirited them away from her garden after finding them one morning. He'd had to look at her house, he'd walked all round it, passing his hands over the rough brick, almost swooning. Even his headache had not diminished his joy. Julia had left Magnus, and she would be his.

She was his. He moved dazedly through Holland Park, nearly alone on the paths, chiming with this knowledge. He had flown deep into her; he knew her bones and joints. Julia was light and vision. And a creature of blood, a furnace of it. *Be*, the bird had said to him. Traveling toward Julia, he was traveling toward blessedness. A pure greedy joy smashed drunkenly at him. Queenly, she was waiting. *Be*. He staggered under the impact of it.

A girl walking slowly in front of him lowered her umbrella with a motion of such grace that he nearly sobbed aloud. He recognized the back of her head and neck, where black hair fell down over a brown leather jacket. Mark quickly crossed the ground between himself and the girl and linked his arm into hers, laughing. When she twisted toward him, startled and a little frightened, he kissed her familiar mouth and felt his soul expanding with a scream of happiness.

"I can't believe this," Magnus said, still holding the telephone. "I tried to persuade you that there might be something to Julia's story, recall that? And you were certain that it was all a delusion. You convinced me. I cannot be convinced back again, Lily." He set the receiver back in its cradle, very gently, a sign Lily knew quite well: he was rapidly reaching the demarcation between annoyance and outright irritation.

"Perhaps not," she said. "It makes little difference whether or not you are persuaded. But do think back, Magnus—what did you see on that day you thought you saw Kate?"

"How can I answer that? I don't know what I saw. The reflection of a cloud, a flash of sun on the window. . . ."

"No. I mean, what did you think you saw?"

He looked at her in disgust. "I am not going to be made a fool of, Lily."

"Tell me. Just tell me what you saw."

"Kate. Standing in the window of Julia's bedroom."

"How do you know it was Kate? Was she facing you?"

"She needn't to. In fact, the girl I thought I saw was facing the other way, and I saw only the back of her head."

"It might not have been Kate! It might have been the other one!" Lily half-started from her chair. "Magnus, that's it. You saw Olivia Rudge. She wanted you to see her, and to think that she was Kate. She wanted to hurt and confuse you."

"Lily," Magnus said slowly, "I have never interfered with your enthusiasms, and I have never jeered at them. But if you are telling me that I saw an apparition in that window—"

"What did you feel when you went into her house that day? Didn't you tell me that you were terrified?"

"I was spooked. You told me that yourself. I was also drunk."

"No, Magnus. You felt her. You felt her evil. She hates you too."

"My God," Magnus said. "This is a nest of ninnies. What reasoning is behind all of this? Why

should this little demon out of the past suddenly
appear again?"

"Because of Julia," she said. "She needed Julia to
free her. Both of your daughters were stabbed to
death by their mothers. Julia was what she needed."

First I gave birth to Kate, Julia thought, and then
I gave birth to Olivia. But part of Olivia is still in me.
I complete her. The sleeping pills and lack of food
made her mind swim about a general focus, which
was her awareness of the noises from the ground
floor. Things were still being smashed. The suffocating heat that dried her throat and burned her eyes
seemed to carry her some inches above her bed and
leave her floating above a vast, undefined space into
which she could be spilled at any moment. Julia
knew that this was due to a warp, a wrinkle in her
mind that was a part of Olivia. She wished to read,
to bring herself back into gravity, but she was too
weak to pick up any of the books on the bedside
table. A wind seemed to blow through the house,
hot and African. The glass across one of the
McClintocks' paintings shattered, accompanied by
screams of laughter. Then she heard the thunking
noise of the painting's being kicked in.

Maybe all this is just in my head, she thought.
Would that make it less true? Indeed, everything in
the world seemed crowded into her head. The smell
of beasts and burned skin settled about her.

"A rape, Mark? Not in your style, I should have
thought." Annis stood before him, breathing a little
heavily, her face flushed. He could see the place on
her full lower lip where he'd bitten it. "I thought I
was being sent away, anyhow," she said.

"Lovely, sweet Annis," Mark said, holding her

again, "darling, lovely, gorgeous, sexy Annis, how could I send you away?" He laughed at both her absurdity and his own, bubbling up within him.

"Is meditation responsible for these moods? I think I'd advise a little rest. Are you up on something?"

"On you, Annis, on you," he chanted, and swung her around.

She pushed at his arms. "Mark, put me down. Mark, I don't like this."

He whooped with laugher, seeing himself from both within and without, and nearly fell down. "Are you going somewhere? Let's go to a pub. Let's go to a pub and hold hands. I was just noticing how the sky looks like a Turner. Don't you think?"

She looked at the sky half with genuine interest, half with bemusement. "It looks like a slate roof, if you want my opinion. You know, you don't have to act like this with me. I'm perfectly willing to start seeing you again. But I thought you had some new interest in your life."

"On the contrary, dear Annis, I am shedding some of the old interests. I decided to quit teaching. I'm just going to travel for a while. Travel with me, Annis. You'd look lovely on a boat." He began to laugh uncontrollably, and fell onto a bench. Annis and Julia shared one substance, and Mark giddily witnessed Julia's features shining through the other's face. When she turned away from him in irritation, he caught her wrist and pulled her down beside him. "I'm serious, let's have a drink and talk about it." He looked into her wide, beautiful, hungry face and felt himself turn on all the voltage he possessed. Annis' face broke over him like a wave.

"Well," she said. "I'm going somewhere now. How about lunch at one?"

"Lunch at one, what fun," he sang. "Only an hour away." Joy seemed to smash at his ribs again, and he gripped her hand. "Name two places you want to go to, Annis."

"Well, I've never seen California," she said. "I can't think of any other place I'd like to go."

"Europe?"

"Europe is boring. I'd settle for California."

"You'll have it."

"Doesn't it take a lot of money to get there?"

"Doesn't everything come through meditation? Lord Buddha provides, Annis, Lord Buddha provides."

"We're going to have everything," Magnus said, having by now passed firmly into outright anger, "we're going to have the lot, and you decide to get mysterious and orphic. Aren't we going to have everything you wanted? I have a mad wife who's going to be locked away for God knows how long, but you'll have the bleeding lot, Lily. What do you think you're trying to do to me?"

"Self-pity isn't your most attractive trait," she said. "What I think I am trying to do, as you put it, is to tell the truth at last. Look, Magnus. Suppose that Julia came to you with some idea about a point of law that you'd been thinking about for months? Suppose she said something about it at breakfast?"

"Bugger the analogies," he said, even angrier, and causing her more fear than she knew she could afford to reveal.

"I'll tell you what you'd do. You'd ignore her, and resent her incursion on your special territory. That's the way I felt."

"The law is not a ridiculous bundle of lies and fantasies!" he shouted.

She merely looked at him, not daring to speak further.

When he turned away and slammed his fist into the counter top, she waited for him to settle down again—she could see his shoulders sinking back to their normal level, and his neck lose its swelling, as if it were shedding layers of tissue—she said, "Try to ring her again. I am afraid for her, Magnus."

"Damn you," he said, but said it quietly.

She said to his back, "Someone killed those two men. Julia knew about it before they were in the papers."

"Are you sure? She's no fortune-teller."

Lily thought back to her last conversation with Julia. "I *think* so. She told me about the second one, certainly. The Swift man. She was in his flat."

"Then I'm glad he's dead."

"She was there to warn him about Olivia Rudge—I think that's what she said. Or I may have gathered it."

"That's two things you're vague on. You're not terribly persuasive."

"And Mrs. Fludd was killed because she saw Olivia."

"Nonsense. Wait. Did you imply that Julia was in the Swift man's flat when he was killed?"

"That's what she told me."

"She told you that she saw him—what? Die? Be killed? What did she say?"

"I can't remember. She said that she was there."

"*Damn,*" Magnus said loudly. "Didn't she inform the police?"

"I shouldn't imagine that she thought they had much chance against a ghost."

"Ghosts don't murder people," Magnus said and

went quickly back to the telephone. After dialing and listening intently, his lips working in and out, he said, "Still no answer."

"Then she has either drugged herself to sleep or she's gone out," Lily said. "We must do something quickly, Magnus. Olivia is after her. I know it. She's already tried to kill her once."

"I wonder if Julia is actually madder than you. You should both be put away." He considered a second, containing his anger, and said, "Think about this, Lily. If Julia was right, then aren't we all endangered? You and I as well as Julia? After all, we know about Olivia too."

"We're all touched by it, we're all soiled," she answered him. "Mark too, I should imagine. We may be in as much danger as she is."

"Rubbish."

"Remember how you felt inside that house," she said. "She hates you too, Magnus. She's enjoyed torturing you."

Julia was carrying Kate, a bundle no heavier than an armful of leaves and twigs, to the hospital. Kate was injured, and it was urgent that Julia find the hospital immediately: she could feel some warm fluid soaking into the sleeves of her blouse. Down grimy, vacant streets she was wandering, looking up at barred doorways for the name of the hospital. It was her fault that she could not find the hospital, that instead she was trudging through these gritty hopeless streets, looking exhaustedly into one filthy sunless court after another, dirty cobblestones . . . she had failed, and she knew that Kate had already died, that the merest breeze would lift away the feather of her body. Soon she would be on the bare

rooftop, surrounded by failure and loss, carrying them within her. She saw herself turning the knife from Kate's body and turning it toward herself.

Footsteps ran through the house, raising the smells of heat and lions.

She wandered through these hopeless streets, looking for the hospital that could undo what already had been done.

"Where are you going?" She watched tensely as he rushed around her flat, gathering up his raincoat and umbrella.

"I have to get out of this room," he said as calmly as he could. "Before I deliberately break something, I am going to take a short walk. *You* ring her."

"Will you be back? Magnus, please. . . ."

"I'll be back," he said harshly, almost barking the final word. As she watched, half-cowering by the door to the kitchen, he turned away from her and thundered across the floor like a bison. When he left he banged the door with such force that he split a section of the jamb.

Julia moved fractionally toward consciousness, her heart thudding, aware that the hand she had turned toward herself had not been Magnus'. It was a woman's hand, like hers. It was hers. Her mouth flooded with pain and a residue like tar, and she realized moments later that she had bitten halfway through her tongue. She had recognized her hand from the dream. She swallowed a trickle of blood, not really feeling the pain for longer than the time that lay between the vision of the woman's hand with the steak knife in its fingers and the recognition that it was hers. Instead of pain, there was a drumming sensation through her tongue. Her entire body

seemed as dry as a cracked riverbed. Kate's twig-light, leaf-light body lifted out of her arms. Her lips went numb.

In the next instant she had fled back into the condition of the drugs, and was walking up filthy stairs to the bleak rooftop. She knew every discoloration and stain on the walls, every warp of the stairs.

Mark lay sprawled on wet grass, feeling the ground damply claim his shoulders and buttocks. He was dimly aware of the burnished tips of his new boots, gleaming a dark rich brownish gold all the way down the length of his body. His head was filled with birds. That he had just met and spoken to someone appeared miraculous to him, an unbelievable effort of coherence and will.

But I've seen her too, thought Lily, still facing the door and listening to Magnus go noisily down the stairs. It was the day I saw Rosa Fludd sitting on the park bench. She led me across the park. Was Rosa really there, or did she conjure her? She wanted me to see Magnus breaking into Julia's house. She wanted me to feel that sick disappointment. Perhaps Rose came to me as a warning. She had warned Julia, and that day she was warning me. Lily sagged against the counter, felt the metal strip along the top of the wood dig into her hip.

Mark was moving at the center of a golden, glowing haze, a bowl which had settled down over him as he lay on the wet grass. He knew that this humming golden aura was the outward form of his headache, given him by his most successful meditations, and that it was transformingly beautiful

proved the rarity, the absolute value of his mind. It proved also the absolute value of his exercises, even of the headaches, since they had transported him bodily into euphoria. Into paradise.

The trees past which he moved burned at him, the bark blistering in his vision and the leaves rattling like gold. He had felt like this before, but he could not remember when. His boots made the path shiver. If he hit hard enough with his heels, he could open a crack all the way to the planet's red, seething core.

Asleep now, Julia reached the opening to the roof and walked out onto baking tar paper that adhered tackily to the soles of her shoes. The sky into which she moved was a flat field of gray striped with vibrating, humming pink. The strange union of colors gripped the pit of her stomach and made her bowels full and watery. Her mouth drummed, lined with a bitter substance like tobacco juice. A pine needle pierced her tongue. She wanted Kate, but Kate was dead. Olivia raged beneath her in the empty house screeching with laughter. Even up on the flat roof, hopelessness pouring into her like salt, she could hear the noise from downstairs: hoarse screams, shouts, loud breakage. It no longer made any difference. She was watching herself as in a mirror. Her skin burned in anticipatory shame.

Lily pushed herself away from the counter and went unsteadily into the living room. She knelt before the telephone and with a shaking hand dialed Julia's number. Now instead of the ringing she expected, she heard only the bottomless space, filled with the echoes of static, which precedes the dial tone. She punched the button and the gray depthless

space hung in the receiver. When she struck the button again, the depthless sound mercifully gave way to the dial tone. She tried Julia's number again, and heard the digits slot into connection; then a sound like that of a man falling through deep space, spinning away from life.

Lily banged the receiver down, waited until she felt safe enough to lift it again, made sure of the reassuring, chunky dial tone, and then dialed 100. She gave the operator Julia's number and waited.

"I'm sorry," the operator's twanging voice came back a minute later. "That number appears to be temporarily out of service."

"Why?" asked Lily. "What do you mean, out of service?"

"We are not permitted to offer that information," the operator disdainfully said. "You may speak to the supervisor."

"Yes."

"Hold, please."

Lily licked her lips and waited again. The silence in the telephone was furry and dense, more solid than the other. She listened to it for what seemed entire minutes before she could bear the waiting no more and hung up. Then she paced nervously in her living room, waiting for Magnus to return. She would not go to Ilchester Place alone.

Something flew along the upstairs hall, something infinitely despairing.

Slowly, with merciful intent, the knife in her hand slid into Kate's blocked throat. Her hand, the hand she had dreamed of turning toward herself, gripped the sleek little knife between thumb and finger, blade up. Kate uttered a half-conscious, choking

noise and opened her eyes at the instant Julia began to carve into her throat. Kate's eyes were clouds. As in a mirror, the scene glinted at her from where it was happening at the flat edge of the roof, two figures bent together in a clumsy parody of love. She heard the door to her room bang open, and the hot wind gusted about her, making the scene before her and the pink-striped sky mist over, like a mirror. The one who wanted her was with her, and she whirled about on the roof and saw only desolation, dirty tar paper and a ruined sky. A white column of air blew toward her. She could see dust and scraps of paper whirl about inside it, spinning crazily. From somewhere below in the streets or from another side of the bedroom came a chortling sound she knew was the suppressed laughter of a small dark-skinned child whose name she could not remember. Strong arms braced her, and Olivia's smoldering odor invaded her nostrils and the white column of air whirled her into it, caught up with dust and scraps of old newspapers, dust and paper.

November

"You said you'd heard from Mark at last."

"Yes."

"Still in California?"

"Still in California, yes. Los Angeles."

"With that girl?"

"What was her name?"

"Annis."

"Odd sort of name for a girl. Or is it her patronym?"

"I don't know. He said that he was working at last. He'd found a job as maintenance man at something called a free school. Annis apparently has a little money each month."

"Do you think he will marry her?"

"I don't know whether she would marry him."

"I suppose that means you are becoming liberated, Lily."

She sniffed, and returned to her novel. When she was certain that he was not looking at her, she peeked across the room to the Sisley. Magnus had bought it for her in October. It hung in the place of the Stubbs drawing of the horse, although she had actually preferred the Stubbs horse. That had been relegated to the dining room.

"Mark has found his level at last," Magnus was saying. "Maintenance man. That means cleaner. I'm

surprised that in the city of the angels the position is not referred to as maintenance engineer."

"He said he is also taking classes at a yoga institute."

"And belongs to the Che-Mao-Lumumba Revolutionary Tactics Chess League, no doubt. Didn't he tell you sometime before the inquest that it was yoga—those damnable exercises—which had finally pushed him over the edge? I should think he'd stay away from that sort of thing."

"You know very well it wasn't that. I don't imagine I need particularize."

"Please don't," said Magnus, sounding rather wounded. "But even he said that it played a part in his crackup."

"Julia played a larger part," Lily said maliciously.

"I think I just said that I did not require reminding. A very nasty shock, finding that my wife spent her last night before committing suicide in another man's bed. Especially that lunatic's bed. And the bloody fool didn't even possess the wit to see what Julia was going through." Magnus stared at his hands, which he had clasped tightly in his lap.

"We can be very grateful she left that—letter," Lily said substituting the last word for "note." "It really did make things much clearer. I did think the coroner was right, don't you? To think that it proved instability of mind and was a clear indication of suicidal intent?"

"It offends me to see any man lead a jury to that extent," Magnus growled. "Coroners have far too much power in this country. Little gods. But yes, Lily, for the thousandth time, yes. I do think the coroner was right. Of course he was bloody right. There's no doubt about it. Any fool looking at the condition of that house and her car would know that

her mind was gone. Now do you suppose we might have some tea? Actually, I'd rather have a drink. Would you get me one? No, I'll get it myself." He rose and moved toward the drinks trolley.

"Do have some cheese and biscuits, Magnus. There's a bit of Stilton on the sideboard."

"One cannot get a real Stilton anymore," he said. "Only supermarket rubbish. And have you seen or, heaven forbid, tasted what they have the gall to refer to as Sage Derby? It should be fed to birds. A decent pig wouldn't touch it."

"I just thought you might like a bite of some nice cheese and bikkies," she said, watching him splash whiskey into a tumbler. He took even more than she had expected. "I didn't mean to upset you."

"I . . . am . . . not . . . upset."

"Magnus, you know that I am deeply, truly grateful to you for not being affected by my silliness on that last day. Your steadfastness was simply remarkable. I lost my head, I was an utter fool, and you were so strong, you wouldn't be shaken, not in the least, and I am enormously grateful to you for that. I am grateful for your clear head and for your strength."

He glanced at her, and took a long swallow of his drink. "You shouldn't be grateful that I avoided being an ass. That's a negative sort of compliment." But she saw that he was calmer.

"And I shall never cease to be grateful that she wrote that note," she said. "If she hadn't given the game away by naming two of you, well . . ."

"Well," he said. "Tellingly put, Lily." He went back across the room and sat carefully in his chair. Magnus seemed to Lily to be gaining weight with every day. "I should have been in the soup, at least until they tried to 'pin it on' Mark."

"Do you know, I think that I appreciate how she felt. Not about you or even Mark, of course, but how she must have felt about *life*, when I was being so foolish on that day, I experienced the most remarkable sensation of utter hopelessness and despair. It was quite total. I felt utterly gray and washed-out, as though everything bright was long behind me. Julia must have felt something of that kind."

"Julia was not in a rational frame of mind. None of us can know what she thought about anything, much less something so vaporous as *life*." He looked at her sourly. "You didn't see the condition of that house."

"I couldn't go in there," she said. "I just couldn't do it." She switched to a safer topic. "Have you had any luck with the house?"

"Nobody is buying houses now, especially not houses as criminally expensive as that one. That officious twerp at Markham and Reeves told me the market is worse than it's been for fifteen years."

"Have you been to the cemetery yet, Magnus?" She had been earlier in the week, to see to the flowers.

"No, not really. Not since the funeral. I can't abide Hampstead cemetery. It looks like a suburb of Melbourne."

"Julia never liked it either."

"Rot. Utter rot. How can you claim to know such a thing?"

"Because she told me on the day of Kate's funeral. She said that she wished Kate could have been buried in an older cemetery. In Highgate."

"I don't believe that Julia held a firm opinion on a boneyard she saw only once, and then so exhausted she could scarcely stand upright."

Lily shrugged, irritated with him.

"Anyhow, nobody seems to want the damned house," he said. This was an oblique apology to her, and she peeked again at the Sisley painting. He was still talking, of course. "People look at it and they don't like it, for some reason. Did I tell you that that McClintock person wrote wondering if Julia would sell him his furniture back? Said he couldn't find any furniture like it in Barbados. He'd have had a shock if he could have seen his precious furniture."

"That frightens me," she said. "Please don't dwell on it."

"I wasn't about to dwell on anything," he said and gulped at his drink again. "Anything good on the goggle box tonight?"

"Nothing," she said. "I thought I might try reading one of those books Julia had. I'll be finished with this novel by tonight, and I thought I'd try one of hers. That's an odd coincidence, isn't it? I didn't have time to look at them for ages, and then I didn't want to. But it seems a pity to let them go unread. There's a nice long one about a rainbow. I think I'll begin with that, it looks a lovely read. She did have a lot of books, didn't she?"

"It was because she was friendless," Magnus said flatly.

"How can you, Magnus?" she said, genuinely surprised. "Julia had friends. You and I were certainly her friends. And I suppose Mark was a friend of a sort."

"Bloody Mark. I hope he falls under a bus."

"Mark has suffered a great deal."

Magnus turned away in impatience. "Are you sure there's nothing on the box? I'd like to watch something tonight."

Lily knew that this meant that he wished to spend

the evening with her, and that he would fill it by insulting the television and all who watched it. She wished that he would leave—Magnus was in one of his carping moods, which lately annoyed Lily more than they once had. "Nothing you would care for, Magnus. You despise the television, as we both know. But," she added more from habit than desire, "you might stay for dinner. This is one of my vegetarian nights. I'll make a big salad."

Magnus shuddered. "I could get something from a restaurant and bring it back. I don't like these meatless Tuesdays of yours."

As neutrally as possible, she said, "If you wish."

"Right, then."

In exasperation, she thrust down her book and went over to the window on the terrace. Her flowers still bloomed vigorously, and were dazzlingly, violently colored in the damp gray air. To Lily, they looked like little flags of contentment—they said *we, at least, have no problems*.

Behind her, Magnus cleared his throat. "Just out of curiosity, my darling, do you still go to those groups of yours?"

Lily looked into the deep green of the treetops.

"Not as often as before," she said.

"Why is that? Don't you fancy the new swami?"

She let her gaze travel down the rough, pitted bark of the trees. On this cold, cheerless November day few people lingered in the park, and the men and women on the long path rushed by, their hands deep in the pockets of their coats. They looked gray and insubstantial before the great trees, like smoke blown past.

"Oh, Mrs. Venable is acceptable," she said, not paying much attention to what she was saying. "I don't feel the same about the meetings." Now she

was watching a child in a blue hooded coat recklessly ride a bicycle down the path, which was forbidden. None of the people on the path seemed to care, as if their opinions were smoke too. "But I don't like to disappoint the others," she said. The child swung off the bicycle and propped it against one of the trees. A girl's bicycle, Lily noticed. "Rosamund Tooth is such an old dear, and Nigel Arkwright can be quite charming when he doesn't babble on so," she said. The child on the path had turned around and was now apparently scrutinizing the ground, her cowl making her look like a dwarfish monk. "But I'm not as interested as I once was," Lily said. "Mrs. Venable's speciality is communing with the departed, through a control named Marcel, and I've always thought that was a shade—you know." Irritatingly, Magnus snorted, lumping her with the class of people who sought information from controls named Marcel. She could now see the pale glimmer of the girl's face. The child was staring straight ahead, as if counting to herself. Then she tilted up her face and looked right at Lily. Her eyes were blue and expressionless. With both hands, still holding Lily's eyes with her own, she swept back the hood and revealed hair the color of white gold.

Lily jumped back from the window, whirled around, and uttered the first sentence to appear in her mind. She said, "We should never have buried Julia in Hampstead cemetery."

Magnus said, "What?"

I

THE BOOTS

MANY YEARS AGO there lived a man called Laurids Madsen, who went up to Heaven and came down again, thanks to his boots.

He didn't soar as high as the tip of the mast on a full-rigged ship; in fact he got no farther than the main. Once up there, he stood outside the pearly gates and saw Saint Peter—though the guardian of the gateway to the Hereafter merely flashed his bare ass at him.

Laurids Madsen should have been dead. But death didn't want him, and he came back down a changed man.

Until the fame he achieved from this heavenly visit, Laurids Madsen was best known for having single-handedly started a war. His father, Rasmus, had been lost at sea when Laurids was six years old. When he turned fourteen he shipped aboard the *Anna* of Marstal, his native town on the island of Ærø, but the ship was lost in the Baltic only three months later. The crew was rescued by an American brig and from then on Laurids Madsen dreamt of America.

He'd passed his navigation exam in Flensburg when he was eighteen and the same year he was shipwrecked again, this time off the coast of Norway near Mandal, where he stood on a rock with the waves slapping on a cold October night, scanning the horizon for salvation. For the next five years he sailed the seven seas. He went south around Cape Horn and heard penguins scream in the pitch-black night. He saw Valparaiso, the west coast of America, and Sydney, where the kangaroos hop and the trees shed bark in winter and not their leaves. He met a girl with eyes like grapes by the name of Sally Brown, and could tell stories about Foretop Street, La Boca, Barbary Coast, and Tiger Bay. He boasted about his first equator crossing, when he'd saluted Neptune and felt the bump as the ship passed the line: his fellow sailors had marked the occasion by forcing him to drink salt water, fish oil, and vinegar; they'd baptized him in tar, lamp soot, and glue; shaved him with a rusty razor with dents in its blade; and tended to his cuts with stinging salt and lime. They made him kiss the ocher-colored cheek of the pockmarked Amphitrite and forced his nose down her bottle of smelling salts, which they'd filled with nail clippings.

Laurids Madsen had seen the world.

So had many others. But he was the only one to return to Marstal with the peculiar notion that everything there was too small, and to prove his point, he frequently spoke in a foreign tongue he called American, which he'd learned when he sailed with the naval frigate *Neversink* for a year.

"*Givin nem belong mi Laurids Madsen,*" he said.

He had three sons and a daughter with Karoline Grube from Nygade: Rasmus, named after his grandfather, and Esben and Albert. The girl's name was Else and she was the oldest. Rasmus, Esben, and Else took after their mother, who was short and taciturn, while Albert resembled his father: at the age of four he was already as tall as Esben, who was three years his senior. His favorite pastime was rolling around an English cast-iron cannonball, which was far too heavy for him to lift—not that it stopped him from trying. Stubborn-faced, he'd brace his knees and strain.

"*Heave away, my jolly boys! Heave away, my bullies!*" Laurids shouted in encouragement, as he watched his youngest son struggling with it.

The cannonball had come crashing through the roof of their house in Korsgade during the English siege of Marstal in 1808, and it had put Laurids's mother in such a fright that she promptly gave birth to him right in the middle of the kitchen floor. When little Albert wasn't busy with the cannonball it lived in the kitchen, where Karoline used it as a mortar for crushing mustard seeds.

"It could have been you announcing your arrival, my boy," Laurids's father had once said to him, "seeing how big you were when you were born. If the stork had dropped you, you would have gone through the roof like an English cannonball."

"*Finggu,*" Laurids said, holding up his finger.

He wanted to teach the children the American language.

Fut meant foot. He pointed to his boot. *Maus* was mouth.

He rubbed his belly when they sat down to eat. He bared his teeth.

"*Hanggre.*"

They all understood he was telling them he was hungry.

Ma was *misis,* Pa *papa tru.* When Laurids was absent, they said "Mother" and "Father" like normal children, except for Albert. He had a special bond with his father.

The children had many names, *pickaninnies, bullies,* and *hearties.*

"Laihim tumas," Laurids said to Karoline, and pursed his lips as if he was about to kiss her.

She blushed and laughed, and then got angry.

"Don't be such a fool, Laurids," she said.

IN 1848, WAR BROKE OUT between the Danish crown and the rebellious Germans across the Baltic in Schleswig-Holstein, who wanted to cut their ties with Denmark. The old customs steward, de la Porte, was the first to know because the provisional insurgent government in Kiel sent him a "proclamation," accompanied by a request to hand over the customs coffers.

All of Ærø was up in arms, and we immediately formed a home guard led by a young teacher from Rise, who from then on was known as the General. On the highest points of the island we erected beacons made of barrels filled with tar and old rope, attached to poles. If the German came by sea, we'd signal his approach by setting them alight and hoisting them up.

There were beacons at Knasterbjerg and on the hills by Vejsnæs, and all around our coast, guards watched the horizon closely.

But all this war business soon became too much for Laurids, who never had much respect for anything to begin with. One evening, as he was on his way home from Eckernförde Fjord, he passed Vejsnæs, where he neared the shore and yelled, "The German is coming!" His voice rang out across the water.

A few minutes later the barrel at the top of the hill was set alight, then the one on Knasterbjerg, and the others followed all the way down to Synneshøj, almost fifteen miles away, until the whole of Ærø was illuminated as on bonfire night.

As the flames rose, Laurids lay in his boat, laughing his head off at the mayhem he'd caused. But when he reached Marstal, he saw lights everywhere and the streets teeming with people, even though it was late evening. Some were shouting incomprehensible orders; others were whimpering and praying. A belligerent crowd was marching up Markgade armed with scythes, pitchforks, and the odd gun, and terrified young mothers rushed around the streets, clutching wailing babies, sure that the German would skewer them on his bayonet. By the well on the corner of Markgade and Vestergade a skipper's wife was arguing with a servant girl. The woman had got it into her head that they should hide in the well and was ordering the girl to go first.

"After you, madam," the girl insisted.

We men were ordering one another about as well, but there were too many skippers in our town for anyone to heed anyone else, so all we could agree on was a solemn vow to part with our lives only at the highest possible price.

The upheaval reached the parsonage in Kirkestrædet where Pastor Zachariassen was entertaining guests. One lady fainted, but the pastor's twelve-year-old son, Ludvig, grabbed a poker, ready to defend his country against the advancing enemy. At the home of Mr. Isager, the schoolteacher, who also doubled up as parish clerk, the family prepared for imminent attack. All twelve sons were on hand to celebrate the birthday of their mother, the portly Mrs. Isager; she equipped them with clay pots filled with ashes and commanded them to throw the contents in the face of the German, should he dare to storm their house.

Our flock moved on through Markgade toward Reberbanen led by old Jeppe, who was waving a pitchfork and yelling that the German was welcome to come and get him if he dared. Laves Petersen, the little carpenter, was forced to return home. He had bravely slung his gun over his shoulder and filled his pockets to bursting with bullets, but halfway down the street, he suddenly remembered he'd left his gunpowder behind.

At Marstal Mill the miller's hefty wife, Madam Weber, already armed with a pitchfork, insisted on joining the fight, and because she appeared more intimidating than most of us men, we instantly welcomed her to our bloodthirsty ranks.

Laurids, who was an emotional man, was so fired up by the general fighting spirit that he too ran home to find a weapon. Karoline and the four children were hiding under the dining table in the parlor when he burst in and proclaimed cheerfully, "Come along, kids, time to go to war!"

There was a hollow thud. It was Karoline, banging her head against the underside of the dining table. She crawled laboriously out from under the tablecloth, stood to her full height, and screamed at her husband, "Have you completely lost your mind, Madsen? Children don't go to war!"

Rasmus and Esben started jumping up and down.

"We want to go! We want to go!" they yelled in unison. "Please, please, let us go."

Little Albert had already started rolling his cannonball around.

"Have you all gone stark raving mad?" their mother shouted, boxing the ears of whichever child came near. "You get back under that table right now!"

Laurids ran into the kitchen to find a suitable weapon. "Where do you keep the big frying pan?" he called into the parlor.

"You keep your hands off it!" Karoline shouted back.

"Well, I'll take the broom then," he announced. "The German will be sorry!"

They heard the front door slam behind him.

"Did you hear that?" whispered Rasmus, the eldest, to Albert. "Father wasn't even speaking American."

"The man's insane," their mother said, shaking her head in the darkness underneath the dining table. "Have you ever heard of anyone going to war with a broom?"

Laurids's arrival in our militant crowd stirred great delight. True, he had a reputation for being cocky, but he was big and strong and good to have on your side.

"Is that the only weapon you've got?"

We had spotted the broom.

"It's good enough for the German," he replied, brandishing it aloft. "We'll sweep him right out of here."

Feeling invincible, we roared with laughter at his joke.

"Let's leave a few pitchforks behind," Lars Bødker said. "We'll need them for stacking the bodies."

By now we'd reached the open fields. It was half an hour's march to Vejsnæs, but our pace was brisk and our blood was up. At Drejbakkerne, the sight of the flaming beacons further fueled our fighting spirit. But at the sound of horses' hooves in the darkness we froze. The enemy was upon us!

· · ·

We had hoped to surprise the German on the beach, but here on the hill the terrain still favored us. Laurids positioned himself for battle with his broom and we followed suit.

A voice rang out behind us. "Wait for me!"

It was the little carpenter, who'd gone home for his gunpowder.

"Shhhh," we warned. "The German is closing in."

The hoofbeats grew louder—and it became clear that there was only one horse. When the rider appeared out of the darkness, Laves Petersen raised his gun and took aim. But Laurids pushed down on the barrel.

"It's Bülow, the controller," he said.

The horse was dripping with sweat, its black flanks pumping in and out. Bülow raised his hand.

"You can go home. There's no German at Vejsnæs."

"But the beacons were alight," Laves called out.

"I've spoken to the coast guard," Bülow said. "It was a false alarm."

"And we left our warm beds. For what? For nothing!"

Madam Weber folded her arms across her chest and fired us all a warning glance as though looking for a new enemy, now that the German had failed to show.

"At least we've proved that we're ready for him," the controller said soothingly. "And surely it's good news that he's not coming at all."

We mumbled in agreement. But although we saw his logic, we were sorely disappointed. We had been ready to stare the German in the face, and death too—but neither had made it to Ærø.

"One day that German will be sorry," Lars Bødker said.

Starting to tire, we decided to head home. A chilly shower had started to fall. In silence we reached the mill, where Madam Weber parted company from us. Turning to face our miserable flock, she placed her pitchfork on the ground as though presenting a rifle.

"I wonder," she said in an ominous voice, "which one of you jokers got decent folks out of their beds in the middle of the night to go to war."

We all stared at Laurids, towering there with his broom on his shoulder.

But Laurids neither flinched nor averted his eyes. Instead he looked straight at us. Then he threw his head back and started laughing into the rain.

SOON WAR BROKE OUT in earnest and we were called up for the navy. The naval steamer *Hekla* anchored off the neighboring town of Ærøskøbing to pick us up. We lined up on the wharf and as our names were called, one by one we jumped into the launch, which took us to the steamer. We'd felt cheated out of war that evening in November, but now the wait was over and we were in high spirits.

"Make way for a Dane with his life, his soul, and his sea bag!" yelled Claus Jacob Clausen.

He was a small, sinewy man who liked to boast that a Copenhagen tattoo artist called Frederik the Spike had once told him he had the toughest arm he'd ever stuck a needle into. Clausen's father, Hans Clausen, had been a pilot, as had his grandfather, and Clausen wanted to follow in their footsteps; what's more, the night before we embarked he'd had a dream that told him he'd emerge from the war alive.

In Copenhagen we were inspected on board the frigate *Gefion*. Laurids was separated from the rest of us and was the only one to join the *Christian the Eighth*, the ship-of-the-line, whose mainmast was so tall that from top to deck, it stood one and a half times the height of the church tower in Marstal. We had to crane our necks to take it in, but the dizziness it induced filled us with pride about the great deeds we'd been summoned to perform.

Laurids watched us as we left. After a year on the American man-of-war *Neversink*, the *Christian the Eighth* suited him. He'd soon feel at home on her deck—though when he saw the rest of us disappear up the gangway to the *Gefion*, he must have briefly felt abandoned.

So off we went to war. On Palm Sunday we sailed along the coast of Ærø, past the hills at Vejsnæs, where Laurids had turned the island upside-down with his cry "The German is coming!" Now the Dane was coming, and it was the German's turn to light his tar barrels and take off like a headless chicken.

We moored off Als and waited. On Wednesday we set course for Eckernförde Fjord and reached its mouth late that afternoon. There we followed the order to line up on the quarterdeck: in our homespun shirts and cloth trousers of blue, black, or white, we were a motley crew. Only the ribbons on our caps emblazoned with the name *Gefion* and a red and white cockade announced that we were members of the king's navy. The captain, who was dressed in his finest uniform, complete with epaulettes and a sword, gave a speech in which he ordered us to fight like brave men. He shouted three cheers for the king and waved his tricorn, and we joined in with all our might. Then he ordered the cannons to be fired so we raw recruits could hear how they'd sound in battle. A formidable roar rolled across the sea, accompanied by the acrid smell of gunpowder. A strong breeze was blowing, carrying the blue haze of cannon smoke off on the wind. For several minutes we couldn't hear a thing. The noise from the cannons had deafened us.

Two steamers arrived, and we recognized the *Hekla*, the ship we had sailed in from Ærøskøbing. We were now a full squadron. The next day we geared up for battle, settling the cannons in their ports, positioning the pumps and hoses where they could be put to immediate use if fire broke out on board, and placing case shots, grapeshot, and boxes of cartridges by each cannon. Over the past few days we had practiced this drill so many times that we knew most of the naval commands by heart. We were eleven men to each cannon, and from the moment the first command sounded—"Get ready!" followed by "Fuse powder and paper!" and "Insert cartridge!" to the command "Fire!"—we scrambled around one another, terrified of making a mistake. We were used to working in threes or fours on our small boats and ketches but now suddenly we were to be masters of life and death.

All too often we'd stand there, baffled, while the gun captain screamed something like "Tend the vent!" or "Search the piece!" What the hell did that mean in plain Danish? Whenever we succeeded in performing a complicated routine without errors, the captain would congratulate us and we'd erupt in cheers. Upon which he'd look first at us, then at his cannon, and finally down at the deck, and shake his head.

"You bunch of puppies," he said. "Just do your best, damn you!"

·   ·   ·

We weren't entirely sure which German we were supposed to be shooting. It surely couldn't be old Ilse with the crooked hip who sold us our beloved schnapps when we moored our boats at Eckernförde Harbor. Nor Eckhart, the grain trader: we'd struck many a fine bargain with him. Then there was Hansen, the innkeeper at Der Rote Hahn. What could be more Danish than the name Hansen? And we'd never seen him anywhere near a gun. None of them could be the German; that much we understood. But the king knew who the German was. As did the captain, who had been cheering with such bravado.

We approached the fjord. The enemy batteries on the coast started to thunder, but we were outside their range and they soon grew quiet. We were given schnapps rather than the usual tea. At nine o'clock came the beating of the tattoo; it was time to turn in. Seven hours later we were roused from our slumbers. It was Maundy Thursday, April 5, 1849. Again we got schnapps rather than tea, and a barrel of beer awaited us on the deck. We could drink as much as we wanted, so morale was high by the time we raised the anchor and headed into the fjord.

We had no complaints about the victuals on board His Majesty's ships. Food had been scarce when we'd had to supply it for ourselves. They said you'd never see a seagull in the wake of a Marstal ship, and that was true enough: we never wasted a crumb. But on top of tea and beer, the navy gave us all the bread we could eat and more. Lunch was a pound of fresh meat or half a pound of bacon, dried peas, porridge or soup; in the evening it was four weights of butter, and a schnapps to go with it. Long before we smelled our first whiff of gunpowder smoke, we loved the war.

Now we were inside Eckernförde Fjord, where the shores were closer and the cannons' positions clearly visible. Kresten Hansen leaned over to Ejnar Jensen and confided in him, yet again, his conviction that he wouldn't survive the battle.

"I've known it since the day the German demanded the duty coffers. I'm going to die today."

"You know nothing," Ejnar replied. "You had no idea the battle would be on Maundy Thursday."

"I've known a long time: the hour is upon us!"

"Shut your trap," growled Ejnar. He'd suffered Kresten's bleating ever since they'd packed their sea bags and laced their boots.

But Kresten was unstoppable. Breathing in rapid gasps, he placed a hand on his friend's arm.

"Promise me you'll bring my sea bag back to Marstal."

"You can bring it yourself. Now stop it, before you scare the living daylights out of me too."

Ejnar threw an anxious glance at Kresten. We'd never seen our friend in such a state before. Kresten was the son of the skipper Jochum Hansen, an official with the harbor authority. Kresten took after him, right down to the freckles, the strawberry blond hair, and the silent manner.

"Here," Ejnar said, handing him a pitcher of beer. "Get that down your neck."

He held it to Kresten's lips, but the beer went down the wrong way; he spluttered and his eyes grew glassy. Ejnar slapped him on the back, and Kresten gasped and wheezed, the beer pouring from his nostrils.

"You dumb oaf," Ejnar laughed. "You won't drown if you're meant to hang. You nearly finished yourself off there. You're doing the German out of a job."

But Kresten's eyes remained distant.

"The hour is upon us," he repeated in a hollow voice.

"Well, I for one am not going to be shot." Little Clausen had joined in the conversation. "I know, because I dreamt it. I was walking down Møllevejen, going into town. There was a soldier on either side of me, ready to shoot. Then a voice called out, 'You shall go!' And so I did. The bullets whizzed past my ears, but none of them hit me. So I'm not going to get shot today. I'm certain of it!"

We looked across the fjord: the surrounding fields were clad in spring green, and a thatched farmhouse lay snuggled in a small grove of lime trees in bud, with a road flanked by stone walls leading up to it. A cow grazing by the roadside turned her back to us and flicked her tail lazily, oblivious to the war approaching by water.

The cannon batteries to starboard were closing in; we saw the smoke, then heard their thunder roll across the water like a storm gathering from nowhere.

Kresten leapt up.

"The hour is upon us," he said.

A tongue of fire flashed from the *Christian the Eighth*'s starboard stern. We exchanged puzzled glances. Had she been struck?

Being unfamiliar with warfare, we did not know what a direct hit might entail. There was no reaction from the ship-of-the-line.

"Why don't they shoot back?" Ejnar asked.

"Because they're still not crosswise to the battery," Clausen answered knowledgeably.

A moment later a cloud of pewter smoke on the starboard side of the *Christian* announced that they were indeed responding. The battle had begun. Fire and earth exploded on the shore and tiny matchstick men rushed around. A good easterly wind was blowing and soon it was *Gefion*'s turn to deliver a broadside. The roar from the huge sixty-pound cannons made the whole ship shudder. Our stomachs lurched. We pressed our hands to our ears and screamed from a mixture of fear and elation, astounded by the force of the impact.

Now the German was getting a real hammering!

After some minutes, the firing from the battery on the point ceased. By now we had to rely solely on our eyes because we couldn't hear a thing. The shore looked like a desert landscape, with sand shoved up in piles. The black barrel of a twenty-four-pounder stuck up in the air, flipped over as if by an earthquake. No one was moving.

We slapped one another's backs in mute victory. Even Kresten appeared to forget his grim premonitions of doom and surrendered to the general ecstasy: war was a thrill, a rush of schnapps that fired up your blood—only the joy was wider and purer. The smoke drifted away and the air cleared. Never before had we seen the world with such clarity. We stared like newborn babies. Rigging, masts, and sails formed a canopy above us like the foliage of a fresh-sprung beech forest. Everything bore an otherworldly sheen.

"Christ, I feel all solemn," Little Clausen said, once our faculties had returned. "Damn, damn, damn." He couldn't stop swearing. "Damn me if I've ever seen the like."

We'd heard the thunder of cannons being tested the previous evening, but actually witnessing their effect—that did something to a man.

"Yes," Ejnar reflected. "Those cannons make Pastor Zachariassen's hellfire seem tame. So what do you say, Kresten?"

Kresten's expression had turned almost pious. "Fancy me living to see this," he said quietly.

"So you've stopped thinking you're going to die?"

"Oh, I'm more certain of it than ever. But I've stopped being scared."

We couldn't claim this incident as our personal baptism of fire, because the sixty-pound cannons that we manned were mounted on the top deck on the port side, and the fighting was to starboard. Our turn would come soon, when we sailed deeper along the fjord toward Eckernförde, where two more batteries awaited on either bank. But this was no great threat, as we saw it. It wasn't yet eight in the morning and the battle was already half won; we even began to fear the war would end before it had begun. We'd just had a taste of it, and now it looked as if the German might be beaten before lunch.

The *Gefion* continued toward the head of the fjord; the northern battery lay straight ahead. We were only two cable lengths from the southern battery when we shivered the topsails so they spilled the wind. We struck the jib and let go a drag anchor on the port side so that we lay facing the enemy with our broadside, and the *Christian the Eighth* did likewise. It was time to fire.

Our blood sang. We were like children waiting to see Chinese fireworks. Fear had melted away completely and only anticipation remained. We hadn't yet recovered from our first victory, and a second one awaited us.

Then the *Gefion* started to move. The drag anchor was failing to hold her and the strong current propelled us toward the southern battery. We looked across to the *Christian the Eighth*. The huge ship-of-the-line was adrift too and already coming under intense fire from the shore. Its sailors lowered the heavy anchor to stop her from drifting and let off a violent salvo, which burst from her side, from stem to stern. Cannon smoke erupted from the ports, floating across the fjord to form a rapidly growing cloud. But there hadn't been time to adjust the cannons before the ship's unexpected drift toward the shore, and they'd fired too high, hitting the fields behind the batteries.

A moment later it was our turn. We were now close enough to the coast to be within firing range of the German rifles. The current and the wind continued to torment us, and we were crossing the fjord with both broadsides facing the empty water. Only our four stern cannons had a chance to respond to the vicious fire from the battery on shore.

The first hit cleared our aft deck of eleven men. We'd been calling the cannonballs "gray peas," but the thing that shot low across the deck, tearing rail, cannon ports, and people apart in a shower of wooden splinters, was no pea. Ejnar saw its approach and registered every meter of its journey as it swept across the deck, shearing the legs off one man and sending them flying in one direction while the rest of him went in another. It sliced off a shoulder here and smashed a skull there. It was hurtling toward him, with bone splinters, blood, and hair stuck to it. He let himself fall backward and saw it shoot past. He later said that it took off his bootlaces in passing; that's how close it came before it tore out through the quarterdeck aft.

To Ejnar that cannonball was a monster with a will of its own. It showed him what war was: not a battery that exploded and sent matchstick soldiers fleeing, but a dragon that breathed hot fire on his naked heart.

The deck was in chaos; a wild-eyed officer screamed at him to go to the mast with the helmsman and a soldier. The order made no sense, but he did as he was told. The soldier collapsed straightaway in a pool of blood. It looked as if he'd imploded: a hole had opened in his chest and blood gushed out. Ejnar saw a man's eye explode into a red mess and another man's skull torn off. That was a strange sight: pink brain matter exposed and splattered as if it were porridge, and someone had slammed a wooden spoon into it. Ejnar had not known that such things could happen to human beings. Then a second cannonball struck and killed the lieutenant. As he witnessed Armageddon, Ejnar went hot and cold and his nose started bleeding from the shock.

Another officer with blood pouring down his face ordered him to cannon number seven. Ejnar had originally been assigned to number ten, but that one had taken a direct hit and now stood lopsided by the cannon port. Around it lay a roil of motionless bodies in a slowly spreading pool of blood. Small streams of urine formed deltas between their legs. He could not see if Kresten or Little Clausen was among them. A severed foot lay a short distance away. Like the dead men, Ejnar had wet himself. The roar of cannons had caused an earthquake in his intestines, and he'd filled his trousers too. He knew that people emptied their bowels at the moment of death, but he hadn't imagined that it could happen to the living as well. The notion that war made a man of you vanished as he felt the stickiness slide down his thighs. He felt half corpse, half baby, but soon discovered that he was not the only one. The stench of upturned privy buckets wafted across the deck. It wasn't just coming from the slaughtered. Most of those still fighting had soiled pants.

The gun captain at cannon number seven was still alive, bleeding from a cut above his eyebrow where he'd been hit by a flying splinter. He screamed at Ejnar, who could hear nothing, but when he pointed at the cannon, Ejnar understood that he wanted him to load it. His arms were too short to reach, so he had to climb halfway out of the cannon port in order to stuff the cannonball into the muzzle, exposing himself to the enemy battery. As he worked, only one thought occupied him: when was the next round of schnapps?

Meanwhile, the *Gefion* had managed to reposition herself so her broadsides were aligned with both shores. But the steamer *Geiser*, which had tried to come to our aid with a hawser, had taken a hit to her engine and was being pulled out of the battle, and so was the *Hekla*, whose rudder was shot to pieces. The wind was due east and the loss of the two steamers, which were supposed to tow us, meant that we were unable to retreat if things went wrong.

However, our luck was about to change. The northern battery took one direct hit after another, and we saw the matchstick soldiers on the beach run for cover. Their cannons were undamaged and new soldiers kept running to man them, so there was hardly any respite from their fire, but still, it was halfway to victory. The quartermaster came around with a pail of schnapps, and we accepted the outstretched mug solemnly, as if it were communion wine. Fortunately the beer barrel had survived intact and we paid it frequent visits. We felt utterly lost. The constant bombardment and the randomness with which death scythed us down had exhausted us, although the battle was only a few hours old. We kept skidding in sticky pools of blood and there was no avoiding the spectacle of all the horrifically maimed bodies. Only one sense was spared: our deafness prevented us from hearing the screams of the wounded.

We were afraid to look around, for fear of staring straight into the face of a friend, snared by eyes that might plead for relief one moment and burn with hatred the next, as though the fallen blamed us for our luck and wanted nothing more in this world than to exchange fates with us. No one could offer a single word of comfort; it would pass unheard in the din from the cannons. A hand on the shoulder would have to do. But already those of us who were still uninjured were keeping to ourselves and avoiding the stricken, even though they were the ones in need of consolation. The living closed ranks against those marked for death.

We reloaded the cannons and aimed as the gun captains ordered us, but we'd stopped thinking in terms of victory or defeat. Our battle was to escape the sight of the wounded, and questions rang in our heads like an echo of the destruction around us: Why him, or him? Why not me? But we didn't want to heed them: we wanted to survive. Nothing existed beyond what we could see through the barrel of a gun.

The schnapps had worked its blessed magic. Drunk now, we surrendered to a blankness born of terror. We sailed on a black sea and we had only one goal: not to look down and drown in it.

Ejnar climbed in and out of the cannon port. It was a beautiful spring day and every time he appeared in the mild sunshine, he expected a bullet to his chest. He was muttering to himself, though he'd no idea what he was saying. He was a sight to behold, smeared in soot and blood, with a bleeding nose, which from time to time he would wipe with his sleeve before tilting his head back to try and stanch the flow. There was an acrid taste in his mouth that only repeated swigs of schnapps could relieve. Eventually his tension loosened into lethargy and his movements became mechanical. But he was in no worse a state than the rest of us, with his bloodstained appearance or his soiled trousers: none of us looked alive anymore. We resembled ghosts from a battle fought long ago: corpses on a muddy battlefield where we'd lain for weeks, forgotten in the pouring rain.

Three times we saw the men on the northern battery relieved, and not one of the shots fired by the matchstick soldiers appeared to miss its target. It seemed that the batteries on both sides of the fjord had concentrated their fire on us.

At one o'clock a signal flag was hoisted on the mangled rigging of the *Gefion*. Its message was intended for the crew of the *Christian the Eighth*: we can do no more. Most of our cannons were now abandoned and the ones firing were undermanned. Those of us still standing were working amid piles of corpses and the dying, who reached out for us in their delirium, pleading for company in the mire of guts, blood, and voided bowels.

The signal we sent was in code. The enemy on the shores of Eckernförde Fjord couldn't understand it, but the *Christian the Eighth* knew exactly what it meant.

On the ship-of-the-line there was no significant loss of life as yet. Early that morning a quartermaster from Nyborg had been killed and since then two men had been wounded, but the vessel had been spared any major hits. At the same time, Commander Paludan was forced to acknowledge that our squadron's bombardment of the batteries on the northern and southern shores had inflicted no significant damage. The battle had now been raging for more than six hours and there was no prospect of victory. Retreat was impossible; anyone could see that.

The two steamers, the *Hekla* and the *Geiser*, were out of action, and the wind was set against us. So when Commander Paludan decided to raise the flag of truce, it was not a surrender, not yet: merely a pause in the battle.

A lieutenant was rowed ashore with a letter and returned soon after, with the message that a reply would be forthcoming in an hour. *Christian the Eighth*'s top and lower sails were fastened and the crew given bread and beer. There was still order on deck, and though everyone had been deafened by the cannons, there was no mood of resignation. At most the crew felt a vague unease about the course of the battle. They could see that the *Gefion* was in a bad way, but there was no way they could imagine the bloody chaos on our deck.

Laurids Madsen sat by himself with his bread, busy satisfying his hunger and as yet unaware of his fate.

By now thousands of people had spilled out of the town of Eckernförde and were crowding both shores. Watching them as he munched his bread, Laurids soon realized that it was not curiosity that had brought them out. They were lighting huge fires in the fields and collecting the cannonballs that lay scattered on the beach, then shoving them in the fires and heating them until the iron glowed red before transporting them to their own cannons. Horse-drawn land artillery appeared on the high road from Kiel and spread out behind the stone walls that bordered the surrounding fields.

Laurids recalled his father's account of the war against the English, when Marstal came under attack. Two English frigates had anchored south of the town; they had come to hijack the town's ships, of which there were roughly fifty in the harbor. The English sent out three launches crammed with armed soldiers, but the inhabitants of Marstal, together with some grenadiers from Jutland, managed to drive them off. They could scarcely believe their own eyes when the English started retreating.

"Well, I never did understand what that war was really about," his father said afterward. "The English are good sailors, and I've no quarrel with them. But our livelihoods were at stake. If they took our ships, that would be the end of us. That's why we won. We had no choice."

On the deck of the *Christian the Eighth* Laurids sat beneath the flag of truce, watching the teeming crowds on the shores. He wasn't sure he understood war any better than his father had. They were defending the Danish flag against the Germans, and that had sufficed for him up until a moment ago. War was like sailing. You could learn about clouds, wind direction, and currents, but the sea remained forever unpredictable. All you could do was adapt to it and try to return home alive. Here the enemy was the cannon fire in Eckernförde Fjord. Once it had been silenced, the way home would lie clear. That was the war, as far as he was concerned. He was no patriot, nor was he the opposite. He took life as it came. His horizon was one of mast tops, mill wings, and the ridged turret on the church: the skyline of Marstal, as we saw it when we approached from the sea. Here were ordinary people throwing themselves into war: not just soldiers, but people from Eckernförde, a port where he'd often docked with cargoes of grain, the very place he'd sailed from on the evening he'd turned all of Ærø upside-down. Now the Eckernfördeners stood shoulder to shoulder on the beach, just as the Marstallers had once done. So what the hell was this war all about?

A boat was launched from the beach. In it sat the lieutenant from the *Christian the Eighth*, returning from a third round of negotiations. On each occasion the battle had been deferred. The ceasefire had lasted two and a half hours and it was now half past four. From the furious way the sailors were tugging at the oars, it was clear that something decisive had happened. Then out of nowhere the cannons on the beach burst into a roar. The flag of truce was still fluttering from the mast, but the war had resumed.

The *Christian the Eighth* returned fire immediately, while the *Gefion*, silent as a ghost ship, tried to get out of the way. We had given up and were using our last strength to inch ourselves forward with the kedge.

Now the enemy changed tactics, aiming the batteries on both sides of the fjord at the *Christian the Eighth* rather than us, in an attempt to set her alight. Many of the cannonballs that struck her were red-hot from lying on the field fires half the afternoon. The Eckernfördeners had made good use of their time.

Within seconds, the deck was covered with fallen and wounded men. The attack had come out of the blue. Fires flared in several places, and we immediately deployed pumps and hoses to swill death off the deck, but the crackling flames had already taken hold.

Commander Paludan now saw that the battle was lost. The *Christian the Eighth* swayed to escape the line of fire, but the wind was still set against her and all she succeeded in doing was traversing the current, losing the advantage of facing the shores broadside-on. Second-guessing the commander's plan, the Germans immediately aimed at her sails and rigging. They weren't going to let us cut and run.

The heavy anchor was raised, but to huge losses. Firebombs landed on the bows; grenades exploded between the legs of the poor souls manning the capstan. They called for reinforcements and the new arrivals kicked aside the dead and the wounded with their boots. Then fresh grenades blew off the bars of the capstan, leaving ragged wood stumps, shattered bones, and mangled fingers. Finally the anchor was pulled up, dripping with mud and seaweed. This feat alone cost the happiness of ten families. Their sons and fathers would never return home.

The jib was raised, the topsail sheets secured, and the sails hoisted. As a top-man, Laurids went up with the others and clambered onto the yardarm, from which he had an excellent view of the battle.

The sun was setting on the horizon, casting its soft light across the fjord and the landscape. Wisps of cloud fanned out across the blushing sky; only a few hundred meters from the fjord everything was peaceful and springlike. But the shores were black with armed people and the artillery was firing away from behind the shelter of the stone walls. From the beach, red-hot cannonballs flew in an endless cannonade, while civilians in the thousands raised their guns and took aim.

Once, Laurids had hung off the far end of a yardarm through a whiteout south of Cape Horn, his hands freezing to lumps of ice. He'd had to crawl back to the rigging, clinging to the yard with his arms and legs—but he hadn't been afraid. Now his hands were shaking so badly that he couldn't undo the simplest knot.

Sails, masts, and rigging had been torn apart during the firing. Around him other top-men fell one by one, hit by grenades or fire-balls or spear-sized shards from the stricken masts, tumbling down between half-raised sails, ropes, and halyards, plunging to the deck far below or plummeting into the water. Then he gave up and made his way back to the rigging.

On deck chaos reigned. The sails couldn't be hoisted because the halyards and braces were shot to pieces. Some of the crew were pulling like mad at the cross-sail and had almost managed to raise it when suddenly the blocks and tackle—heavy enough to crush any man in their path—came hurtling down.

Every attempt to rescue the *Christian the Eighth* had failed. Sailing her had become impossible and in any case the wind blew directly toward land. A severe gale was brewing and the mighty ship drifted helpless to the shore, where she foundered just east of the southern battery, which continued its ferocious shelling of the now defenseless ship. Only her stern cannons could have been used in this position, but she'd tilted so violently that nothing would hold in place.

Then the cry went up: "Fire on board!"

The earliest shouts had been cries of wolf compared to this. A fire-ball had pierced the innermost battery and lodged in the starboard hold. The blaze spread quickly, threatening the powder magazines. Other areas had caught too. The men worked the pumps, but in vain. The flames had the upper hand.

At six o'clock the flag was lowered and the *Christian the Eighth* ceased firing, but the bombardment continued for another quarter of an hour before the enemy's lust for victory—over a battleship that only hours before seemed invincible—was assuaged.

Commander Paludan was rowed ashore as a sign of surrender, and it was at that point that the crew's courage finally plummeted. They gave up fighting the fire and shuffled around, filthy and foul-smelling. Their seamanship was of no use to them now, and they had no experience of war or of defeat: they'd imagined the battle would be a laugh, and now their souls were drained of energy and their heads empty of all but the echo of cannons. This last shameful part of the battle had lasted one and a half hours, but it felt like one and a half lifetimes. They could see nothing beyond this. They were utterly spent.

Some sat down on the deck in the midst of the sea of flames, as if clergymen's pulpit warnings about the fires of hell had become reality, while others stood motionless, staring straight ahead, their inner mechanisms broken. Lieutenants Ulrik, Stjernholm, and Corfitz rushed around, screaming into the men's faces: they must act, they were needed more than ever, if complete disaster was to be prevented and the honor of Denmark saved after a battle that they could hardly pride themselves on. But they'd been deafened by the cannons, and only pushing, shoving, and kicking would stir them.

Laurids let himself be herded to the powder magazine farthest astern, but it was slow work throwing the kegs into the water. They were only five men, and whenever a new crewman was forced into the chamber, he'd rush straight back out.

Suddenly came the cry "All men up!"

They knew instantly what that meant. Exchanging looks of alarm, they dropped the bombs and the kegs and raced up the ladder to find sheep, calves, pigs, hens, and ducks out of their enclosures, running on deck among the terrified sailors. A pig rummaged about, sticking its snout into bloody piles of guts, slurping things up.

The men raced about, each on his own urgent mission. Some hunted for their clothes and sea bags, while others climbed onto the rail as though contemplating jumping into the cold water. No one paid heed to the wounded men, who got in the way and were carelessly trampled. Their screams of agony went unheard; most of the crew were still deaf after the hours of intense shelling.

Laurids rushed downstairs to the sickbay, concerned that the wounded might be abandoned. Smoke seeped up through the heavy oak planks. Covering his mouth with his hand, he stepped into the murky room, where an orderly, covering his face with a cloth, came up to him.

"Is anyone coming?" Laurids realized his hearing had returned. "We've got to get the wounded upstairs. We're choking down here!"

"I'll go get help!" Laurids shouted back.

On deck there was no sign of the officers who had kicked the crew and whacked them with the flat side of their blades; instead he saw a crowd of men flocking to an open gangway with a Jacob's ladder, and ran over to them. The evacuation was already in full force. He spotted a couple of the lieutenants slashing through the crowd with their swords as they tried to reach the gangway. The ship's second in command, Captain Krieger, stood to one side, watching it all with an odd, distant gaze, his binoculars slung across his back, a gilt-framed portrait of his wife tucked under one arm, and the other raised in salute.

"You have shown yourselves to be brave men," he muttered over and over again, as if blessing his woeful flock. "You have done your duty. You are all my brothers."

No one took notice of him; each man was focusing on the most important obstacle in his path to salvation: the back of the sailor ahead of him, blocking his access to the open gangway. Laurids made his way to Krieger and screamed into his face:

"The wounded, Captain Krieger, the wounded!"

The captain turned to him, but his gaze remained distant. He placed a hand on Laurids's shoulder. Laurids felt it tremble, but the captain's voice was calm, almost sleepy.

"My brother, once we are ashore, we shall speak like brethren."

"The wounded need help!" Laurids screamed once more. "The whole ship is about to blow sky high."

The captain's hand stayed on Laurids's shoulder.

"Yes, the wounded," he said in the same monotonous tone of voice. "They too are my brothers. When we are ashore, we shall all speak like brethren." His voice disintegrated into mumbling, and then he began again, reeling off the same phrases. "You have shown yourselves to be brave men. You have done your duty. You are all my brethren."

Giving up on the captain and turning to the men who were struggling to reach the open gangway, Laurids grabbed them by the shoulder one by one, shouting his message about helping the wounded into their faces. The first man reacted by punching him on his chin. The second shook his head in disbelief and then threw himself with renewed energy back into the brawl.

The evacuation had picked up pace. Fishing boats set off from the beach to rescue the crew from the battleship that only a few hours earlier had been bombarding them, while the ship's own main launch shuttled continuously between ship and beach. Laurids leaned over the rail and spotted the roaring fire leaping out of the stern cannon ports. It was only a matter of time.

Smoke was pouring out of every hatch, making it just as difficult to breathe above deck as below. Once again he rushed down to the sickbay but was soon forced to abandon the idea: the smoke was now so dense and suffocating that it seemed impossible that anyone might have survived.

"Is anyone here?" he called out, but there was no reply.

The smoke seared his lungs and a fit of coughing sent tears streaming down his cheeks. He hurtled back up to the deck, squeezing his burning eyes shut in pain, temporarily smoke-blinded. He slipped and fell on the deck, slick from human excretions and spilled organs. His hand touched something soft and wet, and he shot to his feet, rubbing his palm on his soiled trousers in terror. He couldn't bear the thought that he'd touched another human being's blood and guts. It felt as though his soul had been scalded.

He staggered to the rail, where the smoke was thinner, and tried to regain his vision. Through a mist of tears he made out the launch, which had run aground on a sandbank, forcing the crew to jump into the water and wade ashore, where the enemy soldiers were waiting for them. Then the launch came unstuck and immediately set course for the *Christian the Eighth,* while several of the fishing boats close to the ship started heading back to the shore. The launch too turned around. Howls of protest erupted from the open gangway.

Laurids stepped back from the rail into the billowing clouds of smoke.

"I SAW LAURIDS," Ejnar would always say later. "I swear I saw him."

Ejnar was standing on the beach when the *Christian the Eighth* blew up. He'd been taken ashore from the *Gefion* under guard and grouped with the other survivors from the frigate, waiting to be led off. The German soldiers seemed taken aback by their own victory and looked as if they had no idea of what to do with us. Our numbers kept swelling as men from the two vanquished battleships filled the shore.

Then the warning cry rang out across the water.

Most of us, tired and disheartened, had been sitting on the beach with our eyes fixed on the sand as the soldiers pointed their bayonets at us with hands that trembled. But now we looked up. At the stern of the ship-of-the-line, a pillar of fire shot up with a deafening boom. Then more: column after column of flame broke through the deck as the powder magazines ignited. In seconds, the masts and yards were reduced to charcoal, while the sails fluttered off in huge flakes of ash and the great oak hull became a weightless toy in the brutal hands of the blaze. But the worst was yet to come. The immense heat had set off the vanquished ship's cannons, which at the moment of capitulation had been loaded. Now, simultaneously, they discharged their deadly contents toward the shore.

Screams of horror rose from the crammed beach when the cannonballs started crashing down on us. Death was arbitrary. Burning debris rained from the heavens, wreaking destruction wherever it landed, so that the hour of victory was marked only by the sound of men screaming. This, then, was the dying ship's final salute to the victors and the vanquished: a murderous broadside that attacked both friend and foe alike. War showed its true face out there in the fire shower on Eckernförde Fjord.

. . .

For a moment it looked as if everyone on the beach had been killed. Bodies were strewn everywhere and not a single man was standing. Many were lying face-down with their arms outstretched as if they were praying to the flames that leapt on the water. Here and there a piece of wreckage lay burning in the sand. Slowly, some of the prostrate figures got to their feet, anxiously eyeing the burning ship. Cries came from the water. Several of the boats that had hurried to rescue the ship's crew had been struck and set ablaze. Lieutenant Stjernholm and four men had been heading for the beach with the ship's coffer, but their launch's stern had been blown off when the *Christian the Eighth* exploded. The coffer was lost, but the lieutenant managed to save himself. Only one of the men from the launch was with him when he staggered ashore, drenched. The rest had drowned.

The beach was quiet except for the faint moaning of the wounded and the crackling of the still-burning wreckage, when suddenly a loud yell echoed across land and water.

"I've seen Laurids! I've seen Laurids!"

We raised our heads and looked around. We'd recognized Ejnar's voice, and most of us presumed the poor man had lost his mind. Then chaos erupted across the entire beach and everyone began shouting, as if the only way to feel alive was to kick up all the ruckus you could. In the confusion we could have escaped our captors, but we'd lost our nerve—and with it our ability to act. We had to content ourselves with having simply survived: we could run no more.

Our captors weren't much better off. They led us away from the beach, their faces frozen, mute witnesses to the destruction they'd so closely avoided themselves. Our march looked more like a wholesale retreat from the theater of war than an organized transportation of prisoners.

The Germans had routed us, but their faces showed no signs of triumph. Horror at the unthinkable forces that war had unleashed united both victors and vanquished.

THEY TOOK US TO Eckernförde Church. Straw had been spread across the floor so we could collapse and rest our weary bodies. We were soaked through and shivering with cold. Once the sun had set, the April night grew chilly. Those of us who'd managed to save our sea bags changed our clothes and lent our less fortunate comrades what they needed. Soon food rations arrived: whole-grain bread, beer, and smoked bacon collected from the town's grocers. No one in Eckernförde had expected to see the town filled with prisoners of war. On the contrary, they'd been expecting Danish soldiers to be patrolling their streets before the day was out. Now, instead of being under guard themselves, the town's citizens were playing host.

Old women appeared in the church to sell white bread and schnapps to those with money. One of them was Mother Ilse, with the crooked hip. She stroked one prisoner's cheek with a sooty finger and muttered, "You poor lad."

She'd recognized him from his previous visits to the town. We'd all bought schnapps from her in our time. The man grabbed her hand.

"Don't you call me a poor lad. I'm alive."

It was Ejnar.

In the long pause that had followed the hoisting of the signal flag, Ejnar had wandered the deck looking for Kresten, but he could find him among neither the living nor the wounded. Many of the dead were lying face-down, and he'd had to turn them over. Others had had their faces shot off. But Kresten wasn't among the bodies around cannon number seven.

Torvald Bønnelykke, who'd been standing by one of the other cannons, came up to him.

"Are you looking for Kresten?" he asked.

He was a Marstaller and had been party to Kresten's grim premonitions.

"He's lying over there," he said, pointing. "But you won't recognize him. A cannonball took off his head. I was standing next to him when it happened."

"So he was right," Ejnar said. "Bloody awful way to die."

"Death is death," Bønnelykke said. "I don't know if one way is better than another. The result's always the same."

"I'd better go find his sea bag. I promised him I would. Have you seen Little Clausen?"

Bønnelykke shook his head. They asked around, but no one had seen him.

By now it was around ten o'clock. Exhausted, we were getting ready to sleep when the church door opened and yet another prisoner was led in, wrapped in a huge blanket. He sneezed incessantly, and his whole body shook.

"Damn it, I'm cold," he said hoarsely, then gave another explosive sneeze.

"My God, if that isn't Little Clausen!"

Ejnar struggled to his feet and went over to his friend.

"So you're still alive."

"I damn well am. I told you I would be. But this bastard cold will be the death of me instead: I'm sick as a dog." He sneezed again.

Ejnar put his arm around him and led him to the straw bed he'd prepared for himself. He could feel Little Clausen shivering beneath the blanket, and his white face was mottled with feverish red.

"Do you have some dry clothes?"

"No, damn it, I didn't manage to save my sea bag."

"Take these. I hope you don't mind wearing Kresten's stuff."

"So he—"

"Yes, it turned out he was right. But what happened to you? We looked everywhere. I thought you ..."

"Don't they say that you don't drown if you're meant to hang? Seems the Lord has decided I'm to die from a cold, rather than in combat. I spent the whole battle suspended in an old bosun's chair along the side of the ship. I was supposed to be mending the holes with lead plates. They kept shooting at me, the bastards. But somehow they missed."

"I didn't think you were a weakling," Ejnar said. "How come a bit of fresh air made you sick?"

"The rest of the crew damn well forgot about me. I was stuck there the whole day with my legs in the water, freezing my butt off." Little Clausen sneezed again. "It wasn't until the ship was evacuated that I managed to flag down a boat. By then I was blue all over. I couldn't even walk when I got back on shore." He'd put on the dry clothes and now slapped himself for warmth as he glanced around the church. "How many were killed?"

"You mean how many Marstallers?"

"Yes, what else would I mean? I don't know the others."

"I think we've lost seven."

"Was Laurids one of them?"

Ejnar stared at the floor. Then he shrugged, as though embarrassed about something shameful. "I can't answer that."

"You don't mean he ran away?"

"No. Not exactly. I saw him shooting up into the sky. But then I saw him come down again."

Little Clausen stared at him in disbelief, then shook his head.

"My eyes tell me that you've not been wounded," he said. "But my ears tell me that you've lost your mind."

He let off another sneeze and sat down abruptly on the bed of straw. Ejnar sat next to him and stared into space with lost eyes. Perhaps he really had gone mad. Little Clausen leaned toward his friend and put his arm around his shoulder.

"There now." He comforted him. "It'll come back, you'll see."

He lapsed into silence. Then added, softly, "But I suppose we might as well write off Laurids."

They sat for a while longer, saying nothing. Then they lay down and fell asleep, utterly spent.

At seven in the morning they woke us and treated us to more bread, bacon, and warm beer, and an hour later there was a head count. When an officer arrived to take down our names and our hometowns so that our families could be informed, we fell on him, yelling out our details so clamorously that by ten o clock, when the order came to march us to the fortress in Rendsburg, he'd noted only half our names.

Outside the church they lined us up in ranks. The mood had shifted: it seemed that Eckernförde was turning against its vanquished enemy, and our guards were losing patience with us. Many of us were still half-deaf from yesterday's cannon fire and couldn't hear orders even when they were shouted right into our faces. So they shoved us around and beat us. The town's citizens hustled around us, whooping at our humiliation, while a crowd of sailors with cutlasses swinging from their belts hurled out coarse oaths—which, to our great irritation, we had to endure in silence.

The high road ran along the shoreline, affording us a final glimpse of our inexplicable defeat: the wreck of the *Christian the Eighth,* floating on the water. She was still smoldering, with smoke wafting from her charred hull, and the beach was littered with the debris of masts and yards flung ashore by the explosion. Like ants stripping the carcass of a lion, the Germans were already busy securing the flotsam from what had recently been one of the Danish navy's proudest vessels. We passed the southern battery, which we'd spent a day bombarding and that in the end had sealed our fate. Not even the most unschooled among us needed to count fingers to calculate the enemy's firing power. Four cannons! That was all. David had fought Goliath. And Goliath had been us.

Several vehicles overtook us, carrying officers from the *Christian the Eighth* and the *Gefion.* They too were heading for prison in Rendsburg. We exchanged salutes, and they were gone in a cloud of dust. Then came the rumbling of yet another cart and the sound of laughter. Some Holstein officers drove past us. Among them towered a man. He was bareheaded.

Little Clausen and Ejnar looked at each other.

"The devil take me," Little Clausen said. "That was Laurids!"

"I told you so. He went shooting up into the sky and came back down again."

Little Clausen's face split into a grin.

"Well, I don't care how he did it! The most important thing is he's alive."

The cart stopped a short distance ahead, and the officers got out and shook hands with Laurids. One of them shoved a bottle of schnapps into his coat pocket, and another thrust a wad of bank notes at him. Then they raised their arms to salute him, and left. For a while Laurids just stood there, dithering. Little Clausen called out his name. He looked in our direction and lifted his hand hesitantly. A soldier took hold of his arm and nudged him into the ranks next to the two men from Marstal.

"Laurids!" exclaimed Little Clausen. "I thought you were dead."

"And so I was," Laurids said. "I saw Saint Peter's bare butt."

"Saint Peter's bare butt?"

"Yes, he pulled up his tunic and flashed his ass at me."

Laurids fished the schnapps bottle out of his coat pocket and took a swig of the clear liquid. He handed the bottle to Little Clausen, who drank deeply before passing it on to Ejnar, who still hadn't said a word.

"Didn't you know," Laurids said, "that when Saint Peter shows you his ass, it means your time's not up yet?"

"And so you decided to return to earth."

The explanation illuminated Ejnar's face, and he spoke with the relief of someone who has just been let off a criminal charge.

"I saw it," he said. "You were standing on the deck when the *Christian the Eighth* blew up. You were flung high into the air, ten meters at least, and then you came back down and landed on your feet. Little Clausen said I must have lost my mind. But I saw it. You did it. Isn't that right?"

"It was hot as hell," Laurids said. "But cooler higher up. I saw Saint Peter's ass and I knew I wasn't going to die."

"But how did you get back ashore?" Little Clausen asked.

"I walked," Laurids said.

"You walked? You're not telling me you walked on water?"

"No. I'm telling you I walked on the seabed."

Laurids stopped and pointed at his boots. Somebody in the column behind him bumped into his broad back, and the ranks became muddled. A soldier rushed over and shoved Laurids with the butt of his gun.

Laurids turned around.

"Gently, gently," he said with the tolerance of a drunk. He made a calming gesture, then fell back into the ranks and picked up the rhythm of the march.

The soldier kept pace alongside him.

"I didn't mean to hurt you," he said in Danish. He had a South Jutland accent.

"No harm done," Laurids replied.

"I've heard about you," the soldier continued. "You're the man who was blown up with the *Christian the Eighth* and landed right back on his feet, aren't you?"

"Yes, that's me," Laurids replied with considerable dignity, straightening up. "I landed on my feet, thanks be to God and my sea boots."

"Your sea boots?"

Now it was Ejnar's turn to be mystified.

"Yes," said Laurids in a tone of voice you'd use to explain something to a child. "It's because of my sea boots that I landed on my feet. Have you ever tried wearing my sea boots? Damn heavy. No one wearing them could stay in Heaven for long."

"It's like the Resurrection." The soldier gawked.

"Hogwash," Laurids snorted brusquely. "Jesus never wore sea boots."

"And Saint Peter didn't flash his bare ass at him either," Little Clausen added.

"Too right," Laurids said, offering the bottle around.

The soldier too was offered a drop. Glancing quickly over his shoulder, he took a big swig.

But our merriment soon abated. It was thirty kilometers to Rendsburg and we had to walk all day to get there. When the farmers came out to stare at us, we didn't look back at them; our bravado had faded. As we staggered on, most of us just kept our eyes on the highway dust. A leaden weariness had us all in its grip, but whether it stemmed from our sore feet or from our sunken spirits we couldn't tell. Past caring, we jostled one another like drunken men, though only Laurids was enjoying the privilege of actual intoxication. He, for his part, was unmoved by our predicament. He marched along, humming tunes to himself—despite his visit to the Lord, none of the songs he chose were godly. Finally even he too fell silent and trudged on with his eyes turned inward, as if beginning to sleep off his inebriation while on foot.

From time to time we would stop at a pond for a drink of water. The soldiers would keep an eye on us, bayonets at the ready, while we filled our caps with water and passed them around. Then the marching resumed. Halfway to Rendsburg, our guards were relieved, and Ejnar and Little Clausen bade goodbye to the friendly soldier. Laurids was still in a world of his own. The soldier took one last look at him and swapped a few words with his replacement, a Prussian. The Prussian threw Laurids a doubtful look and shook his head. But throughout the rest of the march, he kept eyeing him.

We reached Rendsburg at dusk. Rumors of the battle had preceded us, and the highway and ramparts were teeming with people who had come out to gawk at the prisoners. We passed through the town gate and crossed a bridge before going through the inner portal, then found ourselves in the narrow streets of the town center. Here thousands more had gathered to stare, and our guards had to show their guns to make way for us and keep curious onlookers at bay. There were plenty of pretty girls among them, and it was an ugly thing to know that their eyes rested on us with contempt.

They held us in a spacious old church whose floor had been strewn with so much straw that it looked more like a barn than a house of God. We had eaten nothing all day, but now they distributed sacks of biscuits and warm beer. The biscuits must have been several years old, they turned to dust in our mouths, but the beer was welcome, and soon we lay scattered across the broad church floor, fast asleep.

The next day, Holy Saturday, we milled about, assessing the accommodations and sleeping options, rediscovering some friends, and noting the loss of others. There were men from both the *Gefion* and the *Christian the Eighth*. Some rooms in the church had chairs, and curtains in the windows; these quarters were quickly occupied, and possessing one was considered a privilege. We men from Marstal gathered in a room by the chancel. The others stuck with those from their hometowns too: men from Ærøskøbing here, men from the island of Funen there, men from Lolland, men from Langeland. There in the straw-carpeted church, we redrew the map.

We knew nothing of discipline. We hadn't been in the navy long enough to value any formal systems of order beyond those we'd come up with ourselves. When our battleship had been set alight beneath our feet, we'd been separated from our officers. Now we obeyed only one command: that of the stomach. When the church door opened in the morning for the guards bringing bread, there was a stampede, each man thinking only of his own hunger. In the end the soldiers flung the bread over our heads and we fought over it like wild animals. Someone tore Ejnar's loaf from his hands, and Little Clausen got kicked in the shin. It was a shameful episode, but whatever discipline the navy had instilled in us had vanished. In the new hierarchy we were forced to create, fighting was a useful skill. Only Laurids remained above it all, as though untouched by hunger or thirst.

The next meal was distributed as though it were a military exercise, with a major and a sergeant bellowing commands at us. They had brought the bosuns from the *Gefion* and *Christian*, who divided us into the same groups of eight as on the warships, so we could be fed in an orderly way. We were each given a spoon and a metal bowl and made to line up by the altar. And it was, in its way, a form of communion, because it took every last scrap of imagination to transubstantiate what was in our metal bowls into something edible, and we consumed the sorry-looking mess of gruel and prunes only out of sheer necessity. Afterward we lay down on the straw to sleep. The exhaustion that had overwhelmed us the day after the defeat still held sway.

Late in the afternoon the church door opened again, and a group of officers entered, along with some well-dressed men, doubtless prominent citizens of Rendsburg, and the Prussian soldier who had eyed our fellow townsman so suspiciously on the second leg of the march. While the guests waited by the door, the Prussian began walking around in the church as if looking for someone. Finally spotting Laurids, he ordered him up from the straw and led him over to the party of officers and gentlemen. When they began talking, it became obvious they were questioning Laurids. Then, after a while, they did the same thing that the departing Holstein officers had done on the way to Rendsburg: they handed Laurids bank notes before politely taking their leave. A few of the well-dressed folk even tipped their hats.

Laurids, the heavenly traveler, had become a celebrity.

The story was now circulating around the whole church. It turned out that Ejnar wasn't the only one who'd seen Laurids shoot up into the sky when the *Christian the Eighth* exploded, only to miraculously reappear on the burning deck once the column of fire had subsided. They'd all believed it to be a kind of mirage, an apparition brought on by the nervous strain of mortal danger during battle, and had mentioned it to no one—but now they came forward to bear witness to the rest of us, and soon a large crowd had gathered in front of Laurids.

We wanted to know why his clothes and hair weren't scorched.

"My boots are," he said, sticking out a leg for inspection.

"And your feet?" We wanted to know.

"They stink," said Laurids.

Ejnar couldn't take his eyes off Laurids. He looked at him the way you'd look at a total stranger—which was precisely what Laurids had become to him. He started treating him with a bashful subservience and couldn't seem to act normally around him. Little Clausen, meanwhile, accepted what had happened. Or rather, now that Laurids was standing in front of him as large as life, he accepted that others believed in his ascension. Personally he had been a skeptic right from the start, so when he became an official believer, it was mostly for the sake of comradeship, like joining in the laughter of a shared joke. In his eyes, Laurids was a born prankster. First he'd made the whole island believe that the German was coming. And now he'd made the German believe that he'd been to Heaven and back. Little Clausen felt a jaw-dropping respect for this achievement. That Laurids was one hell of a guy!

While Laurids held forth on the subject, the church filled with women who'd been given permission to come daily with their baskets to hawk coffee, cakes, sour bread, eggs, butter, cheese, herring, and paper. The men from the *Gefion* had money to spend: before throwing the ship's coffer overboard to prevent the enemy getting hold of it, the officers had opened it and given each crew member a couple of coins, and most of us had managed to save our sea bags.

We Marstallers considered ourselves privileged: we'd all been on board the *Gefion*, except for Laurids, who'd recovered nothing from the *Christian the Eighth* except the clothes on his back and, of course, his reputation as an astral traveler. However, the latter was enough to secure him a considerable income. His pockets were stuffed full of five-mark coins given to him by curious Germans. When he saw that we had everything we needed, Laurids bought extra provisions and distributed them among the crew from the *Christian the Eighth*, who, like him, had been forced to abandon ship without their possessions. They received his gifts with gratitude and this enhanced his reputation even further.

When we woke up, it was Easter Sunday—and we were to spend it locked up in a church without a clergyman in sight. We lay on our backs on the straw, gazing up at the soaring, pinnacled arches high above us. All around were dark paintings with heavy gilded frames, and carved wooden figures, and from the ceilings, which were as high as masts, hung chandeliers: all a far cry from Marstal's church, with its blue-painted pews and plain, whitewashed walls. But we weren't in any mood for worship, lying there in the straw. Straw was for farmyard animals, and we felt like pigs in a sty: the church's grandiose arches prompted not so much a feeling of religious contemplation as a sense of humiliation and mockery. For we were beaten men, robbed not only of our freedom but also—far worse—our pride. We hadn't fought with honor. Later we would probably be informed otherwise—and perhaps one day some of us might end up believing it. But right now, the events of Eckernförde Fjord were fresh in our minds, and they told the story straight. We'd been confused and panicky—and yes, even drunk too—and those of us who were skilled sailors weren't trained as soldiers, and those with military expertise knew nothing of seafaring.

Captain Krieger had been blown up, together with his wife's portrait (and the Lord have mercy on his soul, the poor bewildered wretch) while Commander Paludan had been the first to board the lifeboat and be rowed ashore to safety. Was this conduct becoming of a commander? An act an honest seaman could respect?

Sitting there on the straw like the pathetic creatures we were, we gazed up at the arches. And from high above, they jeered back.

Pails of schnapps could be found in several corners of the church, and we were offered all we could drink, for free. The hawkers didn't sell strong liquor, but from the very first day of our captivity, the German army doctor had decreed schnapps to be good for the health, and we headed for the buckets like pigs to the trough. Yes, we were indeed like pigs, sleeping and rolling around on the straw: pigs that had temporarily avoided the butcher's knife. We might be alive, but we were no longer human.

And we stank too. We'd soiled our clothes during the battle, and we reeked of fear and uncontrolled bowels. For isn't it a secret common to all men that if you go to war, you'll fill your pants like a frightened child? As seamen, we'd all feared drowning, but none of us had ever crapped his pants when a gale ripped off the mast and rigging, or a wave crushed the rail and cleared the deck.

What was the difference? The difference was that the sea respected our manhood. The cannons didn't.

"Hey, heavenly traveler," we called out to Laurids, and pointed to the pulpit. "It's Easter Sunday. Give us a sermon! Tell us about Saint Peter and his bare ass!"

Stumbling slightly, Laurids climbed the stairs to the pulpit. His elation had subsided and he was drunk again, like the rest of us. The pulpit was no mast top, but once up there he grew dizzy all the same. It was the schnapps. He'd been shipwrecked twice in his life. The second time he'd stood a whole night on a flat rock in the sea off Mandal, where his ship had gone down. There he'd felt both grief and terror, and he'd been within an inch of death. The water had slapped at his feet until dawn, when a pilot boat came and threw him a line. He'd felt no shame on that occasion, for it was no shame to be defeated by the sea. He wasn't a bad sailor. He knew that. The current, the wind, and the dark had simply got the better of him. But in the battle on the fjord, where his seamanship had counted for nothing, a lesser enemy had defeated him, and that defeat and his commander's unmanly conduct had left him without honor.

When he stood on the pulpit, he found he had nothing to say. His gullet stung. Then he leaned forward and threw up.

We greeted this with cheering and applause.

Here was a sermon we could all appreciate.

Laurids remained silent the rest of the day. Once again, officers and local bigwigs turned up to visit him and hear the story of his ascension, but he turned his back to them in the straw, like a hibernating bear. They offered him money, but nothing could tempt him out of his retreat and in the end they had no choice but to leave. His fame dwindled in the days that followed. It would have been lucrative to put himself on display, press the flesh, and expound his views of the Hereafter. But he was in the grip of a foul mood.

He lay on the straw or paced up and down with his arms folded across his chest, frowning.

"He's thinking," Ejnar said, filled with awe.

Ejnar was Laurids's only remaining disciple. But he could have spawned a whole sect if he'd wanted to.

· · ·

As for the rest of us, our mood had improved; we gathered in small groups, and soon music and singing echoed from various corners of the church. At first we'd grouped according to our home districts, islands, or towns and looked at one another almost as enemies. But music united us. Here was a man from one of the islands next to a man from Jutland, here a man from Lolland next to a man from Seeland. As long as our voices were in harmony, it didn't matter that our accents were at war. That said, all the melodies came courtesy of the schnapps pail.

A few days later Little Clausen received a letter from home. It was from his mother, who gave him her version of the fateful Maundy Thursday when the battle took place. Ejnar and Laurids settled down beside him on the straw, and Torvald Bønnelykke joined them. We were all eager to hear news from home. Little Clausen read aloud in a stumbling voice, with long pauses.

His mother wrote that they'd heard the cannon fire in Marstal from early morning, and it was loud enough for you to think the battle was being fought at the end of the breakwater, rather than on the other side of the Baltic. The thundering had been especially fierce during Pastor Zachariassen's sermon in the church; the ground had literally trembled beneath their feet, and the minister had been moved to tears.

Around noon it grew quiet, but no one could relax. Instead of going home for lunch, the citizens of Marstal wandered the streets, discussing the course of the battle. A few men with combat experience, such as Petersen the carpenter and old Jeppe, and even Madam Weber—all veterans of the great mobilization, the night we thought the Germans were coming—had insisted that there was no way we Danes could lose. A ship-of-the-line could never be defeated by a coastal battery. The Germans must have got a good thrashing: what they'd been hearing all day was unquestionably the sweet music of victory.

Toward evening came a boom so gigantic that it collapsed the cliffs at Voderup. No one in Marstal got a wink of sleep all night, tormented by a creeping unease about the battle's outcome. News finally reached them well into the afternoon of Good Friday, a day that must have been as tough for them as it was for our savior. For now their worst fears were confirmed.

"I was completely beside myself with despair, though I should have put

my trust in the Lord. I prayed to Him all night to keep you safe and He heard my prayers, though there were others He did not heed. Kresten's mother walks around with a tearful face and blames herself for not forcing him to stay behind. I tell her that Kresten foretold his own death and that no one cheats fate, but she says that Kresten had lost his wits, and it is a mother's duty to shield her son from his own lack of sense, and then she starts to cry again."

Little Clausen read all of this in a monotone. The strain of deciphering the letters required every ounce of his concentration; he had none left to understand the meaning of the words he was repeating.

"What does it say?" he suddenly asked.

We gave him a blank look.

"You're the one doing the reading," Ejnar said.

Little Clausen looked helplessly at them, unable to explain his predicament.

"Well, it says that we lost," Laurids snapped. "But we don't need her to tell us that. And then it says that Kresten's mother has lost her wits from grief. And that your mother has been praying for you."

"My mother has been praying for me?"

Little Clausen looked down and with some difficulty found the line where his mother described her sleepless night. Then he read it again, his lips moving silently as he did so.

"Read on," Ejnar implored him. "What else does she say?"

Marstal had been issued a royal decree to send all its large vessels to the navy immediately, in order to transport troops across the Great Belt. But although every sailor in town had gathered in the schoolroom to listen to the order, not one volunteered to comply. Eighteen vessels were then commandeered—but when the day of their departure dawned, the ships were gone. From the pulpit, Pastor Zachariassen lambasted the people of Marstal for their lack of self-sacrificial spirit, after which the townsfolk began to talk of replacing him. Everything was in confusion. There was a war on, and times were harsh, but if only the good Lord would protect Little Clausen and the rest of Marstal, all this misery would surely have to end someday, and things could return to normal. Little Clausen's mother ended her letter by conveying her most fervent prayers and loving thoughts to her captive son, and expressing the hope that he was getting enough to eat and keeping his clothes neat and clean.

"Lack of self-sacrificial spirit!" Laurids fumed when Little Clausen had concluded his reading. "That pastor's got a nerve! Seven men are dead and the rest of us are prisoners. We're prepared to give up our lives. But is that enough for him, the devil? No: he wants our ships too. But he won't get them. Never!"

The others nodded their agreement.

The mornings began with warm beer, with bland gruel and prunes one day, split peas and meat the next. Our stomachs soon adapted to the pattern; they had no choice, and besides, we'd had worse at sea, working for stingy skippers, so we complained mainly for the sake of complaining. They'd confiscated our knives, so we had to tear our bread or gnaw at it like horses. For one hour, morning and afternoon, we were allowed to stroll around the churchyard and smoke, while the sentries watched over us with loaded guns. There, we'd let our eyes wander from headstone to bayonet and back again, and if we fancied it, philosophize about the meaning of life. That was as much variety as our captivity afforded.

A FORTNIGHT LATER they woke us at five in the morning and ordered us into the churchyard, where they lined us up in ranks. We were six hundred men in all, and we were joined by the junior officers, whom the Germans had been holding in a riding school. Our guards felt we were in need of discipline, and who better to knock it into our heads than our own cadets?

We marched out of Rendsburg with our sea bags on our shoulders and our food bowls tucked under our arms. Our arrival in the small town of Glückstadt was met by thousands of onlookers. No longer covered in powder residue and at last wearing clean clothes, we almost resembled human beings, so it wasn't our appearance so much as our quantity that made an impact on the townsfolk.

We marched down to the harbor, where we were to be billeted in a grain warehouse. Inside there was a lower and an upper loft, with a separate room in each where the cadets were housed. In these vast open spaces the men slept on the floor, 150 to a row; it seemed that one wall was to serve as our headboard while some planks hammered together would be our footboard. Our bedding, once again, was straw. But there were also tables and benches, and a yard at our disposal, so overall it was a change for the better. There was a second grain warehouse across the yard, connected to ours by wooden fences, so we were locked up on all sides.

A small pond that lay between the warehouses made our yard seem a complete landscape in itself. The eye rests easier on a fence than on a bayonet, and the pond fired our imagination much more than the headstones in Rendsburg, so outside too we found something new to enjoy: we built model ships, fixing scraps of fabric to masts made of sticks and staging naval battles on the smooth surface of the pond. Half the ships sailed under the Danish flag, while the other half—which appeared to be stateless—represented German rebels, whom we could not bring ourselves to honor even with their own colors. During our battles we bombarded the flagless German fleet with pebbles, and we Danes won every time, suffering losses only when one of our fleet took an accidental hit from a stray pebble.

We clustered in our hundreds around the ponds, cheering every time a pebble struck its target and a toy ship tipped over. This was our hour of restitution.

But Laurids turned his back on us, fuming with contempt.

"Yes, that's all we're good for. If only we could win when it really matters."

Laurids spent most of his time in the straw, staring out a window that faced the river Elbe, watching the ships sail to and from Hamburg. His eyes followed them as far as they could, and his heart went even farther. He longed for the sea.

After his trip to Heaven, he'd become a different man.

During the day we'd relax in the sunshine. Benches had been put out in the yard, and some of us played cards. We dictated our letters home to a literate seaman from Ærøskøbing, Hans Christian Svinding. He was never without a notebook in his hand and his eyes were always on the alert; he wrote everything down. But most of the men just stared vacantly into space, halfway to a schnapps-induced haze. In the evening there would be singing and dancing, and the heavy floor planks would creak under our weight. The cadets made the most noise. They didn't mix with the crew but stayed behind the closed doors of their rooms, their drunken shouting drowning out even our music. They were mere boys and couldn't hold their drink. Not one of them was older than sixteen; most were thirteen or fourteen. The youngest was twelve. Many of us had sons their age or older, yet as junior officers the cadets were our superiors, though they knew nothing and could do nothing either. We had to stand to attention to a bunch of cabin boys.

Speculation about Commander Paludan's desertion at the moment of greatest peril remained rife. Why had our commander got into the boat before everybody else? A soldier from Schleswig started the rumor that Paludan had claimed a German officer arrived on board the *Christian the Eighth* and commanded him off the ship before the wounded could be brought ashore. Paludan protested bravely but was told that if he disobeyed, the bombardment would resume. However, no one on board the *Christian the Eighth* had known anything about this officer, whose name was supposed to be Preuszer, and the German rebel army denied any knowledge of him. The soldier from Schleswig said he thought that Commander Paludan had invented Preuszer as a cover for his own cowardice.

When Little Clausen heard this story, he opened his mouth to defend his commander: his own honor, as a Dane, was at stake. But he couldn't think of a single argument to make. In fact, the story sounded all too plausible. We'd been led by dishonorable men. Ejnar too stayed silent, but his eyes filled with tears of shame. Laurids swore.

Commander Paludan's treason didn't light the fire of rebellion in us; instead, it sent us more frequently to the schnapps pail. As our disgust at our captivity grew, our manners coarsened.

The cadets became a target for our anger. We'd already cracked plenty of jokes about their smooth chins, but only behind their backs. Now we told the little men to their faces, "Pull down your trousers so we can see if you're hairless there too."

The cadets' leader was a fourteen-year-old with the surname Wedel. He'd been the first cadet of the *Christian the Eighth* to board a rescue boat, and we'd all noted his triumphant expression as he sat next to Paludan—a close friend of his father—on the main launch. He led the drinking sessions the cadets held behind closed doors. But now he became the most frequent target of our increasingly aggressive bullying.

In response to a particularly cruel reference to the size of his genitalia, Wedel slapped an able seaman, Jørgen Mærke from Nyborg, hard across his face. The fact that Wedel had to stand on tiptoe to do it fueled our mirth—but the slap was a proper one. The seaman stood dazed with shock before hesitantly putting his fingers to his stinging cheek, as though unsure that he'd really been struck.

"Stand to attention, God damn you!" little Wedel roared.

The seaman grabbed Wedel by the shoulders and flung him to the floor, then thrust a heavy sea boot into the boy's chest. A crowd quickly formed around them—not because anyone wanted to rescue the kid, but because here, finally, was a chance to vent our frustrated rage. Wedel was saved only by his screams. Two soldiers from Schleswig-

Holstein came charging up the stairs, brandishing their bayonets, but before they reached the boy, Laurids had dispersed the combative crowd, pulling the boy to his feet by the collar while holding off the bystanders with his free hand.

Wedel dangled limp, like a rag doll, fear buckling his legs.

"Now behave," Laurids said in a calm voice.

He'd rediscovered the authority he'd lost on the deck of the ship. The menacing crowd dissolved, and the soldiers led the cadet away.

We heard Wedel sobbing all the way down the stairs.

Later the same evening the cadet recovered his courage. Another loud drinking session was held in the closed room, and from a corner of the loft someone began cursing the noise. It wasn't bedtime yet, but everything about the cadets was beginning to rile us.

We banged on their door, demanding silence. A brazen, high-pitched boy's voice immediately told us to shut up. "Or we'll cut your prick off, you peasant oaf!"

"What did you say?" the seaman roared back.

The drunken men who sat clustered on benches around the sturdy central table staggered to their feet en masse. Hefting a bench, they swung it back and forth as if calculating its weight, then rammed it right into the cadets' door. On the other side, all went quiet.

"Right," shouted one of the men. "Bet you're not feeling quite so cocky now, are you?"

They stepped back for another salvo, then rammed the door again. This time it gave way and they poured into the room, knocking over a table and sending a bottle smashing to the floor. Someone screamed, and the crowd that was gathering outside the cadets' room started cheering the brawling men. Ejnar and Little Clausen stood at the back on tiptoe to catch a glimpse of the fight but could see nothing through the narrow doorway.

Then the German soldiers turned up, alerted by the uproar. Smashing their way through us with the butts of their guns, they broke up the fight.

The brawlers emerged one by one. The cadets' heads hung low, and it was obvious who had borne the brunt. Wedel's nose was bleeding. Another boy had a swollen eye that had already begun to close up. A third spat out a tooth as he came through the door; blood was streaming down his chin.

A cry rang out from the crowd. "Someone's lost a milk tooth!"

Then Commandant Fleischer arrived. He was a sturdy man, with a high forehead and soft curly hair on the back of his neck. His cheeks were flushed and his lips moist; he had gravy on one corner of his mouth, as if he had just left a dinner party and had forgotten to wipe his face.

He was a major, but he instantly disappointed us all with his jovial tone of voice.

"Listen, men, this won't do. You've got to show your officers a bit of respect. Otherwise I'll have to be very strict with you and I don't really want to do that. So let's all try to get along. You'll be exchanged soon and there's really no need for us to fall out while we wait."

We stared at one another, slack-jawed. Was this supposed to be the enemy? The German, who had blown the deck from under our feet and was now holding us prisoner?

The next few days passed quietly. The pails of schnapps were kept full and we carried on drinking. Jørgen Mærke never missed an opportunity to needle the guards. Monkey asses, he called them. Dogshit. Snakes in the grass. Prickless pygmies. He insulted them with impunity, protected by his entourage who, if a guard approached, instantly formed a protective shield around him.

One day the soldiers finally decided they'd had enough. They'd been keeping an eye on Mærke, and two of them came up to the loft to nab him at the table where he was sitting with his gang. They were arresting him, they said, for drunkenness.

Jørgen Mærke's men laughed out loud at the charge and offered their wrists.

"Better arrest all six hundred of us, then."

One guard grabbed Mærke by the shoulders. He clung to the edge of the table, yelling the usual insults and adding a few fresh ones for good measure. Leaping up, his men jostled the two soldiers, rendering their guns useless, then started shoving them toward the stairs. Scared, the soldiers made little resistance. One stumbled and fell backward down the steps, while the other got a shove that sent him flying. He lost his gun as he fell. It landed a few stairs down.

The rebels looked at one another, then at the gun, then back at one another.

No one moved. It had all gone very quiet.

The soldier on the landing scrambled to his feet. He was too dazed from his fall to notice that he'd lost his gun. When he looked up there was no menace in his eyes, only confusion.

Jørgen Mærke took a step forward.

"Boo!" he shouted, tugging at his caveman beard.

The guard jumped, then turned and hurtled down the stairs. His companion got to his feet and followed him. The men laughed and slapped their thighs. Then their eyes rested on the gun and they fell silent. It was lying so near them! All they had to do was walk down a few steps and pick it up.

"Take me." It seemed to beckon. "Shoot, kill, be a man again!"

The men stood spellbound, mute, listening to the gun's whisper. Then one of them broke the silence.

"We could—" he began, taking a step toward it.

He looked at Jørgen Mærke. He was waiting for a nod, approval, an order: Yes, do it!

But Mærke's eyes were empty, and the mouth behind the caveman beard stayed closed.

The man who'd spoken began to waver. The others took a step back, as if he were no longer one of them. Then he bent down and picked up the gun. He didn't look at anyone as he walked down the stairs, bearing the weapon in outstretched hands with the greatest of care, as it if were a sacrifice. When he reached the lowest landing, he leaned the gun against the whitewashed wall. Then he turned and went back up.

We drank heavily that night and shouted "Hurrah!" countless times. The cadets came out of their room and joined us. We were all brothers now.

The next day we made more model ships, decorated them with tiny paper flags in the Danish colors, and launched them. Bobbing there proudly on the scum of the pond, they reminded us of our nation's power.

We started doing drills in the yard, marching in closed ranks as though preparing for a major battle. Holding three fingers high, we swore that we would never "retreat or desert," but "preserve and defend"—puzzling phrases we barely understood. Nonetheless, they sounded impressive, and we proclaimed them out loud, there in the middle of the yard. Anxious-looking faces appeared above the wooden fence from time to time. They belonged to the townsfolk of Glückstadt, who were spying on us. It was in their honor that we staged these little dramas.

And sure enough, the rumor soon started spreading in Glückstadt that the Danish prisoners were gearing up to conquer the town, and the commandant informed us that from now on we were banned from equipping our model ships with the Danish colors. The people of Glückstadt were upset, it seemed, by the sight of the enemy flag.

We regarded that as a victory.

Now the German had learned to fear us!

Many victories of this kind were won in the weeks to come, and we celebrated every one of them with large quantities of schnapps.

We were more than four months into our captivity, when, at the end of August, it was decided that we would be exchanged for German prisoners of war. It took us ten days to get to Dybbøl, where the exchange was to take place. We suffered many delays and humiliations on the way, but we took them all in stride because we'd regained our honor by alarming the people of Glückstadt. And when we saw the Danish ships anchored in Sønderborg Harbor, we knew that we were free men. On board the *Schleswig*, the steamer bound for Copenhagen, they gave us white bread and butter, schnapps, and as much beer as we could drink.

We spent the night on the bare deck, with the ship rolling gently and the wheezing engine vibrating the planks we slept on. It was a cloudless night, and the starlit sky stretched high above us. August 21, 1849, was a good night for shooting stars, and the bright tails of the comets conjured a cannonade very different from the one that heralded our miserable captivity. Laurids breathed a deep sigh. Prison had cut him off from the stars.

When you can't see land, and when the wind, the current, and the clouds tell you nothing, when your sextant has gone overboard and the compass won't work, you navigate by the constellations.

Now he was home.

"Hurrah" was the word we heard most often in the days that followed. On the Baltic Sea we passed a steamer filled with Swedish troops, and from the deck of the *Schleswig* we shouted three cheers for the brave Swedes. At the Customs House in Copenhagen the crew of the frigate *Bellona* welcomed us with a triple cheer, to which we immediately responded; soon the entire harbor had erupted in answering hurrahs.

Then it was the turn of the officers. They too were celebrated with applause. Commander Paludan took the lead as they walked ashore, just as he'd done when he abandoned the wounded on board the *Christian the Eighth*. Through his incompetence he was responsible for the loss of two ships, the deaths of 135 men, and the captivity of a thousand. But now he was greeted with respect because he was a hero. We were all heroes. It seemed as if the clapping would never end.

With our sea bags in hand, we went our separate ways to look for lodgings for the night. Soon we were seated in the city's pubs, drinking and cheering. We missed the schnapps pails; since we were now footing the bill ourselves, our drunkenness didn't reach the extremes it might have.

The following morning we were due to meet at Holmen. The naval minister had announced that four months' captivity merited two weeks' wages. Afterward we were to draw lots to decide who would return to the navy's ships and who would be sent home. Laurids, Little Clausen, and Ejnar returned to Marstal two days later. Here, a celebration arch of spruce branches was constructed in Kirkestræde, where the homecoming men were applauded and the dead mourned.

A terribly deformed creature stood in the midst of the crowd that greeted us. One eye was missing, and the bones of his right cheek and his lower jaw protruded from his skin, which leaked constantly. Even those of us who had witnessed so much on that dreadful day on Eckernförde Fjord had to avert our eyes.

We didn't know who he was until he greeted us.

It was Kresten.

It emerged that not all of his head had been shot off, as Torvald Bønnelykke had told us: only half. He'd been in a hospital in Germany until recently and had been sent home some days before the rest of us. The army surgeon had tried patching him up, but his damaged jaw refused to heal. Now he was back home with his mother—who still hadn't recovered her senses and kept asking after her missing son. When poor Kresten assured her that he was standing right before her, she stuck her finger into the hole in his cheek, just as doubting Thomas had stuck his into the savior's wounds. But unlike Thomas, she didn't turn into a believer. Her Kresten didn't look like this. It was a cruel thing for him to hear: he'd been expecting comfort and joy from the reunion with his mother, despite his ruined face. Tears trickled from the one eye he had left. It would have been better, he said, if he really had died as he'd predicted.

Laurids temporarily regained his fame as a heavenly traveler because Ejnar had described the wondrous event in a letter, and now we all wanted to hear it from the horse's mouth—except for Karoline, who was convinced that it was just another of her husband's tall tales.

The children formed a circle around him, calling out, "*Papa tru,* tell us a story, tell us a story!"

Albert, the youngest, yelled the loudest and gazed at his father with shining eyes. The two of them were like two peas in a pod.

But Laurids simply looked at them with this new, strange expression he'd acquired in captivity, as though they weren't even his children and the notion of having ever produced them was unthinkable.

So Ejnar had to tell them the story instead, and he did it so well that everyone thought he must have been practicing it for ages. The house filled with people who'd come to see Laurids. Karoline stood out in the kitchen, boiling water to make coffee, and turned her broad back to us, clattering the cups, as she was in the habit of doing whenever she was angry with her husband. But she finally succumbed and joined us in the parlor to listen to Ejnar.

"We will never forget how we fought for Denmark's glory," Ejnar said.

Everyone nodded, suddenly consumed by ardent patriotism.

But what Ejnar said next startled us. "We fought for Denmark's glory," he repeated. "But we found only disgrace. We willingly risked life and limb, and showed undaunted courage, to save the honor of our country. But thanks to a lousy leader, we lost it. I'll never forget how those cannonballs hailed down on us on Maundy Thursday. How we fought and fell and died in smoke and flames, and how that evening we were carted off to Eckernförde like slaves and locked up in God's house. How we lay there on the straw, exhausted and dazed. I won't forget how the *Christian the Eighth* was blown up and how so many poor souls died; how on Good Friday we were marched to Rendsburg, to another church, and how again we had to sleep on straw and eat stale bread for our Easter lunch. How the house of God became a cage for slaves, full of degradation and blasphemy, and how our captivity was a stretch of dark, miserable days. I'll never forget any of that, as long as I live."

"I saw Laurids," Ejnar continued, "and that became my only hope and comfort in captivity. I saw Laurids fly toward Heaven from the deck of the burning ship, as high as the main, and I saw him come back down again and land on his feet. And that's how I knew we'd be seeing our loved ones again."

"I've told you before, Ejnar, and I'll tell you again, it was the boots."

Laurids stuck out his foot so everyone could see his sturdy leather sea boots.

"The boots saved me. That's all there is to it."

"Didn't you see Saint Peter's bare behind?" asked Laves Petersen, the little carpenter, for this rumor was already spreading like wildfire. Little Clausen had been unable to keep his mouth shut.

"Yes, I saw the behind of Saint Peter," Laurids said.

But his voice sounded weary and distant, as though he'd already forgotten the episode. We knew immediately that this was all we'd get from him. Most of us believed that just as each man has his own private hell, he also has his own private heaven. And it's his right to keep it to himself.

Those of us who'd been left behind in Marstal couldn't help noticing that Laurids was a changed man. We understood that the war had been a bad time for him and that he'd witnessed things that do a man no good. But he'd already been shipwrecked twice without its affecting him in the slightest. Little Clausen said that the fighting had been like a ship going down, only worse. But Ejnar retorted that Little Clausen had spent most of the battle with his feet in the water and had escaped with nothing more than a cold, while others' heads had been blown off.

As none of the rest of us had experienced battle, we didn't know what to make of Laurids's attitude, and so we left him alone.

Karoline thought that her husband should find himself a job on land, so that both she and the children would get to see more of him. She worried about the change that had come over him and preferred to keep him close by.

Little Clausen and Ejnar were each called up several times during the war, but they always came home in one piece, and we soon grew tired of erecting celebration arches and applauding their return, and started treating them like any other sailors who made it back.

Laurids too was recalled, but by then he had already quit Marstal.

He hadn't taken a land job, as Karoline had wanted, but had instead traveled to Hamburg along the Elbe, the same river he'd stared at every day during his imprisonment in Glückstadt. In Hamburg he was hired as third mate on a Dutch ship bearing immigrants bound for Australia; the other crew consisted of three Dutchmen and twenty-four Javanese. There were 160 passengers on board and it was Laurids's task to hand out provisions and keep the accounts. After a six-month voyage, the ship arrived at Hobart Town in Van Diemen's Land, where Laurids signed off. And that was the last we heard of him.

KAROLINE SAW no reason to worry during the first two years of Laurids's absence. He'd been away from home before, for two or three years at a stretch, and letters sent from the other side of the globe don't always reach their destination. Our women, who have no choice but to stay behind in Marstal, live in a state of permanent uncertainty. Even a letter is no proof that the sender is alive; it can be on its way for months, and the sea steals men without warning. But we're all so used to enduring periods of anxious waiting that we never share our unease with one another. Which is why there was no visible change in Karoline for the first three years, until the day when her neighbor in Korsgade, Dorothea Hermansen, asked her, "Isn't it about time Laurids came home?"

"Yes," Karoline answered. And she said no more. She knew Dorothea had been working up to putting the question for a long time, and that she wouldn't have done it without first consulting the other women in Korsgade. It was in fact a statement, rather than a question: Laurids wasn't coming back.

That night, once she'd put the children to bed, Karoline cried. She'd wept before, but always tried to suppress it. Now she allowed the tears to flow freely.

The next morning the local women crowded into her parlor to ask if she needed help.

Laurids's demise was now official.

They sat around her dining table, each with a cup of coffee. At first their voices were pragmatic and matter-of-fact as they assessed Karoline's circumstances: when it came to help, she had little in the way of family, having already lost five brothers at sea, and with Laurids's father gone too. Then their voices softened and they started praising Laurids's qualities as a husband and provider.

Karoline started crying again. He came alive for her in these moments, resurrected through the words of others.

The oldest woman, Hansigne Ahrentzen, embraced her, and let her dampen her gray dress with her tears. They stayed until she was all cried out.

Thus ended the first meeting, which introduced Karoline to her new status as a widow.

A message was sent to the Dutch shipping company, but they reported no lost ships, nor did Laurids's name appear on any of their crew lists.

The merciful comfort of a grave to which you can take your children and tell them about their father in front of the headstone that bears his name, the possibility of distracting yourself by clearing weeds or perhaps disappearing into a whispered conversation with the man who lies underground—a sailor's widow is denied all that. Instead, she'll receive an official document declaring that the ship her husband was working on, or perhaps skippered and owned, has been "lost with all hands," gone down on this or that date, in this or that place, often at a depth beyond salvaging, with fish as the only witnesses. And she can put that piece of paper away in a drawer of the bureau. Such are the funeral rites awarded to the drowned.

She can hold her own memorial service in front of that bureau, the only grave she can visit. But at least she has the document and with it, certainty: a conclusion, but also a beginning. Life isn't like a book. There's never a final page.

But it wasn't like that for Karoline. No official message reached her. Laurids was gone, but how or where he'd disappeared no one could tell her. Hope can be like a plant that sprouts and grows and keeps people alive. But it can also be a wound that refuses to heal.

It's said that if the dead aren't buried in consecrated ground, they'll haunt us, and Laurids soon began to haunt Karoline. He became the ghost in her heart, and he never left her in peace, because he did not know the difference between day and night, and finally neither did she. There was her yearning during the day, when she should have been busy with domestic matters. There were the practical concerns at night, when she should have been sleeping or crying herself empty from loss. Without rest or relief, she grew gaunt and gray, as if she were made from the same substance as the ghost in her heart.

Only her hands never lost their strength. She'd draw water from the well, light the fire in the kitchen every morning, wash and mend clothes, weave, bake bread, bring up four children, and box their ears hard enough to remind them of the missing Laurids.

THE THRASHING ROPE

THE SUMMER HAD just ended, but the sun's warmth was still in our blood, and we longed for the water. After school we'd run down to the harbor and jump right in, headfirst, or walk out to the long strip of beach known as the Tail. Once we'd swum, we'd lie on the warm sand to dry off and talk about Mr. Isager, our teacher. The new pupils thought he wasn't all bad. Having your ears pulled or getting a slap on the side of the head was no big deal; it was no different from home.

But some of the older ones warned, "Just you wait. He's in a good mood right now."

"He said something nice about my dad," said Albert Madsen.

"But what did your dad say about him?" Niels Peter asked.

"He said that Isager was a devil with the thrashing rope."

His mother had then declared that they were not to call the school-teacher a devil and his father had retorted, "Well, that's easy for you to say. You girls never had Isager."

Remembering his father brought tears to Albert's eyes. He blinked and looked down. His nose thickened and he wiped it with an angry movement of his wrist. We saw his tears, but none of us teased him. Many of us Marstal boys had lost a dad at sea. Our fathers were often away. But then sometimes, out of the blue, they'd be gone forever. *Often away* and *gone forever*: the two phrases marked the difference between having a living father and a dead one. It wasn't a big difference, but it was big enough to make us cry when no one was looking.

One of us slapped Albert on his shoulder and jumped up.

"Race you!"

And we tore across the sand and threw ourselves into the water.

Every summer we went to the beach, with its border of dried seaweed that crackled and pricked under our bare feet, its carpet of crushed mussel shells, its luminous green seabed, and its swaying submerged forests of bladder wrack and eelgrass.

When we turned thirteen we went to sea. Some of us never returned. But every summer new boys came out to the Tail.

One day in August we lay on our stomachs in the warm sand, licking our salty skin, still tanned from the summer, and talked about Jens Holgersen Ulfstrand, who during the reign of King Hans had defeated the Lübecks in a naval battle; about Søren Norby, Peder Skram, and Herluf Trolle, who had all fought on the sea we'd just emerged from; about Peder Jensen Bredal, who was killed at Als by a musket bullet to the chest; about King Christian IV, who boarded his own ship, the *Spes,* and chased the Hamburgers away from Glückstadt, a town that had been built on his orders. It was also where our fathers had once been held captive, but we never talked about that.

Our favorite naval hero was Tordenskjold, who spent a whole night off the shores of Ærø and Als chasing the *White Eagle,* a Swedish frigate equipped with thirty cannons, though his own ship, the *Løvendals Galej,* had only twenty. We knew all about his triumphs at the battles of Dynekilen, Marstrand, Gothenburg, and Strömstad, where so many of his brave men perished, while he survived, safe and sound, though he always gave his utmost.

"Not this time!" we yelled, recalling the day when Tordenskjold found himself alone on Torekov beach in Scania, surrounded by three Swedish dragoons: he'd hacked his way past them and swum through the surf, with his sharp rapier clenched between his teeth.

Then there was the story of how, having fought an English captain for nearly twenty-four hours, with just a brief pause between midnight and dawn, Tordenskjold announced to his wounded foe that he'd run out of gunpowder and coolly asked for the loan of some more so the battle could continue. Upon which the English captain had appeared on deck, raised a glass of wine, and saluted his Danish opponent with seven hurrahs. Then Tordenskjold too found a glass and they'd toasted each other.

Another story we liked was about the time he'd lost the foremast overboard on the *Løvendals Galej* in a howling storm, but managed to stoke fresh courage in his men by yelling "We're winning, boys!" through the gale.

We walked home across the headland, on the other side of which lay the wide inlet we called the Little Ocean. In the distance you could see the ships tied to the black-tarred mooring posts in the harbor: a couple of old luggers, two cutters, a ketch, and the fore-and-aft schooner *Johanne Karoline*, affectionately known as the *Incomparable*. Distinguishing one type of ship from another with the skill of an experienced sailor was something we'd learned long before Isager started drumming the alphabet into our heads. We often swam in the harbor, egging one another on to dive deeper and deeper, right down to the shell-encrusted ships' keels. Then we'd surface with our hands full of mussels.

Behind the harbor wharf rose the town, where from the church rose the thin spire that reached skyward like the bare mast of a ship. Just then, the church bells started tolling a long-drawn-out farewell; a funeral procession was coming down Kirkestræde, led by girls strewing greenery across the cobbles. They were burying old Ermine Karlsen from Snaregade. She'd outlived her husband and both her sons. Death was a certainty for all of us, but whether the bells of Marstal would ever toll for us, there was no knowing. If we drowned at sea, there'd be only silence.

THE FIRST WEEK OF the new school term, Isager paid us little attention. His movements and speech gave him the automatic, dazed quality of a man who has risen before truly waking and is floating in a pleasant dream. Still in dressing gown and slippers, he'd shuffle to the school from his house, the thrashing rope coiled in his pocket like a viper drowsy from the heat. Isager had been a schoolteacher for thirty years, so most of our fathers had felt the snake's lash, and many still bore the scars, like marks of their initiation into manhood.

The good weather lasted well into September—and so did Isager's benign mood. He didn't bother us with revision questions and on the rare occasions when he hit us, it was never hard enough to draw tears or blood, and the infamous thrashing rope stayed in his pocket. He read aloud from *Balle's Textbook,* heedless that some of us had only just started school while others had been there five years. He'd concentrate on the first three chapters: "God's Powers," "God's Works," and "Mankind's Corruption Through the Fall," but he'd stop at the fourth chapter, "Mankind's Redemption Through Jesus Christ." There was no need for all that, he said. It was hogwash—as was everything that followed. Then he'd move on to the Old Testament. His favorite story was that of Jacob and his twelve sons, and it always made his eyes soften. "I too have twelve sons, like Jacob," he'd murmur.

We knew all about Jacob: we'd paid attention. We knew that he was an impostor who stole from his own brother, the hairy-armed Esau, and lied to his father, the blind Isaac, and sired children by four different women, Rachel, Leah, Bilhah, and Zilpah, and that when one proved barren, he would simply move on to the next, and that he had a fight with an angel that left him with a limp, but that later he was blessed by God. It was a peculiar story, but none of us dared point out its oddness to Isager.

Two of Isager's twelve sons were still at the school: Johan and Josef—the latter being the only one Isager had actually named after a son of Jacob. When we told the Isager brothers that their father's Bible hero was a liar, a thief, and a fornicator, Johan burst into tears (he cried a lot anyway because Josef beat him up daily), and teardrops as greasy as candle wax dripped from his bizarrely huge eyes, while Josef, thumping his brother on the head with a clenched fist, merely retorted that their father was no fornicator: he was just a drunkard and a fool.

We never spoke about our own fathers that way. But from then on we left the Isager boys in peace.

We knew that the mild weather was over one day in the middle of September, when an east wind brought looming clouds that covered the entire island with a lid of slate gray. The same day, we noticed that Isager's steel spectacles were sitting higher than usual on the bridge of his nose and pressing tightly against its flesh. Some of us had a theory that Isager's swings of mood related to the weather, so we'd developed the habit of glancing at the sky on our way to school, looking for indications in the cloud formations. But it wasn't an exact science, and even its most ardent proponents had to concede that Isager and the clouds weren't always in concord.

On this mid-September day, however, they were. Dressing gown abandoned, Isager appeared in a black tailcoat, commonly known as the Combat Uniform—and in his right hand he brandished the thrashing rope. His boots clacked on the cobbles as he crossed the yard that divided his house from the school. Then, positioning himself by the school door, he lashed each of us across the back of the neck as we entered, catapulting us over the threshold.

There were seventy of us in his class and we had to pass through the entrance one by one, tensing our scalps for the lash as we went. The older boys among us were used to violence and could take a beating, but no one could quell the fear in his heart as he waited for it. Pain that you anticipate is always worse than the kind that comes out of the blue. Before they even came close to Isager, the youngest boys' lips started quivering. A blow to the back of the head was their school baptism.

But worse awaited us in class.

. . .

We always started by singing "Gone Is the Dark, Dark Night," with Isager leading, in his braying voice. He doubled up as parish clerk, but he had to pay the assistant teacher, Mr. Nothkier, to lead the hymns in church on Sundays because half the congregation had vowed that if Isager led, they'd march out as soon as he opened his mouth—and this was too much for his vanity. But we schoolboys had no such choice, and indeed, we learned to appreciate his voice and to wish that the lengthy, turgid hymn would go on forever, because as long as he was singing, he couldn't clobber us.

He'd pace restlessly up and down while in full flow; although he knew the hymn by heart, he held the open hymnbook right up to his nose, while his predator's eyes roamed the room over the top of the page. As he reached the last few lines, "God grant us happiness and guidance, may He send us the Light of His Grace," you'd usually catch the sound of someone crying. The hymn always served to drown our sobs—but only until it ended. It was the blow across the back of the head that brought on the tears. And it was fear that kept them welling.

Albert Madsen pressed his lips together firmly and fixed his eyes on Isager's spectacles, fighting his terror through concentration.

The teacher's face took on a vigilant expression as he scanned the room again, this time in an exaggerated manner, as though he were in a stage play. He went over to Albert and stared hard into his face. Albert was one of the younger ones, and they were always the first to crack. But Albert just stared ahead stiffly, and Isager let him off and moved on.

There were a lot of us. He never addressed us by name. He just called out, "You there!" or hit us. His rope knew us better than he did.

The class grew silent. Those still crying covered their mouths, terrified of summoning a catastrophe with even the smallest squeak. Then from somewhere in our group a raucous sob emerged (clapping your hand over your mouth didn't always work) and Isager jumped, his eyes narrowing behind his spectacles as he looked around and roared:

"Shut up!"

"Mr. Isager," ventured Albert, "it was wrong of you to hit us. We haven't done anything."

Isager paled. Even his red nose lost its color. Then he unbuttoned his tailcoat. That was the sign we'd feared. All through the hymn he'd been holding the rope: book in one hand, tool of punishment in the other. Just a moment ago he'd been singing about joy and good tidings and the light of grace; now he uncoiled the rope with a practiced hand. If it were a whip, he'd have cracked it.

"You'll get your punishment now"—here his breath caught—"upon my most sacred honor!" And with a single movement he yanked Albert up by the sweater, hauling him from his desk and ramming him down to the floor. Then, trapping him between both legs, he grabbed the lining of his trousers. He'd been saving his strength for this: for an entire long, leisurely summer, he'd had only Josef and Johan to thrash. His moment had come. Deploying skills he had honed over three decades of practice, Isager prepared to land his rope with full force.

Albert cried out in terror. He'd never been flogged before. Laurids had rarely hit him, and his mother mainly boxed his ears. He was used to that. But now he was being thrust down onto his knees. He squirmed to free himself from Mr. Isager's grip.

"So, you're being disobedient, eh?" Mr. Isager hissed and hefted him back to his feet by the hair. He looked Albert right in the face.

"Disobedient," he muttered again, and whipped him across the cheek.

Then he moved on to his next victim.

By now, some boys had climbed up onto the windowsill at the back of the classroom and were struggling with the window catches. By the time Isager was aware of it, the window was gaping open and the boys had jumped out onto the playground and escaped through the gate. Isager had the thrashing rope poised for the next flogging, but the boy between his legs wriggled loose and hurtled round the classroom in a blind panic. At this, Isager began storming across the room, lashing out with the rope, left, right, and center.

"Hurry up, hurry up! He's coming!" we screamed.

Another boy squeezed through the window just before Isager reached it, thrashing those who remained before hauling them down from the sill. The rope flayed our legs, our backs, our arms, and our bare faces. One boy curled up in a ball on the floor, protecting his head with his hands while Isager whipped his back and booted him in the ribs.

Hans Jørgen grabbed hold of Isager's arm. He was a big, strong boy who was due to be confirmed the following spring.

"How dare you lay a hand on your teacher, you lout!" Isager yelled as he struggled to free himself.

Even though there were enough of us to overpower Isager (and if all seventy of us had mobbed him, our sheer weight would have suffocated him), we simply didn't dare come to Hans Jørgen's aid. Indeed, it never crossed our minds. After all, Isager was our teacher. Most of us stayed in our seats, too frightened to move, even though we knew our turn was coming. But Albert approached the still-scuffling duo and looked our teacher up and down. Isager, busy freeing himself from Hans Jørgen's grip, was oblivious to him. Albert watched the two with the same scrutiny he had applied to Isager's spectacles earlier on. His cheek was red and swollen where the rope had landed. Suddenly, he kicked out with his wooden clog, catching Isager on the shin. The teacher howled in pain and Hans Jørgen seized the opportunity to twist his arm. Groaning, Isager sank to his knees.

That was the moment we should all have jumped him. But it was beyond contemplation. Isager was a monster you could never slay, even now, when he was on his knees, howling like a wounded animal. We all knew from our own skirmishes that the battle was over now. When you had someone kneeling with one arm twisted behind his back, you'd order him to plead for his life, or apologize, or otherwise humiliate himself. And since you'd never actually break anyone's arm deliberately, the unspoken rule was that the fight would end there. But with Isager the thing was murkier. There was nothing you wanted more than to break the hated arm he hit you with, but you couldn't do it. If an adult in our group had ordered us to finish him off, then we'd have done it. But Isager was the only adult around. And so we let him go, without even forcing him to plead for mercy, however briefly.

Hans Jørgen took a step back. Isager didn't dare touch him now. Without looking at him, he brushed the dirt off his trousers, then lunged out at the nearest boy. It was Albert, who for the second time that day ended up trapped between the teacher's legs.

Isager was to experience a few more brawls because not everyone put up with his brutality. But the majority of us ended up, like Albert, in the vise of his legs, gritting our teeth and taking a flogging.

Isager returned to his desk, panting and short of breath; he was no longer a young man, and flogging seventy boys was hard work. But he'd managed it. He put his left hand on the desk for support. The other still clutched the rope.

"You vile louts, you've just earned yourself another flogging," he snorted.

But he was too exhausted to deliver it.

His spectacles were still in place. Not once during his skirmishes with the bigger boys did they abandon their position on the bridge of his nose.

It was Albert who deciphered the code of the spectacles. If they perched low toward the tip of Isager's nose, he announced, the day would be a calm one, with only minor, quick-healing injuries to faces and hands. If they were positioned halfway down, things could go either way. But if they were pressed against the bridge, that day's education would be provided by Mr. Thrashing Rope, focusing on the tenderest parts of our bodies, which were also the ones least likely to learn anything.

This discovery earned Albert a certain amount of fame and was perceived as a tactical advantage in our ongoing war with Isager.

It was a war that left its mark on us. Our scalps were scarred from the sharp edge of Isager's ruler, and our fingers—which would get a lashing if our handwriting offended him—would often be so swollen, we could barely hold our pens. He called this practice "the distribution of ducats"—and it was the currency he dealt out generously even on the days when his spectacles sat low. Limping and bleeding, our skin black-and-blue with livid bruises, we were always aching in some exposed place. But that wasn't the worst of what Isager did to us.

He left his mark in another far more frightening way.

We became like him.

We committed appalling acts and only realized the horror of what we'd done when we stood gathered around the evidence of our atrocity. Violence was like a drug we couldn't relinquish.

He planted a thirst for blood in us. One that could never be quenched.

ONE AUTUMN DAY when the wind had torn the last leaves off the trees, we stood, flogged and sore, in Kirkestræde, looking for something to distract us, when suddenly it waddled by: Isager's dog, a stumpy-legged, bloated creature of indeterminate breed. Its short coat was white and gray, and its belly pink as a pig's. We'd seen Karo before, clasped in Mrs. Isager's arms. She was as shapeless as her own dog and had eyes like a Chinaman's, squeezed to slits by the pressure of her fat cheeks.

We didn't know much about her, though we suspected she was the root cause of our woes. People said that she regularly pummeled Isager with her huge, hamlike fists and that it was this humiliation that sent his spectacles high up on the bridge of his nose.

Now here was the dog trotting down the street, with the easy air of a creature at home in its own drawing room, and perhaps that's where it thought it was, since none of us had ever seen it in town on its own before.

"Karo," Hans Jørgen called, clicking his fingers.

The dog stopped. Its jaw hung and its tongue protruded between its teeth. We could feel the rage building inside us; suddenly we hated that dog. Fat Lorentz kicked out at it, but Hans Jørgen held up his hand and started singing the old nursery rhyme we'd chanted when we were little and wanted a snail to stick out its horns. Holding hands, we danced around Karo in a circle.

> Snaily, Snaily, show us your horn,
> Here we come to buy your corn.
> Are you a man or are you a mouse?
> Come outside or we'll burn down your house!

Karo jumped about, yapping.

"Come here, boy, come here." Hans Jørgen enticed him and started running.

The obese animal lumbered after Hans Jørgen in happy anticipation. We circled him and started racing up Markgade. Anyone passing us would have seen nothing but a gang of boys on the move. We passed Vestergade. Ahead of us lay Reberbanen. Farther out, the fields started, and it was here we'd roam when the town got too small for us and we needed to let off some steam. The road was flanked by ancient pollarded poplars, split by old age. We'd marked our ownership of them with wooden planks and nails, transforming them into tree houses with steps, rooms, and attics. These were the castles from which we lorded it over the fields. But we had to recapture them constantly because the farmers' sons claimed them too. They were children of the soil, sturdy and sullen, and they felt that the wide-open fields were their birthright. But we outnumbered them. We only turned up here in gangs, always ready to do battle, and we'd always leave the field victorious. The farm boys were the natives and they defended their soil with the passion of savages. But we were stronger and we showed them no mercy.

"Can he run this far?" Niels Peter asked.

Saliva hung in strings from Karo's black lips as he bounded along, struggling to keep up with us. This was better than life as a lapdog with the teacher's fat missus.

"If Lorentz can do it, so can Karo," Josef said, and slapped Lorentz on his chubby shoulder. Lorentz was already puce from the strain of running: his shoulders and chest heaved, and he wheezed as though something inside him had punctured. His face was thick with fat and when you slapped his cheek hard, it would quiver hilariously: even his lips shook, and only his pudgy nose stayed still. His eyes would assume a pleading expression, as if to apologize for his shameful size.

"Look at him, he's disgusting," said Little Anders, pointing at Karo. "He's dribbling, yuck!"

"And he's got legs like a chest of drawers. What kind of a dog does he think he is?"

Karo responded by yapping merrily. He had company, and he had no idea of what lay in store for him. Why should he, the blameless creature? But in our eyes, Karo was no innocent. He was Isager's dog, and he couldn't escape the hatred we felt for our tormentor. As we ran alongside Karo, we pointed out the many similarities between the animal's ugly squashed face and our teacher's.

"All that's missing is the spectacles," Albert said, and we all laughed.

We were heading for the high clay cliffs before Drejet, but Karo, used to only the short journey between his basket and his food bowl, was soon defeated: his stumpy little legs gave out and he collapsed on his belly, drooling from exhaustion.

But he was going to have to stick with it. What we had in mind wasn't something for the open fields.

Hans Jørgen picked him up and cradled him in his arms; Karo licked his face happily and Hans Jørgen grimaced.

"Eurk!" we shrieked in unison, and ran on, our excitement mounting. Down the first slope and up the next we ran, then along a field boundary and up the hillside. The cliff edge, with its dizzying drop to the beach below and the sea stretching in every direction, had always entranced us. As we stood there, gazing out at the water, it seemed that a great mystery lay before us: the mystery of our own lives, spread before our eyes. No matter how often we came here, it was a sight that always rendered us speechless.

The drop wasn't sheer everywhere. The cliff face was steep, but there were ledges where western marsh orchids, yarrow, and golden buttons grew in the rich clay soil. You could hurl yourself off the edge and into the void, and land just a few meters below. You couldn't walk down the cliff, but you could conquer it ledge by ledge if you descended with care. Not always without injury—but then, cliff climbing was all about putting yourself in mortal danger.

We reached the edge and surveyed the Baltic. Hans Jørgen was still carrying Karo, who yelped again. He probably thought we wanted to show him the whole wide world. We hadn't agreed on a plan. There was no need to. We all knew what was going to happen.

Hans Jørgen gripped Karo's front paws and began swinging him to and fro. Karo, in pain, tried to snap at him, but his thick neck was too short. He bared his tiny teeth and bit at the air, half whining, half growling, his hind legs flailing as if grappling for a foothold.

"Snaily, Snaily, show us your horn!" Hans Jørgen shouted, and we joined in.

"Here we come to buy your corn!"

Then he let go. Karo sailed up toward the overcast autumn sky, making a wide arc as he plummeted toward the stones on the beach far down below, his fat torso twisting and turning in midair. How funny he looked! We jostled right up to the edge so we could see him slam into the beach. At first he just lay motionless and silent, on his side, but then a sort of whine started up: the groan of someone losing strength. He twisted laboriously until he lay on his belly. Then he tried to stand up, but couldn't. His hindquarters wouldn't budge, although his front legs kept clawing. He tried again and again, and all the time we could hear him. His cries sounded more like a child's than an animal's, a haunting, frail, yet penetrating sound.

Our triumph died instantly within us.

We didn't look at one another as we climbed down the hillside separately. Suddenly, we weren't a group anymore. Most of us wanted to turn around, run home, and forget all about Karo. But Hans Jørgen led the way and we followed, stumbling. Little Anders lost his footing and rolled down several meters before hitting a rock, then scrambled to his feet, crying. We were battered and bruised by the time we gathered around Karo, who was still whimpering in this scary way we couldn't bear to listen to.

He gazed up at us and licked his nose with his tiny pink tongue. At that moment he almost looked happy, as if unaware that we were the cause of his plight, and was simply waiting for us to make everything all right again. His tail wasn't wagging, but that was only because his back was broken.

We gathered around him in a circle. None of us felt like kicking him now. He looked so innocent. He hadn't done anything wrong, and now there he lay, whining, with his spine snapped.

Albert squatted beside him and started stroking his head.

"There, there." He comforted the dog, and suddenly we all wanted to cuddle Karo.

If only he'd started wagging his stubby tail at this moment. But he didn't, and he never would again. We knew that.

Swiftly, Hans Jørgen moved across to Albert.

"Stop it," he said, grabbing hold of Albert's arm to pull him away.

Albert got to his feet and faced him. Hans Jørgen was still holding on to him. He was the biggest of us and the most fair-minded. He was the one who bravely stood up to Isager when he paced up and down the classroom with the thrashing rope. He always defended the youngest children. Now he stood there, his shoulders sagging, just as lost as the rest of us.

"We can't leave Karo here," Albert said.

"Well, cuddling him won't do him any good either," Hans Jørgen snapped.

"Can't we take him back to Isager?"

"To Isager? Are you out of your mind? He'd kill us!"

"What are we going to do then?"

Hans Jørgen let go of Albert and shrugged. Then he started walking up and down the beach.

"Help me find a big rock," he said.

None of us stirred. Anders was still crying. Karo had gone very quiet, as if Hans Jørgen's words had made him pensive.

"Listen," Albert said. "He's stopped whimpering. Perhaps he's feeling better."

"Karo isn't going to get better," Hans Jørgen said darkly. That's when we understood there was no other way.

"You can go if you want to," he said.

He'd found a rock. He was clutching it in both hands.

We wanted to go, but we couldn't. We couldn't leave Hans Jørgen. If we did, it would be like being left alone with Isager.

Hans Jørgen knelt in front of Karo. The dog looked up at him expectantly, as though he thought Hans Jørgen wanted to play.

"Turn him on his side," Hans Jørgen said.

Niels Peter put a hand under the dog's hairless pink belly and turned him over. That's when Karo screamed. He didn't whine. He didn't moan. He screamed. We were all so terrified, we started screaming with him, because it was all so sad: sad that he was so stupid, and sad that he couldn't understand a single thing about this world.

Afterward, when we climbed back up the hillside, each of us carried a stone in his hand. We didn't really know why. We walked home without speaking, clasping our stones.

Lorentz met us, wheezing. He had given up on the first slope.

"What's happened?" he asked in his usual sucking-up way. Then he saw our faces.

"Where's Karo?"

"Shut your gob, you fat pig."

Niels Peter walked right up to him and punched him in the stomach, and Lorentz sat down in the middle of the road with that begging expression on his face that we all loathed. No matter what you did to him, he always put up with it.

Later we met two boys from one of the farms in Midtmarken. They stank of cow shit, so we chased them, pelting them with our stones. They howled as they scampered home to their dung heap. We didn't care what they told their parents. Our mood hadn't improved. We had a feeling that once again, Isager had won.

The next day we were sure that Isager would have vengeance on his mind. Sure enough, his spectacles sat high on the bridge of his nose, and he paced the schoolroom with the springy, elastic steps we had learned to fear. The thrashing rope too seemed to have acquired a life of its own. We sensed it twisting and turning in his hand, ready to lash out at its first victim. We were already cowering.

This was it.

Karo's failure to return home must have caused an upset in the schoolteacher's house, and whether or not Isager thought we were involved, we knew he'd make us pay the price, the way he'd made us pay for every other disappointment in his life.

Isager marched up and down, muttering "Bad boys, bad boys" as usual. But no one was ordered to kneel on the floor: when he struck, there was no warning. He started on Lorentz, who was sitting by his desk, taking up two spaces. He attacked him from behind, swiping him across his broad back. Then, quick as lightning, he whipped around to the front of the desk and hit him first across the chest and then the face. Lorentz squealed in a mixture of pain and fear and covered his head with his massive arms. Isager tugged at them to gain clear access for the rope, but Lorentz held fast, so Isager pulled him to the floor—he landed with a loud thud—and started kicking him. We'd all tried hitting Lorentz, even the smallest of us. His obesity had something fascinating and irritating to it, a feminine softness that attracted and provoked us at the same time. Word had it that he didn't have any balls and that his tiny white worm hung between the fatty masses of his thighs with an empty scrotum dangling behind. This feature made him a born clown in our eyes. We believed that his fat protected him, and even when he wailed from our blows, we thought he was crying because he was a sissy and not because it really hurt. So we hit him harder to make him stop whining.

Lorentz never hit back. He'd put up with anything to avoid being shunned. And we strung him along because we needed someone we could bully without the risk of punishment. Perhaps he thought we tolerated him. But we didn't; to us he was nothing but the thing we called him when we wanted him to do something: the fat pig.

Sticking together was the only thing Isager had taught us. He never,

ever succeeded in turning us into snitches. We'd each rather take the blame than betray a comrade, and Isager knew it. That's why he regarded us all as equally guilty and beat us all equally hard.

Lorentz lay defenseless on the floor while Isager kicked at him. Of all of us, Lorentz was the least guilty, yet even so, not one of us raised his voice to protest the boy's innocence.

Was it solidarity that made us keep silent now too?

Then we heard the familiar wheezing that usually accompanied our excursions when we ran faster and fat Lorentz began to lag behind, struggling for breath. Fighting to sit up, he forgot to shield himself—and Isager, who so far had relied on his boots, now raised the thrashing rope, ready to bring it down on his victim's unprotected face and his fat-girl chest. But something halted him in his tracks. Lorentz's arms were flapping, as though he were facing a new but invisible enemy. His face was turning blue and his eyes bulged in their sockets. He gurgled and gasped. He seemed to be choking.

Isager, at a loss, took a step back, then shoved the rope back into his rear pocket as though nothing had happened and headed for his desk.

By now Lorentz, shoulders still heaving in an agonizing struggle for breath, had managed to sit up. Isager did nothing but watched from the corner of his eye. We could tell that he was scared. Lorentz remained on the floor for the rest of the lesson, in a world of his own, his eyes sightless. Then slowly, his huge body began to relax and his wheezing died down. When he fully regained his breath, he looked around at the rest of us with eyes that seemed to beg that he might be one of us at last.

We looked away. None of us wanted to answer.

ISAGER HAD BEEN a schoolteacher for thirty years. His predecessor, Andrésen, had taught for fifty-one years, but only the old folks remembered him. Isager had met two kings. The first was Crown Prince Christian Frederik, who later became King Christian VIII. Escorted by the schooner *Dolphin,* his ship had dropped anchor at a stone bridge in the harbor—henceforth renamed Prinsebroen. On his way to Kirkestræde, he'd strolled up Markgade—which was promptly rechristened Prinsegade. Whatever street Crown Prince Christian Frederik put his feet on got a new name. The girls came dressed in white frocks and the pastor gave a speech, but Isager was the star attraction of the visit because the crown prince had come to inspect his pupils.

Twelve years later came another royal visit, this time from the future King Frederik VII, who arrived by ferry in a northerly gale. We were standing on the wharf, debating which passenger might be the prince, when a man in knitted gloves and a cap with earflaps leapt ashore and secured the hawser, saying, "Cold today, isn't it, lads?" That was Crown Prince Frederik.

At school we sang, "We want to be sailors, as long as we live!" (the words were supplied by Isager) and then we were subjected to the teacher's grilling—upon which the crown prince turned to his adjutant and asked him if he could do sums as difficult as those faced by the children of Marstal. The adjutant replied no, and the man who would one day succeed to the throne as Frederik VII announced, "Neither can I."

The calculation that had generated such admiration from the crown prince came from page forty-seven of *Cramer's Arithmetic* and went as follows: "The Earth goes through its annual course of 129,626,823 geographical miles in 365 109/450 days. Given that the Earth moves constantly at the same speed, how far does it travel in one second?"

This question was enough to make anyone dizzy, especially since Isager had omitted to tell us that the Earth circled the Sun. However, he'd drilled the answer into us. It was at the back of the book: four geographical miles—plus a fraction that no one would have known how to pronounce, had it not been for the thrashing rope. A boy called Svend gave the answer on this occasion. From that day on he was known as One-Second Svend, and he went on to take the famous fraction with him to his watery grave at the age of sixteen.

Isager bowed deeply in response to the crown prince's compliment, and Frederik patted him on the back. One-Second Svend had been ordered to keep his hands behind his back so that Frederik wouldn't catch sight of his damaged fingers.

That was all the wisdom Isager ever imparted to us: that the thrashing rope and the ruler could achieve what a teacher's skill could not. Isager's knowledge didn't extend far even with *Cramer's Arithmetic* in his hand. But the rope did its work. If we learned to count, it was only to keep track of the number of strokes we were dealt.

Marstal School was later named Frederik School in honor of the occasion. But they might as well have named it Isager Establishment. Crown Prince Frederik's pat on the back had turned the school—and our bruised limbs—into Isager's personal property. He'd bowed to two future kings, and two future kings had given him a pat on the back: that put him beyond criticism.

An education committee consisting of a wholesale grocer and two skippers had been set up, and our parents could complain to them if we came home looking worse than usual after an encounter with Isager's rope. But the committee members were simple people, who dumbly deferred to the learned schoolteacher. After all, he'd been praised by not one but two kings. So no complaint was ever upheld.

Besides, everyone remembered what it had been like in old Andrésen's time. There had been 350 pupils at the school in those days, but only two classes, with 175 pupils each. Andrésen couldn't possibly remember so many names, so he gave the boys numbers instead and directed them with the aid of a whistle. Pupils would sit wherever they could find space, including on the windowsills, in the kitchen, and even out in the yard. This meant that the windows had to stay open until the weather grew too severe. But long before that happened, the pupils all caught colds and bronchitis from the draft. Then, once the windows had been closed for the winter, the atmosphere became suffocatingly close, and children fainted daily. And there were no black-boards or writing implements: the pupils stood in front of a tray of sand and scratched in it with a stick. A single gust of wind could blow their combined knowledge clean away.

With such memories, the three members of the committee regarded the new school, with its inkwells and its blackboards and its headmaster who had been praised by two future kings, as progress. There was only one remedy for children's reluctance to learn, and that was more thrashing.

But then again, we rarely complained, because another aspect of the solidarity that Isager had taught us was that we couldn't even snitch on our tormentor. We'd return home with bald patches on our scalps where a furious Isager had ripped out clumps of hair; with black eyes; with fingers incapable of holding knife or fork. And we'd say we'd been in a fight, and when parents asked who with, we said, "Nobody."

We swore that when we grew up, we'd give Isager what he'd been asking for. We couldn't fathom our fathers' tacit consent to our ill-treatment: they knew full well who Nobody was because they too had been victims of the rope. But they turned a blind eye to our suffering.

Our mothers suspected that something was wrong, but they were always at a loss when dealing with the authorities. It wasn't that they lacked strength: they had considerable supplies of it, with so many children and their husbands away at sea. But when faced by the minister or the schoolteacher, they started doubting their own judgment.

"You're sure it wasn't Mr. Isager?" they'd ask.

And we'd shake our heads. We hardly knew why, but we never pointed the finger at him as the cause of our daily injuries. Instead, we blamed ourselves.

"Well, perhaps this will teach you to stay out of trouble."

And we would get a clip on the ear.

"Look at your sister, she comes home neat and tidy every day."

It was true. But then again, our sisters had Nothkier, the assistant teacher, and he never beat them.

This was another malign effect of Isager. He followed us home unseen and sowed discord.

WINTER ARRIVED, and with it the frost. The boats were laid up in the harbor, the harbor froze over, and an ice pack formed on the beach. Island and sea became one; we inhabited a white continent whose infinity both beckoned and terrified us. We could walk as far as Ristinge Klint on the island of Langeland if we wanted to, marching across frozen ships' channels between sandbanks that lay like white hills, collecting snowdrifts fringed by ice packs. It looked so wild, windswept, and deserted.

This new landscape even forced its way into our streets, where a blizzard of snowflakes whirled and danced on the heavy drifts, then leapt back into the air to obliterate the world once more. We were desperate to get outside and join the dance, to take our skates down to the harbor or trek out across the fields to the hills at Drejet to fight the farmers' sons with snowballs and hurtle down the slopes on our toboggans.

Isager was an obstacle to this, but winter was on our side: without a stove in the classroom, we couldn't cope with the cold—but the stove-pipe was easily obstructed, and once the room filled with smoke, he had to send us home. On these occasions he'd stand in the doorway, treating us to a clip on the ear by way of goodbye as we filed out.

"You rascal," he would mutter to each of us. By now he could barely breathe and his eyes would be red behind his spectacles. But like the captain of a sinking ship, he was always the last to leave the class-room: if he could still see well enough to strike us, even though he was hacking and coughing, he'd stay on to do it. He hated us so much that he'd rather choke than miss out on a single blow.

So only on Sundays could we devote ourselves to the snow without paying for it with a sore neck.

· · ·

One day Niels Peter deftly dismantled the stovepipe and stuffed his entire sweater inside, whereupon the stove duly started to smoke as planned—but the sweater too caught fire. Isager stifled the blaze immediately. But the flames that burst briefly from the pipe wouldn't be forgotten in a hurry: even Isager was silenced by the episode.

If we could smoke him out, what else could we do?

On cold winter evenings Isager would go visiting. He frequently called on Christoffer Mathiesen, the grocer, his most fervent supporter on the education committee. A few other local people sat with him around the grocer's mahogany table, but not Pastor Zachariassen. Isager wasn't on good terms with the pastor, who was embarrassed by his poor teaching. Mr. Mathiesen, on the other hand, was honored to entertain the learned gentleman who had been patted on the back by royalty.

"And as the king said to me—" was Isager's most frequent remark in that company. He would sit there in his tailcoat, with a two-finger toddy in front of him. Describing his royal encounters served as a form of payment for the steaming brew, which he never raised to his lips without referring to it as "the best medicine against the cold the good Lord ever created."

As the medicine took effect, his lower lip would begin to sag and his spectacles slide toward the position Albert described as "fair weather," revealing a face we never saw at school: not amiable exactly, but relaxed.

When Isager left Mathiesen's house in Møllegade that night, he was unsteady on his legs. It had snowed all evening, and now there were drifts against the stone steps and all across the street. There was no street lighting in Marstal, so the town lay dark in the whirling snow. The wind was easterly, blowing up from the harbor straight into Møllegade.

We saw his face in the light from Mathiesen's window. For a brief moment his slack expression gave way to the same look of rage he wore on a punishment round, and we fully expected to hear him scream "Rascal!" at the snowstorm. Instead his lower lip drooped and his eyes returned to their vacant look.

Now, outside, he was nothing but a shadow against the snowdrifts.

We followed him for a while to make sure that he was heading home via Kirkestræde. He made progress laboriously, getting stuck in drifts and shoveling himself free frantically with his hands. This might have helped him warm up, but it didn't speed him on his way.

We could have got him right there and then.

Only the oldest of us were out that night. Niels Peter had sneaked downstairs from his attic room and left via the back door. Hans Jørgen had lied and said he was visiting a friend. His father was away on a long voyage that winter and his mother had started treating him like a grownup. Josef and Johan Isager were not with us, obviously.

We all knew that our plan would mean trouble in some form or other the next day. But an extra beating made no difference to us.

Lorentz begged to be part of it.

"Please, please let me," he said.

"Haaaaaaaaaa," we said, imitating his wheezing when he was out of breath. "We'll be running fast. You're no good."

In fact, if we'd really loathed him, we would have let him join us. He had no idea what we were saving him from that night.

We waited for Isager on the corner of Kirkestræde and Korsgade, the crystals in the falling snow reflecting the starlight above us. Then we spotted him, a shadowy figure slowly growing in size among the glimmering snowflakes. The darkness protected us, and we had tied our scarves around our faces so that only our eyes were visible. Our breath felt hot behind the wool. We were shadows ourselves, a pack of wolves in the snowy night.

We started bombarding him with snowballs. We came up close, hitting him hard and with precision. But it was only fun and games. So far, at least. Just a gang of boys throwing snowballs.

One knocked his hat off. He staggered forward to pick it up. Then another, crusted hard with ice after being lovingly molded in a hot and vengeful hand, slammed right into his ear, which was already burning in the severe cold. It might as well have been a stone. He touched his head.

"Rascals!" he screamed. "I know who you are!"

He took a step toward us, and a snowball smashed him right in his face, blinding him. Then a direct hit to his neck. He raved in pain.

"Rascals!" he screamed again.

But the power was gone from his voice. He was moaning now—and he was scared.

That was what we wanted. We'd moved on from fun and games. Now he'd see us for what we really were. With every backward step he took, our fear shrank; we'd tasted our own strength and it had whetted our appetite. Outside the classroom he was nothing but an old drunk, alone in a winter storm. But we didn't see him like that. We had Satan himself in our grasp. And having captured the bringer of all evil, we'd show him no mercy—for if we did, we'd stay scared the rest of our lives. Hans Jørgen had once brought Isager to his knees and twisted his arm behind his back, but even then, he'd kept his power over us, and Hans Jørgen had let him go.

But this time there'd be no escape.

We backed off briefly and he cleared the snow from his eyes. Still he didn't see us. He seemed to think he was safe, but that was our plan. He gave up looking for his hat and stumbled on through the drifts, mumbling to himself. We knew he was cursing us. Then we attacked again. Harder snowballs this time. Pure lumps of ice. And there was no missing at such close range. It was like pounding him in the face, first one cheek, then the other, forcing his head to jerk from side to side. This was our thrashing rope. We stayed silent while he grunted and moaned. We would have loved to break every bone in that detested face, but we held off because we didn't want him to collapse here in Kirkestræde, where he might be found before the frost finished the job for us.

We let him get as far as the corner of Nygade before we surrounded him again, forcing him to flee down the street. We wanted to drive him out to the deserted area down by the harbor, where no one came at night. We'd almost got him down to Buegade: by now he was swaying and faltering. From time to time he'd fall into a snowdrift, headfirst. Then we'd wait until he got back on his feet and start again.

He was blubbering.

It was a dreadful thing to hear, but it stirred no pity in us. The snowstorm muffled all other noises, so the only sound was our tormentor's weeping. The tears ran down his cheeks, where they froze to ice. Snow hung in his sideburns, which made them seem longer, and frayed. Sobs, mumblings: was he still cursing us, or was he pleading for his life? We weren't sure, nor did we care. Finally, we had Satan under our thumb.

Isager sought shelter by the wall of one of the tall half-timbered houses at the bottom of Nygade. He tripped over the doorstep, collapsing onto stairs that were half-buried by snow. When he raised himself with his hands, Hans Jørgen hit him on the nose with a rock-hard ball. It was dark, but the snow lit everything up, and we saw the blood drip onto it, first a small stain, then a bigger one. Isager turned his head toward us and brayed with fear, blood dangling from his nose in a snotty strand.

Hans Jørgen launched yet another shot at him, but he missed, and the snowball smashed into the door instead.

A lamp was lit inside, and a light flickered behind the frost flowers on the icy window.

"Who's there?"

We heard scrambling in the hallway.

Then we legged it. In Buegade, Kresten Hansen was coming along, swinging his lamp in the snowstorm. The glowing wick cast a flickering light across his mutilated face. He was a night watchman now. He slept during the day and worked at night to spare the town the sight of his face. He looked horrific. He made way for us, and as we raced past, he dropped his lamp in a snowdrift and darkness descended.

The next day, Isager wasn't there to greet us in the doorway of the school. Silently, we entered the empty, ice-cold classroom. But we felt no relief. It was so strange. We couldn't imagine a world without Isager. Was he dead?

Nothkier, the assistant teacher, arrived and told us Isager was ill. We were all to go home and come back tomorrow. The next day the classroom was empty again, but the stove had been lit. Nothkier arrived and informed us that "Mr. Isager's illness will be a long one" and that in the meantime he'd attend to our education, though our hours of instruction would be reduced, as he also had to teach the girls.

Nothkier was no better at teaching than Isager: he, too, stuck to *Balle's Textbook*, which made very little sense to us, and *Cramer's Arithmetic*, which made no sense to anyone including him. But he never hit us. Sometimes he'd ask us whether we understood what he'd had just explained—and relieved, we'd answer no, we didn't. He didn't get angry or call us donkeys or give out "ducats": he just started again from the beginning.

The snow was still there, but we didn't block the stove or pour sand into the inkwells. Fewer of us played truant. It was as though we wanted to reward him.

Isager had pneumonia, it was said, and at home our parents talked about how he'd lost his way in the storm.

"He was probably drunk out of his mind," the men said. The women hushed them.

All the children knew what had happened, including those of us who hadn't been there. But we never said anything, not even to one another. As long as Isager didn't turn up for school, we were happy. Our failure to kill him the way we'd planned barely crossed our minds. Had anyone asked us if we really wanted him dead, we'd probably have replied that we didn't care, so long as we were rid of him.

Christmas came, and with it the holidays. Isager was still bedridden, and this year we spared him the torments we normally subjected him to on New Year's Eve, in thanks for the year gone by. We didn't smash his garden fence or shoot the school's forty windows to bits, or offer our trademark New Year's greeting in the form of clay pots full of ashes and stinking waste lobbed through his windows.

After New Year's Day, Isager returned, and everything was back to normal.

His skin was as white as the snow outside, and even his nose had lost its color. But he wore his black tailcoat and his spectacles were high on the bridge of his nose, and the thrashing rope swung in his right hand like a viper roused from its winter hibernation, ready to attack. We stared at him as though he'd risen from the dead—not least because we'd already pictured him in his grave.

We sang "The Dark Night Has Ended" as usual, but the words on our lips belied the feeling in our hearts. The dark night had begun anew, and a ghost walked among us.

After the hymn, Isager strode over to Little Anders and grabbed him by the ear. That was all it took for Anders to position himself obediently on his knees between the schoolteacher's legs. Isager raised the thrashing rope, ready to strike.

"Sinning is a disease of the soul. That's why it causes the soul to experience anxiety." The calmness of his voice spooked us. Normally, even at this early stage of a punishment, he'd be in the grip of a mad rage. "This anxiety we call conscience." He looked up. "Do you understand?"

The schoolroom fell silent. The only sound was the crackling of the flames in the stove. We nodded. When Isager finished with Anders, he moved on to the next boy. Albert too knelt obediently, and Isager gripped him by the lining of his trousers.

"The purpose of conscience is to judge and to punish." Isager's lash made Albert jump: the stroke was unexpectedly painful on a backside that had toughened during the autumn but regained its normal sensitivity during the long break. "Lie still," Isager ordered him in the same calm voice as before, renewing his grip on the lining of Albert's trousers. "But how does your conscience punish you? Through the inner unrest you experience when you have committed a misdeed. Does your conscience trouble you? Do you feel the punishment?"

He laid off Albert and looked around the schoolroom. Again we nodded. "You're lying," he said, without raising his voice, then moved on to his next victim, Hans Jørgen. We anticipated that one of their regular confrontations might erupt—but Hans Jørgen too knelt to await his punishment. Oblivious to this unexpected triumph, Isager continued his lecture while raining down more blows. "You know nothing of remorse. And do you know why? Because you have no purpose. Do you know what purpose is? Probably not. Purpose is God's plan for us. But God has no plan for you. You have no reason and you have no conscience. You don't know the difference between right and wrong."

He straightened up and paced about the schoolroom. He made Niels Peter his next choice—but instead of thrashing him right away, he paused next to the boy's bowed back and brandished the rope.

"Take a good look at this," he said, before laying into him. "This is your conscience, and it's the only one you'll ever have. Only the rope can teach you about right and wrong."

When school was over, we walked across the snow-covered fields beyond town. None of us said anything. We were looking for some farmers' boys to start a fight with. Every now and then we'd steal a glance at Hans Jørgen. Had he let us down? We'd all presented our backs to Isager. But we hadn't expected him to.

Today the snow had none of the glittering surfaces and bluish shadows it took on when the sun shone. The dull weather cast everything in a uniform gray, and only the bare poplars provided any perspective. There wasn't a soul about.

"There's no one here," Niels Peter grumbled.

We stole another glance at Hans Jørgen. He was walking slightly ahead of us, but suddenly he stopped and turned to face us.

"I don't want you to think that I'm afraid of Isager," he said. "Because I'm not."

He sounded angry. We didn't say anything and looked down at the snow. A snowflake fell from the overcast sky, and then another. We expected him to add something, but he didn't.

"Why did you let him hit you?"

Niels Peter put the question without looking up, almost as if he were talking to himself. Hans Jørgen hesitated. Then he shrugged, as though defeated in advance.

"It doesn't matter now," he said.

Albert looked up, squinting into the falling snow.

"I don't understand."

Hans Jørgen paused. "Well, we didn't get him," he said. "And now he's come back and he's worse than ever. It's all"—again he flung out his arms—"hopeless."

"But he was bleeding," Albert protested. He hadn't seen it, but he'd heard detailed, almost painterly descriptions of Isager's dripping blood.

"Yes," Niels Peter said. "He did bleed."

"And so what?"

Hans Jørgen turned around and started heading back to the town. The snowflakes came thicker now. We followed. For the first time, we disagreed with Hans Jørgen. He'd always been our leader. But now we had to answer for ourselves.

We'd killed the dog, but we'd failed to kill the master. He'd thrashed our fathers and he'd go on thrashing us. We did the math on our fingers. We stayed in school for six years. Albert had five and a half years to go. Hans Jørgen had six months, the rest of us something in between. If Isager claimed six years of our lives, how many more would it take us to forget what he'd done? It sounded like a problem from *Cramer's Arithmetic,* but whether you solved it through addition, subtraction, or multiplication, none of us knew.

We had seen Isager bleed one winter's night, and the sight of his blood on the snow had filled us with hope. We'd seen fire lick through Niels Peter's sweater in the schoolroom stove, and we weren't through with contemplating what those flames meant.

At which point we began to see the potential of fire.

Hans Jørgen took confirmation with Pastor Zachariassen and went to sea. Eight months later he returned with the winter ice, having saved up his wages and bought himself a tall hat of the kind the older sailors wore.

Now was the moment for taking his revenge on Isager, we told him, because he was an adult, and no one could hurt him. But Hans Jørgen said he got thrashed just as much on board ship, so nothing had changed, and now that Isager was no longer his teacher, he'd lost the urge to smash him to pieces. In fact he'd bumped into him in the street, and Isager asked him about life at sea and they'd chatted as though Hans Jørgen had never forced him to his knees by twisting his arm, or lain on the floor being flayed: one adult to another.

"Do it for us, then," Albert pleaded. "You're big and strong. You're stronger than last year. You can take him on."

"I've already forgotten him," Hans Jørgen said. "He's of no interest."

"You're full of it because you've just been paid."

"You're not listening."

Hans Jørgen squatted down so his face was level with Albert's.

"They thrash you on board ship too. It never ends. It goes on and on. You might as well get used to it now."

"It's not fair!" Niels Peter fumed.

"No"—the others joined in—"it's not fair!"

"What's the point of teaching us to do sums, or to read and write," asked Hans Jørgen, "when all we need to know is how to take a beating, if we want to get ahead? And when it comes to that, there's no better teacher than Isager."

We looked at him uncertainly. Was he mocking us?

"Did the great Tordenskjold complain when a wave snapped off the foremast? No. What did he say to his men?"

"We're winning, boys," Niels Peter mumbled, and looked at his feet.

"There you are. We're winning, boys! Just remember that and stop whining."

"He's gone really strange," Albert said afterward.

We nodded. We felt more alone than ever. Hans Jørgen was no longer one of us. He'd become a grownup and he knew more about the world. But we didn't like what he told us. We decided not to believe him.

However, from that day on, it seemed that we were readier to put up with things. When Isager went on a thrashing round, there was less rebelliousness in the classroom, and fewer of us jumped out of the window to escape.

Christmas and New Year came around again. Isager had escaped our torments the previous year because he'd been bedridden, fighting for his life, but he'd won, and now it was time for more seasonal fun. We suspected we'd never be rid of Isager, but we couldn't forget those classroom flames, the day Niels Peter used his sweater to obstruct the stovepipe, and it caught fire. Having seen the flames bursting out, we knew that once fire had taken hold, nobody could stop it.

This too was Niels Peter's idea. How had the big fire of 1815 started? Had men with torches set fire to the thatched roofs at night? No: a candle had been knocked over in a house in Prinsegade. That was all it took! And the blaze had jumped from house to house, until every third house in town was reduced to ashes. The glow could be seen all the way from Odense.

Albert's grandmother Kirstine still spoke about the fire with terror in her voice.

"Granny, tell us about the Great Fire!" Albert pestered her, when she came to visit. So as she sat by the stove, Granny would tell the story of Barbara Pedersdatter, the maid who'd been hackling flax on Karlsen's threshing floor in Prinsegade with the tallow dip lit, but then had taken it into her head, the silly girl, to read a letter from her sweetheart because he'd landed her in trouble and she was keen to know what he intended to do, given that it was all his fault. But in the process of opening the letter, the befuddled girl had knocked the candle over and the tow caught fire and soon it wasn't just Barbara Pedersdatter but the whole town that was in trouble. "Whoosh,"

Granny said, and flung her hands in the air to indicate how the hungry flames shot out through the thatched roof. She'd seen that fire and she'd never forget it.

"You pray to God that you'll never have to live through what we did," she'd say, as she finished telling the tale.

But Albert prayed to God that fire would be unleashed again.

It was New Year's Eve and we did what we always did: we ate our traditional dinner of boiled cod with mustard sauce, and then ran out into the dark winter's night, banging on doors and wreaking havoc. We smashed fences and threw clay pots. We caught a dog and tied a bit of old rope around it and hung it upside-down from a tree until its howls attracted the attention of its owner, whom we then bombarded with more clay pots.

And now, having stuffed straw into our sweaters, we were waiting for it to get dark enough to surround Isager's house. There was still light coming from the inside, so we threw a couple of clay pots through the windows into the drawing room. We heard his fat wife squeal and, shortly afterward, more noises came from the hallway. Then Isager appeared in the doorway, a stick in his hand.

"Louts," he yelled.

"You can shout as much as you like," we called back, and aimed a few more clay pots in his direction. One hit him on the shoulder and sent its foul, stinking contents running down his black tailcoat. His yelling ended in a strangled cough as if he was about to throw up. Another pot flew past him into the hallway. Josef and Johan stood looking out the window, laughing at their father. They were never allowed to go out mischief-making on New Year's Eve, so this was their revenge. But they had no idea what was to come, because we hadn't told them.

We legged it down Skolegade with Isager chasing after us, his stick raised, ready to attack. The sound of smashing glass now came from the other side of the house: Niels Peter and Albert Madsen had broken a bedroom window and thrown burning straw inside. The fire had started.

"Come out now or we'll burn your house down."

We turned into Tværgade and raced up Prinsegade. We could still hear Isager shouting. We were back at the schoolhouse by this time; we'd tricked him by running in a circle. We felt the wind grow stronger. The day before it had begun to thaw, and most of the snow in the streets was melting, warmed by the mild western wind that always sucked winter away from us. You could hear it howling across town.

We'd broken the windows on both sides of the house, and Isager had left the door open behind him when he chased us, so now the wind rushed straight through the building, blowing through the burning straw in the bedroom. Flames began to lick the walls. We'd never seen fire like this before, and the sight of it sent shivers down our spines: so this was what a hungry fire looked like! Wilder and fiercer than we'd ever imagined, it shot straight through the roof and lit the house like a thousand tallow candles. Then it burst out of every opening.

Isager screamed, and we saw his fat wife stumble through the door. She slipped on the stairs and plonked down on her fat bottom. She stayed there, sobbing loudly and plaintively, like a child.

Isager ran over to her and thumped her with the stick, as if the calamity that had befallen them was her fault. Meanwhile Josef and Johan watched the scene as if it was no concern of theirs. Jørgen Albertsen, from the house across the street, came running.

Our group, which continued to grow, stood on the other side of Kirkestræde. We wanted to cheer loudly, but we knew it was definitely not a wise move, so we just whispered the Snaily Snaily rhyme, glancing furtively at one another and giggling.

Our tormentor had got his comeuppance.

The adults raced over with buckets full of water, but that made no difference at all, because the west wind was blowing in earnest now. And it wasn't just through Isager's house that it stormed like the devil, setting alight curtains, wallpaper, furniture, and the loft; no, it carried on. Flames jumped on the wind's back and rode it from Isager's house to Mr. Dreymann's house, from Mr. Dreymann's house to Mr. Kroman's.

Little Anders wasn't chanting the Snaily Snaily rhyme anymore: he was screaming. It was his house that had caught fire. He watched his mother rush out with the soup tureen of tin-glazed English earthenware, which was the finest thing they owned. Soon all of one side of Skolegade was ablaze. The snow began to fall again, but this had to be Satan's snow, for it fell black rather than white.

The fire didn't stop until it reached the corner of Tværgade. Here the streets were wider apart, and the houses on the other side had tiled roofs. But from the near side, glowing embers rained down on the cobbles, and anyone who ventured there came away with burn holes in their clothing. Meanwhile, all along Skolegade, smoke and flames whipped into the sky, like the lashing tail of a fiery dragon.

Finally, the fire engine arrived. The horses were neighing with fright; they'd never seen a real fire either. The heat prevented them from entering Skolegade, so the fire brigade left the engine on the corner by Tværgade and tried to stop the flames rampaging through the town. Meanwhile efforts to extinguish the fire in Skolegade had ground to a halt, though Levin Kroman had shouted at us to join in, and we had. But the heat was too intense. We couldn't get near the Isager house and could only press ourselves against the houses on the opposite side of the street, clutching our buckets, while we watched the mighty sea of flames through stinging eyes.

It never crossed our minds that we were the cause of this unimaginable thing. No: the fire itself was the cause. It had a force, a consuming purpose all its own. It had nothing to do with us.

Our hour had finally come. All our bitterness, fear, and hatred—passions too huge to stay contained in the narrow chests of children—had fueled this fire, whose flames had the awesome capacity to purge us of everything hateful or unnecessary. Entire houses had been turned into sooty carcasses by those flames, and tomorrow that would be a sad and terrible sight to see. But tonight it was a stupendous spectacle. That's what we felt: nothing more.

But a western wind always heralds rain. High above the flames the storm clouds burst, and a torrent of rain tipped down and drowned both the fire dragon and our joyful excitement.

The next morning we wandered around and inspected the remains of the burned-down houses. Skolegade was one huge scene of devastation. The walls were still standing: the empty windows gaped darkly, and the townsfolk gaped back. January 1 was a holiday. Men wore top hats and examined the damage with expert faces, as though they were assessors accustomed to major fires—even though almost forty years had passed since the last one. The women, including those who'd lost nothing, wore black shawls over their heads and wailed loudly. It seemed that fear had claimed the women of Marstal just as the fire had claimed the houses the night before. It was the same fear that the sea instilled in them, the fear of losing everything: brothers, fathers, and sons. But the fire had shown more mercy than the sea. It hadn't taken a single life.

In the midst of all this, we heard Mrs. Isager calling out for Karo. She seemed to forget that the dog was long gone. The other women spoke to her, but she shook her head and went on calling.

Though the lives of dogs and humans had been spared, many families had lost the things that help us through life, such as furniture and clothes and memories and kitchen utensils. The Albertsen family found a cast-iron pot that could still be used, and the Svanes unearthed a frying pan. The handle had burned away, but Laves Petersen, the carpenter, said he could make a new one.

The fire had started while we were bombarding Isager's house with clay pots. We did this every year and we were all—even those who had not taken part—punished for it annually. Since we never snitched on one another, we were all regarded as equally guilty. But this year there was no punishment—because set against the scale of the inferno, our clay-pot larks seemed like small beer. They were forgotten, and so were we. Isager had been in the street when the fire broke out and simply didn't connect us with what had happened. Unable to conceive that we might be responsible for such a disaster, he'd underestimated us. Likewise he was unaware of the wickedness he had sown in us. His stupidity was our protection.

In the days that followed, we learned that his fat wife had lost her reason. She kept wandering around, calling for Karo. She thought that the flames had scared him away, and she put his bowl out every day to entice him out of hiding.

"She's improved," Josef said. "She keeps forgetting to thump us."

THE FLAMES HADN'T touched the school, and the teacher's home was rebuilt. Before long, new houses had appeared on Skolegade. But at school, nothing had changed. Isager had been bedridden and fought off death. His house had burned down. And we, his pupils, were behind it all. But he kept coming back. We'd lost. It was hopeless.

Again we counted the remaining years on our fingers. Sooner or later we would be old enough to leave the school. That was the only hope we had.

Lorentz was confirmed and became apprenticed to the baker in Tværgade. Appropriate, we thought, given his obese, unmanly body. As he grew older it had become increasingly feminine: he'd developed breasts, and the Isager boys had once taken him out to the Tail and made him strip so they could see what a girl looked like. Then Josef had held Lorentz in a viselike grip while he twisted away at his fat, quivering flesh, and Johan, who was sensitive and cried greasy, waxy tears at every opportunity, had done things to Lorentz that afterward made them both shoot us knowing glances, as if they possessed a secret that we could share if we begged them hard enough. But we didn't want to know what it was. No. We didn't.

Lorentz worked for the baker in Tværgade at night, kneading dough. But he lasted only a few months. The clouds of flour next to the hot oven got into his lungs, he said, and he couldn't breathe properly. But that was a load of rubbish. He'd always had breathing trouble because he was fat, and he and his mother were to blame for that. He was an only child and she was a widow and she fed him from morning till night like a goose she was fattening for Christmas. No: the baker didn't want Lorentz because Lorentz was useless; all he could do was hunch his shoulders and wheeze. So Lorentz went to sea and came back that winter with a black eye. Hans Jørgen was right, he said. They hit you on board ship too. And again he gave us that pleading look, which asked, Can I be one of you now?

But we looked away, as we always did. Afterward we thought that he'd never stand a chance if he looked that way at the crew of the *Anne Marie Elisabeth*.

No one respects a weakling who crawls.

Hans Jørgen wasn't around to say "I told you so!" when Lorentz reported that they hit people on board ship too. He'd gone down with the *Johanne Karoline*, which vanished without a trace one autumn day in the Gulf of Bothnia.

The future that lay ahead of us consisted of more thrashings and death by drowning, and yet we longed for the sea. What did childhood mean to us? Being tied to life ashore and living in the shadow of Isager's rope. And life at sea? We had yet to learn the meaning of it, but a belief that nothing would ever change while we stayed on dry land took root in us. Isager was still Isager. His sons hated and feared him, and so did we. No one knew whether his wife hated and feared him too, but she'd stopped beating him up. She lived in a world of her own now. We'd robbed him of his dog, his house, and his wife's reason, but he remained unchanged. He thrashed us as he'd always done, and taught us nothing. We battled back as we'd always done, and learned nothing. We no longer persecuted him when he walked home on a winter's night after his two-finger toddy with Mr. Mathiesen, the grocer, or threw foul waste into his drawing room on New Year's Eve. But we still filled the inkwells with sand, blocked the stove, jumped out the windows, played hooky, and stole his books. Soon it would be Niels Peter scuffling with him on the floor, and one day it would be Albert.

Isager was immortal.

JUSTICE

WE KNEW THE ROPE. But now it was time to meet the sea.

Was it true, as Hans Jørgen had said, that the thrashing would never stop?

Laurids Madsen had once told Albert about punishment on board the *Neversink*, the naval frigate on which any wretch who transgressed was tied to the mast and whipped till he bled. They beat seven kinds of shit out of him, Laurids said. It was not an expression we were familiar with, but Laurids told us it was American. "Seven kinds of shit": we couldn't help but think that the world beyond our island was like that. The great America was like that. They had more of everything—shit included. We'd never noticed much variety when it came to our own shit. The color might change, and the texture might be either on the runny or on the lumpy side, but shit was shit, wasn't it? We ate everything—cod, mackerel, herring, sweetened gruel, pork sausage and vegetable soup, cabbage—and we knew of only one basic type of shit. So this was what the wide world would do for us. It would change our diet, so we'd be eating deep-sea monsters that our local fishermen never caught: squid, shark, jolly jumpers, bright coral-reef fish; and fruits unknown to our farmers, like bananas, oranges, peaches, mangoes, and papayas; curry from India, noodles from China, flying fish in coconut milk, snake meat and monkey brains. And when they thrashed us, we too would shit seven kinds of shit.

But in those days we mainly sailed grain to the German and Russian ports on the Baltic Sea, calling at Norway and Sweden for timber. No foreign spices, strange fish, or new fruits for us: peas, porridge, salt cod, and sweetened sago soup with barley dumplings and prunes were our daily fare. All our sauces and soups contained syrup as well as vinegar, the sweet with the sour, but we struggled to find the sweet side to life at sea. And when we were beaten, the same kind of shit still came out of us.

We said goodbye to our mothers. They'd been around all our lives, but we'd never properly seen them. They'd been bent over washing tubs or cooking pots, their faces red and swollen from heat and steam, holding everything together while our fathers were away at sea, and nodding off every night on the kitchen chair, with a darning needle in hand. It was their endurance and exhaustion we knew, rather than them. And we never asked them for anything because we didn't want to bother them.

That was how we showed our love: with silence.

Their eyes were always red. In the morning, when they woke us up, it was from stove smoke. And in the evening, when they said good night to us, still dressed, it was from exhaustion. And sometimes it was from crying over someone who would never come home again. Ask us about the color of a mother's eyes, and we'd reply, "They're not brown. They aren't green. They're neither blue nor gray. They're red." That's what we'd say.

And now they've come down alongside the wharf to say goodbye. But between us, there's silence. Their eyes pierce us.

"Come back," their stare pleads. "Don't leave us."

But we won't be coming back. We want out. We want to get away. Our mother sticks a knife in our heart when we say goodbye on the wharf. And we stick a knife in hers when we go. And that's how we're connected: through the hurt we inflict on one another.

Some elements of our new life we'd already learned at home. We knew how to splice a rope's end and strike knots. We could climb the rigging, and the height of a mast didn't scare us. We knew our way around a ship. But we'd stood on the deck only in the harbor, in winter. We had yet to learn how big the ocean is, and how tiny a ship can feel.

We started out as cooks.

"Here," the skipper said, shoving a tarnished copper pot at us.

This pot was the entire equipment of our galley, and in those days the galley was nothing but a clay stove in the fo'c'sle, with a flue made of four boards nailed together, poking up through a hole in the deck. When it rained, the water swept inside, and in stormy weather, when the waves washed over the deck, seawater would cascade down and put out the fire; there were times when we were up to our knees in water. The slightest wind caused the ship to pitch, and then we had to hold the pot in place to stop it from sliding across the floor; we pulled down the cuffs of our sleeves to protect our fingers from the hot handles and watched the sago soup with smoke-stung eyes. Nothing we did was ever good enough. Someone had to be the whipping boy on a ship, and if there wasn't a dog on board, then it was us.

We were roused at four in the morning and had to be ready with coffee at any point during the day. There'd be time for only a quick nap between any two cups, and then a kick would wake us: "Damn it to hell, you sleeping again, boy?"

We never had a single hour ashore to visit the towns where we loaded and unloaded. After a year at sea we'd been to Trondheim, Stavanger, Kalmar, Varberg, Königsberg, Wismar, Lübeck, Antwerp, Grimsby, and Hull. We saw rocky coastlines, fields and woods, towers and church spires—but we came no closer to them than to castles in the air. The only land we ever felt under our feet was near the wharf, and the only buildings we entered were warehouses. The wide world we'd come to know consisted of the ship's deck, the smoky cabin, and the permanently damp berths.

Every night when we were in port, we had to wait until after midnight for the skipper, just to pull his boots off.

"Are you there, boy?" he'd say in a thick voice as he sat down on the berth, blotchy and panting, with his legs outstretched.

It was not until then that we could turn in—only to be roused a few hours later.

We met every winter, when the ships came home to wait for spring and waters free of ice.

"Do you remember what Hans Jørgen said?" Niels Peter asked. "That the most important thing Isager taught us was to take a beating?"

"He should have taught us how to keep awake," Josef said.

He was Isager's son, but he'd gone to sea anyway, while Johan had stayed home to take care of his mother—who since the fire had taken to wandering the fields dressed in rags and calling out for Karo. He was hoping to become a schoolteacher like his father.

We nodded in agreement. This was roughly the sum of our experiences during our first year at sea: beatings and the never-ending night vigils.

"The coffee ran out," Albert said. He had sailed on the cutter *Catrine* for a year. "I was given a quarter pound. It was supposed to last three men for seven days, and the skipper said it had to be strong, and they were always shouting at me because it was too weak. But I got my own back in the end."

"What did you do?" Niels Peter asked. He'd sailed a year longer than Albert and was still wrestling with the coffee problem.

"We've got plenty of dried peas, so I burned some and mixed them in with it, and the skipper said, 'That's a fine cup of strong coffee; this will keep a man on his feet,' but then he and the second mate got the bellyache, and that's how they found out. I used four measures of peas to one of coffee, but I never told them that. Anyway, then I had to come up with something else, so I burned a pot of rye instead. And now I'm getting praise for my strong coffee."

"We always get the blame," Josef said, "when the porridge is burned or the peas won't soften or the rye bread goes moldy."

"My skipper thinks I should eat the food if it's spoiled. 'Eat that moldy bread,' he goes to me one day. 'Swallow those raw peas.' And I said to him, 'No, I'm not some pig that you can just throw any old swill at.'"

Albert straightened his back. We could tell that he was proud of his reply, but we knew what it would have cost him.

"So what happened?"

"I got no breakfast or dinner for two days."

Lorentz turned up. Johan stepped back and stared at the cobbles, but Josef sent him a challenging look, which Lorentz returned: his days of sucking up to us were gone. He was still huge, but there was a strength to his bulk that hadn't been there before. We had never fantasized about his fat white body the way we'd fantasize about women, though a warm tickling had gone through us when we thrashed his soft flesh. If you were to hit him now, you'd damage your knuckles.

He said nothing, and we retreated a step. Did his balls finally drop, once he'd climbed the rigging of the *Anne Marie Elisabeth*?

Albert sailed another two years on the *Catrine*. He landed at Flekkefjord, Tønsberg, Fredrikstad, Gothenburg, Riga, Stralsund, Hamburg, Rotterdam, Hartlepool, and Kirkcaldy—and saw nothing. So he signed off. He wanted to get away from the copper pot and the coffee war. The sea was ever-changing, and yet it left him with an impression of sameness. In the autumn he saw it congeal beneath low-hanging layers of stratocumulus cloud. The water moved sluggishly, like liquid mercury. The temperature fell, and when winter announced itself, he saw his own life reflected in the slowly freezing surface of the water.

The clouds above the frozen sea changed, but he was already familiar with them all. There was plenty for the eye to feast on, but nothing for the soul. He had a hunger for something that no sky could satisfy. Somewhere on the planet there had to be a different kind of light. A sea that mirrored new constellations. A bigger moon. A hotter sun.

The skipper offered to sign him on as an ordinary seaman.

"You're a sailor now," he said one night in Stubbekøbing, as Albert helped him pull off his boots. "You can fix a flying jib and a topsail. You know the compass and you can sail by the wind and run before it."

But instead, Albert did as his father before him: he went to Hamburg to find a ship that would take him farther out into the world.

Before he left, he went up into the loft at home. Here, among the sacks of potatoes and grain, sat the sea boots his father, Laurids, had abandoned when he left home for the last time. That had been an omen: they'd realized it later. In stormy weather, when the roof shook and the gable quaked, Albert's mother thought she could hear the empty boots stomping about up there on their own. But no one ever dared go up and look.

Rasmus and Esben had never touched the boots. Out of fear, perhaps—or simply because they'd never matched their father's considerable height and their feet weren't big enough. Only Albert took after Laurids.

He came down the stairs holding the boots, their wooden soles still scorched from Laurids's famous trip to Heaven.

"What are you doing with those?" his mother asked. Her eyes were anxious, as though she both hoped and dreaded he'd be throwing them out.

"I want to wear them," said Albert.

"You mustn't!"

Her hand flew to her mouth. Did she fear that bad luck would follow him if he put them on? Was it superstition or premonition? It was hard to tell. There was a mother's worry, certainly. Perhaps she sensed that this time he would be going far, and would be gone many years. Which for her was the same as death.

"I'm going to" was all he said.

He had to stoop now to walk through the doorway, and his shoulders filled it.

"You promised my father to make them like new again," he said, when he arrived at the workshop of Mr. Jakobsen, the cobbler, in Kongegade.

"That was twelve years ago. You've got a good memory," Jakobsen said. "But a promise is a promise. You can pick them up on Saturday."

Albert worked seven months as an ordinary seaman on board a Hamburg brig that sailed to the West Indies. He saw palm beaches and flying fish. He saw people whose skin was black and brown. He saw the cowed look in their eyes and their bowed backs and needed no one to tell him that that they knew the thrashing rope. Men like Isager weren't schoolteachers here. They were rulers of these sunny isles, including those where Danish was spoken, and they all ruled by the rope.

He drank coconut milk and ate alligator meat, which tasted like chicken. He shat seven kinds of shit, but none of it was beaten out of him.

He'd escaped.

"It never stops" was what Hans Jørgen had said. But it does. When you become an able seaman, when you're seventeen years old and big and strong enough to defend yourself, then it stops. Albert watched the black and brown men who loaded and unloaded the brig. They didn't have ownership of themselves, and they were forever in thrall to the rope. He wondered what would have happened if he'd been born one of them, to be flayed all the way to the grave. Would he have broken eventually? Or would he have looked for someone he could pass his humiliation on to, just so that he could feel vaguely human? Would he have found a dog to kill, a house to burn down, a woman to drive mad?

When we met every winter in Marstal, we sized up one another. We were becoming men. Our eyes seemed deeper-set, and our cheekbones jutted: it was as if the beatings we'd suffered over time had led to something permanent. Our hands had grown big, our palms were tough, our biceps bulged, and sinews and veins fought for space on our forearms beneath the blue spider webs of tattoos. We'd grown bigger and stronger, to spite the rope.

Albert didn't come home. He returned to Hamburg and left again, this time for South America. On his return, he signed off in Antwerp and joined a Liverpudlian bark going to Cardiff to load coal. He wanted to learn English.

When the bosun yelled, *"All hands up anchor!"* and *"Heave, my hearties, heave hard!"* he heard his father's voice, and felt his *papa tru* close by him once more. He remembered the American words that had so irritated his mother and so delighted him and his brothers.

"Hanggre," he said in the mess.

They shook their heads and laughed at him.

"Monki," they said.

It was a good while before he realized that his *papa tru* hadn't been speaking American but pidgin, the Chinese and Kanak version of English. That was what his *papa tru* had taught him. Pidgin English: the language of cannibals.

Albert crossed the equator and was baptized, as his *papa tru* had been before him. They forced him to kiss the ocher-colored Amphitrite, from whose pockmarked cheeks sharp nails protruded. They covered him in tallow and lamp soot, and mermaids and nigger boys held him underwater until his lungs were close to bursting. They shaved him with a rusty razor and gave him a scar that he hid under a beard from then on.

He learned a song that he sang to us for many years. He said it was the truest song ever written about the sea:

> Shave him and bash him,
> Duck him and splash him,
> Torture him and smash him,
> And don't let him go!

He sailed south around Cape Horn, where he heard penguins squawk in the pitch-black night and was finally made able seaman. He called at Callao and Lobos, the guano island, just south of the equator. He sailed back to Europe and signed on to a three-masted Nova Scotian full-rigged ship headed for New York. There he went ashore, looking for a job on an American vessel, where the wages would be higher. Perhaps *papa tru*'s dreams of America haunted him.

But it wasn't his *papa tru* he met on board the *Emma C. Leithfield*. It was something else: Isager and his rope, all over again. And this time the battle would have to be settled.

Later, he told us that he would never forget the moment he first set foot on deck.

But, we asked him, had he really not heard about conditions on board American ships? Didn't he know that the crews would often mutiny, and that first mates were chosen not for their sea skills, but for their physical strength and their fighting prowess? And that the fist or the revolver gave the orders more often than the captain? Had he not known this?

Albert looked away and chuckled a little, as if deep down he had known, but couldn't bring himself to admit it.

He looked us in the eye.

"No," he said, "I didn't know it could be that bad. It was ten months in hell. I'd been there before. But finding the exit was one thing that blasted Isager never taught us."

THERE WERE SEVENTEEN men before the mast of the *Emma C. Leithfield*, of whom six were Scandinavians—and in Albert's opinion, the only decent sailors on board. It didn't seem odd to us that he felt this way because we always prefer our own. But he based his opinion on a single observation: they were the only ones who didn't keel over when they boarded the ship.

When the launch brought the newly shanghaied sailors alongside the *Emma*, a bunch of dead-drunk Frenchmen had to be forcibly shoved onto the deck, an operation performed by two brutal-looking crimps—land sharks in cahoots with a boardinghouse, where the Frenchmen had already been relieved of their cash. A party of boozy Italians and Greeks followed, while a third boat brought some drunken English and Welsh. Each sailor bore under his arm a small parcel of clothes. That was all he owned. Their hair was unkempt, their faces scarred, and half-empty bottles of whiskey poked out of their pockets. They may have jabbered and shouted in a chaos of languages, but they all came from the same place. They were the dregs of every port on God's earth.

They were all incapable of doing any work that day. They stared at the anchor chains but clearly hadn't the slightest idea where they led, and after gazing up at the rigging and grinning dizzily, they simply staggered to their quarters. Disappearing down the ladder to the fo'c'sle, they threw themselves on their berths or on the bare floor, where they fell asleep, snoring.

Captain Eagleton was a young man with bushy whiskers and shifty eyes. As soon as he ordered Albert down to the sleeping quarters to bring back the men's half-empty whiskey bottles and throw them overboard, Albert knew he'd never gain the crew's respect. Eagleton should have thrown out the whiskey himself, and in front of the whole crew, rather than behind their backs while they slept it off: it was obvious. Albert eyed the bottles as they bobbed up and down on the waves. He'd already noticed the big solid armchair bolted to the deck, like the throne of an absent king. Albert knew enough about seamen to recognize Eagleton as the type who'd stay clear of the deck and isolate himself from the crew, so it wouldn't be his. It might belong to the first mate, he speculated, but for now there was no way of telling, as the man had yet to make an appearance.

Meanwhile a terrible racket had started in the fo'c'sle and the captain ordered Albert to investigate. From out of the darkness came angry shouting.

"You've nicked my whiskey, you bloody dog," yelled an English voice.

A reply came in Italian, followed by another in a language that could have been Greek. In between were sentences that contained a few words Albert recognized, but he couldn't work out their meaning. These men had lived in international crews for so many years that they now all spoke a tongue straight out of Babel.

One thing was clear: the fight was over the missing whiskey. Albert heard the sound of a blow and then of a body crashing into a bulkhead. Glancing down the hatch, he saw a knife flash in someone's hand; it was followed by groaning and the kind of labored breathing you hear when men are raising the anchor. But it was something else they were hauling up. It was dark and terrifying and it came from the depths within.

Though Albert was still safe on the deck, he took a few steps back. There was nothing he could do down in that dark hole, and the brawl would eventually exhaust itself. He'd seen fights like that before, and they rarely ended in a killing. The men would emerge from the fo'c'sle the next day, bruised and cut and severely hung over, and begin work, mute and reluctant, with bloodshot eyes. Today they were animals. But tomorrow they'd be sailors again.

It wasn't the savagery down in the fo'c'sle that worried him. It was the captain's lack of authority.

"Out of the way!"

Someone grabbed Albert's shoulder and shoved him violently aside; he turned to see a monster of a man towering over him. His face was dominated by a bulbous red nose and disfigured by scars that crisscrossed it as if his head were a pumpkin someone had slashed at.

Half-drowned in this mass of battered flesh sat his eyes, their pupils like black stones on the bottom of a deep lake. Underneath a filthy, torn shirt, his vast muscular body too was riven with scars, as though someone had gone for the giant's heart with a sharp knife but given up—it would be like trying to stab a steam train.

Albert instantly understood who was standing in front of him. This was the man to whom the throne belonged, the true ruler of the ship.

The first mate had made his appearance.

The giant didn't use the ladder but jumped straight down into the fo'c'sle, his huge body tumbling directly into the midst of the brawling men. There came another crash and some roaring from below, and the tumult intensified, with intermingled howls and groans of pain, the thudding of punches, and a strange whimpering that seemed quite unrelated to fighting. It went on for a while before starting to subside, until only one voice—that of the first mate—could be heard.

"Have you had enough? Have you had enough then?"

More of that whimpering sound. Then the thud of a few more blows—or were they kicks? Then silence.

The first mate emerged from the fo'c'sle, panting. He'd acquired the makings of a few more scars down there in the darkness. There was a deep cut to his forehead, and blood ran from his neck, but he wiped his face absent-mindedly, as if the blood that welled in one dense eyebrow was no more inconvenient to him than sweat.

Albert hadn't shifted from the spot where the giant had first thrust him, but now he was swept aside once more, as the bleeding first mate shoved past him again to scrutinize the rest of the crew, as if contemplating how to continue the punishment he'd begun below deck.

"The name's O'Connor."

At this, the men on deck nodded as if responding to an order.

O'Connor went to his throne, sat down heavily, and belched. The blood that he'd smeared across his forehead gave him the look of a heathen idol that demands nothing but human sacrifices. Albert wondered if O'Connor would call for soap and water to clean his injuries, but he just sat there while the blood congealed, as though his scars were tattoos and he'd just added fresh details to the gruesome work of art that was his face and body.

Then he gave a sudden whistle, and a long-haired black monster of a dog that no one had seen before padded over with the skulking gait of a wolf and hunkered down at his feet. Pulling a heavy-caliber revolver out of the pocket of his nankeens, O'Connor started spinning the barrel pensively.

That night Albert ventured down to the fo'c'sle, but he soon came back up again. By the glimmer of his tallow dip he'd seen men lying on the floor in oddly contorted positions, while a few sat on benches, cradling their heads in their hands. He couldn't tell whether they were sleeping. But there was blood on the bulkhead, and vomit covered the floor. He'd prefer to sleep on deck.

The next morning the men emerged, bearing the traces of yesterday's brawl. Some were limping while others moved about slowly and deliberately, as if their bodies ached beneath their clothes. Their faces were bloated, with livid swellings around the eyes. One man had a broken nose — though its shape suggested it wasn't his first. These were tough men, used to beatings and the aftereffects of prolonged drinking — men who could take practically any treatment without complaining. But they wore an expression you rarely see in a sailor. They looked cowed. They didn't so much as glance at one another and never lifted their eyes to O'Connor when he roared his orders. Instead they stared at their hands or let their eyes drift toward the rigging.

There was a proper cook on board the *Emma C. Leithfield* — and we understood Albert well when he pointed out the difference between a proper one and the kind we'd been on the Marstal cutters, when we'd all started out as galley boys, barely mastering any cooking skills beyond steadying the water pot in a storm to ensure the supply of hot coffee and satisfying the appetites of men more interested in filling their bellies than in the pleasures of the palate.

But Giovanni, said Albert, was nothing like that. He was an Italian and he made sure that every day, both fore and aft, there was freshly baked bread, a hot lunch and dinner, and plenty of pies and pastries. We ate better than at the best boardinghouse: not even Frau Palle in Kastanien Allée in Hamburg could compete with Giovanni.

All told, the *Emma C. Leithfield* was an odd ship. Despite the men's linguistic differences, they understood one another well enough to agree that of all the vessels of the American merchant navy, the *Emma* had the worst first mate and the best cook. The galley was heaven, and the deck was hell.

· · ·

Giovanni was the last man to board, but he didn't arrive alone: with him came two suckling pigs, ten hens, and a small calf, for which he built a pen on the foredeck. O'Connor's dog grew restless and left his place at his master's feet to roam, with its huge jaw hanging open and a hungry look in its eyes. Spotting the dog, Giovanni stepped right up to the beast, which bared its teeth and growled menacingly: it seemed to think the whole ship was its territory. But Giovanni stared straight into its eyes and slowly raised his hands—not to strike it, but to explain. Hypnotized, the dog lay down on its belly and whined pitifully, before starting to shuffle backward. The sight of the ferocious monster, its belly to the floor, backing off from the small, agile man, was so funny that the sailors watching the incident started laughing.

O'Connor saw it too. But he didn't laugh.

O'Connor never ate with the other officers. Instead, he sat on his throne on deck and had his food brought to him there. The weather never bothered him; his body seemed immune to everything. He never changed clothes, but always wore the same tattered shirt, barely covered by a waistcoat with no buttons and ripped buttonholes. By day, only a blizzard or a hailstorm could budge him out of the chair, while at night, they said he slept in another chair, bolted to the floor of a cabin that stank like a wild animal's lair. He was always on guard. Word had it that he kept his muscles tensed even while he was asleep.

When Giovanni brought him his food the next day, instead of placing the plate on his own lap, O'Connor lay it on the deck and signaled to the dog, which immediately came and wolfed down the whole beautifully presented meal. All the while O'Connor kept his eyes fixed on Giovanni, and Giovanni met his stare. He was no more afraid of O'Connor than he was of the dog. He could control the animal with one simple gesture. But O'Connor was beyond his control—and he'd acquired a mortal enemy.

And that's how he first came among us.

The next day Giovanni brought O'Connor his food in a dog bowl and placed it on the deck at the first mate's feet.

"Enjoy your food," he said, and turned to leave.

"Where's my dinner?"

O'Connor's voice was low and menacing.

"There." Giovanni pointed to the bowl. "If I were you, I'd hurry up before the dog gets to it."

In that moment, he sealed his fate.

Giovanni was far more than a mere cook. When a ship is at anchor in New York, it's not just tailors, shoemakers, butchers, ship's chandlers, and fruit sellers who come on board—all those practical men no ship can do without before she sets sail. No, along with them comes a motley crew of fences, offering false gold rings and pocket watches that stop at the slightest knock; tattoo artists with filthy needles whose every tattoo becomes a weeping infection; beggars and magicians; jugglers, fakirs, and fortunetellers; procurers, pimps, and thieves. Giovanni, standing on the deck with a red bandana around his ink-black hair, juggling four eggs at a time without dropping a single one, seemed more at home with this crowd than with the crew of the *Emma C. Leithfield*.

No one had the faintest idea how he'd ended up at sea, but he'd begun as a circus performer. He'd been a knife thrower as well as a juggler, and sometimes when we were off duty we'd linger in the doorway and watch him practice. He could juggle three or four sharpened knives until they whirled about in a deadly spinning wheel. He never dropped one, he never missed a catch, and he never cut himself.

"Giovanni's setting the table," someone would shout on deck, and the crew would rush to the mess to grab a front-row view as he set the table without moving a single inch from where he stood. Knives, forks, and tin plates would fly through the air—and land exactly in the right spot, right next to each other. It set his audience dizzy with excitement. He never broke anything—but no one could understand how.

"How do you do it, Giovanni?"

He smiled and shook his head. There were no secrets. "It's all in the wrists," he said, flexing them.

The men winked at one another. They were proud of their cook. With the whiskey thrown overboard and the ship at sea, it was Giovanni who got them straightening their backs and going about their work feeling like a crew.

It was a fortnight since they'd left New York. The *Emma C. Leithfield* had just passed the equator, heading for Buenos Aires, and the men were admiring Giovanni as usual when O'Connor suddenly appeared.

The cook was busy setting the table, and the plates were sailing accurately through the air en route to their destinations, when O'Connor stuck out his giant fist and intercepted one, sending it crashing to the floor. Tin plates don't break, but the effect of O'Connor's sabotage was greater than if it had smashed into a thousand pieces.

Giovanni's reaction was instant. When he performed, he was at once focused and dreamy. But now, his expression switched to something new: wariness. When O'Connor's fist came at him, he dodged it with the same lightning agility with which he threw cutlery and plates, and O'Connor's fist, which would have turned his narrow, delicate-featured face into a bloody mess, slammed into the bulkhead, with an ugly crunch. When he regained his balance, his knuckles were bloody.

Giovanni stood his ground, his face showing not hostility, fear, anger, or panic, but the concentration of an acrobat high in the circus tent, preparing for a tricky jump, with no safety net. And when O'Connor lashed out again, he ducked with the same accuracy as before.

O'Connor stumbled forward as if he'd lost his balance. But those playing close attention sensed something was up. His eyes, narrowed to slits in his swollen, scarred face, bore a calm chill, which indicated the stumble was premeditated.

Giovanni leapt to one side and out of the path of the toppling giant. But instead of thrusting his hands out to break his fall, O'Connor flung out an arm and grabbed the little Italian, pulling him down to the deck. Guessing that O'Connor would straddle Giovanni and beat him up, the men began crowding in to pull him away. But the two fallen men just lay next to each other for a moment, motionless—until Giovanni uttered a sudden cry of pain and clasped his wrist. His hand was dangling from it in an odd way. It was all limp. O'Connor had snapped it with a single quick twist of his strong hand.

Calmly the first mate got up. Standing next to his victim, he fixed the men hard with his eyes. Then, without even looking down, he raised his foot and stomped his boot down on Giovanni's injured hand. They heard the sound of his fingers break.

When O'Connor walked away from the mess, the men stepped aside for him. But if they'd had one of Giovanni's sharp kitchen knives, they'd have buried it in his back, deep enough to prick his rotten heart and extinguish the hellfire that burned inside.

They flocked around Giovanni and helped him to his feet. He was still clutching his ruined hand, and the tears rolled down his cheeks. It wasn't the pain that made him weep, but the loss of his ability. They looked at his broken fingers, which stuck out at unnatural angles. They'd seen enough accidents on board to know that he'd never use that hand again. Minutes earlier, he'd been an artist. Now he was barely a man.

The men took him to Captain Eagleton, who had the hand bandaged. Much good that would do. Even a doctor couldn't have saved it. And when they protested about what had happened to Giovanni, Captain Eagleton looked the other way, as if it had nothing to do with him.

"O'Connor," he said, "has his reasons."

And that was all he'd say on the matter.

Giovanni had turned the men into a united crew. But O'Connor wanted the opposite of solidarity: he wanted each one of them to face him alone. Not because he lacked the strength to beat up more than one of them at a time, but because he knew they feared him most when they had no one to share their fear with.

The captain had lied when he said that O'Connor always had his reasons. And the lie was a huge one. Nothing O'Connor did had a reason. He hit and punched and broke men's bones for the pleasure of it, rather than as punishment for anything they'd done. He toyed with them as a god toys with his worshipers, leaving them to reason their own suffering. It was this unpredictability that turned him into a monster. Whatever his dark motivation was, expressed in his hatred of everything that stirred on board, it lay deep within him. The men ducked, or tried to make themselves small and invisible, in order to escape his motiveless malice—but that wasn't always enough. His eye worked like a falcon's, searching for mice in the wheat.

They had nowhere to hide. What place of safety is there for those who live under the thumb of an all-powerful ruler? What choice but to do everything correctly and second-guess his slightest whim?

"What did Giovanni do wrong, apart from being the best cook who ever sailed, the best juggler who ever wasted his talent on a drunken and thick-headed crew? Apart from making each of us a better man than the Lord ever planned? What did he do to deserve a broken hand? What offense was he being punished for?" Albert asked.

. . .

A boy by the name of Isaiah had to take charge of the galley. He was from America and fourteen years old, with black skin that was so shiny and smooth, it looked permanently wet. When he lit the fire in the morning, his dark cheeks reflected the oven's glowing embers. He did his best. But gone were the fresh-baked bread, pies, and cakes.

Giovanni had been sitting in the fo'c'sle for some days, staring at his bandages in the half-light. Despite all that had happened, he'd not been broken. Soon he reappeared on deck, entered the galley, and started bossing Isaiah around. Then his left hand woke up. It was, after all, the hand of a performer, and was just as deft as his right. He might be only half a man, but he was still more capable than most whole ones. Soon the plates were sailing across the table again. But there was a new air of defiance about him. He knew he was playing a dangerous game. His eyes shone. The crew guarded him, ready to defend him, though they were more terrified than he was.

But the falcon always spots his chance.

It was when Giovanni was briefly alone with Isaiah that O'Connor attacked him next. They came running at the sound of his screams—but it was too late. O'Connor had got hold of his left hand. Giovanni grabbed a knife with his right, but the pathetic bundle of broken fingers had lost all its strength and precision and he could barely lift it. He knew he was fighting for his life, and all he could manage was a scratch across O'Connor's chest.

How desperate Giovanni must have been to use the knife like that. When the men in the fo'c'sle had encouraged him to take his revenge and promised to cover for him—and yes, even take the blame themselves—he'd replied, "I'm a knife thrower, not a murderer."

The plates sailing across the table again, the reawakening of our taste buds: those had been Giovanni's revenge. Only now he'd gone for the knife. Isaiah said later that he'd seen tears in the artist's eyes as he clutched the weapon in his damaged hand—as if in that moment, forced to share the coarse language of his enemy, his honor was lost.

O'Connor laughed and offered up his chest.

"Come on," he snarled.

But Giovanni put the knife down on the table.

When they got there it was too late. The killing blow had been struck.

. . .

Wrapped in sailcloth, Giovanni's body was swallowed by the sea the same day. Captain Eagleton wasn't present at the funeral. O'Connor represented him. The crew suspected he'd turned up only to relish his meaningless triumph.

Isaiah arrived with a shovelful of ash from the galley.

"Ashes to ashes, dust to dust," the cook's boy said, and scattered the ashes over Giovanni's body as it lay on the deck in its sailor's shroud.

At that very moment, a gust of wind came like an avenging hand and flung the ash right into O'Connor's maimed face, where it settled into every line and crack, including the slits of his eyes. It burned and stung. He roared and thrashed about as if a real enemy had attacked him, and the men scattered: nobody wanted to be hit by the random flailing of his fists. From a distance they saw him commit a final act of sacrilege against the deceased as, cursing and shouting, he lifted Giovanni's frail corpse from the deck and tossed it over the rail like a piece of rubbish.

They were watching the funeral of a mutineer. That, at least, was the message that Captain Eagleton passed on to them.

But below deck, they plotted O'Connor's death.

Everyone volunteered for the job. No one had any scruples when it came to killing O'Connor. If they hadn't all been hardened men when they signed on to the *Emma C. Leithfield,* they were now. They'd been abused daily, and there wasn't one of them who didn't bear the mark of the first mate's fist. He even beat his fellow officers. The second mate, a Swede by the name of Gustafsson, went around with a closed-up eye that might never regain its sight.

With no rule of law on board the *Emma C. Leithfield,* they'd have to create one themselves. It wasn't mutiny: it was justice.

Their only concern was technical. How to do it?

O'Connor was stronger than any of them: they'd learned that much. They'd never defeat him in an open fight. But the thought of their own weakness merely added fuel to their anger.

"When he's asleep," said a Greek who went by the name of Dimitros.

Could that be the answer? They exchanged glances. There were two problems. The first was the loaded gun that O'Connor always carried, and the second was the dog. When the first mate dozed in his chair on deck, the dog always lay at his feet, and the minute anyone approached, it raised its massive head and growled menacingly. No one could figure out how to get close to O'Connor without waking the dog first. At this point their rebellion began to crumble. They discussed the dog at length, but it wasn't really the dog they were scared of. The revolver, then?

No. It was simply O'Connor.

Even without his dog and his gun, he seemed invincible. What terrified them most was whatever went on inside that scarred, pumpkin-like head of his. They could never confess that openly, though. After all, they were seventeen against one. They sat in silence, some of them staring at the table, others at the bulkhead.

It was Albert who broke the silence. "Anyway, isn't it wrong to kill another human being?"

They stared at him as though the idea had never crossed their minds. And perhaps in some cases it hadn't. They knew very little about one another's past, but they also knew that anything could happen in port or out at sea. A man's drowning wasn't always an accident—and O'Connor may not have been the only unpunished killer on board the *Emma C. Leithfield*.

"Would Giovanni have wanted to be avenged like that?" Albert continued.

"I don't care what Giovanni would have wanted," said the Welsh seaman Rhys Llewellyn, surveying the hairy hands folded in his lap. The first mate had given him a bruise on one cheek—and it was a greeting he dreamt of returning. "I'm speaking for myself," he added, looking around the group. "But I'm thinking about us too. It's him or us. It's not revenge. It's survival."

The others muttered their approval.

"Giovanni didn't want to pull the knife," Isaiah said. "I saw him put it down again."

His voice was hesitant, and we could hear him breathing between the words. He was only fourteen, and it took courage to speak up in a gathering of men who were senior to him in rank and age. "Do you remember that he said he was a knife thrower and not a murderer? Are we murderers?"

"Shut up, you black dog!" retorted the Welshman.

"No, I won't!" The words erupted unexpectedly. Isaiah had found his courage now. He'd spoken out, and the damage was done. "I get beaten by him just like you. So I've got a right to speak. And I don't think we should kill him."

"The boy's right," Albert said. "We don't want to become like him. He's just waiting for us to become as desperate as Giovanni and pull a knife on him, because that's the game he plays. It's what he wants. Do you think he's stupid? At this very moment he's probably hoping that we're plotting to kill him because then he's got us. Do we really want to be like him?"

They mumbled and looked down again. Undoubtedly some of them did want to be like O'Connor. But they never could be. They'd have to find other ways of matching his power.

"I think I know how we can win, but it'll take patience," Albert said. And he laid out his plan.

At first they didn't understand what he meant.

"It can't be done" was the universal message—uttered in almost as many languages as there were men. No matter where they came from, none of the sailors had ever seen justice dealt in the way Albert proposed. The idea wasn't just unfamiliar; it flew in the face of all experience.

"But this is America," Albert kept repeating.

"It's not America, it's a ship," they said. "And a ship has its own rules."

But Albert dug in his heels and refused to back down. Every time he refuted one of their objections, they saw his certainty grow. And every time he spoke, he finished with the same question: "Does anybody else have a better idea?"

No one did, apart from killing O'Connor—and in their hearts they knew they couldn't. They didn't have the courage, either individually or together.

So what was that strange, indefinable imperative that finally made them change their minds and agree to Albert's proposal? Might it be conscience? It was. But it was so mixed up with other things, like fear, and deviousness, and caution, and the clannishness of men in a pack, that in the end no one particular urge could be singled out. "So to simplify it, we'll just call it conscience," Albert always said when he told the story later.

They'd sailed for eight months with O'Connor by the time they called at St. Iago in the West Indies to load sugar for New York. There'd been no shortage of opportunities to jump ship, but the crew had resisted because if they deserted, their plan would never bear fruit and their suffering would have been in vain. The real test of their strength would come here in St. Iago. It would have nothing to do with muscle power—a commodity that had long been tried and tested and whose shortcomings were daily confirmed when they endured O'Connor's violence. But they stuck it out and began to look at O'Connor with an increasing boldness. For they'd discovered a force that the brutal first mate knew nothing of. Its name was fortitude.

The more experienced among them had already figured out that this was the place where Captain Eagleton would try to make them jump ship. They'd been through this before on other vessels. When a voyage nears its end, a bad captain will treat his crew so atrociously that they'll throw in the towel. And invariably, once they're branded as deserters, they'll forfeit their unpaid wages—thus increasing the profits of the trip. And so it was on the *Emma C. Leithfield*. First of all, O'Connor reduced their water rations while they sweated in the tropical heat. And then the provisions grew scarce too. Isaiah had picked up some cooking skills since Giovanni was murdered in his own galley, but now his limited knowledge was entirely superfluous: the crew's daily rations dwindled to three small ship's biscuits per man, while on Saturdays they were given rice and a single piece of salt meat. Their stomachs screamed for food. O'Connor's dog ate better than they did. The whole strategy was so damn clever. So devilishly, fiendishly cunning. You spend eight months with a brutal and malicious jailer, and then he opens the door to your cell.

Yet they refused to come out. They still had a score to settle with him. But oh, how they longed to escape from his brooding presence and from their own terror.

They stayed because they had a plan. They stayed.

Faint with hunger and thirst, they scrubbed the deck and the deckhouse with sand and stones under the tropical sun. They were roused from bed a full hour before any of the crews of the other ships anchored in St. Iago, and couldn't turn in until long after the rest of the port was asleep. Shaded by an outstretched sail, O'Connor sat in his chair, with a loaded revolver in his hand and the huge hound at his feet. But he wasn't there to ensure they worked hard. Indeed, if one of the men had left the murderously hot deck, bolted for the gangway, and rowed himself ashore, he wouldn't have lifted a finger to stop him. Instead he'd have grinned in raw triumph and wished him a fair wind.

When the washee-washee girls sailed by in their canoes, with their pinned-up hair, bare shoulders, and flared dresses, calling out flirtatiously, "We're coming on board!" O'Connor rose and threatened them off with his revolver.

The battle of wills weighed the men down, and they became more exhausted, silent, and emaciated with each day that passed. But by now, the sum total of their injuries constituted a victory. They saw O'Connor's gaze become evasive and a puzzled expression begin to disturb the restful calm of his mangled face.

On arriving at New York they did two things. First, they signed off from the ship where their only consolation in the face of daily abuse and humiliation had been the limited triumph of passive endurance. Then, all together, they marched to the nearest police station and reported the first mate of the *Emma C. Leithfield*.

This had been their plan. It was Albert's idea, and it had helped them endure. They'd discussed killing O'Connor, but something—perhaps their own terror more than anything—had held them back. Albert had realized that if a captain fails to intervene with someone as out of line as O'Connor, then his ship is lawless. The crew can't make the rules on a ship just because the captain fails to, unless through mutiny—which is no more than a cry for help and does nothing but add to the general lawlessness. So if justice can't be found on board, it must be found ashore.

And that was why they marched together to the police station: not to get revenge on O'Connor, but to seek justice.

They came to ask if there was any to be had.

And they received their answer.

They walked up the Lower East Side until they reached the police station on Twelfth Street. Grouped close together, they filled the width of the sidewalk, and passersby had to step aside to make way for them. Deep down they still felt ashamed that they'd failed to deal with O'Connor themselves. Here were seventeen large, broad-shouldered men, used to hard work, coming to beg others for justice—on one man.

Was the law something only the weak resorted to?

They reached a grimy yellow building whose sign proclaimed it to be the home of the law. When they entered and saw men not unlike themselves being dragged in from the street by policemen, for a moment they weren't sure which side of the law they belonged on. But they went over to a counter and stood there, nudging one another hesitantly. Albert ended up doing the talking. He told the police officer about the murder of Giovanni, and the Swedish second mate showed him his blinded eye.

The officer wrote a report. The moment they saw their words being committed to writing, something changed. They could look one another in the eye again and stand up straight. They were no longer a group of frustrated men whose complaints merited no more than a disdainful shrug.

Two police officers accompanied them back to the ship. O'Connor was sitting in his chair on the deck, his dog lying at his feet. They knew he had a loaded revolver in his pocket—but you don't shoot the law. If you shoot a police officer, ten more will take his place.

They saw O'Connor's astonishment. He glared at the crew of the *Emma C. Leithfield* one by one. And when none of them looked away, he understood. They'd done the unthinkable. They hadn't beaten him up, or arranged a counterattack, or tried to murder him—all of which would have met with his approval. Indeed, he'd have wanted it, because that was the language he spoke and understood. But now they'd acted in a way that was incomprehensible to him, in which *might* and *right* didn't share a meaning.

For a moment he hesitated as he took head-to-toe measure first of them, and then of the policemen. The officers' faces betrayed no reaction upon seeing the giant with the grotesquely scarred face, the tattered clothing, and the obvious bulge in his nankeens that revealed the presence of a revolver. But the crew saw them stiffen as their hands sought the butts of their own weapons.

O'Connor spotted it too, and displaying a cunning they would not have credited him with, asked the police officers what the problem was. They replied that he'd been accused of murder and assault and that the witnesses were the men standing next to them. They informed him that he was under arrest.

O'Connor handed over his revolver voluntarily. The men saw him trying hard to look smaller as he was led away between the two policemen. O'Connor!

They exchanged glances.

The law was so strong that a mere snapping of its fingers could reduce even the most bloodthirsty monster to a lamb.

They'd never have believed that O'Connor had the gift of the gab. He'd certainly never provided them with evidence of an extensive vocabulary. Grunting and roaring had been his favorite forms of expression. But now he revealed a completely new side of himself. They'd noted a flash of deviousness in his eyes when he agreed to go with the officers voluntarily. Now, in court, they began truly to understand what sort of calculating fiend was lurking within that brutal mass of flesh.

When the charge against him was read out in court, O'Connor

grabbed the Bible and kissed it with a passion that he'd hitherto reserved for outbursts of rage. He held up his hand and swore that he'd never, in all his life, laid a finger on any man. Then he clasped his maimed head and turned it from side to side, as if his neck were a socket and he was attempting to unscrew it.

"Look at this face," he cried. "Is this the face of a killer?"

He stared directly at the judge and then at the public gallery.

Had his latent violence not been visible in every bulging sinew, some members of the public might have burst out laughing, so grotesque was his claim to innocence. It was hard to imagine a more fitting face for a ruthless killer.

However, even the judge himself looked down when O'Connor stared hard at him, and they began to wonder who was stronger: the law or O'Connor.

Again O'Connor turned his head.

"Look," he said. "Look at my ruined face. This isn't the face of a man who fights back. It's the face of a man who turns the other cheek even when he's wrongly attacked." He looked directly at the witness box, and not one of the crew met his eyes. He showed the court first one scarred cheek, then the other. "Do you really think that I would let anyone come near me if my blood was as bad as people say?" He ripped his tattered shirt, which he wore even here, with a theatrical movement, baring his scarred chest. "This," he said, his voice turning hollow from emotion, "this is the body of a martyr. This is the body of the lamb."

"He's going to win," Gustafsson said, fingering his ruined eye as they sat in the nearest bar after the session. "Did you see how scared the judge was of him?"

"But the law isn't scared of him," Albert objected.

"What good's the law if the judge is small and weak and the criminal is big and strong?" asked Rhys Llewellyn.

Albert was the only one who still believed in the law. Every day they turned up in court, to be called as witnesses one by one. O'Connor contradicted them brazenly every time, looking at the judge, who averted his eyes. Their cuts began to heal, and their blue and yellow bruises were fading: only Gustafsson's eye stayed ruined, but even on his blind side he didn't have the courage to meet O'Connor's stare.

They'd had to put off looking for new work until the trial was over.

They grew restless and lost faith. They drifted around the bars and drank their savings away.

"We should never have reported him," they said to Albert.

"The law's stronger than O'Connor," he replied.

"Look at the judge," they retorted.

They didn't believe in shore justice. Albert had talked them into this. Soon O'Connor would be freed and he'd take his revenge. They should have swallowed their defeat and never sought the help of the law. It always sided with the strongest anyway.

"Look at the judge," they repeated. "He's small and he stoops. He's bald. He's barely bigger than a child."

"So don't look at him," Albert said. "And listen instead."

"So, what did you hear?" Albert asked them after the next session.

They mumbled something and looked away. Well, he had a point. When you listened to what the man actually said, you got a different impression. He sank his teeth in like a bull terrier. He was impossible to shake off: he kept asking questions until he got to the heart of the matter, until the giant snapped and banged the counter in front of him with his fist as he roared across the courtroom, "I'm a man of peace; everyone will testify to that!"

"Everyone except the crew of the *Emma C. Leithfield*," the judge commented. He looked away again, but his voice stayed calm.

"It's the law that comes out of his mouth," Albert said.

"No, he's speaking for himself," Rhys Llewellyn said, "but he does it well."

After sixteen days of questioning, the judge convicted O'Connor, sentencing him to five years in jail for assault and manslaughter. Since it couldn't be proven that he'd intended to kill Giovanni, though no one doubted it, he wouldn't be branded a murderer and hang by his neck until he was dead. But they hadn't expected that. They'd expected him to walk free.

O'Connor roared like a wild animal when the sentence was pronounced.

"Serves you right, you brute!" Gustafsson shouted.

The judge turned and sent him an angry look, the first they'd seen throughout the trial.

They congratulated one another as they left the courtroom, but instead of triumph at the defeat of their enemy, they were filled with simple relief. It was as if they'd been on trial themselves. And now they'd been set free.

"I finally got rid of Isager," Albert said many years later.

"But we don't want to hear about him," we said. "We want to hear about the boots."

THE VOYAGE

I SIGNED ON for Singapore and from there to Van Diemen's Land, to Hobart Town, the last port where my father had been seen. But it wasn't just his final port: it was everyone's dead end—and if it wasn't yours, it soon would be, if you didn't get yourself out in time. Picture the workhouse in Marstal: that's what Hobart was like.

The year was 1862. I met a man with one eye who'd been there since 1822 and never had a day of freedom for the better part of forty years. He'd counted every lash they'd given him during his imprisonment: three thousand in total, he said. He was free now, but his will was as broken as the skin of his back, which had more ridges than a washboard. He wasn't the only one. He'd tell you his story in exchange for a glass of gin, and with forty years on the wagon to make up for, he'd happily tell it ten times a day. But in Hobart Town there weren't many to listen. The place was full of outcasts and ex-cons like him, who'd murder for the price of a drink.

Hobart had been a penal colony since the first house was built there in 1803. Now they called it a town of free men, but since everyone was either a former convict or a guard, the distinction didn't mean much. They were all men used to either giving beatings or receiving them. The option of living together like men with their heads held high didn't look like it had occurred to anyone. No one there ever looked me straight in the face. They'd keep their eyes on the ground, and if they looked up, it was to judge the depth of your pocket and whether what you had in it was worth killing for. People said they'd steal the joey from a kangaroo's pouch. Kangaroos carry their young in a pouch, did you know that?

There were plenty of old men in Hobart Town, but few young ones. Anyone who had the strength or the slightest hope left in him fled for greener pastures. Whole flocks of filthy children ran wild, with no sign of any fathers. The mothers were left in peace though, because, they say, convicts lose their appetite for women when they're long in the clink and go for other men instead. Whether that's true or not I don't know and don't care to know. But one thing's for sure: I wasted my wages on those scumbags.

I started my search at the police station, but they just said the same thing that all the other authorities I spoke to said: "If a man wants to lay low and vanish without a trace from the surface of the earth, then he'll pick Hobart Town."

But *papa tru* hadn't had any reason to disappear, I knew that. The officers just shook their heads and said they couldn't help me.

So I walked up and down Liverpool Street. Every second pub was called the Bird-in-Hand. That made sense to me. In Hobart Town alcohol sang sweeter than any other bird, and if you've nothing else to believe in, then you'll believe in whatever you can grab hold of.

I bought gin for anyone who looked as if he might have a story to tell. And they all did. They'd start by asking me about *papa tru:* height, nationality, what he looked like. Then, oh yes, they remembered him well, they'd say, and they'd scratch their filthy hair until the dead lice dropped out, and look mournfully into their empty glass and tell you in this humble voice that another gin might just jog their memory. And sure enough, now they remembered him: the tall Dane with the big beard and the distant eyes! He'd stayed at the Hope and Anchor in Macquerie Street. Then he'd signed on to the ...

Oh, but the name of the ship escaped them. They'd give their empty glass another wistful look and as soon as they'd had a refill, the name of the ship would come out.

Within a few weeks it was clear there'd been a thousand Laurids Madsens in Hobart Town, and my *papa tru* had signed on to a thousand ships sailing to a thousand destinations. I didn't have a single bird in my hand, but I had thousands in the bush. Laurids Madsen wasn't a man. He was an entire race.

Even so I went to the Hope and Anchor to ask about the lost man. I'd come this far and I wasn't ready to give up. The man behind the bar was called Anthony Fox. He was an ex-con like the rest of them, but unlike them, he'd thrived—by making a profit from their misery. He stood behind his brass counter, rubbing it with a cloth until it shone. When I leaned over it to question him, I could see my face in it and I wondered if it had ever reflected my father's beard.

I ordered a gin—for myself this time—and mentioned my father's name. That was all I did mention, because by now I'd learned my lesson. I could have said that Laurids was a Hottentot with fiery red, woolly hair that stuck out on all sides and three legs instead of the usual two and they all would have said yes, we remember that Dane well. So I left it at the name.

He stood there for a while. "What was that name again?" he asked. "And the year?"

"Fifty or fifty-one," I said.

"Just a minute."

He ordered a waiter to take over behind the bar and disappeared into a backroom, returning with a large ledger tucked under his arm.

"I never remember a face," he said, "but I do remember a debt."

He put the ledger on the counter and started leafing through it.

"There!" he exclaimed triumphantly and pushed the book across to me. "I knew it."

He pointed to a name. Laurids Madsen, it said.

I can't claim I recognized my father's signature. I still hadn't learned to read when he disappeared, and he wasn't a man to write his name down too often.

"What does he owe you for?" I asked.

"He owes me for two beers," Anthony Fox said.

I found the money and paid him.

"We're quits now."

"Don't tell me you traveled halfway around the world to pay Madsen's debt?"

I shook my head.

"He's disappeared. I'm looking for him."

"Sailor or convict?"

He gave me a searching look.

"Sailor."

"Then I suppose he must have drowned, like sailors do. Or jumped ship."

He flung out his arm in a vague gesture that might encompass the Pacific Ocean, with its tens of thousands of islands, as well as the ice-covered pole south of us, where no one had ever set foot.

"It's a big world. You'll never find him."

"I found his debt," I said.

"People who disappear don't always want to be found. Where does a sailor belong? On deck, or with his missus and kids? Sometimes he gets confused. Then he starts living like his life's a spinning top that he can spin again and again. He drowns ten times, and he comes back ten times—and each time he's got a new woman in his arms. Back home, his family's mourning him, while he's sitting next to a cradle on another continent, chuckling away. Until he gets fed up with that family too. Trust me. I've seen it happen."

"I didn't know that sages tended bar here in Hobart Town."

He grinned at me. "You're his son. Am I right?"

"I thought you said you never remember a face. Do I look like Laurids Madsen?"

"I've no idea. I don't remember him. But I recognize an offended man when I see one. Only a son would pull a face like that when his father's accused of being a cheat."

I turned to leave.

"Wait," Anthony Fox said. "I'm going to give you a name."

"A name?"

I stopped in the doorway of the Hope and Anchor.

"Yes, a name. Jack Lewis. Remember it."

"And who's Jack Lewis?"

"The man your father drank a beer with."

"And you remember that man ten years on? I suppose he owes you for a beer too."

"He owes me for a lot more than a beer. Find him for me, and jog his memory about that debt."

I turned back to the bar, where my half-empty glass of gin was still waiting. Fox hadn't cleared it away. He'd known he could pull me back. It was early in the day, and I was the only guest at the Hope and Anchor.

"Do you want something to eat?" he asked.

"Not if it's lamb." I was sick of lamb. It was the only meat they ate in Hobart Town.

"I've got sea bass." We sat down at a table. "There's plenty of room here," he said. "Australia's bigger than Europe and it's still needing more citizens. The Pacific Ocean takes up half the globe. I call it the fatherland of the homeless."

"Did you ever sail?"

"I've done everything. Farming, carpentry, sailing, being a con. Because that's a trade too. Two kinds of men come to the Pacific. The ones who just want to lie under a coconut palm and never do a day's work, and the ones who are following the money."

"The money?"

"Jack Lewis was one of them. Opium from China, arms, human trafficking, name whatever vice you can think of—and I don't just mean cargo that can be weighed and measured—and Jack Lewis will step forward as your humble supplier. If you follow the money, you need to stick to certain routes. On one of those routes you'll find Jack Lewis."

"Give me the name of his ship."

"The *Flying Scud*. But you need to make up your mind about something before you start. You need to decide what kind of man your father was. Was he the coconut palm type, who wanted to spend his life lying on his back in the shade, or was he after money? If he was a coconut man you'll never find him. Melanesia, Gilbert Islands, Society Islands, Sandwich Islands: ten lifetimes aren't long enough to visit them all. But if he's the other kind, you've got a chance. Jack Lewis doesn't come here anymore. But he's out there somewhere."

"And how do I find him?"

"Not in any register. Jack Lewis is the kind of man the authorities don't know about. But he's lodged in a lot of men's memories. Including mine."

"Tell me about his debt."

"Just mention my name. Anthony Fox. And the sum of one thousand pounds."

"One thousand pounds!" I exclaimed. "But why did you give a thousand pounds to a notorious swindler?"

"Greed is the correct term, I believe," Anthony Fox said without flinching. "Besides, I hadn't acquired the money lawfully myself. Call it a loan between swindlers. Nowadays I wander the narrow path of virtue. But purely due to lack of means."

"It's a topsy-turvy world," I said. "Most men become thieves out of necessity."

"As did I once. Well, I was more than a thief. I'll leave you to guess what. Today I live an honest life. People keep their eye on an ex-con. The *Flying Scud*. Now you've got the man's name—and the ship's too."

"And if I find it?"

"I can't promise that you'll find your father. But you'll find Jack Lewis. I've no hope of seeing my money again. But now you know that Jack Lewis is a crook. Do whatever you want to him, and you'll have my blessing."

That was how men in Hobart Town spoke to each other: as one

con man to another. I thought of the vast surface of the Pacific Ocean, which I'd already crossed once. Who could keep an eye on what happened on a deck thousands of miles from shore—or on an island no bigger than a ship?

The word *freedom* was something the world had taught me recently and I'd had to sail far to grasp its meaning. In Hobart Town I heard that word from men who'd chained themselves to their own greed. Freedom had a thousand faces. But so did crime. The thought of what a man might do made me dizzy.

"Honolulu," Anthony Fox said. "I suggest that you start your search in Honolulu."

"If you know where I can find him, why don't you go there yourself and collect your money?"

"I've become an honest man. Only the stupid steal from the rich. The clever steal from the poor. The law usually protects the rich."

"So you're not stealing from the poor?"

"No, I'm just exploiting their weakness." He pointed to the bar and its battery of bottles.

"It's more profitable and less risky. A bottle in the hand is better than money in the bank. That's how the poor think."

"Ah! So you own all the Bird-in-Hand pubs?"

"Indeed I do."

I got up to leave.

"One moment." It was a trick he had, holding back information until the end. "I do remember one thing about your father." I looked at him. My heart was pounding in my chest. "He looked like a man who'd lost something. Do you have any idea what that might be?"

"No," I said, my heart still banging. "I was only a child when he disappeared."

I went out the door and heard Anthony Fox's voice for the last time.

"You forgot to pay!" he called out. "You're going in my book."

I WAS ONLY too pleased to be leaving Hobart Town. I'd slept with my head on my sea chest with the door locked, but even so, on more than one occasion I'd had unexpected visitors and had to fight someone off in the dark.

Now I was headed for Honolulu. It took me a year to get there. I had to sign on and sign off several times: no routes led directly from Hobart Town to Hawaii. I saw a lot on that journey, and there was more than one shore where I was tempted to settle. If Anthony Fox was right about there being two kinds of men who came to the Pacific Ocean, I knew which kind I was: the kind looking for the shade of a coconut palm and a view of a blue lagoon.

Yet I always moved on. I had nothing on my mind but the name Jack Lewis.

I had to wait fourteen days in Honolulu, and if I hadn't been looking for Jack Lewis, I would have stayed there for the rest of my life.

The women wore red ankle-length dresses with bare shoulders, and they wriggled their hips in a way Marstallers would have called indecent. But their lives were governed by a different, more fertile kind of nature than the one at home. The air was thick with perfume. At first I thought it was the ladies, tempting my nostrils in the same way they tempted the rest of me. But the scent came from the flowers. Jasmine and oleander were the only ones I knew the names of, but they grew everywhere—in front of the houses, in the shade of the trees, and along the roads. Instead of gin, the drink of choice here was bourbon, and I'd down it on a shady terrace, watching life go by on the promenade in front of me, listening to the surf.

The houses in the town were white with green shutters, and the roads were straight and wide. Instead of cobbles, I walked on a carpet of crushed coral, shaded by tall trees with leaves that grew so thick, no sunlight came through. The men wore the color of the town: white jackets, white waistcoats, white trousers. Even white shoes—they'd chalk the canvas every morning. And the women wore gypsy hats decorated with flowers.

The Micronesians have light skin, and they like to tattoo their faces. It was the men who struck you the most. They shave their heads and they're tattooed from the neck up, so their faces are just blue shadows, lit up by lightning flashes of white from the glint of their eyes.

Hobart Town and Honolulu lie at opposite sides of the Pacific Ocean, and I've never been to two places more different. I'd first heard Jack Lewis's name in Hobart, but every time I mentioned it here, it was as if I'd brought some of its filth with me. People would eye me suspiciously and make me feel like undesirable company. One man even spat on the ground and turned his back on me altogether. It felt like the whole of Honolulu was shunning me.

An American missionary shot me a look of pity from beneath his broad-brimmed straw hat. He said to me in a fatherly tone, "You look like an otherwise decent young man. Why do you want to talk to that dreadful person?"

I couldn't explain my business, so I just stood there mute. He misunderstood my silence and thought I had something to hide. He walked away, shaking his head.

I felt unclean.

In the end, though, I got the information I was looking for. I learned that Jack Lewis was expected within the next few weeks. But I paid a price for my interest in the *Flying Scud*. I drank my bourbon alone.

The *Flying Scud* dropped anchor outside Honolulu, and I was waiting on the beach when Jack Lewis was rowed ashore by his crew, which consisted of four Kanaks. Their faces were covered in blue tattoos and I noticed one had an ear missing. I took the fact that Jack Lewis chose to surround himself exclusively with natives as a sign that he didn't trust anyone. I reckoned this was the kind of company a man preferred if he had a secret to keep. What did he talk to these blue-faced men about? Nothing, I guessed. They had their goals in life, and he had his—and their paths need never really cross.

Jack Lewis was a small, withered man, with skin burned the color of mahogany by the trade winds and the noonday equator sun. His face was wrinkled and his eyes were set deep, like an old monkey's. He wore a washed-out cotton suit with stripes that had all but faded away. A straw hat kept his face in shadow, except when he tilted his head back to look at whomever he was talking to, which he did with the air of a nabob holding court.

At first glance he seemed unremarkable. He didn't look like a captain: far from it. A modest merchant, maybe. And yet all sorts of rumors stuck to him. I'd already learned that just the mention of his name made you untouchable.

His crew pulled the boat up onto the beach, and he stood next to it, studying the sand, seemingly deep in thought. I went over to him and told him my name. He looked up at me. I watched his face, but it seemed my name rang no bells—or if it did, he wasn't letting on.

Then I mentioned Anthony Fox, and he turned his back to me. His men didn't seem to be listening to us, but they were clearly waiting for orders.

"I'm not here for the money," I said. "I'm here for something else."

He swung around to look at me.

"Everyone comes here for money. What other reason is there?"

"I'm looking for someone."

He sized me up with his close-set monkey eyes. "Madsen," he said. "You're Laurids Madsen's son."

"Is it that obvious?"

"It's easy to work out. Only a son would look for a man like Madsen."

"What's that supposed to mean?"

I stepped up to him. I could feel my anger surge. But it was mixed with a fear of what I might discover. And when anger and fear get mixed up, anything can happen.

Jack Lewis didn't move. He kept staring me in the face. His eyes were inscrutable. I could tell this was a man who'd taught himself to control others with just a look.

"Listen to me," he said. "You're young. You're looking for your father. I've no idea why and it's not my business. Nor is morality. I'm not interested in good and evil and I judge no one. I'm only interested in whether a man is suited for work on board."

"And my father wasn't?"

There was still anger in my voice: a ridiculous feeling of hurt pride on my father's behalf had swept through me. After all, the man passing judgment on him was no more than a criminal.

"The first time I met your father he seemed like a man who'd lost everything. As a rule, men like that are useful in my line of business. They have no illusions. They're survivors and life has taught them what really matters: money. I ask this out of curiosity, and you don't have to answer—what had he lost?"

I shook my head. "I don't know."

"His family? His fortune? Or some quaint notion of honor?"

"He had my mother. He had three sons and a daughter. He could get all the work he wanted. He was a respected sailor."

Jack Lewis made a gesture of invitation. "We're standing on a beach. Let's go into town and have a drink."

When we parted a few hours later I discovered, to my astonishment, that I'd grown to like Jack Lewis. He reminded me of Anthony Fox. In Marstal I would probably have avoided him like the plague, but when you're far from home you learn to appreciate the strangest people. He was a man who considered things. He was direct and he never pretended to be anything he wasn't. He invited me on board the *Flying Scud* the following day, and I accepted his invitation.

Neither of us mentioned my father.

Sunshine filtered through a skylight onto the table in Jack Lewis's low-ceilinged cabin. At the center sat the empty shell of a sea turtle, laden with a strange fruit—the Kanaks called it a pineapple—that I'd never seen before coming to Hawaii. A whale-oil lamp was burning, but it seemed that the real light came from the fruit. It was gold and it glowed like a slice of sun.

On the bulkhead a spear and shield shared space with two miniature portraits, which I studied closely. One was of a portly gent with sideburns and bushy eyebrows; the other showed a pale, weak-looking woman with a sharp nose, whom I took to be his wife.

"You're wasting your time," Jack Lewis said. "I've no idea who they are. I found them in a wrecked ship. I thought my cabin could do with a few ornaments. A couple of portraits like that give a man some respectability. Make him look as if he has ancestors and a family history. But I haven't and I don't want any, either. That would be stupid for a man in my position. Take a look at him," he continued. "A big man with a big appetite for life. And then take a good look at her: a sad sack. I bet that pointy nose of hers was always red from crying and whining. He can't have had much fun out of her. I look at them every now and again to remind myself why I'm here. Take the Pacific as your bride, and she'll bring you money and all the fun you could wish for."

I pointed at the weapons.

"And those?"

"A gift from the Pacific. A healthy brawl with cannibals on a remote island that no one ever visits. A fight like that makes you feel alive. Especially afterward, when you're wandering the beach, looking at the enemies you've slain. Those weapons are trophies. They remind me why I'm here."

He opened a wall cabinet and took out a bottle. It was an unusual shape and held a white liquid that seemed to whirl around like mist or boiling milk. I thought I saw something dark stir inside it. Jack Lewis shook his head and put the bottle back, then selected another one.

"Scotch?"

I nodded. We sat down, facing each other.

"And my father?"

"He looked at things differently. He didn't share my view of a good time. He didn't want the same as me. But I didn't know what he was after, so we went our separate ways." He raised his glass to me and we drank. "Pity," Jack Lewis said. "He had it in him. He could have done well out here. I liked him."

He got up and drew the curtain of the bottom berth. He was looking for something and a moment later he straightened up. In his hand he held a small parcel wrapped in a cloth that had once been white but had yellowed with age. He grinned at me.

"Now that we've got to know each other, there's something I want to show you. Initiate you into the inner sanctum, so to speak."

He placed the parcel on the table and started to untie the string around the yellow cloth with slow, careful movements, almost as if this were a ceremony he'd invited me to witness. Then he whipped off the cloth with a quick tug.

Before me lay the most disgusting sight I've ever seen.

At first I couldn't even have found a name for it, but my eyes were faster than my brain. Even before I'd understood what was on the table in front of me, my stomach started to spasm and my heart felt as if it had stopped. The thing wasn't much bigger than a clenched fist.

The filthy, smoky hair, which must once have been white, was gathered in a pigtail at the back.

I clasped my mouth with my hand and staggered to my feet. Jack Lewis sent me a look of approval, as if my reaction had lived up to his expectations.

"You've gone pale," he said.

I grabbed the table for support, then withdrew my hand as if a scorpion had stung me: the revolting thing was still on it. A terrible thought struck me. I had only vague recollections of my father's face. We'd no pictures of him at home, and whenever I tried to recall his features, my imagination seemed to be conjuring something as shifting and unreliable as a cloud in the sky.

"My father?" I whispered.

I'd never have expected to see Jack Lewis erupt in laughter. But at this, his hard mask cracked and he guffawed—not a warm or hearty sound, but one as dry and harsh as his appearance. Still, he was laughing.

"For God's sake," he hiccuped between fits. "Of course it's not your father. What kind of a man d'you take me for?" Then he burst out laughing again. It was only when he'd finally stopped that it dawned on him that I was standing with my fists clenched. My fear had turned into rage.

"Don't be angry," he said, holding up his palms to calm me. "I'm only trying to contribute to your education."

He picked up the head from the table.

"Do you know how to make a shrunken head like this? Clearly you have to start by scalping it. Now the redskins in America take only the scalp and the hair. For this, you have to slice off the whole face, because you can't shrink the skull. Then you dry it over the fire. Not much left by way of a resemblance. A shrunken head's hardly a fine example of portraiture." He held up the head before my face and scrutinized it, turning it about so that I too could fully appreciate the sight.

"But still, something remains. His old mother would recognize him, don't you think?"

"It's a white man," I said.

"Yes, of course it's a white man. Do you think I'd keep the head of a cannibal? No, a white man's head is a great rarity. I had to pay five rifles for it on Malaita. They're all headhunters there. It was a bargain. I handed over the guns and taught the cannibals how to shoot. Then they aimed them at me, so I shot all five of them before they had time to count to three. Which incidentally they wouldn't have been capable of. I was a more experienced shot, of course. But I'd failed to mention they needed to release the safety catch before pulling the trigger. Sadly, I can't put the shrunken head of a white man on public display. But when I'm alone or in company I trust, I'll take it out and contemplate it." He placed the thing back on the table. I stared at its horribly distorted features. They were still recognizably human, and that was the worst of it. "If I have a religion, then it's him. He can't say a word, but he tells me everything I need to know about life. Look! What are we? A trophy for others? An enemy? Yes, that too—but above all, a commodity. There's nothing that can't be bought or sold. I paid with rifles. If those miserable cannibals had known about money, I'd have paid the right price and we could have avoided all that unfortunate shooting. Which, by the way, I don't regret. That too was a trade. In my favor. Another drink?"

I wanted to say no, but I needed another one. So we sat there drinking in Captain Jack Lewis's cabin with a shrunken head on the table between us. I glanced at it out of the corner of my eye until slowly I grew used to its presence.

"Who was he?" I asked.

"Even if I knew, I wouldn't tell you. Let's just say that I call him Jim and leave it at that. Do you ever look at yourself in the mirror?" Jack Lewis fixed his eye on me.

We had a small mirror at home, but it was hidden away in one of my mother's drawers and it rarely came out. I'd seen myself reflected in a windowpane more often than I'd stood before a mirror; none of the ships I had sailed kept one in the fo'c'sle.

"Not often," I replied.

The question didn't interest me, nor could I grasp where Jack Lewis was going with it.

"A wise decision. You should never study yourself in a mirror. It tells you nothing but lies. When a man looks at his reflection, he starts getting all sorts of wrong notions about himself. I'm not talking about what a mirror does to a woman. A man doesn't look to find out how handsome he is. A man's vanity isn't in his face; it's found elsewhere. Still, the mirror gives him the idea that he's unique, totally different from everyone else. But it only looks that way. Do you know how we come across to others, in this mirror, here?"

He pointed to his eyes.

"Let me show you."

He grabbed hold of Jim's pigtail with his clawlike hand and dangled him in front of my face. Startled, I jumped up.

Jack Lewis laughed triumphantly.

"That's you," he said. "That's how you look to me. And it's me. That's how I look to you. That's how we seem to each other. The first question we ask ourselves when we meet someone is this: what use is he to me? We're all shrunken heads to one another." He sat down again and poured himself another drink. He gave me an encouraging look. "Another one?"

I shook my head. All I wanted was to get away from this man as quickly as possible. But it wasn't an option. I'd traveled too far to meet him, and without him I'd never find my *papa tru*. I had yet to ask him where he was, but Jack Lewis beat me to it.

"I know where your father is," he said. "And I'm offering you a deal. I'll take you to him. But there's a price, of course." He looked at Jim and laughed again. "This is the deal. You don't get something for nothing. I'm bored with having only Kanaks for company, but it's difficult for me to hire crewmen of my own race. You'll be my first mate—which is a promotion, I'd imagine, for a man as young as you. You won't get paid, but you'll get free passage. Now here comes the most important bit." He raised his index finger and stared at me with what seemed like an artificial gravity, though I didn't know him well enough to interpret his expression. "I'm your captain and you'll obey my orders."

"I obey only my conscience."

"And what does your conscience bid you do?" he asked mockingly.

"My conscience doesn't care about the course we take, or wages, or time off. I'm not afraid of hard work. But there are some things it forbids me."

"We'll see," Jack Lewis said. "It's your choice. Your father or your conscience."

"Where is he?"

"I'm not going to tell you. The Pacific's a big place, and he's far away. The trade winds blow as they will, but I promise not to travel there the long way round. So, what shall it be? Yes or no?"

And I replied, "Yes."

WE SAILED a fortnight later. The hold was full—but what with, I didn't know. Captain Jack Lewis had deliberately kept me away from the loading.

"The usual," he replied, in answer to my question.

I knew it was pointless to ask again: I could see his urge to mock me resurfacing.

"Remember your conscience. What you don't know won't hurt you."

Our course was southwesterly, but that told me nothing. Hawaii was in the eastern Pacific, and the course merely confirmed what I already suspected: that my *papa tru* was somewhere across that vast expanse of water, on one of the thousands of islands.

I was at the helm and we were being carried along by a light breeze. Jack Lewis was standing next to me. He was a man of his word and he must have been serious when he told me how lonely it was with nothing but Kanaks for company, because now he rarely left my side.

"You may not be aware of this," he said, "but you're crossing the Pacific for the wrong reason."

"How do you mean?"

He could always arouse my curiosity, though I rarely enjoyed his philosophy.

"If I ask someone like you where he's headed, do you know what you're meant to say if you're a young man with a zest for life? I'm headed for the whole world, you should say. For the oceans and all their islands. A young man goes to sea to escape from his father. But you're looking for him. That's the wrong way around. Is it because of your mother?"

"It would be better for her if he were dead, and she had a grave to visit. It would do her no good to know that he's still alive."

"So you're not doing her a favor. Are you sure you're doing yourself one?"

"I need to know the truth."

"What do you want from your father?"

"A man needs a yardstick."

"A yardstick? Find another one. A ship, your own actions. Let the Pacific be your yardstick. Look at the swell. You'll not find a bigger swell anywhere. It has half the globe for its run-up. You're young. You have the whole world. Don't bother yourself with the past."

I made no reply. What I wanted from my father was none of Jack Lewis's business, so why was he interfering? Besides, we'd struck a deal, and I wasn't questioning him about our course.

I thought about my *papa tru*. Once upon a time I missed him so much that my heart ached every day. Then I grew up and a feeling of bitterness crept in. I never doubted that he was alive—and I assumed he'd gone missing because he wanted to. I had to know why. That was all. What kind of life was he living? What would I say when I met him? I didn't know. I hadn't prepared a speech. I just had to see him. And then what?

I couldn't answer that either. I only knew that while I was searching for him, he'd changed into a different man. And that was the truth about him. He'd become a stranger. Perhaps that was what I wanted confirmed. I needed to find him so I could say goodbye.

It was a year since I'd left Hobart Town. I had been back and forth across the Pacific, but I hadn't seen it, because Jack Lewis was right: I'd been traveling with my back to it. But now I saw it for the first time. I saw its long swells, which were the remnants of storms past; I saw the dolphins leap and the sharks' fins cut through the water; I saw huge shoals of tuna churn the water to foam. Only rarely did I see a seagull; land was always far, far away—though I saw the albatross glide past on its massive wings. It didn't need to be near land.

They said the Pacific was just like any other ocean, only bigger. But I learned that was nonsense. It could be gray and rough like the North Sea, or calm like the South Funen Archipelago, but I never saw the sky as blue or as vast over any other sea, and though the earth isn't flat and has no edge, I discovered that the Pacific was its center.

On clear nights when I was at the helm on my own and even the constantly philosophizing Jack Lewis had surrendered to the demands of sleep, the stars were the only geography, and I felt like one of them, adrift in the center of the universe.

The Kanaks sat on the deck, silently watching the constellations, and I knew that as a seafaring tribe who'd once navigated by the most remote suns of the universe, they too felt at home here. Suddenly I understood my *papa tru*. There comes a time in the life of a sailor when he no longer belongs ashore. It's then that he surrenders to the Pacific, where no land blocks the eye, where sky and ocean mirror each other until *above* and *below* have lost their meaning, and the Milky Way looks like the spume of a breaking wave and the globe itself rolls like a boat in the midst of the sinking and heaving surf of that starry sky, and the sun is nothing but a tiny glowing dot of phosphorescence on the night sea.

I was filled with an impatient longing for the unknown, and there was a ruthlessness to it; perhaps this was what Jack Lewis had meant when he spoke about that need for adventure that makes young people yearn to see the whole world, the oceans and all their islands. Mystery emanated from the Pacific's vast surface. My *papa tru* must have felt it once. And when a man has felt it, he doesn't return.

I was reminded of a summer's evening on the beach back home. The wind had died down and the water was completely calm. In the dusk light, sea and sky had taken on a violet tinge and the horizon had melted clean away, leaving the beach as the only fixed point, its white sand marking the farthest edge of the world, beyond which lay endless violet space. When I took my first stroke, I felt as though I was swimming straight into the immensity of the universe above me.

That night on the Pacific I had the same feeling.

The *Flying Scud* smelled of copra from stern to bow. There was nothing strange about that in itself. Dried coconut was the most important commodity in these parts. But given Jack Lewis's reputation, it occurred to me that the copra smell might be masking something else. It wasn't through dealing in copra that Jack Lewis had become notorious—though I couldn't work out what else he might be trading.

Anthony Fox had used the word *slavery*, and when I repeated it to Jack Lewis, for once he failed to reply in his usual direct way.

"I do what all sailors do," he said. "I take things to the places they're needed. That's the way of the world. I don't make it better and I don't make it worse."

"Slave trading?" I asked.

"In case you don't already know, I can inform you that the slave trade's illegal in this part of the world. I'm a law-abiding man."

He gave me a wry smile.

"Plantation workers?" I asked.

It was a well-known fact that there was widespread traffic in Kanak laborers, who were tricked into working on the large plantations where, instead of earning money, they ended up in bottomless debt. Their employers owned everything, including the houses the workers rented and the shops where they bought their food. A plantation worker's contract might be for two years, but he'd end up working ten before he returned to his native island, penniless and broken. If he ever found his way home across the sea, that is.

Jack Lewis shook his head.

"This is an amusing game we've started. But don't think that I'll provide you with the answer. You're not a practical man. And then there's that sensitive conscience of yours. With one of those, it's best to turn a blind eye."

Jack Lewis always relieved me at midnight, precisely when the middle watch began. I wondered about it at first, then decided there had to be a secret side to him that forced him to be alone with the stars. One warm evening, when the sails hung limp and the calm surface of the sea mirrored the Milky Way, making its white starlight seem like surf breaking over a submerged reef, I fetched my bedding in order to sleep on deck.

Jack Lewis immediately ordered me below, his voice sharp.

"Kanaks sleep on deck. It's not appropriate for a white man." I hesitated. I felt no urge to return to the muggy cabin below. "All right, stay here and get some fresh air." His voice was conciliatory now, and I could tell he wanted to talk. I seated myself on the rail. It was very quiet, apart from the squeaking of the rigging. "I've lied to you," Jack Lewis said. I could hear him chuckling to himself in the darkness. "I know very well who Jim is. But you won't believe me."

"Out with it. I'll believe you. But tell me, why do you want to tell me the truth now?"

"Oh, so I've got your blessing, have I? Lucky me. Why do I suddenly feel like telling you the truth about Jim? Because the story's too good to keep to myself. That's the strange thing about a good story. No pleasure if you can't share it. So listen to this: Jim's real name is"—here he paused for dramatic effect—"James."

I gave him a disappointed look. "So what?"

Jack Lewis laughed. "I'm guessing his surname will mean more to you than his first name. Cook. James Cook."

I gasped. "*The* James Cook?"

"Yes, *the* James Cook. Captain of the *Resolution* and the *Discovery*. The man who discovered the Tonga Islands, the Sandwich Islands, and the Society Islands. That James Cook."

"But that's impossible!"

"Show me his grave, then. Go on, tell me where he's buried." I shook my head. I didn't know. "James Cook was killed on Hawaii. In Kealakekua Bay. He was strict but fair. You have to be if you're dealing with Kanaks. When one of them stole a sextant, James Cook cut off his ear." He fixed me with his eyes to make sure I'd understood what he'd just told me. I had. One of his own Kanaks had an ear missing, and I didn't doubt who'd inspired him. "James Cook shot a chief on Hawaii who'd tried to steal a boat from him. Thousands of natives surrounded Cook and his men, but he could have been all right. The natives thought he was their missing god, Lono, making a return."

"He shouldn't have shot their chief."

"I thought you might say that. But the opposite's the case. Shooting the chief was vital. By making an example of him, Cook showed his strength. His mistake was that he showed them his weakness too. The natives were scared of attacking—though they had Cook and his men well outnumbered. But then one of them fired an arrow. Maybe it was an accident. No one knows. But the arrow hit James Cook. It didn't cause any serious injury. That wasn't what killed him. He died because he blundered." Jack Lewis sent me the look he always used when he wanted to educate me. Though I couldn't see how James Cook had blundered, I guessed that some cynical remark about mankind's wretchedness was about to follow, and I wasn't mistaken. "In the eyes of the Kanaks he was a god, and gods don't flinch. But Cook screamed when the arrow hit him. That gave them their signal to attack. Fifteen thousand men came at him and tore him to pieces. Literally. They roasted his flesh over an open fire—except for the nine pounds they sent back to the *Resolution*. They hung his heart inside a hut, where three children found it. They ate it, thinking it was a dog's. Some of his bones were discovered later by his officers, and they buried them at sea. But his head was lost."

"So how did you find it?"

"It wasn't easy. The Kanaks kept it secret, you see. It became a trophy in their internal wars. Finally the head left Hawaii and started wandering the Pacific—almost as if it was copying its owner's voyage all those years before. At one time no fewer than five heads were rumored to exist in the Pacific region, all attributed to James Cook. But I found the real one. I've got sources. I finally tracked it down on Malaita. The chief who sold it to me was an educated man. He spoke and read English. He'd been taught by a missionary. Whom he later ate with great relish, or so he claimed. He knew exactly who Cook was and what his head was worth. Besides, he saw nothing barbaric in headhunting. "I've read in your Bible," he said, "about David, the great warrior. After he defeated Goliath, didn't he cut off his head to show to King Saul?"

Shortly after this conversation I returned below deck, and soon I'd fallen into a restless sleep on my narrow berth, inhaling the sultry air and dreaming about Isager's house in flames that New Year's Eve, all those years ago. I was in the street, looking through the window—and I saw the schoolmaster's severed head sitting on the dining room table, staring back at me.

Then I heard the murmur of voices and the sound of bare feet against the deck. Confused about whether or not it was just a new dream taking over from the previous one, I woke with a tight feeling in my chest. I swung my legs out of the berth. The ship groaned and the waves heaved: the wind was no longer calm, and I decided to return to the deck to feel the fresh breeze on my face. I found the door to my cabin was closed—though I could have sworn that I'd left it open when I went to bed. I turned the handle—but the door was locked from the outside.

There was something going on that I wasn't allowed to see. And I now had a good idea what it might be. I banged on the door and called Jack Lewis's name, but no one came. I couldn't break it down, so eventually I gave up and returned to my berth, where I surprised myself by falling asleep again.

When I woke, light was streaming in through the open door. I found Jack Lewis in his cabin with a cup of coffee. He looked as if he had been expecting me and smiled broadly when I entered.

"Coffee?" he offered, and gestured to a chair opposite him. I made no reply. "Are we about to go another round? How about one of our

Socratic dialogues about ethics? Trust me. Everything I do, I do purely to protect your delicate conscience."

"An unused conscience is no conscience at all."

"How philosophical we are this morning. Nothing makes a man more reflective than a locked door. If it weren't for this delicate conscience of yours, your door wouldn't be locked. But you're always welcome to come up on deck and enjoy the night. As long as you remember that I'm your captain and that my word is law on board."

"So it is slaves? The *Flying Scud* is a blackbirder?"

"Certainly not. There are only free men on board the *Flying Scud*."

"Who are locked in the hold during the day?"

"They can leave the ship whenever they want. Only I don't want them jumping overboard into the middle of the sea. They'll drown. Not even the strongest swimmer could ever get as far as any land. But the Kanaks are superstitious, and they're afraid to swim in the dark. So at night they're safe on deck."

I understood nothing at all.

"Leave the ship whenever they want?"

My voice was thick with anger and disbelief. Jack Lewis was making a fool of me.

"Yes. Once we reach land, they're free to leave the ship."

He got up and held out his hand. "The captain of the *Flying Scud* gives you his word."

I remained standing, with my hands at my sides.

"If they're free men, why have them on board? I presume there's a purpose?"

"Everything has a purpose."

"Yours or theirs?"

I glanced at the cupboard behind him, which contained the Winchester rifles. I knew he had no need to give me an answer.

That same evening I was at the helm when he came on deck to relieve me.

"I'll do a couple of hours of the next watch," I said.

"As you wish."

In the moonlight his face looked like a carved wooden mask.

Nothing happened during the first hour. The Kanak crew were sleeping around the deck, for the nights were still warm. Then Jack Lewis roused them. They got to their feet without complaint, though it was the middle of the night and the moon was the only source of light. I could see that this was their routine. They disappeared into the galley and returned with jars of water and bowls of cooked rice, which they placed on deck before lifting the hatch. A black hole appeared in the center of the deck and I wondered if all my questions would finally be answered. At last I was about to clap eyes on the "free men" who spent their days locked in the hold.

One of the Kanaks hollered down the hole and a chorus of voices responded. One by one they emerged. I tried counting them, but it was hard in the dark. I don't know how many there were, but I think they were all male. Their skin was as dark as a moonless night, and their faces were hidden behind great clouds of woolly hair. In the moonlight they looked like Negroes from Africa, but I knew they had to be Melanesians from the eastern Pacific—the darkest of all the races spread across this vast sea, and notorious among white men for being not only the most bloodthirsty warriors but also the keenest of all headhunters.

Now they were wandering peacefully around the deck, where scenes soon unfolded that I imagine you'd experience in their villages. Some sat down around the bowls of rice. Others drank from the water jars or poured the water into their palms to wash their faces. Others went to the rail to relieve themselves. Soon they were all sitting on the deck in smaller groups and a monotonous murmuring spread among them.

One started singing, and others joined him until soon they were all singing a song that seemed to use the Pacific as a metronome, rising and falling with a slow dignity that matched the immense swelling rhythm of the waves. Then, as abruptly as it had begun, for no apparent reason the song ceased and silence descended over the deck again as the *Flying Scud* sailed across the sea toward a destination known only to Jack Lewis.

I looked around for him. He was leaning against the deckhouse with a Winchester rifle.

The same scene was repeated each evening. The hatch was opened and the black shadows, otherwise known as free men, moved around the deck, going about their everyday business. Then they'd disappear. I had no idea what fate had in store for our free men. But Jack Lewis had told me too much about his philosophy for me to believe it would be anything good.

Why did he so adamantly refute the suggestion that they were going to be sold as slaves? After all, he was no hypocrite: I had to give him that. So what were they doing there?

"I've told you before, Madsen, and I'll tell you again: they're not slaves and they're not plantation workers. They're free men, like you and me."

That was his answer the next time I pressed him on it. After that I gave up asking.

A few days later he sought me out. The look on his face told me I was in for a surprise.

"It'll do no harm to reveal it now, Madsen," he said. "We're heading for Samoa. That's where your father is."

"So now I know," I said, though I'll admit I felt no urge to thank him. Instead I said, "So what's stopping us from going our separate ways? There's nothing to keep us together now."

He laughed and flung out his arms as if to embrace me. "Of course there is, my dear boy. Look around you. The sea! That's what binds us. How will you get to Samoa on your own? Swim? Get off on one of the desert islands that don't figure on any sea chart, and hope to obtain passage from there? No, you're tied to this ship. Just like the free men in the hold."

Jack Lewis was right. Knowing where my father was—knowledge that I feared I'd paid for dearly even if I benefited from it—changed nothing.

"We'll make a single stop along the way," Jack Lewis continued, in the same triumphant tone. "But I trust you won't feel the need to desert me."

"And why wouldn't I?" I retorted.

"Don't be insubordinate, my boy. Because you're too smart to live out your days on a desert island."

"If the island is deserted, what are we going to do there?"

"The same thing I always do wherever I go: trade."

"Who with, if there's no one there?"

"A good question, my boy, more profound than you can imagine. Yes, who with? That question I can answer only with a new one. What's a human being? Yes, what?" He looked directly at me. "Can you tell me that?" Jack Lewis laughed in a way that signaled he was uninterested in my answer and that our conversation was at an end.

TWO DAYS LATER we spotted a seagull: our first in three weeks. But there was no land in sight. I took out my chart and found not a single island mapped in our vicinity.

Jack Lewis sent a man up the rigging. Shortly afterward an affirmative shout came from above—and some hours later a palm-fringed coastline appeared on the horizon.

"Your desert island?" I asked Jack Lewis, who was standing alongside me by the rail.

He nodded but said nothing.

Once we got closer, I could see that there was another ship off its coast. I pointed toward the island.

"Someone seems to have beaten us to it."

"She's a wreck," Lewis said. "She's stuck on the reef. Been there for years. The *Morning Star*. That's where I got the portraits of the red-nosed lady and her husband."

"And the crew?" I asked.

"The crew was long dead when I found the ship."

"What happened?"

Jack Lewis shrugged. "Only they know. And as they say, dead men don't tell tales."

"Mutiny?"

He turned to give one of the Kanaks an order. I realized that I wouldn't learn more, but I couldn't tell from looking at him whether he was holding something back.

We crossed in front of the reef, looking for a way in. Jack Lewis steered toward the wreck. Just before we reached it, we saw a gap in the thundering surf—which the crew of the *Morning Star* had clearly been aiming for. They'd paid a high price for their lack of perfect accuracy. The ship sat high on the reef, as if she'd been flung there with great force. And her position explained why she still appeared undamaged, so that at first I'd assumed she was anchored off the lagoon. She barely heeled, and all three of her masts were intact. Her name was still legible on the stern. A weather-beaten figurehead in flowing white robes held out her hands beseechingly toward the shore, the sole, stiff survivor of that wreck.

The next minute we'd negotiated our way safely into the translucent water of the lagoon, where we could see every fish that darted across the seabed. Beyond the reef's white surf the water was a deep blue, as if in shadow, but in here it was emerald, so dazzling you'd think the sand below contained a source of energy as strong as the sun. The beach was white and fringed by lush undergrowth, which melted into jungle. I sensed that this dense vegetation was the wall behind which Jack Lewis kept his secret.

My thoughts must have been drifting because I didn't notice we'd dropped anchor until Jack Lewis suddenly reappeared next to me, clutching a pair of binoculars. He was searching for something on the beach. I saw nothing—but he grunted in contentment.

"Now's the moment."

"What moment?"

"The moment when I prove to you that I'm a man of my word. You didn't believe me when I told you that the men in the hold were free men and not slaves. Now you can judge for yourself."

"You've got a gun in your hands."

"A man needs to take precautions. But I don't plan to use it."

He ordered the Kanaks to remove the hatch from the hold and then make themselves invisible in the fo'c'sle in front of the mast. It was a strange command, but they didn't look ready to question it, so I guessed it wasn't the first time they'd participated in the ritual, or whatever it was I was about to witness.

Jack Lewis signaled to us to hide behind the deckhouse and pressed a finger against his lips. He looked tense, and I noted that his other finger rested on the trigger of the rifle. Soon we heard voices and footsteps on the deck: the "free men" were emerging from the hold. Lewis gestured at me to keep still, and for a while we just stood listening. Then I heard splashing, and his face lit up in a smile, as if everything was going according to plan. He nodded and grinned silently at me. A second splash followed, and then a third.

I could see from the way Lewis moved his lips and fingers that he was taking some kind of tally. When he'd counted through all the fingers on one hand four times and reached twenty, he slapped me on the shoulder in high spirits.

"So, my boy," he said. "Any questions?"

I glanced across the lagoon where the men, who until a few minutes ago had been trapped in the hold, were now making for the beach. They all reached it almost simultaneously—and then disappeared into the jungle. None of them looked back.

I didn't know what to say. I felt more baffled than ever. Jack Lewis cocked his head and studied me. "Look," he said. "Free men. Did you see anyone trying to stop them from running off?"

"You're a practical man, Mr. Lewis," I said. "And I don't understand why you've fed these men for so many weeks only to see them disappear. What's in it for you? And what are the men doing on a desert island?"

"Surely that's their own business. I don't know what they're doing there and it's not my concern. All I know is that they had the choice. You saw with your own eyes that I ordered the hatch opened."

"Who wouldn't have fled, if the alternative was to stay in a dark hole? Is that a real choice?"

"It's a choice," Jack Lewis said. "And I offered it to them. But that's enough talking. Let's get down to the real reason we're here."

He went over to the fo'c'sle and shouted an order to the Kanaks, who immediately appeared on deck and started readying a boat.

"I think you should come ashore with us. You'll find it a worthwhile experience."

Across his shoulder he slung an old-fashioned musket with a powder horn and a ramrod, and I gave him a puzzled look. In his hand, he held a Winchester rifle.

"Don't ask," he grinned. "I'm a superstitious man. This old gun is my talisman."

I climbed down into the boat, together with two Kanaks, who manned the oars. The beach was deserted. On a desert island, what else could it be?

We dragged the boat ashore, and Jack Lewis walked up and down the beach while he scanned the thicket as though in search of something. Then he waved at me. Behind a flowering hibiscus I spotted a row of calabashes. In the sand next to them lay a hide filled with something that looked like pebbles, but I was too far away to see it properly.

Jack Lewis went over to the hide and tied it into a parcel with some leather string while the Kanaks started carrying the calabashes to the boat. They made a sloshing sound, and I realized that they were filled with supplies of fresh water. Jack Lewis weighed the parcel in the palm of his hand. I heard a rustling sound, and if his masklike face had ever been capable of expressing an emotion such as happiness, then that's what it was doing now.

Just then a gunshot rang out across the island.

Lewis froze.

"Damn it to hell!" he exclaimed. "Damn, bastard hell!"

He clutched his leather parcel and turned to me.

"Quick!" he said. "Take as many calabashes as you can carry!"

He yelled an order at the Kanaks, who immediately started pushing the boat back into the water. He gripped the packet tightly as he ran. I could tell from his face that our frantic flight was to save that, rather than our lives. Whatever it held was clearly his pirate treasure.

By now the boat was in the water, and I had to wade out thigh-deep before I could climb aboard. The Kanaks started rowing immediately, while Jack Lewis stood in the middle of the boat, cocking his rifle. He aimed at the shore and I heard a thundering crack. I turned toward the beach and saw it was teeming with natives. Several of them had guns and they were firing back, a whole salvo of bullets that hit the water around us. Jack Lewis returned fire, and I could see he was a good shot. One of the natives already lay outstretched in the sand. Soon another one tumbled.

"Ha," he snorted. "Fortunately for us those devils don't know how to aim."

"I thought you said this was an uninhabited island."

"I never said it was an uninhabited island. I said no humans lived here. If you call those devils humans once more, I'll order you off the boat. Then you can join your own species if that's what you want."

He grinned cruelly at me and carried on shooting. Yet another native collapsed, but the rest kept firing.

"So, what's your decision?"

I shook my head.

"I think I'll stay here."

I didn't understand any of this. Who were the natives, and why were they shooting at us? They couldn't be the free men from our hold. Where would they have got the guns? And the calabashes of water and the mysterious pebbles that had made Jack Lewis's rigid face crease with joy? What was their significance? He'd called it trading—but the deal appeared to have gone badly wrong.

No, I didn't understand anything. All I knew was that my heart was beating as it never had before and that the minutes I spent under this hail of bullets, with no task to distract me because the only oars in the boat were in the hands of the Kanak crew, felt like hours and days. The *Flying Scud*, which was probably a couple of cable lengths from the shore, seemed as far away as ever. Fortunately, the two Kanaks who'd remained on board ship saw our predicament and started to raise the anchor, but this didn't lessen the danger we were in: a second group of natives had pulled a long canoe across the beach and launched it not far from where the first group was positioned. They were still keeping up a heavy barrage of gunfire, though Jack Lewis's marksmanship had by now reduced them to half their original number, and the beach was strewn with bodies.

The canoe gained on us rapidly. Half of the men paddled while the rest stood shooting at us, so Lewis was forced to cover two targets at once. He fired a final shot toward the shore as a farewell and another native fell. Then he focused his attention on the canoe and I saw the foremost of the crewmen thrown sideways into the water just as our own boat suddenly slackened its speed.

Until now I had watched the dreadful spectacle in mute fear, my role reduced to that of the spectator of a drama whose outcome had not yet been written. And if fate was cruel enough, the spectacle would cost me my life. Just then, one of the Kanaks collapsed over his oars with a howl of pain. I pushed him from the thwart to the bottom of the boat, where he stayed, clutching his wounded shoulder. Blood bubbled out of it in a glistening stream barely visible against his dark skin. With a part to play at last, I rowed as I'd never rowed before. As soon as my hands had found something to do, I felt I'd seized some control over my own fate: my dark thoughts vanished and time—which a moment earlier seemed to stand still—resumed. The *Flying Scud* quickly grew closer. Her mainsail and foresail were already raised, thanks to the nimble fingers of the Kanaks aboard. I thought we were saved. But then came a burst of obscenities from Lewis.

"Oh, bloody hell!"

I thought that for once he'd missed his target. Then I realized he'd stopped shooting. He'd run out of ammunition.

I looked up. He tore open the leather purse and started rummaging in it. Then he fished out a small object and held it up to the light. As Jack Lewis twirled it in his fingers, the sun caught it, changing its color from white to pink to purple to blue, and back again to white.

It was a pearl!

I can't say that it was the most beautiful pearl I'd ever seen because I hadn't seen many, let alone held one in my hand. But it was wondrously lovely, and for a moment I was completely floored by the sight of it. Somehow, it was an invitation to dream. And despite the dire situation we were in, I let myself be whisked somewhere entirely different from an undermanned launch pursued by a canoe of bloodthirsty natives, who were swiftly gaining on us with brisk strokes. Jack Lewis knocked me brutally out of my reverie.

"Row, damn you, row!"

I'd been sitting immobile, the oars in my hands, while I stared at the pearl. Now I watched as Lewis took the old musket from his shoulder, poured gunpowder into the barrel, shoved the pearl down after it, and tamped the whole thing tight with his ramrod. Then he raised the gun he'd called his talisman and took careful aim. Before the noise of the blast died down, one of the natives flew backward, as if flung by a giant hand, and disappeared into the water.

"I'll send you the bill, you devil!" Jack Lewis screamed, his face distorted by rage.

He reloaded the gun. His fingers shook as he pushed yet another precious pearl into place. I could barely believe my own ears when I heard the strange sound that escaped his compressed lips: I could have sworn it was a sob. The gun went off with a bang.

The Kanak behind me jumped. I thought he'd been shot, but it turned out that his oar had taken a direct hit close to the oarlock and snapped in two. Now I was the only one rowing.

Our lives were riding on the pearls, Jack Lewis's aim, and the strength of my arms, and I rowed until they felt ready to drop. Desperation lent them a power I'd never known, and the gap between our pursuers and us began to widen. There were fewer of them now. Lewis's precision with both bullets and pearls had taken every second man. Our enemy's victory song echoed in our minds just as menacingly as before—but its chorus had diminished. Finally we reached the *Flying Scud*, where a rope ladder awaited us. I slung the injured Kanak over my shoulder without feeling his weight, climbed the side of the ship, and hefted us both over the rail, heedless of what kind of target we might present as I did so. Several shots rang out behind us, but neither one of us was hit.

The Kanaks on board had prepared everything for our departure: the anchor was hung from the bow, the sails were set, and if they'd had access to the captain's cabin and his stash of guns, they'd undoubtedly have been handing him loaded rifles so he could continue shooting down our pursuers uninterrupted. But access to those guns was a taboo they dared not break.

We were barely back on deck before Jack Lewis had dashed to his cabin and reappeared with a box of cartridges and a new rifle. Then he knelt behind the rail and resumed firing. His face was that of a man settling a personal score, rather than putting a dangerous enemy out of action. For every precious pearl that he'd lost, he was making the natives pay, not just with the life each pearl had ended, but with interest. He greeted every clean kill with a cry of triumph.

"Take this, you devil!"

He spat contemptuously over the rail.

I had to take the helm: the captain was too preoccupied with his blood lust. It was up to me to get us across this lagoon and out through the opening in the reef. My success had nothing to do with seamanship, but with the fortunes of wind and tide, both of which were on our side. The wind had picked up and it filled our sails even before we were out of the lagoon. The tide was low and the current raced out through the gap in the reef. A believer would have said Our Lord was giving us a helping hand. But since I don't believe that the Lord, if He exists, would have been on Jack Lewis's side, all I'll say is that during one lucky hour, Nature ordered the sea and wind to side with him.

The feeling of being miraculously saved at the very last moment never quite left me, though I can't speculate who would have been worse off if Nature had decided to trap the *Flying Scud* in the lagoon, ourselves or the natives. There were many of them, but Jack Lewis's marksmanship was—to use a word that would undoubtedly have flattered his vanity—fiendish.

We sailed past the wreck of the *Morning Star* at a smart speed, at which point Jack Lewis took a break from shooting natives and turned his rifle on the wreck instead. I heard a bang and saw the face of the figurehead disappear in a cloud of splinters. It seemed that Lewis's rage could no longer be quenched by the blood of his enemies—and in that moment I sensed that we had not escaped danger. It had just changed shape. Now it was on board with us.

HAVING REACHED the open sea, I might have felt it was safe to breathe a sigh of relief—had I not seen that savagery in Jack Lewis's face. He'd finally put the gun down and left his position by the rail, and was now pacing up and down, muttering to himself.

"It's all ruined . . . who is the bastard . . . if only I could find that accursed bastard."

He scowled at me as if I too were suspected of a crime, the nature of which I couldn't fathom. His plans, whatever they were, had been thwarted. He owed me an explanation for the nightmare we'd just lived through. But I realized that now was the wrong time to ask him. If I valued my life, there might never be a right one.

I glanced over at him anxiously, trying to gauge the mood that accompanied his stream of muttered expletives. So when his face lit in a sudden smile, it caught me off guard.

"Well, I never," he exclaimed, as though he'd just spotted a much-missed friend whom he'd soon be welcoming with open arms.

I turned to see what had caught his attention and there, half a cable's length astern, the natives' canoe was bobbing up and down in our gleaming wake. I could barely believe my eyes. How could they possibly think they had a chance of defeating us now?

They worked their paddles feverishly. They were all sitting down; not one of them stood to aim a gun. There were seven or eight of them left: perhaps they wanted to be sure in advance they'd hit their target this time. They might even be planning to board us. Had they learned nothing?

I didn't for one moment worry about their attacking us. I simply pitied them and their naive folly, for it seemed they were not just dicing with death, but positively inviting it. Their daring filled me with deep sadness on their behalf.

No, I didn't fear the natives and their suicidal attack. I feared Jack Lewis's reawakened blood lust.

"What a delightful surprise," he declared. "And I was just thinking that the fun was over."

He grabbed his rifle and placed it on his shoulder. Then he lowered it.

"They're too far away," he said, sounding disappointed. "Let them catch up a bit. Sail closer to the wind."

"But Captain," I objected, "they've no chance of reaching us. Surely enough blood has been shed by now?"

He looked at me dispassionately. "We were attacked and we defended ourselves. That's all."

"But we're not being attacked now. And as long as we stick to our course, we won't be."

"Sail closer!"

My hands still hesitated on the wheel. He stepped up close to me, and his small eyes widened with rage.

"Mr. Madsen, I'm the captain of the *Flying Scud* and I have just given you an order. If it doesn't please the young gentleman to obey, he will be regarded as a mutineer, and mutineers get short shrift from me."

He poked the barrel of the gun into my face and for a moment we stared into each other's eyes.

It wasn't his stare or the menacing closeness of the gun barrel that made me follow his order. The weapon was shaking in his hands, and I sensed that although his voice was calm, he was in an uncontrollable rage—not at me or the natives who had spoiled his plans, but at the entire world. And he didn't care who paid the price: the natives or his first mate. It was all the same to him.

"Aye, aye, Captain," I said, and turned the wheel.

He lowered the rifle and returned to the stern. The ship dropped speed until we lay still, with the sails flapping in the breeze. The natives' canoe came closer. Jack Lewis raised his rifle and began picking them off one by one. With each direct hit, he emitted a short, contented grunt.

The canoe kept gliding forward. One after another, the natives stood up with their guns, aimed, fired, and fell dead.

At last there was only one left—but he kept paddling toward us. Jack Lewis paused in his shooting, and his attention seemed to drift momentarily. It was clear that his rage had abated.

"Leave him be," I said. "It's enough."

He looked up and gave me a small, sleepy smile, and in that moment his face had the strange gentleness of a newly wakened child.

"You're right," he said. "It's enough." He joined me.

"Aye, aye, Captain, straight ahead."

Once more the wind filled our sails and we raced ahead at the same speed as before. Neither of us spoke for a while. I'd escaped death only to have my life threatened by the very man who'd saved me—and now he was standing next to me, pretending that nothing had happened.

"Fine weather," he said suddenly, and inhaled deeply. "Sea air! Nothing like it. Makes a sailor's life worth living."

Of all the things I'd heard Jack Lewis say during the months I'd spent with him, this unremarkable comment seemed the strangest. I didn't believe for one moment that he meant what he said—and yet I welcomed his words. The terror I'd felt these past few hours had eased and we were once again a captain and his first mate on our way across the ocean.

"Yes," I said, and imitated Jack Lewis by inhaling deeply. "Sea air does a world of good."

Our idyll was interrupted by an agitated Kanak who ran up, pointing backward. We both turned. And there was the solitary native in his canoe, a black silhouette against our glittering wake. He wasn't far behind. How he'd managed to gain on us, on his own, in a canoe built for several oarsmen, was incomprehensible.

We watched him for a long time. The distance between our unequal craft remained constant. I glanced sideways at Jack Lewis but said nothing. I expected him to grab his rifle again and put an end to the life he'd spared in a moment of kindness. But he didn't.

Eventually he turned to the helm and ordered me to adjust our course. From time to time I'd look back across the water. The native was still there. The distance remained the same. He neither gained on us nor lagged behind.

A couple of hours passed in this manner, and as I watched our pursuer, my perception of him shifted. Now what I saw was a man all alone in a canoe on the sea. He wasn't a native any more, part of the savage group that had recently attacked us. I no longer knew who he was or what he wanted from us, whether he was a pursuer or someone in need. All I saw was the vast ocean and his lost figure at the center of it. I felt he had to be some kind of messenger, but I had no idea what he was trying to tell us.

"This has got to stop," Jack Lewis said at last.

I knew then that there was nothing I could do.

He went back to his rifle and picked it up. I didn't look at him but kept staring at the solitary oarsman in the middle of the sea. Somehow I wanted to say goodbye to him in the minutes he had left and make sure I wouldn't forget him. My memory would be his only tombstone.

He must have seen Jack Lewis aim his Winchester, because he suddenly stood up and flung his own gun onto his shoulder. A bang sounded from Lewis's rifle, and at the same time a red flash shot from the muzzle of the native's gun. They'd fired simultaneously. Our pursuer crashed backward into the canoe, and it turned sideways in the wake, where it bobbed up and down. Quickly, the gap between us widened. Soon the canoe and the dead man would be gone from view.

So preoccupied had I been with the native's fate that I'd paid no attention at all to what was happening on the *Flying Scud*. But now I heard a loud groan. It came from Jack Lewis. When I turned around, he was sprawled on the deck, a red stain spreading across his shirtfront. The native's bullet had also found its target.

Bewildered, the Kanaks knelt around their captain, as if awaiting his orders. Could they not see that Jack Lewis lay dying right in front of them?

For a moment I wondered if they considered him immortal because his actions were guided by the same unpredictable cruelty shown by their own gods. He'd sliced an ear off one of them, and I'd never heard him address them in anything other than a tone of command. He'd used them as pawns in a game that brought them no profit yet might have cost them their lives, and he'd sacrificed them without explanation. So why not consider him a god? After all, this was how gods behaved, wasn't it? With an inscrutability that was indistinguishable from arbitrariness? Believers might offer prayers and even sacrifices, but none ever found a method of worship that ensured their prayers were answered.

When I saw Jack Lewis stretched out on the deck, with the bloodstain blossoming across his shirtfront, I realized that he'd become my god too. He'd promised to deliver me to my *papa tru*. Instead, he'd taken me to an uncharted island where I witnessed mysterious transactions and a terrible massacre, on a ship with a cargo of human beings he insisted were free men.

I'd sailed with him to solve one puzzle, only to discover another.

I was just like one of his Kanaks. But I was also a white man, and I felt he owed me an answer to the riddle. He was about to die, and I wanted that explanation before it was too late.

I ordered one of the Kanaks to take the helm, and went over to Jack Lewis. I'd never seen a human being die before, unlike my *papa tru*, who had been to war and seen men all around him blasted to pieces as the *Christian the Eighth* headed for disaster. I'd seen men fall overboard and disappear into the sea, but that was different. Swallowed up by the waves, they were already lost from view by the time they began that lonely journey into the depths. They didn't die in front of your eyes. They just left your field of vision.

Jack Lewis was about to die, I was certain of it. Just as I was certain that now, as he lay on the deck like the statue of a deity toppled from its plinth, his stony façade would crack and reveal the naked human inside. Bleeding from his wound, he'd soon be exposed as human just as James Cook was in Kealakekua Bay.

But as he stared at me, I realized that I'd been wrong to think that. Jack Lewis might be a toppled god, but he was still a god. There was no fear in his eyes, and I didn't know why I ever thought I'd see it. Was there grief, then, at all he'd have to bid farewell to? Or regret, for all he'd no longer achieve? Or was there just pure rage?

I'd seen him lose his self-control when he was forced to use his precious pearls as bullets. Was that how he viewed his own death? As the waste of a pearl?

I was young and I'd never given death a second thought. Can the feelings that another's death prompts in you provide a forewarning of what you'll experience when you draw your own last breath? I was about to find out.

"Fetch the whiskey." He had to swallow between each word, but Jack Lewis's voice still retained its old authority. He patted the deck with a feeble hand, as though inviting me for a final drink in his cabin. "And Jim."

I stared at him.

"Are you deaf?"

Perplexed, I shook my head and went to his cabin to carry out his order. Unwrapping the ghastly head from its cloth, I placed it next to Lewis. Then I opened the whiskey and poured some into my palm. I'd never treated a gunshot wound before, but I vaguely recalled that you cleaned them with alcohol.

"What do you think you're doing?" Jack Lewis snarled.

"I'm going to wash your wound."

"My wound!" he exclaimed. "My wound isn't thirsty. I am. Fetch two glasses."

When I returned with the glasses, Jack Lewis was scrutinizing Jim, as though he'd just asked him a question and was now awaiting the reply.

The Kanaks stood rooted to the spot in the middle of the deck. The helmsman had let go of the wheel: I shouted at him and he returned to his post. But he kept turning around. It wasn't the dying captain his eyes kept roaming toward, but the shrunken head in his hands.

"Is this wise?" I said to Jack Lewis.

"That's none of your business." His voice was thick with contempt. "Of course, it's bloody stupid to show a shrunken head to a bunch of cannibals whose blood's just been roused. But I'll be gone in a moment. And then it's your problem, not mine."

A gurgling noise came from his chest, and he bared his teeth in a grimace that might have been a smile.

"Fill up the glasses. Let's toast our onward journey. Mine's to the unknown. And yours will be as the newly fledged captain of a cannibal ship."

I poured and passed him the glass, but he didn't have the strength to hold it: I had to support his head and raise the glass to his lips. He drained its contents with a groan, but it was impossible to tell whether it was from pleasure or pain.

"The free men," I said. "I want you to tell me about the free men."

"The free men were just like Jim here."

"So they were a commodity?"

"Yes," Jack Lewis said, and his eyes took on a remote expression, as though the conversation didn't interest him and his journey into the unknown had already started. I was going to have to hurry.

"But what was the deal about?"

"Grains of sand," he whispered. "Pebbles. Toys for children."

His head slumped to one side and his eyes closed, as if he was falling asleep. For a moment I feared that he had died. Then he opened his eyes and looked at me.

"We despise the natives because they allow themselves to be mesmerized by glass baubles. I don't know what they must think of us. We'll kill over a grain of sand covered in oyster scum."

"What did you give them in return for the pearls?"

"I paid with the free men."

"So they weren't free. They were your prisoners."

"No," Jack Lewis said and shook his head; again his shattered chest gurgled. "You still haven't got it. They weren't my prisoners. They were my students."

"You're right. I still haven't got it. I think you've been telling me a pack of lies."

"Listen to me." Jack Lewis was still lying with one cheek against the deck. When he glanced up at me again, it was with a teasing look that was hard to associate with a dying man. "The savages have no concept of freedom. They're free, but they don't know it. So before they can learn to value their freedom, they must first lose it."

"And so you trapped them in the hold?"

Jack Lewis grimaced, but whether it was in response to my slow wits or because he was trying to smile again, I couldn't decide.

"No, I didn't trap them in the hold. I merely left them to their own fear. I made sure they never saw the light of day, and in the dark they conjured up all sorts of ideas about the terrible fate that was waiting for them. When I opened the hatch and allowed the daylight in, their education was complete. They understood instantly what freedom was, and they grabbed it."

"What's that got to do with the pearls?"

"The answer lies with the *Morning Star*," Jack Lewis said. "She was a blackbirder, a slave ship. She foundered and the slaves in the hold rebelled, killed the crew, and took over the island, which was uninhabited. There were women and children among them, so as far as they were concerned they weren't stranded on a desert island. They'd been given a whole new world, where they could start over. Their paradise was only missing one thing, and that's where I entered the scene."

His face lit up in triumph, and it suddenly dawned on me why he was confiding all this to me. He was so proud of his cruelty that he couldn't bear the thought of dying with it unwitnessed. He'd turned his entire life into a mystery, but now he needed someone to know the full extent of a crime that he personally regarded as final proof—not of his cunning so much as his own unique insight into the human mind.

He turned ugly in his triumph, and I let my eyes slide toward James Cook, with his flared nostrils and stitched-up eyelids. In that moment, I preferred his horribly distorted face to Jack Lewis's. Yet I had to continue with my questioning. Even if I feared that by listening I might end up complicit in his crimes, I couldn't stop myself. I had to know the secret of the free men.

"So what were the savages missing in their paradise?" I asked.

"A change of diet," Jack Lewis replied, and his face contorted in a terrible grimace, which I took to be the dying man's attempt at laughter. The sound quickly curdled into a hollow, gurgling cough. He seemed to be choking, and blood leaked from his cracked, narrow lips. Slowly I realized what he'd said. My disgust must have been obvious.

"They're cannibals, you see," he explained, as though to a child.

"So you sell human flesh," I said. Again I was looking at Jim.

"The world isn't a straightforward place," Jack Lewis said. "I don't sell human flesh. I sell the opportunity for victory. That's what's lacking in paradise, you understand. In every paradise. That's the flaw in its construction. The serpent isn't the enemy; he's just the tempter. I'm thinking of a real enemy, whom you have to fight or else be vanquished. I'm thinking of the chance to test yourself in battle, to win or die. That was the opportunity I gave those damned cannibals: not a shipload of human flesh, but a chance to prove their worth. For God's sake. They're savages. And they're men. They can't live unless they fight. I visited them once a year. I offered free men the opportunity to escape. And who won the battle once they'd swum ashore was none of my business."

He fell silent, and again for a moment I thought that he'd died. His eyes were closed.

"And then they discovered a new and better enemy," I said out loud, but I was talking to myself as much as to him.

Jack Lewis opened up his eyes and gave me a reproachful look, as though I'd just reminded him of something unpleasant.

"Some idiot sold them guns and ruined my business." He snarled and attempted to spit on the deck, but what came out was blood. "I had a good operation running there. It could have carried on for years. They got someone they could fight, and kill, and eat. And I got the pearls. And then that bastard turns up."

"Who?" I asked.

"None of your business." He spat more blood. "Get me another glass."

I poured him another whiskey and held it to his lips. He coughed, and the whiskey trickled down his lower lip and mingled with the blood, which was now flowing in a constant stream. He sighed.

"You'll inherit all this. A bag of pearls and a ship. A good start for a young sailor. More than you deserve."

I didn't know what to say. I didn't want to take charge of this ship, which, regardless of what her owner said, was nothing but a black-birder. Nor would I touch the pearls. Their pink sheen put me in mind not of grains of sand, but of dried blood.

I said nothing. Though I had no respect for Jack Lewis, I respected the hole in his chest. He was dying, and you owe the dying your attention.

"Paradise," he mumbled. "A paradise complete with everything, including enemies, ready to kill you." He glanced at the Kanaks and bared his yellow teeth. Blood was seeping out between them. "The moment your back's turned, they'll stick a knife in it. They can see me lying here. And they've met Jim. If they didn't know it before, they know it now: white men can die too."

Jack Lewis closed his eyes again and sighed. He didn't move, and after a while I realized that he was never going to open them again. Despite those last words of warning, which echoed in my ears, there was no way that I could keep his death a secret from the Kanaks.

I couldn't keep him on board, so I went down to his cabin to look for something to wrap his body in before surrendering it to the sea. A flag was what I had in mind, but I couldn't find one, so I took an unused strip of canvas. His shirtfront was soaked with blood, but I had no way of sending him overboard in clean clothes, and no urge to touch his body, with its sticky blood. So there he lay, wrapped in canvas bound by a piece of rope. A life had ended—though hardly a beautiful one, in my opinion. I didn't know much about Jack Lewis, but I knew enough not to mourn his death.

I summoned the Kanaks, and together we eased Jack Lewis over the rail. He bobbed up and down in our wake for a while. And then he sank. No sharks circled his body before it went under. He'd regarded his fellow human beings as no more than meat on a butcher's slab, and I had no idea if he'd been a Christian, but I did him the honor of folding my hands and reciting the Lord's Prayer.

I said the words in Danish. The Kanaks watched in silence. When they saw me fold my hands, they folded theirs too. I interpreted this as a gesture of respect, toward me as much as the deceased. I was their captain now. What they thought beyond that, I had no clue. Their dark, blue-tattooed faces gave nothing away. Was this the start of another Kealakekua Bay? Would the fate that Jack Lewis escaped befall me instead? Would they tear me to pieces, eat my heart, and smoke my head over an open fire? I wanted to hide in my cabin while I went through my options, but I felt that if I entered its protective darkness, I'd never emerge again, for fear they'd be waiting outside the door with their knives.

So instead I took the wheel.

I REALIZED THAT the first thing I had to do was overcome my fear of the Kanaks, which Jack Lewis had planted so cleverly. As long as I was in thrall to it, Lewis was still on board and in control. I had to issue my own orders and assume they'd be executed. I had to enter my cabin without dreading an ambush and to go to sleep safe in the knowledge that I'd wake up again. In short, I had to do what men have done on ships for thousands of years: I had to be the captain.

But I was young and I'd never commanded a ship before. I was alone with four Kanaks, one of them out of action, and we were in the middle of the Pacific Ocean. I knew very little about the destination we'd been headed for, and I was aware that even if I skippered the *Flying Scud* to a safe haven, that wouldn't solve my problems. Who would believe my story?

I was still weighing my prospects when I happened to look at the deck. There lay the shrunken head of James Cook, just where it had been when Jack Lewis bade it farewell. I steadied my voice and ordered one of the Kanaks to take the wheel. Then I picked up the shrunken head, carried it down to the cabin, and settled it on Jack Lewis's berth.

I can't explain why I didn't throw it overboard immediately, because I had no desire to keep it or ever cast my eyes on it again. But when I cupped it in my hands and gazed out over the shimmering sea, something held me back. I'd unwrapped the head for Jack Lewis when he'd asked to see it for the final time, but I'd been so preoccupied by his imminent death that I forgot I was handling the horrifying remains of a human being.

Now I became more conscious of the feel of James Cook's leathery skin and straw-dry hair, and the physical contact seemed to link me to the man he'd been before he'd been shrunk into a symbol of barbarism. I could ease my captain's dead body over the rail. But I couldn't do the same to James Cook.

It wasn't just because Jack Lewis had told me Jim's true identity. Did I believe him? Yes and no. But ultimately it made no difference: the whole thing seemed completely unreal anyway. If this was indeed the head of James Cook, it should probably be returned to England—though I had no idea what the people of England would do with it. Keep its existence a secret because the whole business was somehow embarrassing? Hold a ceremony to lay it to rest? Even provide it with its own coffin, perhaps? But how many times can you bury a man? What if a foot was to turn up someday? Would the funeral have to be staged a second time?

Naming this shrunken head Jim in the first place had seemed a malicious joke. But now the joke involved James Cook too. I thought it best to let him rest in peace, but his head was still here, the last vestige of a man who'd suffered a horrific death. I couldn't just toss it overboard like some broken object or a piece of meat that had started to smell.

It was at that point that I understood the difference between me and Jack Lewis. To Lewis, Jim was a shrunken head. To me, he was a human being.

I've often wondered whether Jim appeared more human to me than the Kanaks, whose individual features were hidden in the unfathomable darkness of the blue tattoos etched across their faces. I looked for something human in their eyes, but I found nothing but foreignness, as if their eyes were also tattoos. I never heard Jack Lewis talk to them, and I was never to do so either. I gave my orders and they carried them out. When I bandaged the wounded Kanak, I noticed he was the one with the missing ear. He looked away when I tried to clean his wound, and continued to look away while I bandaged it. A line lay between us and it was never crossed. But as the days passed, my fear of them faded. The ship told us who we were: I was the captain, they were the crew, and the trade wind, which always came from the same direction and blew with the same strength, assured us every day that all was as it should be.

It was under these circumstances that I started behaving in a way that I realized was strange. I started talking to Jim. I'd go down to the cabin, light the whale-oil lamp, and unwrap him from his cloth.

Then I'd place him on the table in front of me, where the flickering light from the lamp lent his face an attentive expression. I could feel him concentrating, behind his stitched-up eyelids. But he never once talked back to me and I was glad of that. It would have been ultimate proof that I had lost my mind.

I'd place the bag of pearls in front of him and take them out, one by one, to show him. Then I'd ask him if he thought I ought to keep them.

My first impulse had been to throw them into the sea after Jack Lewis's body. Indeed, at times I regretted that I hadn't done so right in front of him, while he still breathed. That missed moment might have represented some sort of victory over him and the amorality he clearly believed he'd infected me with. But I'd hesitated too long. One moment had turned into several, and now I kept the pearls hidden next to Jim. Before long I would probably tuck the bag under my shirt and start guarding it with my life, giving the Kanaks a good reason for taking both from me. Why wouldn't they know the value of pearls, or want some of what the money could buy—freedom especially?

I felt that I was holding my entire future in my hands when I felt the weight of the swollen bag. I didn't even need the *Flying Scud*. I could buy my own ship. I could buy three ships, become a shipowner, and have my own house. Perhaps even the big, beautiful house built after the fire in Øvre Strandstræde, across from the parsonage. In my imagination I started peopling this house with a wife and children: yes, servants, even. I saw my future wife in a violet dress, picking roses in the garden.

I never described these fantasies to Jim. Instead, I asked him to be my judge. He must make the decision for me. It wasn't the suffering he had endured before he became a shrunken head that qualified him. Rather, it was his silence. I could put any reply I wanted into his mouth.

"So, Jim," I'd say in the twilight of the cabin, "should I keep the pearls? What do you think?"

Jim never said yes or no. He just looked at me through his stitched eyelids, and I felt that the answers to all my questions were hidden behind them.

I began thinking a lot about my *papa tru*. I'd never asked him for advice and he'd never given me any. We'd parted far too early for that. But now I was looking for him. That was my mission in the Pacific:

to find my missing *papa tru*. But what did I want from him, and what would I do when I found him? Ask him for some good advice? Rebuild our lost relationship? The last time I saw him, I was a child. Now I was an adult and I couldn't turn the clock back. So what did I want to do? Show him that I could stand on my own two feet? Had I looked for him across half the world just to prove to him how easily I could manage without him?

I realized that I'd never thought past the moment when I stood face to face with him again. I was a skilled sailor. I'd crossed the great oceans, but when it came to this, I felt like a newcomer to the world—not because I didn't know its busy, overcrowded ports, its palm-fringed coasts and wind-lashed rocks, but because I understood so little of my own soul. I could navigate from a chart; I could determine my position using a sextant. I was in an unknown place in the Pacific on a ship with no captain and I could still find my way. But I had no way of mapping my own mind or the course of my life.

I emptied Jack Lewis's cupboard of bottles and went on deck to throw them overboard. I didn't open a single one before chucking them into the water—not even the mysterious one with the white fluid in which the outline of a dark shape could sometimes be seen. The doors Jack Lewis had opened to me had led to rooms filled with horrors. I watched the bottles fall astern and disappear beneath the waves.

I knew that I ought to have thrown out Jim as well. But he continued to keep me company. And so did the pearls.

The days passed. I fantasized about my future. I regarded the pearls at one moment as an unexpected stroke of good fortune, and at the next as a curse that would make me an accomplice in Jack Lewis's crimes, should I ever sell them.

All the while we held our course for Samoa.

As long as Jim didn't answer me, I felt I was still free and that nothing had been decided yet. I'd stopped time and I caught myself wishing that I could remain forever in this fuzzy inner world that I'd created with Jim in the twilit cabin, a world where dreams could come true and there was no price to pay for them. I forgot where I really was.

· · ·

I spent most hours of the day alone, but my solitude was no burden. I took my meals in the cabin while the Kanaks ate on deck. They prepared the food: rice and steamed taro. From time to time they'd throw a line over the rail and catch a yellowfin tuna.

I appeared on deck only to correct the course and adjust the spread of the canvas.

After a week the trade wind died down. It disappeared one evening with the sun, which sank into the horizon like a red ball while the clouds fanned out on all sides.

I took that as a bad omen and prepared for a hurricane, but when the next day dawned, the opposite confronted us. The sea was dead calm, as if a heavy lid had been pressed on top of it. The overwhelming heat suggested that a thunderstorm was approaching, but the sky was as blue as a gas flame, and no menacing clouds loomed on the horizon.

I was still convinced that something was about to happen, but my imagination stretched no farther than my fears of an imminent hurricane.

The days passed and we stayed put. The sails hung slack and we rigged an awning amidships to provide shade. For a while I had to part from Jim; it was too hot to sleep in the stagnant air of the cabin, and I didn't want to bring him up on deck with me. Should I leave the pearls down there too?

The dark thoughts I'd nursed down in the cabin wouldn't leave me. I began carrying the leather purse—which contained my entire future—under my shirt, against my bare chest. But it clung to my body in the heat, which had grown so oppressive that I struggled to breathe; I felt as though a gauze bandage gagged my mouth. So I locked the pearls in the cabin with Jim and went bare-chested. From time to time I'd lower a bucket into the sea and pour lukewarm salt water over my body, but neither that nor the arrival of night brought any relief from the heat.

One night, unable to sleep, I headed for the deck. The Kanaks had attached hammocks to the rigging and were murmuring quietly. For the first time my loneliness felt like a burden, but I knew it would be a sign of weakness to approach them or try to strike up a conversation.

We'd secured the wheel. There was no course to stick to. With no current on which to hitch a ride, we weren't going anywhere. I gazed up at the sky. There were still no clouds, and the twinkling of the stars had grown faint, as if they'd given up signaling to us. I understood then how utterly cut off we were from the rest of the world. The *Flying Scud* was like a planet torn from its orbit and about to vanish into the deepest, darkest corner of the universe.

A groan came from one of the hammocks. I stepped closer. It was the Kanak with the bandaged shoulder. His wound had been healing over the past few days. Did his groaning mean that the fever had returned and that his wound had become infected? I knew what an infection looked like, but I had no idea how to treat it, apart from the primitive method of regularly pouring whiskey over it. It was too dark to do anything, so I decided to wait until morning.

I didn't sleep that night; it was too hot, and I felt restless and irritable. Not because this dead calm had brought our voyage to an unexpected halt and cut us off from the world, but because it had severed me from something far more important: the interior world of the cabin, where I ran the pearls through my fingers and chatted to Jim on the table in front of me. That was where my life had been unfolding—and now it was closed to me.

I examined the Kanak's shoulder the following day. There were yellow stains on the white bandage and pus oozed from the gash. It had almost closed, but its edges were red and swollen. I cleaned it as well as I could. The Kanak's blue face stayed passive, but his shoulder twitched every time I touched the swollen wound. So I poured whiskey over it and left it to his fellow Kanaks to change the bandage. I knew they fiddled with his wound too. They had their own medicines, which I wasn't going to interfere with: I already doubted the value of my own methods.

The Kanak's infection gave me the frightening impression that the stagnant air around us was somehow poisoned. We were in the middle of the sea, yet it felt as if we were in a dense jungle, surrounded on all sides by the toxic breath of rotting plants. Was I the only man here who felt that a giant hand was squeezing his chest?

I watched the Kanaks. Their movements too seemed more sluggish. Were they suffocating too? Did this calm, which had nailed us to the vast floor of the ocean, sit on them too, like a dead weight? Were anxious questions beginning to show in the dark eyes behind the blue masks? Were superstitious terrors rising in them like bubbles from the bottom of a stale swamp, demanding some explanation for our cursed immobility? And might their answer be me, the stranger, who didn't belong among them and who could be used as ransom in the face of the inexplicable?

We cast lines, but no fish bit. Again I got the feeling that all life around us had vanished. The depths of the sea had become just as still as its surface. It wasn't the fear of sharks that prevented me from seeking refreshment in a swim. It was the notion that the sea would suck me down the moment I came into contact with it, and I'd disappear into its darkness forever.

On the fourth day I checked our provisions. We had half a sack of taro roots and a few kilos of rice left. I wasn't afraid we would starve, for I had enough common sense left to expect that the sea would, at some point, give up some of its riches and land a tuna on our deck. Our big problem was fresh water. We hadn't picked up sufficient supplies on the island and we were about to run out. A good rainfall would have fulfilled our needs, but the sky remained mercilessly blue. I had to ration the water, but I feared that this in itself might trigger a mutiny. So I decided that from now on we'd all eat our meals together on the deck: that way the Kanaks could see that everyone received the same amount of water.

We weren't equals, nor should we be. A ship's written and unwritten laws must be obeyed. But we had to be equal in our sufferings; otherwise we'd never get through them together. Slowly it began to dawn on me that being becalmed like this could, for a newly fledged captain, prove a far greater challenge than any storm.

Every day we continued to cast our lines but caught nothing. The fish shunned our ship, and I could see a perplexed look on the faces of the experienced Kanaks, who'd spent their entire lives on these waters. We were in the middle of the sea and there wasn't a single fish to be had! Were we cursed?

I handed out one mug of water to each man at every meal. One day I peered into the last water barrel and saw that it was close to empty: enough for two more days, at most. Our only hope was that the trade wind would start to blow and bring rain with it.

On the seventh day, the water ran out. Soft moans came from the hammock where the wounded Kanak was drifting in and out of his fever. No more relief came to his cracked lips, and his eyes rolled upward, as if he hoped to escape via the rigging. When he closed them again, he carried on whimpering. No other sound broke the silence on board. It was at once a sign of life and an omen of the fate that awaited us.

THE SECOND DAY after the water ran out, we were eating our taro roots, which we'd boiled in salt water, when suddenly one of the Kanaks pointed at the horizon. I looked up and saw a cloud. It hung low above the water, and it was moving rapidly and oddly, like steam coming from a boiling pot except that it didn't rise like steam, but spread in all directions at once, like the flocks of migrating starlings that gather in autumn above the fields outside Marstal. Sunlight shone right through this cloud, which was slowly approaching us, though there was still no wind. It seemed to pulsate, as if there was a whirlwind inside it, shaking the leaves of a dense forest.

Then the cloud was upon us, and fleetingly we felt as though we were being showered with the withered leaves of an autumn forest. Then I realized it wasn't dead foliage, but living creatures whirling around us, fluttering silky yellow wings. We were at the center of a vast swarm of butterflies.

There had to be millions of them. A storm, raging far away from the tyrannical calm in which we found ourselves, must have swept them off an island and out to sea. They must have been seeking land—and thought they'd found it on our doomed ship. They settled everywhere, on the ship's rigging and on every single one of its countless ropes, covering the slack sails and transforming them into bright tapestries of yellow. Within minutes this living, breathing mass of exhausted insects had changed the *Flying Scud* beyond recognition.

And the butterflies settled on us too, apparently unable to distinguish between wood, rope, canvas, and human skin. Sharing our desperate thirst, they stuck their tiny proboscises all over our skin, to suck the sweat from it. It wasn't painful in the same way as a bee sting or a mosquito bite, but it was soon followed by an unbearable prickling itch that drove us out of our minds. The moment we relaxed, the creatures descended on us again in droves, going for the moist corners of our lips and eyes, which we had to squeeze shut for protection. If we opened our mouths to scare them off with an angry roar, they instantly clung to our teeth, covering our tongues and tickling our palates with their fluttering wings.

We staggered around, blind and hacking, lashing out at them, but we were their last chance and nothing was going to keep them off. We smashed them against our cheeks, foreheads, and eyebrows, but they kept coming at us, even though they were flying to their doom. I think we'd all willingly have jumped into the sea to escape them, had the water around the ship not been swarming with them. The *Flying Scud* sat like a coffin on a church floor littered with flowers.

When I briefly opened an eye just a crack to find my way to the rail, I caught sight of one of the Kanaks, his blue face and head half swallowed by butterflies. For a moment I forgot the danger and let myself be lulled by the lovely sight of his beautifully rounded blue skull clad in lemony insects slowly flapping their half-open wings, his dark eyes staring out from behind those shining fans. But unlike me, he seemed completely at ease. Whether this was simply because he'd accepted and surrendered to his fate, I never discovered, for at the next moment I was hit in the face by a slosh of water: a quick-witted Kanak had lowered a bucket into the sea and started dousing himself and the rest of us. We followed suit, and it was only then that we succeeded in ridding ourselves of the fluttering parasites.

For a while after that, the butterflies continued landing on our faces and naked torsos, searching for moisture, until finally they gave up. We collapsed on the deck, which now was covered with a sticky mess of trampled and drowned butterflies. It was as if every living thing on board the ship had surrendered to the same lethargy.

I happened to glance at the hammock where the wounded Kanak lay. In his exhausted state he'd been defenseless, and now he was buried beneath a vibrating mountain of paper-thin wings. We brought the bucket, poured water over him, and scraped handfuls of insects off his skin, not even knowing if he was alive underneath. He'd done the only sensible thing he could, which was to bury his face in his arms, and this was how we found him. His chest was heaving. He was still breathing.

We cleared a space for him on deck and laid him down. I fetched a sheet for him from my cabin and brought clean shirts for the rest of us. On the ladder and the bulkhead and the floor of the tiny corridor in front of the cabin door, butterflies lay in heavy drifts: I had to brush them off the door handle to get in. As I did so, others immediately took off from the bulkhead to swarm into the new, unclaimed territory. Jim lay in the middle of the table just as I'd left him. They'd settled on his white hair, and it seemed, as they decked him with their beautiful wings, that they were paying some kind of tribute to him—though he was the one human here who could offer them nothing. But at least he was indifferent to their intrusion and didn't beat them off.

I left Jim and returned to the deck, where I rid myself of the new layer of butterflies that had settled on my face in the cabin. Then we—the captain and his crew—sat down together. We were all wearing shirts I'd taken from Lewis's drawers and my own sea chest.

We stayed on deck for the rest of the day and slept there the following night. The butterflies no longer stirred. There was no more water, and we'd eaten the last taro roots. The world was exhausted not just of wind, but of everything. There were only us and a million butterflies left. Everything else had died. The sea had stopped breathing, and we were resting our heads on its lifeless breast. Soon our hearts would stop too.

I'm not superstitious, and I don't know whether the Kanaks are. Most likely they are, though what they'd call faith, we'd call superstition. Yet I felt that the dead calm that smothered us was some kind of punishment—not for something Jack Lewis had done (because if there's a judge in the Hereafter, which I doubt, then Jack Lewis was now facing him) but for a crime that was mine.

Chance had made me captain of the *Flying Scud*. I was unprepared and I was young, but that was no excuse. A captain is a captain, and I'd failed as one.

I'd sat in the cabin with Jim and a bag full of pearls, thinking about myself rather than my crew. If the Kanaks even crossed my mind, it was only because I feared that they'd stand in the way of my plans.

But what should I have done? I couldn't command the wind and make it obey my orders. So how could I be responsible for the calm that had descended on us like a curse?

It must have been fever, and thirst, and the oppressive heat, and the dying butterflies, and the sight of the leaden lid of the sea, and the gas-flame blue of the sky by day, and the growing remoteness of the stars at night, that had affected my brain and driven my thoughts down this mad path.

Does anyone fully understand nature? Why does the wind suddenly stop blowing?

Could it be that nature doesn't care whether we live or die?

It seems so much less frightening to blame yourself.

I stood up, went down to the cabin, grabbed the bag of pearls, returned to the deck, and hurled it as far out to sea as my diminished strength allowed.

I believed this was the only way I could atone for my guilt and finally free myself from Jack Lewis, because I knew he was still on board. I'd been traveling with shadows and living in a world of ghosts. Superstitious as it was, I feel to this day that my action made complete sense. When my hands were finally empty of something I'd never had any claim to, and my mind was liberated from frivolous dreams, I'd earned the right to call myself a captain. Now I remembered a captain's honor and his only duty: to bring his crew back alive.

I'd thrown all my dreams for the future overboard, and I had only one wish left: that a storm would come and tear us loose from the becalmment we sat trapped in as if in hardened lava.

I stayed at the rail, scouting across the sea, but its surface stayed unchanged. I turned to look at the Kanaks, slumped on the deck with their wounded friend prone between them. They gazed at their hands and dozed in the oppressive heat.

I don't know if they saw me throw the pearls overboard, and if they did, they must have thought that I was making a sacrifice to a god not much different from theirs.

But I hadn't done it to appease any god. I'd done it for myself, out of a sense of duty.

The sun set just as it had every evening since the dead calm gripped us. That first night it had looked like a red bullet heading for my heart. Now it was even darker—not like blood, but like the bullet hole itself. The whole world was prey, killed by an unknown hunter.

A crackling sound woke me. At first, still surfacing from sleep, I guessed fire had broken out on board, the heat having caused the *Flying Scud* to ignite spontaneously. Then I realized that it wasn't the crackling of dry wood ablaze but something slamming hard on the awning stretched above us. I raised myself on my elbow and felt a puff of air on my face. The wind was rising. And it was bringing rain.

I stood by the rail and opened my mouth. Cold, heavy drops of water fell onto my face. They hit my shoulders and naked chest and a shudder passed through me, as if everything inside me was returning to life.

I heard movement behind me and turned around. The Kanaks came over, supporting their wounded comrade. Together we stood along the rail and let the rain soak us. I'd never known real thirst before, and I've never felt grateful the way I did when those first drops of rain wetted my lips. I snapped at the air for more, and for a moment I forgot who I was.

The sea began to stir and when the first waves lapped tentatively against the side of the ship, she reacted with a slight swaying, as if she had been long awaiting an invitation to start moving again. The first wave broke, its top glowing white in the moonlight, and the gaff above us flapped heavily in the wind. A storm was brewing.

We bustled about, preparing the ship. The awning was sagging beneath the weight of the rainwater that had already collected in it: before we took it down, we filled our barrels. Our throats were no longer parched, but we hadn't eaten for days, and as we worked it was clear how weak we'd become. But no matter: not even the prospect of facing a storm with no provisions could dampen our joy at the return of the wind and the rain. Every time I yelled my orders through the resurrected wind that howled in the rigging, the Kanaks replied with the only words I ever heard them say in English—"Aye, aye, sir!"—like a chorus responding to a solo.

It might sound strange—even reckless—to say that we sailed into the storm with exhilaration, but there's no other word to describe our mood as, utterly drenched, we watched the waves toss around us, sending up huge sheets of flying foam that merged sea and sky. We'd double-roped the flying jib, but soon we had to drop all but the foresail to prevent the mast and rigging from going overboard. I lashed myself to the wheel as the vast waves thundered over us, clearing the deck, from bow to stern, of anything that wasn't strapped down. I stayed there for two days. I could have ordered one of the Kanaks to relieve me every four hours, but I didn't. Not because I didn't trust them, but because I had something to prove to myself. I think they understood that.

They'd stretched ropes across the deck to cling to when they moved around the ship, but most of the time they were lashed in place, like me. They'd tied the wounded man to the rigging where the waves couldn't reach him, and from time to time they'd climb up with a mug of water to wet his lips. One of them brought me water too.

When a wave washed a tuna fish onto the deck, I took it as a sign. Before, the fish had stayed away; now they came to us. The sea was generous. In a brief break between two waves, one of the Kanaks hurled himself at the fish, slashed it with his knife, and brought me a hunk of live meat that still trembled in his hand.

During the two days the storm lasted, I remained in a state of undiminished rapture. I stayed on my feet with the wheel in my hands, tied to my post by the rope. If I was tired, I never noticed.

Finally, on the third day, the wind died down, so I untied the rope and allowed myself to be relieved. For a little while I just stood swaying on the deck—until suddenly exhaustion overwhelmed me. I thought I'd faint, and I had to return to the wheel to support myself, fixing my eyes on the deck as I tried to regain my balance.

When I looked up again, the Kanaks had formed a circle around me. The wounded Kanak had come down from the rigging and was standing unsupported, as if his stay up there had done him good. I held out my hand. They stared at it. Then they stuck out theirs too, and one by one we shook hands. They didn't speak, and no smiles lit the darkness of their faces. They just shook my hand. I don't know whether it was something they'd learned from white men or a gesture they also used among themselves. But I knew what it meant at that moment. We'd sealed a pact. These were sailors, not savages.

Below deck I lay down in Jack Lewis's berth. I felt I'd earned the right to it. It wasn't until the next morning that I discovered Jim was missing. I remembered that I'd left him on the table—but now he was gone. I looked for him in the bottom berth and the locked cabinet, but he was nowhere to be found. It wasn't until I crawled around on the floor that he reappeared. He'd rolled into a corner, and somehow finding him in that humble position on the not very clean floor stripped him of the horror that had both attracted and repelled me. I wiped the dust from his hair, wrapped him in his frayed cloth, and locked him in the cabinet.

Not for one moment did I consider sending him the same way as the pearls. He was no longer a threat. Jim was a witness to the darkness in Jack Lewis. But I'd been there too, and I'd come back.

IT TOOK US a week to reach Samoa, but during that whole time I never thought about the purpose of my journey: I was too busy with my duties as a captain. I measured the height of the sun, plotted our course, kept an eye on the sails, and issued my orders. We had plenty of water and we lived on fish. We saw no other ships, and the trade wind blew constantly from the same direction.

When I stood in the bow and watched the never-ending break of waves and the white foam flecks glinting like pearls spilling onto a stone floor, I remembered Jack Lewis's words: a young man should travel the whole sea and every island in it. But when my gaze slid astern toward the white stripe of the wake sparkling in the sunlight, it struck me that it was a kind of chain, and I knew that the moment I became captain of the *Flying Scud* I was free but at the same time bound.

The ocean was so infinitely vast. It could take you anywhere, and yet it shackled you.

The port of Apia is shaped like a bottleneck: a big bay encircled by two peninsulas. The western one is called Mulinuu, the eastern one Matautu. Beyond that lies a reef that looks a bit like the breakwater around Marstal. Here the thunder of the surf is so loud that it's difficult to hear yourself speak: even five kilometers away, high in the green mountains that soar up behind Apia, you can hear the waves roar. And no one in Apia will call a captain a bad sailor if he wrecks his ship trying to pass through the gap in the reef during a storm, because it's regarded as well-nigh impossible. Instead they'll call him irresponsible or ignorant, for everyone knows that in foul weather, the open ocean is a safer bet than their shelterless bay in an oncoming wind.

· · ·

But I knew nothing of this when I bent over the chart in Captain Lewis's cabin. To me, Apia was no more than a name on a map. But since that time, I've learned that a shipwreck can be a welcome thing, if the ship's loss saves a man's honor.

And as we neared Apia, my honor was very much on my mind. How could I ever explain the way I'd ended up as captain of the notorious *Flying Scud*? Who'd believe my story about the free men in the hold, the cannibals from the *Morning Star,* the death of Jack Lewis, and the leather bag of pearls thrown overboard?

Yet I was bound to this ship, for I could not reach my destination without her. Jack Lewis and I were inseparable. He'd plotted the course and I could do nothing but follow it. From now on, regardless of whether people saw me as his killer or his accomplice, my reputation would be connected to his.

I'd considered changing course, but it wasn't just myself I was responsible for. And where else would we go? We couldn't last on fish alone, trusting the weather gods for our supplies of water. I felt that my fate was already cast—and inescapable. I had only one thing left to hold on to: my duty as a captain. I had to guide the ship and its crew to safe harbor.

But in making my calculations, I'd forgotten one factor: the sea.

Every sailor knows this bitter feeling: the coast is near, but you'll never reach it. Is there anything more heartbreaking than drowning in sight of land? Is there a single one of us who hasn't at least once felt haunted by the fear of slipping away within sight of a safe haven?

I imagine that drowning is less devastating when a gray, raging sea has wiped out the horizon completely. But to close your eyes for the last time on something precious—a hope, a hand reaching out for you—that must be the worst. Even terror needs a yardstick, and surely the yardstick for the unknown is the known?

We could see land. The green mountains of Samoa appeared on the horizon just as the gale blew in at us—as though it had been lurking behind the island, awaiting our arrival. We held out for twenty-four hours. One moment we'd be flung to the top of a mountainous wave, and we'd get a view of Samoa; the next, another wave would plunge our bow underwater, and it would be just us and the sea again. We never came any closer to our destination, but nor were we dragged farther away. Then a huge wave came and knocked the ship onto her beam ends, and the shrouds and stays that had strained to support the mast gave way with a groan, sending both mast and the rigging tumbling down. It felt as if one of my own limbs had been partially severed and now dangled from my body by a few sinews.

And yet I still believe we could have ridden out the storm. I wasn't short of self-confidence on that deck. But I realized that the real threat to our survival came not from our crippled ship so much as our own fatigue. We were still weak and exhausted from our recent ordeal, and in that state, we were no match for the storm. We had to get to land.

Even though I'd never called at Apia and didn't know the dangers of trying to force the small gap in the reef during a storm, I was aware of exposing all of us to considerable risk. What if we struck the reef and sank? We'd lost our launch during the battle with the natives in the lagoon. Were we about to drown so close to our destination?

I told the Kanaks to chop the mast into pieces and lash them to the yards, to make a makeshift raft that could carry us the final distance across the bay into Apia, in case our attempt to pass the reef failed. Meanwhile I turned the *Flying Scud* so that she lay cross-wind—a maneuver fully as risky as anything else we were about to do. If a huge wave had crashed on top of us at that moment, that would have been it. We all knew our lives were at stake.

The Kanaks worked hard, concentrating on their axes, and soon the raft was secured to the deck. I'd long since packed my sea chest with my father's boots and Jim. Ordering the Kanaks to tie it to the raft, I straightened up the ship and steered toward the reef.

From the crest of a wave I caught sight of Samoa again, beneath a stormy sky of poisonous purple. The sun had broken through above the island's emerald mountains, suddenly lighting them—but I can't say this heartened me. More, it gave me the feeling that the elements were mocking us and jeering at our vain wish to survive.

As I clasped the helm, I felt the ocean's power: the wheel jerked in my hands as if it were arm-wrestling me, while the waves drove the ship in the direction opposite to its course. Suddenly I felt a new and violent force seize the ship. It was the current, taking our side against the storm and sucking us straight into the bottleneck of the bay. The wheel shook again. And in that moment I lost control of it. Or of myself.

Had I let my guard down? Did I fail in my responsibility? I can't answer that question, and it haunts me still.

A massive wave seized us and flung us at the reef, making the entire ship shudder and flinging the last mast overboard. I found my-self with my back against a rail, my shoulder and arm in such pain, I thought I'd broken them. Then a second wave pounded the ship and nearly overturned her; a cascade of water flooded the deck before streaming back into the sea—and washing me overboard. I grabbed at a piece of the broken rigging, then screamed in pain as it tugged my arm, but I managed to hang on, so at least I knew it wasn't bro-ken. The ship never righted herself. Each fresh wave hit her like a fist bashing a defenseless face, smashing everything to smithereens. Soon there'd be nothing left of us but a wreck on the reef. Clinging to the shreds of rigging, I crawled back up onto the skewed deck and saw that the Kanaks had cut the ropes to the raft—which now slid along the deck and vanished into the bubbling foam. The Kanaks jumped in after it.

I hesitated for a moment, then leapt. The sea was heaving across the reef in a continuous motion that sucked me right down: I felt sharp coral slash my feet before the water's pressure forced me upward again. When I broke the surface, I spotted the raft a couple of meters away. Within a few strokes I'd reached it, and the Kanaks helped me clamber on.

We clung to our raft, hoping the surf would carry us into the la-goon. The reef, which had snared the ship, allowed our flat-bottomed craft to pass, but I'd miscalculated when I'd thought we'd find safety in the bay. Here too the sea was in uproar. The reef broke the rhythm of the waves, but it didn't stop them. They were just as mighty within the bottleneck as they were outside it.

The raft and its makeshift lashings groaned.

And yet it wasn't fear that consumed me now; on the contrary, I was aware of a huge, spreading sense of relief. I'd got rid of the *Flying Scud*. When I reached land, I'd be leaving Jack Lewis behind. Trust-ing that the sea would erase all traces of the *Flying Scud*, I'd already set to work rechristening the splintered ship with a new, but for me familiar, name: the *Johanne Karoline*, after the old fore-and-aft-rigged Marstal schooner that we'd all dreamt of sailing in before she sank with Hans Jørgen in the Gulf of Bothnia. This was my new version of events—and who would be there to deny it? It wasn't that I wanted to avoid being answerable for my actions. I just wasn't prepared to take the blame for misdeeds that weren't mine. It was a way of sidestep-ping Jack Lewis and the ugly taint that came with him.

We were still clinging to the raft, which shuddered from the blows the sea pummeled us with, one whack after another. The green mountains were very close now, but they'd darkened to shadows: the poisonous violet clouds had blocked the sun, and the rain seemed to be lashing the mountainsides as violently as waves on a reef. The storm was at its peak, and though the coast was near, it offered no respite.

We could hear the thundering surf. Hoisting myself up on one elbow, I could see how close we were to the white beach. From my perch on the cresting waves I seemed to be level with the tops of the swaying coconut palms. That's when I saw the futility of my hopes, just as clearly as if I were sitting on the roof of a collapsing house: the wave we rode was about to crush us all under a mass of water. When it broke with the roar of a thousand waterfalls, the raft shot away beneath me and I was in whirling free fall, with the sky below and the sea above.

I can't say everything went black: in fact it went as green as the tropical sea itself. But I was off in some place lost to memory: full of nothingness. When I came to, I was in the arms of one of the Kanaks. Behind us another giant wave crashed down, and I saw we were in the middle of the roiling spume, where the huge waves spent themselves before surrendering to the suck of the sandy shore. But we could gain no foothold. I was gulping and choking, while the blue face of my rescuer remained immobile, fixed on the job of dragging us both the last few meters to the shore. From his missing ear, I recognized him as the Kanak I'd borne back to the ship from the lagoon and later nursed. So now we were quits.

Another wave washed over us. Kicking out blindly in panic, I felt one of my feet touch bottom. I managed to stand but lost my footing again immediately, and tried instead to crawl on all fours through the raging foam. The surf had exhausted itself and the water retreated in a violent undertow, spraying my face and tearing at my limbs from beneath. I was just about to be dragged out to sea again when the Kanak grabbed hold of me. I walked the last few meters upright, leaning against him for support.

The beach was so deserted, it seemed we'd arrived in an abandoned world. I wanted to throw myself on the sand from sheer exhaustion, but a prickling sandstorm was whipping at my half-naked body. Then I heard a loud crack and saw a palm tree snap in half. Its top tumbled through the air and landed on the roof of a hut, which promptly collapsed. We couldn't stay here: if we wanted shelter, we'd have to walk farther inland.

A shout rang out behind us. I turned and saw two more Kanaks struggling in the surf and then staggering onto the beach. Then a third appeared. The entire crew was now safely ashore. Their blue faces made them look like mermen born of the boiling foam.

I felt enormous relief. I'd wrecked the *Flying Scud,* but I'd not lost a single man. True, they'd saved both themselves and me, so I couldn't claim the credit, but their survival made the loss of the ship easier to take.

The nearest huts were all empty, and as we passed them, the wind at our backs shoved us forward so we could barely walk upright. Soon we gave up running and stumbling, went down on all fours, and simply crawled. All around us we could hear the heavy thud of coconuts hitting the ground, and the storm howling through the wildly swaying palm trunks. I concentrated on my hands and knees, my only contact with the ground in this insane weather. It felt as if we'd all end up being blasted off into the endless universe.

Then at last our cries for help were answered, and someone let us into a hut. There was no fire burning, and the inhabitants sat silent and cowed, as if they hoped to avoid the rage of the storm by making themselves invisible. The hut quaked and the roof trembled ominously, but it was holding. I was too exhausted to consider the impression I must have made on them. I was a shipwrecked sailor seeking shelter. It made no difference to them that I was a white man. The storm had made equals of us all.

I fell asleep shortly afterward. When I woke, it was quiet. It was night, and I heard the breathing of sleeping people around me. I stared into the darkness for a while, then drifted back to sleep.

The next morning I took my leave of the Kanaks, and for the second and final time we shook hands. My one-eared rescuer placed a hand on my shoulder and from the bottomless blue of his face, fixed me with his eye. As I returned his look, I felt there was a bond there, though I don't suppose it could be called friendship. We'd never exchanged a word. But now, as we parted, each of them said something, and I still remember what: "Palea," "Loa'a," "Kauu." The fourth word was longer. Something like "Keli'ikea," but I'm not sure. At the time

I assumed they all meant goodbye. Later it struck me that they had been telling me their names.

I went down to the beach. There was still a heavy swell, but the air was no longer filled with flying foam. Everywhere there were smashed palm trees and ruined huts torn apart by the wind and rain, and it struck me how lucky we'd been that the hut we'd sheltered in had withstood the storm. I went as close to the surf as I dared and scouted anxiously across the battlefield of the beach, terrified that I'd see wreckage from the *Flying Scud*, which might belie the story I'd prepared. A yard, a plank, or a ship's wheel would be fine. A nameboard, though, would ruin everything. But when I scanned the horizon and the reef, I saw not a single trace of the ship. The sea had annihilated the *Flying Scud*, and wherever its wreckage might have ended up, it certainly wasn't here on the beach in Apia.

My sea chest had been on the raft, but I abandoned all hope of seeing it again. Its loss was the price I must pay for severing my connection with Jack Lewis.

I was in the western part of the bay, close to Mulinuu, which I'd seen on the map. I followed the shore eastward in the hope of coming across buildings that would indicate the presence of white men. Soon I spotted some brick houses with red-tiled roofs behind the palm trees and I headed for them. They too had not escaped storm damage: one house had a collapsed gable, and another's tiles were ripped off, exposing the bare rafters.

It was a sparsely built area, with houses scattered amid the palms rather than packed together in street formation. I got an impression of wealth and order: large airy estates, with whitewashed walls, covered verandas, and broad eaves, afforded their inhabitants the shade that people long for so keenly in the sun-baked tropics. Whites and natives were going about their business, with a well-organized cleanup operation already under way.

I wandered about aimlessly, feeling superfluous and alien, which, of course, was exactly what I was. No one paid me any attention or called to me. Many were merely passing through too, I guessed: merchants, sailors, and adventurers like me.

I stopped to look at a freshly polished brass plate that shone against the white wall of a house, hoping that behind the wall might be some kind of authority I could approach with my false report of the loss of the *Johanne Karoline.*

DEUTSCHE HANDELS- UND PLANTAGEN-GESELLSCHAFT, it said.

I had just finished reading the words when I heard someone behind me clear his throat. I turned to see a gentleman dressed all in white, his suit immaculately clean and newly pressed. He wore a fresh hibiscus in his buttonhole and looked as if he had spent the night of the storm preparing for a fancy dinner engagement. His pale eyes observed me from beneath the wide brim of his hat, while his hand stroked a mustache that unfurled in two impressive semicircles on either side of his suntanned, slightly lined cheeks.

"May I help you?" he asked, in English. Instantly recognizing his accent, I replied in German.

"I'm a Danish sailor. I'm here to report the loss of my ship, the *Johanne Karoline* of Marstal, which ran aground on the reef outside Apia in the storm. Please, can you tell me if there might be a consulate or another authority nearby, where I can go?"

"Ah, you're Danish. In that case we're almost compatriots. Obviously you won't find a Danish consulate here. And as far as any authorities go—" He shrugged as if the word didn't mean much in these parts. He let go of his mustache and surveyed the ground for a moment as though in search of something. Then he folded his hands behind his back and his face grew pensive. "Well, *I'm* a consul of sorts; I mean, I'm the German consul. So I suppose I'd be the most appropriate person to deal with your case. I did hear that a ship had run aground on the reef, but the storm made any rescue mission impossible. Staying alive ourselves was challenge enough." He held out his hand. "Heinrich Krebs."

"Albert Madsen."

"Madsen? The name sounds familiar." He took off his hat and wiped his brow with a handkerchief. "But this heat does something to a man. Ruins his memory."

"He's a fellow Dane," I said. My mouth had gone dry, and my heart was pounding. "There's supposed to be another Madsen here on Samoa. I'd like to meet him."

"Yes, I'm sure that's possible. I'll ask around. But I must warn you. Meeting a fellow countryman in these parts isn't always a pleasant surprise."

He placed his hand on my shoulder and gave me a searching look.

Then he smiled. "Do come inside. You look exhausted. But you've had luck on your side, eh? Not many men emerge in one piece from an encounter with the reef at Apia. What about the rest of the crew?"

"Captain Hansen didn't make it," I responded curtly, feeling a pang of conscience at my second lie.

"You could probably do with a bath and some lunch. You can make your report afterward."

A native servant dressed in whites as immaculate as his master's prepared me a bath. When I'd removed my filthy, torn clothes, I examined myself in the full-length gilded mirror. Its frame was far too elegant for the sight that greeted me. I'd grown lean and angular, and my body was covered in bruises. My face too bore witness to my recent trials: it was scored with half-healed cuts and scratches. One bisected my right eyebrow, while another made a blood-red line across my cheek. I looked like a drunken sailor fresh from a brawl rather than a man who'd been shipwrecked, and I wondered why the consul hadn't told me to clear off at once. I'd got the impression that my report on the shipwreck would be purely a matter of form: that no inquiry would be held, and no official authorities would become involved. It would have been easy enough for me to blend in with the other inhabitants of Apia, where no one would have noticed an extra vagrant on the beach.

The lie I was telling wasn't even necessary. Having told it, there was no withdrawing it now—but Heinrich Krebs was unlikely to unmask me, or even try to. I guessed that he simply wanted confirmation of his own importance. My role now was to enable him to play the benefactor and provide him with some distraction—for clearly a hurricane was not novel enough in these parts to count as excitement. That said, he gave the same impression as most of the other white men I'd met in the Pacific: behind the façade of civilization and order, you sensed they all had something to hide.

Not that Heinrich Krebs's secrets were of any interest to me. I'd made enough discoveries recently to last me a lifetime.

As I stepped out of the bath, I noticed that a white suit had been laid out for me on a chair, and on the floor beside it was a pair of chalked white canvas shoes. Heinrich Krebs was lending me his own clothes—but as I was considerably taller than he was, both the trousers and the jacket were too short, and I couldn't even button the shirt. I had to forgo the shoes entirely and appeared at lunch barefoot. I still looked like a vagrant—but a lucky one.

The dining room was pleasantly cool. Floor-length white curtains filtered the light from outside. The table had been set with a damask cloth, china, silver, and crystal glasses. I've sat at many dining tables since, but never one that could match that of Heinrich Krebs.

Then he appeared. He'd taken off his hat, and his sandy hair was combed back and held firmly in place by a viscous pomade.

The table was set for two.

"You live alone?" I asked.

"I'm in the process of establishing myself. My wife and our three children will join me later." The food was brought in. "A little surprise," Heinrich Krebs said.

When the china serving dish was placed in front of me, I blinked in disbelief. Not knowing the name of the wonderful dish in German, I said it in Danish: *"Flæskesteg."*

"Yes, *flæskesteg*," my host said, in almost flawless imitation of my Danish. "I have, of course, visited Denmark, and found that the Danes and the Germans share a fondness for pork. The crisp crackling, which I know you Danes value so highly, you'll have to do without, I'm afraid. The talents of my otherwise excellent cook do not extend that far." Krebs was studying me. He gestured at the food. "You can take many things with you. You can re-create your home, surround yourself with your treasured objects and your native culture, read familiar authors, eat the dishes of your childhood, and speak your own language, just as we're speaking mine now. And yet it isn't the same, because there's something you can never re-create. Perhaps even the very thing you once wanted to escape. Why does one leave in the first place? I often ask myself that question. Why are you here? You have been shipwrecked, endured all sorts of hardships. It's written in your face. But why?"

"I'm a sailor," I replied.

"Indeed. But why did you become a sailor? Surely God didn't point His finger at you and command you to go to sea? It was your choice, I presume?"

I shook my head.

"My father was a sailor. My two brothers are sailors. My sister's married to a sailor. All my friends from school sail."

"The Baltic wasn't big enough for you? It would suffice most men. Why the Pacific? What are you hoping to find here?"

I resented Krebs's curiosity, if that's what it was. Perhaps he just enjoyed the sound of his own voice. But he'd got too close, and I had no intention of confiding in anyone. I looked down at my plate again and concentrated on eating.

"This really is delicious," I said.

"I'll pass your compliments on to the chef."

I could tell from his tone that he was insulted. I'd rejected his invitation to confide in him, and a chasm had opened between us.

"This Madsen," he said eventually. "Is he a relative?"

I was already regretting having mentioned my father's name. But this was a big island, and I had to find him one way or another.

"No." I lied. "We're not related. We just happen to come from the same town."

"And share the same surname?"

"A lot of Marstallers do. I promised his family I'd find out how he's doing. Since I'm here anyway."

"Since you're here anyway. Since you happened to pass by Samoa."

His voice was thick with contempt. He didn't believe me, but rather than say so directly, he mocked my reply.

I didn't care. I'd had my bath and my hot meal. He could kick me out now if he wanted to, and I'd manage without his help. I wiped my mouth with my damask napkin.

"That was lovely, thank you," I said, feigning politeness.

I could see that Krebs was reconsidering his position.

"There's dessert too," he said. "Don't get up, please."

Venetian blinds, made from thin bamboo, were swaying in the light breeze on the veranda. It was just as pleasant here as indoors, though the tropical sun blazed from its zenith. The natives were still busy clearing up after last night's destruction. The surf pounded the beach. In the distance I could see the foaming barrier of the reef where I'd nearly lost my life the day before.

Krebs questioned me about the circumstances of the shipwreck. I mentioned the raft and Captain Hansen, who'd gone down to his cabin to rescue the ship's papers and failed to reappear when the *Johanne Karoline* gave a last lurch and a wave washed us overboard. He asked about the Kanaks, and when I told him that they'd reached the shore alive with me but then disappeared, and that apart from that I knew nothing about them, he shrugged as though it was an insignificant detail.

He looked at me again and smiled the ambiguous smile that I'd quickly come to recognize.

"It's amazing what a good meal can achieve. Wouldn't you agree?"

I nodded.

"Take me, for example," he continued. "My memory has returned. Madsen: yes, I recall him now. If you feel sufficiently rested, I can provide you with a native to show you the way. Then you can see him as early as this afternoon."

"I really can't turn up looking like this," I said. Even I could hear the panic in my voice.

"Of course not." Krebs continued to smile. "You're a stickler for etiquette, I see that now. Which attire would you prefer to wear when you meet this Madsen?"

"My own," I said.

I could hear the falseness in my voice, and it seemed to me that we were play-acting for each other. But truth be told, I could see nothing remotely funny about this comedy. In fact, I was afraid. I was afraid to meet my *papa tru* after all these years, and I was afraid of Heinrich Krebs because he seemed to know something about my father that he didn't care to reveal. He'd sensed how eager I was to meet him—and he'd sensed my fear. He was toying with me, but I didn't know why. What was he after?

Krebs excused himself and left the veranda, and I spent the rest of the day wandering around the beach, looking out at the ocean and reflecting on my situation and all I'd been through. Should I have stayed away from *papa tru*? Should I have left him—as I would have left the dead—in peace? For if I had not gone looking for him, he would have been just as dead to me as any other man in Marstal's long list of drowned fathers, brothers, and sons. What did I want from him, when he so clearly wanted nothing to do with me? He could easily have returned home to Marstal, but he hadn't. He'd rejected us. What do you say to a father who's stood with his back to you for fifteen years? You tap him on his shoulder. And what do you do when he turns around?

Punch him?

•   •   •

I returned to Heinrich Krebs's house toward the evening. He'd invited me to stay the night and I'd accepted his invitation because I didn't want to sleep on the beach. The dining table had been set for me, but Krebs was absent.

When I entered the room where I was to spend the night, I took it at first for a room that Krebs had furnished for himself and a wife whose arrival he longingly awaited. It was like entering a tent or being under the awning on a ship. Everything was in the same airy style as the dining room: the canopied bed was big enough for two or three people, and the huge mirror on one of the walls added a whole extra dimension.

It was the strangest place I'd ever spent a night, and I hesitated before climbing into the bed. The floor seemed more appropriate—but then again, I'd never slept on a cloud before, and I felt I deserved some comfort after all I'd suffered, so in the end I threw myself into this paradise of goose down.

I woke up during the night when someone tentatively touched the door handle. It was pushed down, and then it went up again. Shortly afterward I heard a plank squeak on the veranda. Then silence returned and I drifted back into my slumbers.

I was awakened the next morning by a knock at my door, to which I gave a drowsy reply. The servant had come with a pile of neatly folded clothes draped over his arm. In his hand he held a pair of high boots.

"Your clothes, *masta*," he said, and disappeared.

I unfolded the clothes and gazed at them in wonder. They were indeed mine—but they weren't those I'd worn the previous day. These were my shore clothes: dark blue trousers and jacket, white linen shirt with a collar, and the gray wool socks that I'd darned myself. The boots, which I'd dragged around half the world, were *papa tru*'s. I'd been sure I'd lost my few belongings when the raft sank in the bay outside Apia. But now here they were, in my hands.

I dressed and pulled on the boots. I hadn't worn them for months. They felt heavy and uncomfortable in the heat, and my feet hurt as I walked to the dining room, where Heinrich Krebs was waiting for me with breakfast. As usual, he was immaculately dressed, with a fresh hibiscus in his buttonhole and pomade in his hair. My sea chest sat right there on the damask tablecloth. It looked like a large moldy stain in the neat room. And there was my name on it. I'd painted it myself.

"It drifted ashore last night," Krebs said. "One of my men found it."

I said nothing.

"I presume the shrunken head isn't a member of your family?"

"No," I replied. "His name's Jim."

"Well, that explains everything. Is he from Marstal too?" I shook my head, having reached the conclusion that it was best not to answer. "You're a very interesting young man, Albert Madsen," Krebs said, and looked at me over the rim of his cup. "Very interesting."

"And you sneak a peek at another man's property without asking for permission." I stared back at him without blinking. I was hoping he couldn't tell how outraged I was.

"If one doesn't, one never learns anything" he said, without looking away.

"What is it you want to know?"

"Many things," he said. "You come crawling out of the surf like some merman, all alone in the world, with this story about where you come from and who you are. A story that no one can confirm or deny."

"My name's on the sea chest."

"Which contains a shrunken head. Of a white man."

I reached for the silver coffeepot.

"That's another story. It doesn't concern you."

"There's no need to get upset. You're quite right. It doesn't concern me. By the way, you'll be relieved to hear that your friend has suffered no damage from his time in the sea. Remarkable when you think about it, wouldn't you say?"

Krebs stirred his coffee. I couldn't make him out. He was toying with me and I hated it.

My host tilted his head and examined me. Then, without warning, he started whistling a tune I didn't know.

"So distant," he said finally, sounding almost as though he was addressing himself. "So young, so angry, and so very unapproachable. How sad." He shook his head. "Tut, tut, tut." Then he continued. "By far the most bizarre thing about you is your interest in your namesake. You see, that interest—and you can trust me on this one—is shared by no one else here in Apia."

He got up abruptly. "Right, let's get going."

He nodded in the direction of the sea chest, which was still on the table. "You'd better take that. I presume you'll be staying with your"—he hesitated before tasting the word—"friend."

I nodded, but I was at a loss. I hadn't even thought that far ahead. But I supposed that Krebs was right. I would stay with my father. Fifteen years with his back to me, I tap him on the shoulder—and he turns around and invites me to stay? I could feel my earlier anxiety return. It was all so ill-considered. I really had no chart for this part of the voyage.

I stood and took the sea chest.

"Of course you're always welcome to return here, should the stay with your friend fail to work out. I would be only too happy to renew our acquaintance." Krebs bowed theatrically and gestured me toward the door with a sweeping movement. "Do you ride?" he asked, as we stepped down from the veranda. Two horses, already saddled, awaited us.

"Well, I can try," I replied, and stuck a foot in one stirrup with a movement that I hoped looked practiced. Then I swung myself up onto the horse. For a moment I thought I might slide down the other side, and I could feel how bruised and battered I was. I secured the sea chest to the saddle.

"You're doing pretty well," Krebs said, sizing me up.

With a light tap of his whip he got his horse moving at a walking pace, and I copied him as best I could. A white-clad servant trotted alongside me on foot: I presumed he was there to take charge if my horse decided to cause me any trouble. We followed the beach for a while. Here the pounding of the surf made conversation impossible, but when we turned toward the interior of the island and the ocean's din subsided, Krebs launched a torrent of speech, which didn't end until we reached our destination. I was too preoccupied by my own thoughts to pay much attention to his words, but I recalled them later—along with the warning that lay buried in them.

"Take a look around," he said. "We have big plans for this area. We don't own much land at the moment. But that's going to change." As he pointed his whip here and there, his posture straightened in a way I'd not seen before. "Come back in ten years and you'll see the difference for yourself. Then all this chaos and lack of discipline will be gone."

He snorted in contempt as he said this, and I recalled his house. Yes, it was light and airy—but it was also so neatly arranged that a sea chest on his dining table, and a man like me sitting next to it, looked like pieces of dirt. I followed the movements of his whip, and at first

I thought that the chaos he was referring to was the mess left by the storm. Then I realized that it was nature itself that he saw as being out of control.

"Straight rows," he said. "In ten years there will be straight rows everywhere. Stone walls at right angles, and behind them, pineapple, coffee bushes, and cocoa trees—in formation! Copra plantations, yes, but with the palms properly aligned. Areas for grazing, leveled out. Cattle. Horses. Avenues of palm trees, like soldiers on parade! Fountains!" His voice grew staccato as the list of future delights grew longer. Then he paused and became pensive. "Of course, we'll have to import labor. The locals are utterly useless."

"Why?" I asked—though mostly to demonstrate an interest in his impassioned words, because my thoughts were elsewhere.

"Oh, it's not because they're lazier here than anywhere else in the world. A native is a native. I can mention several individual examples of hard work, of course. But it never lasts." He looked at me as if to signal that what he was about to say was of particular interest. "Their families are their curse. When my servants go home for a visit, I make them leave their nice clothes behind. Take Adolf—yes, I give them German names, it makes it easier." He pointed at the servant walking next to my horse. "I gave Adolf permission to visit his family, wearing his fine clothes. He was so proud of them. But he came back in rags. His family had taken over his uniform. I meet them, from time to time, prancing about. There's a cousin wearing the waistcoat, there's a brother in the jacket, an uncle with the shirt, and his dad's wearing the trousers. They'll wear one item of clothing at a time and nothing else—oh, it's a sight all right, eh, Adolf?" He poked the servant with his whip, but Adolf stared straight ahead as if he hadn't heard what Krebs had said, or didn't understand a word. The latter seemed the most likely. "The Samoan doesn't work," Krebs said. "He goes visiting. He's not your industrious ant type. More of a grasshopper."

"A grasshopper?"

"A grasshopper. You see, if a Samoan suddenly grows rich, whether through hard work, which is rather unlikely, or through luck, then his entire clan will instantly come and visit him. Even the most distant branches of the family tree will arrive. I've seen it. A whole village might move. And they'll behave like a swarm of locusts. They won't leave until they've stripped him of everything. Your Samoan has the same word for *visit* and *misfortune: malanga*. And you can figure out the consequences. It's a system that rewards the beggar and penalizes effort. Hard work is nothing more than an invitation to be robbed. It's impossible to save. So what does the smart man do? He makes sure he earns enough to cover the bare necessities, so he can put food in his mouth and the mouths of those closest to him, and nothing more. A man like that's no use to me. No: imported labor. Single men who don't need much and, most important, don't have a big family."

While Krebs had been speaking we had left the last houses behind, and only native huts surrounded us. The road had ended and we had to ride around a crisscross of woven fences behind which black, hairy pigs grunted in the mud. A crowd of children encircled us. Adolf gave a warning whistle as though chasing away dogs and the kids shrieked and retreated—but they soon reappeared, and every time they did, their chattering numbers had swelled. Women stared at us from the opening of their huts.

"Well, this is where Europe ends," Krebs said. "Now we're among the savages."

A gust of wind swept through the tall coconut palms and set their tops rustling. I looked up. Their large leaves opened and closed like sea anemones, and I caught a brief glimpse of a man perched in one of them. He was white, with a naked torso and a large gray beard. Then the leaves closed again and hid him from view, as if the palm tree was his home and he was now shutting its door against curious onlookers.

For a moment I doubted my own eyes. Most of all, I wanted to ignore the strange apparition, which seemed to belong to a dream world. Krebs had seen it too. He stopped his horse and turned to me.

"We're here," he said. "So I'll be turning back." He gestured to me to get off my horse. I took hold of my sea chest and dismounted, and he leaned down to shake my hand. "I hope you won't regret it. You're always welcome at my house." He squeezed my hand and turned his horse around. Then he looked back at me. A mocking smile appeared on his face. "Good luck with your father." Then he spurred his horse and galloped away.

I STOOD THERE, with my sea chest under my arm. The children gawked and gestured, but I ignored them until eventually they calmed down and squatted around me, looking curious and expectant. Women continued to stare at me from the surrounding huts. There were no men in sight.

I looked up at the palm tree where the hidden man, who might be my *papa tru*, had briefly appeared. I felt hot and uncomfortable, standing there in my shore clothes and knee-high boots, not saying anything, so I shouted up at the tree:

"Laurids!"

I didn't call him *papa tru*. I couldn't bring myself to. The whole business seemed bizarre enough as it was. I didn't want to be the man standing on some remote Pacific island, yelling for his dad. At first nothing happened.

"I've seen you," I shouted. "I know you're there!"

I grew annoyed, and then furious. But it was a form of rage that didn't know what to do with itself. "Now come down! What do you think you are? A damned monkey?"

My own voice frightened me. I was addressing him as though I was the captain of the *Flying Scud* and he a primitive Kanak.

The palm leaves rustled, and then the man appeared between them. He was strong-limbed and bearded, with one of the natives' colorful cloths wrapped around his waist. Had it not been for his lighter skin and his gray beard, I'd have taken him for a Samoan. He grabbed the trunk with his large hands, planted his naked feet firmly against its rough surface, and came down, using a native climbing technique that made it look as if he almost walked down the tree. He landed with a bump and stood opposite me.

He stared at my feet.

I studied his face, with its dense beard. If I'd had a moment's doubt, it had vanished completely. I can't say that I recognized him after all these years, for what do the memories of a four-year-old count for? But I recognized myself. I don't often have an occasion to look in a mirror, and if someone was to ask me to describe myself, I'd lack not just the words, but the interest. Yet now I stood face to face with my mirror image. Time had drawn its marks across my father's face. Deep lines ran along his sunken cheeks, and wrinkles spread from his eyes like the marks a bird's claws leave in wet sand. But it was me. We were father and son, and now I saw how Heinrich Krebs had known what he'd known. All it took was one look at me.

I had no idea what to say or do; it was *papa tru* who broke the silence. Tearing his eyes away from my boots, he now fixed them on me.

"I see you've brought me my boots."

"They're mine now."

I gritted my teeth and made my voice as hard as his. But he held his gaze. The only thought going through my mind right now was that there wasn't a chance in hell of his getting my boots. Then he said a few words in a native language, and three of the boys in the circle around me stood up.

"Say hello to your brothers."

Behind his beard, his lips formed a vague smile. He pointed at the boys one by one. "Rasmus. Esben." He hesitated in front of the youngest one, whom I guessed to be about the same age I'd been when he left us. "Albert."

I don't know what he said next to the three boys, but none showed any sign of wanting to get to know me better, nor did their father encourage it. They just rejoined the circle of kids and started giggling.

To begin with, I couldn't take in what he'd just said. He appeared to be living with a new family, just like his old one—and it included three sons he'd christened with our names. The whole thing felt like an idiotic and vicious dream. But if it was, it had gone on far too long. Fifteen years had passed since *papa tru* left us. The dream had swallowed up my whole life, turning night into day, until I no longer knew where I belonged, in the light or in the darkness.

I don't know what my face looked like just then—whether it was astonished, baffled, angry, or blank. At any rate, *papa tru* made as if there was nothing unremarkable about what he'd just said. And out of pride, I did the same. But I could feel resentment welling inside me, and I knew that it would keep growing until it changed into something far more dangerous.

I should have turned on my heel and left him at that moment. Made him call out after me, plead with me to stay, beg my forgiveness for all the years that had passed while he'd stayed away. But I already knew that he wasn't going to do that. He'd managed without me for all these years, and the only thing that interested him, when he finally saw me again, was his boots.

So instead, I stayed. I knew exactly why.

Because I wanted him to embrace me. Just the once.

"Right, let's go home and get a bite to eat in Korsgade," he said.

Had he completely lost his mind? Korsgade! Rasmus, Esben—and Albert! And it followed that there would have to be a sister called Else too somewhere. It felt like staring into an abyss. Here, in the shade of the palm trees, my father had re-created the family he'd turned his back on. I might have been able to take the betrayal if he'd been living an entirely different life—if, I don't know. But this!

The small dark-skinned boy trotting alongside me was claiming to be Albert. So what did that make me? A first draft?

My heart was unmoved by the sight of the boys darting after *papa tru*. They were my half brothers—but I felt no kinship to them. All I could feel was sudden, fierce bitterness that overwhelmed me. Now I understood Heinrich Krebs's warning. Hell, I even approved of his mockery. I watched my father's muscular back above his sarong. My father! No, he wasn't my father. He was the father of the little dark-skinned boys. Our blood tie was gone.

I watched the red dust beneath my feet; the hens, wandering freely; the woven fences with the snorting black pigs behind them; the airy huts. I heard the rustle of the palm tops. In the days when I'd dreamt of the Pacific, that sound had called to me. Now here I was, reunited with my father, and it was no dream come true: it was a loss of hope. I'd rather have found his grave than the man himself.

"*Papa tru*," I called out to his back.

He didn't even turn around.

"*Papa tru*." I mocked him. "That's what you taught me to call you. Do you actually know what that means? *Papa tru*—my true father. But what kind of father are you? One big lie—that's what you are!"

I should have turned and left at that point. But I followed him to his hut.

· · ·

He shouted something and I understood that he was demanding food for his guest and himself. A woman appeared in the opening to the hut. I didn't look at her. I didn't want to know anything. I had no idea whether she knew about me. We sat there, waiting. The children formed a circle around us.

Laurids looked at my boots again.

"Give them to me," he said.

"You're not getting them!" All of my disappointment was expressed in those words. "You're not getting them!" I repeated.

He gave me a baffled look, as if he hadn't anticipated a refusal.

Then I looked him in the face and saw a peculiar lethargy in his eyes—and I knew that he was lost. He was no longer my father. Nor was he Laurids Madsen anymore. He'd left everything behind, including a part of himself. I saw now that all the names from home that he'd strewn around him were nothing but a desperate attempt to grasp at something that was gone forever. My rage gave way to horror. I wanted to get up and leave. I looked around for my sea chest, which I had set down, but it was nowhere to be seen.

"The boots," Laurids said again.

He'd recovered his commanding tone, but I'd seen evidence of something else in his eyes. So I ignored him and began looking about for my sea chest, which I found over by the woven fence: the boys had dragged it there and were just opening it. They giggled in anticipation. The oldest one put his hand inside and rummaged around.

Then he froze. His eyes widened as though he'd discovered a poisonous snake, and he screamed. His brothers scattered. A word, whose significance I didn't know but could easily guess, echoed through the palm trees and across the whole village.

Laurids froze too, and the lethargy in his eyes gave way to terror.

I can't explain how, but I knew instantly what was going on in his addled brain. The boy had found Jim—and Laurids now believed that I was a ruthless killer who wandered about with his victims' heads in his sea chest. Maybe he even thought I'd come to wreak revenge.

It was so ludicrous that I started laughing. If I hadn't, I'd have howled like a wounded animal.

My father gawked at me, paralyzed with fear. Then he started to crawl backward in the dust like a crab. He thought my laughter was triumphant, that I was about to get my own back. He shook with fright, the poor shadowy creature.

In the hot midday sun the sight of him had stirred up all sorts of feelings in me: anxiety and panic, bafflement and rage. For a brief moment I was even prepared to feel sorry for him. Now any compassion I might have felt turned into contempt. I got up and went over to my sea chest. A fiendish impulse made me grab Jim by his hair and dangle the shrunken head in the air. I took one menacing step toward the man who'd once been my father.

Papa tru was still crouched in the dust. A wet patch appeared on the sand between his legs. In his petrified state he'd lost control of his bladder. His children pressed themselves against him. Had I known their language, I'd have yelled at them that they shouldn't seek comfort in a father as miserable as this. The boys' mother, big and heavy, appeared in the doorway. Her eyes were wide with fear like her children's.

I put Jim back in my sea chest, tucked it under my arm, raised a finger to my cap in farewell, and went on my way. The first few steps I took were measured. Then I started to run. As I ran, I felt the tears cascading down my face. The natives watched me cautiously. I'd interrupted their midday rest.

Laurids must have got his courage back at the sight of my retreat, because behind me I heard the sound of his voice one more time.

"My boots!" he shouted.

But I didn't turn back.

I never saw my father again.

I WENT BACK to Hobart Town, where this cursed voyage had begun. It was no happy return, for there was nothing in this wretched place that could inspire joy in anyone. But this was where it had all started, and so this was where it must end.

I went to the Hope and Anchor to say hello to Anthony Fox. When I left, he was black-and-blue. That was my conclusion to the story.

Fox hadn't been pleased to see me: he had no reason to rejoice at our reunion. But he did his best to conceal it. To him, I must have looked like someone back from the dead.

I told him that I was like him: I never forgot a debt. That wiped the fake welcoming smile from his face. He reached for his revolver, which he kept under the brass bar counter, the smartest in Hobart, but I'd anticipated that, and I was quicker than he was. We ended up in the backroom. He fought well. He was an experienced fighter who knew plenty of dirty tricks from his prison days. But I was younger and bigger and I finally floored him. He stayed down for a long time. I kept pounding him even after he'd given up. My rage demanded it.

When I'd kicked and broken his last rib, I said, "And Jack Lewis says hello."

Not because I owed Jack Lewis anything, but to finally balance the books. We'd both been victims of the same fraudster. It was Anthony Fox who'd sold the guns to the natives on Jack Lewis's island, and when he told me his name, he must have calculated that I wouldn't be coming back alive.

I don't know what had happened between him and Jack Lewis. Nor do I give a damn. Each was as bad as the other. If anything, Lewis was probably worse, and no doubt Fox had had much to avenge.

He played with my life. The idea of my death only added a touch of spice to his game. So there was an outstanding debt between us. In fact, there were two. I owed him for the gin from our previous meeting, when he sent me on the voyage he expected would be my last. Before I left the Hope and Anchor, I tossed a coin at his pulped face.

There was once a time when I thought that I'd learn something if I found my *papa tru*. But I hadn't. I hadn't grown wiser.

I'd just grown harder.

THE DISASTER

IT WAS MANY YEARS before we heard further news of Laurids Mad-sen. Albert never told his mother anything, and we all agreed that was the kindest thing to do. She'd died by the time Peter Clausen returned home, so Karoline Madsen never found out what had happened to the man she'd hopelessly yearned for all those years.

Peter Clausen was the last Marstaller to see Laurids. He was the son of Little Clausen, who had taken part in the battle at Eckernförde Fjord and been held captive with Laurids in Germany. After that, Little Clausen became a ship's pilot and moved to a house in Søndergade, in the southern part of the town. He built a wooden tower on its roof, so he could watch the comings and goings of ships that might need his expert knowledge of local waters.

Peter Clausen arrived on Samoa in 1876 when he and a fellow sailor jumped ship, and Peter took up with a native girl. In the be-ginning he lived by sponging, *malanga*-style. Then he bumped into Laurids and realized what could happen if you forgot who you were. Laurids had started to change after his German imprisonment. He hadn't grown any more genial with age. On the contrary: whatever the reason, he'd become even blunter and more closed off. He'd de-veloped a fondness for the local palm wine—which was why you'd often find him in the treetops, where he'd use a machete to hack at the palm trunk to get the sap. But he had to do it in secret because palm wine was banned on Samoa during those years. Laurids had ended up a queer fish, respected neither by his fellow whites nor by the natives he'd chosen to live among.

Peter Clausen decided to become a merchant. He set up his own lit-tle trading station and ran the Danish flag up the pole outside. Around that time he took a native wife and and soon had children with her. He followed Laurids's example and gave them Danish names, but he never managed to teach them any Danish. Several years passed. He was just about making ends meet.

His Samoan family, as was the local way, considered his trading station to be a common source of income and settled on his lawn like a swarm of locusts, until he put them in their place. If there was one native habit that Marstallers never shook off, it was thrift. Peter Clausen didn't object to entertaining his relatives on festive occasions—that was entirely appropriate—but not daily. No way. And so he chased them off. If they failed to get the message, he was happy to threaten them with his gun.

Their problem, he said, was that they didn't understand the meaning of *daily*. They saw every day as one long party and never missed an opportunity to dress up or burst into song. An ordinary day was a concept you had to teach them.

His wife sulked, but when it came to imposing his will, Peter took after his father and eventually—according to him, at any rate—he ended up universally respected. He was no *mata-ainga*—that's a man who is weak and gives in to his family—nor was he a *noa*, which means "beggar" or "layabout."

Then came 1889, the year that would turn Peter Clausen into a man of consequence and restore Laurids Madsen's reason.

One event changed both their lives.

At that time the English and the Americans had joined the Germans on Samoa. They'd all laid claim to the island and ended up filling the Bay of Apia with their warships, taking sides among the Kanaks in their internal disputes, and giving them all the guns they could carry on their broad, brown shoulders.

Heinrich Krebs was now an important man. All his plans had come to fruition, and envious competitors claimed he was the only plantation owner in the Pacific with his own private navy. And it was true that Germany indulged his every whim. He was a statesman and a plantation owner rolled into one. His coconut palms were lined up as if on parade, and the way his whip cracked, you'd think his land was a drill ground. People called his plantation simply the Company, as if there was nothing on Samoa but Heinrich Krebs and his dream of straight lines, though at this point Apia had both an American consul and an English-language newspaper.

There was going to be a war. The natives now had plenty of guns and enjoyed firing them—but they never worried much about taking aim first, so they seldom suffered great losses when they attacked one another.

Then the Flag War started. The great colonial powers had planted their flags around the island, where they had no business being in the first place. First, a shot was fired at a British flag. Then an American flag was burned, and the Germans were blamed for it. German troops came ashore to find themselves surrounded by Kanaks, who made short work of fifty of them. It was said that the house where the Germans held out had more holes than a fisherman's net by the time the Kanaks had finished. The Germans inside had been killed by American bullets, supplied by the British, and all of a sudden the bay outside Apia was packed with seven warships from three nations. Everyone was waiting for the first shot.

It was never fired though, and that was the whole point of the story, Peter said. Because the sea attacked before the cannons had a chance.

The barometer fell to 29.11. Any sailor who knows the Bay of Apia knows what that means: get out to sea as quickly as you can. But the officers on board these naval ships hadn't a clue. They just wanted to challenge one another, and the poor fools didn't realize that their worst enemy was the ocean. The wind built to hurricane force and the waves in the bay grew big enough to frighten even those of us who'd witnessed an autumn storm in the Skagerrak or the North Atlantic.

The next morning revealed a sight to match any horrors of war. Three warships had run aground on the reef, two lay on the beach with their keels bared, and two had sunk to the bottom of the bay. The sea had swallowed cannons and ammunition and wrought its own destruction in their absence. Drowned sailors bobbed face-down in the frothy surf before finally being washed ashore.

The sun rose, and its glorious rays spread across a sky swept clear of clouds. But the beach was a different sight altogether. The recovered bodies were lined up, while mute survivors wandered up and down between the rows, trembling either from exhaustion or from a lingering terror of the sea's power. These were troops, not seamen: they'd been destined for other forms of victory and defeat, death and survival than the kind we knew. They were soldiers who'd tasted a sailor's fate.

They never made history. No one would remember them. The Battle of Samoa was not won by the Americans, the British, or the Germans. It was won by the Pacific.

Laurids walked among the waterlogged bodies placed face-down in the sand. No one knew why they'd been arranged that way. Perhaps those who laid them out thought it too gruesome to look so many dead people in the face at once. The day before, these people had been ready to shoot one another. Now it was impossible to tell who was German, American, or British. Laurids kept pointing at them as though taking a tally, and each body he counted seemed to cheer him.

"When I saw that, I thought he really had lost his mind," Peter Clausen said later.

He too had come down to the beach that morning. But unlike Laurids, he wasn't counting the dead; he was counting the survivors. Every one of them was a potential customer, now that the fleets of three nations had been smashed to pieces and all provisions had been lost, along with a whole swath of crew.

"Fortunately, there were more living than dead," Peter Clausen said. Whether he meant fortunate for them or for his business wasn't clear, but at any rate, the disaster in the Bay of Apia proved to be a turning point in the fortunes of his trading station.

"All I know," Clausen said, returning to the subject of Laurids, "is that if he really had once lost his reason, he got it back that day. I can't say whether he became his old self again, since I've no idea what he was like before. But he turned up at my door, asking if there was anything he could do. That was new. In the old days he showed up only when he wanted something—which he always did. Don't get me wrong. I was happy to help him, within reason. I never refused him a meal and a cup of coffee. After all, we were both from Marstal. But he wasn't someone whose company I enjoyed. He never thanked me when he left with a full stomach. But if there was ever a different Laurids, it was the one I saw when he'd finished counting the dead on the beach. I couldn't help but remember that he'd been on the losing side in a naval battle too and spent time in captivity. That must have given his pride a hard knock. Now it was as if he'd been redeemed."

His father, Little Clausen, said, "Laurids saw Saint Peter's bare behind. He went to Heaven and stood at the Gates of Paradise. But then he came back down again, and his mind probably suffered some damage from that. Standing on the threshold of death and then turning back can't do a man any good."

"Well, I wouldn't know about that," said the son. "I don't have a clue what mad people think. But the upshot was he became almost human again. He'd been a palm-wine drunk who'd gone native. His life had been one big *malanga*. He wasn't exactly respected by the whites on Samoa. Not that they thought much of me either because I had children by a native woman too. Even though they've got good Danish names, they're still called half-blood or half-caste and that's no compliment. The British are the worst when it comes to labels like that. But now I'm a rich man, and the American navy is my customer, so I don't give a damn what they call us. My children will inherit the shop, so they'll be all right.

"The Germans are keeping a low profile these days. Heinrich Krebs has become a quiet man. Not much Bismarck in him now. He's a businessman again. While Laurids grew almost respectable. He trimmed his beard and stopped drinking. I even let him look after the shop from time to time. He built himself a smack and sewed his own sails. He'd sail through the surf and return with fish, just like a local: no more twiddling his thumbs in a palm treetop for him. I only once asked him if he missed his family back home. Perhaps it was stupid of me. What's family, when you haven't seen them for forty years? He turned his back on me and disappeared with a face like a thundercloud. I thought he'd go off on another *malanga*. But he came back a few days later and he was still the new Laurids. The next day he sailed across the reef in his smack and never came back. The boat was never found. Most people would probably say that was the end of Laurids. But I had the strange notion that he'd set off to start a new life for himself."

Albert hadn't wanted to listen to Peter Clausen's story. We told him anyway, once Clausen had left. He listened in silence and said nothing. He leaned forward and rubbed his boot with the sleeve of his jacket.

"I kept the boots," he said. "The rest is of no interest to me."

He got up. He was still wearing the same boots, thirty years after his visit to Samoa.

II

THE BREAKWATER

WE DIDN'T KNOW for sure that Herman Frandsen was a murderer. But if he was, we knew what drove him to it.

Impatience.

No one in our town has such a thing as privacy. There's always an eye watching, an ear cocked. Each and every one of us generates a whole archive of talk. Your slightest offhand remark takes on the weight of a lengthy newspaper commentary. A furtive glance is instantly returned and pinned on its owner. We're always coming up with new names for one another. A nickname's a way of stating that no one belongs to himself. You're ours now, it says: we've rechristened you. We know more about you than you know about yourself. We've looked at you and seen more of you than you'll catch in the mirror.

Rasmus Asswhipper, Cat Tormentor, Violin Butcher, Count of the Dunghill, Klaus Bedchamber, Pissy Hans, Kamma Booze, how can any of you imagine we don't know your secrets? Hey, Question Mark: we call you that because you're a hunchback! And Masthead: well, what better name for someone with a tiny head, a long body, and no shoulders?

Everyone in our town has a story—but it's not the one he tells himself. Its author has a thousand eyes, a thousand ears, and five hundred pens that never stop scribbling.

No one saw what Herman Frandsen did. A moment came and went, and with it went a human life, snuffed out forever. There's no telling what happened, or how. It's all guesswork. And because we don't know for sure, we can't seem to let it go.

We know his motive, though. We found it within ourselves.

·   ·   ·

It was a summer's night in 1904, and Herman was twelve years old. As he sneaked out the front door of his house in Skippergade, you could hear the noises that emerged from within. His mother, Erna, and his stepfather, Holger Jepsen, were groaning and sniggering away on their creaking mahogany bed. Herman walked south until he left the last houses behind and then continued out toward the beach. Above him the Milky Way lit up. It was headed the same way as he was, spreading out of the night above the rooftops of Kongegade and disappearing somewhere on the other side of the Tail. In the endless universe there are no maps, yet the Milky Way still gives us Marstallers the impression of being a real road: a road that leads out to sea.

Herman did not stop until he'd reached the water. He took off his shoes and stood with his feet in the foaming surf and watched the Milky Way stretch away from him into the distance, and a feeling that could easily be mistaken for loneliness washed over him. It wasn't the kind of abandonment an orphaned child feels so much as the sense of loss you experience when the older boys go off on their adventures and leave you behind. You're full of anguish and you don't realize that it's a feeling born of impatience. You long to grow up, right there and then. You realize that childhood is an unnatural state and that within you there's a much bigger person, one you can't be right now but who'll come to life somewhere beyond the horizon.

Herman never spoke about that night to a single one of us.

But we knew: we've been there ourselves.

Herman lost his father early. That's something quite a few of us experience, but this loss was especially cruel. Frederik Frandsen from Sølvgade went down with his ship, the *Ofelia*, on the Newfoundland route in 1900. Herman's two brothers, Morten and Jakob, were on board too. Herman was only eight years old when he was left alone with his mother. Erna was a big woman, who'd matched her husband in height and in girth: he'd always had to bow his head and enter doors sideways, both in his modest captain's cabin on the *Ofelia* and at home in Sølvgade. The ceiling was so low there that if anyone in the family wanted to stand up straight, they had to go outside and do it in God's fresh air. Herman excepted, of course.

Erna soon remarried, and this earned her a rather unfair reputation for cold-heartedness—though you could well argue she was the opposite. Was her swift remarriage due to the fact that she had no need to mourn—or that her heart was so frail in the face of loneliness that she had to seek comfort where she could? Her new husband was captain of the *Two Sisters,* Holger Jepsen from Skippergade, a quiet man who long since seemed to have settled into a bachelor's life. He was so sinewy that his bones looked as if they were bound in string, but he was small and slight of build, and standing next to big Erna he practically disappeared: it was almost comical. After their marriage he was nicknamed the Boy.

But you could see that Jepsen stirred something in Erna. She became a blusher, which she'd never been before. What's more, her mustache disappeared. Until Jepsen turned up she'd always had a shadow on her upper lip, though whether it was prickly no one could say, as she wasn't the type to go around kissing people, least of all her own sons. Frandsen had been a coarse man and everyone had agreed that the manly, broad-shouldered Erna had been a good match for him. But now she grew almost tender, if you can imagine tenderness in a woman with hands the size of shovels. It was as if Jepsen had discovered, within the giant woman, a wisp of a girl his own size, and lured her out.

But Herman was none too pleased. He'd already lost his father and two brothers, and perhaps he sensed that he was losing his mother as well. He must have felt homeless in Jepsen's house, as if he'd come to a strange country with a different language—though Jepsen treated him decently: it wasn't long before he presented his new stepson with his very own boat and taught him to scull, set sails, tie knots, and everything else he needed to know to handle himself at sea. But in Herman's eyes, Jepsen had committed the unforgivable sin of turning Erna into a simpering fool. All that touching and holding hands is bad for your health, he'd tell anyone who'd listen. He behaved like Erna's rightful owner, watching his property being mismanaged. The way he puffed himself up and got all indignant like a right little man, you'd think he considered Erna's mustache her best feature.

Herman would also come to blame his stepfather for his mother's sudden death. Erna succumbed to blood poisoning after gutting a codfish. A hook, buried in its flesh, had pierced her middle finger, but she hadn't been concerned and simply pulled the hook out without so much as a wince. That was the old Erna, the one Herman liked. But two days later she was dead, even though Jepsen had fetched Doctor Kroman, who'd done all he could.

Herman's view was that his mother wouldn't have died if his father had been alive. At home in Sølvgade she'd have survived, as the big, tough-as-nails woman she'd once been, not the quivering, blushing, mustacheless, lovesick jellyfish Jepsen reduced her to when he moved them to Skippergade. The fact that Herman still said "at home in Sølvgade," long after his father's death, despite the fact that he lived in Skippergade for most of his childhood, should have served as a warning to his stepfather.

Erna and Jepsen never had children of their own. In the convivial company of Weber's Café, our favorite joke was that Jepsen was too short to conquer Erna's majestic thighs, which were as tall and as thick as the mizzenmast on the *Two Sisters*. But when Erna was gone and Herman was left alone with no family in the world, Jepsen, who was more softhearted than was good for him, gave the boy all the affection he'd once given Erna, convinced that he needed a father's love and guidance more than anything in the world.

But Herman was of the opposite opinion. There was nothing he wanted more than to get rid of his stepfather.

And he did get rid of him, sooner than anyone had expected.

The way it happened both stirred our admiration and planted a strange, vague feeling of fear.

As soon as Herman Frandsen was confirmed, he was off to sea. Holger Jepsen, who wanted only the best for the boy, made the mistake of signing him on to the *Two Sisters* rather than another ship. They had some good times, and some bad too—though their disagreements never actually ended in fisticuffs. Jepsen had more authority on the deck of a ship than he did on land. Although he was slight, he had a powerful voice, and he used it to order Herman up and down the ratlines and out on the footropes of the yards.

"Never trust your feet," he shouted at the overgrown Herman, dangling up there like a seasick gorilla. "Feet can slip and ropes can fail, and then you're falling sixty feet and learning the most useless lesson of your life. The sea won't spit you back up, and if you hit the deck we'll be scraping you off it with a shovel."

Herman looked at his feet. If he couldn't trust them, what could he trust? Up on the yard, Herman stalled like a clockwork toy somebody had forgotten to wind. Not from fear or panic, but mistrust. He didn't understand what Jepsen meant.

Jepsen had to climb the rigging himself to get his stepson down. He clambered onto the yard and held out his hand.

"Come here," he said, gently.

Herman scowled and tightened his grip on the ropes.

"Don't be scared," Jepsen said, placing a hand on Herman's arm.

But Herman wasn't scared. He was simply rigid with reluctance.

Jepsen had to prise open his fingers, one by one. It was a test of strength, but Jepsen was the stronger. "There we go. Slowly. One step at a time. One hand at a time." He spoke to Herman as if he were a child learning to walk. Herman looked down at the deck. The able seaman and the first mate were staring up at him. They too thought he'd panicked.

"I can manage on my own. Leave me alone," he hissed.

Jepsen pulled away, still facing him.

"Now remember," he said. "Hold on tight with your hands. And if you can't use your hands, use your teeth. And if your teeth fail you, use your eyelashes." He gave Herman an encouraging grin and winked at him. Herman scowled back.

A year passed and we asked ourselves if it was time for Herman to sign off. There was bad blood between them now.

Then one spring day, shortly after Herman turned fifteen, the *Two Sisters* sailed out of the harbor with nobody on board but Holger Jepsen and his stepson. They were off to pick up a first mate and two able seamen who were signing on in Rudkøbing before the ship headed for Spain. It wasn't far to Rudkøbing, but we still thought Jepsen was running a risk sailing there with just a cabin boy on board. Perhaps Jepsen had pictured the crossing as a kind of initiation for his adolescent stepson? Or perhaps his tenderheartedness had worn off, and he felt the need to show Herman who was in charge on board, once and for all?

The trip did indeed turn out to be a test of manhood—but not the one Jepsen had in mind.

Jepsen and Herman set off early in the morning, and we didn't expect to see the *Two Sisters* again for another seven to eight months, when she would return via Newfoundland and dock in Marstal for the winter. But that very afternoon the ship reappeared, with her course set straight for the harbor. A crowd quickly gathered on Dampskibsbroen. What was going on? Her sails were set and a brisk wind was blowing: we could tell, even from this distance, that she was going too fast. She was headed for collision—either with the breakwater at the harbor entrance or with one of the ships moored to the black-tarred posts just inside it.

There was one man at the wheel, and he appeared to be the only one on board. As the *Two Sisters* came nearer, we could make out that the lone helmsman was Herman, wearing yellow oilskins and a sou'wester. For a moment it looked as if the ship would crash straight into the wharf. But just then, at the last minute, with a movement whose elegance none of us missed, Herman turned the wheel and the ship glided along the edge of the wharf, with only a few inches to

we, the drowned

spare. But she was still moving at top speed and in danger of colliding with another ship. If the situation hadn't been so unusual—not to mention desperate—we'd have believed that the boy was simply trying to show off.

Suddenly a broad figure shot out of the crowd on Dampskibsbroen and landed on the deck of the *Two Sisters*. It was Albert Madsen. He was in his sixties by then, but he was the one who did what the rest of us much younger men should have done. He'd spotted that something was terribly awry, with the boy alone on deck, all sails set, the ship on a collision course.

Albert may not have set sail in ten years, but the captain inside him was still alive.

He strode straight across the deck and landed a hand on Herman's shoulder. At this, Herman looked up and then did something that made no sense. He tried to hit him. The big boy and the stout old man were about the same height and equal in bulk. But while the boy had the energy of youth, Madsen had the experience—and he responded instantly. His famous open-handed blow had the power to send a grown man flying several feet across the deck. And now was no exception.

Not a word had passed between them: there'd been no time for that. By the time Albert grabbed the wheel and turned the ship sideways, the *Eos,* moored to one of the posts in the middle of the harbor, was only feet away. When the stern of the *Two Sisters* hit the bow of the *Eos,* her speed had dropped enough to avoid any major damage.

Herman scrambled back to his feet, his hand clasped to his burning cheek. He'd lost his sou'wester. The way he glared at Albert Madsen, you'd think the old captain had spoiled some game he had been playing, rather than averted a wrecking. As soon as we'd moored the *Two Sisters* to the wharf and inspected the damage, it was clear to all that Herman felt humiliated. No one told him off. But no one praised him either, though he probably deserved it. He was only fifteen, and he'd steered a ship single-handed. Perhaps this was when things turned sour: when Albert hit him and we remained silent. But perhaps something had gone wrong with Herman long before. Perhaps he'd misunderstood the silence of the stars the night he stood staring at the Milky Way.

We don't know.

In any case, adolescent sensitivities were not uppermost in our minds at this point: a ship had arrived at the port with only the cabin boy on board. Where was the captain? Had he gone ashore in Rud-købing, and had Herman run off with the ship?

"What's happened to Captain Jepsen?" we asked him.

Herman was still nursing his sore cheek. "He fell overboard."

He sounded absent-minded, as though he needed time to recall who Captain Jepsen was.

"He fell overboard? No one falls overboard between Marstal and Rudkøbing in a light wind."

"Maybe I didn't put it the right way," Herman said. It was then that we first sensed a terrible arrogance in him. "What I meant was, he jumped."

"Jepsen? Jumped overboard?"

All we could do was stupidly repeat Herman's words like a bunch of parrots. It was that impossible for us to grasp what he'd said.

"Yes," he said. "He was always whining about missing Ma. In the end I suppose he couldn't take it anymore."

You could hear his arrogance grow with every word, and we felt like asking him whether he too hadn't "whined" about Erna, and whether her death hadn't been a blow for him, as well as his stepfather. Then, finally, the truth dawned on us. Herman had lost his mother long ago, on the day she'd married Jepsen. By the time she died for real, he felt nothing but contempt for his stepfather's despair. Maybe he even had a morbid feeling that things had fallen into place. Had his stepfather's grief and anguish given him satisfaction? Did he feel avenged when Jepsen jumped overboard? Or—and here we hesitated, we never voiced it, but we thought it privately (and when enough Marstallers privately think the same thing, it's as good as spoken aloud)—when Jepsen was "given a hand"?

"Where did he jump?" we asked—though we sensed that the way we phrased the question would take us farther from the truth.

"I dunno," the boy replied brazenly.

"You don't know? But you've got to. Was it in Mørkedybet? Outside of Strynø? Think. It's important."

"Why?" He shot us a defiant look. "Water's water. And when you're drowned, you stay drowned. Makes no difference where."

We got nowhere with him.

Sooner or later Jepsen's body would drift ashore on one of the archipelago's many little islands, on Strynø, Tåsinge, or the coast of

Langeland, perhaps as far in as Lindelse Nor. And there it would lie, sloshing about in the seaweed, half eaten by fish and crabs. But it wouldn't be your regular washed-up body. Or so a lot of us reckoned. Because the forehead would be caved in by a marlinspike. Or a swinging boom. Or one of the many other weapons a would-be murderer might find on board ship.

But Jepsen was never found. Perhaps he sank to the bottom, with a stone around his neck to keep him down. Or perhaps, a long-distance traveler to the very end, he drifted with the current and went south, deeper into the Baltic. Either way, he never came back to testify.

And that's why we never voiced our thoughts, though some of us would hint at them in a whisper: "There's something not quite right about that Herman, isn't there? And Jepsen—could he really have jumped?"

A space grew around Herman. He was only a fifteen-year-old boy, but he was something else too, something different and alien. We slapped him on the shoulder and praised him, eventually, for having steered the *Two Sisters* safely back to Marstal. We had to, because he'd done something spectacular, something no other boy his age could have done. Another kid would have panicked or simply given up. Yes, Herman had the makings of a good sailor. But the toughness that we applauded in him also kept us at a distance.

Herman inherited the *Two Sisters* and Jepsen's house in Skippergade. He wasn't old enough to be the legal owner of either the ship or the house, so Jepsen's brother, Hans, was appointed his guardian. Hans Jepsen found a new captain and a crew for the ship, but when Herman demanded to be signed on to it as an ordinary seaman, he refused.

"You haven't been at sea long enough," he said.

"I sailed a whole damn ship on my own," Herman shouted. Red in the face, he took a menacing step toward Hans—who reacted by taking an equally menacing step toward the kid.

"You're only a boy and you'll sail as a boy."

"It's my ship!" Herman roared.

Hans Jepsen had been a first mate for many years so he was unimpressed by rebellious cabin boys, no matter how tall they were or how loudly they shouted.

"I don't give a damn who owns the ship," he growled in a low, savage voice that was more terrifying than any yell. "You'll be an ordinary seaman when you're old enough and no sooner, you upstart pup!" He jutted his unshaven chin. He'd sailed on an American ship as a young man and used threatening expressions like "You're dead meat, buddy" and "You're history." We were never quite sure what they meant, but we got the gist when he ground his teeth and spat out more American cuss words as if they were gristle. Now he stared at Herman, his jaw working. "I don't know what you did to my brother, but if you so much as look at me wrong, you can kiss your fat ass goodbye."

Herman had his pride. If he wasn't allowed to sail as an ordinary seaman on a ship he regarded as his own, he didn't want to sail on her at all. He did the rounds of the harbor, but no one wanted to take him on as an ordinary seaman, or as anything else. So he went off to Copenhagen and signed on there.

For some years we heard nothing from him. Then he returned, and everything changed.

THERE ARE MANY WAYS to tell a man's story. When Albert Madsen first began writing his diary, it contained very little personal information but concentrated instead on our town and its progress. He wrote about the school in Vestergade, which was now the biggest building in town; about the new post office in Havnegade; about improvements to street lighting and the removal of the open sewers; about the network of roads that extended in all directions; and about the new streets that appeared in the southwest outskirts of the town and were named after Danish naval heroes: Tordenskjoldsgade, Niels Juelsgade, Willemoesgade, Hvidtfeldtsgade.

A sailor's often asked why he goes ashore. Whenever anyone put that question to Albert, he'd always reply that he hadn't gone ashore, he'd just swapped a small deck for a big one. The whole world was moving forward just like a ship at sea. And our island was just a ship on the endless ocean of time, heading for the future.

He always reminded us that the island's first inhabitants hadn't been islanders. Ærø had once been one of many hills in a rolling landscape. Then the huge northern glaciers had started melting. Rivers had plowed their way through the country, and the vast freshwater lakes to the south had expanded. Then the sea had poured in, and what was once a range of hills became an archipelago. Which came first? Albert would ask. The wheel or the canoe? Which would we rather do, master the weight of burdens too heavy for us to carry or conquer the distant horizons of the ocean?

The harbor rang with the cries of seagulls, the banging of shipyard hammers, and the rattle of ropes in the wind. The roar of the sea rose above it all, a noise so familiar it seemed to have been born in our ears. Those were the years when everyone was talking about America.

And many left. We left too, but not for good. In earlier days, we'd had to cram our houses right on the shoreline because there'd been no room anywhere else: the gentry and the peasants owned the fields. With no other choices open to us, we'd turned our gaze seaward. The oceans were our America: they reached farther than any prairie, untamed as on the first day of creation. Nobody owned them.

The orchestra outside our windows played the same tune every day: it was nameless, but it was everywhere. Even in bed, asleep, we'd dream of the water.

But the women never heard its music. They couldn't—or they didn't want to. Outside the home, they never looked toward the harbor, but always inland, across the island. They stayed behind and filled the gaps we left. We heard the sirens' song while our wives and mothers blocked their ears and bent over the washtub. The women of Marstal didn't grow bitter. But they grew hard and practical.

Albert Madsen didn't miss the sea. How could he, living in a world capital like Marstal? He could sit on a harbor bench and chat with Christian Aaberg, the first Dane ever to walk right across Africa. Or with Knud Nielsen, who'd just returned after seventeen years on the coast of Japan. Half the male residents of the town had rounded Cape Horn, a perilous rite of passage for sailors the world over, and done it as casually as they'd take the steamer to Svendborg. Every street and lane in Marstal was a main road leading to the ocean. China was in our back garden, and through the windows of our low-ceilinged houses we could see the Moroccan shore.

There were a few cross streets in our town, but none of significance. Tværgade, Kirkestræde, and Vestergade didn't lead to the sea but ran parallel to it. At first we didn't even have a market square. Then a butcher opened in Kirkestræde, followed by an ironmonger, two drapers, a chemist, a savings bank, a watchmaker, and a barber. The sailors' hostel was torn down. We were to have a market square just like any other town. Suddenly we had a main street, but going the wrong way: instead of taking you to the harbor, it skirted the coast and then veered toward the heart of the island. Heading away from the dangers of the sea, it was a women's street.

Our streets all met and crossed. Some were men's and some were women's, and together they formed a network. The ship-brokering and shipping companies were situated on Kongegade and Prinsegade, while the women did their shopping on Kirkestræde. But that balance was about to shift. At first no one paid much attention to it or saw what it might lead to.

The 1890s were Marstal's heyday. Our fleet expanded until only the one in Copenhagen could beat it: 346 ships! These were boom times, and we all caught investment fever. Everyone wanted a share in a ship, even cabin boys and housemaids. When a ship returned from a voyage and was laid up for the winter, the streets teemed with children delivering sealed envelopes containing the dividends that were paid out to practically every household.

A ship broker needs to know how the Russo-Japanese War will hit the freight market. He doesn't need to be interested in politics, but he has to pay attention to his skippers' finances, so a knowledge of international conflict is essential. Opening up a newspaper, he'll see a photograph of a head of state and if he's bright enough, he'll read his own future profits in the man's face. He might not be interested in socialism, in fact he'll swear he isn't: he's never heard such a load of starry-eyed nonsense. Until one day his crew lines up and demands higher wages, and he has to immerse himself in union issues and other newfangled notions about the future organization of society. A broker must keep up to date with the names of foreign heads of state, the political currents of the time, the various enmities between nations, and earthquakes in distant parts of the world. He makes money out of wars and disasters, but first and foremost he makes it because the world has become one big building site. Technology rearranges everything, and he needs to know its secrets, its latest inventions and discoveries. *Saltpeter, divi-divi, soy cakes, pit props, soda, dyer's broom*—these aren't just names to him. He's neither touched saltpeter nor seen a swatch of dyer's broom. He's never tasted soy cake (for which he can count himself lucky), but he knows what it's used for and where there's a demand for it. He doesn't want the world to stop changing. If it did, his office would have to close. He knows what a sailor is: an indispensable helper in the great workshop that technology has made of the world.

There was a time when all we ever carried was grain. We bought it in one place and sold it in another. Now we were circumnavigating the globe with a hold full of commodities whose names we had to learn to pronounce and whose use had to be explained to us. Our ships had become our schools. They were still powered by the wind in their sails, as they had been for thousands of years. But stacked in their holds lay the future.

Albert Madsen came ashore when he was about fifty, as most of us did. If you'd saved up thirty thousand kroner by then, you could put it in the savings bank, where they offered you 4 percent interest per annum, and you'd get a monthly payment of one hundred kroner: enough to live on. But Albert had earned much more than that, and he didn't put his money in the bank. Instead, he invested it in ships and became a shipowner and broker. Many of those who bought shares in ships in those days, including farmers from the interior of the island, knew nothing about shipping and needed advice from someone who himself had once sailed and understood the sea. This called for someone known as a corresponding shipowner, and Albert became a corresponding shipowner like no other. During his many travels he'd become acquainted with a Jewish tailor in Rotterdam who went on board ships docked there to make clothes for the sailors, and they'd become friends. Luis Presser was an astute businessman. After Rotterdam he'd settled in Le Havre and set up his own shipping company, with a fleet of seven large barks. He had them registered in Marstal and made Albert, who'd just come ashore, their corresponding owner.

In Le Havre Albert had fallen in love with Presser's wife, a beautiful Chinese lady called Cheng Sumei. And she'd fallen in love with him. They'd looked at each other, realized that they'd met too late in life, and decided on friendship instead. When Luis Presser died suddenly of pneumonia, his widow took over the business and continued it with even greater success than her late husband. Perhaps she'd always been the woman behind the man. At any rate, she now became the woman behind Albert. It was she who advised him as he went from being captain on the brig *Princess* to managing ten ships.

Their two businesses eventually became so closely intertwined that Cheng Sumei's company in Le Havre was hard to distinguish from Albert's in Marstal. Albert too had a talent for making money. Once, when he was a young man, he'd stood on the deck of a ship in the Pacific with a bag of pearls in his hand that could have made all his dreams come true, and he'd flung it into the sea because he felt that the wealth they could buy him would bring a curse. Now a woman from China had placed a new bag of pearls in his outstretched hand. And this time he'd opened it.

We don't know whether Albert Madsen and Cheng Sumei were entwined as closely on a personal level as they were on a business one. Life had demanded so many changes from both of them: first they'd had to snuff their growing love and replace it with friendship. Now the possibility of love was open to them once again. Did they grab the chance?

Cheng Sumei never had children of her own, but she always referred to the company's huge, elegant barks, such as the *Claudia*, the *Suzanne*, and the *Germaine*, as her "daughters." She was now too old to bear a child, though you wouldn't know it from her strangely ageless features. The two held hands in public. They probably slept together too, the slim Chinese lady with the smooth, polished skin stretched beautifully across her high cheekbones and the big, coarsely built Dane who could easily fill a double bed. But they never married.

She'd been born in Shanghai. She'd never known her parents and had survived on the street by selling flowers. Many of us had met her in Rotterdam when Presser was still alive and coming on board our ships to measure us up for clothes. But she'd also been seen in Sydney and in Bangkok, in Bahia and in Buenos Aires. Some claimed to have met her in a brothel; others had known her as the manager of a boardinghouse. We all believed we knew something about her, but none of us knew anything for certain. She'd have needed nine lives, like a cat, to have appeared in all the places we thought we'd seen her. She was as well traveled as any long-haul sailor.

But she never came to Marstal; it was always Albert who went to Le Havre. Until one day he stopped. At first we thought they'd fallen out. But then we learned she'd died—quite unexpectedly. Albert didn't tell us any of this; we pieced it together ourselves. Why had they never married? Why hadn't they lived together? Had Albert not loved her enough? Had she not been enough in love with him?

If any of us got up the nerve to ask why he'd never married her or anyone else, he'd reply, "I was in so much of a hurry that I clean forgot." That made us laugh. He'd had plenty of opportunities.

When Albert first came ashore, he bought the old merchant's house on the right-hand side of Prinsegade as you come up from the harbor. Later, he moved across the street, into a brand-new house he'd had built for himself, with high ceilings and a first floor. From its large east-facing balcony he could see the breakwater and the archipelago. A bay window gave onto the street. On the small pane of glass above his front door he had his name painted in gilt letters: ALBERT MADSEN.

Diagonally across from his was the house of Lorentz Jørgensen, who'd set up shop as a shipowner and broker many years before Albert. As a boy, Lorentz had been fat and wheezing, with a permanent pleading look in his eyes. Then the sea had hardened him until we forgot that we'd once thought of him as nothing but a flabby sissy with no balls. He hadn't stayed long at sea, and had come ashore after sitting his navigation exam. Though he'd not been able to save up much from his modest wages, it turned out he had a talent for making money. He bought shares in ships and knew how to talk business with Marstal Savings Bank. He entered into a kind of partnership with the biggest shipowner in town, Sofus Boye, who was nicknamed Farmer Sofus because he came from Ommel, a village three kilometers inland from Marstal.

Lorentz Jørgensen hadn't yet turned thirty when he convinced us to have a telegraph cable laid from Langeland. He spoke of the *world market* and the *telegraph*. The words meant little to us, but he managed to convey that the world market was to the sailor what the soil was to the farmer, and that without a telegraph we'd never make contact with it.

The government turned us down when we applied for financial assistance for the telegraph. So Lorentz went to see Sofus Boye. Farmer Sofus was a modest man who despite owning the biggest shipping company in town could still sometimes be found waiting by the ferry dock, hustling a few coins as a porter. He had no office as such: he'd just tap his forehead with his index finger and say he kept everything in there. But Farmer Sofus listened when Lorentz described the speaking cable that could shrink distances to nothing.

"It doesn't matter whether you live in a big town or a small one. Even if you live on the tiniest island in the middle of the ocean, as long as you have a telegraph, you're at the center of the world."

This kind of talk sounded fanciful to most people, but not to Farmer Sofus, whose ears quite readily went deaf on other matters. He came along with Lorentz to Marstal Savings Bank and told him to repeat what he'd said about the telegraph to Rudolf Østermann, the manager.

"The center of the world," Lorentz insisted.

The bank manager, who considered himself something of a wit, was on the verge of asking if there was any chance of using this telegraph thing to contact the good Lord God—but one sharp look from Farmer Sofus wiped the grin right off his face. As it turned out, Rudolf Østermann soon became the most zealous of the invention's converts, frequently declaring, "The telegraph office is the heart of a town, a pure blessing. They should have it in the church." He'd completely forgotten the joke he'd been ready to crack the first time Lorentz told him about it.

Once Marstal Savings Bank and the biggest shipowner in town had backed the telegraph, other Marstal investors emerged. If the government wouldn't help us, we'd just have to help ourselves.

It was also Lorentz who came up with a plan for the town's own mutual marine insurance. At first we insured only small ships, and then as Marstal's prosperity increased, we took on big vessels too. In 1904 the Marine Insurance Company acquired its own building on the corner of Skolegade and Havnegade, a splendid red-brick house with a relief on its façade depicting a schooner in full sail. The building served the same function as the breakwater: it protected us.

Nothing escaped the attention of the meticulous and imaginative Lorentz. When he was appointed harbormaster he ordered the construction of the four-hundred-foot-long steamer wharf, the Dampskibsbroen. He was also one of the cofounders of the whitewashed Marstal Dairy, with its tall chimney, in Vestergade. He bought a horse, and he cut an impressive figure as he rode through town with the beast's iron-shod hooves ringing on the cobbles. He was the real master builder of the town—though the wall he built around Marstal was an invisible one, designed to shield us from all the unforeseen accidents of life at sea.

Lorentz married a woman two years his senior, Katrine Hermansen. It was a late marriage, but the couple managed to have three children. The eldest immigrated to America, the middle one he sent to England to learn the shipping trade, and the youngest, a girl, stayed at home and married a sail maker, Møller from Nygade. They had four children, who turned up at their grandfather's office in Prinsegade every day to sing to him in their gentle, clear voices. On Lorentz's desk lay telegrams from Algiers, Antwerp, Tangier, Bridgewater, Liverpool,

Dunkirk, Riga, Kristiania, Stettin, and Lisbon. In his later years he ran to fat and began to resemble his old self in the days before he went to sea. But no one teased him about his big body anymore. As he sat in the swivel chair of his office, listening to his grandchildren singing, he reminded us of one of those chubby, contented Buddhas you see in Chinese temples.

The cemetery where Lorentz would one day be laid to rest was new, like so many other things in Marstal in those days. Previously we'd all been buried in the churchyard between Kirkestræde and Vestergade, in the shadow of the beech trees. But now we were put to rest in a completely new cemetery outside the town, which sloped toward the beach from Ommelsvejen and provided a view of the archipelago. In it we planted a long avenue of rowan trees that would last at least a hundred years. There was room there for many dead.

Certainly we were hoping to be just as numerous in the future as we were then. Perhaps we even thought there'd be more of us. We must also have hoped we'd no longer die in foreign ports or at sea, but instead draw our final breaths in familiar surroundings.

A cemetery that fills up slowly sends out a comforting message: You'll die in the place where you were born, the place you love, the place where you belong. You'll see your children grow up. You'll sit, bent with age, while your grandchildren sing to you and your life stretches out behind you like a slope that begins on the narrow, white edge of the beach and ends on a hill with a view of the archipelago.

When one of us was once asked why, when his ship was floundering in a storm, he'd refused to give up even though death seemed like a certainty, he'd given an answer that would seem strange to anyone but a Marstaller. It was Morten Seier, the first mate of the *Flora*, which was skippered by Anders Kroman. It was December 1901, and the ship was bound for Kiel with a load of English coal. A west wind rose and grew, and for six days the *Flora* was adrift in a hard gale, covered in frost, with only the reefed mainsail and the staysail set. Then the storm turned into a hurricane and swept off the longboat, the galley, and the wheelhouse. The men could venture on deck only if secured to a line, while waves as big as houses crashed down on them from all directions. On the tenth day a huge wave took away the rigging, and the cargo shifted. When the *Flora* rose out of the raging water again, she'd taken a severe list. Masts, rigging, and all the superstructure had gone, and the wreckage floated on the waves, covered with white foam from the pressure of the hurricane.

They gathered in the cabin and Captain Kroman, who was a plain-speaking man, informed them that they shouldn't expect to see Christmas.

Then another huge wave crashed over the ship and flung them against the bulkhead. Now they were convinced that the *Flora* had been dealt her final blow. Knowing she would soon sink, they braced themselves for a watery grave.

But the badly damaged hull stayed afloat.

And that's when Morten Seier had the idea that saved them: sling the entire cargo overboard so that the stern could lift above the waterline. They couldn't open the hatches for fear of flooding the ship with seawater, so instead they used their axes to chop through the bulkhead and into the hold. And from there they began heaving out the coal. None of them had got a wink of sleep since the rigging was swept overboard three nights before. Nevertheless, freezing in the howling snowstorm that swept the bare deck, and soaked by the icy water that washed over them incessantly, the six-man crew of the *Flora* used buckets and sacks to shift forty tons of coal and tip them into the sea. In one night: nearly seven tons, or seven thousand kilos, per man.

Afterward, according to Morten Seier, they were all dead on their feet. They soon fell into a deep sleep—the men in the now empty hold, Captain Kroman and Seier in the cabin.

When they woke it was early in the morning of December 24, and the storm had died down. They calculated that they were approximately sixteen sea miles from the Orkney Islands, but as the storm had taken their lifeboat, the sight of land made doom just as likely as salvation. So they shackled the two anchor chains together to avoid drifting into the murderously rocky coast.

Finally help came. A Dutch fishing boat appeared on the horizon, and soon the crew of the *Flora* was on board.

"What made you keep going?" we asked Seier.

It was a stupid question, but we asked it anyway, though anyone could work out the answer. Morten Seier wanted to see his house in Buegade again. He didn't want to be parted from his wife, Gertrud, or his children, Jens and Ingrid, who needed him just as much as he needed them. He wanted to be back for Christmas. And like any other sailor, he wanted to end up captain of his own ship before he came ashore for good. To sum it up: it was too early for him to die.

But Morten Seier didn't offer any of those explanations. Instead he gave us something completely different: an intelligent answer to a stupid question.

"I kept going because I wanted to be buried in the new cemetery," he said.

You might think this was a strange reply. Perhaps only a sailor could understand it. But our new cemetery represented hope.

It was something to come home to.

What would we have done if a stranger had told us that the burial ground would remain half empty, and that only a few gravestones would testify to the lives that were once lived here, or that the avenue of rowan trees we'd planted along the high road would one day be half-buried by tall grass, so that only a trained eye could discern the landscape we'd planned in that wilderness?

What would we have done if a stranger had told us that the ancestral chains binding us to Marstal would soon be broken, and forces stronger than the sea would carry us away?

We'd have laughed at him, the fool.

ALBERT MADSEN DIDN'T believe in God and he didn't believe in the devil either. He believed, a little, in mankind's capacity for good; as for evil, he'd seen it for himself on board the ships he'd sailed. He also believed in common sense, but even that wasn't his strongest belief. Above all else, Albert Madsen believed in fellowship. As far as he knew, those who believed in God had no proof that He existed. But Albert had proof of his own belief in fellowship—and it was a solid reality. He saw it every morning when he looked out of his gable window, past the broker's office in Prinsegade, and he could see it from the bay window of his office below too: in fact, it was the reason he'd added the window to the house. And when he descended the three stone steps at his front door and turned right down Prinsegade toward the harbor, there it was again, laid out before him.

The mighty breakwater had taken the town forty years to build. It lay in the middle of the bay, more than a thousand meters long and four meters high, built from boulders each weighing several tons. Like the Egyptians with their pyramids, we'd built a vast monument of stone. Ours, though, was not meant to preserve the memory of the dead, but to protect the living. Which made us wiser than them. The breakwater was the work of a pharaoh, Albert told us: a pharaoh with many faces. Together they represented what he called fellowship.

This was Albert's morning worship: his sailor's eyes would roam the sky and its cloud formations, full of messages for those who could read them, and then settle on the breakwater. It brought him a feeling of serenity. There it lay, a dormant power stronger than the sea, capable of calming the tides beyond it and providing shelter for the ships: living proof of human fellowship. We don't sail because the sea is there. We sail because there's a harbor. We don't start by heading for distant shores. We seek protection first.

Albert rarely went to church. But he attended services on festival days and special occasions because the church too was part of man's fellowship, and he didn't want to be isolated from it. He had no particular respect for the ritual. But a church is like a ship. Certain rules apply and once you come on board, you have to adhere to them. And if you can't, you should stay away.

For years a succession of ministers had complained that the church was badly maintained. But when Pastor Abildgaard, with whom Albert was on otherwise good terms, went so far as to argue that money earmarked for the school should be spent on the church's façade, he was given short shrift. When it came to choosing between education and religion, Albert said, he'd choose education every time. The school represented young people and the future—and the church didn't. If the school in Vestergade was bigger than the church, so much the better. Any town that believed in the future should take note.

"But what about issues of morality?" Abildgaard objected. "Where will the child learn about those if not in the church?"

"On board his ship," Albert replied tersely.

"And in foreign ports, perhaps?" the pastor retorted.

Albert said nothing.

Where life at sea was concerned, Albert had no illusions. He'd lived the unprotected life of a cabin boy, working like a dog and being treated worse, as he put it. However, times had changed. Living conditions on board ship had improved and become more humane. The children were better taught, and in time they became better skippers. Albert believed in progress. He also believed in a sailor's sense of honor. Fellowship stemmed from that. On a ship, one man's negligence could have fatal consequences for everyone. A sailor was quick to see that. The minister called it morality. Albert called it honor. In the church you were accountable to God. On a ship you were accountable to everyone. That made a ship a better place to learn.

In his experience, ultimately everything came down to the captain. The captain knew the function of everything on board, down to the last sail and rope, and so did the crew. By the same token, each man also had his function, and if the captain failed to make the role of each and every one clear from the start, the crew would settle it among themselves by fighting. And then the weakest—though not necessarily the least able—would find himself at the bottom of the heap. He'd seen that happen on the *Emma C. Leithfield,* when Captain Eagleton let his brutal first mate, O'Connor, take over the authority of the ship. The strongest isn't always the best suited to lead. A captain has to know the human mind as well as he knows the layout of his ship.

When Albert became a captain himself, he'd had crew members jump ship from time to time. But he'd never seen this as disobedience or evidence of the sailor's bad character, so much as a failure of his own insight into human nature. He hadn't paid enough attention to set the man on the right track. He believed there was good to be found in everyone. He knew that there was evil as well. But his basic view was that evil too could be disciplined and kept in check.

Once, in Laguna, Mexico, sometime in the 1880s, an able seaman pulled a knife on him. Albert, who was unarmed, held out his hand for the weapon. He never thought for a moment that he was doing something unusual or courageous: he just did what he had to do in order to remain in charge. The seaman froze, frowning at Albert's outstretched hand, struggling to understand. Seizing the moment, Albert punched him in the jaw with all his strength and floored him. Then Albert put his boot on the man's wrist, twisted the knife out of his grappling fingers, pulled the dazed man to his feet, and calmly proceeded to beat the living daylights out of him—while taking care not to cause permanent injury. He was both inflicting punishment and enforcing his authority.

In the midst of this, he was aware that he didn't represent good any more than the seaman with the knife embodied evil. The two of them were simply opposing forces. Nobody sailed into a raging gale with all sails set. You didn't confront a storm head-on. You adjusted the sails and found a balance. All genuine order depends on that kind of balance, not on one man's suppression of another. No rule deserving of the name is writ in stone.

When James Cook faced a band of furious natives at Kealakekua Bay in Hawaii, in the moment before a club struck the back of his head and a knife slashed his throat, he waved to his crew to come and help. But the boat that might have rescued him turned back to sea. And the men on shore who could have rushed to defend him threw down their muskets and fled into the surf. On his last voyage on board the *Resolution*, Captain Cook had had eleven out of seventeen of his able seamen flogged, giving them a total of 216 lashes. So when he needed their help, they simply turned their scarred backs on him. He'd pulled the wrong ropes.

Every sailing ship has miles of rope, scores of blocks, hundreds of square yards of canvas. Unless the ropes are constantly pulled and the sails endlessly adjusted, the ship becomes a helpless victim of the wind. Managing a crew is the same thing. The captain holds hundreds of invisible ropes in his hands. Allowing the crew to take charge is like letting the wind take the helm: the ship will be wrecked. But if the captain takes complete control, the ship will be becalmed and go nowhere: he strips his men of all initiative; they'll no longer do their best and go about their work with reluctance. It's all a question of experience and knowledge. But first and foremost it's about authority.

When Albert had finished beating up the mutinous seaman and the man lay battered on the deck, he helped him to his feet, then called the galley boy to fetch a basin of water so the man could wash the blood off his face. And that was the end of the matter. The man was again part of the crew.

Albert had once been beaten himself, with the thrashing rope. But he never became anything like Isager, who neither punished nor rewarded his pupils, but just hammered them repeatedly instead. Nor was he like O'Connor, the first mate who'd used his rank to indulge his murderous impulses. As for the captain who'd resorted to flogging to enforce his shaky authority, well, Albert was no James Cook either. Instead he was something Captain Eagleton on the *Emma C. Leithfield* had never managed to be, and it wasn't about obeying or disobeying rules. Life had taught him about something far more complicated than justice. Its name was balance.

IN 1913 ALBERT decided to construct a monument to his personal doctrine in the form of a memorial stone to be erected close to the new Dampskibsbroen. He'd already picked out the stone and knew its provenance. It was about four meters long, three meters wide, and two meters tall. It lay in the Baltic Sea out by the Tail, and in an off-shore storm you could sometimes see it from land. In the summer boys would swim out to it and stand on it, their small blond heads just reaching above the surface of the glittering water.

The light would play on the waves and flicker across its massive flank and sometimes Albert would sit in his boat, resting his oars, and simply contemplate it. It lay so solidly down there in the pale green, shifting waters. But even this boulder had come here on a voyage, millions of years ago, moving down from the north with the ice. Now it must be moved again, this time to a permanent location, to remind Marstal of the construction of the breakwater and man's power over nature.

He even came up with the inscription it would bear: STRENGTH IN FELLOWSHIP.

Then one sunny day in June, as he sat leaning over the rail, gazing into the lapping water, a severe bout of dizziness overcame him, and he got the sudden feeling that the world was losing its cohesion and that everything he believed in was doomed. He felt the shadow of a menace that went beyond the fury of the wind and the pounding of the waves: a foreboding of looming disasters from which even the unyielding boulders of the breakwater couldn't protect Marstal. The sensation was so vague and dreamlike that he thought he must have briefly nodded off in the afternoon sunshine. Then, fixing his eyes on the boulder in the water, he made out his own shadow on its scarred flank, and his sense of reality returned.

It was then he got the idea. It came over him with a kind of urgent haste, in a flurry of inspiration. It was time to take stock, he decided: to make a big, strong, permanent mark to counterbalance his own sudden premonition of doom. The stone.

Only a few days after this epiphany, Albert called a meeting in the rooms of the Marine Insurance Company in Havnegade to present his idea to a circle of invited guests. His proposal for the memorial met with general support, and a committee was set up to carry out the preliminary work. The stone was to be put in place that very year, before autumn set in.

A week later Albert joined the chairmen of the harbor commission and the Marine Insurance Company to inspect it. A strong breeze was blowing from the west, baring its top as the waves broke against it.

On a mid-July morning, two crane barges were towed out to the boulder. On board were Albert Madsen, the chairman of the harbor commission, the harbormaster, a fisherman, and a rigger from one of the shipyards in town. A circle of the town's ladies brought sandwiches and refreshments to the white sandy beach, and these were ferried out to the sweating men on the two rocking decks. By two o'clock the stone had been lifted and secured between the barges. When the returning convoy passed Dampskibsbroen and sailed into the harbor with the stone tethered between them, the flag went up and the large crowd waiting on the wharf cheered.

We were celebrating ourselves: ourselves and our flourishing town.

Two days later the boulder was hoisted ashore. Albert had telephoned Svendborg and asked them to send a flatbed trailer to transport it, and this arrived on the ferry the following day. A huge crowd turned up and everyone volunteered to pull. Shipyard owner and rigger, able seaman and shipowner, merchant and clerk: even the manager of the savings bank turned himself into a human mule and got hold of the rope, while schoolchildren ran around making a racket until they too found a place in the line. Even old, long-retired skippers interrupted their chatting on the benches by the harbor to offer a helping hand, their pipes still stuck firmly in their mouths. But Josef Isager, now known as the Congo Pilot, stuffed his hands in his pockets pointedly and scowled: he was way above this kind of work. Lorentz Jørgensen too kept to the sidelines, claiming age and bulk as his excuse. The marine artist's widow, Anna Egidia Rasmussen, drawn to the harbor by the noise, which could be heard as far away as Teglgade, also looked on, clasping the hand of a grandchild. Anders Nørre, the village idiot, was jumping up and down in great excitement at the edge of the crowd. Spotting him, Albert nudged him into the flock. Once Anders had slung a rope over his shoulder, he grew strangely serene, and seemed to become calm and concentrated like the rest of the crowd.

Then Albert himself grabbed hold of a rope, raised his hand in the air, and turned to the gathering.

"Right, let's pull!" he called out, thumping the air with his fist.

That was the starting signal. Albert put his whole weight into it. He was sixty-eight years old, but he didn't feel his age. It was as if his powerful body had been saving itself for this moment his whole life, as if anything he'd done up to now had just been preparation. His face reddened in the sun, and he felt a surge of happiness that seemed to come straight from his pulsing blood and tensed muscles.

Slowly the flatbed trailer shuddered to a start. They hauled it one meter at a time—until it stopped. The ground was too soft, and the weight of the stone had sunk the trailer's wheels into the gravel, so it was impossible to move it. The legs of two hundred men strained in vain. They leaned forward into the ropes as though testing their combined weight against the stone. But it resisted them.

Albert straightened up and turned to the gathering.

"Come on, folks," he called out, and punched the air a second time. "One, two, three—pull!"

But the trailer wouldn't budge.

Somewhere in the sea of people, a sailor started up a chantey. The others joined in, and soon they were all singing, swaying rhythmically to the old working song that had rung across the sea for centuries. But it did no good.

Albert called out to a boy and asked him to run to the Navigation College in Tordenskjoldsgade and bring back some students. The boy raced off, and it wasn't long before thirty young seamen came marching together down Havnegade. They rolled up their sleeves to reveal their tattoos and shouldered the ropes. That's our youth and our future, Albert thought. That boulder doesn't stand a chance now.

And sure enough, the flatbed trailer started rolling again, its wheels groaning in protest, as if the whole vehicle was being torn apart by the enormous pressure. There was a tense moment when they rolled over a curb; the stone wobbled, but it stayed put, and the chantey resumed. It wasn't until now that Albert had properly listened to its words.

> I will drink whiskey hot and strong.
> Whiskey, Johnny!
> I will drink whiskey all day long.
> Whiskey for me, Johnny!

Young boys sang along cheerfully at the top of their voice. The words held the promise of manhood. The trainee navigators led the singing. They'd sailed for long enough to feel like fully qualified seamen, and this song belonged to them: their years before the mast confirmed their right to it. For the old seamen, it was just a memory. It struck Albert that there were few men here who'd never hoisted a sail or heaved against a windlass to the tune of the whiskey song—the national anthem of all sailors. It made no difference what language it was sung in; the message was in the rhythm, not the words. It didn't preach; it traveled to men's hearts via their muscles, reminding them what they were capable of, so that forgetting their exhaustion, they'd toil in unison.

STRENGTH IN FELLOWSHIP would be the message on Albert's stone—but in the sweaty exhilaration of heaving it onto the trailer, he realized it could just as easily, though more crudely, be WHISKEY, JOHNNY! That too spoke of fellowship.

He raised his sweating face to the sun and smiled.

The stone had reached its destination.

Albert had held several public meetings at Hotel Ærø about the memorial stone, or the Fellowship Stone, as he'd privately named it. It would be financed in the way that anything major and important in Marstal was always financed: through the collection of small contributions. Through fellowship. When he stood on the podium, warming to his theme, he happily forgot that there was something important he'd never explained. What was the occasion for erecting the memorial stone? The seventy-fifth anniversary of the construction of the breakwater had been 1900, the year the century changed, but no one had organized anything back then. Its centenary was twelve years away. He couldn't count on being alive then; he'd be eighty-one years old, and he wasn't one of those arrogant men who assume they'll live forever. But why now? Why in the year 1913?

Fortunately, no one ever put that question to him. "Of course," everyone had said, the first time he suggested it. Of course the town should have a memorial stone—and what better event to commemorate than the construction of the breakwater? So he was never called on to explain that one day in June, he'd grown dizzy on the water south of the Tail and had premonitions whose meaning was unclear to him. He could hardly stand on a podium and talk about that. Indeed, he couldn't even have confided to a friend that this was his reason for having 230 men drag a fourteen-ton boulder around on a flatbed.

Why now, why in the year 1913?

Before it is too late, before we forget who we are, and why we do what we do.

Too late? What do you mean?

No. He could barely answer these questions himself. All he knew was that he'd been overwhelmed by a sense of doom, and to counter it, he'd thrown himself into organizing the raising of the boulder.

Again and again, from the podium in the ballroom at Hotel Ærø, Albert recounted the history of Marstal's breakwater. He explained how the harbor had once been at the mercy of winds from the north and the east, and yes, from the south too, where the sea often broke through the point that we call the Tail. How even ships in winter dock could get tossed ashore. And how, when we all faced ruin, because our harbor was so vulnerable, one man had stepped forward. You could consider him the actual founder of our town as we know it today, Albert would say, even though he didn't build on land, but in the water. He was the creator of our fellowship, the force we're now erecting a stone to commemorate. Skipper Rasmus Jepsen was his name. He encouraged our town's residents to commit themselves in writing to the construction of a breakwater. Three hundred and fifty-nine people signed that document. Some provided their labor, some the stones to build it with, and some money. But everyone gave something—all except one, who declined for the shameful reason that you should put your own needs first and not gamble on posterity.

"I will refrain from mentioning his name, for the sake of his living relatives," Albert said from the podium.

At which point everyone turned and stared at Skipper Hans Peter Levinsen, who was to become one of the keenest and most generous of the contributors to the memorial stone because it finally gave him the chance to erase his family's eighty-eight-year-old shame.

Continuing his speech, Albert recalled how, on January 28, 1825, which happened to be the birthday of King Frederik VI, one hundred men had gathered on the ice under the banner of fellowship to lay the first boulder of the massive building project. Even nature had been on their side, because if that year and the next few hadn't been ice winters, they'd never have been able to lay down the boulders. But they'd succeeded, and now here was Marstal's breakwater, an eternal symbol of what men can achieve through fellowship and hard work.

"When you look at the breakwater," he addressed the gathering, "you see a line of boulders. But never forget the real building materials. Strong arms and unbreakable will."

He concluded by reminding them that the pioneering Rasmus Jepsen had been awarded the Order of Dannebrog for his achievement. All sailors, regardless of how unruly and wayward they may appear, are monarchists, and any reference to the Dannebrog flag makes an impression on them. So sure enough, it was always at this point that the spontaneous applause erupted. Occasionally, Albert allowed himself to accept a little praise as the originator of the memorial stone, but in his heart he felt he hadn't earned it, since what he'd undertaken in these hectic, triumphant days had emerged from unstable mental territory, and from visions as ephemeral as clouds.

On the morning of July 19, the sculptor Johannes Simonsen arrived on the postal service steamer from Svendborg to inspect the boulder. He declared it fit for the purpose, made a series of drafts, and before he returned to Svendborg left instructions for cleaning off the moss and algae. The stone was dusted with chloride of lime and then washed with hydrochloric acid diluted in water. We dug a hole two meters deep for the base and filled it with concrete. At the beginning of August the plinth and iron fencing were cast. The stone was set in place in the middle of that same month. Albert Madsen himself joined in the work, together with several other committee members.

The day it was set on its plinth, six torpedo ships entered the bay. Like the ships in the harbor, they were garlanded in bunting and they'd hoisted their flags. The wharf was soon teeming with spectators. It was the first time that warships had called at Marstal, and even Albert's committee stopped its work to walk down to Dampskibsbroen to take a look. That same evening, a festive gathering for the officers from the warships had been arranged at Hotel Ærø, and Albert attended the dinner. The sight of the narrow steel-gray hulls at Damp-skibsbroen earlier had filled him with a strange unease, and now he succumbed to a dizzy spell similar to the one he'd experienced the first time he studied the boulder in the sea. He spent the entire meal in an odd state of absent-mindedness, which several of those present commented on, attributing his distraction to the huge pressure he was under during the final phase of the memorial's erection. There were moments during the dinner when he felt that the whole evening was taking place at sea. The tables seemed to be floating on the water, with the chairs bobbing around them on the waves. He saw black shadows dart across the blue-gray depths beneath him.

He was called back to reality by a voice addressing him directly. It was the commander of the six torpedo boats, Gustav Carstensen, who wanted to present his compliments.

"I heard about the memorial stone. I heard you're in charge of it and that you mobilized the whole town to put it in place. Well, the young have the energy. It's just a question of coordinating it. As a captain, you know more than most about the importance of discipline."

"I believe in balance between forces, and I believe in fellowship," Albert said.

"Fellowship is certainly important," the commander responded, looking pensively into the distance. Albert's remark had clearly provided him with a cue to proceed with his own thoughts on the matter. "But fellowship must be created. That's why we need a great cause that people can rally round. Right now, people think only about themselves. We haven't had a war to unite and focus our young people for several generations. A war's what we need."

Albert looked at him, his eyes still unfocused from the dizziness.

"But many perish in war, don't they?"

"Well, obviously, that's the price of it."

A note of hesitation had entered the commander's voice. He gave Albert a searching look. It was as if he hadn't noticed the person he was talking to until now, and was wondering if he'd been wrong about him.

"And anyway, the dead will have a grave and a headstone, won't they?" Albert continued, regardless.

"Of course, of course, that goes without saying."

It was now clear to Carstensen that the conversation had taken a wrong turn.

"Go visit the cemetery here, Commander. You'll find many women and some children. You'll also find farmers, a merchant or two, and the odd shipowner, such as myself. But you won't find many sailors. They stay out there. They never get a headstone. They've no grave that their widow and their children can visit. They drown in distant seas. The sea's an enemy with no respect for its adversary. We fight our own war here in Marstal, Commander Carstensen. And that's enough for us."

Someone proposed a toast to the navy, and the commander seized the opportunity to get away from his conversation with Albert, who left alone, fell back into his brooding.

That same night the memorial stone worksite was vandalized. The wooden fence that had been put up for protection while the sculptor finished his inscription was knocked down by a gang of drunken shipyard workers. Albert immediately reported the incident to Chief Constable Krabbe in Ærøskøbing, and received a response within three days: the chief constable informed him that the vandals had been given fines in the police court totaling 315 kroner for drunkenness and breach of the peace.

As the day of the unveiling approached, Albert's unease grew. Fortunately, there was still plenty of work to be done. He'd already written a detailed history of the breakwater and had it sealed in a lead pipe, which was sunk into the cement foundation of the memorial stone. Now he began composing a speech to read aloud when the stone was unveiled. He portrayed the stone as though it were a human being with human disappointments and hopes, and he referred to life as "a place where joy, sorrow, and failed hopes intertwine, and where the best-laid plans don't always bear fruit."

He stopped.

What do you think you're writing? he asked himself. You were supposed to celebrate the breakwater and human fellowship. But you've written yourself into a corner.

He shook his head and switched off the desk lamp. Where had these doubts come from? He had no reason to question his life's work. The town was flourishing as never before, and that was precisely what the memorial stone was being erected to celebrate. This blasted dizziness was troubling him again. Premonitions, a swimming head, visions. Old wives' tales.

He got ready for bed. Sleep might offer some respite.

He stamped his foot angrily as if to scare off the unsettling spirits. The last thing he needed was to grow afraid of the dark, like a child.

Finally the day arrived: September 26, 1913. Hundreds of people had turned up, and Albert once more recounted the story of the breakwater's construction. A choir of young girls sang a song whose words Albert had written himself, and he'd succeeded in keeping free of pessimism, to the tune of "I Pledge to Guard My Country." Then he pulled off the huge Danish flag that draped the stone and as he did so, the spectators flung bouquets. The chairman of the harbor commission gave a thank-you speech, and the event concluded with three cheers for King Christian X, whose birthday it also was.

Afterward there was a dinner at Hotel Ærø for a hundred invited guests, including Chief Constable Krabbe from Ærøskøbing, whose wife Albert escorted in to dinner. The menu was roasted hare, cake, and a selection of alcoholic beverages. Albert gave the main speech and finished by inviting the guests to stand and give His Majesty three cheers. Then they sang "King Christian Stood by the Tall Mast," and Albert read out the birthday telegram that he'd written to the king, which he asked those present to endorse. Afterward there were numerous toasts to Denmark and the Danish flag, and several of the town dignitaries gave speeches in praise of one another. At eleven-thirty a telegram arrived from His Majesty, thanking them. Dancing followed.

As far as Albert was concerned, the evening went off without a hitch. He was present the whole time and had no sense of foreboding. Nor did he suffer any visions of guests in their finery floating around in the sea among the flotsam of well-laid tables.

After saying good night to the last guests at about two in the morning, he walked around the corner to Prinsegade and returned home to a dreamless sleep.

When he awoke the next morning, he felt at peace with himself at last.

Albert Madsen was sixty-nine years old and he'd achieved what he wanted. Although he hadn't had children, which was a regret, the town he belonged to continued to prosper. The shipyards were busy as never before, and the town's leading shipyard would soon switch to building modern vessels, investing in the construction of steel ships instead of wooden ones. Last spring His Majesty the King had paid a visit to the town, which had been decked in bunting in his honor, and the navy's six torpedo ships had been there too. There were plans for a new post office and a copper spire on the church to replace the turreted section of the roof.

The memorial stone at the harbor commemorating the breakwater showed that the townsfolk remembered their history and acknowledged their debt to their ancestors. STRENGTH IN FELLOWSHIP ran the words carved in Johannes Simonsen's neat lettering. Now Albert Madsen's creed had become the town's too.

He knew that the reason for his sense of well-being that morning wasn't just the successful conclusion of his grand project, with the unveiling of the memorial stone and the party that followed. It was something much bigger: the harmony he felt between himself and the continuously prospering world he was part of. He opened the gable window and there in the soft sunlight of an early September morning, beyond the latticework of mast tops, it all lay: the breakwater and the archipelago. The cries of seagulls drifted up, mingling with the clang of hammers and the rasp of saws from the town's shipyards. He knew that these same sounds were heard in every port on every continent, and with a kind of triumph he felt himself to be a part of a much wider world.

Later he would think of this day as "the end," though he never articulated exactly what had been concluded. Not his life, certainly, for he went on to live for several more years. But they were years spent half in reality and half in a world of dreams, and the two were linked by a bridge of terror, for in his dreams he acquired knowledge he couldn't bear alone and yet could share with no one. He ended up living in a town peopled by the dead, and he became death's silent witness.

VISIONS

WHAT DOES A ship broker write about in his log? He'll write about the ups and downs of the freight market, about cargo deals he's made, about ships that never returned home, about crews that were rescued, about insurance questions, about profit margins and the fate of his company. But these days, Albert Madsen didn't write about either business matters or his vessels at sea. Nor did he write about his feelings, and he only rarely made a note of his thoughts. It's true that he recorded certain things that were going on inside his head. But mostly these were things he didn't understand.

A stranger lived inside his head, and he wrote about that stranger.

Albert wrote about his dreams.

But not all of them.

Like most people of a practical nature, he'd once regarded dreams as things made possible only by the hibernation of the rational mind, a confused summary of accidental and half-forgotten events that might once have had a clear meaning but were now lost in a foggy half-world. Like the rest of us, Albert could make little sense of most of his dreams, and didn't try to.

Then one December night in 1877, when he was captain of the brig *Princess,* he'd dreamt of a voice calling out to him, warning that he was heading for danger. He'd leapt out of his berth and run up to the deck, and seen that the ship was indeed about to run aground on a large flat sandbank, where it would inevitably founder. The dream had warned him. It seemed that his head contained knowledge he'd been unaware of. A mysterious guest had moved in.

Two years later he had a similar experience, when he dreamt that the *Princess* went down in a hard gale. But on this occasion, even though he suspected that this dream too was a warning, he decided to ignore it and left Grangemouth early the next morning, just as a southwesterly storm was gathering outside the harbor. After sailing the ship along the coast the whole morning, he finally had to drop anchor and chop down the masts to avoid being beached. As he clung to the tilting deck and watched the rigging fly overboard, it dawned on him that more than one kind of reality was possible.

Albert's gift was not one that everyone possessed. He knew he must keep it to himself. We've read about that in the notes he left us, along with his other papers. He wrote that if the premonitions in his dreams were to become public knowledge, they would almost certainly harm him, or at least tarnish his reputation.

How often have we sat in a fo'c'sle, listening to tales of the *klabautermann*, the grim reaper who hangs in the mizzen shroud, with his white face and his dripping oilskins? Or of the *Flying Dutchman*, or the ship's dog that howls in the night, searching for its lost ship? Albert too, when he was a ship's boy, had listened and been terrified and strangely fascinated, yet deep down he'd remained a skeptic. An explanation existed for every unusual event: science simply hadn't discovered it yet. That was always his conclusion, as we sat there in the dusk, exchanging tales that illustrated how there was more between heaven and earth than we could dream of.

If he'd revealed his ability to see the future in his dreams, most of us wouldn't have hesitated to accept that he had supernatural powers. His reputation on board ship would have been strengthened, and possibly his authority too. But the awe would have been mixed with fear, and he didn't want that. Albert believed a captain's authority should be based on trust in his skills, not on mumbo jumbo.

In the period that followed the unveiling of the memorial stone, a gray emptiness opened up in front of Albert. He had dreams in which people he knew died, and the next day he'd be startled to see them walking around in the street, as large as life. His dreams were full of riddles: he didn't know the times of the deaths he visualized, but the visions were always dramatic and terrifying. He saw people shot down on the deck, he saw ships burst into flames, he saw black shadows in the sea, and he understood nothing of what he saw.

But he never doubted that these dreams were telling the truth. He knew that all the people he'd just greeted, whose hands he'd shaken, to whom he had spoken recently but now increasingly tried to avoid, would die in horrifying and inexplicable circumstances. And they didn't have a clue.

He was walking around in a town of doomed men.

ALBERT'S FIRST DREAM about future disasters occurred the night between the 27th and the 28th of September, in 1913.

He saw a ship he knew, the *Peace,* a three-masted schooner from Marstal—and then he heard a shot. The crew appeared on the deck immediately, bracing the yards and lowering the topgallant sails, then preparing to launch the lifeboat. For reasons he didn't understand, they seemed to have attached huge importance to that one shot. But there was no visible damage to the ship.

Then more shots rang out and one of the men suddenly clasped his shoulder. His arm was dangling. The head of another was blown backward as though an invisible hand had pulled his hair, sending a jet of blood gushing from his forehead as he collapsed on deck. The shooting was constant now. Several projectiles hit the descending lifeboat, and when it reached the sea's surface, it started to leak. The men were soon up to their waists in water as they worked to seal the leaks. Intense firing continued. Then one by one the masts went overboard, and the ship itself disappeared into the deep.

The weather was stormy and the sea was heavy. Clouds raced across the sky. The lifeboat lay low in the water. The men worked the oars hard. At first there was terror in their faces, then exhaustion. The light was dimming. It grew dark, and a long time passed before the light returned. Albert realized that it had been night and now it was morning. It was still stormy and the waves ran high underneath the torn, racing clouds. Two of the men lay stretched out in the boat. The others lifted them up and eased them overboard. He caught a glimpse of a pale face, sunken in death. It was Commander Carstensen. He'd clinked glasses with him at the party to celebrate the memorial stone just two nights ago.

The following night he saw the schooner *H. B. Linnemann* send out a distress signal. As in the previous dream, he saw the crew scrambling around on the deck, trying to launch the lifeboat. Again he heard shots and was unable to tell where they were coming from. He instantly recognized the ship's captain, L. C. Hansen, standing on the half-deck, right under a flapping Danish flag. Captain Hansen sank down as he pressed his hand to his thighs, where a large, dark patch was spreading. A moment later he was hit in the head and wiped from the ranks of the living. Afterward three of the crew were shot in quick succession.

Finally it dawned on Albert what it all meant: the brutality, the mercilessness, the inexplicable killings of peaceful seamen, and the sinking of ships.

He was foreseeing a war.

He thought about Commander Cartensen: he was about to get the war he wanted. And what would Albert get? He sensed darkly that in these dreams he was witnessing more than just the deaths of people he knew. He was witnessing the end of an entire world.

He couldn't explain this feeling in any more detail, only that it gripped him like a deep sorrow and sucked the light out of the panoramic view from his gable window. What use would the breakwater be in a few years' time? Yes, the sailor was at war with the sea, but soon there would be another, crueler war that no amount of seamanship could win.

Albert had neither the imagination nor the political insight to envisage who might start this conflict, nor did his dreams tell him. But he thought about the battleships he'd seen on the sea, and the torpedo boats in the harbor, and the submarines, which he'd read about but never seen. To what object on earth can you compare a sailing ship? None. A ship has her own wondrous architecture. But what about the new floating war machines? The submarine seemed to be made in the image of a shark, while the torpedo boats looked like armored amphibians. It was as if the entire modern war industry had taken as its templates the prehistoric monsters that had lived on earth millions of years ago.

He'd heard enough about the Englishman Darwin's theories on the origin of species to know that life evolved; it did not regress. But surely regression was precisely what mankind was aiming for with these war machines: a return to the brutal and simple life forms of bygone eras.

Was this what his dreams were showing him, a future in which humanity returned to its amphibian stage and became its own worst enemy?

The dreams continued. He saw schooners go up in flames. He saw them blown to pieces by sudden explosions at the bow, vanishing into the sea in minutes. He saw men drifting in sinking lifeboats. He saw the terror in the seamen's faces and heard their cries for help as they were sucked down into the deep. Finally, all he could see was the sea itself and its relentless waves. For a long time he felt as though he were floating on that iron-gray water, all alone beneath a clouded sky. He thought that the world must have looked like this soon after its creation, before life began.

He started keeping lists of the ships he saw go down in his dreams. He also wrote down the names of the dead, when he recognized a face. He wrote all this in the left-hand column in his office account ledger, leaving the right-hand column blank, reserved for the day when his dreams started coming true. He reflected that these must be the strangest accounts ever kept and that he must be the oddest book-keeper, because he was treating an imaginary world as if, like the real one, it must answer for its accuracy.

Albert was a strongly built man, with a short beard and a head of hair that age had not thinned. For many years he'd remained unchanged, still exuding the same controlled strength. He didn't cut a youthful figure so much as a timeless one, as though he existed in a place where age didn't exercise its tyranny. But now he started to age visibly. He saw it himself, and he knew that people were talking. He still trimmed his beard and kept his thick hair neatly cut, but his broad shoulders began to droop and all of a sudden he seemed smaller. He kept to himself and made no excuses when he declined invitations. People could think what they liked. He found it especially difficult to be in company with men whose death he'd seen in his visions. How could they live their lives so lightly when such a terrible fate awaited them?

How could Captain Eriksen stop him in Prinsegade, just as he left his office, and converse about nothing but freight markets and the dredger lying just outside the harbor as it scooped out Klørdybet channel? Didn't he realize his days were numbered?

Albert greeted him tersely and disappeared toward Havnegade. Then he regretted his brusqueness. Soon people would start saying he had grown strange. Well, never mind about that. What else could he do? Embrace Eriksen and weep for him? Warn him? Yes, but against what? Against the sea, the war?

"What war?" Eriksen would ask, and then decide—with reason—that Albert was deranged. An unbearable burden had settled on Albert's shoulders. He witnessed calamities and disasters whose origin and nature he could not understand. Would it have been easier if he'd been a man of faith? Would he have found comfort in Jesus? But it wasn't comfort that a man needed. It was the chance to act. And that was why the dreams were like a disease. They attacked the core of his being. They sapped his energy and willpower. For the first time in his life, he perceived himself as helpless, and this sensation corroded his soul, draining him of strength.

As Christmas approached a severe snowstorm arrived from the northeast, and the water in the harbor started to rise. He went down to watch the crews attach extra moorings. Over a hundred ships were docked in Marstal, and a howling concerto rose over the town from the many riggings raked by the northeasterly wind. There was the slapping and slamming of ropes against wood, and the sound of hulls bashing against each other and the wharf as they waited to be re-moored by the crews. The water level continued to rise and the ships rose higher and higher, their menacing twilight shadows looming in the snowfall, like a fleet of *Flying Dutchmen* come to announce the destruction of the town. But then the water stopped. The only damage done was to Dampskibsbroen, where the waves had smashed up the paving.

In his ledger, where he continued to keep accounts of the still-living, Albert noted of the breakwater that "the great achievement of our fathers still stood the test." He wrote it in defiance, as if in rebellion against his dreams. The breakwater had prevented the water from rising any farther.

All the same, he knew that the age of the breakwater was over. Other and stronger enemies were coming, which the breakwater couldn't protect us from.

SOMETIMES YOU'D SEE poor Anders Nørre hurrying through the streets, pursued by a gang of jeering boys. He walked in rigid strides that kept getting longer, as if he was desperate to escape but too afraid to run. He probably feared that an obvious attempt at flight would trigger something alarming in his pursuers. In any case he didn't stand a chance of outrunning a gang of boys.

The chase always ended with Anders forced up against a wall, where he'd cower, rubbing his cheek against the rough bricks and moaning softly. Then an impotent rage would take over, and roaring like an animal, he'd turn and chase after the boys, who'd scatter in all directions, like squirrels, shrieking with laughter.

Mostly the adults would intervene, but not always. There were those who found these incidents amusing.

It was on one such occasion that Albert Madsen actually got to know Anders Nørre. Anders was older than he was, but apart from the white hair and beard, which bought him no respect from the badly behaved children, he was strangely unmarked by age.

The day Albert saw him, they'd chased Nørre all the way from Market Square down Skolegade and Tværgade and had finally cornered him up against the garden wall across from Weber's Café in Prinsegade. Albert raised his stick as though to strike them, and shouted menacingly. They fled.

"Let me walk you home," he said to Anders Nørre.

Nørre had been standing with his hands covering his ears and his eyes tightly shut. Now he opened them and looked at Albert. He lived just outside the town, on Reberbanen, where he had a little hut. He'd sit there all day long, spinning rope on a wheel, and when the rope was finished, he'd make rope yarn. He'd followed this dreary occupation for as long as anyone could remember. The general opinion was that he was an imbecile.

Albert took him by the arm, and Anders succumbed willingly.

"Have you been to church recently, Anders?" Albert asked.

Anders Nørre nodded. "I go there every Sunday."

Anders Nørre's reputation for being slow-witted wasn't based on an inability to speak. On the contrary, he had a soft, pleasant voice and always expressed himself clearly and intelligibly, and there were never problems engaging him in conversation. No: it was more the blankness of his face, which seemed incapable of expressing any emotion, and the sad, tedious existence he led. He'd lived with his mother until her death, and it was said that before that, he'd slept in her bed every night, long into adulthood. When she died, the women who laid out the body decided to leave her in her bed until she could be placed in her coffin the next day—and in the morning they'd found Anders Nørre sleeping right next to her, because when bedtime came he'd done what he always did and climbed in with her. At her funeral he showed no signs of grief. In fact the only emotion he ever showed was an overwhelming stubbornness, if you can call that an emotion. If you contradicted him or stopped him from doing something he'd set his mind on, he'd leap up and start shouting nonsense words and waving his arms—not to hit anyone, that much was obvious—but in a kind of desperation. Then he'd storm out of his tiny hut and disappear across the fields. He might be gone for days before reappearing, worn-out and bedraggled.

But there was sense somewhere inside him, and it wasn't just a little, but in fact quite a lot. The only problem was, it didn't seem to serve any useful purpose. If he was told a man's age and his date of birth, he could instantly calculate the number of days he'd lived, even making allowances for leap years. Someone once asked him how many days had passed since the baby Jesus was placed in his crib, and he'd answered promptly. When he left the church he could recite the minister's sermon word for word, for the benefit of those sailors in town who on Sunday mornings preferred the bench by the harbor to the pew.

On the first day of spring he'd take off his shoes and socks, and he'd walk around in bare feet until winter returned. In the cold season he'd root around in waste heaps and garbage bins for food. No one would have let him starve to death, but he seemed to prefer this way of life, and for that reason we'd passed sentence on him and judged him an imbecile.

Albert had always greeted Anders Nørre, but there was nothing unusual in that. Village idiots were public property. We spoke to them in a good-natured and patronizing way, were on first-name terms with them, and patted them on the back. Not that they had the right to behave that way with us.

On this occasion Albert continued to question him about the Sunday service, and Anders Nørre answered all his questions willingly. His tone of voice didn't for one moment reveal what thoughts or emotions the service might have stirred in him. Even his ability to solve complex mathematical equations had a soullessness about it. Yet there was a soul somewhere inside him, Albert was convinced of it: the embryo of a human being whom no one had ever thought to nurture and develop. Now it was probably too late.

Anders Nørre had dropped Albert's arm, no longer in need of his support. He'd not been injured when the boys attacked him, and if he was upset, his passive features certainly gave no hint of it.

They passed Market Square, walked up through Markgade, and continued up Reberbanen until they reached Anders Nørre's hut, close to the fields. On the last stretch Nørre entertained his companion with a word-for-word repetition of Pastor Abildgaard's Sunday sermon. Suddenly Albert froze: it seemed that the parrot by his side was addressing him directly with an urgent message.

He stared into Nørre's face. The old man didn't seem to notice anything. His voice was unchanged, continuing at the same pitch. The difference was in his words. They were unusual. Was Pastor Abildgaard really their author, or were these words coming from a completely different place, and if so, where? From Nørre's soul, which had finally awakened?

"You were at the height of your powers," the man said. And because Nørre wasn't looking at anyone and his tone remained the same, the words really did seem to be coming from another place, gracing their speaker with the dignity and authority of an oracle.

"You sensed that the world needed your strength and you rejoiced in that. But then it changed. Your strength vanished and the world withdrew from you, and you felt alone. The world was like a big smile that enticed and beckoned you. But then it changed. Dark and hard times arrived and the smile of the world vanished behind menacing clouds. You were in the midst of a life filled with love. But then it changed. The treasure of your love was taken from you."

Albert felt his throat tighten. The words affected him strangely. He felt that someone was talking directly to him, and to him alone. He thought, Where there's a mouth, there'll be an ear too. At long last he could relieve himself of the burden of his loneliness. At long last he could share with someone all the things he'd been keeping to himself. Every word Nørre spoke was the truth. His strength had been taken away from him. And so had his enjoyment of life: a life in which he'd found things to love, and had lacked nothing. He could share his anguish with the author of these words. But who was he? Pastor Abildgaard? He refused to believe that. Nørre? That was even more unlikely. Or a third party? In which case, who might that be?

For a moment he was lost in his own contemplation. Then he became aware of Nørre's voice again. The Sunday sermon was reaching its conclusion. Old familiar themes now emerged, identical from one Sunday to the next: God's mysterious ways, the crucifix on Golgotha, the love of Christ, and this Sunday the word *love* had been repeated over and over: Christ's thoughts of love, His loving help, redemption through His love. The same convenient trivialities that religion always peddled in response to life's hardship. So it was Abildgaard after all.

For a brief moment the minister had succeeded in talking straight into Albert's soul. But it wasn't religion that Albert needed. It wasn't sugary words of comfort. What it might be instead, he could not articulate. Perhaps it was just this: a listening ear. But not the minister's.

What did Abildgaard know of Albert's predicament? Nothing, however much he might preach. How could he be aware of his banishment from the world of the living, his shipwreck on a dark and unknown shore of bones, peopled by the dead?

Albert shivered like a wet dog. He felt cold. Something inside him was trembling. He entered the hut along with its lone inhabitant. Nothing in Nørre's face revealed whether he welcomed his guest or would prefer to be left alone. As there was no other furniture, Albert sat down on the bed next to him. There was no heating in the hut, and though the winter chill kept the most unpleasant smells at bay, it was still hardly an inviting place.

"Do you ever dream, Anders?"

Albert looked at Nørre and tried to catch his eye. But as usual, he got nothing back. Albert leaned forward and looked at the floor. He began as if he was talking to himself or to the invisible ear he had searched for so long.

"The thing is," he said, "I've been having these strange dreams."

His sense of relief was palpable. It was the first time he'd mentioned the dreams to anyone, and he could feel the pressure diminishing already.

"I keep dreaming about death. I see ships go down and men being shot or drowned. People from this town, people I know."

There was no reaction. What had he been expecting? This was no confession, unless you regarded unburdening yourself to empty space or a blank wall a confession. How could he have hoped for a reaction from this half-wit? He already knew the answer: because he felt that he too was entering the dark land of fools, an unknown territory where the mad moved with familiar ease, but where he was a new arrival. In a way, he was asking for help.

Albert was overcome by the other man's silence and had no idea how to go on. Yet he sensed that something had happened. Anders Nørre's hands were still lying quietly in his lap and his stare was blank as ever, but now something loomed behind it, something other than endless mechanical calculations.

"Do you have dreams like that?"

Albert made his voice as gentle as he could, as if trying to reach the hidden soul of Anders Nørre. But he knew that he was fumbling to find his own.

For a moment Anders Nørre sat frozen. Then he leapt up with a roar, a thick, inarticulate bellowing. He ran to the door and flung it open. He turned and gave Albert one wild look, then disappeared into the twilight.

Albert stayed on the bed. Going after Nørre was pointless, he knew. Anders would be off on one of his long trips across the fields, and he wouldn't reappear for a couple of days. As for Albert, he couldn't even rise from the bed. Nørre's reaction had paralyzed him. He really was in a bad way, he thought, if the village idiot ran away from him in horror. Even in the dark country where Anders Nørre moved with familiarity, he was seen as a monster.

Does he dream the way I do, Albert wondered, or is he like the animals that sense an earthquake long before humans do and howl in fear the night before the earth splits open?

WHEN THE WAR started, Albert was relieved.

That's how it is, he told himself. If you dread something enough, even your worst fears coming true brings comfort.

He didn't know how he'd react once the town's sailors began dying. But for the moment he felt less lonely. Now he could discuss the war with others.

Denmark had declared herself neutral, but nonetheless, the war had serious consequences for our town. All freight traffic was canceled immediately, and Marstal's fleet went into winter harbor as early as August. It was strange to see the schooners filling the harbor with their forest of masts while the sun was still high in the sky and the children still splashed around in the water, playing among the laid-up ships. In recent years, prosperity had risen to ever greater heights, so the seamen had plenty of money. You could see evidence of that in the bars. The restlessness caused by sudden unemployment and the uncertain future led to a rise in drunkenness.

Toward October, offers came in for grain freights to north German ports, but no one dared sail. Marine insurance didn't cover losses caused by war, and the Germans had peppered the Baltic Sea with floating mines. The smaller investors couldn't afford to risk their money.

"At least that's one good thing about this town," Albert wrote. "There are no ruthless shipping magnates who will risk the lives of their crew for a quick profit."

His own ships were far from Europe when the war broke out, and he kept them there for its duration.

Everyone feared the mines because everyone had shares in the ships. The North Sea too was filled with them.

Albert immediately began keeping accounts of ships blown up by mines. For a while the people of Marstal were safe, thanks to their caution, but just three weeks after Germany had declared war on France, two Danish steamers, the *Maryland* and the *Christian Boberg*, were sunk in the North Sea. Only two days later a trawler from Reykjavik was blown up. On September 3, yet another Danish steamer disappeared.

Albert continued his list until the end of the year. Sometimes a ship's name matched a name from his dreams, and each time that happened, it had the same terrible impact on him. He'd been there and he'd seen it happen. If the left-hand column on the list of his nightly visions was longer than the right-hand one, it was only because the war was still new. There were those who speculated about a quick breakthrough on all fronts and an imminent end to the conflict—talk he dismissed with a shake of his head. For obvious reasons, he couldn't tell us the cause of his certainty.

"There's still much death to come," he said.

This unexpected pessimism from a man who had put such faith in the future was seen as the weakness of old age. Albert Madsen had lost his nerve.

In the end, he kept his opinions to himself.

A few months after the war broke out we held a collection in aid of the suffering population of Belgium. It was a sign of how remote the war still was that we had compassion to spare for the woes of others. Albert was persuaded to join a committee responsible for preparing a special public exhibition of items related to the town and its seafaring history; the entrance fees would go wholly to the Belgians.

The exhibition was a success, attracting a great many visitors. On display were old costumes from Ærø, intricate lace and embroidery work, brass candle-scissors, and some beautifully carved cupboards and bureaus. We admired these things, but they didn't stir any nostalgia in us; on the contrary, they proved that the present was better than the past, and the future better still. Our continuing progress was especially evident in the section that documented the development of the shipping trade.

"Look," we said to one another, pointing to the model of a Marstal cutter. "Only twenty-four registered tons. And next to it, a three-masted schooner built at Sofus Boye's shipyard, with a carrying capacity of five hundred tons. And it's already twenty-five years old."

Albert was mainly interested in the collection of curiosities that the town's seamen had brought back from all parts of the world. The conches, the stuffed hummingbird, and the set of teeth from a sawfish took him back to the days of his youth. But when he came to the telegrapher Olfert Blach's Chinese hoard of rugs, embroideries, and a complete and very precious Mandarin costume, he stopped to reflect.

"Yes," he said to Pastor Abildgaard. "A sailor knows from experience that there's no such thing as tradition. Or rather, that there are many kinds of tradition, not just his own. This is how we do it here, says the farmer on his ancestral land. Well, that's not how they do it there, says the sailor. He's the one who's seen more. The farmer provides his own yardstick. But the sailor knows that won't do for him. Right now the whole world is at war; it's not even two weeks since Russia, England, and France declared war on Turkey because Turkey became an ally of Germany. Many millions of people are fighting one another, but does the world get any bigger because of it, or any smaller? The ships lie still. The sailors can't go to sea and come back with tales of new things. All we can do now is sit here on our little island and grow as stupid as the farmers."

"You shouldn't say that. You're being unfair to them."

The minister wasn't from the island. He had an outsider's curiosity about anything local that he considered to be an amusing oddity, and he'd been responsible for that part of the exhibition. Albert knew that the pastor was even writing an account of the town's local history because every now and then Abildgaard would ask for advice. A friendly, if not warm, relationship had developed between them. But Albert had often thought that the minister would have been better suited to a rural parish than a shipping town like Marstal. Given his shackled life, the farmer, after all, fit the basic Christian vision better than the sailor did. All those messages about bowing your head and throwing yourself on the mercy of fate were made for him. Of course a sailor was also subject to the whims of nature, but he challenged the weather and the sea; he was something of a rebel.

Still, there was no conflict between the minister and the rest of us. The inner circle of his congregation was made up of old women who devoutly slept through his sermons, and there was no hint of rebellion in its outer ranks either. We felt it was right and proper to have a minister, and as Abildgaard never questioned our way of life, our relationship was characterized by mutual tolerance.

"You really shouldn't call the farmers stupid," the minister persisted. "The farmers support the notion of public education, which I know you also favor. Just look at the adult high schools. But sailors—well, is anyone more superstitious? And the new radical newspaper in the town—why isn't that prospering if the sailing profession is, as you say, so very enlightened and informed about international affairs? And at election time, haven't you noticed that people here inevitably vote conservative? How do you explain that?"

Pastor Abildgaard's tone had become teasing.

"It's the concept of ownership," Albert said. "If the cabin boy has a hundredth share in the ship, that's enough to make him feel like a captain. He believes that their interests are the same."

"And what's wrong with that?" the minister went on. "Look at your own dictum. You've gone to the trouble of having it chiseled into fourteen tons of granite and unveiled to the sound of patriotic songs. Its message is precisely that there's strength in fellowship."

"I meant that in a socialist sense." Albert had grown irritated with the minister and wanted to rile him. "Where would this town be if its inhabitants didn't know how to unite? We have the second-largest fleet in the country, though the town itself, in terms of population size, is in hundredth place at best. We have mutual marine insurance, financed by the town's sailors. And we have the breakwater. No outsider built it for us. We did it ourselves. I'd call that socialism."

"Which is something to mention in my next sermon. I'll inform the staunchly conservative citizens of Marstal that they are, in fact, socialists. I normally find laughter in church inappropriate; however, I'll make an exception next Sunday."

Albert was aware that he wasn't acquitting himself well, but he refused to give up. For a moment it seemed as if his old fighting spirit had been rekindled.

"Take a sailor," he said. "He signs on to a new ship. He's surrounded by nothing but strangers. Not only do they come from other towns and parts of his own country, but often from completely different nations. He has to learn to work with them. His vocabulary's broadened, he learns new words and grammar, and he comes across new ways of thinking. He turns into a different man, unlike the one who spends his life plowing the same old furrow. These are the men the world needs, not nationalists and warmongers. I fear that this war will cut to the heart of a sailor's life."

The minister laughed again, ready with a new riposte.

"Yes, and then this cosmopolitan returns to Marstal, speaking in a broader Marstal dialect than ever, and claims that the farmer, simply because he lives a few field boundaries away, speaks a foreign language that no one understands. And therefore must be stupid. Yes, you've created a proper world citizen, Captain Madsen. I still prefer the nationalist. His sense of solidarity is more inclusive. It embraces high and low, farmer and sailor, as long as they share a language and a history. And I see no sign of this fellowship being destroyed in these unhappy war years. On the contrary, I think it's growing stronger."

Such a long time passed before Albert spoke again that Pastor Abildgaard, with a little feeling of triumph that he did his best to conceal, assumed that the conversation was over and prepared to continue his inspection of the exhibits. But Albert, who'd been standing with his hands behind his back, contemplating his toe caps, finally cleared his throat and looked Abildgaard firmly in the eye.

"In the years before the war, you'd often take a walk to Dampskibs-broen to see the ferry leave, wouldn't you?"

"Yes," Abildgaard said. "Dare I say it, it's the only entertainment the town has to offer. Well, apart from the ferry's arrival, obviously. Which surpasses the excitement of its departure. So, yes, of course I did."

"Did you notice anything in particular?"

The minister shook his head. "Not as far as I can remember."

"The unusually large number of farmers, weighed down by baggage?"

"Ah, I see where you're going with this."

Abildgaard smiled disarmingly, as though he knew he was about to be robbed of his earlier minor victory and was willing to be a good sport about it.

"Yes, I'm sure you do. But there's no harm in my pointing it out anyway. Those farmers were immigrating to America. There they were, the country's spiritual and cultural backbone, with ancient family farms whose soil their ancestors have cultivated for hundreds of years, saying a faithless farewell. Whereas the sailors, the rootless, restless, stateless freebooters—"

"I never said that." Abildgaard interrupted him.

"—brawlers and vandals, ruffians and half criminals, drunkards and debauchers with a girl in every port, whose Danish is so mixed up with words from every continent that not even their own mothers can understand them when they come home, with their arms and chests as tattooed as a deck of cards—hearts, diamonds, spades, clubs—"

"I must protest," the minister said. "My respect for the breadwinners of this town is too great to speak of the seafaring profession in such terms."

"In that case you have good reason. Because you've never seen Marstal sailors lining up on Dampskibsbroen, with chests of valuables on their backs, to immigrate to America. We might be gone for years. But we always come home again. Because us sailors, we stay."

WHEN SPRING CAME the harbor emptied because a new insurance policy had been established to ensure that shipowners wouldn't suffer financially if a vessel was lost through war. After that the freight market went only one way, and that was up. We sailed like never before, not just to Norway and western Sweden and Iceland, but to Newfoundland, the West Indies, and Venezuela, even right across the war zones to England and the French ports in the Channel. Everything was back to normal, only better, although we moaned about the English, who introduced endless complicated sailing restrictions and charged exorbitant prices for piloting and towing. In this respect the Germans were far more reasonable. There was free piloting and towing assistance in German ports along the Baltic coast. So far, Marstal had yet to lose a single ship.

Then the submarine war began.

Our first loss was the schooner *Salvador*, which went down in flames on June 2, 1915, in the middle of a warm day. Albert made a note in the right-hand column in his account ledger. Now it would start to fill up.

No one had died. The crew returned home and behaved as if they'd achieved something important. Ha, they chuckled in the bars and streets, where curious onlookers crowded around them. It had been a picnic. All right, so they'd lost their ship, but the U-boat responsible had towed their lifeboat for a while. Their first mate, Hans Peter Kroman, had been presented with a pipe and some tobacco—Hamburg brand tobacco, very good quality, incidentally—and Captain Jens Olesen Sand had received two bottles of cognac for the voyage home. The German U-boat crew? Very nice people; a bit on the pale side, perhaps, from being down deep for so long, but otherwise very respectable sailors.

"What a shame," Sand had remarked to the U-boat captain, as they stood on the sub's deck, watching the *Salvador* burn up.

"That's war for you," replied the German, shrugging apologetically.

True, he was no Englishman, but a gentleman all the same. When the submarine crew finally unhitched the tow rope, they asked politely whether the crew from the *Salvador* were sure they had sufficient provisions on the lifeboat. The cook who had lost his cap was given a sou'wester in its stead. Then, after exchanging mutual assurances that this misfortune really was nothing personal, the Danes and the Germans parted. The next day the lifeboat was picked up by an English trawler, whose crew also turned out to be nice people.

Some months later a letter arrived from the German government, stating that the sinking of the *Salvador* had been unwarranted. Captain Sand received an apology from Kaiser Wilhelm himself, along with twenty-seven thousand Danish kroner, the amount for which the ship had been insured.

A few months later, another schooner went up in smoke, and Albert wrote the name *Cocos* under *Salvador* in his right-hand column.

Again the crew returned home, speaking of the war as nothing but high jinks. The U-boat had sailed them to another Marstal schooner that happened to be in the vicinity, the *Karin Bak*, which was allowed to pass through unharmed after its captain, Albertsen, agreed to take the shipwrecked men on board. Then the U-boat sailed away, only to return with the crew's clothes, which in their hurry they'd left behind.

"Well, I must say! The level of service isn't bad when you're dealing with German U-boats!"

"Why didn't you ask them to wash your underpants while they were at it?" Ole Mathiesen joked, and laughter erupted once more.

Telegrams stuttered with news of terrible losses on all fronts. But in Marstal we all agreed that the war was a hoot.

Albert Madsen continued to keep his accounts, and as the war progressed they became his obsession. He believed they contained a message, as yet undeciphered. Convinced that figures had the power to prove things, he made lists of the prices of life's necessities in Marstal: rye bread, butter, margarine, eggs, beef, and pork. He knew the crews' wages, their war supplement, their bonus for European or overseas voyages, and their accident insurance in case of death or disability. He kept an eye on the freight market and the price of ships, on exchange rates and quotations.

A shipowner needs to do all of these things to carry out his job properly. But does he also need to keep long lists of ships sunk by mines, of ships destroyed by torpedoes and fires, of the number of fallen men from North Schleswig, and English losses as of January 9, 1916? Of 24,122 officers dead and 525,345 killed among the junior ranks? The numbers Albert jotted down are incomprehensible. And that's precisely why they make no impression. So why, then, did he write them down? Why did he constantly mention them in his conversations with us?

Why did a ship broker and owner in a small coastal town, in a country that wasn't taking part in the world war and was thus, in a sense, not taking part in the world, keep a two-column list of lost ships, a left-hand column of ships he saw sinking in his dreams, and a right-hand column showing the same ships sunk on real seas? What was he trying to prove?

In the first year of the war, the town lost six ships, and in the second year only one. No Marstaller had been killed, though millions were dying elsewhere, beyond our field of vision. Within that field there were no dead; on the contrary, what we saw, and found so easy to understand, was that the freight market shot up so high that newly built ships earned back their startup capital in a year, and sailors' wages trebled. The price of ships started to rise as early as 1915. Even older wooden vessels, battered from their many years at sea, could be sold for almost double their prewar value. By the end of the year prices had tripled; they continued to rise throughout the whole of the following year. The *Agent Petersen,* the most famous ship in Marstal, which in 1887 had completed the fastest voyage ever recorded between South America and Africa, was valued at twenty-five thousand Danish kroner but sold for ninety thousand.

Marstal had started to lose its fleet, but not to the U-boats.

Albert realized that between his right- and left-hand columns a third column was called for, one that his dreams had never warned him about: the list of ships that had been sold. It filled faster than the other two columns, and soon outstripped them. But there was no drama in this particular list. It contained neither dreams nor dead, but instead marked the strangely frantic wealth that flooded our town. Houses were repaired and painted, women who once dressed modestly now wore their Sunday best every day, and the shops stocked new and more expensive goods. The people of Marstal, once renowned for their thrift, were living as if there were no tomorrow.

This wasn't some frenzy brought on by the mortal fear of war. It was the dizziness that comes from having too much money.

THEN, FINALLY, the war came to Marstal with a face that wasn't cheerful. *Finally:* that was the word Albert used in his notes. The wall between him and the rest of us was about to topple, and we'd all soon know what he knew. It was no longer just in his lonely dreams that people would perish. In real life they'd be shot down, drown, freeze to death, and die from exposure and thirst. Survivors came home and brought his visions to life with their stories. Others vanished without a trace.

A message came from the royal envoy in Berlin: the *Astræa* had been lost. There was no information about where or how. Seven men were missing, including two from Marstal, the skipper, Abraham Christian Svane, and the first mate, Valdemar Holm. A man from the Faroe Islands and an able seaman from Cape Verde were among the others.

Albert had seen them die. He'd seen them jump for their lives through flying shards from a lifeboat under fire. It had been a calm, overcast day. The sea lay like gray silk. He'd seen the water close over them as their lungs gave out and the last air bubble burst.

Germany had declared unrestricted submarine war. Marstal, which had lost only seven ships in the previous two years, now lost sixteen in a single year, then four in a month. The returning survivors didn't get drunk and brag of their experiences; instead, they avoided attention. The crew of the *Peace,* who'd seen their captain and their bosun shot down in front of them and afterward drifted for days in a sinking lifeboat while two more men perished, stayed at home with their families. If an acquaintance approached them in the street, they'd quickly veer down the nearest alley.

The *Hydra* disappeared without a trace, with six men on board. Not all of them were from Marstal, but the losses could be felt across the town.

Gaps began appearing in our ranks.

PASTOR ABILDGAARD went to Jørgensen's grocery shop in Tværgade. The owner, whose full name was Kresten Minor Jørgensen, was a former first mate who'd come ashore and now sold groceries and ship's provisions. He manned the large wooden counter himself, a small stooping man with a bald head that shone as if polished; on a summer's day when he strolled around in his short khaki jacket, it would reflect the sun, forcing passersby to squint.

The small bell that hung above the door rang out, a noisy, irritating sound, as Abildgaard entered the shop. A couple of old skippers were chatting on a long wooden bench to the right of the door, but Abildgaard never learned what they were talking about, because the moment he closed the door behind him, a deathly silence descended.

Deathly was indeed the word, for death itself might have entered the shop with him. Jørgensen took a step back behind his wooden counter, his jaw dropping and his eyes widening. Abildgaard turned around, thinking that the grocer must have seen something shocking in the street through the open door. Meanwhile the two skippers eyed the minister and the grocer alternately, as if waiting for an incident of immense significance to unfold.

"Good morning," Abildgaard stuttered, hesitating to utter such a pleasantry in this laden atmosphere.

Jørgensen didn't answer.

When the pastor approached the counter, ready to order his goods, Jørgensen took another step back and splayed his raised hands. His mouth was still open, and he looked as if he'd stopped breathing. They stared at each other, the grocer seemingly on the verge of fainting, the sensitive Abildgaard paralyzed.

Then one of the skippers on the bench shot a long blob of spittle into the polished brass pot in the corner, and the sound snapped Jørgensen out of his trance.

"Just tell me, please, please just tell me!" he begged.

"A pound of coffee. But I want it freshly ground," Abildgaard said, mechanically repeating his wife's instructions.

Jørgensen buried his face in his hands, and a strange snorting sound, halfway between laughter and tears, escaped him.

"Coffee, coffee, he only wants some coffee!" he choked from behind the lattice of his fingers.

Laughing uncontrollably, he went over to the coffee mill and began filling it with beans. His laughter made his hands shake, and he spilled beans all over the counter and the floor.

Then he pulled himself together.

"I won't be charging you for your coffee today, Pastor."

But Abildgaard was by now outraged. "Would someone kindly explain to me what is going on here?" he demanded, in the thunderous tone he employed in the pulpit.

"Jørgensen is just feeling lucky," one of the skippers behind him piped up.

Abildgaard glared at Jørgensen with all the authority he could muster. "If this is some kind of joke, I can assure you that I don't find it in the least bit amusing."

Jørgensen looked down, abashed, but at the same time a blissful smile spread across his face. He rubbed his bald head as though giving it an extra polish in honor of the minister.

"I do beg your pardon, Pastor. You see, I thought you were here because of Jørgen."

"Jørgen?"

"Jørgen, my son. He's an able seaman on board the *Seagull*. Well, I don't mind telling you, I was worried that you'd come to tell me the ship had been torpedoed and that Jørgen . . . Jørgen . . ." He gulped as if even now the fear still gripped him. "Well, I thought that Jørgen had"—the grocer cleared his throat—"had been lost."

After that incident, Abildgaard grew afraid to show himself in the streets; it dawned on him that every time he left the parsonage in Kirkestræde, people thought he was coming to announce a death. He had a naturally sunny disposition, and he couldn't bear it. He'd become a harbinger of death, a black raven with a starched collar, imprisoned in the low-ceilinged rooms of grief. He struggled to breathe normally, and when he talked to the bereaved about God's mercy and help and comfort through the love of Jesus Christ, he felt he'd choke.

The words came out of him in a strangely helpless, hesitant way, as though they no longer contained real answers to the questions of the bereaved.

He'd often brought the consolation of faith to a family who'd lost a father or a son. What made it unbearable now was the sheer number of dead. Like a huge flock of migrant starlings, they hovered above the town, and one by one the announcements—the death of a father, a brother, or a son—fell onto the roofs of Marstal in a downpour of wrecked hope.

Pastor Abildgaard became a recluse. He stayed indoors as much as he could, emerging only on Sundays, when he was forced to walk the hundred meters to the church, and to officiate at funerals. Fortunately, there were no more of those than usual. After all, the war dead did not return home.

Anna Egidia Rasmussen, widow of Carl Rasmussen, the marine painter who had decorated the altarpiece in the church, began visiting the stricken families when news of a death had to be broken. She was well acquainted with grieving homes. She'd lost her own husband under mysterious circumstances on a voyage from Greenland, and since then she'd had to part with seven of her eight children, all of whom had died as adults. Only one daughter, Augusta Kathinka, was still alive, but she was in America.

Anna Egidia Rasmussen lived in Teglgade, in a large house with tall windows, which her husband had designed and where he'd made his studio in the attic. For many years she'd been a source of help and comfort to neighborhood families who'd been hit by losses at sea, and who suddenly had to say goodbye to a father, a brother, or a son. She had a strange skill. She could lead crying the way some people can lead singing. She'd made it her art. Contrary to what most people think, weeping isn't an uncontrollable emotion that spills into tears. It's the opposite, a channel for feelings, a way to divert them in a healthy direction. Serenity was Anna Egidia's life mission. She'd needed it to deal with her husband, a man of a nervous disposition and a sensitive mind, introverted and prone to brooding. Carl Rasmussen would stand on the beach for hours, staring out to sea, indifferent to the weather and his own health. Finally she'd have to drag him back to their house, chilled to the bone, while between coughing fits he begged her to leave him in peace. Afterward he'd lie feverish in bed, his teeth chattering. At times like that her calm was essential, though it made him accuse her of lacking the imagination to understand his character and failing to share his enthusiasm and vision.

This widow became a second visitor to many houses. Death would be the first, and she would follow in its wake. She was a source of comfort not only to her own family, with its many grandchildren, but to a wide circle around Teglgade. When someone died, the family sent for Anna. She'd arrive in her worn black silk dress, sit down in the middle of the room, send the adults away, and take the children by the hand. When a mother fell ill and was admitted to the hospital while her husband was away at sea, Anna would care for the children in her own home. She was constantly invited to be a godmother to the newborn, as if she'd been charged with keeping watch at life's entrance as well as its exit.

Now the parsonage too has foundered on the coast of bones, Albert thought, when he heard about Pastor Abildgaard's reclusiveness. He could preach about death in a way that moved even me. But he'd never met it. Now that he has, he's fallen silent.

Albert went to the parsonage to volunteer to assist the widow Rasmussen in her work. He felt his dreams obliged him to. He was shown into the minister's study, where Abildgaard was sitting by the window, staring out into the garden. There was a purple beech outside, dark and somber, like a tree that knew neither spring nor summer but grew in an eternal autumn, its leaves burned black around the edges by the frost. Nearby, the rose beds, which were Mrs. Abildgaard's pride and joy, were in bloom.

Abildgaard got up and shook his hand, then returned to his position by the window. When Albert announced the purpose of his visit, the minister didn't speak for a long time. Then all of a sudden he buried his face in his hands.

"My nerves!" he exclaimed.

His narrow shoulders trembled. He took off his steel spectacles and placed them on the desk in front of him. He dug his fists into the hollows of his eyes like a child surrendering to its crying, and the tears rolled down his smooth-shaven cheeks.

"Please, please forgive me," he stammered. "I didn't mean to ..."

Albert rose and went over to him. He placed his hand on the minister's shoulder.

"You've got nothing to apologize for."

The minister clasped Albert's hand with both of his and pressed it against his forehead as though he was seeking to ease a pain inside.

Neither of them spoke for a long time. Abildgaard cried himself dry, then put his steel spectacles back on his nose. As Albert rose to take his leave, he noticed a black object on the minister's desk that reminded him of a claw, but not a bird's. No, it looked more like the curled fingers of a severed human hand, with nails as yellow as old bone.

"What's this?" he asked.

"That's the awful thing. I've no idea what to do with it."

Abildgaard sounded as if he might break out in a fresh attack of tears. Albert took the object and peered at it closely.

"No, you mustn't touch it. It's vile."

It was indeed a human hand. Albert was instantly put in mind of the shrunken head. But here the preservation technique was different: the hand seemed to have been smoked and dried in the heat of a fire.

"Where does it come from?" he asked.

"You know Josef Isager? They call him the Congo Pilot, I believe." Albert nodded. Josef Isager had been a pilot on the Congo River many years ago. He'd worked for the Belgian king, Leopold, and had returned home with a medal for faithful service. He was reluctant to speak about his years in Africa, but the neighbors said that they'd sometimes be wakened in the night by screaming. It was Josef Isager. Once he'd kicked the headboard of his bed to pieces: a loud crack had sounded as the large mahogany frame fell apart. He'd leapt up and thrown the furniture around as if it were an enemy and he was fighting for his life. His bed linen, which fell in a messy heap on the floor, was soaked in sweat. It was malaria, so he told us.

Albert, who'd heard the stories about these nocturnal upheavals, had his own theory. These weren't malaria attacks, but nightmares. Josef Isager was dreaming about Africa.

"And then he comes to me with a severed hand. A hand—a human hand! 'What do you want me to do with it?' I ask him, once I've recovered from my shock. 'Give it a Christian burial,' he replies. 'Who is it?' I ask. 'I don't know,' he says to me. 'Some nigger woman. Damn you, Pastor!' he says. And he gives me a furious look. Perhaps I shouldn't burden you with such things, Captain Madsen, but the man scared me."

Albert nodded. The Congo Pilot had the same effect on him. Josef Isager was a tough customer. But there were many of those. Life had kicked them around and they'd kicked back. The son of the old schoolteacher, he and Albert had been at school together, and Josef had been trapped in the war between the boys and their brutal tor-mentor, unable to take sides because he'd be a traitor no matter whom he supported. He'd taken out his frustration with his fists, beating up his brother, the ever-whining Johan. Then he'd gone to sea and no one knew what he'd seen there: new abuses, with fresh victims, no doubt, where he himself had an outlet, for that was how things were. But perhaps he'd also found a way out. That, at least, was what Albert reckoned. The sea was a vast space where a boy could leave the ill-treatment of his childhood behind and rediscover himself.

After Josef shipped out, we saw nothing of him for several years. We heard he'd gone to the Congo via Antwerp, and sailed on its great rivers. He returned to Denmark, but not to Marstal. Then he left again. Africa had got into his blood. We didn't know why. After many years the fever left him, and he came ashore and worked as a loss assessor, first in Copenhagen and then in Marstal. His wife, Maren Kirstine, whom he'd married in his youth, was a Marstaller, and they'd settled down in Kongegade.

At first he didn't even mention his years in Africa. When we ques-tioned him, he'd shake his head dismissively as though he couldn't find the strength to describe it and because we wouldn't understand anyway. One day he'd asked Albert if he could see the shrunken head. For a while he sat holding James Cook in his hands, turning the head while he assessed it. He looked at it with expert eyes.

"Well, that's not how we used to make them," he finally said.

"We?" Albert frowned.

"Yes," Josef replied casually. "We preferred to smoke them."

He laughed—Albert couldn't determine whether from disgust or cynicism.

"They have put an effort into this one." Josef went on. "We only made sure they dried out. They looked like they were sleeping. Closed eyes, their lips rolled back a bit so you could see a thin white line of teeth." He looked at Albert. His eyes grew distant, as though he was dwelling on the memory.

"Who are you talking about?" Albert asked.

The Congo Pilot snapped out of his trance.

"The niggers, who else?" He sounded disappointed. "We had to show them who was boss, you see. There was this Belgian captain. He used Negro heads as decorations around his flower bed. To each his own."

He laughed again, and this time Albert thought he detected a hint of embarrassment. He sensed that it wasn't the mention of the severed heads that had triggered this embarrassment, but his own ignorance. It was as if Josef had taken him to be a fellow conspirator and was only just realizing that he'd been mistaken. Albert stared at his old schoolmate and didn't know what to say.

"I know that look you're giving me." Josef's voice was suddenly harsh. "But it's the only language they understand. It was for their own good. Otherwise we'd have had to shoot the whole lot of them. They didn't want to work. They'd lie stretched out on a mat, soaking up the sun like crocodiles in the sand. They could do that, all right. Proud and vain, they were. But otherwise they were just like animals."

"I thought you worked as a pilot?"

"Yes, I was a pilot, port captain in Boma, *commissaire maritime*. I took the *Lualaba* all the way up to Matadi, along a narrow and tricky branch of the river. Before I arrived, the ocean steamers could get only as far as Boma. Later they went all the way to Matadi too. But I was the first."

There was pride in his voice. He raised his head and looked Albert straight in the eye. For a moment it seemed as if Josef was observing him from a great height, though they were both sitting down and Albert was taller. Josef had deep-set eyes, a protruding, straight nose, and a mustache whose ends reached all the way down to his strong jaw. His gaze became arrogant.

"I was the best pilot on the Congo River. I was the port captain in Boma. I did it all. But that wasn't what swung it. This is the most important thing . . ." He poked his cheek with his index finger. "Your skin color. That's what decides it. I was a white man. And I was master of all I surveyed. It's as hot as hell in Africa. But that's nothing compared to the fire you feel flare up inside you. That's Africa's gift to you. To finally teach you your own strength. Only one man in four comes back. Fever takes the other three—the fever or the blacks. But it's all worth it."

He leaned forward and fixed Albert with his gaze. His arrogance had gone. He seemed to appeal to Albert for understanding. His voice grew pleading. "I've tried to explain it to people I meet at home. But they don't understand. No one can unless they've tried it themselves. Everything you've seen before—it's nothing. Everything that follows—nothing. Mirages. You bring only one thing back with you from the Congo, and it's not those trinkets that I've got lying about at home. We had this song. No, I'm not going to sing it to you." He cleared his throat.

"Congo," he recited. His voice suddenly quivered with emotion. "Even the strongest man will shut his mouth and lie down for good. Even the hardest, wildest man soon ends up as rat food. They died like flies in the Congo." His voice became more and more urgent, almost thick with passion. "But I didn't die. I lived. Yes, I lived." He slammed the table with the palm of his hand. "Not like here! This is no life!"

Albert still hadn't spoken. He wanted to look away. But they kept staring at each other and Albert knew what he'd seen in Josef's eyes. The Congo Pilot had learned to look at other people as only a god can: the look that asks, Should this man be allowed to breathe, or does he deserve to die? This was the look that Josef Isager, the schoolteacher's son, had brought back from Africa.

Josef was an old man now. He was as tough-minded as ever, but he was old, and in Africa they needed youth and vitality. So Josef had returned to Marstal, where he came from, and where he was now living like a king in exile. Nobody bowed before the threat in his eyes, apart from Maren Kirstine, who was a mute and terrified witness to his nightly rages.

"Did he say why he suddenly wanted the hand buried?"

Abildgaard shook his head. "I asked him how he'd got hold of it. He said it was a kind of souvenir, like an elephant tusk, a necklace, or a spear—he'd come back with plenty of those sorts of things. It was common, he told me, as if he was discussing something quite ordinary, for Belgian soldiers to chop off the hands of natives they'd killed, so they could prove that they hadn't wasted their cartridges. It was on such an occasion that the hand had fallen into his possession. I didn't know what to say." The minister gave Albert a look of despair. "I didn't want the hand. But he left it here. 'You're a minister,' he said. 'The dead are your field.' I can't make myself throw it out. But I can't put it in a coffin and bury it in the cemetery either. There isn't even a name attached to it. I'm at my wits' end."

"Pastor Abildgaard, in one of your sermons you spoke about feeling how the world withdraws and your strength disappears precisely when you need it the most."

Abildgaard looked up with a smile of surprise.

"You were there, Captain Madsen? I'm delighted that you can remember my sermons. Yes, that was an excellent choice of words."

Albert had been going to say something more, but now he fell silent, and Abildgaard relapsed into despondency.

"What am I going to do with that hand?" he wailed. Again he looked out of the window, as though the garden could provide him with an answer to his question.

THE MONEY KEPT rolling into Marstal. The freight market had never been so favorable, nor had seamen's wages. Ship prices too continued their incomprehensible rise. Every other house in one street might be grieving, yet the merriment of those families that remained untouched couldn't be entirely suppressed. Women in their Sunday best mingled with widows in black. Shop fronts were decorated as if Christmas had already come. And no hearses drove to the cemetery, with girls strewing flowers before them: the dead sailors politely kept away. They didn't disturb us, and the elderberry hung low and blossomed over the streets that summer.

Every spring, before the fleet left the harbor, all of Marstal would smell of tar. Sailors armed with sticky brushes would coat the stone foundations of their houses as if they were ships whose bottoms needed caulking in preparation for the summer's sailing. On the house gables were numbers in cast iron, painted black, announcing the year each house had been built: 1793, 1800, 1825. When we hammered away at the tarred plinths, the black peeled off in layers like the rings of a tree trunk. But the numbers never fit. The layers of tar recorded not the years, but the absences. The plinths were tarred only when the men were home.

Now the men were disappearing, one by one, and the women would have to take on this masculine job, along with many others. Soon we'd see them in springtime, tarring away, with brushes as black as their fresh widow's weeds.

Excited students from the Navigation College cycled through the town and pretended to mow down children playing in the streets, who squealed at them in mock terror. The young men were going back to their boardinghouses to eat their hot lunches. Albert froze at the sight of them. He'd seen them too. The U-boats were waiting for them.

They thought the future would bring them money and adventures. They had the fever of youth in their veins and feared nothing. Albert was the one who carried fear on their behalf.

He had odd thoughts about the war and its causes. He visited the church regularly these days. They were just laying the copper lining of the new spire, and the nave echoed all day with the sound of hammering, so Albert visited in the evening, when the day's work was done. He was looking for tranquility. Behind the thick walls, in this cool, white room where dusk arrived early—almost a different version of the rhythm of day and night—he felt he had time to think.

And what he contemplated was death. Some people complained when death came too early and claimed a child, a young mother, or a sailor with a family to provide for. He'd never understood that. Of course, it was a tragedy for those left behind and for the person who'd been robbed of the greater part of life. But it wasn't unfair. Death was beyond such notions. It seemed to him that the bereaved often forgot their grief at a death in favor of railing fruitlessly against life's injustices. After all, no one would dream of saying that the wind was unfair to the trees and the flowers. True, you might feel uneasy when the sun switched off its light, or ice gave your ship a dangerous list. But indignant, outraged, or angry, no. It was pointless. Nature was neither fair nor unfair. Those terms belonged to the world of men.

He was well aware of why he felt this way. He was thinking ahead and looking back at the same time, and he didn't focus on anyone in particular. He thought about the generations, living on from fathers and mothers to sons and daughters, who in turn grew up to be fathers and mothers who had sons and daughters. Life was like one big marching army. Death ran alongside and picked off a soldier here and there, but that didn't affect the army. Its march continued, and its size didn't seem to diminish. On the contrary, it grew on into eternity, so that no one was alone in death. Someone else would always follow. That was what counted. Such was the chain of life: unbreakable.

But this war had altered everything. He'd take a walk along the harbor and see how few ships were lying idle along the wharves or moored to posts in the middle of the harbor entrance. There were still shipowners who weren't prepared to risk lives, but most ships sailed. There were mines and unrestricted submarine war, and still they sailed. Six ships might go down in one month, four the next. Never before had the sea demanded such sacrifices, but owners and captains who'd have kept their ships in the harbor while a storm raged sent them into the far greater storm of war.

Where did this contempt for death, this total heedlessness, come from? Surely ten lost ships and two missing crews in two months was a lesson already dearly learned?

Along the one and a half kilometers of Marstal's harbor hundreds of ships were laid up for winter, bobbing on the water, waiting for their spring departures. That was our town. It was a sight no one would see again. The chain had been broken.

What had happened to fellowship and to what he thought of as kinship, in whose spirit he'd erected the stone only four years earlier? He'd thought at the time that he was erecting a monument to something living. Now he understood that it was a gravestone, marking the end of the spirit that had created the town. And the cause of death was in the third column in his account ledger: profit. The high prices, the high wages, the freight that had risen tenfold, the premium on ships. Responsible owners who kept their vessels in the harbor had to watch their crews sign on elsewhere. Everybody wanted to take part in the spoils of war.

And so we sold our ships. What was the point of having them lie idle when they could be sold for three to four times their worth? The cost of building them could be recouped in a year, and so it wasn't just old, worn-out ships we disposed of, but also those freshly launched. We all spoke in pious terms about the dreadful war and vowed that this would be the last one. And dreadful it was for the millions who were killed in battle. But we, who were spared, benefited from it.

Denmark kept out of the war, taking no sides. But did we really think we'd be spared just because the Danish flag was painted on the side of our ships? A sailor needs a cool head—but this was recklessness. Marstal lay in the heart of the war zone. There were fronts on dry land, but the sea had its fronts too, and half the town's sailors were at them every day.

What drove us? Was the prospect of profit the heartbeat of this war? Was it bare greed that Albert now saw, even in people he'd thought he knew well? Had he simply grown old? Had something definitive changed? Or had it always been this way, without his realizing it?

Albert suddenly felt ridiculous. He'd worried about losing his mind because of dreams that contained information so terrible, he dared not convey it to others. So what if he'd told us what he knew? Would we not have laughed at him and dismissed his words, even though we didn't doubt the truth of what he was telling us?

Die? Well, maybe.

Him and him, a first mate, an able seaman, a skipper. We might have pointed to others. But not to ourselves. Greed made us think we were immortal. Were we thinking about tomorrow? Our own, perhaps, but not that of others.

Skipper Levinsen had protested when the breakwater was going to be built, saying, "You should provide only for yourself, not for posterity." Once, the whole town had heaped shame on those words.

But now the shortsighted Levinsen had become our role model.

HERMAN RETURNED home with a walking stick of white bone in his hand, made from the vertebrae of a shark. He wasn't the first man in Marstal to come back from the East Indies or the Pacific with a shark's spine, but he was the first to stroll around with it in the streets as though it were a scepter, and he a king. Self-importantly greeting old acquaintances, he'd use it to swipe the air with a fancy flourish.

It was with the same stick that he knocked on the door of his guardian, Hans Jepsen. As he did so, a group of boys watched him from a safe distance, chanting, "The Cannibal's loose! The Cannibal's loose!"

When Hans opened the door, Herman waved his sailor's record book in his face. He was an able seaman now, and he wanted to show that he was entitled to respect. Without greeting Hans, he announced his age: twenty-five. He spoke it like a punch. He'd come of age, and he was announcing the dethronement of Hans Jepsen as the official owner of the *Two Sisters* and the house in Skippergade.

But Hans Jepsen didn't seem to be listening. He observed the white stick that Herman was waving.

"I see you staged an eating contest with the sharks," he said. "And that you won. Shame it wasn't the other way around."

Herman's stick sliced the air, but Hans had already slammed the door. The shark's spine struck the green-painted wood and snapped, its vertebrae flying in all directions. The boys shrieked with laughter, scattering and yelling, "The Cannibal's loose! The Cannibal's loose!"

Some time later they returned and picked up the remains of the stick, which Herman had discarded. We didn't know why they called him the Cannibal. Boys have their own reasons. They were probably scared of him and so they did what boys do around any object of fear: they went up close, pointed a finger, gave it a nickname, and masked their terror with roaring laughter. They kept the salvaged vertebrae in tins and boxes and brought them out to use in secret rituals or to decorate their hiding places inside the hollow poplars that bordered the high roads outside the town.

Every day for a whole week Herman bought a round at Weber's Café to celebrate his new status as a man of property. His cheeks were flushed and he had a combative, I-dare-you look: he was constantly testing us, as if preparing to demand some oath of loyalty, a solemn agreement to submit to his whims or face the consequences. A quick glance at the way his huge hands impatiently clenched and unclenched, as though eager for something to grab and crush, gave you an idea of what those consequences might be. He'd grown even bigger since the last time we'd seen him, with broader shoulders, impressive biceps, and a chest like the front of a truck—but he'd also grown a belly. Although still young, he was already running to fat.

We asked him if he ate at Larsen's Chops or Nielsen's Pancakes, places we frequented for stew and mixed hash when we were looking for work in Copenhagen.

"I'm used to better things," Herman said.

At Inky-Hans in Nyhavn, he'd had a crouching lion, ready to attack, tattooed on his right arm. The banner above it read SMART AND POVERFULL in English.

He ordered another round.

"Just you wait and see, damn it," he said. "Just you wait and see!"

Something about his voice made us think that he might surprise us the same way he'd surprised Holger Jepsen that day when, somewhere between Marstal and Rudkøbing, he fell, or jumped, or was helped overboard.

Herman had traveled far. We all had, but he'd been to one place we'd never gone: Børsen, the Copenhagen stock exchange. When he talked about that, the man we'd known as a boy, with a fixed scowl and a sullenness that possibly concealed a crime, burst into an unfamiliar eloquence. But it seemed just as suspicious as his shiftiness over his stepfather's death a decade earlier.

Of course, we knew what Børsen was. It was a place frequented only by the rich and those skilled in arithmetic, where everything could be measured in money that could grow or shrink; where people could be victorious one hour and vanquished the next; where life could shift from triumph to tragedy in the space of a second. Oh, we knew that. We also knew that we too were subject to the laws that governed money, and that the rate of freight was not simply determined by its weight and the number of nautical miles it had to travel, but also by supply and demand. And what we didn't know, Madsen, Boye, Kroman, Grube, and Marstal's other ship brokers and owners did. But though we knew the laws that controlled all this circus existed, we also knew that they were beyond us, and that any one of us was more likely to survive a typhoon than to stroll out of Børsen with money in his pocket. Yet Herman seemed to have spent half the years he'd been away sailing the maelstrom of money and bonds, where people and fortunes were swallowed up and spat out again. He called it the New America.

"You don't have to travel all the way to America to get rich. Just drop anchor in Copenhagen. Even the milk boys speculate on the stock exchange. You can deliver churns one day and be a millionaire the next."

He spoke to us as though we were a bunch of illiterate, bare-assed savages and he was a missionary come to enlighten us about the promised land. His voice was larded with a condescension that didn't suit him, and which annoyed us. Thorkild Folmer, first mate on the *Ludwig*, grimaced and retorted defiantly, "Marstal housemaids have shares in ships too." Herman laughed.

"Ha-ha! Yes, a hundredth share. A hundredth of what? How much can one miserable old tub earn in one season? Who can become a millionaire from that? A tightfisted man from Marstal, probably, if he lives to be two hundred and doesn't eat or drink in the meantime."

And he renewed his unpleasant laughter, which supposedly proved him smarter than the rest of us.

New words were forever on the man's lips. *Margin, bull, bear*—magic spells for those who understood their meaning, but to the rest of us pure unfathomable gibberish. He mentioned the names of his friends at Børsen, who were visionary men of courage: indeed, pioneers in this new country. The Negro Thug, the Rolling Sidewalk, the Tooth Extractor, the Red Jew, the Track Changer: these men, as informal and straightforward as their happily worn nicknames implied, welcomed anyone into their club as long as he had the right attitude and wanted to get rich quick. Including an ordinary seaman. Or indeed a cabin boy.

"All I had to do was mention my inheritance and they lent me money. On the strength of my blue eyes. Me, a cabin boy." Herman's face darkened briefly, and he looked around the circle at Weber's Café. "Unlike others I could name."

He hadn't forgotten that no one in Marstal had been prepared to sign him on as a cabin boy, let alone an ordinary seaman. But Børsen hadn't rejected him. He was good enough for the fine moneymen of Copenhagen, who included him in their circle. We'd shunned him. But now he was back.

"Just you wait and see," he repeated for the umpteenth time, narrowing his eyes to slits. "Just you wait and see, damn you!" He took a swig from his beer and spat it onto the floor. "Beer—ha! No one drinks this dishwater in Copenhagen. We drink champagne for breakfast there."

Weber's Café was packed, and Herman was the star attraction. He'd rolled up his sleeves, and we stared at the lion on his right arm. SMART AND POWERFULL. Perhaps he was a murderer. Perhaps he was just a fool. But then again, perhaps everything he told us was the truth, and we were the fools, and he was the SMART AND POWERFULL one. We weren't like the boys who'd trail him through town, ridiculing someone they secretly feared. None of us grownups dared laugh at Herman; we were too scared of becoming the butt of his derision. Instead we nodded and looked knowing and hid our disgust. Champagne for breakfast! Damn it! Champagne was served on the patios of Buenos Aires whorehouses, the kind with palms, fountains, and dirty paintings on the walls. It was the syrup of pleasure girls. No self-respecting man would choose to drink it except when he had a hard-on. It was the lubrication required to moisten a señorita. *"You nice. Please buy vun small bottle champagne."* Champagne was part of the tariff.

We gazed at the bubbles rising from the bottom of our glasses. They looked like the last air squeezed out from the lungs of a drowned man. We could have spat on the floor. But we didn't. We drained our glasses and thought the beer tasted strangely flat and bland.

A GROUP OF men, young and old, were gathered on Dampskibsbroen one warm summer's evening when the water and the sky were like a pastel drawing, all light blue and pink, and the sea was as flat as a floor you could walk on all the way to Langeland. The young men were the new breed who spoke boldly and frankly in the presence of their elders. They'd only dipped their toes in the ocean, but they regarded themselves as experienced because of the war and the money in their pockets. But today their attention was fixed on a stranger in their midst.

For once even Herman was silenced. He stared intently at the stranger: a tall, energetic man with a wide-brimmed straw hat and a light-colored summer jacket that hung loosely from his broad shoulders. He had full lips and reddish blond hair that flopped casually across his forehead. Only his bloodshot eyes told you that he wasn't just another of the summer residents who came here for some coastal relaxation. Ever smiling, he flung out his arms, his voice rising with excitement as he spoke, clearly delighted with the attention he was receiving from his young audience. Meanwhile the older skippers had withdrawn to the periphery: whether this was due to their instinctive dislike of Herman, who stood within it, or the fact that the stranger was so obviously Herman's ally (and indeed even resembled him in his large physique and bragging manner) was impossible to tell.

Herman's face wore an expression we'd never seen on it before: admiration. Not only did he never take his eyes off the speaker's lips, but his own started to move, as though silently echoing the stranger's words and preparing to repeat them at the first possible opportunity.

Herman wasn't in the habit of looking up to anyone. Albert Madsen had once saved his ship from a serious collision, but the incident had made Herman feel resentful rather than grateful, because on the same occasion Albert had struck him, and he'd borne a grudge ever since. Spotting Albert now, out on his customary evening stroll along the harbor front, he invited him to join the circle, but his intentions weren't friendly. "Good evening, Captain Madsen." It was immediately clear that his politeness was only in honor of the outsider. "Allow me to introduce Mr. Henckel, the engineer."

"Edvard Henckel," said the stranger, offering Albert his hand, with a broad smile.

Albert had never forgotten the look Herman gave him the day he'd jumped onto the deck of the *Two Sisters*. He hadn't expected the boy to lash out at him, but he'd easily dodged his blow and saved the ship. It wasn't the first time he'd made short work of a useless helmsman by landing him one. He might have believed that Herman, then fifteen, had lashed out at him in panic, but the boy's eyes had betrayed nothing but reckless fury, and Albert didn't doubt that Herman was capable of murder. There was a harshness about him. That in itself wasn't a bad thing, but beyond the harshness, something about Herman seemed dead to the core. Like fossilized wood, no shoots would ever sprout from him, and his life wouldn't blossom in unexpected ways. There was no vitality there. Just brutality.

Albert was well aware that the young man saw him as an enemy. The feeling wasn't mutual. He felt an almost physical unease in the younger man's presence, but he felt pity too. Most of all, though, he felt old and resigned. He approached Herman with the wariness he'd feel toward a dangerous animal stuck in a trap, with a bleeding paw.

He shook Henckel's hand, then turned to Herman.

"You've sold the *Two Sisters*, I hear. What a shame; she was a good ship, a joy to behold, and she did the town proud." He heard the pomposity in his own voice and felt annoyed with himself.

"Possibly," Herman replied, "but I made a good profit. That's the important thing."

"To a businessman, yes, but not to a sailor. Surely other things bind us to our ships besides the prospect of short-term gain."

"Now you listen . . ." A note of impatience entered the young man's voice, as though he was talking to someone hard of hearing. "I could sail the *Two Sisters* to hell and back again, and even with the recent rise in the freight—tenfold—I'd never earn the same amount by sailing as I did by selling."

"You're only thinking short-term," Albert repeated.

They were clearly the principal players now, and their audience encircled them as if they were two duelists. Henckel clasped his restless hands behind his back, an expectant smile playing on his lips.

"Who says I even want another ship? Oh, *shipowner* sounds grand as hell. But perhaps it'll soon be an empty title."

The lack of respect wasn't lost on Albert. How dare this upstart tell him his time was over and his experience worthless? He felt a brief surge of anger as he eyed the young man who stood in front of him, his legs planted apart and a contemptuous look on his face. His shirtsleeves were casually rolled up in the warm summer evening, so you could see the lion getting ready to attack, and the words SMART AND POVERFULL.

"There are two spelling mistakes on your tattoo."

Albert instantly regretted his words. He'd allowed himself to get carried away. It was pointless, rising to the bait. Herman was hard, callous. But his brutality was that of the era they lived in. And Albert? His time was over. But so was the town's. That was what no one seemed to realize.

Herman took a step forward. His huge fists were clenched, but Henckel placed a hand on his shoulder. He immediately froze, as if obeying a secret order. Albert was preparing to take his leave when the engineer spoke.

"There's a great deal of truth in what you said earlier. Am I right in thinking that these are the words of an old sailor? I grew up in Nyboder myself and my first apprenticeship was at the naval shipyard. I recognize a sailor when I see one, and I know what it means to love the sea."

Herman stiffened. A dangerous scowl appeared in his eyes, as if he'd been ambushed. Ignoring him, Henckel continued. "It's true that Danish shipping is experiencing a renaissance. The war has brought us prosperity, and we need to maintain that growth." He nodded toward Herman. "More ships! Shipyards! That's what this country needs. Marstal is to have its own yard for building steel ships. You've heard of the Kalundborg Steel Shipyard, and the Vulcan yard in Korsør? Well, allow me to inform you that I'm the man behind them. Now it's Marstal's turn. And it was Herman here who gave me the idea. He's already agreed to be the yard's joint owner. Of course, he's far too modest to mention that himself. But he's put in the considerable sum he raised from the sale of the *Two Sisters*. Which makes him our first investor. We're building Marstal's future, and the future of Danish shipping." His large freckled hand, with its dense cover of reddish blond hair, gave Herman's shoulder a comforting squeeze. "Indeed, Herman, Marstal has reason to be proud of you. You're a true son of the town."

Albert looked at Herman, who placidly allowed Henckel's hand to rest on his shoulder, and he understood that the engineer from Copenhagen had succeeded where everyone else had failed: he'd tamed Herman Frandsen. How had he done it? Perhaps, when the young dreamer had bragged about his grandiose schemes, he'd simply nodded his head instead of shaking it. But there was more to it than that, Albert reflected. Henckel had tamed Herman by appealing to his recklessness. Mentor and pupil were cut from the same cloth.

Albert raised his stick by way of goodbye. He wanted to be alone with the summer evening before returning home to his bed and his tormented dreams.

As he left, he heard the engineer invite the men to come and drink champagne at Hotel Ærø. They responded with enthusiastic laughter. He didn't turn around, but continued up toward the memorial stone. He suddenly had the feeling that he'd lived too long.

He didn't believe in Henckel's promises or Herman's boasts, but Henckel and Herman belonged to the land of the living.

He belonged with the dead.

ALBERT SAT IN the church, composing himself, preparing to deliver more bad news because Pastor Abildgaard had cried again. In his days as a captain he'd often be called on to bear tidings of a sailor's death. Back then, he'd have been personally acquainted with the deceased and could speak of him knowledgeably, without resorting to empty generalities. And even though as a captain he kept his distance from his crew members, he knew enough about human nature to notice the men's quirks and tailor his words to the occasion. Albert knew that the captain's utterances mattered a great deal—even more than the minister's. The minister was closer to God, but he wasn't closer to life and death and the line that separates them. And that was what it was about. The captain's words, not the minister's, were on the invisible gravestones people erected in their memory; as for funerals, the minister was always underemployed in a town of sailors.

Marstal was a small town, so even when Albert hadn't known the dead man well, he'd know enough about him. When the war took a young man, he'd know the father, and could place him that way. If the man was older, he'd know him too. Albert might even have had him as a crew member. So Albert became a presence, a fixed point in the void that yawned open when death came. And in a way, he blocked death, standing in the doorway as a buffer that absorbed the initial shock and anguish of the bereaved, enabling them to succumb to their grief the sooner, and in grieving begin to heal.

But there was one thing he knew about the dead that he couldn't share with anyone: their final moments, as he'd witnessed them in his dreams. He'd seen them surrender to the foaming waves. He'd seen them shot to shreds by bullets. He'd seen them with frostbitten faces, slumped lifeless across the thwart of an open lifeboat after a day on a winter-chilled sea. This knowledge he kept to himself, yet even as he concealed it, his words of comfort were informed by it. He lied as only a man who knows the truth can lie. He lied away the horror and the pain, but he didn't lie away the death. He didn't speak of the Hereafter because he wasn't Pastor Abildgaard. And that was why they believed him. He was old and he'd been born in Marstal: he'd been one of the town's fixtures, with his broad shoulders and neat beard, ever since he came ashore. Even in the presence of death, he kept his captain's authority. He sat in a family's parlor, where he might never have sat before, and his presence gave death a meaning the family might not otherwise have felt. He helped the mourners guard themselves against the darkness. They didn't feel alone, for it wasn't just Albert who sat with them, but the whole town and all it represented: fellowship, kin, the past and the future. Death was already half-beaten, and life would go on.

No one asked to hear about Jesus when Captain Madsen was there, or about where the deceased was now, or whether he was happy. The captain's message was simple: this is the way things are. He taught us a vast, all-embracing acceptance, which allowed life's realities to come at us directly. The sea takes us, but it has no message to convey when its waters close over our heads and fill our lungs. It may seem like strange consolation, but Albert's words offered us a foothold: things had always been this way, and these were conditions we all shared.

Albert knew that some couldn't get through their crisis without the savior, and he left those to Carl Rasmussen's widow. He didn't regard their faith as a sign of weakness. He knew that people have different ways of coping, though personally he had none. His dreams were haunted. He felt alone, his faith in fellowship shattered. He walked tall when he left the grieving homes, but inside he'd shrunk.

He didn't know what he needed, so he sat in the church, gathering his thoughts. Most of the time he studied his hands, but every now and then he'd look up at Rasmussen's altarpiece depicting Jesus calming the Sea of Galilee. Outside, the war raged on. More sailors were being killed than ever before and he noted the losses in his ledger. At times he thought he was just like Anders Nørre, an imbecile whose only hold on sanity was the endless lists of numbers that flashed like lightning through the dark night of his mind. What would Jesus have done in the midst of a world war? One crucified man with a spear in his side seemed a trifle when millions were trapped in barbed wire, dying, with their intestines hanging out.

For his own part, Albert wrote down numbers. In what other way could he contain all this incomprehensible destruction? If anyone ever found his ledger, what would they think? That it had been written by a madman?

He got up from the hard blue-painted wooden pew, shivering. It was chilly inside the whitewashed church. He glanced again at the telegram in his hand, officially notifying the shipping company of the loss of the three-masted topgallant schooner *Ruth:* "Location: Atlantic Ocean, traveling from St. John's to Liverpool. Description of loss: missing. Wind and weather conditions: unknown. Since she left Newfoundland, the *Ruth* has not been seen. The ship is presumed lost with all hands."

His job was to translate that terse verdict into human speech. A ship had been sunk somewhere in the vast Atlantic, within a radius of a thousand nautical miles, by ice, or a storm, or a freak wave. Or by an ironclad prehistoric monster rising out of nowhere, spitting torpedoes, mercilessness incarnate: a reminder that the sea wasn't the only enemy. The result: a young Marstaller gone missing, never to be seen again, and this news about to be thrust in the face of Hansigne Koch, a sailor's widow who two years previously had lost another son, a seven-year-old, in a boating accident in the harbor. This was Albert's task: to guide the woman safely to port, ensure that she wasn't swallowed by the depths as she received the message.

Earlier, from his bay window, he'd watched Lorentz cross the street with the telegram in his hand. He'd let him in. Having hung his overcoat in the hall, Lorentz eased himself painfully onto the sofa. His many active years had taken their toll. He'd already had one heart attack, and his childhood frailty had returned. He was often short of breath, especially during the cold winter months. His shoulders heaved, and he breathed in rasping, wheezing gasps, exhausted from crossing a single street in the stiff, sleet-filled wind. He'd forgotten to put on his hat: his wet, thinning hair clung to his scalp and his Buddha face was flushed red. He'd brought his indispensable walking stick with him into the drawing room.

"This time it's the *Ruth*" was all he said.

He'd lost two ships before her, and each time he'd informed the bereaved families personally. He probably intended to do so now, but in his condition a walk through town would be a feat of strength that might cost him dearly, and he'd become too old to mount his horse.

"You've forgotten your hat," Albert said. "Let me do it."

· · ·

So Albert had walked up Kirkestræde to inform Pastor Abildgaard, then gone to the church to compose himself. And now, finally, he stood in front of the house in Vinkelstræde. Hansigne Koch opened the door to him herself.

"I know why you're here," she said, when she saw Albert's towering figure outside. "It's Peter." When she uttered her son's name, a shock seemed to run through her. The skin beneath her eyes paled and her lips began to tremble. "Don't just stand there," she said suddenly in a brusque tone, and he knew it was to stop herself from collapsing. She disappeared into the kitchen to make the coffee no visitor could escape, no matter how bad the news he bore. Albert entered the parlor and sat down. The room wasn't in daily use and the stove was cold, but he knew that this was where she'd wish to serve him. From the kitchen he heard the clatter of the coffeepot, the *scritch* of a match, the *whoosh* of the gas flame. But nothing from Hansigne. If she was crying, she was doing it silently.

She entered with the coffee cups. They were English tin-glazed earthenware, a gift from her husband perhaps, or an heirloom. When she bent to light the stove, he didn't offer to help, nor beg her not to bother, nor suggest that they drink the coffee in a room that was already heated. He knew that the small household task was holding her together in this moment, just as other daily routines would help her survive the times to come. Coffee was a ritual, as significant as the funeral she'd never be able to give her son.

She sat down opposite him and poured the coffee. He accounted for the circumstances of the lost ship as well as he could. There wasn't much to say. "Missing" meant only that it had failed to arrive at Liverpool, but it was important that she not draw hope from this uncertainty, for then her mourning would never end. Perhaps it never would, anyway. But hope stops time, and time only heals when it passes. He knew that much.

He hadn't mentioned the war.

"Do you think it was a U-boat?" she asked.

He shook his head. "No one knows, Mrs. Koch."

"I got a letter from him two days ago. Posted in St. John. He wrote that a lot of sailors had jumped ship. The *Ægir* couldn't even sail—there wasn't a single hand left. Men deserted from the *Nathalia* and the *Bonavista* too, even though they had rye bread on board. On the *Ruth* they had only ship's biscuits. 'If only I had the crusts that

Granddad gives to his hens,' that's what he wrote to me. Oh, I always worried that they weren't feeding him properly."

She still wasn't crying.

"A mother never has peace of mind." She went on. "Sometimes I think I won't stop worrying till the day I die. I've been scared since his first minute at sea." She fell silent. Then she said suddenly, "Why does it have to be this way? Always the same fear. But a U-boat's the worst."

Albert took her hand. He knew it had been a U-boat. He'd seen it himself, in his dreams. The crew had been shot down before they could leave the ship. Peter had been on deck, preparing the lifeboat, when a bullet ripped his chest open and he collapsed. Then the U-boat crew had boarded the ship, doused it with petrol, and set it alight. The rigging and sails flared into a blazing pyre, and the *Ruth* vanished into the waves with a hiss.

This was always the hardest moment. He had to stop his hand from trembling too as he clasped hers. He was lonely. But his loneliness was nothing compared to hers; she'd lost her husband and two sons.

She looked directly at him. Still she held back her tears, as if subjecting herself to some terrible endurance test.

"Captain Madsen, I feel nothing." There was disbelief in her voice, the disbelief of an accident victim who has been paralyzed from the waist down and suddenly discovers that she can no longer feel her legs. "I knew it," she said to herself.

"What did you know, Mrs. Koch?" His voice was gentle.

"When little Eigil drowned, I knew I'd never cry again. I'd never worried about him. What can happen to a child out playing? And then he drowns in the harbor. Oh, Captain Madsen, my heart stood still that day. I think I counted the seconds, and nothing happened in my heart. Not a beat, or a pounding—absolutely nothing. It was completely still inside my chest. Peter was at home. He hugged me and held me close the way I'd done with him all those years ago when he was little. 'Mama, I'm so glad that I've still got you,' he said, and though he couldn't take away my grief, my heart started beating again. He never ever wrote without asking me to say hello to Eigil at the cemetery." Still her eyes were dry. "And now he's gone too," she said. Her words came out disjointed. "Now there's no one I can remember to little Eigil."

She bowed her head, and her tears fell onto Albert's hand.

Time passed. Albert said nothing.

"Well, it turns out I haven't run out of tears after all," she said eventually.

He could hear the relief in her voice. Her endurance test was over. She'd recovered feeling.

"There's something else you haven't run out of," Albert said. "Don't forget that there's still someone who needs you."

Mrs. Koch gave him a perplexed look, then jerked upright as if someone had just called her. "Ida!"

Lorentz had told Albert something of the family; Ida was Mrs. Koch's middle child, a girl of eleven. Today she'd be at school in Vestergade.

"Ida," Mrs. Koch said again, and rose with a bustling movement. "I must go and get her."

Quickly she put on her coat and was soon standing in the hall, ready to go out. They walked together up Vinkelstræde and along Lærkegade. Albert offered to accompany her to the school, but she declined.

"You said something very true a moment ago, Captain Madsen."

She shook his hand as they parted.

"There's always someone who needs us. We might forget it sometimes. But it's what keeps us alive."

Albert turned into Nygade and shuddered. The sleet blew directly into his face. Was he useful? Did anyone need him?

He stamped the slushy ground in irritation and wiped his wet face.

THE WIDOW OF the marine painter often visited the church too. She sat alone on a pew, staring up at Jesus and the troubled sea. Perhaps she was thinking about the savior, or about the children who had been taken from her, one after another, until only one remained. Or perhaps she was pondering her late husband. It was impossible to know. The first time Albert entered the church and found her sitting there, with her back to him, he'd left quietly, not wanting to intrude. He'd even checked the time—perhaps she had regular habits—and started coming earlier in the day. If he stayed long enough, she'd always turn up. She didn't leave when she saw him; she simply sat some distance away and began her own quiet worship. He could hear the rustling of her dress and the scraping of her shoes. Once, when he rose to go she looked up, and he nodded briefly to her on his way out. After that he arrived every day at the same time. Eventually, she too would appear. Two old people, sitting quietly at opposite ends of the church.

Albert wasn't a man who knew how to seek solace. He knew how to be useful to others, and sometimes the two things are one and the same. But the burden he bore was something he couldn't discuss with anyone, and since he didn't believe in God, it followed that he couldn't talk about it at all. Yet he still came to church every day, half an hour before Anna Egidia Rasmussen, and he sat there as though waiting for her arrival.

If he didn't visit the church to find God, perhaps he went to find a human being.

One day she sat down next to him. He wondered if that was what he'd been waiting for. He looked up from his hands and greeted her.

"So you're here again, Captain Madsen?" she said.

He nodded, not knowing what to say next. The *Hydra* had been reported missing and he had another message of death to deliver, for the widow of Captain Eli Johannes Rasch. Mrs. Rasmussen had one too.

"Will this dreadful war never end?" she sighed, as she sank into her usual contemplation of her late husband's altarpiece.

"No. It'll never end." He spoke in a burst of anger. Suddenly he was doing what he had sworn never to do in the presence of the bereaved: voicing his opinion about the war. "It'll never end as long as someone profits from its continuation."

"How could anyone profit from such horror and death?"

"Take a walk down Kirkestræde. Look at the shops. This town is flourishing as never before."

"Are you seriously suggesting, Captain Madsen, that the inhabitants of a little town like Marstal are keeping the mighty engines of war in motion? Can't you see the grief it's caused this town? You must. Like me, you announce a death to someone almost every week."

"Yes, Mrs. Rasmussen, I see the grief. You and I see it because we visit the homes where death strikes. But the others are pressing their noses against the shop windows. It's human nature to worship the golden calf, and that's the main cause of the current war."

"I know nothing of politics," she said, looking down. "I'm just an old woman who's lived too long."

"You're eight years younger than I am, as far as I know."

"I suppose I am. But as a widow ..."

She stopped, too bashful to continue.

"Well?" he encouraged her.

"As a widow you no longer have your own life. You live through others. It's as though old age arrives in one fell swoop. I've felt old ever since Carl died, and that was twenty-four years ago."

"I've noticed that you come here often. I suppose you're thinking about him."

"I'm here for the same reason you are, Captain Madsen. To contemplate the savior." She gave him a quick, critical glance. "You are a believer, I presume."

"I was," he said, "but not in the savior. I believed in other things. I believed in this town and the forces that built it. I believed in fellowship, in a community of people. I believed in being hardworking and diligent. But I've lapsed now, I'm sorry to say. And I too feel I've lived too long. I don't understand this world anymore."

"You sound like an unhappy man, Captain Madsen. I don't understand the world either. I don't think I ever did. Yet I have faith."

"Perhaps that's precisely why you believe."

"How do you mean?"

"You say yourself that you don't understand the world. Surely that's why you have to believe. Faith's a mystery. It's not a mystery I share. Whether or not that's a limitation, I can't say." He gave her a questioning look, as if he expected an answer. He sensed that he was about to unmask himself to this woman, yet it didn't frighten him. There was an accepting gentleness in her and he felt that he no longer had anything to lose. "I have these dreams," he heard himself say. The urge to confide in her was overwhelming.

"What dreams?"

For a moment he hesitated. Then he made the leap.

"The drowned sailors," he said. "I see them drown. I see them almost every night. It's as though I'm there. I see it long before it happens. If you don't believe me, you can ask me the names of the people from Marstal who are going to die. I can give you their names, every single one of them." She was staring at him as though she didn't understand what he was saying, but he could no longer hold back. "For years I've been walking around this town like a stranger. I feel like a messenger from the land of the dead. The *klabautermann*—that's me."

He halted and gave her a pleading look. Did his words mean anything to her at all?

She was silent for a long time. Then she took his hand.

"It must be dreadful for you," she said. "It's more than a person can bear."

For one moment he feared that she would start talking about the savior. But she didn't.

"So you believe me? You believe I have this special ability?"

"If you say it's so, Captain Madsen, then I do indeed believe it. You've never struck me as a man prone to fantasies, or one who needed to make himself appear interesting."

"I've seen the war, Mrs. Rasmussen." He spread out his arms. "All these deaths. I see the pleading in the widows' eyes. How did my Erik or my Peter die? And I know. I could give her the answer. And yet I can't. There's a terrible helplessness in that. Helpless, yes, that's how I feel. I'm a spectator both asleep and awake. Day and night I witness suffering and grief, and I'm stuck. There's nothing I can do."

Her hand was still resting on his. For a while they sat that way, without speaking. Then she withdrew her hand and stood up.

"Come, Captain Madsen, it's time for us to pay our visits."

On their way out of the church she turned to him.

"I believe in your dreams. But I don't wish to hear about them. I prefer to live in ignorance of God's plans for us."

THEY BOTH CONTINUED to visit the church, but now they sat next to each other. Sometimes they were silent, each lost in their own thoughts, but most of the time they conducted a whispered conversation. There was no physical contact. Her hand on his that day had been a sign of acceptance; there was no need for her to repeat it.

December came, and in the twilight the damp winter cold seemed to concentrate itself inside the unheated church.

"We're freezing here," she said one day. "Let's go to my house and have a cup of coffee."

He looked around as they entered the drawing room of the house in Teglgade. A couple of Rasmussen's paintings hung on the walls. He knew she'd sold most of them, but clearly she'd kept a few as well. One was a portrait of a little girl from Greenland. Rasmussen had been one of the first Danish painters to travel to that icy wilderness, but the portrait wasn't typical of his work. His real subject was the sea and its ships; he'd made his name as a marine painter. The other painting showed a man wearing a gown, kneeling in prayer on the desert sand. In the background were a woman and a donkey. The man's face was strangely blurred, as if the painting was unfinished or Rasmussen's talent for human portrayal had fallen short.

"It's the Flight into Egypt," the widow said, entering at that moment with the coffeepot. Albert nodded politely. There had been no need for her to tell him that. Though he was not a believer, he did know his Bible. "It was rare for him to be inspired by stories from the Bible. Such a shame. I think it might have led him in a new direction. But toward the end it seemed as though nothing would come right for him. At any rate, he was very dissatisfied, very dissatisfied indeed. He was a tormented man. Please don't think that I was blind to his real character."

Albert had first met the painter, who'd been a few years older than him, when he was just a boy. Back then Carl Rasmussen had made an indelible impression on him, not just because of his remarkable talent for drawing but also because of his peculiar innocence. He was from the neighboring town of Ærøskøbing, and the first time he showed up in Marstal a hostile gang of boys had instantly surrounded him: he was an outsider and he'd be made to feel it. But something about his attitude kept them at bay. He'd seemed unaware that he was in danger. Instead, a friendship had developed between them, and they'd all spent one long summer roaming the island together. When Carl did his drawings, a crowd of admiring boys would watch. He'd also read aloud to them, awakening a hunger for a world beyond the dead rote-learning of Isager's lessons. Albert could still recall the impact *The Odyssey* had made on him, with the story of Telemachus who waited for his father for twenty years, never doubting that he was alive. Who knows, perhaps the path of his own life was set that day.

But the idyll had ended with a confrontation. Albert no longer recalled what caused it, only that Carl had left with a bloody nose, and he didn't see him again until as an adult Carl came to settle in Marstal with his family. In the meantime Carl Rasmussen had made a name for himself as a painter and earned plenty of money by it, which he invested in the town's ships. He'd painted the altarpiece in the church and used local skippers as the models for Jesus' disciples. Jesus himself was modeled on a carpenter who ran an illicit pub opposite the church. It was an audacious choice, but Rasmussen got away with it. There was no end to the town's enthusiasm for his talent. His likenesses were uncanny.

He'd asked to paint Albert too. But when Albert brought out James Cook and asked for a double portrait, the sight of the shrunken head had turned Rasmussen's stomach, and he'd had to lie down on the sofa.

Albert always had a feeling that the painter had come to Marstal in search of something he never found. Rasmussen's death was said to have been a suicide. That wasn't malicious rumor, but a conclusion reached through basic sailing knowledge. It was inconceivable that anyone could fall overboard in fair weather. One moment Rasmussen had been standing on the deck, painting; the next, he was gone.

· · ·

Anna Egidia Rasmussen poured coffee into the blue-patterned china cup.

"Do have a cookie," she said, pushing a bowl in his direction. "I baked them myself. Well, I mostly do it for the grandchildren," she added, smiling.

Albert took a cookie and dipped it in his coffee.

"Your husband and I had many discussions about his paintings," he said. "But not about the religious ones."

"Yes, I remember that well. You thought he was limiting himself by just painting life on Ærø and the other islands. I think in the end he agreed with you."

"I'm no painter," Albert said. "I was probably the wrong person to be giving advice. I believe in progress, or at least I used to. But how do you paint progress? I can't answer that one."

"By painting steamers with smoke coming out of their funnels?"

He heard the irony in her voice and laughed.

"You're right, Mrs. Rasmussen. We laymen should keep our noses right out of art. Once I believed the breakwater symbolized everything the people of this town were capable of achieving. But a big pile of stones like that would never have been much of a subject for a painter. And now I realize that there's one thing the breakwater can't protect us from, and that's our own greed. I must admit the way the town's livelihood is being sold off frightens me just as much as the war."

"You mean the sale of the ships?"

"I do indeed. We make our living from the sea. If we cut our connection to it, then what will become of this town? It's as though the times have gone soft. Suddenly being a sailor isn't good enough anymore. Better education plays its part too, I suppose. Children learn more and they begin to see options other than simply going to sea, like their fathers and grandfathers. But I think the mothers play their part in it too. They never miss the chance to tell their sons about their father's tough crossings, and all the sorrow and anxiety they put up with when he's away. That kind of whining kills a boy's desire to go to sea. And why hold on to the ships when the market's favorable? There's no one to carry on the tradition."

"Have you ever considered what it's like to be the child of a sailor?"

"Yes, of course I have. I come from a family of seamen."

"So let's imagine a fourteen-year-old boy who's off to sea. How much do you think he has seen of his father, when he leaves the home he grew up in?" He could hear the obstinacy in her voice and he knew she wasn't presenting it as a question. She was going somewhere with this, and his job was to follow her.

"I'll tell you, Captain Madsen. His father will probably have been at home roughly every other year, and never stayed more than a few months at a time. So when it's the boy's turn to go to sea at the age of fourteen, he'll have seen his father seven times. One and a half years in total, at the most. You call Marstal a sailors' town, but do you know what I call it? I call it a town of wives. It's the women who live here. The men are just visiting. Have you ever looked at the face of a two-year-old lad, toddling down the street holding his father's hand? He looks up at his dad, and it's all too clear what's going on inside his little head. He's asking himself, Who is this man? And just when he's got used to this man he's just met, the man is off again. Two years later it's the same story all over again. The boy's four, and even his happiest memories of his father have faded. And the father has to reacquaint himself with a boy he hardly knows too. Two years is an eternity in a child's life, Captain Madsen. And what sort of a life is it?"

Albert said nothing. He drank his coffee and ate another vanilla cookie. His own father had failed him in a way he'd never been able to forgive. Yet he realized that he'd always regarded the absence of fathers as part of the natural order, even though men in other trades never left their homes for years at a time.

"Yes, what sort of life is it?" the widow repeated. "For the father who barely knows his own children, and for the children who grow up as orphans even though their father's alive somewhere on the other side of the globe. For the mother who's left alone with full responsibility for them, living in constant fear that the ship will be reported missing. Why wouldn't she try to talk her sons out of going to sea? We have electric light, the telegraph, and coal-burning steamers; why should women and children be excluded from that kind of progress and live as they did in the past century? You believe in progress, Captain Madsen. So why don't you welcome this development? Because it changes the world you know so well? If I've understood it correctly, that's the nature of progress. It doesn't just make the world a better place, it makes it an unrecognizable one."

Albert wasn't a parent himself. He'd never held a living child in his arms, a baby animal who, when it learned to speak, would call him Father. He was completely out of his depth here. At times he'd felt there was a void in his life, but he had no regrets. That was just the way things had turned out.

When he came ashore at fifty years of age, it had been too late to start a family. Besides, who could you get at fifty? Not even a spinster, unless she came equipped with a serious defect. A widow? Oh yes, there were plenty of those. They were keen to marry too, though mostly for practical reasons. But they were hardly capable of having more children: their wombs were withered, their breasts were dry. And a young woman burdened with an old codger like him wouldn't have much of a future, would she?

That was how he'd explained it to us, in those casual, slightly contemptuous terms that can be so revealing for those who know how to listen. Now he told the widow, "Well, I can't really comment. I never did have children of my own." He took another cookie. "Strange, really. I was so absorbed by matters of kin that I forgot to ensure the continuation of my own."

"I've never really understood that, Captain Madsen. You should have married."

The widow knew nothing of the Chinese lady.

"Despite my long voyages?" he quipped.

"Those are the terms. You'd have made a good husband all the same. You have a sense of responsibility and you have vision. Those qualities aren't as common as we'd like to think. Children are a great gift. You declined that. You shouldn't have."

"And you say that, even though you've had repeated experience of how that gift can be reclaimed?"

She looked down at her lap. "More coffee?" she asked.

He nodded. He felt he might have gone too far by referring to all the children she'd lost. He lifted the china cup to his lips and looked at her through the steam.

She looked up and caught his eye.

"No, Captain Madsen, you don't regret having had a child simply because you lose it. Having a child isn't a deal you strike with life. As I said: a child is a gift. And what remains after a child is gone is the memory of the years it was allowed to live. Not its death."

She stopped and he could see that she was moved. He wanted to do what she'd done for him that day on the pew: place his hand on hers.

But in order to do so, he would have to get up and walk around the table. He felt clumsy and shy, and the moment passed. He remained where he was, keeping a silence that might be interpreted as respectful but which he knew was caused by awkwardness.

"I've learned to bend." Again she looked directly at him. "I believe God has a purpose for everything that happens. If I didn't believe that, I could never have endured it. I have my Jesus."

Again he was at a loss for words. There was something in her he couldn't fathom, a gulf between them. He wondered if their contrasting ways of seeing the world were simply something to do with men and women and the differences between them. While he sought meaning in everything and became agitated if he couldn't find it, she accepted life—even when it struck in the hardest possible way, through the loss of a child. There was a fortitude in her that was beyond him. Perhaps he'd never had to be strong in the way she had, though he believed that his dreams gave him an intolerable burden. He'd always respected Carl Rasmussen's widow. Now he admired her as well, even though something in him rebelled against her outlook on life.

Silence had descended upon them once more, and again she was the one to break it.

"I still have many children around me. My grandchildren—and then there are the children from the neighborhood."

"Yes, I know you step in when a family's in need."

"At times I look after a child for a while. I want to feel useful. If I didn't feel useful, I don't think I could go on living."

Again she looked directly at him. "Do you feel useful, Captain Madsen?"

"Useful?" he echoed. "Do I feel useful? I don't know. I can't tell anyone about my dreams. Even you feel repelled ..."

He hesitated for a moment. Once again he felt he'd gone too far. It was unfair to blame the widow. After all, she'd listened to him without fleeing, as Anders Nørre had done. He gave her an apologetic look. She looked calmly back at him.

"None of us is superfluous, Captain Madsen."

"But, you just said ..."

"I admit that I may sound pessimistic from time to time. When I think of this endless separation from my Carl, I feel I've lived too long. But when you've lived for too long and yet you can't die, then you have to invent reasons to go on. You're of no use, very well! That may be so, but only in your own eyes. There's always someone who needs you. It's just a question of finding out who."

Albert said nothing. He'd used almost exactly the same phrases when speaking to Mrs. Koch, when he told her of the loss of the *Ruth*, but he didn't feel that the words applied to him. He and Anna Egidia had different ways of looking at life. She'd found a purpose to it. He'd lost his, and in his opinion, that was that.

She leaned toward him.

"Listen," she said. "I happen to know a little boy in Snaregade. He lost his father not so long ago. He never knew his grandfather; the man died at sea long before he was born. He hardly ever sees the other men in his family because they're all sailors. His mother's from the island of Birkholm. She's an orphan, by the way, so there's no family to help out on her side. Don't you think a little boy like that might need someone to take him for a walk along the harbor, even take him rowing in a boat and get him used to the sea?"

"Yes, I'm sure he might," he replied, wondering what her point was.

Suddenly Anna Egidia smiled. It was a beautiful smile that made you forget her thin, bloodless lips. "And then there's you, Captain Madsen, an older, experienced sailor who complains that he's of no use to anyone." Her voice was teasing. She paused and gave him an encouraging look, as though expecting a reply.

"And then what?" he asked, slow on the uptake.

"You really have no idea what I'm talking about?"

Her sunken face grew almost round from smiling. Albert shook his head. He felt dim-witted. She was playing games with him.

"I imagine that you might be the man who would take a little boy by the hand and go rowing with him in your boat."

"But I don't even know the family. I can't just turn up and impose."

"I assure you that the boy's mother won't think you're imposing at all. She'll be both grateful and honored."

"I've absolutely no experience of children."

He made his voice brusque to mask his confusion. He felt betrayed. She'd laid a trap for him and he'd walked right into it. In a moment of weakness, of unbearable loneliness, he'd opened up to another human being. He'd been under the impression that they were two old people talking about their lives. When old men met, they talked about the sea—but he had an inner life he couldn't share with anybody. He'd shared it with her. But behind what he had taken to be her sympathy, there'd been a hidden agenda, which she'd now revealed. He was just a pawn in her charity work.

As he stood up to take his leave, it wasn't the boy he was rejecting. It was her.

"Don't you want to know his name?" she asked, as she showed him out into the hall.

"No," he said, "it's of no interest to me."

THE BOY

THE NEXT DAY she turned up outside his front door, holding a boy by the hand. Albert stood in the doorway, not knowing what to say. He was bad at estimating a child's age, but he supposed the lad to be six or seven years old. He had blond hair, and his ears, which stuck out, glowed red in the December frost.

"Aren't you going to ask us in, Captain Madsen?"

The widow smiled at him. Yesterday he'd loved the way her smile lit up her face and made it round and mild; now he was convinced it had been false. He stepped back, gestured them inside, and helped the widow with her coat while the boy took off his own.

"Say hello to the captain," the widow said.

The boy stuck out his hand and bowed stiffly.

"Aren't you going to tell the captain your name?"

"Knud Erik," the boy said, frozen in mid-bow, staring at the floor in embarrassment. Albert was moved by his shyness.

"How old are you?" he asked.

"Six," the boy said, turning scarlet.

"Let's not stay here in the cold hall."

He escorted them into the drawing room and called his housekeeper.

"Coffee?"

The widow nodded.

"Yes, please."

"And what would you like to drink?"

"I'm not thirsty," the boy said, and blushed even more deeply.

"But I imagine you'd like a cookie?"

The boy shook his head. "No, thank you. I'm not hungry." He shrugged and tried to make himself invisible. Albert took a large pink conch from the windowsill.

"Have you seen one of these before?"

"We've got one at home," the boy said.

"And where does it come from?"

"My dad brought it back."

The boy's hunched shoulders looked like the wings of a bird. He bit his lower lip and stared at the Persian rug as if he was deeply interested in its swirling arabesques. He was trembling slightly. Now Albert grew awkward; he looked at the widow. She shook her head silently. He felt like a fool.

"I might have something you haven't seen before," he said, to break the silence. "Come here." He took the boy by the hand and led him to his office next door. In the window was a wooden model of the *Princess,* over a meter long and almost as tall. Albert carefully carried it back into the drawing room and placed it on the carpet. "I don't normally let anyone play with this. But you can, if you promise to be careful."

"I promise."

The housekeeper entered with the coffee and Albert sat down opposite the widow. The boy was busy examining the model's anchor. Then, very carefully, he turned its wheel. Slowly he pushed the *Princess* across the rug. With both hands on the hull he rocked the ship from side to side while imitating the sound of waves and the singing of the wind in the rigging.

Albert kept an eye on him. When he could see that the boy was completely absorbed in playing, he turned to the widow.

"I told you I don't know anything about children."

Mrs. Rasmussen laughed.

"Oh, don't you worry about that. Just treat him as one of your crew. The youngest member. And you just be the captain, like you used to."

"He doesn't want to be with an old man like me."

"Of course he does. You'll be like God to him. Just start telling him about your travels and your experiences, and you'll find you have an audience like you've never known. And now you must stop making a fuss because I'm not giving you any more compliments."

The next day he went to Snaregade to fetch Knud Erik. The boy's mother, Klara Friis, was pregnant, and the time for her confinement couldn't be far off: her body was big and heavy under a black shawl. He couldn't remember seeing her before, which surprised him.

Marstal was a small town, and he had lived in it for a long time. Yet he no longer knew it.

She invited him in for coffee, but he declined, not wanting to inconvenience her. Besides, he wanted this visit over and done with. He felt he'd been tricked into it and he still felt resentful toward Mrs. Rasmussen.

The boy walked silently beside him down to the harbor. It was a clear, sunny day. The boy had no mittens on and his hands were red with cold.

"What happened to your mittens?"

"I lost them."

They walked along Havnegade to Dampskibsbroen and looked at the water. A thin layer of ice had formed during the night, and the sun sparkled in the white frost around it. Albert felt he should speak but didn't know what to say. What did you talk to children about? His irritation with the widow increased.

"Come," he said to the boy, who looked lost in thought at the sight of the frozen water. They walked on along the wharf, past the coal depot, and down toward Prinsebroen.

"What's it like to drown?" the boy asked.

"Your mouth fills up with water and then you can't breathe anymore."

"Have you tried drowning?"

"No," Albert said. "If you drown, you die. And I'm here."

"Does everyone drown at the end?"

"Most people don't drown."

"My dad drowned," the boy said in a tone that implied that this kind of death gave him a sense of pride, and elevated his father. Then his voice grew more hesitant. "If we drown, do we ever come back?"

"No, we never come back."

"My mama says my dad's an angel now."

"You must listen to what your mother says."

Albert was feeling more and more uncomfortable. He dreaded that the boy might suddenly burst into tears. What would he do then? Take him back home? He couldn't return with a sobbing child. That would be like losing your cargo and letting the sea take your ship. He tried to distract the boy. The harbor was full of moored vessels, some kept back by their owners because of the war and others simply home for the winter. There was nothing to indicate that Marstal's days as a seafaring town were coming to an end. Albert pointed to the ships.

"Are you going to sea when you grow up?" he asked, and instantly regretted it.

"Will I drown then, like my dad?"

"Most sailors come home again. Then they grow old like me and die in their bed one day."

"I want to be a sailor like my dad," the boy said. "But I don't want to drown and get eaten by a fish, and I don't want to die in my bed, either, because my bed is for sleeping in. Is there any way not to die?"

"No," Albert said. "There isn't. But you're very young. You have plenty of years left to live. That's almost the same as not dying."

"Would you like to die?"

"I wouldn't mind now. I'm very old. So it doesn't matter if I do."

"So you're not sad?"

"No, I'm not sad."

"My mama's sad. She is always crying. Then I comfort her."

"You're a good boy," Albert said. He pointed across the water. "Look, there's a steamer. When you go to sea, it'll probably be on a steamer."

"Can steamers sink?" the boy asked.

Albert looked at the black-painted steel hull. THE MEMORY was written on the bow in white lettering.

"Yes," he said. "Yes, they can."

He'd seen the *Memory* go down in a dream.

"A fire always burns at the bottom of a steamer and it's as hot as a washhouse when the kettle's heating up. Men feed the fire. They feed it day and night, and only come out to sleep or eat. They never see the sun or the moon. But high up in the wheelhouse the first mate stands with his hands on the wheel, steering the steamer safely across the sea."

"That's who I want to be," the boy said.

"Yes, that's who you want to be. But then you need to pay attention at school. Otherwise you won't get a place at the Navigation College."

They had passed the boat harbor and walked down to the ship-yards. Rhythmic hammer strokes rang out through the red-painted plank walls of the buildings. The only quiet place was Marstal Steel Shipyard's newly constructed building near Buegade. Whenever Mr. Henckel visited, he would boast about all the orders he'd secured in Norway. But so far, nothing had been built.

The boy seemed lost in thought. He peered up at Albert.

"What does it look like when a steamer goes down?"

Albert scanned his memory. He had never seen it happen in his waking life, but his dreams had shown him every detail of the *Memory* being tossed about before vanishing into the depths.

"You can hear explosions from the core of the hull," he said to the boy. "That's the cold seawater seeping into the glowing heart of the huge boilers. Then boiling hot steam bursts out through every opening of the ship. Big lumps of coal fly up through the funnel and the skylight. There, and there," he said, pointing at the *Memory*. "The ship keels over and lies bottom up for a moment."

"Bottom up!" the boy exclaimed. "Such a big steamer—with its bottom in the air!"

"Yes," Albert said, astonished at the effect his story had on the boy.

"Tell me some more," the boy said, looking at him expectantly.

"The steamer starts to sink stern first. Finally the stem stands almost vertically. The last thing you see before the waves close over the steamer is its name."

Albert stopped. The boy tugged his sleeve.

"More."

"There isn't any more."

The boy looked at him, disappointed. Albert realized that he'd retold one of his dreams in detail for the first time: a closed door had unexpectedly opened. As far as the boy was concerned, the story was all one great big adventure. You could see it from the way his eyes lit up. Albert could tell him everything. He could even tell him about the source of his knowledge: his inexplicable nightly dreams. And the boy would accept it all as part of the same fantastic world, where nothing needed to be explained and no one would be branded as odd just because he could see the future.

No, he hadn't known anything about children, but now he'd learned something: a child's mind is open to everything. There was so much death in his dreams; there was practically nothing else. But he sensed that to the boy, death in a story was one thing, while death in the real world another. He'd told him about a ship that had been sunk by a U-boat, and although Knud Erik's own father had disappeared at sea without a trace, along with the rest of the *Hydra*'s crew, the boy had apparently failed to make the connection. As for himself, Albert didn't know precisely why he'd recounted one of his dreams for the first time, but he knew that it was important.

"There's no more," he repeated, "but I can tell you another story some other day."

"Do you know lots of stories?"

"Yes, I do. When spring comes I'll teach you to row. Come on. Time to go home now."

The boy's face glowed red from the cold. He skipped for a couple of paces, then stuck his icy hand into Albert's. Together they walked back down Havnegade.

ALBERT STARTED going regularly to Knud Erik's house. Anna Egidia couldn't keep acting as their intermediary, so he fetched and returned the boy himself. In fact, the boy could have made his own way to Albert's house and back home again: the town was small enough for that, though they lived at opposite ends of it. But he felt that Knud Erik had been entrusted to him. With that came responsibility, so he stuck to formalities. He collected him from the front door in Snare-gade, and that was where he returned him.

When he came, Knud Erik's mother answered the door, though shy-ness rendered her almost mute. She'd given birth by now, and when he appeared she clutched the baby in her arms as if to protect herself from an unsettling presence. The first time he'd declined her offer of coffee because he didn't want to inconvenience her, but the second time he accepted out of concern that she'd interpret his refusal as a sign of snobbery.

There were differences on board a ship. There was fore and aft, and then there was the captain's unbreachable preserve, which Albert privately referred to as the island of loneliness. But the differences were practical necessities, enforcing rank and authority: he'd never regarded them as a class divide. His eyes were opened in Knud Erik's home. Knud Erik's father, Henning Friis, had been an ordinary sea-man. He'd married early and then hadn't been promoted. Most men waited to get married until they were in their late twenties, when they could afford to, once they'd finished Navigation College and owned a share in a ship. But Henning Friis had been head over heels in love. Or possibly just plain careless.

When someone hadn't got very far in life, Albert had always re-garded it as evidence of personal incompetence. Now he became aware that there might be something else. The boy's mother came from a social rank different from his own, one without expectations. He saw that in her almost mute self-effacement. Nothing but half-strangled sentences came from her lips—"There's no need," "It's far too much," "You shouldn't have." Her eyes always sought the floor or the baby. This paralysis in the presence of rich folks was rooted in the behavior of generations.

Her house was clean and tidy. There were geraniums and wall-flowers on the windowsill. But the furniture was a random collection from all sorts of places. No pictures hung on the walls: the discolored patches on the wallpaper had been left by the damp. No amount of cleaning could keep those stains at bay: they came from within the walls, caused by the poor construction of the house, a house built for poor people. Such a house did not become neglected. Neglect was its essence.

During winter it was either freezing inside or as humid as a greenhouse, depending on whether there was money for coal. On days when he showed up unexpectedly, his breath would linger like white clouds in the cold; on days when she knew he was coming and invited him for coffee, the overstuffed stove glowing in its corner turned the room into a steambath. Heated or unheated, the atmosphere was equally unhealthy and unpleasant.

They'd never had a serious conversation. Her gratitude was expressed in her shy deference. She didn't look him in the eye or say anything that came from the heart. The divide between them remained.

When the water in the harbor froze, Albert took Knud Erik for a walk among the trapped ships. Between them stood wooden stalls where vendors sold apple pancakes and warm elderberry cordial. Business was brisk, thanks to the crowd of people who'd come out to test their skates, and the clear winter air echoed with cheerful voices. Albert taught the boy to recognize the various types of ships. There were small cutters and ketches with round, fat curves and flat sterns. There were all the different sorts of schooners: fore-and-aft schooners, topsail schooners, topgallant schooners, schooner-brig combinations, and then the huge brigantines, which were the boy's favorite, undoubtedly because of their size. How the sails might be set was one big mystery to him, especially now, with all the canvas removed. Only the black lines of the yards and the rigging against the winter sky hinted at their secrets.

"It's just like learning to read at school. The layout of sails is the sailor's alphabet," Albert told him.

"Tell me a story," the boy would say.

So Albert did. He took one from his own life, or from his dreams. It made no difference to the boy and, eventually, to Albert either. He felt as though something inside him that had been violently forced apart had started to grow back together.

From time to time the boy's eyes drifted to the skaters, and Albert could tell that he was in another place.

"Do you know how to skate?" Albert asked.

The boy shook his head.

"Well, we'd better teach you then."

Their excursions always concluded with a visit to Albert's house in Prinsegade. Once Knud Erik had deposited his wooden-soled boots in the hall, he'd settle in front of the stove, where he'd take off his woolen socks and wriggle his toes in its heat. Albert would place his boots next to Knud Erik's. In winter he was still known to wear Laurids's old boots, which had plenty of room for an extra layer of woolen socks. There they stood, with their knee-high leather shafts and their metal caps, right next to the boy's.

The housekeeper would bring them hot chocolate with freshly whipped cream, and Albert would sit at the table, drawing. He was a good, meticulous draftsman, and in his sketches he'd carefully detail the canvas and rigging of different types of ships. He added seagulls and a fair wind, so the ships would heel slightly, offering a view of the deck. Behind the wheel he'd put a man smoking a pipe. There was a galley, a hood, and hatches. In front of the ship he always drew a spiral.

"What's that?" the boy asked one day.

"A maelstrom."

"What's a maelstrom?"

"It's a whirlpool that sucks everything down. The ship will disappear in a moment."

The boy looked up. Then he pointed to the matchstick man behind the wheel.

"The helmsman will save the ship. He'll just sail it somewhere else."

"He can't," Albert said. "It's too late."

The boy stared at the drawing of the doomed ship. Tears welled up in his eyes.

"That's not fair," he burst out. He quickly snatched the drawing and started tearing it to pieces. Albert was about to grab his arm, then stopped himself.

"I'm sorry," he said.

"You always do that," the boy said, "you always draw that . . ." He couldn't get hold of the word. "That thing. Why do you do that?"

"I don't know," Albert replied, realizing that he was telling the truth. He'd never wondered why he drew a maelstrom in front of the bow every time he drew a ship. The spiral simply pulled his pencil along, like an irresistible force. He drew according to a secret command that only his pencil, but not he, could follow.

"I feel sorry for the ships," the boy said.

"Yes," Albert said. "So do I. But their time is over. The age of sailing ships has gone."

"But there are plenty in the harbor," the boy objected.

"Yes, that's right. But no one wants to go to sea anymore."

"I do," the boy said. "I want to be a sailor." He turned and gave Albert a defiant look. "Just like my dad."

THE GRIEF no longer showed in Klara Friis's face these days, and she seemed carefree: Albert thought that it was life, calling her back. Her husband had died, but she held a living child in her arms, and as time went by, the balance of her feelings had to shift from one to the other. The child, a girl christened Edith by Pastor Abildgaard, needed her. And her grief had to surrender to that need. She didn't grow any more talkative, but her eyes were no longer fixed stubbornly on the floor.

Knud Erik had broken the ice between them. He'd long since abandoned his own shyness in Albert's company, though it returned somewhat when his mother was present, as though she and Albert were two different worlds that he couldn't bridge. But now he would report to her in a loud, clear voice the many adventures each day had brought. In the beginning his mother would hush him. However, as she had no conversation of her own to contribute, she eventually let him speak.

At times Albert caught her glancing furtively at him, and then she'd instantly look down again. But her face was no longer tear-swollen, and the shine had returned to her hair. She also made an effort to dress nicely for his visits. This too he thought had something to do with the difference in their social rank: she was smartening up for the gentry.

"I can skate now, and Captain Madsen will teach me to row and swim. Then I won't drown. And then I can become a good sailor."

Knud Erik made this announcement one day as they sat in the parlor, drinking the obligatory coffee.

"I won't hear of such talk! You're not going to be a sailor!" His mother's voice was sharp; her face tightened visibly under the soft curve of her cheeks. Knud Erik looked down. "Go to the kitchen right now!"

The boy disappeared, his head still bowed. Klara Friis turned to Albert. He had stood up.

"I think it's time for me to get going."

"Please don't go," she said. Her voice was suddenly filled with anxiety.

Albert remained standing.

"Don't be too hard on him," he said.

She got up from the chair and came over to him. "Please don't misunderstand—I wasn't trying to . . ." She stopped, unable to continue; she did not know where to look. Then tears welled in her eyes. He placed a hand on her shoulder. She took a step forward and stood close to him. Then she rested her forehead against his chest. Her shoulder trembled under his hand. "I'm sorry," she choked. He could hear her swallow as if trying to suppress her sobbing. "It's just so—difficult."

He let his hand stay on her shoulder and hoped that the weight of it would calm her somehow. She remained standing as she gave in to her tears. He could feel the heat from her body. She held on to the lapels of his jacket as though she was afraid he'd push her away. He towered above her; she seemed to disappear between his huge shoulders. The forgotten feeling of being a man standing opposite a woman surged up in him.

He gave her an awkward pat on the back. "There, there," he said, "sit down. Have some more coffee, you'll see it'll all . . ." He took her gently by the shoulders and steered her back to her chair. She slumped forward and buried her face in her hands. He poured a fresh cup of coffee and held it out to her; then, overcome by sudden tenderness, he stroked her hair. She looked up, but instead of taking the cup, she clasped his other hand in both of hers and gave him a beseeching look.

"Knud Erik needs you so much. You can't possibly know what it means to him—to us. I didn't mean to . . ." She stopped, and Albert seized the opportunity to free his hand. He sat down opposite her.

"Believe me, Mrs. Friis," he said. "I do understand you. I know how hard your situation is. I'll do everything I can to help you." The final words came as a surprise to him. He'd always drawn a clear distinction between the boy and his mother. He'd got involved with the boy. But now another barrier had fallen away.

She'd found her handkerchief and was wiping her eyes. Her voice was thick. "No, that's not it," she said. "We can manage. It's just . . ."

Again she struggled to stop herself from crying. "It's so difficult . . ." The tears slid down her cheeks. The hand holding the handkerchief lay in her lap. She had forgotten it was there.

Suddenly Knud Erik appeared in the doorway to the kitchen. His eyes were wide with fear.

"What's wrong, Ma?"

Incapable of speech, she gestured to him to let her recover. But he ran over and she pressed her face into his chest. He flung his arms around her.

"Don't be sad, Ma."

There was an adult tone to his voice. Albert realized that Knud Erik was a child when he was with him, but at home with his mother, he was a grown man, with a grown man's responsibility and duties.

"I'm going now," Albert said quietly. Neither of them looked up.

As he closed the door behind him, he heard Knud Erik's voice.

"I promise you, Ma, I promise. I promise I'll never be a sailor."

IF THE WEATHER made going for walks out of the question, Albert and the boy would pay visits instead. Before, Albert had been an eccentric who kept himself to himself. But now we saw him everywhere. One day he knocked on Christian Aaberg's door, and when the captain, who was in his midfifties, opened it, Albert introduced the boy.

"This is Knud Erik. He'd like to hear about Africa."

The boy bowed and stuck out his hand, as he'd once done with Albert, but this time he didn't stand staring at his shoes but followed the men cheerfully into the drawing room, where Captain Aaberg recalled the time he traveled right across Africa and was put in charge of twenty-two Negroes in a boat on Lake Tanganyika.

"D'you want to see my Negro spear?" he asked.

Knud Erik nodded.

Aaberg had two iron chests in his drawing room. "They've traveled with me all the way to Africa and back home again," he said, pointing.

"Did you carry them yourself?" Knud Erik asked.

Aaberg laughed. "A white man doesn't carry anything himself in Africa," he said. He opened one of the chests. "Look, a Negro spear. And a shield. Why don't you try holding them?" He handed Knud Erik the spear and showed him how to grasp the shield. "You're a proper Negro warrior now."

Knud Erik straightened up and raised his arm as if to throw the spear.

"Watch out," Christian Aaberg warned him. "That spear can kill a man."

Mr. Blach, the telegrapher who had been to China, showed them Mandarin costumes and chopsticks. But they didn't visit Josef Isager: Albert was of the opinion that severed hands were unsuitable for children. Instead, they called on Emanuel Kroman, who'd rounded Cape Horn and could do a terrifying imitation of the howling of a storm in the rigging in the world's most dangerous sea.

"I heard penguins squawk in the pitch-black night," he said. "We were at sea for two hundred days. The water ran out, and we drank melted ice in wineglasses. When we got to Valparaiso, we ate a whole sack of potatoes. We didn't even bother cooking them first. We were that hungry."

"Really? You ate raw potatoes?" The boy gasped.

Everywhere they visited, there were sea chests filled with strange objects: shark jaws, porcupine fish, sawfish teeth, a lobster claw from the Barents Sea the size of a horse's head, poisoned arrows, lumps of lava and coral, antelope hides from Nubia, scimitars from West Africa, a harpoon from Tierra del Fuego, calabashes from Rio Hash, a boomerang from Australia, riding crops from Brazil, opium pipes, armadillos from La Plata, and stuffed alligators.

Every single object told a story. Each time the boy left one of the low houses with its high roof, he was dizzy with excitement at the world's infinite variety. Everything whispered in his ear: a leather tom-tom from the Calabar River, amphoras from Cephalonia, an Indian amulet, a stuffed mongoose fighting a cobra, a Turkish hookah, a tooth from a hippopotamus, a mask from the Tonga Islands, a starfish with thirteen arms.

"Half a kilometer in that direction," Albert said, and pointed up Prinsegade toward the Market Square. "That's where the countryside begins. The people who live there know only their own soil. They know nothing about the world beyond the boundaries of their fields. They'll grow old there, and when it's time for them to die, they'll have seen less than you already have."

The boy looked up at him and smiled. Albert could feel how his longing stretched in all directions. Knud Erik was fatherless, but Albert was giving him new fathers. The town and the sea.

Spring came and Albert taught the boy to sail.

"What a good sound," Knud Erik said as he sat on the thwart, listening to the gurgling of water lapping against the side of the clinker-built boat, where the narrow planks had been layered on top of one another. He'd heard it before, but only from the edge of the wharf. Now he was surrounded by it on all sides. That was something else.

Albert took his hands and placed them on the oars.

Albert was well aware that he was encouraging the boy, but surely he was only promoting something that was natural for a Marstal boy?

Things couldn't be otherwise. But he couldn't tell Klara Friis this to her face. He saw how vulnerable and uncertain she was in the unfamiliar role of widow. Perhaps he was cowardly not to champion Knud Erik's cause, but he simply thought it was too soon. Life would have to be Klara Friis's teacher. She'd said goodbye to her husband. And then one day she'd have to bid her son goodbye too. It would be a different goodbye, though: not a farewell to a dead man, but a parting with a living one who was going out to stare death down.

So Knud Erik lived two lives. One was at home, where he had to promise his mother that he'd never go to sea. The other was with Albert, where he lost himself in dreams of following in his father's footsteps. The blue of the sea and the white of the sail were the only colors in the boy's mind. He was going to be a seaman. You might as well shorten that to "man." It was the promise of manhood that drove a boy seaward.

Why did a woman fall in love with a sailor? Because a sailor was lost, bound to something distant, unobtainable, and ultimately unfathomable, even to himself? Because he went away? Because he came back home again?

In Marstal the answer was straightforward. There were few other men to fall in love with. For poorer people in Marstal, there was never any question about whether a son would go to sea. He belonged to it from the day he was born. The only question was which ship he'd first sign on to. That was all the choice there was.

Klara Friis came from Birkholm. It was a small island; we sailed past it when we left the harbor in springtime and went to sea through Mørkedybet. Albert remembered those spring days, when the sky was high and the wind brisk, when the ice broke up and a hundred ships left from Marstal. It was as if the whole town greeted the spring by setting its sails, as white as the scattered, rapidly thawing ice floes. It felt as if the sun, rather than the wind, filled the canvas: its bright, stirring warmth propelled us. We could fill half the archipelago with our spring parade. We sized each other up from deck to deck. We were on our way to a hundred different ports, but this moment united us. There was a sense of fellowship that swelled until it broke into a kind of joy.

Farmers on the small islands would come down to the beach and wave as we passed them. They stood there, tiny, rapidly dwindling specks on the white sand, tied to their own limited plots of earth, surrounded on all sides by the endless sea that beckoned them daily and whose invitation they daily declined, happy just to wave instead.

Was this how Klara Friis had found her sailor? Had she wanted to escape her little island, and so had fallen in love with someone who wanted out even more than she did? Had she seen promises in those white sails, but failed to understand that these promises were for the men, not the women?

As they drank coffee, he asked her about Birkholm. She hadn't been born on the island and it was unclear when her family had arrived there. He asked about her parents. Anna Egidia had told him they'd died, but she'd not said when.

She bit her lower lip. "Our teacher was a real monster," she said, sounding as if she'd felt pressed to tell him something about Birkholm and had found a way to stop him from getting too close. "My ears were always aching. He loved to twist them."

Albert nodded. He knew a bit about educational provisions on the island, which had to share a teacher with the neighboring island of Hjortø. There'd be two weeks of school, then two weeks off. Precious little knowledge was imparted to Birkholm's young minds.

She studied her hands for a while, brooding. She looked up and he saw darkness in her eyes: not her earlier grief, but something deeper, like the terror in an animal that fears for its life but doesn't know the nature of its enemy.

"Have you ever been to Birkholm?" she asked.

He shook his head. "I've sailed past it. There's not much to see. I believe the island's very flat."

"Yes, its highest point is just two meters above sea level."

She smiled briefly, as if to apologize for this. Then her eyes darkened again.

"There was a storm surge," she said, and shuddered. "I'll never forget it. I was eight. The water kept on rising and rising. The land disappeared completely. We couldn't see it at all. Only the sea. Sea everywhere. I hid in the loft. But I got scared—it was so dark there. So I climbed onto the roof. The waves were crashing against the house. The spray soaked me right through. I got so wet. I felt so cold."

She shivered as if she was still chilled to the bone.

As she spoke, she curled up and her voice faltered: she was a helpless, terrified child, confiding in him. And although he was unaware of his own change of tone, it was that helpless child he addressed. In his mind, he didn't so much ask about her parents as summon them: where on earth were they in this story? Surely someone had been looking after her? He wanted a rescuing hand to appear, a father to clasp her in his strong arms, a mother to hold her tight and warm her with her body. But she spoke as if she'd been up there on a roof in the midst of a flood all alone.

"Wasn't there anyone else on the roof?"

"Yes, Karla was there."

"Was Karla your sister, Mrs. Friis?"

He still addressed her as Mrs. Friis. Anything else would have been patronizing. But at this moment it was like being formal with a child.

"No, Karla was my rag doll."

"But what about your parents?" he finally asked.

"I sat on the ridge of the roof, clinging to the chimney. And it grew dark. I couldn't see anything at all. It was like someone had pulled an empty coal sack over my head. In the whole world there was just me and Karla. The wind was howling in the chimney something awful. The waves crashed against the house like it was a ship. I thought the walls would come down. But still, I must have fallen asleep. It could only have been for a minute. But when I woke up, Karla had gone. I must have let go of her, and she must have slipped down the roof. I kept calling and calling. But she never came back."

Suddenly she smiled. "What a chatterbox I am. You make me tell you the silliest things. It must sound like pure nonsense to you. All those years you've been at sea—I'm sure you've had far worse experiences."

He looked at her solemnly. "No, Mrs. Friis, I haven't. Nothing has ever happened to me that comes even close to your night alone in that flood."

She blushed. He'd seen the terror in her. And in that moment a bond was forged between them that he'd never be able to break. She'd given him something precious, told him a secret from the very heart of herself. He still knew very little about her, but the fear she'd shown him sufficed. It bound him to her.

"Karla," he said, pondering, almost speaking to himself. "That's very similar to your name. As if she were your twin."

"Yes" was all she answered. "Almost like Klara."

She gave him a look of gratitude. Now he would leave her in peace and intrude no further into her privacy. He knew about Karla and Klara; he didn't need to know any more. She no longer had anything to prove, to explain, or to answer. With him she could be something she'd never been before: a blank page. She got a fresh start.

He never asked about her parents again.

SUMMER CAME AND the war continued. Albert had fewer dreams these days, and those he had didn't affect him the way they used to. He had Knud Erik now.

"Have you had another dream?" the boy would ask him when they met.

"Not last night," he would reply.

"Not last night," the boy would repeat, sounding disappointed. "I hope you start dreaming again soon."

Knud Erik's own dreams were distorted and strange, as most dreams are. But he always told them with the same happy wonder in his voice.

One dream was different, though. He dreamt he was about to drown.

"I called for my dad. But he didn't come."

His eyes grew blank as he told it. For a moment, he sat just the way he had when Albert met him for the first time, with his shoulders hunched and his head hanging. "And so I drowned." He finished in a dull voice.

They sat facing each other in the boat. Albert took the boy's face in his hands and looked him straight in the eye. "You're not going to drown. It was just a bad dream. If you're ever about to drown, then you'll call out for me. And I'll always come."

The tension left the hunched shoulders. The boy's relief was palpable. A moment later he'd forgotten all about it. He pulled at the oars, not expertly yet, but with enthusiasm. His eyes sparkled.

"Where am I rowing us today?"

They were in the middle of the harbor, and they watched the *Memory* pass Dampskibsbroen, a black ribbon of smoke pouring from her tall, narrow funnel. Albert stared at the steamer long and hard. He knew she wouldn't return. The boy waved to the town's deaf sand digger as he rowed past them.

"Keep your rhythm steady," Albert ordered.

That night he had his final dream. He knew it was the final one because it began the same way as the first he'd had, thirty years earlier. It was the same voice speaking. "You're heading for danger."

But this time he didn't wake. He wasn't on a ship, as he had been on the first occasion. It was years since he'd last been on one. He could have leapt out of his bed and run onto the balcony and stared into the darkness, but there'd be no shipwreck outside, no people needing to be rescued. He was on dry land, though he no longer knew if dry land was safe. It was an unsettling dream, filled with terrifying episodes. And like the dreams that had announced the coming of the war, he had no idea what it meant.

The next day he told the boy. "Last night I had the strangest dream," he began.

The boy looked up at him expectantly.

"Go on, tell me," he urged when he saw that the old man was hesitating.

"I saw a phantom ship," Albert said. "Well, I saw lots of phantom ships. But that wasn't the oddest part of it."

"What's a phantom ship?" the boy asked.

"It's a ghost ship."

"How did you know?"

"Well, everything on the ship was gray. There were no other colors. Just gray."

"Like a warship?" the boy asked, though he wasn't old enough to remember the day the torpedo boats called at the harbor.

"Yes, like a warship, only it wasn't one. It was a freighter, a steamer, a bit like the *Memory*, only gray all over."

"And then what happened?"

"Well, now here's the odd thing. It was the middle of the night. But it was as bright as day. There were dazzling lights high up in the black sky. They didn't hang still like stars. They moved slowly down toward the water and when they hit the sea, they went out. But new ones kept coming. On the shore there were buildings on fire, but they weren't buildings like the ones we know. They were big and completely circular, with no windows. And the flames that shot out of them were even taller than the buildings themselves. Big guns were being fired all over the place. You can't imagine their thunder. And airplanes. Do you know what airplanes are?"

The boy nodded. "What did the airplanes do?"

"They dropped bombs and the ships caught fire and sank."

The boy sat very quiet. Then he asked, "Was it the end of the world?"

"Yes, maybe."

"Do you know something?" the boy said. "That's the best story you've ever told."

Albert smiled at him. Then he looked away, out across the sea. There was a part of the dream he hadn't told the boy. He hadn't been able to see the name of the phantom ship in the dark. But he knew, with the strange certainty his prophetic dreams had taught him to recognize: the boy was on board. Knud Erik was there. Right at the end of the world.

ALBERT HAD THE feeling that something in his life was nearing a close. It wasn't just because of the war. He had accounts to settle. The Negro hand on Pastor Abildgaard's desk kept haunting him. Albert too had the remains of what had once been a human being in his care, and it seemed to him that Josef Isager, who was so contemptuous of his fellow men, had acted with more morality than he had. After all, he'd requested a Christian burial for the hand, which he'd once packed in his suitcase like a cheap souvenir, undisturbed that it had been brutally chopped from a human being.

A severed head in a box—was that any different? Surely he owed James Cook a funeral too?

He walked around to Josef Isager's house in Kongegade and knocked on the door. He heard noises inside, but no one came to answer it. Albert knocked again. The noise continued. It was muted by the door, so he couldn't make out exactly what it was, but it sounded like fighting. Someone was running. Then there was gasping, and the sound of a body smashed heavily into a wall. Albert grabbed hold of the knob, and the door opened instantly. He entered the small, dark hall and knocked hard on the door to the drawing room.

"Is anyone there?"

The noise stopped. He pushed the door handle down. Josef was in the middle of the room, with his stick poised, ready to strike. Maren Kirstine was standing on the sofa, looking like a little girl who'd been caught doing something she shouldn't. She'd clearly scrambled there out of fear. Her hair, which she normally kept under a net, was disheveled; gray strands hung down across her distorted face. She was clasping her mouth with one hand as though trying to suppress a scream.

Josef turned to his unexpected guest.

"Are you next?" he shouted, and stepped forward menacingly.

His face, with its heavy, drooping mustache and cold, arrogant eyes, was as formidable as ever, but his aging body was bent and slumped. Albert snatched the stick from his hand and broke it in two across his thigh. A small feeling of triumph went through him. He still had his strength.

"We don't hit women here," he said, and forced Josef onto the sofa with one hand, while holding out the other to the stunned Maren Kirstine. She took it and clambered off.

"Are you hurt?" he asked.

She shook her head, but her old red-rimmed eyes were brimming. Unsteadily, she dragged herself to the kitchen and closed the door behind her. The sight of her cowed back as she left made Albert incandescent with rage. Josef was too dazed to get up from the sofa, so Albert grabbed him by the lapels and started shaking him, backward and forward.

"You beat your own wife?" he yelled.

Josef's hawklike head lolled. His eyes remained cold, but Albert could see how frail the former pilot had grown. If he had any strength left, it lay in his will, not in his hands.

"Ha!" Josef Isager snorted. "I've grown too old, damn it. When I hit her these days, she can't even feel it."

Behind them the door to the kitchen was cautiously opened.

"Please don't be hard on him," Maren Kirstine begged in a pathetic voice.

Albert let go of Josef and straightened up, then stood there helplessly, not knowing what to do next. Josef collapsed on the sofa. He didn't look up. His face was drained, as though his confession of diminished muscle power had sapped the last of his strength and he was unprotestingly surrendering to old age.

"Sit down, please, Captain Madsen. I'll make us some coffee."

Maren Kirstine's voice had returned to its normal pitch, as if all visitors roughed up their host before taking coffee.

Albert and Josef sat facing each other silently while Maren Kirstine moved about in the kitchen. Eventually she came in and set the dining table. Then she returned with the coffee and some pastries. She'd gathered her hair back under the net and wiped her eyes, though they were still red. Once she'd poured the coffee, she vanished back into the kitchen.

Josef's mustache dipped in the coffee as he slurped it. He stuffed a piece of pastry in his mouth and started chewing, spraying crumbs as he did so.

"Why are you here?" he asked. He was still eating. He wanted to show his contempt for the man who'd just put him in his place.

"The Negro hand—" Albert said.

Josef interrupted him. "Yes, what about it?"

"Why did you give it to Pastor Abildgaard?"

"None of your business." Josef pressed his lips tightly shut and sucked them in. He was still chewing. Despite his drooping mustache, he suddenly looked like a toothless old crone, munching away on her sore gums.

"Is that all you have to say?"

"Yes, and you'd damn well better believe it!"

Josef had finished the pastry and, with his mouth empty, his speech became clearer. He stood up abruptly, pushing the table so his coffee cup toppled, sending its contents flying across the embroidered tablecloth.

"Maren Kirstine!" roared the Congo Pilot. "Maren Kirstine! Your coffee's as thin as piss! I want proper man's coffee!"

Holding the coffee cup in one hand, he flung open the door to the kitchen and slammed it shut behind him. The noise of the cup smashing onto the floor followed soon after.

Albert stared at the door, seemingly making his mind up. Then he rose from the table and left the house.

The next day he lowered the head of James Cook into the sea.

Mørkedybet seemed a fitting place of rest for the great explorer. So many voyages had started here, where the Marstal fleet set sail with the first spring. A grave in the local cemetery would have been too complicated, and he didn't think Abildgaard's nerves could handle a funeral.

He decided to invite Knud Erik to come along for Cook's last voyage. He'd never shown him the shrunken head. It wasn't appropriate for a child, he'd thought. But now he brushed all such considerations aside. He'd filled the boy's head with horror stories about sinking and burning ships, and Knud Erik had loved it. He'd probably enjoy the ghastly head too.

However, the real reason for inviting the boy along was that he intended to give the shrunken head a proper sendoff and wanted the boy as his witness. He suspected there was a moral linked to the story of James Cook—though the more he thought about it, the vaguer he felt about what it might be.

On his first two voyages, James Cook had treated the natives he encountered with respect. He'd regarded them as his equals, but they'd reacted with scorn. So he learned from his mistakes and became brutal and callous instead. In a way, he'd ended up like Josef Isager and the white men in Africa.

Where was the balance in the life of James Cook?

On a ship it was the captain's job to find balance. But a ship wasn't the world: the world was far bigger. Where was the world's balance? Did he even know himself? Was there anything at all he could pass on to a seven-year-old boy?

James Cook had lived under enormous pressure, constantly having to prove his worth to himself and to others. Though Cook had been the great mapmaker of the Pacific, there'd been no chart to help him navigate his own life.

Albert had looked for a father and found none. He'd had to make his own way, and so would Knud Erik. Perhaps he could tell him that. Or perhaps he should say nothing at all. Perhaps it was all the same in the end.

Yet he brought the boy along.

He'd placed the bag with the shrunken head in a makeshift coffin, a wooden casket filled with stones. He positioned the casket on the thwart between himself and the boy.

"It's a surprise," he told the boy. "We'll open it once we get there."

They took turns rowing. Albert did most of it. When it was Knud Erik's turn, he gave it his all. Soon they were in Mørkedybet, looking toward the flat island of Birkholm.

"That's where your mother's from." Albert pointed to the shore. "One spring day she was standing there when your father came sailing. And then she fell in love."

He was making this up. Klara Friis had probably never told the boy about her first meeting with his father, but it wouldn't hurt the boy to add some color and scenery to his parents' love.

"So she knew he was a sailor?"

Albert nodded.

"Then why won't she let me go to sea?"

"She will one day. Your mother just needs some time. She's still upset about your father."

The boy sat for a while. "I want to see the surprise," he said at last.

Albert opened the casket and took out the shrunken head. It was just as he'd inherited it from the captain of the *Flying Scud* fifty years before, and still wrapped in the same crumbling cloth. Removing the cloth, he held up the head.

Knud Erik stared at the dark face, as wrinkled and lined as a walnut.

"What is it?" There was no fear in his voice.

"It's the head of a man. He died many years ago."

"Do you go that small when you're dead?"

Albert laughed and explained the technique of making shrunken heads.

"How did he die?"

"He died on a beach in Hawaii. He was fighting for his life, but the natives outnumbered him. In the end he was defeated."

"And then they turned him into a shrunken head?"

Albert nodded. Knud Erik looked at James Cook for a while.

"Can I have him?" he asked.

"No, it's time for him to go to the bottom of the sea."

"And he won't ever come back up again?"

"No. He was the greatest explorer in the world. But now he needs a rest."

"Can I hold him?"

Without waiting for a reply, Knud Erik took the head of James Cook and cupped it in his hands. "You died in the end," he said to the shrunken head. "But you fought first." He patted the dry, faded hair of Captain Cook as if applauding his accomplishments.

They wrapped the head in the cloth again and put it back in the casket.

"I want to say a few words," Albert said. And then he said the Lord's Prayer, as he'd done when Jack Lewis, captain of the *Flying Scud*, had been eased over the side of the ship, wrapped in canvas, still wearing his blood-soaked shirt. He'd not prayed since then.

The casket bobbed briefly on the surface of the water. Then the weight of the stones dragged it down. A few air bubbles rose before it disappeared into the green-blue depths.

Albert contemplated the boy's words to the shrunken head. Knud Erik had extracted his own moral from the little that Albert had told him. There was a kind of wisdom to it. Perhaps the most basic. "You died in the end, but you fought first." As long as the boy held on to this, things couldn't get that bad. Life could throw in its own complexities later.

When they moored the boat at Prinsebroen, the boy tried to leap from the boat to the bridge, but miscalculated his jump and fell overboard. Albert stuck a hand into the water and pulled him out.

Knud Erik laughed. "Let's do it again!"

"You've been baptized now," Albert said. "Once in the church and once in the sea. You're a sailor now."

"Did I nearly drown?" the boy asked, trying to look important.

"Yes, you can boast about that. But not to your mother. Once underwater, twice underwater, but never three times. Remember that."

"What happens the third time?" the boy asked.

"The third time's the shortest journey," the old man said. "The journey that leads to death. It only takes two minutes. Always take the longer journey when you become a sailor. Never the shorter. Remember that."

The boy looked at him and nodded gravely. He hadn't understood any of this speech, but he sensed that something important had been said.

Albert pulled the boy's clothes off him and hung them to dry on the front thwart. "Come on," he said. "Let's do some more rowing. It'll warm you up."

"IT CAN'T GO ON," we said about the war. "It has to end."

We didn't know anything and we didn't understand politics.

"The good times will be over soon," the old skippers said, as they sat in the summer sun on their benches by the harbor. Their lined faces, tanned to leather, gave nothing away. With their eyes hidden beneath the shiny brims of their caps, it was impossible to tell whether this was gallows humor or whether they really meant what they said.

Albert too sensed that the war would be over soon. The right-hand column was now nearly as long as the left-hand one. September came. The boy started school, but they continued to meet in the afternoons, as they always had. Seven more ships were lost. The last to go down was the steamer *Memory*. Then it ended. Albert delivered his last messages to the bereaved. The war lasted a few more months, but as far as Marstal was concerned, it was done with.

Albert sat down next to the skippers in the harbor who were soaking up the September sun, giving their old bones a last warm-up before the winter. The group shifted uneasily. They weren't used to his company.

"Yes, the good times are indeed over," he said, and he didn't hide the sarcasm in his voice. They shifted again.

"Four hundred and forty-seven Danish sailors were lost," he said. He knew his figures. "Fifty-three of them came from Marstal. That means roughly one in every nine men who drowned came from this town."

He paused to let them digest this fact. Then he continued with the figures.

"The number of Marstal inhabitants is only a thousandth of Denmark's total population. And what's the bottom line of our sum, gentlemen? Does our total amount to good times?"

He got up from the bench, touched his cap with his finger, and left.

They looked after him as he swung his stick and walked up toward Havnegade. Yes, he knew his math, did Albert.

"Fifty-three hands lost," Albert thought, as he continued along Havnegade. "Perhaps I'm being unfair. A town quickly forgets. A mother, a brother, a wife, or a daughter won't. But a town will. A town looks ahead."

Mr. Henckel still visited Marstal. Tall and broad, with his light coat-tails flapping behind him, he'd stride down Kirkestræde on his way to the Hotel Ærø, where he kept a room permanently at his disposal. His arrival was celebrated with grand champagne galas for investors and other interested parties, of which there were always plenty. Herman, meanwhile, had sold both the *Two Sisters* and his house in Skipper-gade. This had left him homeless, and so he'd moved into Hotel Ærø, where he soon ran up an enormous bill. With his entire fortune sunk in Mr. Henckel's engineering projects, he was unable to settle it right away. But that didn't matter, said Orla Egeskov, the proprietor; he was happy to extend credit to him and Mr. Henckel. Orla Egeskov was an investor himself. He knew that every penny would come back tenfold; each bottle of champagne would be paid for out of future profits. And champagne was all Herman drank.

Henckel had built lodgings for the workers at the shipyard at the end of Reberbanen, where the village idiot, Anders Nørre, had once had his hut. Compared to the miniature proportions of most of the town's houses, it was an impressive structure, with two stairwells, eight apartments, and a mansard roof. And instead of crouching in a narrow street as though sheltering from the wind, it stood on a bare field, open to all sides, with a view of the Baltic, as if the engineer meant to challenge both wind and sea. After the school in Vestergade and the stately post office in Havnegade, with its granite foundation and swirling cement garlands below each window, Henckel's work-ers' house was the biggest building in Marstal. Here, ordinary people would live one on top of another, with no back gardens or front doors leading directly to the street.

"It's for an army of working men," said Mr. Henckel, who was a fiery soul. "It's just the beginning. The day will come when we'll tear down all the old rubbish in this town and make proper use of the space." In addition to the shipyards in Marstal, Korsør, and Kalundborg, he also owned a brickyard. "I've enough damn bricks to build a whole new Marstal if you want one. Just say the word," he bragged in the bar at Hotel Ærø, as his eyes grew bloodshot and large patches of sweat formed on his shirt. Then he'd buy another round, and we'd toast the new era that was storming in. We'd grown accustomed to champagne. The bubbles rose to the surface and burst in little pops that tickled your lips. There was no end to them, just as there was no end to the engineer's ideas.

Herman raised his glass too. He no longer went about with his sleeves rolled up, and he wore cuff links on his shirt these days. We'd all heard about the two spelling mistakes on his tattoo.

All we'd had before in Marstal was a savings bank: now we got a proper one. The Commerce and Credit Bank from Svendborg, on the island of Funen, opened a branch. The building stood across from Albert's broker's office and it was even taller than the school, the post office, and Henckel's workers' accommodation, with a large façade facing Prinsegade. Broad granite steps led up to a big varnished oak door with a brass handle. It looked like the entrance to a castle.

From time to time you might hear the noise of a rivet hammer from Marstal Steel Shipyard, but no ships had been launched yet.

Albert nodded to Peter Raahauge, the boat builder, as he made his way home through Buegade at the end of the day. Raahauge raised a finger to his cap and stopped.

"When do we finally get to see one of your ships?"

Raahauge set his toolbox down on the cobbled street. He folded his strong arms across his chest and snorted contemptuously into his mustache, before he shook his head. "Damn strange way they do business," he said. "If laying down the keel is the same as building a whole ship, then I've built an awful lot of ships lately. I've yet to see any frames or shell plating."

"So how does that work?" Albert asked. "It doesn't make any sense to me."

"Or to the rest of us mere mortals. But that's because we're not as smart as Henckel. You see, Captain Madsen . . ."

Raahauge leaned close to Albert. His voice became a confidential whisper. "He's arranged it so that the Norwegians pay the first installment as soon as the keel's been laid. Then he invites them down here, offers them champagne, and shows off the keel, and they think the ship's as good as built. How are they to know that the last set of customers were shown the same keel? It's the same one we show all of them."

"So Henckel's taking large sums of money for ships he'll never deliver? But that's fraud!" Albert was outraged.

"You might say so, Captain Madsen. I couldn't possibly comment. Still, I'll be having to look for new work soon. Because there's no way in hell this can last."

Peter Raahauge touched a finger to the brim of his cap once more and disappeared up the street.

FOR SOME YEARS now, Albert had gone out fishing for shrimp. Many of us did that when we came ashore. Some did it out of necessity, but for Albert, it was a way of passing the time. The local waters belonged to boys and to old men. He'd learned his way around the archipelago as a child, exploring all its islands, bays, points, sandbanks, and invisible currents. In between childhood and old age he'd sailed the world's oceans; now he'd returned to the smallest print of the sea chart, seeking out the old familiar places. He'd begun in the good years before the First World War, and when his prophetic nightmares descended on him, he escaped their reign of terror by fishing for shrimp. Tending to his nets beneath the drifting clouds, he'd found, if not peace, then at least a ceasefire.

Albert was thinking about shrimp one evening after he'd left Knud Erik and his mother and was strolling along Nygade to his house in Prinsegade. Shrimp. He'd take Knud Erik with him the next time he went to check on his nets. He'd teach the boy how to do it and give him a bucketful to take home to his mother. They could sell the rest at the harbor, and Knud Erik would get a bit of money in his pocket and bring in some earnings like a good little man. It would be half play and half real help for the hard-up widow, who was unlikely to accept assistance in any other form. Normally he'd just give his shrimp away to anyone who happened to turn up at his office or to Lorentz across the street.

That summer he'd laid his nets along the coast of Langeland, starting at Sorekrogen and working his way toward Ristinge. In the light summer nights when he fished, the water's surface was like a mirror. The first glow of the sun blazed northeast as he rowed out through the entrance to the harbor, and the sound of the oars traveled far across the water.

He asked the boy if he wanted to come along.

· · ·

The summer holidays had started. With school over, Knud Erik hung about during the long, empty days when the weather didn't tempt him to swim at the beach. After some hesitation, Knud Erik's mother consented to a shrimp outing. A bond had grown between Albert and Klara. He felt it keenly but he didn't explore its nature, though he found himself spending more and more time in front of his mirror, and sometimes a smile—one of recognition—would appear behind his dense, graying beard. It was an old friend he was greeting in the mirror, one he hadn't seen for many years: his own younger self.

He was to pick up Knud Erik in the evening and take him home. The boy would sleep on the sofa in Albert's drawing room until three in the morning, and then he'd wake him and they'd head for the harbor. Klara was baking thick pancakes when he arrived. They were a local specialty; as she made them, she brought them directly out from the kitchen, so they could be eaten piping hot. He stood in the doorway, watching her as she deftly poured batter into figure eights in the hot pan, where they quickly rose into small compact mounds. When they turned golden, she placed them on brown paper to drain. Knud Erik stood next to her, eagerly awaiting the first pancake, which he immediately sprinkled with sugar.

No words passed between them as she worked on the pancakes, but the silence was a comfortable one. Standing in the doorway with his arms folded across his chest, Albert realized he felt at home in the presence of this young woman.

She'd tied a scarf around her hair to protect it from the greasy fumes: when a lock came loose and fell over her eyes, she blew it out of the way and shot him a cheerful glance. He smiled back at her.

She served gooseberry compote with the pancakes and he asked if it was homemade. She nodded. There were gooseberry bushes in their little back garden. Even the most wretched hovels in the town had a garden. She'd made far more pancakes than they could eat, and she gave them the remaining ones, wrapped in a tea towel, along with a jar of compote.

"In case you get hungry tonight," she said.

She turned to Knud Erik and handed him a woolen sweater.

"It can get cold out on the water."

"I won't be cold," Knud Erik said, in a tone that implied that his newly acquired manhood had been offended.

"Well, I'll be bringing my sweater," said Albert. He placed his hand on the boy's shoulder. "Say goodbye to your mother."

Klara stood in the doorway, waving after them as they walked toward Kirkestræde.

When he roused Knud Erik at three and handed him a cup of warm coffee, the horizon was glowing, but the sky above was still dark, keeping the last stars alive.

"This will help you wake up."

The boy scratched his head with one hand and took the cup with the other.

"Blow on it."

The boy blew and kept his lips tentatively pursed as he slurped his first mouthful. He made a face. Albert took the cup from him and added a teaspoon of sugar.

"Now try it."

The boy took another sip and smiled. Albert pulled the woolen sweater over the boy's head. He'd already put on his own Icelandic one.

They slipped the mooring at Prinsebroen and started rowing out of the harbor entrance. The boy huddled on the thwart, shivering with tiredness and cold. Albert passed him an oar.

"Lend me a hand, will you?" he said.

The boy positioned himself on the aft thwart, then stuck the oar into the water and started moving it between his hands with a rolling motion, twisting it in the water like a screw. He was sculling, a technique Albert had taught him.

They passed Dampskibsbroen and headed for Ristinge. Knud Erik had warmed up and they made good speed across the bright, glassy water. Theirs was the only boat out this early. An hour later they reached Sorekrogen. The nets were brimming with shrimp.

"There'll be some for your mother too," Albert said.

They made themselves comfortable on the thwarts with the pancakes. The sun was now clear of the horizon, igniting a low-hanging stripe of cloud. Apart from that the sky was clear.

"It'll be beach weather today," Albert declared.

"Tell me about the shrunken head," Knud Erik said.

A few hours later they were back at the entrance to the harbor. The sun was higher in the sky and Albert could already feel its warmth, though it was still early in the morning. They passed Dampskibsbroen and approached Prinsebroen. Knud Erik went to the bow and readied the boat for mooring with accomplished ease. Albert filled a bucket with shrimp, then took the boy home to Snaregade. The boy raced through the door with the bucket in his hand.

His mother appeared in the doorway.

"Thank you for the shrimp, Captain Madsen. Now, why are you standing outside? Do come in, please."

She stepped aside to allow him to enter through the narrow doorway. He tried making himself small, but he brushed her with his arm all the same. He knew his way around and walked to the sofa. A cup had already been put out for him. She disappeared into the kitchen and returned with the coffeepot.

"Shrimp fishing is a good business," Albert said. "Knud Erik will be a prosperous man."

Her face tightened. "We can't accept money."

"It's not a gift, Mrs. Friis. He's worked hard and it's only fair that he should get his share."

Knud Erik started jumping up and down in excitement.

"Go find your swimming trunks and a towel. And then you can run over to the beach."

"Really, can I, can I?" By now his jumping had built up a rhythm.

"Yes, of course. Now be off with you."

He rushed to the kitchen and returned a moment later with a rolled-up towel. He was about to tear through the hall with his hand raised in a goodbye gesture, when he stopped abruptly, went over to Albert and stuck out his hand. He bowed stiffly and thanked him for the day. Albert placed his hand on the boy's head and ruffled his hair gently. "You're welcome."

"He's a lovely boy," he said, once Knud Erik was out the door. "Take good care of him."

"You already do that for me."

She smiled again and he looked up. Their eyes met and he couldn't decide if it had been by chance. He felt that he ought to look elsewhere but seemed paralyzed. He was aware of a smile spreading uncontrollably across his face. Klara Friis's cheeks slowly reddened. She too seemed unable to break away from the moment, which kept expanding, from seconds to minutes to what felt like wondrous weightless hours. At last she looked down. He felt a sudden shame, as if he'd molested her. He had to stop himself from apologizing, even though nothing had happened.

He cleared his throat. "Thanks for the coffee."

She gave him a confused look, as though he'd woken her from a reverie. Her cheeks were still red.

"You're going now?"

"Yes, I think I'd better," he said, and hoped his words sounded neutral, so that his leaving didn't become a verdict on the awkward situation they'd just found themselves in.

"Oh," she said, as if his going surprised her.

He remained sitting and waited for her to continue. She stared at her hands.

"Well, I don't mean to impose on you. But would you like to come to dinner tonight? After all, we have the shrimp," she said, looking up at him.

"I'd like that very much. I'll bring a bottle of wine."

"Wine?" Her awkwardness grew.

"Ah, perhaps you don't drink wine?"

She wiped her forehead. Then she suddenly laughed behind her hand.

"I've never tasted it."

"There's a first time for everything. And that time is tonight."

When he left the house, he noticed the thickset figure of Herman striding briskly toward the harbor, with his flat cap pulled down over his forehead. Looking up, Herman gave the Friis house a quick once-over, glanced back at Albert, and touched one finger nonchalantly to his cap. Albert returned the greeting, but there was no exchange of words.

Albert kept walking in the direction of Kirkestræde, pondering the look the young man had just given him. Was he checking up on him? Was he aware of something? Then he shrugged. What kind of nonsense was this? Nothing had happened between him and Knud Erik's mother. But the invitation for tonight? The wine? Not long ago he'd held a weeping widow in his arms. When they'd talked about the wine just now, their tone had been almost coquettish. Her laughter behind her hand. Was she falling in love with him? Or was it the other way around? Was he interpreting everything in a certain light because he'd fallen for her?

He shook his head at himself. The mere thought was inappropriate. He didn't know the exact age difference between them, but it was huge. He couldn't just be her father; he could be her grandfather.

He had his own life and habits. He didn't want them disturbed. He'd seen and heard more than he needed to: his dreams had shaken him to the core. He'd experienced them as a cruel and vicious halting of his life, inflicted by a God whose savagery repelled him, who inspired in him neither the urge to believe nor the impulse to beg for mercy. His faith had been faith in mankind, and he'd lost it, ending up in the darkness, a badly injured, shipwrecked man on a shore of bones at the end of the world.

But, unexpectedly, his life had restarted. A seven-year-old boy had restored his faith. And now the boy's mother had become part of it too, and the appeal of this new life grew stronger all the time. He couldn't deny that he felt strangely exhilarated in the presence of Klara Friis. Knud Erik had knocked the first hole in the wall of loneliness he'd lived behind. But now, when Klara was there, he felt the entire wall was on the brink of collapse.

Yes, it was inappropriate. And yet he couldn't stop smiling.

It was late in the afternoon and he was sitting in his bathtub in preparation for dinner when he felt something like a shooting pain in his mind. A man with a character less proud and stubborn would have called it anxiety. Once again, his thoughts were circling around Klara Friis. Human beings are afflicted by a need to judge. So what might people think if they suddenly saw him in the company of a much younger woman? Some men, like the monstrous O'Connor, lash out with their fists, but there are other ways to do damage, and the tongue can be the most vicious weapon of all: in the courtroom of gossip, there's no appeal. But why should he care? He'd done his duty in life. He'd earned respect and built up a fleet of ships. His work was done, yet he carried on living. What was left? Might there be new, unexpected freedoms awaiting him in these closing years?

He got out of the bath and dried himself. He went over to the mirror and with his towel wiped a porthole shape on its steamy surface so he could inspect himself. He'd rarely viewed his body through the eyes of another. For him it was a tool. Strength and endurance were the yardsticks he measured it by, whether he was on deck fighting the sea or using his thick muscles to enforce his authority in front of an insubordinate crew. How long could he stay awake when a storm demanded his constant presence on the deck? How much power did he exude?

In the mirror he could see that his chest was sunken and long stretch marks ran from his shoulders down to his pectorals, which sagged under their own weight. The curly hair that covered his chest had been gray for many years. Yet once he was dressed, his body seemed as impressive as it had ever been.

One summer evening long ago he'd made love with Cheng Sumei in her large suburban villa in Le Havre, not knowing that it would be for the last time. It had been an evening like many others. Wax candles, flames that stood straight up in the calm evening, the scent of incense. She'd leaned over him and let him loosen her silk kimono, which fell open and exposed her naked body, as white as the petals of a tree peony, with a faint hint of something that was not yellow exactly, but more like cream. Her skin was as smooth as a polished jade figurine. He didn't understand it, the mystery of her agelessness, which he associated not with the Orient, but with her. In all the time he'd known her, only the few lines that appeared around her mouth betrayed her as the mature woman she was. They were like lines drawn on a picture. They only enhanced her beauty.

Cheng Sumei unbound her long hair and let it cascade over her shoulders, and he buried himself completely in its dense darkness. This was the unvarying prelude to their lovemaking. He closed his eyes and surrendered to her hands, which gently caressed his cheekbones. Then her lips landed on his.

The next morning she didn't wake up. She just lay there with her black hair spread out across the white, embroidered silk pillow. She'd died as though she'd merely turned her face away to look in a different direction. She'd never aged and was never struck down by illness. And yet her life had ended.

Cheng Sumei had passed away. That was exactly how he thought of it: she'd risen from the bed in the middle of the night and passed away, away from him. He looked at her dead body on the sheet as though it were a kimono she'd stepped out of. Every night for a long time afterward, he expected to hear the familiar swishing of silk as she undressed in front of him. He closed his eyes, though darkness already reigned in the room, and waited for the touch of her hands gliding across his face.

He worked hard during the day. But not even his daily activities provided distraction or escape. They'd worked together too closely for that. He'd accompany her to her office, and in the evenings they'd bring telegrams and newspapers home with them. Then they'd discuss freight rates and political events around the globe. He learned from her. And she learned from him. He had firsthand knowledge of the sea, and if there were problems with a crew, or if she was dissatisfied with a captain's decisions, she would consult him. If a new market was opening up, they'd make the decision jointly after extensive discussion. They discovered common ground in the brokerage business, and that was fundamentally the strongest bond between them.

He could still recall the moment he'd fallen in love with her. Luis Presser had invited him for the first time to dinner at the villa where he'd later spend so many nights. At the table, he'd been mesmerized by her. He'd had to concentrate on not staring and force himself to pay attention to the conversation, which was in English. After a while even he realized that it was embarrassing—odd almost—that he hadn't yet addressed her, or looked in her direction, except furtively. If he felt anything, it was awe. There was something transparent about her beauty that in his eyes made her enigmatic, almost supernatural. He hadn't expected that she would deign to do something as profane as open her mouth to speak, and so when she addressed him, he was as startled as the devotee of some pagan god would have been, had the lips of the statue he was kneeling to suddenly parted to give him a jovial greeting.

"Monsieur Madsen, would you like me to tell you about the moment I fell in love with the West?" she asked.

She pronounced his name with a strong French accent, but otherwise her English was perfect. She sparkled, full of curiosity and playful teasing, as though she'd sensed his bashfulness and now wished to demystify herself. He hadn't noticed them before. He'd only seen her long, dense eyelashes when she looked down, not the eyes behind them.

"It was the first time I saw a fire being put out," she went on. "You see, in China we believe fires are started by evil spirits. So when a house catches fire, we try to scare the spirits away." She paused, as if to emphasize the words that followed. "With noise. Drums and cymbals. I've seen many houses burn to the ground to the beating of drums. We have a five-thousand-year-old culture, and in all those five thousand years it's never once occurred to us to put a fire out with water.

"The English set up a fire brigade in Shanghai. A house opposite me caught fire. It started in the evening, and the English gentlemen, who were all volunteers, arrived straight from a dinner party, wearing top hats, tailcoats, and starched white shirt collars, which quickly became filthy from the soot. They pointed large hoses at the flames. When the fire hissed and died away and most of the house was still standing—that was the moment I fell in love with the West. Do you understand what I'm saying, Monsieur Madsen? My philosophy is basically very simple. You put out fire with water. That's why I live here and not in China."

She laughed. He laughed back and nodded.

"Well, my philosophy tends to be that water's for sailing on. But I don't suppose that deep down we're so different."

It was at that moment that his awe turned into love. Here was a woman whose attitude to life resembled his. Her cheerful directness liberated him. Her beauty suddenly became accessible. When Cheng Sumei took over her husband's business after his death and carried it on successfully, it came as no surprise to Albert. He'd already spotted that she had it in her.

He wasn't just one man with her. He was several. Any sailor, by necessity, must be one man at home, another on the deck, and a third in a foreign port. But his inner selves are separated in time and space, always by vast distances: just like a ship, he has waterproof bulkheads inside, to prevent sinking. But with Cheng Sumei, Albert found he could be several men at once. He was first and foremost the man he considered his real self, the sailor and captain, and he often thought that the two of them, Cheng Sumei and Albert Madsen, were like two captains on the same vessel—an unlikely couple who nonetheless respected each other's authority and never risked the safety of their ship.

But he was also the man he remembered from the brothel visits of his youth. That self wasn't always rough. In the brothels of Bahia or Buenos Aires, a young seaman was a dumbstruck guest in marble palaces with fountains and palms, silk sheets, and mirrored ceilings and walls. And the girl, yes, she was a compliant spirit put on this earth to grant him his wishes in a brief, faithless moment, but though she was compliant she was also superior. How speechless, how blushing, how shy and ignorant, and at the same time how infinitely grateful he'd felt in her skillful hands, which knew things about his body that he'd never even suspected: that battered body, with its permanently aching muscles, sore from the rigging, covered with saltwater blisters and unhealed cuts, always on guard, always ready to fight back in the bitter necessity of self-assertion.

He'd never felt like anyone's master in those brothels. He didn't visit them to enjoy a master's dubious privileges: he'd felt like a guest and behaved with polite restraint. In them, his permanently clenched fists briefly opened up. But he learned nothing. He wasn't a better lover when he left. He remained the same clumsy, awkward man, made brutal by sheer uncertainty when it came to women.

With Cheng Sumei, it was like the brothel visits of his youth. In the bedroom she was a compliant and yet superior spirit. In their encounters he became his younger self. He didn't know whether or not he was a good lover. Desire had never been a demanding inhabitant of his body: it had never had the power to rearrange his life. It was not lovemaking he missed as he lay awake. It was a human being.

He finished drying himself and ran a hand through his short, trimmed hair, which had begun to dry despite the humidity of the bathroom. He found a pair of scissors and started trimming his beard. He studied his face in the mirror and wondered what it was he'd awakened in Klara Friis. His age and position offered security. He presumed that was what she was looking for. And he'd seen gratitude in her eyes when he listened to her story about the flood on Birkholm.

What did he want from her? Was it just about gratified vanity? Though she wasn't exactly pretty, the traces of grief had vanished from her face, which when they first met had seemed both swollen and sunken. She dressed with more care nowadays: she'd lost the shapelessness of her pregnancy and he could see that she had a lovely figure. But it wasn't her looks that attracted him. Nor was it her personality. He didn't actually know her at all. Her words were few and reticent, stilted by the difference in social rank they were both only too well aware of. It was something impersonal that had stirred this feeling in him, which he still hesitated to acknowledge as desire. No, it wasn't her. It wasn't even the woman in her. It was her youth, a fundamental force of nature that had reawakened in her along with the summer, a last reflection of what she'd once been before childbirth and poverty started to grind her down, and grief struck. It was his own doing, in a way. His attentiveness, which to begin with had been nothing but kindness, had rekindled her youthfulness.

The boy had come first. Then the three of them had sat down together and suddenly they'd resembled a family, the family he had
never had, the family she'd lost. But they could not be that family unless he and Klara behaved like a man and a woman.

He was old. Again, he reminded himself of that. Old men had their
regular orbits like planets that circle a sun. But the sun they circled
was cooling down. He halted his reflections at this point. He ought to
stay in his rightful orbit, around the fading sun. He was in the ice age
of his life, and any open ground not yet covered by snow could only
produce lichen.

But his hands spoke a different language when he tied the laces
on his white canvas shoes and settled a straw hat on his head. As he
passed through the dining room, he stopped and took a white daisy
from the bouquet his housekeeper had placed in the middle of the
table. In front of the mirror in the hall he ran his hand through his
hair once more, and put the daisy in the buttonhole of his summer
jacket. Then he opened the front door and walked down the steps to
Prinsegade, filled with the blind triumph that people sometimes experience when they've conquered their own better judgment.

When albert was asked to step inside the house, Knud Erik was there. Klara Friis had put up her long hair; he noticed that she'd washed it. He rarely paid attention to the seasonal displays of changing fashions in the shop window of I. C. Jensen in Kirkestræde, but he could tell from the cut of her dress, which reached halfway down her calves, that it wasn't new. She must have produced it for this occasion: a garment set aside from the first years of her marriage, perhaps, or even an earlier time, when she was full of youth and expectation.

The table was set for three, which both disappointed and reassured him. Knud Erik's presence ruled out any blunders occurring, and yet Klara Friis blushed when she opened the door to him. She stepped aside, just as she'd done this morning, and bowed her head slightly. Her neck, exposed below her chignon, looked so delicate that he had to suppress an urge to cross the line between protectiveness and possessive desire, and put his hand on it.

Little Edith was nowhere to be seen, and he asked after her. Klara told him that she'd already eaten and had been put to bed.

She invited them to sit down at the table. Knud Erik, whose sun-bleached hair had been combed through wet, was the last to pull up his chair. He sat down with an unnatural stiffness and stared into the distance. A big bowl of freshly boiled shrimp stood in the middle of the table. Albert had brought the wine in a basket, wrapped in a damask napkin. He took it out and opened it with a little pop. He'd had trouble deciding whether to pack wineglasses too. He knew that she wouldn't have any, but feared that if he brought his own, she might interpret it as a criticism, an underscoring of the poverty of both her home and her life. In the end, it was his sense of tradition that won the argument. He didn't fancy drinking good wine from an ordinary glass, so he took his best crystal. Old men and their habits indeed. He'd even brought a corkscrew.

He poured the wine into the glasses, glancing at Knud Erik, who was watching him attentively. "I nearly forgot you," he said, and pulled out a bottle of cordial and placed it in front of him.

The boy laughed. "Just like a picnic," he said. He looked at the condensation on the wine bottle and touched it carefully. "It's cold," he said, and his voice was filled with wonder.

Albert Madsen and Klara Friis clinked glasses. She clutched hers as if afraid of dropping it. He glanced at her over the rim of his own. She blushed, unfamiliar with the rituals surrounding the consumption of wine. Her glance flickered confusedly away from the table, then she threw her head back and swigged from the glass, as though its pale contents were medicine, best downed quickly. She grimaced, then reddened again.

"Please, may I taste it?" Knud Erik said.

"It's not for children." His mother gave him a severe look. Albert could see that her rebuke was an attempt to hide her confusion at this meal, which was unlike anything she'd ever taken part in.

"I'm not a child," the boy retorted. "I earn my own money."

"Then you're allowed a taste." Albert winked at Knud Erik's mother and passed his glass to the boy, who took it carefully with both hands before raising it tentatively to his lips, as though already regretting his nerve.

"Just one small sip," his mother ordered him.

Knud Erik grimaced.

"Ugh," he exclaimed. "It tastes sour."

Albert laughed. "I think your mother agrees."

"Yes," she admitted. "I don't think wine is for me."

"It's always like that to start with. Later you'll learn to appreciate it."

"Not me," Knud Erik declared. "I'll never learn to appreciate it."

Albert wished that time could stop right then. He had a family. He was sitting at dinner with a boy who could be his grandchild and a woman who could be his daughter, and he wanted nothing more. He'd put the loneliness of the war years behind him. He almost felt he had a home that consisted of more than just himself and his memories.

He thought of his afternoon in the bath and his preening in front of the mirror. He'd dressed up, putting on a summer jacket and fixing a flower in his buttonhole. Perhaps there was a spark left in him. But if so, it was the last spark: the one that flares suddenly in the embers of a fire that has burned itself out overnight. Finding no nourishment in ashes, it soon fades. For a moment he'd given in to vanity, but it wasn't a woman he needed. It was this: two people he could be something to and who, by mere virtue of their presence, could be something to him.

He twirled the stem of the wineglass and chuckled to himself.

"What are you laughing at?"

"Oh, I'm not sure I even know, I just feel so comfortable here. Put it down to contentment."

"That's good to hear." She got up. "Time for dessert."

She brought in a bowl of rhubarb compote and a jug of cream. Knud Erik followed her, bearing three smaller bowls, which he placed in front of them.

"You're good at helping your mother, I see."

"Yes, he's a good boy."

She sat down and served them.

"When you've finished you may go outside to play."

Knud Erik wolfed down his compote, sending the cream splashing over the tablecloth. She frowned at him but didn't speak. Then he disappeared out the door. She looked after him and laughed.

"Someone's got places to go."

"It's summer," Albert said.

The low-ceilinged room was semi-dark, but outside, the street was bright as day. He pushed back his chair. "Thank you, that was lovely. I suppose I'd better be off home now."

She bowed her head as though he'd rejected her. "Please stay a little longer," she begged, and looked at him. "See, I haven't even finished my wine. You did promise you'd teach me to enjoy it. So you can't abandon me now." Her voice was coquettish, as if she was permitting herself greater freedom now that her son was absent.

"I'll stay a little longer, then. May I suggest that we go outside into the garden and enjoy the summer evening?"

He could see that she was taken aback by this proposal. Her garden was small, a kitchen garden—more decorative than a bare yard but not a place she'd invite guests or spend a spare hour.

"Allow me," he said, picking up two of the high-backed, dark-varnished dining room chairs. He carried them through the kitchen and set them next to each other in the garden while Klara disappeared into the bedroom to check on Edith, who had slept soundly through the entire meal. When she returned they clinked glasses once more, and this time when he tried to catch her eye across the rim, she responded. The soft evening light transformed her pale skin, giving it an enigmatic, intense glow. She smiled at him. He smiled back. For a moment they were both embarrassed.

He looked across the small garden. At the back he saw black currant and gooseberry bushes. There were also potatoes and rhubarb. A small gravel path led to a flower bed bordered with conch shells bleached by salt water and sun; you'd find the same shells bordering most gardens in Marstal. Growing next to the house was a small rose bed. There was no terrace; he'd had to balance the chairs on the flagstones that had been laid here and there on the soil. There were no weeds between the stones, and he could see that the garden was neatly tended.

From the street came the sound of children's cries, while in the neighboring gardens women were chatting quietly. An outsider wouldn't have noticed the absence of male voices, but Albert did. Summer was the women's season. At the first sign of spring, the ships began preparing to leave the shelter of the breakwater. Some would return at Christmas, but many, bound on longer voyages, would be gone for years. In the absence of the menfolk, it was the women who ran the town. Now he sat in the midst of this female life, surrounded by summer light and the scent of elderberries, and experienced a part of Marstal in a way he hadn't done in years.

He leaned forward and picked up a conch. He put it against his ear and listened to the rush coming from the spiral within.

"Listen," he said, and handed it to her. "They've invented the radio now. But when I was a child, we had these for radios."

Instead of putting it to her ear, Klara replaced the shell in the border, with an expression that suggested he'd disturbed a secret harmony in her garden by picking it up.

The conch had a melody for everyone who listened to it. For the young, the conch sang of longing for distant shores; for the old it sang of absence and sorrow. It had a song for the young and another one for the old, one for the men and one for the women, and the women's song was always the same, as monotonous as the beating of the waves against the beach: loss, loss. The conch offered them no enchantment. When they put their ear to it, all they heard was the echo of their mourning.

They sat in the garden for half an hour. The sun went down behind a rooftop, and a grainy twilight filtered between the gooseberry and black currant bushes as the sky turned an even deeper violet.

"Oh, it's way past his bedtime!"

Klara leapt to her feet. She'd just remembered her boy. It was time for Albert to leave, but before he managed to stand up she'd disappeared through the door to the kitchen. He brought the chairs back inside and put them by the dining table, then waited in the parlor until she returned with Knud Erik.

"I've taken up far too much of your time," he said apologetically.

"But you haven't even had your coffee!" She led him to the table and pushed him down in one of the chairs. Her movements had acquired a new freedom. "Now you stay here while I make it." Pulling out a drawer of linens, she made up a bed for Knud Erik on the sofa and then left. The boy undressed and crept under the covers.

"Are we going fishing tomorrow morning?" he asked.

"No, not tomorrow. We can row to Langeholm and swim there, if you like."

But there was no reply. The boy was already asleep.

Klara appeared from the kitchen with a pot of coffee in her hand.

"It's been a long day."

She sat down in front of him and filled his cup. The lamp in the parlor had not yet been lit, and in the dusk her pale skin shone above the neck of her dress. They sat for a while in silence as the dark intensified around them. They could hear Knud Erik breathing from the sofa, in the undisturbed rhythm of sleep. Somewhere nearby a clock struck ten, deep and sonorous. In the growing darkness her features grew indistinct and began to swim before his eyes, as if making strange grimaces.

"Thank you for a lovely evening," he said, and got up.

She was as startled, as if she'd been suddenly wakened.

"Are you leaving now?"

Her face was a white spot in the dusk, and he couldn't read its expression. Was she tipsy? She'd drunk the first glass and he'd poured her a second. She'd had no more than that, but women have less tolerance for it than men. He felt a sudden misgiving about the whole situation. He wanted to get away.

She rose to her feet and accompanied him to the hall. But she didn't turn on the light, and she closed the parlor door behind them. His heart was hammering at the wall of his chest like a prisoner begging for release. Again he felt the sharp shooting pain in his head. Then he felt her. Her hands fumbled on his chest, apparently unaware of his pounding heart. Then, abruptly, she flung her arms around his neck.

"I need to say goodbye to you properly," she mumbled.

Her lips moved searchingly across his face until they found his mouth and pressed against it. The pounding of his heart grew stronger. A black wave surged inside him and rendered him helpless. He wanted to push her away, but he couldn't. She leaned into him with all her weight; he could feel the soft pressure of her breasts. Her hips rubbed against his. A moan escaped from her, like the prelude to a fit of tears.

"Ma" came a voice from the parlor.

She froze and held her breath.

"Ma, where are you?"

Klara gasped, then flinched.

"I'm here, in the hall."

"You sound so strange. Is anything wrong?"

"No, go back to sleep. It's late."

"What are you doing, Ma?"

"I'm saying goodbye to Captain Madsen."

"I want to say goodbye too."

They heard him shuffle across the floor. Then he stood in the doorway, a dark silhouette.

"Why isn't the light on?"

Klara found the switch and flicked it. Albert ran a hand through the boy's hair.

"Good night, son. I think your mother is right, it's time to turn in."

He turned to Klara but avoided looking at her face.

"Good night, Mrs. Friis, and thank you for a lovely evening."

He shook her hand. Her palm was hot and sweaty. Even this formal contact suddenly felt too intimate. He withdrew his hand and took his straw hat from the coat rack. Then he opened the door.

He heard it close behind him. Too agitated to go straight home, he headed toward the harbor. Turning into Havnegade, he saw a figure get up from the skipper's bench across from Sønderrenden.

"Good evening, Captain Madsen."

Albert nodded briefly from under his straw hat. He had no desire to strike up a conversation. But the other man caught up with him and began walking beside him along Havnegade.

"You're out late."

Albert recognized Herman's thickset shape.

"I don't believe I need to account to you for my movements," he said curtly.

"Nice clothes," said Herman, ignoring the hostility in Albert's voice. Albert increased his pace. Herman did the same. "You seem quite youthful tonight." He smirked, making no attempt to hide the falseness of this remark. Albert stopped abruptly and turned to face the young man.

"Tell me, what do you want from me?"

Herman flung out his hands. "Want from you? What do you mean? I don't want anything from you. I just thought I'd keep you company for a while. But perhaps you prefer to be alone?" Albert made no reply, but turned and continued along Havnegade. He passed the slipways and the shipyard. "Pleasant dreams!" Herman called out after him. "You could probably do with a good night's sleep after this evening's exertions."

Albert jumped, and tightened his grip on his walking stick. He briefly considered going back and punishing the scoundrel, but dropped the thought instantly. Those days were long gone. They were roughly the same height and breadth, he and Herman, but there was half a century between them. It wouldn't be an equal match. Not only would he lose the fight, he'd lose his dignity too. The realization knocked him flat. He might as well already be lying on the ground, bleeding.

He walked up the stone steps to the house in Prinsegade and let himself in. He entered the drawing room without switching on the light and sat down heavily on the sofa. How could that rogue know what had occurred at the widow's? Had he been spying on them, or was he just guessing? Was it so obvious what was going on? But the events of the evening had surprised even him. Had others seen things that he'd failed to spot himself?

Yes, he'd toyed with a few notions when he was getting ready for his dinner with her, he'd admit that much. But he realized too that he hadn't really wanted it enough. He'd entertained the possibility that something might happen. But now that it had, he suddenly felt exposed. If Herman could see it, then the whole town could. He had to stop it now. He understood what it was he'd felt in the hall, when Klara Friis surrendered to him. It was fear, fear of his routine life being knocked out of its orbit, fear of life's unpredictability, fear that everything he'd parted from in preparation for his twilight years would reclaim him. And Klara, he knew, had more strength than him. Just as Herman did. And for the same reason: they were young.

A panting embrace in a darkened hall, a street fight: those were the prerogatives of youth, not of age, and God help the old man who came too near youth and thought he could warm himself by its fire. The price for that was ridicule, and he'd have to pay.

The old should stick to their dying sun. This house, in which he'd built up and managed his business—this was the sun he circled. He shouldn't try to rebel against the laws of gravity that controlled life's end. During the war he'd earned a reputation for being strange. Now perhaps he was stuck with that reputation; well, he could live with that. But he didn't want to be thought of as a fool. To walk around the town fully dressed and yet appear naked to the world was a shame he couldn't bear.

The next day he slept late and didn't venture out. The following day he rowed to Sorekrogen, alone, to tend to his shrimp nets. They were full as always: almost ten pounds. He emptied the nets into the container of the boat well and sat contemplating the myriad tiny creatures. He remembered how proudly Knud Erik had walked home to his mother in Snaregade with his bucket full of them. He heaved the container back onto the rail and tipped it into the water. For a brief moment the shrimp swarmed in a brown cloud, then vanished.

Being on the water brought him no peace. He missed the boy. But there was something else, something stronger, tearing at him: an inner pressure that swelled the more he refused acknowledge it. It hadn't just been fear he'd felt when Klara had pressed herself against him in the hall. There'd been a physical stirring too, one that he hadn't felt in years. Now the mere thought of that episode in the hallway gave him an unexpected erection.

An old man in a boat on the sea on a summer's morning, with an erection. He was furious with himself. And he needed relief at the same time. He'd reached the critical stage of an illness. The only cure for it was time. And distance.

AFTER TWO WEEKS he came home and found Klara Friis in his drawing room. She was sitting on the edge of the sofa when he entered, wearing the same dress she'd worn on that fateful evening. He could see the contours of her body beneath the thin, loose-fitting fabric.

"Your housekeeper let me in. I told her I had an important message."

He remained standing in the doorway, looking at her guardedly. He knew his behavior was rude, but he was held back by the fear that he might do something impulsive if he took another step. The urge he'd refused to name in his restless hours on the water took hold of him again, just as it had that night in the darkness of the hallway. Fear and excitement at the same time.

"It's Knud Erik," she said. "He doesn't understand why we don't see you anymore. He asks after you every day, but he's afraid to visit you. Have you dropped him completely?" She directed her gaze at him. At the mention of Knud Erik his fear seemed to evaporate.

"My dear Klara," he said, and went over to her.

He took her hands in his. She looked at him, and her eyes suddenly reddened.

"There's something else. I miss you terribly too!"

She freed her hands and flung her arms around him, pressing her lips against his. Suddenly he was overcome by rage. He grabbed hold of her waist to push her away, but his hands did the opposite. He pressed her to him as he kissed her hard, without tenderness. She buckled, and he pushed her down onto the sofa. Landing heavily on top of her, he tugged at her dress.

"Wait, wait," she breathed.

She pulled her dress up around her waist and got herself ready for him. His anger hadn't left. When he entered her, gasping, he struck her hard across her face. In the excitement of the moment it seemed to him that he was hitting her in self-defense, in protest at her youth and what she'd lured him into. Then he collapsed, panting, already done, both with his own violence and with her surrendering body, which he'd barely seen or felt. She clung to him, apparently unaffected by the blow, which had left her cheek burning red.

Albert's head lay on her chest. He felt its softness and resented it. In her arms he was a defenseless child. He already knew that he was trapped. He'd come back to her and then he'd hit her again. He grew red with shame. He freed himself from her arms and started rearranging his clothes. She came up to him and rested her cheek on his shoulder. The mark of his hand was still visible.

"Are you fond of me?" she asked. "Are you really fond of me?"

"Yes, yes," he snapped. "Now let me get my clothes in order."

He didn't recognize himself. He felt no triumph in his conquest. Instead, the feeling that a disaster had occurred was slowly spreading through him.

Klara got up and went over to a mirror hanging above a chest of drawers to fix her hair. When she'd finished, she turned to him.

"What do you want me to tell Knud Erik?" He shrugged and turned his head away. "He knows I've been to see you. He'll be very disappointed if you drop him."

"I'll be there to pick him up tomorrow. We'll go out and catch some shrimp."

In the hall they grew formal again, shaking hands when she left. The small dark room was like a lobby entrance to the town outside, and to its ever-curious eyes. Albert remained in the doorway as she stepped into the street. Across the way Mrs. Jensen, the draper's wife, was going up the granite steps to the bank. He nodded to her. She threw a critical glance at Klara from underneath the brim of her black lacquered straw hat and returned his greeting with a curt nod. His public undressing had begun.

When he turned up to find Knud Erik the next day, the boy wasn't there. He'd been sent to fetch milk and was due to return soon, his mother said. Little Edith was having her midday nap. To his horror he saw that one side of Klara's face was swollen and her cheek had turned yellow and blue.

"Don't look at me like that," she said. She took his hand and held it against her cheek affectionately. "It doesn't matter."

Leaning against the kitchen table, she stretched her hands out to him as if to pull him toward her. He turned his face away, but his body gave in to her invitation. He felt it once again, his unmentionable old man's erection. He hated himself as he tore at her dress to get it up around her hips. He entered her again, but this time he quickly grew limp and slid out. He'd forgotten all about the boy, then suddenly remembered him and realized how rash and irresponsible their frantic coupling had been.

But she kept holding him close. He hadn't hit her this time, but he tore himself away with a violent movement. He didn't know what they wanted from each other, and he told her so.

"Nothing good will come of this." She didn't reply, but rested her head against his chest in a kind of deaf-and-dumb surrender, which only increased his anger. "Do you hear?" he said, shaking her.

Her head lolled as if she were barely conscious. Then they heard the boy at the door and quickly let go. Knud Erik carried the milk pail into the kitchen and put in on the table.

It seemed to Albert that the boy's manner was guarded, but soon he realized that the awkwardness was his own. They'd walked down to the harbor and rowed the length of its entrance before he returned to his familiar ease. He'd imagined that he might need to explain his long absence, but the boy didn't ask about it. Instead he sat on the thwart and showed off his rowing skills, his face red with eagerness and exertion.

Albert suspected that the mother had used her son's distress as a pretext for coming to see him. If only he could keep the two emotions separate—love of the son and fascination with the mother. But she wouldn't leave him alone. Who had started it? Should he be honest enough to admit that it wasn't her, but something in him, that had ruptured his tranquility? And what was that? Desire? Or the memory of desire? Was it longing for that part of life he'd failed to grasp before, which was now reoffering itself a final time, in the shape of Klara Friis?

Whatever it was made no difference now. He couldn't endanger his bond with the boy. But how was he to stop it?

Klara and Albert didn't speak much, and when they did it was mostly about everyday matters, as if they'd known each other a long time, and all the important things had already been said. He thought that perhaps they had little to say to each other. In the beginning there'd been a coziness to their silent companionship at the dining table or over a cup of coffee, the four of them. Now their meetings were filled with a tense, electric impatience while they waited to be alone, without the boy.

Little Edith toddled around the floor and spoke her first words. He was always uncomfortable when she yanked at his trouser leg and looked up at him expectantly. He would lift her onto his knee and bounce her up and down. But his face stayed rigid and he didn't know what to say to her. *Gallopy, gallopy*, he supposed. But he remained silent.

"Daddy," she said one day.

He looked over at Klara, who smiled, embarrassed.

"I don't know where she got that from. It's not from me."

Did language grow in a child like milk teeth? Was *Daddy* a natural part of her budding vocabulary?

He stopped bouncing her. No more gallopy, gallopy. He looked sternly at the child in front of him. "No," he said. "Not Daddy. Albert."

Edith began to cry.

No intimacy ever developed between them. They never spent a whole night in each other's company; indeed, they never even lay naked together, exhausted in a moment of tender calm after lovemaking. On the contrary, their encounters were always hectic and semi-hostile. Every time he held her, his chest became a battlefield: he was filled with reluctance, but his attraction won out, and the result was inevitably that he took her with a ruthlessness that he later regretted. When she moaned loudly as he thrust into her, he was never sure whether it was from ecstasy or pain. He would come with the sound of a man being punched in the stomach.

He hadn't hit her again, but he knew that this was only because his first blow had left evidence on her face, which would be visible to the whole town. Only fear for his reputation stayed his hand when the urge to hurt her overwhelmed him. Oh yes, his stiff member could have the same effect as a punch, and be used to inflict pain, but here he was betrayed by his age. He didn't have the stamina he once had.

They made love like two people who are tied to others and can only meet illicitly, briefly, and breathlessly. And that was indeed their situation: he was married to his old age, and she to her youth. The bridge where they were supposed to meet cracked the moment they stepped on it. He didn't understand himself, he didn't understand her, and he knew that if he asked her to explain her feelings for him, he'd get no reply.

Knud Erik returned to school, and a rainy autumn forced them to abandon the trips, but their meetings continued. They thought of other things to do. Knud Erik would visit him frequently in the afternoons, and they'd go through his homework together while the light faded outside. Sometimes Albert would go over to Snaregade, but Klara never came to his house. It hadn't been agreed on formally, but the understanding lay in the air between them. He could enter her world, but she couldn't enter his.

Albert stopped visiting the marine painter's widow, and it felt like final proof of his shame. Did the whole town know what was going on? He was sure it did. He couldn't put his finger on one thing in particular, but the signs were all about him. A passerby would give him a stare, a conversation on a bench would suddenly stop when he passed, a shopkeeper whom he'd long been familiar with would greet him with a new reserve.

Sometimes he'd run into Herman. After their confrontation, the young man no longer spoke to him, but wryly lifted a finger to his hat, or grinned coarsely, as though they were fellow conspirators. Albert ignored him but worried about how often he encountered him on his way to or from Snaregade. Did that layabout have nothing better to do than spy on him?

We saw him sitting late at night in the bay window facing Prinsegade, with a book in his hand, trying to read. Most of the time, though, he simply stared into space.

What was he thinking about? He was old, but he hadn't found peace.

Had he realized that a long life didn't automatically bestow wisdom?

Albert and Klara did have one thing in common: their concern for Knud Erik. She trusted all his views about the boy implicitly, even though he'd never had children of his own. His presence set Klara apart from most Marstal women who, with their husbands at sea, were forced into the role of father as well as mother. Any doubts about their

we, the drowned

ability to achieve this they'd hide behind a strict, almost harsh manner. For many months of every year and sometimes for years on end, they lived life like a dress rehearsal for widowhood.

Klara Friis was now experiencing the rare privilege of having a man around, an unexpected luxury that made her surrender to an inner weakness, which she should have fought. She handed things over to him and stopped making her own decisions. She looked to Albert as though expecting that from now on, he'd organize her life.

She stood firm on only one point: Knud Erik was not to follow in his father's footsteps. She'd listened to the conch and she'd heard the rush of death. Her son must never make a living at sea. When she talked about this, she abandoned the passivity that characterized her behavior in Albert's presence: she straightened up in her chair and her voice took on an unwonted sharpness.

The boy flinched whenever Klara raised the subject. Albert had heard him promise his mother that he'd never be a sailor. But the boy's bad conscience was written all over his face. Albert almost felt guilty himself, though he'd long concluded, privately, that things could go no other way. Indeed, he'd been part of the boy's inspiration. His stories, the endless conversations about foreign countries and ships, the rowing and sculling, all these had pushed the impressionable boy in that direction. But there were other influences too, which lay beyond the control of a mother or a father. The constant roar of the sea beyond the breakwater; the sight of topsail schooners, topgallant schooners, and brigantines, with the early spring wind in their sails, ready for their big migration to the great ports of call: Rio de la Plata, Newfoundland, Oporto, Le Havre, Valparaiso, Callao, and Sydney—legendary places that formed part of every boy's mental geography and pulled at his young soul.

Klara Friis knew this. There was a hint of pleading in her sharpness, and it was directed at Albert. He had the power to wrench the boy in a different direction if he would only use it.

She looked from the boy to the old man and back again, and she sensed a conspiracy between them. "How's your reading going?" she asked her son.

"Well," the boy replied, as unforthcoming as any child questioned about school.

"He's only just started his second year, but he's already reading fluently," Albert said approvingly.

Klara looked at him. "So he's good at schoolwork," she stated. "Perhaps ship brokering would suit him?"

The question took Albert by surprise. He had to admit that he'd never imagined that path for the boy. In his view, the career of a good ship broker didn't begin in an office. It began on deck, then spread into the more abstract world of freight rates. That was how he'd done it, and he'd expect all future ship brokers to do likewise.

"It most definitely would," he said, but his tone was evasive. He couldn't bring himself to explain his principles to her. Sensing his lack of enthusiasm, she took it to mean that he wouldn't be prepared to help the boy. Her mouth became a thin line, and she slumped in silence. "There are many things you can become if you get good marks. Surely it's a little early—"

She interrupted him. "I know what you're going to say. You're going to say that a man with a good education can pass the navigation exam as well. But believe me, that's not the path my boy's going to take." She turned to her son. "Do you hear, Knud Erik?"

The boy nodded mutely and lowered his head. A tear rolled down his cheek and he breathed in with a loud sob. Then he jumped up from the chair and ran into the kitchen. Klara gave Albert an accusing look, as though it was he, rather than she, who'd prompted the boy's tears.

"There are several ship broker's offices in this town," he said. "I can easily get a place for him when the time comes."

"That would be wonderful." Her face softened and she blessed him with a smile. Then she went into the kitchen to bring the boy back. He could hear her voice through the wall. He sat alone, feeling the emptiness of his promise.

"When the time comes," he repeated to himself, and did a quick mental calculation. "When that time comes, I'll be dead."

WHEN KLARA WAS expecting a visit from Albert, she heard an unfamiliar knock on the door. She went to open it and found Herman on the steps. He was an acquaintance of hers dating back to the time when her husband was alive. Henning had sailed with Herman and talked about him. He'd heard the rumors about Herman murdering his stepfather all right, but he hadn't believed them. Henning always said Herman was a good mate. They'd shared a fondness for grandiose talk, and she suspected that for the most part, their comradeship had been forged in sailors' bars.

When Herman reappeared in Marstal, he'd taken the time to stop by and offer his condolences. She'd never forgotten that, and it had disposed her more favorably toward him. She hadn't met him since then, but he always greeted her kindly when they passed in the street, and on one occasion he'd actually stopped to ask her if there was anything she needed.

Now he was standing at her door. She took a step back in surprise.

"I just wanted to see how you were getting on," he said. Without waiting for an invitation, he strode over the threshold. For a moment they stood jammed in the small hallway, before continuing into the parlor. "Hello," he said jovially to Knud Erik, and ruffled the boy's blond hair as if they were old friends. Knud Erik, who didn't know him, took a step back, while Klara remained in the doorway.

"He's tired," she said.

"I won't be staying long." Herman sat down on the sofa and crossed his legs. "I hear you're doing well." Klara didn't reply. He looked at her. "Old Madsen isn't a bad match."

She stared harshly. "What are you talking about?"

"What am I talking about? The same thing everyone in town's talking about. We're hearing wedding bells. You and the children provided for: good thinking."

Klara blushed scarlet. She glanced down and chewed her lower lip. When she lifted her head, she avoided looking at her visitor.

"That's just people talking," she said weakly.

Herman eased into the sofa, as though in his own home. "Now take it easy," he said. "A boy needs a father. I understand old men are good with children. All right, so he's not always very careful. But a bit of water never hurt anyone."

"What do you mean?" Her question came out as a whisper. Knud Erik was watching both of them, but Klara had forgotten his presence.

"Well, the boy fell off the boat one day and nearly drowned. But I expect Madsen told you."

Klara was shocked. She turned to Knud Erik. "Is that true, what Herman says? Did you nearly drown?"

Knud Erik looked at the floor and grew red. "It was nothing. I just fell into the water."

Klara opened the door to the hall. "I think you'd better leave," she said to Herman in a voice that had suddenly recovered its strength.

"By all means, if I'm not welcome." Herman heaved his large body up from the sofa. When he reached the doorway he turned. "I'll stop by another day."

Klara slammed the front door behind him. Then she sat down on a chair and folded her hands. Her knuckles grew white, and her face assumed a look of concentration. The boy peered at her anxiously.

After a while she broke the silence. "Why didn't you tell me that you'd fallen into the water?"

"But, Ma, it was nothing."

"Nothing! You could have drowned. Why didn't you tell me?" Knud Erik pressed his lips together. "Did Captain Madsen tell you not to tell me? Answer me!"

He blinked and looked away. A tear slid down his cheek. He swallowed. And then nodded.

When Albert turned up an hour later, Klara received him at the front door with Edith on her hip. "What do you want?" she snapped, without returning his greeting.

She looked at him directly, and the fury in her eyes gave her femininity a hint of something feral. A mother defending her young, he thought, and understood in that instant that he wasn't welcome inside. She'd answered the door only to deny him access to the house. He wouldn't be allowed in to assert his authority; no, he was to stand in the street and be made to feel small.

Knud Erik appeared by her side. "Go back inside," she ordered him. The boy disappeared into the house. Again she turned to Albert and threw her head back as if she meant to butt him.

Albert instinctively took a step backward. "I don't understand . . ."

"You don't understand what?" Her tone was commanding, as though she was still speaking to the boy.

"I understand that you're angry with me. But I don't understand why."

"You don't understand why? Look at this child, take a good look. Look at me and my child. This child who's never known her father." Her voice grew louder and angrier.

Taking fright, Edith started screaming, and squirmed in her mother's arms to be let down. Then she stretched her arms toward Albert. "Daddy," she cried.

Klara's anger was undiminished. "And you want to turn Knud Erik into a sailor. So he can drown like his father! That's what you want, isn't it?" She sneered at him. "You want him to be like his father, like you, like the whole damned town, and drown like a real man!"

"But the war's over," he said, trying to placate her. Her accusation was by now a familiar one, but he'd never heard her state it with such venom.

"So sailors don't drown anymore? So ships don't get lost? So now everyone can survive a couple of days afloat after a winter storm in the North Atlantic—or even swim home to Marstal, if they're unlucky enough to lose their ship? So no one drowns in peacetime? Perhaps we've all grown gills? Is that what you're trying to tell me?"

He stood dumbstruck by this outburst from a woman whom he'd come to regard as half mute. He shrugged, in self-deprecation. Behind her he saw the boy's face at the window. But sensing Knud Erik's stare, his mother instantly shouted, "Get away from that window!"

"Mrs. Friis," Albert began, with the formality he'd use to address a stranger.

"Be quiet," she yelled. "I haven't finished with you. And then I have to hear it from strangers that the boy nearly drowned. That he fell into the water and that you calmly pulled him out and forbade him to tell me! Well, that's a fine thing. His own mother gets to hear it from others. And all those stories you fill his head with: shipwrecks, destruction, shrunken heads, mad adventures! Do you think that's the way to help a child who's lost his father at sea? Do you?"

She stared him right in the eye. He looked away. He didn't know what to say to her. He supposed she was right. He said so out loud. "I suppose you're right. I don't know anything about children."

"Don't know anything about children." She snorted. "No, you know nothing about children. You . . ." She looked him up and down as she searched for the right word. "You bachelor."

"I did my best," he said. "I was told that the boy needed some adult company and so I came."

"Yes, you came. And now you can leave. *I want to be a sailor like my dad who drowned!* What a fine lesson Knud Erik learned in your company."

The boy's face reappeared in the window. "You get away!" she screamed.

"Daddy," Edith cried again.

Klara Friis turned her back on him and slammed the door behind her.

He lifted his cap to the closed door. Then he turned and walked down Snaregade. He thought he could feel the boy's eyes on his back.

A heavy November rain was falling. A cold drop hit his neck and ran down under his scarf.

ALBERT LET HIMSELF into his house and walked around, switching the lights on. He was restless and didn't know what to do with himself. Still in his coat, he went upstairs and out onto the balcony. He was aware of the rain soaking his hair as he looked across to the breakwater. In the dusk the long line of boulders seemed to shimmer, as though made of fog.

He went back inside and asked his housekeeper to make him a pot of coffee. Then he sat down in the bay window. He watched as the dark deepened outside and felt as if he was holding his breath, and that if he let it out, something violent and unpredictable would happen: he'd start shouting, or crying, or doing something beyond his own imagination.

He was gripped by a feeling that took him right back to childhood: the same feeling he'd experienced on the beach at Drejet as he stared in horror at Karo, lying on the stones at the bottom of the cliff, with a broken back. He'd tried stroking the little dog's fur in the hope that a bit of tenderness might piece him back together. But in that moment, a notion that something irreparable had happened reverberated inside him with a long and terrifying echo. Now it reverberated again.

He took a sip of his hot sugarless coffee and tried to calm himself. He had to clear his thoughts. He'd never lived in a marriage, never experienced a woman's emotional outbursts. His relationship with Cheng Sumei had been ruled by what he'd jokingly called a meeting of souls. It was a meeting that had never existed between him and the young widow. How serious had Klara's anger been? Was her rage really caused by his conduct with Knud Erik? For heaven's sake, all boys fell into the water sooner or later. Someone pulled them out again and that was all there was to it.

No, he didn't believe the boy was the problem. Klara's anger was over something between the two of them, though for the life of him, he didn't know what. Or perhaps he himself was the problem. He both wanted her and didn't. She was a disruptive force in his life. Either way, she'd now rejected him. So wouldn't the wisest course of action be to let this rejection, however hurtful, stand?

Then what about the boy?

If only the two things could be kept separate. But they were hopelessly entangled now and he was the one responsible for that. His thoughts ran in circles, taking him nowhere. He drank his coffee and stared into the darkness.

His housekeeper entered and asked him when he'd like his dinner. He had no appetite and asked her to wait until eight o'clock. He put on his coat again and went back out into the November rain. A few minutes later he was standing opposite Mrs. Rasmussen's house in Teglgade. It was an age since he'd last been there. What did she think of him now? They'd been close, but he couldn't go back to her. She'd scrutinize him, and in that forthright way of hers, she'd target his sorest points. She'd do it with the best intentions, undoubtedly. But good intentions were of no use to him. He felt utterly lost.

He turned down Filosofgangen, then continued south along the harbor, and soon he found himself in front of Klara's house again. The light was on, but the windows were steamed up from the heating and he couldn't see inside. He continued his wandering. An hour later he was back there for the third time, furious with himself.

His longing kept drawing him back, but his fear drove him away again each time.

A period of waiting began. What was he waiting for? He didn't know. But he felt in his bones that his own death was drawing near. He looked at himself in the mirror, and where previously he'd found evidence of undiminished strength, he now saw only the ravages of time. He hadn't known what was lacking in his life until he met Knud Erik and Klara. Without them his old age was like Ithaca without Penelope and Telemachus. But with them? Could it even go on?

It seemed a countdown had started that couldn't be stopped.

He stopped going out while it was still light, for fear of meeting Knud Erik. He wouldn't know what to say to the boy. He'd be unable to handle seeing the lad's face light up. Or—far worse—seeing him turn away in disappointment.

But in the evenings, after a dinner that he mostly left untouched, his restlessness drove him out into the November darkness. We saw him wandering through the streets, icy drops of rain lashing his face.

He stood on Snaregade again, watching the lights glow in the windows of her house.

Then the waiting ended. One day Klara turned up outside his door and asked to come in. Her face displayed no joy at seeing him, but remained hard and closed, as if she'd made an important decision and was here to inform him of it. He helped her off with her coat and escorted her into the drawing room. She didn't look at him as she spoke, but stared down at her lap. Her voice was neutral, almost flat, as though she was reeling off something she'd memorized.

"I think we need to find a solution to what's happened between us," she began, and inhaled deeply. Only her uneven breathing betrayed any emotion. "We can't go on like this. You always visit us, Captain Madsen—I mean Albert. That's not right. I hear things and people stare and I'm well aware of what they're thinking. They think that I'm a kept woman, and I don't want people to think that of me."

She stopped. Her hands, which had lain unnaturally still in her lap during her speech, suddenly clenched.

"But, Klara, dearest . . ." He put out his own hand to touch her. She froze and then recoiled.

"Let me finish. It's no use saying they don't, because they do. I know more about what people think than you do, Captain Madsen." Still she didn't look up; instead, she focused her attention on her knuckles. "I can't live like that." She went on. "Henning's dead. I'm a widow. But Knud Erik and Edith need a father, and if it's not to be you, then it has to be someone else, Albert. That's how it is."

He noticed that she kept switching between his first name and his last. He couldn't follow her train of thought. "I'm an old man," he said helplessly.

"Not too old for us to—well, you know what I mean." She looked away, then took another deep breath, as if about to deliver a message that was not only generally outrageous but also against her own nature. "So I'm suggesting that Knud Erik, Edith, and I move in here and that the two of us get married. So that—so that things can be put right." Suddenly she slumped. Her clenched fists opened up. She'd delivered her message. Now, exhausted, she awaited her fate.

Everything inside him contracted. This he hadn't expected. He sensed that the situation demanded an immediate and unequivocal answer, but nothing approaching it emerged. Instead, he asked, "But do you love me?" He put the question in the dutifully polite tone he'd have used with a stranger; at this moment they didn't trust each other.

"Do you love *me*?" she retorted sharply.

"I've missed you," he said, and his voice grew thick. He couldn't come up with a declaration of love; nor was there any way he could express the chaos inside him more precisely. The way it came out, it sounded like a plea for mercy.

A moment of silence followed. A shiver ran through her, then she grabbed his hands and squeezed them between hers. "I've missed you too." She leaned into him and gave way to tears. Unburdened now, she could surrender. He stroked her back mechanically. His own paralysis hadn't abated. He didn't share her relief. They'd reached a point where he felt he couldn't possibly deny her request. His answer had practically been dictated to him.

Did he want it himself? The question was as unanswerable as whether or not he loved her.

"That's how it'll be then," he said eventually. He tried to give his words the ring of reassurance, but she couldn't possibly have missed their undertone of resignation.

She'd won. But the victory came without joy for either of them.

The next day they appeared together in public. As they strolled down Kirkestræde, she held his arm and he bore himself tall and straight—not out of pride, but to avoid looking decrepit next to her. From then on, she regularly visited his house with Knud Erik and Edith, and all of them dined together. She didn't stay the night. They'd never yet spent a night together and they weren't going to start now. The eyes of the town still rested on them. They both felt there was a line that shouldn't be crossed. They weren't married yet.

Knud Erik's attitude to Albert changed unexpectedly, as if now, for the first time, he realized that his father would never return. Someone else was going to take over the empty space at his mother's side. Before, he'd felt magnetically drawn to Albert. Now the magnet had switched, and it repelled him.

He joined his mother reluctantly on their visits to Albert, and when Albert called on them in Snaregade he acted introverted. It was as though he wanted each of them to himself, separately. When his mother's world and Albert's finally met, he felt he'd lost ownership of both. His old ease with Albert reemerged only when the two of them were alone together.

Albert didn't mention this to Klara. So much remained unuttered between them. The unspoken is sometimes the preferred language of lovers, but for him it was an unknown tongue for which he had no dictionary. He constantly felt a pressure that he couldn't fathom. They neither kissed nor embraced in Knud Erik's presence. They'd never done so before, either, but then they'd had something to hide. Now that everything was out in the open, they didn't exchange so much as a reassuring squeeze of the hand.

Was there really nothing more between them than the raw passion that came only in sudden, illicit bursts? Ejaculation without relief—could that be all they had? He was unfamiliar with the conventions of marriage and could not interpret what was happening between them.

When he'd stayed with Cheng Sumei, there'd been a certain measured respect in their behavior toward each other, which he'd attributed to the Chinese in her—and perhaps to the Dane in him. Yet when they sat at table, telegrams and documents covered with freight rates spread before them, they'd sometimes both look up and break into a sudden surprised smile, as though seeing each other for the first time. They'd never taken each other for granted.

They'd been intimate, but intimacy isn't the same as routine. There was always a spark that glowed.

He missed her.

"Was she beautiful, your Chinese lady?" Klara asked him once, out of the blue. The question startled Albert. He hadn't known that she'd heard the old rumors. He shrugged. He didn't feel like talking about Cheng Sumei with Klara. "Did she have tiny little Chinese feet?"

"No, her feet weren't bound. That was only for the daughters of rich men; poor girls escaped. She provided for herself from a very young age."

Klara stared into the distance. Apparently this piece of information had knocked her off course.

"So she was an orphan?" It was a word she'd avoided when he'd asked about her childhood on Birkholm.

"You could say that."

"So she was all alone in the world," Klara said.

He'd expected more questions, not only about Cheng Sumei's appearance, but also about their feelings for each other. He dreaded the conversation moving into a minefield where each reply might trigger unfavorable comparisons and fits of jealousy. And he knew how he'd have replied: with icy distance in his voice. This was private territory.

Instead, she fell silent. Several days passed before she asked him again. Her questioning now pursued a new direction, as though she'd been thinking something through.

"Was the Chinese lady very rich?" she asked.

He explained that she had become rich by marrying Presser and that she'd carried on his business very successfully after his death. "She was an independent woman," he said. "A businesswoman."

"All alone in the world," Klara said. "And then she became rich and independent." She spoke thoughtfully, as though this brief account of Cheng Sumei was leading her to a conclusion about herself.

Christmas was coming. For Albert, the holiday was a pretext for postponing the wedding to an as-yet-undecided date in the new year. Christmas had to be got out of the way first. Then they could get married and she could move in with him. She wouldn't be bringing much from Snaregade. Compared to his, her belongings were mostly junk. But perhaps they meant something to her?

He didn't ask, but he noticed that she looked at his home in a new light. She wandered about, assessing things; tentatively, she'd move an armchair or a table—just by a few inches—or shift a sofa when she thought he wasn't looking. But her eyes announced changes that no ruler could measure.

His world stood on the brink of a great upheaval. It was the only world he had left, a reduced kingdom, but still a kingdom, built just as much on habits as on furniture and floor space. Now he'd have to give up those habits too.

The distance between them grew. Every time she mentioned a possible date for their wedding, he made an evasive reply. His reluctance was blatant. He'd given his overall "I do," but it had been followed by a long series of small, unspoken "I don'ts."

When he thought about the moment he'd have to visit Pastor Abild-gaard and ask him to read their banns in church, everything inside him cringed. The minister with whom he'd shared so many discussions, the pastor whose duty to call on the bereaved he'd taken over in the dark years of the war because Abildgaard hadn't the strength to take care of his flock as a minister should, the man he'd seen in tears: now Albert would have to stand before him with all his own weaknesses laid bare.

Abildgaard was bound to be ironic, condescending even. He'd undoubtedly have the nerve to play the father figure: oh yes, he'd be unable to resist getting back at him by delivering some lecture to the far older and more experienced man who'd opposed him on countless issues in the past. And though Albert believed deep down that he'd left the power struggles of Marstal behind him long ago, he was still loath to turn up as a supplicant at the minister's office.

He hadn't altered that much. He hadn't surrendered the last of his fighting spirit. He didn't want to sacrifice his own dignity. Yet he knew he had to do it, because the dignity of another was at stake. Klara would have to live longer with a ruined reputation than he would. She had a small boy and an even smaller girl to take care of. She'd still have a life to live, long after he was gone. This was what her visit to him that day was really about. Her reticence abandoned and her self-effacement put aside, she had indeed been a mother defending her young.

They spent Christmas Eve in Prinsegade. The table was set in the dining room with a damask cloth, silver, and china. The Christmas tree stood in the drawing room. Albert had asked Knud Erik to help him decorate it, and the boy had done so, but with his new sullenness. Albert had a hard time getting used to it: he didn't understand it, and he caught himself interpreting it as ingratitude, a reaction that was entirely alien to him: he'd never before believed that the recipients of his gifts owed him anything. The result was that he grew irritated with both himself and Knud Erik, and he scolded the boy several times. He didn't notice that Knud Erik himself was actually ashamed of his own sulkiness and wanted to snap out of it, but couldn't. Albert's sudden reprimands only made it worse.

They carried their bad mood with them to the dinner table. Knud Erik didn't utter a word during the entire meal. Klara had returned to her old, passive self, behaving like a servant who has found herself at the master's table and expects to be sent back to the kitchen at any moment. Albert was gloomy and tense, filled with dark premonitions. His housekeeper waited on them, her face tight with disapproval. When he saw Klara shooting her a furtive glance, Albert knew immediately that his first task as her husband would be to dismiss the servant who'd been with him fifteen years.

Edith climbed onto his lap and started beating the rice pudding with her spoon. "Daddy," she said, and pulled his beard with her other hand. He said nothing. He'd given up trying to correct her.

They rose from the table for the traditional dance around the Christmas tree, but it was too wide for them to link hands around it, and by tacit agreement they avoided trying. Nor did they sing carols. We'll never be a family, Albert thought. We're just the wreckage of other families. She's a widow with two children, and I'm an eccentric hermit who should never have left his cave.

There were few presents under the tree. Klara hadn't bought many, and their new situation had deprived Albert of the joy of giving. He'd bought Klara a pair of leather gloves and Knud Erik a box of tin soldiers. Edith got a doll. There was a tobacco pouch for him. They unwrapped these gifts in silence and thanked one another politely.

When she left to go home to Snaregade, Klara turned in the doorway.

"We need to agree on a date, and you have to talk to Pastor Abildgaard."

They saw more of each other between Christmas and New Year's Day. Albert's sister visited from Svendborg, and later they went to see his friend Emanuel Kroman. Everyone regarded them as a couple now. People took it for granted that a wedding was imminent, but no one was indiscreet enough to inquire about the date.

The oppressive atmosphere between them did not improve, but they eventually agreed on a Saturday in late January. Once the New Year celebration was over, he'd have to pay a visit to the parsonage and make sure their banns were read.

January was relentlessly gray, with temperatures that hovered near the freezing point. Showers of rain and sleet swept through the deserted streets, and the shops kept their lights on all day. The parsonage in

Kirkestræde stayed lit too. Albert often passed it in the rain, but he didn't knock on the door. As with Klara's house in Snaregade in the days of their estrangement, he could neither stay clear of it nor enter. It wasn't just the meeting with Abildgaard. Surely he could survive that, blast it. No, something different and more powerful held him back, but no matter how hard he tried, he was unable to articulate what it was. He felt as if he was standing on the top of a steep cliff, waiting to step into the void. The mute instinct for survival: that was what prevented him from taking the fatal step. Nothing else.

"Why didn't you marry the Chinese lady?"

He didn't have to reply. He could see in her face that she'd already decided on an explanation of her own. "That's what you're like, isn't it?" she said. "You never marry them."

"Have you spoken to Pastor Abildgaard?" she asked the next time he came by Snaregade.

He looked away. "Not yet."

"Why not?"

He said nothing. A feeling of impotence overwhelmed him—shame too. He had no idea how to reply. She bit her lower lip. She didn't know how to open him up. Unaware of his fear and resistance, she focused instead on her own sense of being jilted.

"I'm not good enough for you?" she asked. "Is that it?" He didn't reply. "You promised." Her gaze grew firm.

"I'll do it." He was mumbling, a rare tone of voice for a man used to shouting orders on deck in high winds and who'd not dropped the habit once he came ashore. But this answer was worse than none at all.

"I don't know what to believe," she said, shaking her head. "I don't suppose it matters, anyway. I thought that was what you wanted."

"I'll do it," he repeated.

He hated himself and her because she was addressing him like a child, and it was his own fault.

"So do it, then. Do it tomorrow."

Unable to bear the humiliating situation any longer, he rose and left without saying goodbye.

"You're ashamed of me!" she screamed after him.

ON SHROVETIDE EVE the lamp above Albert's door was lit. To us this was an invitation: according to the traditional, unwritten law of Shrovetide Eve, every lit door was an open door. If you didn't want visits from revelers in fancy dress, you switched off the light.

The housekeeper answered our knocking and let us in. It looked as if she'd made preparations for our arrival. The punch bowl awaited us on a stand. We were just settling on the sofa and the chairs that had been set out for visitors when our host entered. We saw the surprise on his face—unpleasant surprise, disapproval even—and realized immediately that we'd made a mistake.

It could be that Albert and his housekeeper had misunderstood each other. But later we speculated that she'd let us in as an act of revenge. The prospect of another woman in the house couldn't have thrilled her, and this was her way of paying him back.

Obviously, we should have made our apologies and left at that point. But we were full of a particular energy that night. We weren't that easy to control.

Was it our fault that Albert later forgot himself? No, it was mostly his own. The scandal was his, not ours. You have to be prepared to put up with a few japes at Shrovetide. We meant no harm—well, not much. Besides, our host was welcome to give as good as he got, and join in the fun. It was all just high spirits. We certainly bore no responsibility for what followed.

We had nothing but sympathy for Albert Madsen. He'd been good to Marstal and we didn't begrudge him taking a young wife in his old age, if that was what he was up to, and not something worse. Which his procrastination over marrying Klara Friis certainly seemed to indicate.

When he opened the door and found us in his drawing room, one hell of a sight met his eyes. A cow was sitting on his sofa, yanking on a springy coil of yellow paper hanging from its tar-black nose. Next to it, a Spanish señorita was brandishing a fan. Her red lips, painted on the outside of the silk stocking pulled over her head, were parted slightly, as though inviting a kiss. A thickset farmer's wife with a lampshade for a hat stood in the middle of the floor with hands — in gloves sized for a man — planted on her hips. The room had filled with the smell of glue, naphthalene, and other stranger odors. A caveman was leaning his club against the wall, while a Chinese lady with slanted eyes painted in black on a yellow paper mask pulled a huge pair of knitting needles from a ball of wool on the top of her head and clashed them together. In a corner of the room a two-legged pink pig snorted contentedly, while the pirate beside it raised his sword as though proposing to slaughter it with one blow.

"Evening, Li'l Albert," we yelled in unison.

Li'l Albert said nothing. A bad sign.

The housekeeper poured punch from the bowl into glasses, which she passed around to us. We'd made holes in our masks and stockings where our mouths were, and we'd brought our own straws so that none of us would have to take off his mask and reveal his face.

After all, it was Shrovetide.

Most of us present that night were women: great broad-shouldered women with huge breasts. Their weight should have made us topple, but instead we pushed and battered them about like goose-down pillows. We wore woolen skirts with velvet ribbons, tight blouses, embroidered aprons, and shawls long enough to cover head, chest, and back — all from the bottom of the dressing-up box, mended and re-mended over the years, and brought out especially for this evening.

We swayed our hips and fluttered our hands with the giddy abandon that comes not just from emptying so many punch bowls in the course of an evening, but from the odd feeling of freedom that floods a man when he dresses up in women's clothing. Hidden beneath capes and bonnets, caps, lampshades, and wigs, with masks that were nothing but red-painted pouts and wide-open eyes with black lashes the size of fans, we snuggled up to the nearest manly chest, while cooing like doves and delivering daring remarks — as close to outright obscenity as we could get away with in our character of virtuous ladies — in falsetto voices.

. . .

The crudest reveler of all that evening was the bride. She wore her petticoat on the outside, and a flesh-colored garter belt circled her massive waist: two breasts swung in opposite directions behind her cream-colored silk bodice, and every time she swirled coquettishly they'd collide with a loud slap. She wore a blond wig with thick braides sticking out, and her starched veil stood as stiff as a frozen snowstorm of lace.

She went up to Captain Madsen and tweaked his earlobe. He pulled back his head with an irritated movement.

"How's your love life, Li'l Albert?" she asked in the high-pitched keening voice that countrywomen once used at funerals. "When's the wedding?"

Captain Madsen's face seemed to indicate he'd decided this was some sort of endurance test, and that if he stood it long enough, it would end of its own accord.

The bride placed a large gloved hand on his thigh, close to his groin. "Trouble down there?" For a moment she forgot her part and burst into loud, braying laughter.

Then the pig tore itself away from the pirate in the corner and approached them, its two pointy udders sticking out from its pink belly, rigid and fixed as fingers of accusation. "Have you lost your appetite, Li'l Albert?" asked the pig.

The bride made kissing noises and the pig offered him its snout.

It was Shrovetide. Fun and games.

By now the housekeeper had left and the large punch bowl was almost empty. "Li'l Albert," intoned the pig. It must have had a poetic bent because it started improvising on the subject of our host.

> Have you lost your appetite
> For the fun of the night?
> Is the girl too cold?
> Or are you too old?

Captain Madsen stood staring at the floor.

The pig raised its trotter like a conductor calling the orchestra to attention, and we repeated the crude verse in unison: we were in high spirits, and it came to us easily. Then Albert looked up and shot out his huge fist with a speed we'd never had thought possible in a man whose old age we'd just mocked. He slammed the pig right on the snout, completely flattening it. Though cushioned by the mask, the blow was still hard enough to send the pig flying into the stand, and the punch bowl went crashing to the floor. The pig stayed down there amid the shattered glass, blood dribbling from its wrecked snout.

Then the bride, who was still standing right next to Captain Madsen, punched him in the face, and the back of his head smacked against the wall. He staggered, then regained his balance. Tentatively he ran a finger across his split lower lip, staring straight ahead with empty eyes.

The bride looked as if she was getting ready to have a second go at him, but we restrained her and dragged her away. Things had got out of control and we had to put a stop to it, though we didn't understand what had gone wrong. Had we crossed a line? But surely the whole point of Shrovetide was that there were no lines. On this one evening, anything went. And we'd after all done only what we always did, which was to tell a few home truths in an entertaining fashion. There was no need for anyone to get violent.

We put the fallen table back up. There was nothing we could do about the punch bowl. The housekeeper would have to see to that. Then we carried the unconscious pig into the hall and down the steps into Prinsegade.

There we turned and looked up at the bay window. Albert was looking down at us. Our masks were beginning to disintegrate in the cold February rain. The bride waved to the dark shadow in the pane.

"Is the girl too cold? Or are you too old?" she yelled.

One of her sleeves had slipped down to reveal a beefy forearm with a tattoo of a lion crouching to attack. In the dark, you couldn't make out the words.

NORTH STAR

IT HAD RAINED in the morning, but then the weather changed, and the lid of gray clouds that had covered the island gave way to a high, blue sky that warned of frost.

Albert staggered blindly, gripped by despair. "You're ashamed of me!" Klara had screamed after him. No, he wasn't ashamed of her. He was ashamed of himself. He had to get away, take a walk to clear his head and decide on an unambiguous statement, a yes or a no, and then live with it. He wanted to say yes, but couldn't bring himself to. He could have said no, but he didn't want to do that either. This wasn't a case of "where there's a will there's a way." There was nothing but will, but both ways led to a void. He was too old. They were right, these masked Shrovetide revelers who'd so humiliated him, and that was why he struck out at them. He couldn't handle such a big change in his life. He recognized this with savage indignation, a helpless rage that had nowhere to turn but inward.

He headed for the beach. Farther out, a figure appeared. As it came closer, he recognized Herman and braced himself for a confrontation. It hadn't been difficult to figure out who'd played the bride that night, when he'd been ridiculed and struck in his own home.

Despite the cold, Herman's shirt was unbuttoned down to his belt, where his hairy gut, which hadn't shrunk during his many months of the good life at Hotel Ærø, spilled over. His face glowed red from the cold and he was staring ahead with glazed eyes. He passed Albert without so much as glancing at him, walking as if he was set on a distant goal, somewhere beyond the houses of Marstal, and was prepared to walk through every wall in his path to get there.

Relieved to avoid a clash, Albert walked on and was soon consumed by his thoughts again. He wanted to get away from the town, in the hope that out here, surrounded by nothing but sea and sky, a solution would reveal itself. "Ha!" he snorted to himself. "The only answer would be to stay out here forever." He strode forward, half expecting that some refuge really would present itself on the narrow strip of sand, in a limbo where no one could force a decision on him.

Walking on the wet sand was hard work. After some time it gave way to a carpet of pebbles left by the surf, which he stumbled across until he reached the dense shrubbery on the sandy crest of the spit, where well-trodden paths wound through the vegetation. Walking on, he came to the spot where the spit bent like a crooked elbow. Here, between spit and breakwater, the water lay heavy and oily, as if anticipating the arrival of frost and its own imminent crystallization. It was dotted with tiny islands where rushes and bulrushes sprouted from thick, heavy mud. The breakwater lay between him and the town. He could see the masts of the ships in winter harbor. Behind them were the red-tiled roofs of Marstal and the newly constructed copper church spire.

He was staring at the town that spread panoramically along the coast, searching for a solution to the dilemma that tormented him, when he suddenly realized that he was stuck. He'd strayed from the sandy spit and into the shallow water by the shore of one of the little rush-covered islands.

The muddy ground tugged at him. He pulled back, first one leg, then the other, so hard he nearly lost his balance, but he got nowhere. He felt the icy water seep into his boots. He stared down in disbelief. Then he laughed out loud, a brash artificial laughter, to mock his own folly. He tightened the muscles of his right leg and tried again. With the shift of weight, his left leg suddenly sank deeper. This wasn't quicksand. He wasn't about to be sucked down. He was just stuck. It was nothing. He had to try again. He bent to haul himself up by his boots and nearly toppled over. He was a big man in a heavy winter coat, and he'd lost his suppleness long ago. He was aware that he was growing increasingly desperate, but he still refused to accept that he was in a risky situation. Ridiculous, yes, but not dangerous. What if he was to throw himself forward into the rushes? Would he find solid ground there and be able to drag his feet after him? But he didn't know what lay beneath their dense growth. Perhaps they were rooted in water and the same muddy ground he was now stuck in, in which case he'd only make matters worse for himself.

The sun was approaching the horizon, and with the dark would come the frost. The thought didn't fill him with panic. He just felt like a fool who'd carelessly landed himself in a tight spot. Soon it would be no more than an embarrassing memory. The highest price he'd have to pay for his stupidity would be a cold. Then he felt the icy chill creep up from his feet to his legs. He shuddered for a moment, then slapped at his body to warm it up, but he was soon exhausted. Stopping, he let his arms hang limp by his sides. He couldn't stay here. He had to think of something. He tensed his leg muscles again, but it was no use. The mud wouldn't give.

Everything was casting long shadows now. The mast tops and the riggings threw a spider's web across the rushes. The church tower stretched over the sandy spit and reached the water behind him, and his own shadow seemed to straddle the rooftops. Then the sun disappeared behind a house, and the dark shape of the town swallowed him. Marstal was nearby, but it might as well have been on another planet.

It struck him that for many years he'd observed the breakwater from within the harbor, where it lay like a protective wall. This was the first time he'd actually considered it from the outside. It no longer protected him. It was shutting him out.

He looked around. The darkness seemed to rise from the ground and the sea itself, and he thought of Homer's description of the twilight land of the dead, where all joy is frozen, and realized that this was where he was. He felt the frost as a sharpness against his skin. Soon it would reach all his limbs. For the first time it struck him that he might be about to die.

The stars appeared, and the mud froze between his feet until he was standing in a concrete block of cold. He looked up and saw the North Star, and he thought about Klara Friis. In the last moments before old age closed in on him, he'd reached for youth. But youth was as unreachable to an old man as the North Star on a winter's night. Now he was certain. It was over. His life was about to end as unexpectedly as a ship wrecked in a freak storm.

Numb with cold, he stood motionless in the mud. It was as if he was planning to die on his feet. He thought about Knud Erik, and a sense of warmth filled him. That was his heart deploying its last resources.

Then the cold moved in and started its blockade of his flowing blood.

WE DON'T KNOW if that's how it actually happened. We don't know what Albert thought or did in his final hours. We weren't there. We only have the notes he left us, together with the columns of figures that spelled out what proved to be the beginning of the end of our town. In telling this story, each of us has added something of his own. Our picture of him is made up of a thousand thoughts, wishes, and observations. He's entirely himself. And yet he's one of us.

We've walked out to the Tail. We've visited the place where Albert died. We've planted our boots in the mud and tried to pull ourselves out of the sucking ground. Some of us say yes, he was stuck. Others say no, he could have freed himself. Or he could have rolled out of the trap that the cold and the mud had set for him. A drenched winter coat and soaked trousers are a small price to pay for an escape from death. Even pneumonia is preferable to a sudden end to it all, and he was a strong man.

We don't really know anything, and we each have our own version of the story because we're all looking for a little of ourselves in Albert. Some of us would like to condemn him. Others regard him as being above all petty-mindedness. We all have an opinion about Albert. We followed him everywhere he went. We watched him through our windows and passed his words on, not always for kind reasons, and possibly they weren't the actual words he'd used, but we attributed them to him because we thought it proper or likely that he'd have said them.

We've gone over his life again and again, just as we always go over one another's lives in our conversations—some whispered, some spoken aloud. Albert is a monument we've all carved and erected.

We thought we knew everything about him. But that's not how life is. When all's said and done, we can never truly know one another.

· · ·

Albert was found the following day.

It had snowed through the night, and in the morning a couple of boys appeared on the breakwater. They'd half rowed, half crashed a boat through the new ice toward Kalkovnen, and they were in line for a major ass whipping from their fathers, or anyone else who caught them doing something so blatantly dangerous. When it comes to boys who flout the rules that apply on the water, every single one of us has a father's rights and responsibilities.

But this time there was no ass whipping.

They saw him from the top of the snow-powdered granite boulders of the breakwater, where they were leaping about like mountain goats.

"A snowman!" shouted one, a boy called Anton. "Who's built a snowman there?"

They ran through the stiff rushes, which rang in the frost like a forest of steel blades, across the rock-hard mud and solid puddles and frozen shallow creeks.

There he was.

They never forgot him. You rarely see such a sight. Some say never.

Between Marstal and the sea, frozen to death in Laurids's boots, Albert stood upright.

THE WIDOWS

IN THE MONTHS that followed Albert's death, Klara sat in her house in Snaregade, staring blankly into space. We saw her when we walked past and glanced inside the lit parlor, where she'd neglected to draw the curtains. It looked as if her brain had stopped. At first we thought she was in mourning. It was a while before we recognized that Klara wasn't numb with grief, but rather in a state of profound contemplation.

Sometimes life unexpectedly throws up a wealth of possibilities, so many that the mere thought of having to choose between them can floor you. Was that Klara's problem? The sudden flood of freedom in which an ordinary person, unaccustomed to making her own decisions, might drown?

Then one day she ordered a horse and cart to move her furniture. She called Edith and Knud Erik, and they all walked hand in hand to Prinsegade, where she took a key from her purse and let herself into Albert's empty house. She had her own furniture stored in the loft and left Albert's where it was. She sat on his sofa and slept in his bed like a guest in someone else's life. The housekeeper dismissed herself.

Klara sat in the bay window facing the street and stared into space again.

Klara Friis, a sailor's widow of modest birth, had inherited an imposing house, a broker's office, and a fleet of ships. In one fell swoop she'd become one of the biggest shipowners in town. With the last glow of youth on her cheeks, she'd reached for the big prize and won it. Albert hadn't married her in life. But he'd delivered in death.

We wasted no time discussing how much she was worth, though we failed to understand that the most fascinating thing about Albert's legacy wasn't its size, but the power it bestowed. It was during these months, as Klara sat frozen in the bay window, that our town's fate was sealed.

One day Klara called a halt to her reflections and went to visit the widow of the marine painter in Teglgade. Since her introduction to Albert was all thanks to Anna Egidia, Klara Friis felt she owed the widow a favor. She now informed Mrs. Rasmussen that she would like to be of assistance in her tireless charity work. But she offered more than that. As they sat in the drawing room with the tall windows and the paintings on the walls, she explained that her plan was to found an orphanage in Marstal.

"It will be an orphanage like no other," she said. "Where children will feel loved. They won't feel they're in the way—or at best, that they deserve to live only because they'll be of use to others. No: they'll feel they're entitled to be on this earth for their own sakes. It'll be a place where the least wanted children will feel welcome." Her voice ought to have been filled with light and energy as she described her plans to improve the existence and the future of life's overlooked, but it trembled strangely.

Mrs. Rasmussen observed her for a long time.

"You knew an orphanage from the inside once, didn't you?" she said gently.

Klara Friis nodded and began to weep. This was the unutterable part of her story, the part she'd been unable to tell Albert Madsen, even at their moment of deepest trust, when he'd guessed the secret of Karla, the rag doll lost to the dark waters of the flood.

Under the widow's maternal gaze, she finally confided her story. She'd grown up in Ryslinge Orphanage on the island of Funen. Then she'd been "collected," as she put it. It wasn't an adoption: at least she'd never use that word for it, because the Birkholm farmer who'd taken her in at the age of five had no caring parental impulse. She wasn't a human being to him: just an extra pair of hands, cheap in terms of wages, food—and emotions. She laughed bitterly. No, when it came to feelings, she'd cost nothing at all. Love was a luxury that had been available to everybody except the orphaned girl.

On Birkholm there was no getting away from the sea. It ringed the small island like a wall enclosing her restricted life, but it also represented escape. She didn't dream about a knight riding in on a white charger so much as a knight blown in by a white sail. And every spring she imagined that he'd arrive. Hundreds of sailing ships passed the island—and then disappeared again. They came from Marstal, and the town became a place she yearned for. One day the sea came to her in the form of a flood. Doomsday was paying a visit. Instead of bringing a knight, the waves took away her doll. Now, at long last, with the help of Albert's fortune, she could stick her hand into the water and haul Karla out again.

"Do you want to know how I met Henning?" she asked the widow suddenly. The confidences were pouring out of her now, and before Anna Egidia had time to reply, she continued. "I met him one winter night on the frozen sea."

"On the ice?" The widow looked up in surprise.

"I was so young. Only sixteen. I wanted to go to a dance on Langeland."

The sea had frozen over, and it was as if tiny, flat Birkholm had started to expand, trying to meet and merge with the surrounding islands. On that moonlit Saturday night, snow crystals lit a path into the world, and her longing became irresistible. Having no dresses of her own, she borrowed one from a girl on the farm, then got hold of a bicycle and cycled across the ice toward Langeland. She wasn't running away. She'd just headed toward the lights of the houses on the distant island, hoping for a moment of happiness. Back then, she still dared to dream.

But she hadn't gone far before she reached black water. Suddenly, a rift appeared in the ice ahead of her, plowed by the *A.L.B.*, the ferry between Svendborg and Marstal, whose massive steel hull functioned as an icebreaker. As it went past, sparks flew from its funnel. The ice under her feet shuddered. In the ship's wake came the *Hydra*, homebound, her sails set to catch even the slightest wind that frosty night.

The *Hydra*'s crew crowded along the rail. A girl in a party dress in the middle of the ice was the last thing they'd expected to see.

They hailed her. "Where are you going?"

"To a dance on Langeland," she replied.

They invited her to a dance in Marstal instead, and both she and her bicycle were pulled over the rail.

"You look frozen stiff," said Henning Friis, the handsomest of them. And she was indeed cold. Under her dress her legs were bare. He took her down to the fo'c'sle to warm her up in the top berth. And that was how she became his, with her blue lips trembling and cystitis lying in wait in the wretched block of ice that was her inadequately clothed body. She didn't get pregnant right away. Knud Erik came later. So did Henning's drinking, and pub crawls, and endless voyages.

One year Henning came home with a stuffed guenon monkey.

"The guenon is the most ungodly of all the animals," he said. "The son, grandson, and great-grandson of Injustice." An Arab had told him that.

"And what am I supposed to do with it?" she asked.

"You can look at it when you miss me," he replied, his voice laden with contempt. That was how things had grown between them.

"The worst thing about the sailor isn't that he steals your virtue. The worst thing is that he steals your dreams," she said to the marine painter's widow.

Now the *Hydra* was gone, and Henning with it.

"One day Marstal will be a good place to grow up in," she said, "instead of a place where boys are raised to become fish food, and girls to be their widows."

"Do you really think you can take the sailor out of a Marstaller?" asked the widow.

"Yes, I do. I have the means. And I know how to do it." A new stubbornness had entered Klara Friis's voice, and her face grew ugly with defiance.

Wondering if the younger woman's mind might have become dislocated by grief or her vast inheritance, the widow quickly steered the conversation back to the orphanage, and to her relief Klara Friis became sensible and practical again.

But Klara never mentioned the most important part of her plan.

THE SAME DAY that Albert died, Mr. Henckel was declared bankrupt. At a general meeting of Kalundborg Steel Shipyard Limited, to everyone's astonishment he voted in favor of liquidating his own company; he owned 99 percent of its shares. It was subsequently revealed that the shipyard owed Kalundborg Bank twelve million kroner. The bank collapsed, dragging other businesses along with it. Including, finally, Marstal Steel Shipyard. Peter Raahauge, the ship worker, had warned Albert that there was no way in hell things could last. His prophecy had now been fulfilled. The nearly one million kroner that had been invested in the Marstal enterprise was lost, and the yard was auctioned off for just thirty-five thousand kroner. Mr. Egeskov, owner of the Ærø, would survive. He had his hotel to fall back on. But Herman had ransomed his house in Skippergade, along with the *Two Sisters,* and he was left with nothing but debts.

Court cases followed. Both Edvard Henckel and the manager of Kalundborg Bank were arrested. Not even the devil could make head or tail of their accounts. Henckel had been too smart for them. You could argue that he was a kind of genius who happened to forget the laws of the land and ended up on the wrong side of them. He was quite open in admitting everything. He'd been irresponsible, even thoughtless. But his intentions had been good.

We pictured him standing in the dock, broad and mighty in his wide-brimmed hat, his coattails flapping as though he'd brought the fresh breeze of enterprise into the courtroom with him. His bloodshot eyes were bright with energy, and the way he flung out his arms and confessed to all his mistakes, you'd think he was inviting the judge, the journalists, the defense, and the prosecutor to a champagne party.

It turned out he wasn't an engineer at all. Like everything else about him, the title was a concoction. Now he was off to prison. He took the announcement of his three-year sentence like a man, refusing to let it break him. He'd stormed through life bursting with grand plans for himself and for others; if he had to make a detour to a locked cell, it was only a temporary interruption. He'd come back out again eventually, and then he'd show us.

We no longer frequented Hotel Ærø. Our starched shirts stayed at home, once again reserved only for weddings, confirmations, and funerals. Back in Weber's Café, we reacquainted ourselves with flat beer. We didn't gloat when we heard about the prison sentence. We couldn't even get properly angry with Henckel. Yes, he'd cheated us, but fraud takes two: we should have exercised better judgment. We certainly didn't regard him as evil. His enthusiasm and his spirit of enterprise were genuine. His problem was simply that he'd had too many ideas and he'd lost track of them until they became hopelessly entangled. But the man was willing to take a risk. We respected that. It was what we did all the time. We acknowledged something of ourselves in Henckel: not his fraudulence, but his get-up-and-go.

We toasted him the way we'd have toasted a ship that was lost with all hands.

Herman did the rounds of the shipping offices, looking for work. We'd expected him to run away from it all, just as he'd done when Hans Jepsen put him in his place and refused to sign him on as an ordinary seaman on the *Two Sisters*. He'd come back as a big shot: he'd talked big and had a wallet to match, but then he'd lost it all and ended up where he'd begun. He'd been sold a pig in a poke. But then again, he wasn't alone. Quite a few of us had bought one. In that respect we were all in the same boat.

We never expected Herman to be humbled by his fall. It wasn't in his nature, which was stubborn-minded and arrogant. We just imagined that he'd flee the humiliation and reappear only when he had money in his pocket and was ready to start bragging again. Instead, he stayed in the town that had witnessed his downfall and signed on to the *Albatross*. We couldn't help but think that he must have finally learned his lesson and accepted that life had no plans to treat him differently than anybody else and that a certain amount of humility was therefore in order. Apart from that he was just the same Herman, as aggressive and unpredictable as ever. But he knew his way around a deck, so he had no problem finding a job.

He returned from his first voyage a war hero, though the war had ended long before. He'd fought in the defense of Denmark in a pub in Nyborg, together with two other men from Marstal, Ingolf Thomsen and Lennart Krull, fellow crewmen on the *Albatross.*

He sat in Weber's Café, holding forth about his deeds, while Ingolf and Lennart nodded in affirmation. From time to time they'd interject. But under Herman's stern eye, it never amounted to more than "Yes," "No," or "Exactly."

So they'd been in this pub in Nyborg with the rest of the crew, and they'd started talking to this car mechanic. Ravn was his name: greasy little fellow with a potato nose covered in blackheads, engine oil on his hands. When he learned they were sailors from Marstal, he pulled out his wallet and showed them a photo of a schooner in flames. It was the *Hydra,* which had vanished without a trace in the Atlantic in September 1917. So had the six hands aboard, including two from Marstal: the captain and the ordinary seaman Henning Friis, who left behind a widow, Klara, and a son, Knud Erik. Vanished without a trace: that meant never seen by anyone, no bodies to recover and bury, no flotsam found afterward, not even a life buoy with the name of the ship—nothing.

Ravn was from Sønderborg in South Jutland. He'd been drafted to fight for the Germans and had served on a U-boat. Photographs had been taken of all the ships the U-boats had sunk, and every man got a copy. He had a whole album of them at home.

"I've got the photograph here," Herman said. "Do you want to have a look?"

He passed it across the table and turned to order a new round.

We instantly recognized the *Hydra,* and the sight of it in flames shifted a weight inside us. The black-and-white photograph echoed our own experiences of shipwreck.

"Anyway," Herman said, "Ravn won't be going around bragging about sinking Danish ships anymore."

"Perhaps we were a bit too rough with him," Lennart said. We could hear the uncertainty in his voice.

"It was a fair fight. Ravn could have fought back. We've got nothing on our conscience." Herman sounded like a priest offering absolution. "He got what he deserved," he added, turning to us. "I beat him up for the men who died. And for the *Hydra.*"

Herman paid a visit to Klara Friis, intending to tell her the story of Ravn. We imagined he was hoping to profit from it. Only this time he'd say, "I beat him up for Henning."

Klara opened the door. "What do you want?" she asked tersely, when she saw Herman on the doorstep. The last time he'd paid her a visit, his intentions hadn't been good. "I've got news of Henning," he said.

She listened to his story in silence. She'd paled when he informed her that he had news of Henning; now she reddened as he sat there boasting about having beaten to a pulp the man who sank the *Hydra*. When he concluded by claiming that he'd beaten him up for Henning's sake, her face whitened again and her mouth became a thin line. She stared at him through narrowed eyes. Completely unable to interpret her expression, he felt temporarily at a loss.

"Perhaps you disapprove of fights, Mrs. Friis?" His manner had suddenly become very formal. Still she didn't speak. He shifted in his chair and regretted having come.

Finally she broke her silence.

"I'd like you to accompany me to Copenhagen," she said.

By now Klara Friis had hired a maid who could take care of the children in her absence. She'd been to I. C. Jensen and ordered new rugs and consulted Rosenbæk, the carpenter, about a new bed suitable for her widowed status. She was filled with energy, but no one knew what she planned to do, apart from rearranging her life to suit her new financial status.

She revealed nothing to Herman while they were on the ferry. He'd not expected her to be forthcoming, nor had he speculated about what the trip to Copenhagen might involve. When she asked him to accompany her, he'd sensed no promise on the horizon, so it was purely out of curiosity that he'd agreed. He was on the lookout for new opportunities in life, and although he couldn't determine the nature of this expedition, he felt it held possibilities.

"You know the moneymen in Copenhagen, Mr. Frandsen," she said to him.

She addressed him formally, and he preferred it that way. It established a businesslike tone between them, and he was up for doing business.

"I want you to introduce me to them."

He stared at her. Was she stupid or just hopelessly naive? Was she practically asking to be robbed? He hadn't given much thought to

Klara Friis's intelligence, but there was no reason to assume she was a fool. Was this a test?

He decided to be honest with her—which in turn demanded a rare moment of honesty with himself.

"Are you referring to Henckel? But he was a fraud. Surely you know that he's in prison now?"

"I'm well aware of that. But you must have known others. You've been to the stock exchange. I need to speak with someone who understands finance."

"You mean people like the Negro Thug or the Rolling Sidewalk? I'm afraid they're cut from the same cloth as Henckel. If you value your money, then don't entrust them with any of it."

"They can't all be frauds."

"Possibly not. But it's hard for ordinary people like us to tell the difference."

He looked down at his big hands. For a moment he listened to his own voice. It sounded humble. He wasn't used to talking like this. He spoke about his own defeat in a frank, even regretful tone. Who could say if it was false or not. He was the shooting star who'd crashed and repented and learned from his mistakes.

"I've become wiser," he pronounced, "since I allowed myself to be robbed. Why don't you just leave your money where it is? I imagine it's well invested."

"You don't understand," she said. "I have other plans."

But by the time they arrived at Copenhagen Central Railway Station, her confidence had deserted her. She took Herman's arm like a child grabbing its father's hand, terrified of becoming lost in the crowds. He'd sensed this fear when they boarded the train in Korsør: she'd tossed her head haughtily when she stepped onto the running board, but a shudder seemed to pass through her, hinting at a feral panic she couldn't control. She'd sat straight up on the seat opposite him and avoided looking out the window. Later, as they passed Slagelse, she'd snapped out of her trance and turned to look at the scenery, but she'd had to shut her eyes right away. For most of her life, her only landscape had been the flat meadows of Birkholm. To her, Marstal was "the city." But you could fit its whole market square, church, and high street beneath the vaulted roof of Copenhagen Station, where the buzz of countless travelers gathered into one great shouting echo.

· · ·

The first place he took her was the vestibule of the stock exchange. He deliberately chose late afternoon, when the prices had been set for the day and the brutal circus known as the post-trading period had begun. His intention was quite simply to scare her off. He discovered he had a protective instinct, which, had he been at all interested in his own psychology, he might have described as selflessness. There was no need for her to be conned out of her money, as he'd been. Since he'd been unable to talk her out of the vague plans she was so hell-bent on carrying out, he'd make use of the deterrent power of example.

In the center of the vestibule was a roped-off area resembling a boxing ring. Inside, stockbrokers roared out their offers all at once.

From one end of the vestibule a man came walking toward them with an odd, rolling swagger. Avoiding the swing of his bruising shoulders, the crowd parted to make way for him. He looked like an old sailor trying to keep his balance on a ship in a gale; his colleagues, who'd never stood on a deck, called him the Rolling Sidewalk.

He raised his bowler hat as he spotted Herman. They were old acquaintances. Herman returned the greeting with an inviting smile, and instantly the man stepped up to Herman and Klara.

"Ajax Hammerfeldt," he said, and took Klara's hand with an elegant gesture, pursed his lips, and planted a kiss on it.

The unfamiliar greeting startled her. She looked down and reddened, and forgot to introduce herself. So Herman did it for her, and added, "Mrs. Friis has just inherited a considerable fortune. She's in need of some good advice."

"Then you've come to the right man, my dear Mrs. Friis," the Rolling Sidewalk said, and raised his hat a second time, as though they were about to become very well acquainted. He threw a quick glance at Herman to secure his consent to what was about to happen: when no reaction came, he took it as acceptance and continued.

"The shipping industry is enjoying enormous progress," he said. "Have you heard about the ship with no funnel, Mrs. Friis?"

Klara shook her head, overwhelmed.

"The steamer succeeds the sailing ship. But the ship with no funnel will replace the steamer. That's the future, and you have the opportunity to be among the first to invest your money in it. You're young"—here he threw her a flattering glance, then added, in a tone that suggested that he was now presenting his decisive argument—"and the future belongs to our youth."

Herman looked from one to the other. He couldn't help but admire the Rolling Sidewalk. He certainly knew his trade, even if it was a con man's, peddling a fraudulent blend of truth and lies. The ship with no funnel! It sounded made-up, but it wasn't: a ship with a diesel-powered motor, the *Selandia,* had been launched by B&W Shipyard some years ago. And she was undoubtedly a successor to the steamer. He waited patiently for Hammerfeldt to continue. The truthful part had been conveyed. Now for the lies.

"Kalundborg Steel Shipyard," the Rolling Sidewalk said. "That's where the ship of the future will be launched. They've just issued the shares. The last one will be sold before the day's out. It's about striking while the iron's hot, don't you agree, sailor?" He winked at Herman, whom he still regarded as an accomplice.

Klara looked astonished, as if she couldn't believe her own ears. "Kalundborg Steel Shipyard! But that's Mr. Henckel's company, isn't it? He's in jail!" She appealed to Herman, who nodded.

"Yes," he said. "That's correct."

They both turned to the Rolling Sidewalk. But the cocksure hawker of future riches had already vanished into the shouting crowd.

Klara Friis had learned her lesson.

They crossed the Stock Exchange Bridge and continued down Slotsholmen. The wharf teemed with life: dockers were busy unloading scented cargoes of fresh-cut wood from bark- and brig-rigged ships from Finland. He glanced at her. The anxiety had returned to her face. All he'd wanted was to open her eyes a bit, but now it seemed she'd lost heart. That hadn't been his intention, though he kept asking himself what her true purpose was. What was it she really wanted here?

They crossed the square at the corner of Holbergsgade and Havnegade. She looked up at the huge bronze statue of the naval hero, whose outstretched arm seemed to be directing the traffic.

"That's Niels Juel," he said.

"Just like at home?"

Marstal was her yardstick for everything, so she was probably thinking of Marstal's Niels Juelsgade. Perhaps she even believed this statue was named after a street in their own little backwater. There were no statues in Marstal, only the stone that Captain Madsen had erected in honor of fellowship. Now Klara could compare the two edifices and acquire a realistic sense of her benefactor's true stature.

Copenhagen was the real world. Here, people didn't haul old boulders out of the sea and stick them up somewhere, with a few lines carved into the granite. Here, people thought big and built big.

Suddenly Herman had an idea. He pointed to a foreign-looking building on the corner. It had tall, narrow windows with pointed Oriental arches, and its roof sat like a heavy lid that was about to slide off into the street. A set of steps led up to a solid wooden door set in walls a meter thick. It was a house that looked as if it had turned its back on the rest of the city.

"The man who lives in there could give you some good advice."

She gave him a puzzled look. Then she turned her head and scrutinized the sand-colored building. "Who is he?" she asked.

"He's a completely ordinary man. His name is Markussen. He was once an able seaman. Now he's a friend of the king. There are those who say his word is more powerful than His Majesty's. He'll help you."

They crossed the square and stopped in front of the entrance. She gazed up at the façade: THE FAR EAST ASIA CORPORATION, said the brass plate next to the door.

"It's a big house."

"No smaller than his houses in Vladivostok and Bangkok."

"Should I really go in?" she asked.

He nodded encouragingly, but he was already regretting this whim. Which was all it was, after all. He'd felt magnanimous when they left the stock exchange. Then he'd seen the sense of defeat spreading across her face and felt obliged to do something more for her, to cheer her up. Magnanimity was a new and unfamiliar feeling for him. Finding it to his taste, he'd wanted to bathe in the sunshine of selflessness a little longer. But this was downright ridiculous. If she'd been disappointed earlier, her disappointment would only deepen with the rejection that awaited her. He cursed himself. Damn it all to hell! He should never have come with her on this doomed mission to Copenhagen; in a moment of weakness he'd once again succumbed to the temptation to look important.

"I'll wait for you out here," he said, and smiled cheerfully.

This won't take long, he thought to himself as she disappeared behind the heavy door. But time passed, and she stayed in there. Herman started pacing up and down the sidewalk. Why hadn't they seen her off? He went up the steps and opened the heavy door. A man in uniform blocked his path and asked him what his business was. Herman was taken aback; he hadn't prepared an answer. He looked over the doorman's shoulder, but there was no sign of Klara in the vast lobby. The doorman again demanded that he account for his intrusion. Herman shrugged and went back down the steps.

An hour later she reappeared.

"I'm meeting the commissioner again tonight," she said. Herman's face was one big question mark. "Markussen, I mean. He gave me some excellent advice. I'd like to thank you so very much for your help, Herman."

His jaw dropped. Her tone of voice had changed. She was back to calling him by his first name. Before, she'd briefly addressed him as Mr. Frandsen, and he'd taken it as a sign of respect. But since her audience with Markussen, he'd been demoted to the level of a servant.

She pulled her purse from her handbag. "I'm delighted that you brought me here," she said. "I want to give you something for your trouble."

Out came a hundred-kroner note. His initial impulse was to reject the money. What did she take him for? Did she think he had no pride? Then he reconsidered. He'd done her a favor, after all. And wasted his own time, to boot. A hundred kroner wasn't to be sneezed at. He needed to get drunk. A roll in the hay wouldn't come amiss either. The good reasons for accepting the cash piled up until they tipped the balance. His precious pride forgotten, he didn't thank her, but stuck the note in the inside pocket of his jacket.

"So, what did you and Markussen decide?" he asked with forced casualness.

"The commissioner felt our conversation should remain confidential."

Klara Friis pronounced the last word slowly and carefully, as if making sure that Herman caught every syllable. The word *confidential* was clearly a new one for her too. Then, for the first time, she smiled.

When she'd entered the building, she'd found it just as forbidding inside as out. The heavy door had barely closed behind her when a uniformed man blocked her path, as if to inform her that she'd confused the front door with the tradesman's entrance. She'd sensed immediately that this was as far as she'd get.

A small man holding a black silk hat came over to her and asked her politely if he could be of assistance.

It was Markussen.

She'd been dreadfully confused. When she mentioned Albert's name and her inheritance, his expression changed from politeness to impatience. He was slim, with white eyebrows and a white, well-groomed mustache. His features were sharp, with a jutting nose and a firm chin, but there was a sunkenness to his face that bore witness to the first onslaughts of old age. His gaze grew inquisitorial. The doorman approached again, as if awaiting the signal to show her the door.

The worst thing was that she seemed unable to stem her own nervous jabbering and take off on her own accord, and thereby preserve the last vestige of her dignity. Instead, she fumbled deeper and deeper into her story, which wasn't so much a story as a load of information that poured out helter-skelter. When you came right down to it, she had no actual business there. She just needed someone to listen to her.

Suddenly his eyes changed. She could never afterward describe to herself the expression that appeared on his face, though she'd often try, because she felt it contained the key to so much more than Markussen himself. A suddenly awakened curiosity? Yes, that was part of it. Darkness, pain, longing, and regrets? Perhaps.

At any rate, his impatience with her suddenly and swiftly evaporated. Bending toward her, he looked searchingly into her eyes with an intensity that frightened her. She stopped talking. What did I say? she wondered. Why's he looking at me like that?

Then he took her by the hand. "Come" was all he said.

They took the elevator to his office on the third floor. It was the first elevator she'd ever been in. When the floor wobbled beneath her feet, her hand trembled in his.

He told a secretary to telephone to cancel the meeting he'd been on his way to. He was still holding her hand, as if afraid she'd vanish into thin air if he slackened his grip.

He gestured her into his office. "I don't want to be disturbed," he said to the secretary. He pulled a chair out for her and they sat opposite each other at a large desk of dark wood. Through the window she could see the statue of Niels Juel below.

"Chance is a strange force," he said, stroking his white mustache. "You came to me for reasons that seemed to me quite unclear, and I was close to asking you to leave. But in reality you and I have much more in common than you can imagine."

"It was something I said," she mumbled, and looked down.

"Very much so. But perhaps you don't realize what it was?"

She shook her head. Again she felt her inadequacy.

"I understand that you have some papers you wanted to show me. Let's get that out of the way first."

He held out his hand. Obediently she delved into her spacious oil-cloth bag and handed him the envelope containing Albert's will, together with the relevant deeds and share certificates.

For a while he sat bent over the documents, glancing up at her critically from time to time. She said nothing. Finally he gathered the papers back into a pile on his desk. "It's as I thought," he said. "The shipping company's just the tip of the iceberg. The actual fortune is invested in plantations in Southeast Asia and factories in Shanghai. You're rich, Mrs. Friis. Not quite as rich as I am. But still rich. Your assets in Asia actually constitute a kind of parallel enterprise to my own. It's not as strange as it may sound. The same person created both fortunes, you see."

She looked at him, astounded.

"You mentioned her name yourself. I'm speaking of Cheng Sumei. I understand that she was Albert Madsen's mistress. She was mine once too. She wasn't a woman who left her men empty-handed."

He folded his hands on the desk. For a moment he looked lost in reverie. His gaze darkened. "For many years I knew nothing of what became of her," he murmured. Then he snapped out of his trance and looked at her with new energy. "Now tell me about your plans."

She'd never described them completely to anyone before and as she gave an account of them, she felt unsure how they'd sound to a stranger's ears. She felt she was breaking out of a shell of loneliness, one she'd been trapped in for months. When her flow of words finally ebbed and ceased, he was silent for a long time.

"Have you heard of Xerxes, king of Persia?" he finally asked. "Xerxes got it into his head to punish the sea because a sudden storm arose and destroyed his fleet before a decisive battle against the Greeks. His method was somewhat unusual. He had the sea whipped with iron chains. I'd say, Mrs. Friis, that you're a modern-day successor to Xerxes." He looked at her, but she didn't react. What he said had made no impression on her. "I hope you understand that your plans will have fatal consequences for your little town."

"On the contrary," she said, mustering all her courage. "I intend to save it."

THAT SAME EVENING she dined with Markussen in a suite that he kept at his disposal in the Hotel d'Angleterre. He used it for business associates and important meetings. This evening it was reserved for the story of Cheng Sumei.

"Women," he said, "see themselves as conciliators. They're always diplomatic: not by nature, but by necessity. Women need to have a supple grip. Cheng Sumei did too. But only until she'd found her real mission. Then that grip became as tough as steel."

As he spoke, she understood instinctively that he was confiding something he'd never told another human being. He was like her. She too was unable to open her heart to anyone but a stranger.

She and Markussen needed each other.

He'd met Cheng Sumei in Shanghai. He'd been trying to break into the Chinese market, but being too inexperienced and ill-equipped to weather the losses that a beginner inevitably suffers, he was faring badly.

Cheng Sumei's background seemed unusual to him, as a Dane. But in fact it wasn't extraordinary for the type of woman foreigners met then in a city like Shanghai. She'd been orphaned at an early age and had survived on the street by selling flowers. And flowers weren't all she sold. But that wasn't where he came across her. She'd been adopted by a benevolent Jewish businessman from Baghdad, a Mr. Silas Hardoon, who would almost literally pluck urchins from the gutter and offer them a home, an upbringing, and an education, teaching them English, Hebrew, and Confucian ethics. He'd died relatively young and left a legacy to each of his twelve adopted children. This money had enabled Cheng Sumei to buy a share in a popular bar, the Saint Anna Ballroom. Markussen had first met her at a party there.

Spotting the foreign guest who was clearly feeling like an outsider, she'd approached him.

Her beauty was all too apparent, but it was her intelligence that attracted him more than the perfect curves of her face. They spoke about nothing other than business. "That's all I can talk about," Markussen added coyly.

Klara Friis could tell it wasn't the first time he'd used this line.

He'd come to China to "carve up the melon," as foreign initiative was referred to in those days. But others had carved it up before him, and he found that Englishmen, Frenchmen, Americans, and even Norwegians were in a more favorable position than Danes with no connections. He'd done quite well under the circumstances. He'd established himself on the Bund, chartered out ships for coastal sailings, built warehouses, and founded a shipyard. But he hadn't made a profit from any of it yet.

"Fill your warehouses," Cheng Sumei said.

He gave her a baffled look. What with? Yet more goods he couldn't move?

She shook her head and laughed.

"Just do it on paper, *lao-yeh*. Fill your warehouses, but only in your account book."

"And what if people find out that I forged them?"

"Stack your board with bigwigs from the cream of society. Then no one will know. That's the Shanghai way, *lao-yeh*."

When that crisis was over, she suggested that he move the activities of his shipping company to Port Arthur. There, not Shanghai, was where the Russian expansionists had their headquarters.

"But there's a war coming."

He was well informed about politics: he had to be. And he'd heard the Russian interior minister say that it was bayonets, not diplomats, that would make Russia great. The question of who had the right to plunder the defenseless giant that was China would be decided by weapons, and he had no doubt as to who'd win.

"Exactly," she said. "But there will come a time after the war that you can turn to your advantage."

The war came, and Port Arthur was besieged. Following her advice he stayed on, rather than pull out his staff and dispose of his enterprises.

the widows

Could he bear the loss if the town fell? It fell, and instead of loss he reaped an unexpected reward: Russian troops and refugees were evacuated on board his company's ships, and he was paid handsomely for it. His fleet also transported war matériel to the embattled Russians when the Japanese fleet blockaded Vladivostok; and there was a need for neutral-looking ships that could be loaded and unloaded without rousing suspicion, whose cargo would travel on to the Russian fortifications near Nikolayevsk, at the mouth of the Amur.

"Have you learned your lesson now?" Cheng Sumei asked him. The question was teasing. But as always with her, it was pointed too. "Listen to your little sampan girly. You succeeded in Port Arthur for the very same reason you failed in Shanghai, *lao-yeh*. You failed in Shanghai because the big powers had already carved up the melon. There was nothing left for a little Dane. An English businessman, or a French one, or an American can always support his claim with gunboats. A Dane can't. But that's why he's welcome in certain places. No one suspects he's got battleships to back up his merchant fleet. Being Danish, all you have is your supple grip and your light touch. There are plenty of places in the world where the guest who extends a weaponless hand is the most welcome. A man from a small and weak country is as good as stateless. Just wave your Danish flag. They won't see a white cross against a red background as a crusading banner; they'll just see it as a white cloth. So wrap yourself in its innocence, *lao-yeh*."

He didn't take offense. He wasn't a patriot. His loyalty was to his ledgers, even if they were forged, and he recognized the wisdom of what she said. He used his Danish citizenship to signal his harmlessness before he struck. He acquired the supple grip and light touch of a woman.

"So why did the two of you part?" Klara asked.

The trust between them had already put them on a more familiar basis, without either of them thinking about it.

"I'll tell you one day. But not now. I've told you this story because I want you to learn something from it: not about me, but about what it's like when a woman runs a business. I've got three children, but my daughter's the only one who takes after me. My sons are complete write-offs. If I left the business to them, it would sink immediately. My daughter's the one with the talent—but her sex works against her.

So although she's going to be the real head of the entire company, she'll be working behind a front man. She'll never get any recognition for her achievements. That'll be her tragedy. She'll operate through deceit, which in turn will be her strength. You must do the same thing. From now on, consider yourself a con artist."

KLARA FRIIS RETURNED to Marstal, where she found a new, unexpected ally.

Death.

The Spanish flu had arrived and was making a dent in our population, just as it was everywhere. Influenza was different from the sea, which took only men. This took everyone, but graciously, as they lay in their beds, and it left us graves to visit afterward.

Pastor Abildgaard did his rounds, spoke to the bereaved, and officiated at each graveside ceremony. The flu didn't scare him the way the war had. The cemetery acquired new headstones and flowers that needed watering every Sunday afternoon: the bereaved came along and mumbled to their dead, and from time to time they sobbed, but if they looked up and spotted a neighbor at the next grave, they'd soon strike up an animated discussion of the latest news. Forgetting where they were, children ran around noisily on the newly raked paths until somebody hushed them.

It was tough on the bereaved, but still, that was life. We had to bow our heads and accept it. No one lost control and raged at the heavenly powers or indeed the earthly ones. "We'll manage. We have to," we replied, when we met and asked one another how we did.

Though the Spanish flu struck without regard to age or sex, and made no distinction between rich and poor, it seemed to take a special fancy to the family of Farmer Sofus. Sofus Boye had died many years before, but his shipping company remained in the hands of his descendants. The year after Henckel's bankruptcy, they'd opened a new steel shipyard farther north in the harbor. Every time we heard the boom of hammers knocking glowing rivets into a steel hull, the same thought went through our minds: *We can still do it*. The Boyes, a family from our own town, had created this shipyard. While all else, these past years, had proved fleeting or doomed to failure, what we created ourselves endured. Like the breakwater that shielded the harbor, we built things to last.

However, Poul Victor Boye, who was head of the shipyard, did not endure. He was a tall and dignified man, with a wavy beard down to his chest. As a ship's carpenter and qualified ship's engineer, he'd been equally capable both in the office and at the slipway, where he'd always muck in if the yard was late with an order. But the flu came along with its sick breath and blew out his light.

A month later, his two sisters, Emma and Johanne, bade farewell to their husbands—both solid, sensible men who'd jointly run the Boye shipping company. They'd managed to maintain a precarious balance in their wartime account books; they'd lost men and ships, but never money, and when afterward they felt the time had come to make the big change from sail to steam, they were ready to help launch that future.

But the flu had other plans.

For a second time and then a third, half the town accompanied a Boye coffin out onto Ommelsvejen. Those who died at home rather than at sea got to have a bit of a fuss made of them: in keeping with the old tradition, the funeral procession was led by girls who scattered greenery over the cobbles to prepare the deceased's path to paradise. Then came the hearse, drawn by a black horse.

Within weeks of one another, one by one, Farmer Sofus's heirs were laid to rest. The first time it didn't strike us that anything significant was happening, but by the third time we knew that we'd buried a lot more than three men.

"Well, that's the captain and the two first mates gone," said Petersen the stonemason, scratching his neck with the flat cap that rarely left his head. "So it's only able seamen left now."

We called Petersen the Collector of the Dead, because whenever anyone died, Petersen would carve a little statuette of them in wood. He was always sizing us up from beneath the brim of that cap: not in exactly the same way as the undertaker, but close enough. No sooner had a man been buried than his figurine would appear on a shelf in the Collector's workshop, which was right opposite the cemetery— convenient both for him and his customers, since the shiny stones, with their crosses, doves, angels, and anchors, didn't have to travel far. The Collector's workshop was the cemetery in miniature—except that here you could view the dead themselves, rather than their graves. The Collector never offered his carvings to the next of kin: when asked why, he'd reply that he didn't want to offend anyone. His little wooden figures always resembled their subjects, but in a crude way. In his hands, a big nose grew bigger, a bent back became more hunched, and the bowlegged seemed to carry an invisible barrel between their knees. Almost all of the deceased had had nicknames, and the Collector captured them in his likenesses. Smiling innocently, he said it was through sheer lack of skill, rather than ill will, that his figurines found themselves with slightly exaggerated peculiarities.

"Be patient with me," he said. "It's the best I can do."

The Collector was busy during the influenza. By day he'd carve and polish his gravestones, while at night he'd sit with his pipe in his mouth and carve wood. More and more figures appeared on his shelf.

"Who'll sail the ship now?" he said to Captain Ludvigsen. The captain, nicknamed the Commander, had come to order a gravestone for his wife. Answering his own question, he continued, "The women. Just you wait. Watch Klara Friis. Mark my words. The women will take over."

Ludvigsen shook his head. "Women don't know a damn thing about running a business."

"I didn't say they did. All I said was that they're in charge now."

IN THE NIGHT, when he was alone, Knud Erik cried. He couldn't do it in front of his mother. After all, he was her little man. And men, both big and small, don't cry in front of women. When Albert died, Knud Erik had steeled himself for his mother's tears. He'd be the one to comfort her in her second mourning. He'd be the man at her side, whose job it was to shoulder her worries and her grief. He could do that: he'd prepared himself for it. And her red-rimmed eyes and joyless face always confirmed he was indispensable. He was the only one who understood her, the only one who listened with such attention.

He placed a hand on her arm one day as she sat staring into the distance.

"Ma, are you sad?" he asked, with the usual inviting tone of voice. She could confide in her little man.

Her grief was a burden so heavy, he came close to collapsing under it, and yet he couldn't lay it down. With that burden on his shoulders he was someone. Without it, he didn't know whether he'd be visible to her at all.

"No, I'm not sad," his mother said. "Leave me alone for a while. I'm thinking."

He started playing with Edith. "Where's Daddy? Where's the man?" she asked.

But she wasn't really interested in the answer. She'd seen so little of Albert. Daddy was just a word to her: she probably thought it was Albert's name. She was just a child.

Knud Erik himself no longer knew what he was. Just now, his mother had met his offer of consolation with a blank stare. This was new to him. Had their pact dissolved? Was he no longer her little man? If he wasn't, then what was he?

·   ·   ·

When he was very young, Knud Erik had learned that the world could disappear and reappear all by itself. A blind would be pulled down, and everything would vanish into darkness. Then a few hours later it would roll up again with a clatter, and the world would return. The bright blue canvas of day would give way to the blackness of night, only to come back the next morning.

Loss was like the blind not rolling up again. Loss was a night that never ended.

His father had vanished in the night, but for a long time Knud Erik kept hoping that the blind he'd disappeared behind would roll back up with a clatter. He searched the horizon for a piece of string he could give a quick pull to, so the blind would roll up and his father—a man whose face had already dissolved in a mist—would reappear. He'd tried repeatedly to conjure his father's features, never certain if it was the same face as last time, until nothing was left but the word *Dad*. He'd had one once. The certainty was like a gap in his mind, a white spot on the canvas of his memory.

Now he had to get over the loss of Albert.

He remembered him for all the good things he'd been. They'd been mates, friends, more. Albert was an entire universe that had embraced him, with arms strong enough to protect from everything. And he knew that the old man had loved him, though he'd never said it aloud.

In death, Albert would help him one last time.

With his ginger hair, sinewy body, and sprinkling of rust-colored freckles, Anton was a figure so brim full of fighting spirit that far bigger boys respectfully made way for him. He kept a half-tamed seagull called Tordenskjold in a cramped bamboo cage in his parents' garden, and if you wanted to be on good terms with Anton, you popped a herring into Tordenskjold's hungry beak. He'd found the seagull as a chick at Langeholm Head, where he rowed every spring to plunder the gulls' nests of eggs, which he sold to Tønnesen, the baker to the south. He put them in his sand cakes and his vanilla cookies, which earned him the nickname Seagull Baker.

Anton's own nickname was the Terror of Marstal. He'd acquired it when he'd blown the porcelain insulator at the top of a lamppost to smithereens with an air gun and blacked out half the town. The gun, borrowed from a cousin, was one he normally used for shooting sparrows for a farmer in Midtmarken, who paid him four øre per bird. When the farmer tossed the dead birds onto the dunghill, Anton would simply retrieve them and resell them to his gullible client, presenting them as freshly killed—he often sold the same ones four or five times. As a result, the farmer had acquired an exaggerated impression of the size of the sparrow population plaguing his fields.

Anton was from Møllevejen, on the northern side of town; Knud Erik, who now lived in Prinsegade, belonged to the southern side. The invisible line that separated the two halves of Marstal was one that the boys took as seriously as if it were a front of the recent world war. Two factions, known as the North Gang and the South Gang, engaged in an unending and merciless war. By rights Knud Erik and Anton should have been natural enemies. But while Anton was a respected member of North, Knud Erik, who kept to himself both on the school playground and on the streets to and from school, hadn't bothered to enlist.

One spring day when the wind clipped the crests of the waves beyond the breakwater, Anton sidled up to Knud Erik on his way home from school. Knowing Anton's reputation, Knud Erik braced his shoulders in anticipation of an attack: not being a thug himself, he was unaware that behaving defensively could provoke the very fight he was trying to avoid.

"It was me who found Captain Madsen," Anton announced.

Knud Erik tried to make himself even smaller. Suddenly he wished the other boy would just hit him and get it over with.

"I wanted to tell you that I think he was quite something," the older boy said. "Dying like that with his boots on, standing up. I'd like to die like that." Knud Erik didn't know what to say, but his tension started to dissolve. "You knew him. He was like a granddad to you, wasn't he?" His tone wasn't mocking.

"Yes," Knud Erik said hesitantly. He paused, then asked, "How did he look when you found him?" He wanted to know if Albert had suffered in his final hours. If so, perhaps it had been written on his face. He was afraid the question made him look a sissy.

"He had frost in his beard and his hair. Over his whole head in fact. It looked really good," Anton said.

Knud Erik summoned up his courage. "What else?"

"What do you mean? He looked ordinary, I guess. He was dead, wasn't he?"

They walked in silence for a while. The clouds gathering above their heads began to darken. They walked through Markgade and crossed Market Square. Knud Erik would soon be home and Anton might never seek him out again. He wanted to win the older boy's friend-ship. He racked his brains for something interesting to say. Then came sudden inspiration.

"Have you ever seen a shrunken head?" he asked.

Knud Erik no longer had an adult male in his life. But now he had Anton, who'd gained experience of the grown-up world through his countless clashes with it. Anton knew it in the same way an army spy knows the enemy's camp: with a view to capturing it.

One day after school Anton walked home to Prinsegade with Knud Erik. Under the guise of a visitor, his secret role was that of an ob-server, come to get the measure of his opponent. The maid, with her starched apron and pinned-up hair, received them. Anton looked her up and down as if he was contemplating asking her out that evening, while she in turn glared at his clogs and sharply ordered him to re-move them before entering the drawing room.

Anton's behavior with Klara Friis was exemplary. He politely an-swered her questions about his parents and his school grades, though he failed to mention that he always signed his monthly grade report himself: indeed, his mother didn't even know such a thing existed. Klara was impressed by this model schoolboy whose friendship her son had won, and who'd clearly be an excellent mentor to him. She liked everything about Anton, in fact, except the restlessness of his eyes, which scanned the room as if registering every object it con-tained. And his legs kept swinging back and forth under the table. In the presence of mothers, Anton always found the etiquette of sitting still a monumental effort.

She asked about his plans for the future. Anton was only eleven, but in a couple of years he'd be confirmed and leave school, so it wasn't unlikely that he'd considered the matter. "I'm going to sea." His reply betrayed neither enthusiasm nor reluctance—just mild surprise that anyone would think to pose the question at all.

"Knud Erik isn't going to sea." Klara said this with deliberateness, determined to distinguish her son from his friends. They should know who they had in their midst. Knud Erik was destined for other things.

Anton quickly glanced from mother to son, and then around the room. Again, it was as if he was taking an inventory. This left her with a feeling of unease.

· · ·

"She's tough," Anton said to Knud Erik, the next time they met. He sounded like a boxing coach sizing up his fighter's opponent. Seeing the defenselessness in Knud Erik's face, he placed a hand on his shoulder. "Don't worry, they're all damned tough," he said, by way of comfort. "She wants you to end up in some ship broker's office. You're to wear a starched collar and look ridiculous. No way in hell."

"No, no way in hell." Knud Erik hesitated as he repeated the words, trying to sound like Anton.

"There's a surefire way of avoiding this," Anton advised him. "You just need to do badly in school."

Doing badly in school is harder than you think. Knud Erik was infinitely tempted to stick his hand up when he knew the answer. After all, he'd done his homework, and his instinct was to be a good boy.

Having always belonged to the middle stream of his class, he now deliberately sank to the bottom. This did no harm to his reputation among his friends, but he paid the price in punishment. Most of the teachers were spinsters. Some were fat and others were scrawny, but they all hit, scratched, pinched, and otherwise disciplined the boys with an energy you'd never have guessed they had in them. Miss Junckersen would pull your ears; Miss Lærke would tweak the hairs at the back of your neck; Miss Reimer would slap you with the palm of her hand. Miss Katballe would put unruly children across her knees and smack their backside, something that only Anton was sufficiently hardened not to dread. Rage would turn her face a terrifying blue-black. It was a color we feared—along with her spluttering and her flying spittle—far more than the spanking itself. But the worst was Mr. Kruse. There was no escape from him because he was a man, with a man's strength. He would dangle lazy pupils over the first-floor windowsill and threaten to let go: no one could withstand the all-consuming terror that breathed from the void below. In his lessons, his every question was greeted by a forest of hands.

Knud Erik did his homework but kept his mouth shut in class. He didn't feel comfortable about it, but he trusted Anton's advice and hoped he'd get his reward in the hereafter that followed the years of marking time at school.

In class he sat next to Vilhjelm, who had a stutter. Whenever Vilhjelm tried to answer a question, the teachers lost patience with him—which in turn would make him lose patience with himself, and give up before finishing his answer. Knud Erik took to whispering the right answers in his ear or writing them on a scrap of paper. Soon he'd become a kind of ventriloquist, with Vilhjelm as the dummy through which he channeled the knowledge he refused to show his teachers. Over time a friendship grew between the two of them.

Vilhjelm took home his best school report ever—and Knud Erik his worst.

His mother gave him an accusing look.

"What's happening to you at school?" she asked. In her voice he heard concern, budding panic, and anger. But mostly anger. She was a different person now, and he was glad of the change. If she'd remained permanently close to tears as before, he'd never have been able to pull this off; he'd have been too busy being her trusty little helper. Nowadays she lectured him, and he hardened himself to her just as he hardened himself to his teachers. She was a part of the regiment of women he had to endure before he was granted his freedom.

"You're a strange boy," she said to him.

The words stung him; they felt like a rejection. For a moment he had the urge to throw himself into her arms and beg forgiveness. Part of him still desperately wanted to be reconciled with her, so he could be the big boy again, and she could be the poor little mother who needed him so badly. But she was no longer helpless, and her anger taught him to give as good as he got, and to stand firm.

Anton, meanwhile, remained guarded in his attitude to Vilhjelm. He wasn't keen to amass all the runts of the playground as his followers, and his interest in Knud Erik was mainly due to his connection with the late Captain Madsen, who in Anton's eyes grew into more and more of a hero as Knud Erik retold his tales. Anton had heard about shipwrecks and adventures in foreign ports—such yarns were daily fare in every boy's childhood—but he'd never heard of shrunken heads. Next to stories like that, what did the stuttering Vilhjelm, who could barely complete a sentence, have to offer him?

No, Vilhjelm couldn't compete with Knud Erik when it came to storytelling. But he had physical prowess. The proof of it came one winter day as they were climbing around a laid-up ship in the harbor, and Vilhjelm suddenly scrambled all the way up the rigging, going higher and higher until he reached the brightly polished acorn at the very top of the mast, twenty-five meters above the deck. Then he lay across it on his stomach and balanced there, stretching out his arms and legs as if in flight. They hadn't seen anything like it since the Dannebrog Circus visited the summer before. And even then no one had climbed as high as twenty-five meters.

None of the other boys dared to match his feat. The bravest went as high as the acorn, then hesitated and backed down—even Anton. Some expected the Terror of Marstal to shrug and say it was nothing: if he didn't care to do it, it was because it wasn't worth doing. But Anton wasn't like that. On the contrary.

"Damn it, that was brave," he said. "Me, I just didn't have the guts when it came to it."

He slapped Vilhjelm on the back in approval and Vilhjelm's fortune was made. He was no longer an outsider.

In fact, Vilhjelm was able to tell a story, but it took him a long time—and time was something we didn't have. Once, though, we heard him out, and he told us how he'd nearly died, and it was only luck that saved him.

It had happened on a Sunday morning, quite early. He'd gone with his father to the harbor to repair their boat. His father was a sand digger. He was also completely deaf, and it was his deafness that gave the story its excitement and set it apart from the usual kind of mishap that befell all of us: to explore the depths before you could swim was a rite of passage.

Vilhjelm was only three or four years old, and his father gave him instructions in his slow voice, which always made him sound like someone speaking into emptiness, concentrating on every word as if not quite sure of its meaning. "Sit down there," he told Vilhjelm. "I want you to sit still, and if you need me you'll have to shake me."

Then he turned his back and started mending a plank on the sail deck. Vilhjelm stared at the clear, calm water; he could still describe to us the impression it had made on him. The rocks on the wharf were green and slimy, and as the rays of sun began to penetrate the water, a wonderland of changing colors emerged, filled with starfish, scuttling crabs, and shrimp that hung motionless, with only their whiskers vibrating. Vilhjelm leaned forward, full of desire to explore further—and suddenly fell headfirst into the water. Most of us had done that. But none of us had a father who was deaf as a post as our only protection against drowning.

Vilhjelm bobbed to the surface like a cork, grabbed hold of the boat's rail, and found a foothold on one of the slimy rocks of the wharf, then lost it and was left clinging there above the murky green depths until an icy undercurrent caught him, and began dragging him under the boat.

His clogs had come off and he saw them floating nearby like the lifeboats of a sinking ship. His sodden clothes, so dry and comfortable a moment before, felt awkward and alien. His father was nothing but a huge, blue-clad back turned away from him. It was like the whole world giving up on him. He screamed in desperation, but his deaf father didn't hear a thing. He screamed a second time, so loudly his voice echoed around the deserted harbor.

"Help! Pa!"

Then his strength ran out. His fingers lost their grip on the rail, and he disappeared into the water. He kicked it, he bit at it, he thrashed about in it as if he were fighting a wild animal, and yet it was only gentle, soft water, which pulled its covers over his head as though it were bedtime and the waters were bidding him good night.

And then—his father's huge arm came and dived in after him: a giant arm that could reach to the bottom of the sea if it had to, all the way down to death's door, to pull him back again. "At the very, very, very last minute," he said.

We knew that repetition wasn't related to his stammer. It really had been at the very, very, very last minute.

"And then he gave you a good thrashing, didn't he?" Anton asked, because that's how things were at his house.

But Vilhjelm hadn't been thrashed, not on this or any other occasion, and we didn't understand why until we met his father, who looked more like a grandfather. Vilhjelm had been an afterthought, and he behaved toward both his parents as we normally did toward our grandparents. He was kindly and devoted, and they all spoke to one another very carefully, as if the family's problem was not deafness, but rather sensitivity to any form of noise. By a strange coincidence his mother was deaf too.

Anyone can work out that not much talking went on in this family. When his parents did speak, it was in an earnest petitioning tone, as though they were making a humble plea. But they touched one another all the time, holding hands and stroking one another's hair and cheeks. Vilhjelm didn't just receive physical affection, he gave it to his parents too, all the time. No one ever hit anyone in Vilhjelm's family.

So Vilhjelm got something different from a good thrashing from his father the day he nearly drowned. We didn't realize what it was until Anton asked, as he always did on these occasions, "What would you say was the worst thing about drowning?" and Vilhjelm gave a very strange answer.

Of course Anton, who knew an astonishing amount about the world outside Marstal, thought that the worst aspect of drowning would be missing out on all the adventures he imagined having. He could reel off the names of the most famous red-light districts in the world. It certainly wasn't during our geography lessons in Vestergade that he'd learned about Oluf-Samsons-Gang in Flensburg, Schiedam-sedijk in Rotterdam, Schipperstraat in Antwerp, Paradise Street in Liverpool, Tiger Bay in Cardiff, the Vieux Carré in New Orleans, the Barbary Coast in San Francisco, or Foretop Street in Valparaiso. These were discussed in Weber's Café and, with the flinty expression of a connoisseur hardly appropriate for a boy of his age, he assured us that French girls were the best and Portuguese the worst because they were too pushy, and besides, they stank of garlic. If we asked what garlic was, he'd roll his eyes to indicate that our stupidity knew no bounds. He also knew the names of all the different kinds of booze he looked forward to tasting one day: Amer Picon, Pernod, and ab-sinthe—now *that*, he said, was something to really knock you flat. As for beer, he'd remain a loyal Hof drinker, no matter where on earth he might end up. Belgian beer, which many praised, was nothing but weak piss.

"You can list every red-light district in the world," he concluded, "and every brand of booze, and then you can add them all up and you'll find the bottom line proves mathematically that drowning is a terrible waste."

Knud Erik said that the worst thing about drowning was that he'd never see his mother again. He said this partly out of duty, because he felt he ought to say it, but also because he still longed for her.

Vilhjelm said the worst thing was that his parents would be sad.

"That means that you don't live for your own sake, but for your ma and pa's," pronounced Anton. He elaborated on this theory. If you were obedient, good, polite, well behaved, and dutiful, it meant that you lived for others and not for yourself.

"That's why I'm none of those things," he said. "Because I live for my own sake."

When Vilhjelm had hung, soaked and wriggling, from his father's rescuing arm, he'd looked into his eyes and what he'd seen there was neither anger nor fear, but grief. What kind of grief it was or what had caused it he did not know, but he felt instantly that he had to make sure that his father never had reason to be sad again. He instinctively knew how to help him: by drawing as little attention to himself as possible. Being invisible would be best of all, but second-best was to pass through life as inconspicuously as possible. So he'd turned into a quiet and dutiful child. Perhaps that was why he stammered: the effort of drawing attention to himself was beyond him.

Anton, on the other hand, lived for his own sake, and when Vilhjelm had balanced on the acorn of the top of the mast, with his arms and legs outstretched twenty-five meters above the deck, he'd been living life the Anton way. For a moment, he'd forgotten to be invisible.

Of course, Anton had parents too, though according to him he might as well not have. He could make his mother, Gudrun, believe almost anything. When she found out that he'd been lying about his school reports, she wept and said as soon as his father came home, he'd get a good thrashing—though she was quite big and heavy enough to dole one out herself. In the end his father just gave him a feeble slap: on the rare occasions he was home, he found that punishing his children for old, long-forgotten offenses was hardly a priority. He could deliver a stinging blow, but it had to be cash on delivery, as he put it. He didn't want to mess with something stored in a bank.

"Spanking and banking! Do you get it?" his father roared, laughing idiotically.

At roughly the same time as Vilhjelm, Anton had made a discovery of equally far-reaching significance about his own father, Regnar, whose last name was Hay. Anton's last name was Hay too, of course, but his middle name was Hansen. That was the mother's maiden name.

Regnar, who had recently returned after several years' absence at sea, had just settled his son on his lap, having boxed his ears first, in compliance with his wife's demand that he punish the children for transgressions committed in his years of absence. He hadn't struck Anton very hard and didn't expect that Anton would hold it against him. Encouragingly, he asked the boy what his name was. Presumably Anton's willingness to affirm his paternity would assure him that harmony once more reigned between them. It's also possible that Regnar wanted to assure himself that he'd thrashed the right child, so that, having performed his fatherly duty, he could leave the house and head for Weber's Café.

"Anton Hansen Hay," Anton said.

"What the hell did you say, boy?" his father shouted. His face grew fiery red, and he began shaking Anton, rocking him violently back and forth on the knee he'd sat him on only a moment earlier, in a mood of father-son reconciliation. Then he hurled the bewildered Anton to the floor, where he skidded on its varnished surface until coming to a halt among the chair legs under the dining table.

"Would you believe it?" Anton said, as he told the story. "The asshole didn't even know his own kid's name."

Anton had been christened while his father was away at sea, and Regnar had never troubled to look at his birth certificate or ask about the ceremony. Nor had he imagined that his wife would call the boy by her maiden name, Hansen, for he'd made no attempt to hide his loathing for her family. Anton's fat, compliant mother wasn't made for rebellion. She deferred to her husband just as she had always deferred to her own family and ended by trying to please them all; so she'd squeezed her family name between Anton's and his father's. Anton Hansen Hay became a three-word recipe for a family feud.

Anton himself couldn't care less. He never sided with anyone and described his father as a fool. Most of us called our fathers "the old man." It was a term of respect, because that's how sailors refer to their captain. But Anton respected no one. His nickname for his father was the Foreigner.

However, their relationship could have been worse. The Foreigner, after all, was the source of most of Anton's knowledge of the world, not because he confided in his son about his visits to brothels in foreign parts, but because he allowed him to listen in when the sailors on leave sat bragging in Weber's Café.

Deep down, Anton wanted to be like his father, but no one ever heard him say so, or indeed utter a single kind word about Regnar. Not since the day his father had hurled him to the floor for having the wrong middle name.

That was the day he started living for himself.

IN BOYE'S SHIPPING company only the widows remained: three women stunned not just by grief at the sudden loss of their husbands but also by the task they'd inherited, a task as unfamiliar as it was titanic. Marstal's future lay in their hands. They alone had sufficient capital to switch the town's fleet to steam power, as the times demanded. The age of sail was over; the men had known it and now it was up to them to turn their prematurely deceased husbands' vision into reality. The company owned five steamers already: the *Unity*, the *Energy*, the *Future*, the *Goal*, and the *Dynamic*—names that spoke of a master plan.

In theory the widows knew what had to be done, but they didn't know how to put theory into practice. They'd turn up at the shipping office every morning and have coffee served to them while the day's documents were presented. Munching their home-baked vanilla cookies, they brooded over freight offers, maintenance and crew costs, and proposals regarding acquisitions and sales. The whole world was clamoring for their attention, and every piece of information, every figure, every question mark felt like an insurmountable challenge.

No one ever saw them actually put their hands over their ears, but they might as well have. Every decision was discussed at such length that by the time they'd made it, it was too late. The fact that the *Unity*, the *Energy*, the *Future*, the *Goal*, and the *Dynamic*, built to transport huge cargoes safely across the sea, were mostly laid up in port was due not just to unfavorable market conditions, but to the confusion of their owners.

Poul Victor's widow, Ellen, the oldest of the three, was tall and stately, just as he had been. But any willpower she might once have possessed she'd ceded to her enterprising husband, and he'd failed to return it when he went to his grave. His sisters, Emma and Johanne, were more confident. Despite being thorough matriarchs in their own homes, outside them they were at a loss. They looked to Ellen—and she looked to the cemetery. But the defaulting Poul sent her not the slightest hint.

The women owned a fair amount of land around the town, and they started selling it off. It was Klara Friis who bought it. She sat in Prinsegade and watched the three widows as a vulture watches some miserable animal about to collapse from thirst and exhaustion, and when three of the Boye lots came up for sale, she took her first bite.

All three lots lay along Havnegade, the first on the corner of Sølv-gade, the second at the corner of Strandstræde, and the third, a large field enclosed by a fence, at the end of Havnegade, which was where the town ended too. Farmer Sofus had once grazed sheep in the enclo-sure and raised hens and pigs there, ensuring a supply of live provi-sions for his ever-growing fleet. But those days were long gone, and the field lay fallow. Everyone said Klara had been wise to buy the three lots: she could build on them.

But Klara Friis did no such thing. Stinging nettles still grew tall there, and the apples and pears from the trees Farmer Sofus had planted were still targets for birds and thieving boys. Marstal watched and wondered. What had Klara wanted with them, then? we asked ourselves. But we didn't ask hard enough. If we had, we'd have got an inkling of what lay in store for us.

Klara still dressed modestly, as if unaware of her change in status. This made a good impression on the three widows, who regarded thrift as a virtue. They weren't snobs and didn't look down on her, though their wealth was far more established than hers. They'd been surrounded by servants for several generations, but they still took part in the housework. They baked their own vanilla cookies every Christ-mas, a generous batch that over the course of the year grew rock-hard like the sea biscuits eaten every day on the company's ships—the only difference being that no maggots fell out of the vanilla ones if you tapped them against the table.

Farmer Sofus had been a man of the people, and his children and grandchildren were cut from the same cloth. They didn't make up a caste of their own; like everyone else, they belonged to the town. They knew that their money came from the hard toil of sailors: the boys had had to work their way up from the bottom of the ship's brutal hierarchy before reaching the broker's office or the board of the ship-ping company. Every word spoken in their daily meetings expressed a reality these men had personally experienced. But to their widows, who'd been brought into this new world with neither warning nor preparation, the language of shipping was a barrage of abstract terms that flew about their ears like lethal projectiles on a battlefield.

Sometimes Klara Friis would give them a piece of sound advice or display a sudden decisiveness that astonished them. Their good nature made them regard the young widow as a helpless creature who needed their charity. So they were baffled when the opposite frequently occurred; she was the one who rescued them from their difficulties. As they didn't have much faith in women's business acumen, they imagined that her good advice was pure serendipity, snatched out of thin air.

They didn't know, of course, that Klara Friis was taking her own correspondence course in brokering, ship ownership, and much more. Like the prince's kiss that breaks the witch's spell, the wealth that had come to her after Albert's death had aroused her slumbering intelligence. Before then, her mind had been imprisoned by her own humbleness, a humbleness imposed on her not only by her harrowing childhood but also by her position in adult life, which demanded that she work with her hands, not her head.

Now once more, there was a man in her life—but this one she didn't have to seduce with her already timeworn feminine charms. Unlike poor Albert, Markussen wasn't interested in kisses or cuddles, or what they might lead to. It was Cheng Sumei who bound him to her and to the task that, so late in his life, had fired his curiosity one last time: helping Xerxes find an apt way of punishing the sea.

They exchanged letters frequently and often spoke on the telephone. Every now and then Klara Friis would travel to Copenhagen. She could manage on her own now and didn't need Herman or anyone else to accompany her.

"You're not interested in taking over a shipping company on the verge of bankruptcy," Markussen said, "and you can soon straighten out the shipyard. Give them good advice, but not too good. They shouldn't get confident. You must make sure they keep thinking that disaster's only one wrong decision away. Tell them how dangerous the world is." He wrote all this on a piece of paper, so she'd remember. Klara Friis was getting the support she needed.

But it was she who determined the course.

. . .

The three widows completely misread Klara Friis, both overestimating her character and underestimating her abilities. They thought her helpfulness was altruistic: they were wrong. They thought her often remarkably useful advice was pure luck: they were wrong there too. Deep down, they all thought they were doing her a favor by listening to her. They gave her their company and a little bit of attention—surely that was what a young woman in her situation, stricken by a dreadful loss and alone with two children, really needed.

They offered her home-baked bread to take with her.

"My dear," Johanne would say to her, patting her cheek.

They recognized themselves in her. She was a woman—and by definition just as helpless as they were when it came to the ways of the world.

As they continued to puzzle out the mess in which their own widowhood had landed them, it finally dawned on them. They were in the jungle, and they needed what women had always needed to survive there: a man.

His name was Frederik Isaksen. He was the Danish consul in Casablanca, employed by a renowned French broker's firm. He'd started with Møller in Svendborg, then worked for Lloyd's in London. A number of Boye's skippers who regularly called at Casablanca, including Captain Ludvigsen, had recommended him. Competent, and a man with a vision, pronounced the Commander, who'd been elected spokesman by the other skippers.

"But does he do his job properly? Is he someone you can talk to?" Ellen asked.

"Not too pushy, I hope?" Johanne added anxiously, when the Commander mentioned that Isaksen had vision.

"Yes, I've heard about him," Markussen told Klara over the telephone. "I'd be happy to hire a man like him. He has drive. He wouldn't come to Marstal if he saw it as a provincial backwater. He's spotted an opportunity. Old Boye must have done better than we suspected. Capital in the bank, no debts. An enterprising man could go far with that. Isaksen could very well throw a wrench in the works."

Isaksen was hired on the skippers' recommendation, and he arrived in the middle of August. Avoiding the complicated ferry and train transfers that made the journey from the capital to Marstal so onerous, he'd opted instead for a nonstop trip on the packet boat, which normally carried passengers of humbler origins. He stood on the deck, tossed the mooring line to the people on the wharf with familiar ease, then waved his broad-brimmed straw hat as if he was greeting the whole town.

He was dressed in a white linen suit and wore a fresh carnation in his buttonhole, and when he raised his hat, we saw that his skin was as dark and tanned as a sailor's. Or perhaps it was his natural coloring. His brown eyes were fringed by thick lashes that made him look both gentle and enigmatic.

A man of the world, we concluded as we returned his greeting. We didn't mind men of the world. That's what we were ourselves, and we had no need for any new arrival to go all meek and self-effacing just to suck up to us. He was welcome to show off a bit if he could back it up.

Isaksen could indeed back it up, and as the days went by, his popularity increased. The skipper of the packet boat, Asmus Nikolajsen, who'd chatted with him as they navigated the archipelago, reported him to be a straightforward and informed man, full of natural curiosity. Indeed, after answering all his questions, Nikolajsen reckoned the exotic-looking stranger probably knew more about packet sailing than he did himself. He clearly knew his way around a ship, and he'd very deftly lent a hand on board without once soiling his beautiful suit—something that further raised him in Nikolajsen's esteem: all sailors value cleanliness.

Of course, one big question remained. Would Isaksen know how to talk to the widows?

First he talked to us. He did a round of the harbor and sat down among the old skippers on the benches. He knocked on the doors of the brokers' firms, stepped inside, raised his hat, and said immediately that he wasn't some rival come to spy on them. He'd come because he felt that this town was a community, one that could tackle the challenges of the future only if it set aside rivalries and grudges, pulled together, and, to sum it up, dared to think big.

What he said reminded us of Albert and his speech about fellowship. Only a few years had passed since we'd stood in front of the newly mounted memorial stone and heard those words, but it seemed a lifetime ago. It finally struck us: that day on the harbor in 1913 had marked the end of an era. And not a single one of us had noticed.

Isaksen's words had a magic to them. He helped us see how things looked from the outside. Our multiply owned shipping shares had helped us get this far, but the age of the small investor was over. The money now required was far more than a maid, a cabin boy, or even a good captain could supply. Big investments demanded big money: the capital of a whole town. Marstal had that capital; it was just a question of knowing how to use it.

"My suggestion is that Marstal's capital should be in fewer hands. It's the only way that merchant shipping, and the control of it, can remain here."

What was he hinting at? Some thought he seemed a bit too similar to the enterprising Mr. Henckel, who'd promised us the world and ended up robbing us blind. But it was soon clear that Isaksen wanted something very different. He didn't want to take our money. He wanted to be our compass. He wanted to chart the course, not just for one shipping company but for the whole community.

He had only one hostile encounter and that was with Klara Friis. He'd done his homework, so he expressed no surprise at finding a youngish, modestly dressed woman at the helm of one of Marstal's most renowned shipping companies. He knew all about Albert Madsen and his alliance with the widow in Le Havre; he also knew that Denmark's last great barks, the beautiful *Suzanne, Germaine,* and *Claudia,* were registered in Prinsegade. There was only one lesson he'd neglected. He hadn't looked into Klara Friis's heart, or into her safety-deposit box. He had no idea of the size of her fortune, and more important, he knew nothing about what she planned to do with such a vast amount. She'd have welcomed him if he'd arrived like Genghis Khan, to lay waste to the entire town. Instead, he arrived like Alexander to found a city. So she received him as an enemy.

He wanted to build the new Marstal from the ruins of the sailing trade that had once made the town flourish. He was offering a renaissance, not a funeral. No swan song here: instead, a joyous salute to the future.

He touched something in us. Once before we'd seen progress arrive—sooner than most people—and we'd stood to salute it. Now he was asking us to rise and welcome it again.

Klara Friis had pondered what to wear when she received Frederik Isaksen. Finally she decided to dress in her usual modest fashion, so as not to draw attention to herself in any way. She wouldn't flaunt her wealth or her recently acquired self-confidence, or, for that matter, her femininity. She wouldn't have been able to seduce him anyway—not because she'd lost her bloom, but because she didn't have a sufficiently high opinion of her charms. She thought it safer to reprise the role she'd played effectively for much of her life, which she too had believed in: that of the poor, self-effacing woman who allowed herself no richer emotion than a barely articulated bitterness at the wicked-stepmother treatment that life had given her. She wouldn't act downright dumb, but she'd let him think she was paralyzed by anxiety and an inability to understand the great big world in which men moved; she'd feign the very helplessness that she encouraged in the three widows.

She responded to everything Isaksen said with a hesitant, mechanical smile and a nod contradicted by the blankness of her eyes, which clearly hinted that she hadn't understood a word of what he'd said but was merely acquiescing to it, with the timidity and submissiveness so typical of her sex.

But Isaksen didn't give up. He changed his wording, making his images simpler and more accessible. He even waxed lyrical about the sailor's uncertain existence, to persuade her that his proposal actually involved a whole new style of life, one that would take the sailor's dependents into account and thereby free them from constant anxiety about his fate.

"Imagine the difference a big, well-managed shipping company could make to a sailor's job. Regular leave, safety on board, none of the poverty that currently forces smaller skippers to take risks in dangerous waters."

He fixed her with his thick-lashed brown eyes, which she hadn't met until now. His voice grew urgent. He wasn't satisfied with the empty gaze that was her sole reaction to his words. She felt tempted to surrender and was immediately overwhelmed by a familiar terror: of darkness and flooding, of black waters rising up to reach the roof where she huddled; of Karla disappearing into the torrent; of the ridge of the roof, shaped like the sawhorse that landowners had once used to beat rebellious peasants, pressing against her groin like an instrument of torture

Cold sweat erupted on her forehead. She grew pale and had to ask him to leave, making excuses in a feeble voice about a sudden attack of migraine.

Isaksen left with a frown. He sensed that the performance he'd just witnessed was a peculiar mix of authenticity and pretense, but the point of it was beyond him. He had no reason to suspect that this woman—who reminded him of a timid servant girl—was his main opponent.

In between visits to the town's shipping companies, Isaksen worked on the three widows. He spoke of the sea and ships in a language he thought they would understand, using housekeeping as a metaphor. Shipping too had its shopping lists, expenses, accounts, and servants. He knew these women were skilled housewives and he tried to make them grasp that, viewed in that light, the shipping trade was not so very different from their own everyday experience.

It had just the effect he hoped for. The widows calmed down. They no longer felt that bullets were whizzing past their ears. Isaksen had done what they'd asked him to do: he'd released them from the war zone. The responsibility was out of their hands.

ISAKSEN CALLED A grand meeting of the owners of the Boye ship-ping company: its entire staff, all its skippers and first mates who were currently ashore, and their spouses. He was smart enough to grasp that the wives were a force in maritime affairs as well as in matters domes-tic. He booked the Marine Room at Hotel Ærø, the grand salon hung with royal blue Danish china plaques, Danish flags, and paintings of ships registered in Marstal, and he planned a three-course meal. For the first course, he gave the hotel's kitchen a recipe for bouillabaisse, which he knew most of the skippers would be familiar with from their travels in the Mediterranean. For the main course, he chose tra-ditional roast beef with crispy fat. He addressed the guests between the bouillabaisse and the roast.

It was a speech about the future.

He began by describing his years in Casablanca, the port he'd been summoned from, and where he and so many of Marstal's skippers had become acquainted. Apparently he'd made a good impression on them, and he took this opportunity to thank them for their support. But his heart sank, he said, whenever a Marstal ship left Casablanca. Because he always feared it was the last time he'd see it there. He wasn't referring to the risk that the ship might be lost on her return voyage, although of course that was always a tragic possibility. No, he was thinking of another far more shocking notion: the ship might simply vanish into thin air, never to be seen again. However strange this might sound to his honored guests, this was more likely than a conventional shipwreck. They might well be surprised to hear it, but the fact was, the ship's disappearance was as certain as the sun setting tonight and rising again tomorrow.

By now he had his gawking audience's full attention. Not a single one of us could imagine where he was going with this peculiar statement.

"But listen," he said. "I can explain this strange premonition of mine. What's more, I can help you make sure that it never comes true. The cause of my despondency whenever I see a Marstal schooner raise anchor in Casablanca"—and here he looked down so that his long eyelashes swept his tanned cheeks (visible all the way up the long table, this caused the bosom of more than one skipper's wife to heave and sink in a most unusual way, as if from shortness of breath)—"the cause of my despondency"—he repeated the striking phrase—"is"—and he suddenly assumed a most prosaic tone—"that I happen to know the French authorities in Casablanca plan to build a new port. You'll all understand the consequences of this."

Again he paused, but this time, instead of lowering his eyes, he looked around urgently, as if to remind us of some piece of knowledge we already possessed but had momentarily forgotten or suppressed. One or two women returned his gaze with flashing eyes, as if they'd received an invitation, and several of the skippers looked shame-facedly at the table, as if they knew only too well that they themselves should have said, or at least thought, what Isaksen was about to follow up with.

Resuming his speech, his words now came fast and sharp as whip-lashes.

"It means that Marstal schooners will never again carry freight to Casablanca. The only reason that steamers have kept away from one of the most important ports in North Africa is the lack of a suitable harbor. Now the steamers will come, with their bigger cargo capacity and greater speed. You can time their arrival down to the minute. The compass plots a course, and the steamer follows it, without any devia-tions or delays. And I'm not just talking about Casablanca."

Isaksen's voice, which had grown more and more forceful, now took on a doom-laden significance.

"I'm also talking about the freight to the French Channel ports, where the tide used to let in only sailing ships. The railways are tak-ing over. I'm also talking about Rio Grande in Brazil and the Mara-caibo Lagoon in Venezuela. In both those places, the shallow water over the sandbanks allowed only small vessels through. Now, with the railways, that obstacle to the steamers will be removed as well."

At the mention of each port, the skippers and the first mates started visibly, as though he'd threatened them with his fist and they had no idea how to defend themselves.

"The sea was your America. But now America is closing her borders to you. There will be less and less demand for your services. The freight contracts will vanish into thin air. And that means that your ships will too. You might decide to sell them. But think about it. Who's going to buy them? All that awaits them is the demolition crew. A funeral pyre to an era, *your* era, turned to wood smoke. But not all hope is lost ..."

Isaksen's voice assumed a comforting tone, like the minister who has just described Hell and now offers Heaven as an alternative open to anyone who sees the light.

"There are still places where nobody else sails. Harbors that can't be dredged or where dredging doesn't pay. Or where currents, rocks, and frequent storms conspire to ban the steamer forever." The comforting tone disappeared abruptly from his voice. "Newfoundland. The most inhospitable coast in the world, the most dangerous waters on earth. The Marstal schooner will still be able to load stinking dried cod there. You'll still be welcomed by places and cargoes nobody else will touch. You'll be reduced to living off the leftovers of the world markets. You'll be the pariahs of the seven seas, the rubbish collectors. You'll be those left behind."

We'd thought he was going to give us encouragement. Instead, he had delivered our funeral oration. A deathly silence descended upon the table. Ellen Boye looked down. Her cheeks were burning bright red. Emma and Johanne looked to her for support, but her agonized face pained them so deeply, they nearly burst into tears.

Then Isaksen started speaking again. He'd only paused for effect, but his pause had sounded like a full stop to us. What could possibly follow this annihilating verdict?

"Marstal has a great future," he said, and again we raised our chins attentively, conscious now that we were nothing but puppets dangling from the strings of his artful words. "Marstal has a great future because it has a great past. It's not always the case that one guarantees the other. Traditions can be a burden. If we believe a method will work forever because it worked once, we get stuck in the past and miss out on the future. But it's different here in Marstal. You came up with your own design of ship—the hull with the heart-shaped stern and the rounded bow—and you named it after your town. You kept experimenting until you discovered what best suited your purpose. Your tradition is one of catching the wind. You may think that's an odd expression, and so it is in the mouth of a farmer, who thinks someone

Isaksen had consulted the compass and plotted the course. He'd spoken eloquently about our ability to navigate through life even when it was at its hardest, but he'd overlooked one essential thing about the art of steering a ship. You don't just keep your eye on the compass; you also check the rigging, you read the clouds, you observe the direction of the wind and the color of the current and the sea, and you look out for the sudden surf that warns of a rock ahead. It may not be like that on board a steamer. But that's how it is on a sailing ship, and in this respect its journey parallels that of life: simply knowing where you want to go isn't enough, because life is a windblown voyage, consisting mainly of the detours imposed by alternating calm and storm.

We can debate till the cows come home whether Klara Friis caused Isaksen to fail or whether it was the vanilla cookies. His knowledge of the female sex was certainly incomplete. He'd imagined that a woman paralyzed by anxiety needs to be rescued by a man bursting with the urge to take action. That was how he saw the three widows, the shipping company, and in fact the whole town: we were the bride and he was the groom. He would release us from our state of paralysis. But sometimes a whirlwind of energy can do just the opposite: it can whip up female anxiety.

When their husbands met unexpected and pointless deaths within three weeks of one another, the sailor's wife in each of them, along with what little courage and endurance she possessed, left through the front door. And in the through back door came a woman who, no matter how long ago her family had abandoned the soil, was a farmer's wife to the core. This woman was suspicious, brooding, gloomy, and passive, and she clung tenaciously to her ordained place in life.

· · ·

Isaksen understood nothing of this. He believed he'd got the widows on his side. After all, hadn't they stood there cheering his speech, along with the entire staff of the shipping company? Of course, he'd heard of their inability to make a decision even before he came. The skippers he'd been negotiating with in Casablanca had made no secret of the fact that the women were "difficult" and "tricky to deal with," but they'd concluded unanimously that "all they needed was a firm hand"—and that he was the man to wield it.

Though Isaksen had previously regarded the women as the least of his problems, they were now proving themselves the greatest. They sat there with their coffee and their stale vanilla cookies, dipping and munching endlessly, testing the texture with their front teeth just like beavers. And that was what they were: a family of beavers, building dams around the flow of his ideas and blocking him from getting anywhere.

Out of sheer frustration he turned up for one meeting with a bag of fresh cookies from Tønnesen, the baker in Kirkestræde. But this gesture had precisely the wrong effect. Emma and Johanne exchanged looks. So he was spurning their home-baked treats. That made him wasteful. And then to bring cookies from the Seagull Baker! Did he really think they didn't know that Tønnesen bought seagull eggs from the boys in the town, who collected them on the little islands outside the harbor? What did he take them for!

Those cookies were a diplomatic disaster. Soon Isaksen noticed other signs of discontent.

"It's too risky," Ellen Boye said, when he suggested building a new steamship at the steel shipyard.

He explained that the freight market was recovering and the investment would quickly pay for itself.

"Isn't that terribly uncertain?" Emma repeated, after a long pause, during which they all resumed munching. He could hear that it wasn't a question, but a no. He made his voice firm and said that if they wanted a reward for the trust they'd shown by hiring him, then they'd need to allow him free rein.

"But you do have free rein," Ellen said authoritatively. "Only the times are so uncertain."

"I need power of attorney."

Power of attorney? The three women looked at one another, not following his drift. Again they were on shaky ground. Did he not trust them? "Klara Friis says that—"

"Klara Friis?" Isaksen woke from the lethargy that overpowered him more and more often these days when in the company of the three widows. He'd suddenly spotted a connection.

"What does Klara Friis say?"

It wasn't clear precisely what Klara Friis had said, but she'd said something and it had left an impression: that much was evident. Words like *uncertain* and *risky* were much in her vocabulary. Words like that fed the farmer's wife in them, nurtured their suspicions, and strengthened their simple philosophy that in this life you know what you have, but you don't know what you might get, and so it's better to stick with what you have.

"But that philosophy doesn't hold here," he said in desperation. "If you stick to what you have, you'll lose that too. Such are the times. Only by risking the unknown do you have a chance of achieving anything at all."

"I don't understand," said Ellen, the tall one, in a wounded tone. "We haven't said anything about philosophy!"

He realized that he'd been thinking aloud, and that for a moment he had actually let them hear the inner dialogue he constantly had with them, trying to persuade them to let him get on with the job they'd hired him to do.

He stood up and made his excuses: he suddenly felt unwell. He needed fresh air. He knew they'd be staring after him as he left; the moment he was out the door, they'd begin a discussion far livelier than any they'd ever let him be party to.

He went down Havnegade, turned on to Prinsegade, and knocked on Klara Friis's door. A maid in a starched apron showed him into the drawing room. Klara Friis rose from her sofa, and he saw more than surprise in her eyes. He saw fear, as if he'd caught her, red-handed, being someone other than the person she'd pretended to be.

"What do you want?" she exclaimed involuntarily.

He watched her struggling to assume the vacant expression she'd worn the last time he visited her. But her face signaled vigilance and her eyes stayed alert, confirming his suspicions. So he came straight to the point.

"I want to know why you are working against me," he said. "I don't understand your motives. Do you think of us as rivals? As a shipowner you surely ought to have the town's best interests at heart."

He spoke to her as to an equal and hoped this would make an impression and convince her to abandon her mysterious games.

"You talk like a mayor," she said. "But we've already got one of those."

She gave him a defiant look. Her mask had fallen. Well, that's something, he thought. Now I don't have to put up with the usual feminine subterfuge. Now she can't get her own way simply by pretending not to understand mine.

Aloud he said, "A mayor doesn't have much power. But I would, if you'd just allow me to get on with my work. And you would too. I understand that you inherited a shipping company of your own and that you're managing it quite expertly."

"I'm just minding my own business," she said. "You ought to do the same."

Ah, there it is; the thought rushed through him. We're back where we started. If you won't fight openly, then obstinacy's your last defense.

"That's what I'm trying to do," he retorted. "But every time I try to get the widows to approve one of my proposals, I hear the same things. Times are too uncertain. It's too great a risk. Some say it would be wise to wait. And the same name keeps cropping up. Yours."

He could feel himself growing angry. He thought about the plots of land that she'd bought along Havnegade, sitting unused. A vibrant harbor front could have been built there, buzzing with enterprise. Instead, the plots looked like a wasteland of ideas, destroyed before they'd had a chance to flourish.

"Every day I walk past the plots that you've bought, lying vacant. Shamefully so. Perhaps they reflect all too aptly what you have in mind: laying the whole town to waste. But let me tell you this, Mrs. Friis." His voice betrayed months of frustration. "What you call minding your own business, I call neglecting the business of others. We're talking about a whole town. Its history and traditions."

"I hate the sea," she burst out.

If he'd been listening properly, he'd have understood she'd given him a vital clue, and seized his chance. But anger had got the better of him: he now had no doubt that at last he'd come face to face with the cause of his problems and the increasingly inevitable failure of his plans for Marstal. It would be the first failure of his career. And, he hoped, the last.

"What a strange thing to say," he snapped at her. "It's like hearing a farmer say he hates the soil. In that case I can only tell you that you're in the wrong place at the wrong time."

"No, on the contrary. I'm in the right place at the right time."

She was now just as angry as he was. But he heard something more than indignation in her voice: he heard his own wasted opportunity. He heard the bitterness of someone who feels rejected. He'd failed to listen properly.

"If I've accused you unfairly, I regret it," he said, trying belatedly to rectify his mistake by striking a conciliatory tone. "Please, can we try talking sensibly to each other? I think we have a great deal in common."

"I must ask you to leave," she said firmly.

He nodded briefly at her, turned, and left the room. It wasn't until he was back on the street that he realized that she'd never even asked him to sit down. During the entire confrontation they'd been standing up, facing each other. She had a shocking lack of manners, he decided.

Isaksen went back to the widows a second time to request power of attorney, so he could finally carry out his plans for both company and shipyard.

"I must advise you that my demand for power of attorney is an ultimatum."

They asked him what an ultimatum was. Relations between them were becoming so strained that he'd abandoned his much-admired powers of persuasion and was increasingly resorting to the cold formalities of legal language. He explained that an ultimatum meant that if he did not get what he wanted, he would have to hand in his resignation and look for a post elsewhere.

"But good heavens! Aren't you happy here?"

He replied that yes, thank you, he was happy here, but no, he was at the same time most unhappy. He cared about the town. He could see that the shipping company possessed considerable promising potential, but his work was being sabotaged daily. As he spoke, his anger resurfaced. "I understand that you prefer to take the advice of Klara Friis. But I'm warning you. She does not want what is best for the company."

Ellen shot him an outraged look, and he knew that he'd lost.

"Klara Friis, that poor girl. If you only knew what she's been through. How dare you talk about her like that!"

The verdict had been pronounced. It was written all over their faces. He was a bad man. All right, he'd done his duty. Now he could leave.

But actually, he'd failed to do his duty, and that was precisely what stung him. He'd spotted an opportunity and he hadn't been allowed to develop it. This was a challenge to his most deeply held values: he'd not carried out his task to the best of his abilities. He'd failed. He'd failed the shipping company, the town, and himself. His persuasive skills had been inadequate. His psychological insight had been found wanting. He, the only one among them who knew which course to follow, had been prevented from taking the wheel and steering the ship, and he had no one to blame but himself. He wasn't the type to need scapegoats, though the town had offered him several.

The following day he submitted his resignation.

When Isaksen left town, he took the ferry, like any other traveler.

He didn't fit in—that was the general verdict.

But not all of us agreed. There were those who realized that the prophecy of doom he'd made in his appointment speech during the gala dinner at Hotel Ærø would now be fulfilled. The only person who could have prevented it was the one who'd made it—and he was leaving. It wasn't only Frederik Isaksen's back that was turned on us when he boarded the ferry. It was the world's.

He left on an autumn day of pouring rain. He was clutching an umbrella, but there was a fierce wind blowing from the west and the shoulders of his cotton raincoat had already darkened. A deputation of skippers and first mates had assembled on the wharf to see him off. They'd all been there that night at Hotel Ærø when he gave his grand speech.

Their spokesman, Captain Ludvigsen, stepped forward. He'd been Isaksen's keenest supporter. Personally, he'd never dreamt of setting foot on a steamship. But he regarded himself as a man of vision.

"A damn shame that it had to end like this," the Commander said.

"Don't feel sorry for me," Isaksen said with an encouraging smile, as though it wasn't he but the Commander who needed consoling. "It was my own fault that it turned out like this. I should have been a better listener."

The Commander wasn't sure he understood what Isaksen meant. "Damn women" was all he said.

"You mustn't blame them," Isaksen said. "It's an unusual position for women to be in. They're just doing what they think best."

The ferry gave a warning hoot. It was time to go.

"Where are you off to?" the Commander asked. He'd prepared a short speech, but he'd forgotten the words.

"New York. Møller's opening a new office. Drop by if you're ever in town. There'll always be work for a man from Marstal."

Isaksen shook the Commander's hand. Then he went around and said goodbye individually to each of them. The ferry gave a last warning blast. He raised his umbrella and lifted his hat. Then he disappeared up the gangway.

There was no longer anyone around to prevent us from becoming what Isaksen had predicted we would become: those left behind.

THE SEAGULL KILLER

"WHERE DID ALBERT bury James Cook?"

Anton was making big plans. He'd become the leader of North, but that wasn't enough for him. As far back as he could remember, there'd been just the two gangs, North and South, and they'd divided the town between them. But now boys from Niels Juelsgade and Tordenskjolds-gade had started forming their own gangs. These had yet to split from South, but Kristian Stærk in Lærkegade had already made the break. His surname, which means "strong," had proved apt, and he named the gang after himself: the Strong Gang.

This trend worried Anton. He liked being at the forefront of everything, and now he feared being "left astern," as he put it. He talked Knud Erik into stealing Albert's sea boots, which were waiting in the attic in Prinsegade for someone to build the museum they'd been bequested to. His idea was that his new gang would be named after Albert and it would accept only those of us who were willing to swear that they were prepared to die, like Albert, with their boots on. He laid claim to the first tryout of the historic, rather battered Madsen footwear, but the boots were far too big for him. Still, he planned to don them whenever a new gang member swore his oath of allegiance, before ordering the initiate to kneel down and kiss them on the toe.

Knud Erik and Vilhjelm protested that he'd never get a self-respecting kid to do that, and if the gang was to be worth joining, he'd need decent kids. Personally, they'd both refuse. They surprised even themselves by this sudden defiance. Finally Anton gave in, and together they agreed that instead of the boot kissing, new gang members would just wear them for the swearing-in. It was more dignified; even Anton could see that. The shrunken head of James Cook would be the group's mascot. Knowledge of its secret existence would cement them all as a gang.

There was just the one problem: James Cook's head lay at the bottom of the sea.

Helmer, who lived in Skovgaden and belonged to North, got permission to borrow his grandfather's smack. Seven boys piled on board, but only Anton, Vilhjelm, and Knud Erik knew what the mission was. Anton told the rest of us we were sailing to the part of the sea called Mørkedybet to go treasure hunting. He described the wooden casket but didn't say what it contained—only that it wasn't a sight for the faint-hearted.

Tordenskjold sat on the thwart next to him, surveying us with his beady, inscrutable eyes. From time to time the bird would take off, soar into the blue sky, and dive into the water without warning. Returning to the boat, he'd settle on the thwart again and fling back his head, his sharp beak tilted skyward. We'd see his throat flex beneath the feathers as, oblivious to our presence, he swallowed the fish he'd caught.

"Well done, Tordenskjold," Anton would say. He always addressed the gull as if it were a dog.

"Does the treasure have to do with the English?" Olav asked. He was a big, burly boy whose hair hung low over his brow.

"In a way," Anton said. "That's all I'm going to tell you."

Knud Erik and Vilhjelm exchanged a look.

We started diving in the Mørkedybet. It was a cloudless day in the first week of June. There were no waves, so you could see far down into the water, though not as far as the seabed, which lay hidden beneath an undulating canopy of green and dark blue. One after another we plunged off the side, but the deeper we dived, the harder it became to see anything: the bottom was an impenetrable shadow. It was creepy to feel the seaweed caressing our stomachs; it was as if the water had grown long, soft fingers and was tentatively reaching for you. A swaying colony of jellyfish kept us company, and at one point a flounder suddenly flipped out from its camouflage in the sand. But there was no sign of any treasure. We rowed from one place to another and kept diving, while our limbs got colder and colder. Anton held out longer than any of us, but every time he broke through the mirror of the water, his lips trembled.

Tordenskjold took off and floated high in the blue sky, as if keeping an eye on us.

It was a hopeless enterprise, and soon it was hard to believe we'd ever imagined finding the head of James Cook at the bottom of the sea. We began to lose our enthusiasm along with our breath and our body heat. The sun was shining, but the sea was still tinged with the chill of winter.

The only one who wasn't shivering with cold was Helmer. He sat warm and dry on the stern thwart, picking at the places where his sunburned skin had started to peel and staring skeptically at the water. "Well, the boat's mine," he said. In his opinion, that was contribution enough.

"Chicken!" we yelled at him.

This offended his manly pride, and he swung himself out on the forestay. But when he realized how cold the water was, he forgot all about saving his honor. He grabbed hold of the stay and tried to scramble back into the empty boat, which promptly keeled over.

No one panicked and no one tried to climb onto the capsized vessel. It was too heavy to turn over, so we started pushing and dragging it toward Birkholm, where we'd be able to right it and bale it out in the shallow waters.

Knud Erik and Vilhjelm stayed behind to fish out everyone's clothes—shirts, sweaters, and trousers that floated on the water like a blanket of algae. They hung some things up to dry on the perches that marked the channel; other items they brought ashore. Only Anton kept diving, determined to find Cook's head. It wasn't until the rest of us were lying naked on the sand on Birkholm, trying to warm up, that we saw him heading in toward the beach. He was swimming on his back and clasping something in one arm, as if he was rescuing a drowning man.

"He's found the treasure! He's found the treasure!" Helmer yelled.

Knud Erik and Vilhjelm looked at each other. Could he really have found the head of James Cook?

Anton staggered up onto the beach. His face was pale blue, and his teeth wouldn't stop chattering, so that for a few minutes he was incapable of saying anything. He squatted, breathing deep and gurgling as if he'd swallowed a lot of water, hugging the treasure all the while. He exchanged a quick glance with Knud Erik and shook his head. Then he got up and stretched out his arms triumphantly. His torso was still shivering with cold, but his face was lit up by a grin.

"Look what I've found!" he shouted.

We all stared at the object he was holding in his hands. At first we couldn't make out what it was. Then Helmer gasped.

"It's a dead man!"

The others could see it now too. Anton was holding a skull, green from long years in the water and covered with seaweed, which hung from the cranium like a drowned man's hair. The lower jaw was missing. Where the eyes used to be, two gaping holes stared with the inscrutable glare of the dead. The bared teeth in the upper jaw grinned in malicious triumph, as though the head anticipated the fate that awaited us when we too became sad human remains.

"No," Anton said. "This isn't a dead man. It's much better. It's a man who was murdered." He lowered his arms and held out the skull to us. "See for yourself."

We formed a circle around him. He turned the skull of the murdered man so we could view it from all angles. At the back of it we saw a big hole.

"It's a Stone Age man," Knud Erik said. "Someone whacked him with an ax."

"No, this is no Stone Age man," Anton declared. He looked around at all of us in turn, pausing between each of us to heighten the suspense. "I know who it is."

"Who is it?" we asked at once.

"I'm not going to tell you right now. But this was the treasure I asked you to find."

Knud Erik and Vilhjelm were well aware that Anton was lying. We hadn't found the head of James Cook. But we'd found something, and Anton always knew how to turn the unexpected to his advantage. "I want you to place your hand on the head of this murdered man," he said, "and swear not to breathe a word to anyone. Or I'll never tell you who it is."

We all placed our hands on the skull. The slimy weed that sprouted on it was disgusting to the touch, and we shuddered. "Swear," Anton commanded. And we swore in unison that we'd never reveal the secret.

"Now tell us who it is."

"Later," Anton said, and made a calming gesture, as if asking us not to get too excited.

We rowed out to the perches and retrieved the rest of our clothes. The sun and the wind had dried them, but none of us had remembered to gather the clogs. We supposed that after Helmer capsized the boat, the current had taken them.

Vilhjelm couldn't find his trousers either, and his embarrassment worsened his stammer.

"Give him yours," Anton said to Knud Erik. "That'll make your mother really cross." This remained Anton's recipe for freedom: annoy your ma and pa as much as you possibly can.

People stared at the bunch of barefoot, trouserless boys walking home through the streets. We were clearly in for a thrashing.

But we didn't care.

Nothing could touch us the day we found the murdered man's skull. We had a secret. And a secret meant power.

A COUPLE OF days later Anton went to see Kristian Stærk to suggest they join forces to form a new gang, which, he reckoned, would be the mightiest in town. Though "the strongest" was the phrasing he chose, quite deliberately, to flatter Strong's leader. He'd taken Knud Erik and Vilhjelm with him as deputies. Their most important task was to bear the wooden casket containing the murdered man's skull, which Anton considered to be vital leverage in the delicate negotiations ahead.

With Kristian Stærk, Anton's biggest disadvantage was his age and his height. Kristian was fifteen and much bigger than Anton. He had broad shoulders and a thick neck, with a remarkably small head perched on top. The prominence of his ears once prompted Anton to remark that his head had "unfolded its wings because it was planning to fly off and find a body that fitted better." But no one came out with things like that when Kristian Stærk was within earshot, because he loved nothing more than dealing out horse bites and Chinese burns, gripping the skin of your wrist between his clammy hands and twisting.

He was an apprentice at an ironmonger's, Samuelsen's in Kongegade, and no one understood why he still bothered running around with a gang of boys and getting into fights. The adults didn't think much of Kristian Stærk, but all the children were scared of him. Maybe that's why he carried on behaving like them. He preferred company that guaranteed his position as the biggest and the strongest.

In Anton's case, it was all the opposite. The adults were no fonder of him than they were of Kristian; the mothers, especially, looked askance at the boy who'd blacked out half of Marstal with a single shot. But we town boys idolized him. Anton never minded whether people were bigger or smaller than him because he was always more ingenious, and that was enough.

Kristian Stærk received him more favorably than he'd expected; his reputation preceded him. But Anton was well aware that his strongest card in their forthcoming talks was the contents of the wooden casket borne by his two deputies, Knud Erik and Vilhjelm. He was adamant that the name of the gang should be the Albert Gang, and he'd extended his plans for the initiation ritual: now, potential gang members would not only wear Albert's boots to pledge allegiance but also place a hand on the head of the murdered man. He'd scrubbed off the seaweed and polished the skull, hole and all, till it shone. Anton had decided that the name of its owner should remain a secret to all but the two leaders of the gang: Kristian Stærk and himself.

He asked Knud Erik to lift the lid of the casket, then solemnly took out the skull and handed it to Kristian Stærk. As he took it in his hands, his protruding ears rocked back and forth: we could tell he was frightened of it, but we could also see the cunning boy's brain, trapped in its adult body, racing at full tilt. The head appealed irresistibly to his imagination and he knew instinctively that it would have the same effect on his peers. Whoever owned the head would have the biggest and strongest gang. He nodded wordlessly, signaling that he agreed to Anton's terms.

"And we're not talking about some Stone Age man clobbered with an ax here," Anton said. He made Kristian squat so their heads were level and whispered the name of the murder victim in his ear. Then they looked each other in the eye to seal their pact.

The first task awaiting the newly formed gang was to procure weapons and equipment for the new recruits. The Margarine Man, who sold butter and margarine from his horse-drawn cart, gave us lids from his empty barrels. We attached straps to them and they became our shields. Kristian Stærk proved himself especially useful by procuring bamboo canes from the ironmonger's, which we turned into bows. We used garden stakes as arrows, but they weren't really much use, though they could give you a bruise if you got hit on the forehead with the blunt end. We tried sharpening one with a knife, but the wood wasn't hard enough to take a point. It was Anton who thought of tying sail needles to them. They not only hurt more, but they pierced the skin too: after a battle, some of us looked like hedgehogs. Especially in the summer, when we had less clothing to protect us, the needles went straight into bare skin. This was the life. Our games were becoming dangerous, and danger was what we wanted. We had a name to honor and the skull of a murdered man as a mascot. Only the actual threat of death made fighting worthwhile.

We had certain rules. All members had to be more than ten years old. Knud Erik and Vilhjelm, who'd only just turned ten, were exceptions; other boys their age weren't admitted. The initiation test wasn't for the weak of spirit. You had to jump into the harbor clutching a big stone, sink to the bottom, walk under the keel of a ship, and surface on the other side. If you dropped the stone while you were down there, you could wave goodbye to membership in the Albert Gang. Few adults would have been able to pass, but instead of scaring off applicants, the test attracted us in huge numbers. We all longed to prove our abilities, and we staggered around in the bottle-green darkness with bursting cheeks and eyes popping out of our heads from oxygen deprivation while the keel of a ship, alive with undulating seaweed, mussels, and barnacles, loomed above us like the overgrown abdomen of a sperm whale. We surfaced like bubbles popping from a bed of mud. As soon as we'd filled our lungs with air, we'd erupt in a yell of triumph while struggling not to sink again with the stone, which lost its weightlessness the moment we raised it above water.

Did we ever think that we'd just been down to the place where so many of our fathers had ended up? We swore that we'd die with our boots on. But then, that's what you do when you drown.

We drew members from every street in town, including the half that had always been South's turf. But the test also meant saying goodbye to some of the old members of North. The most important thing was passing the test; it overrode where you were from. South had a hard core that refused to surrender, but this suited us just fine: we needed someone to fight. We gave them a hard time, and mostly, they got thrashed. Sometimes we'd fight on rafts in the harbor or have sea battles in stolen boats. But most of the time we met in a field in Vestergade where the adults never came. We didn't want to be disturbed while we inflicted cuts and bruises, black eyes, and battered skulls on one another.

Until the terrible thing happened to Kristian Stærk, the leader of South, Henry Levinsen was the only one of us to receive a permanent injury. He'd been wearing a copper flowerpot holder as a helmet, and Kristian Stærk gave it a whack with a stake from a fish trap, ramming it right down over his ears and breaking his nose on the way. Groth, the plumber in Vestergade, had to cut the pot free, and Henry's nose was crooked from that day on.

The adults called us pickaninnies. This meant "children" in a language that wasn't English, German, or French, but one they used in a faraway place. And that's just how the word made us feel: as foreign as natives and savages from an undiscovered island.

If we'd ever bothered to count the members of our gang who were fatherless, we'd have realized just how many of us had at some point started blubbering in the street or the playground, suddenly remembering the father we'd lost when a ship went down. Whether in peacetime or in war, it was always the same: death by drowning, and no funeral afterward.

But we didn't bother ourselves with thoughts like that, even though there was undoubtedly a reason why some of us punched harder than others when we got into fights, and didn't care how much it hurt when we got punched back. We clobbered one another the way a blacksmith clobbers red-hot iron. We did it to forge ourselves into some kind of shape.

Anton claimed that the murdered man appeared below his gable window every night and called out to him in a hollow voice that he wanted his head back. We didn't believe it though. How can you shout from the garden when your head's up in the attic?

Hadn't we noticed that his lower jaw was missing? Anton asked us. That was where the voice came from. He showed us the footprints in the potato bed at the end of the garden.

We reckoned he'd made them himself.

Anton sighed and said that being disbelieved by those nearest to him, even though he possessed great and burdensome knowledge, was a cross he'd have to bear. Not only did he know the identity of the murdered man; he knew the murderer too. He gave us a look that sent shivers down our spines. We didn't believe everything he said, but he had the power to unsettle us all the same.

We didn't know it at the time, but a night would come when there really was a man in the garden calling out for Anton. It wouldn't be the dead man wanting his head back though.

It would be the murderer. And Kristian Stærk would have sent him.

IT ALL STARTED when Anton found he had less spending money than usual and had to cut down on his daily quota of Woodbines. Smoking them gave him a manly voice that made him sound much older. He said that the lack of money stemmed from a problem with Shooter, as he called his cousin's air gun. He'd been taking out fewer local sparrows than usual. He dismissed as pure nonsense the theory that he'd finally eliminated the population. Shooter was to blame.

As a result he decided to put the weapon to a conclusive test by bringing down a really big bird. Marstal's biggest, in fact. It was a decision that in our opinion showed his true stature, but at the same time it worried us; indeed, it made us feel uneasy. Everyone in town was fond of this bird; it even had its own name. Of course, so did the many macaws, cockatoos, nymph parakeets, mynah birds, and canaries that sailors had brought back to Marstal over the years. But those birds sat in cages, begging for sugar lumps—and even Anton's Tordenskjold was half tame. This was different. This bird, whose life Anton planned to end, was a free and noble creature that flew just as far, every year, as the men of Marstal sailed. We were honored that it had chosen to nest in our town. It was a stork, and it lived on the roof of Goldstein's house. We called it Frede.

Goldstein's roof was a strange place for a stork to pick for its nest. Storks like being high up, but Goldstein's house, which lay at the end of Markgade, was a low half-timbered building, painted yellow, with a red-tiled roof that looked set to skid right off the sunken walls. Abraham Goldstein was a white-bearded, mild-mannered shoemaker who never looked at you. There was a reason for that: some said he could give you the evil eye. Any skipper who passed him on the way to his waiting ship postponed his voyage until the next day. What's more, Goldstein had been sighted standing in Market Square early one spring morning, hypnotizing sparrows. They'd flown onto his outstretched hands and hopped all the way up his arms and along his sloping shoulders, even settling on his hat. Others said this was all nonsense and that Goldstein was a completely ordinary man who should be judged only on his ability to resole a pair of boots. As far as that went, no one had any complaints.

We went over to Goldstein's house on a Sunday afternoon in July. The heat had driven everyone to the beach, so Anton could shoot the stork without worrying about witnesses. The whole thing felt infinitely sad. And yet we had to watch. We were sure we'd shut our eyes the moment the stork flapped its black and white wings for the last time and tumbled out of its big nest of twigs, its red legs in the air. We had a vague sense that great men and pointless, sad events went together, and we saw the whole business in that light. Convinced that Anton was destined for greatness, we wanted to be there when it happened.

Anton raised the gun and narrowed one eye. He stood like that for a long time, as if unsure of his aim, and we thought we saw his hand shaking slightly. Looking at the stork, we understood. I felt we were bidding it farewell, and Anton surely felt the same. Then he pulled the trigger.

We all shut our eyes tight, as if on command, and kept them shut as the shot rang out. It seemed loud enough to carry all the way to the Tail. Absolute silence followed. Then Anton cursed. We opened our eyes and looked up at the ridge of the roof. The stork was still standing there, motionless on its pile of twigs, as if it had fallen asleep.

Was that how storks behaved when they were shot? The bullet should have reduced the noble bird to a pathetic heap of feathers and long red legs; instead, it stood upright, as if it had been stuffed.

It took several minutes to figure out why. Anton had missed.

Furiously, he reloaded the air gun and fired again and again, until he had no pellets left. The stork didn't so much as twitch. It was like it was deaf. But deaf or not, one thing was sure. Despite Anton's cannonade with the air gun, Frede remained unharmed.

Suddenly the door to Goldstein's house flew open and a man appeared: not the little old shoemaker, but a giant who had to bend to exit the tiny door. Beneath his blue overalls, his tanned torso was bare; we could see his massive biceps and the blue and red tattoos that snaked around his muscles. It was Goldstein's son-in-law, Bjørn

Karlsen, who worked as a rigger at the steel shipyard. He'd been enjoying his afternoon nap and Anton's shooting had wakened him.

"What the hell do you think you're doing, boy?" he shouted, threatening Anton and the rest of us with his clenched fist. "Have you been shooting at the stork?"

But Anton seemed not to have heard. He was staring at the gun in his hand with a look of intense hatred—a look we fervently hoped he'd never direct at one of us. We wanted to scamper, but we didn't feel we could desert him, so we just backed off a few steps. Which left Anton alone on the pavement when Bjørn Karlsen crossed the street with a couple of giant bounds and grabbed him by the neck. He lifted him up by his shirt collar so that his feet dangled in the air, as if he were nothing but a little kid. And perhaps, to a furious, six-foot-five rigger, that's all he was. To us Anton was anything but that. Yet now we began to realize that there were several ways to see Anton. Bjørn Karlsen dragged Anton down Markgade, bawling him out.

"Is this gun yours?" he demanded, and Anton replied that it was. He couldn't be bothered to explain that it was really his cousin's: it was irrelevant now anyway.

"Let me show you what happens to the likes of you," the rigger said.

He crossed Market Square still holding firmly on to Anton. We followed at a safe distance. We couldn't understand why he didn't say anything. No one ever impressed him, and we'd never met an adult the fast-talking Anton couldn't get the better of. Now he seemed indifferent. As for us, a strange, passive curiosity kept our mouths shut. We could have yelled words of encouragement or hurled abuse at Bjørn Karlsen, but we said nothing.

Bjørn Karlsen continued down Prinsegade and along Havnegade and all the way out onto Dampskibsbroen. We met no one on the way. The town was deserted, like a stage waiting for an important and sad event. Perhaps this would be the day we'd witness the fall of Anton.

The rigger stopped at the very edge of the wharf.

"Here's all that this damn gun's good for," he said. Grabbing Shooter from Anton, he slammed it hard against the side of the wharf, splintering the wooden handle. Anton said nothing but continued to stare into the distance. Then Bjørn Karlsen hurled the broken gun out into the water of the harbor, and with a small splash it disappeared below the surface. Karlsen was still holding Anton by his collar; now he grabbed hold of his trousers too, and with a forceful swing he sent Anton hurtling the same way as Shooter.

When Anton climbed back onto the wharf, he pretended nothing had happened, even though he was soaking wet. He looked at us through narrowed eyes.

"Good riddance to that shitty gun," he said.

There was something he wanted to prove, perhaps to us, but mainly to himself. It had to do with the accuracy of his shot. None of us could fathom how Anton, who'd always been capable of hitting a sparrow from a great distance or a hare running in panic, could miss a stationary stork. So the problem had to be Shooter.

As long as it was Shooter that had missed, and not Anton, his honor was intact. We could follow this line of thought, but we could see no farther.

Next, Anton came up with the idea of shooting an apple off someone's head. He'd do it with a bow and arrow, like William Tell. Obviously, it would have to be done on a windless day. An arrow wouldn't let him down. Bows and arrows were ancient weapons and their accuracy depended on the skill of the archer and not, as in the case of the shitty gun that now lay at the bottom of the sea where it belonged, on some random technical issue. Kristian Stærk would provide the head that the apple would sit on. Who else? It wasn't Anton's style to command his gang members to risk their lives unless he too was in the danger zone. But he and Kristian Stærk were equals. All he had to do was drop the hint, and Kristian would volunteer. He was right. Kristian's ears rocked, as they always did when he was scared, but he didn't hesitate. He'd have been finished if he had.

Over and over we debated the possible outcomes. What if Kristian Stærk's courage failed at the last moment? Or what if Anton's aim failed him again?

The big day came. We went to the field off Vestergade where we'd often met for battles against South. They turned up too, with their leader, Henry Levinsen, who stood there with his new nose, crooked but healed, on show. They hadn't brought weapons. Like the rest of us, they were here to witness Anton's triumph or defeat. All in all we must have been about fifty boys.

It had just stopped raining, and the black mud made it heavy going.

Kristian Stærk positioned himself in the middle of the field, and Knud Erik tried to balance the apple on his head, but it kept rolling off. We hadn't held a dress rehearsal, and most of us considered this a bad omen. Kristian had to twist his long, greasy hair into a kind of cushion before the apple would stay put. His ears kept rocking. We were reminded of Anton's joke about them: that they looked like wings getting ready to carry his head off to another body. Without doubt that was precisely what Kristian Stærk's ears wanted to do right now.

Anton faced him and their eyes met, like those of two duelists. Then Anton started walking backward, narrowing his eyes as though in concentration—but he kept going until it was clear he'd have no earthly chance of hitting the apple: in fact we even doubted that an arrow could travel that far. Knud Erik yelled at him to stop and come back a bit. Anton refused, and it took a lot of arguing before he agreed to shoot from a distance of fifteen paces. Kristian, in the meantime, had grown so confused that he'd dislodged the apple again.

Finally, everything was ready. Anton put the shaft to the string and drew the bow, narrowing his eyes until they were almost shut. Quite a few of us thought the arrow would go as wide as the bullets he'd aimed at the stork, because Anton had lost his knack.

But this time, Anton didn't miss. It wasn't the apple he hit, though. It was Kristian Stærk.

We'd barely registered the twang of the bowstring before Kristian doubled up with a howl and buried his face in his hands. The undamaged apple hit the ground, but none of us saw it fall. We could see that the arrow was stuck into something behind Kristian's hands, but not exactly what. Then Kristian straightened up and roared up at the sky as if he'd lost his mind. It sounded scary; after all, he was almost a fully grown man. He threw back his head so he could scream even louder. The arrow stayed attached for a bit, then fell to the ground. Its tip was red.

Vilhjelm was the first to reach Kristian, a handkerchief at the ready. Anton didn't stir. It seemed he needed time to digest his defeat before he could even begin to take in that he'd shot Kristian Stærk. Later we often discussed which was worse: the damage to his reputation or the injury he'd inflicted.

Finally he snapped out of it. He ran toward Kristian but stopped a

the seagull killer

few feet away. "He needs to go to Doctor Kroman," he said, in a voice that he managed to make completely matter-of-fact.

He was still our leader, and when he spoke we all calmed down, though several of the younger boys continued to shriek in fear when they saw how Vilhjelm's handkerchief had gone red from the pouring blood.

Anton went over to Kristian, who was still clutching his face and roaring. "Let me see where I hit you," Anton said, sweeping Kristian's hair back.

"Don't you touch me," Kristian howled. Nevertheless he took his hands away from his face, and we could see that the blood was coming from his right eye, which was now a mess of red.

Anton took Kristian by the hand, just as he'd done with Henry Levinsen when the flowerpot holder got shoved over his ears. Henry would probably have been reminded of it too, if he'd still been present, but the members of South were long gone. "We'll tell them that he got a twig in his eye," Anton said, and looked around the gang with his old authority.

Together, with Kristian still screaming his head off, we walked through town toward Doctor Kroman's. To everyone we encountered, we reported the same thing: "He got a twig in his eye." We didn't feel that we were covering up for Anton. We were covering up for ourselves. It was none of the adults' business how blood came to be pouring out of one of Kristian Stærk's eyes. That was Doctor Kroman's business. He was the only one who could fix it. We'd leave Kristian's fate to him.

We didn't know then that Kristian's wasn't the only fate to be decided that day in Doctor Kroman's surgery. Anton's would be too. Soon we'd lose him as our leader forever.

By the time we reached the surgery, a large crowd had gathered. The Albert Gang had been joined by twenty to thirty other people. It was outside normal doctor's hours, and Anton had to hammer on the door and call out for Kroman. He opened the door. When he saw Kristian, he immediately put an arm around his shoulder and led him inside. Here Kristian quickly calmed down, as if recognizing he was in safe hands—or perhaps he was just putting on a brave face.

"What do you think you're doing?" Doctor Kroman said, as the rest of us tried to follow them inside. "Get out of here."

He let in only Anton, Vilhjelm, and Knud Erik. Then he asked what had happened, never once taking his eyes off Kristian.

"He got a twig in his eye," Anton said.

"Can't you speak for yourself?" Kroman asked.

"I got a twig in my eye," Kristian Stærk seconded. In this moment we liked him enormously.

Meanwhile Kroman had got Kristian to lie on the couch, and he'd started washing the blood off his face. Carefully he lifted the eyelid to examine the eye fully. We turned away. We had no urge to look.

"Doctor Kroman," Kristian said, and his voice was completely calm. "Will I ever be able to see out of this eye again?"

"I'll be honest with you," the doctor said. "No."

"Will I have to have a glass eye?"

Kristian's voice was still calm, as though the information Kroman had just given him was of no particular importance. Our awe of him soared to new heights.

"No, there's no need for that," Doctor Kroman said.

"Good," Kristian said. "Because I'd prefer to wear a patch."

· · ·

Afterward, when we talked it over, we realized what Kristian's game was. He'd worked out that Anton was finished and he'd spotted an opportunity. He could now become supreme leader of the Albert Gang. He'd have a patch over his eye, and the murdered man's skull would pass to him. But in the surgery, the only thing we grasped was that Kristian Stærk had finally lived up to his name. Our admiration of the way he took the harsh blow that fate had dealt him knew no bounds. We'd completely forgotten that Anton was present too.

But Doctor Kroman hadn't. He stared hard at Anton. "Every time someone gets hurt, you seem to be around," he said. "You brought Henry Levinsen here when he got a flowerpot holder stuck on his head, didn't you?"

"Yes," Anton said. "That's right. But I didn't do it."

"And you didn't try to kill the stork either?" Doctor Kroman pursued his point.

Anton said nothing. He stared straight ahead, as if his thoughts were in a completely different place and he wasn't even listening. Again he narrowed his eyes in that irritating manner we'd noted so often recently, as if he was still taking aim with Shooter.

"And you've got nothing to do with this either?"

"He got a twig in his eye," said Knud Erik.

"I got a twig in my eye," confirmed Kristian from the couch.

"No. It was my fault," Anton blurted. "I shot him."

We couldn't believe our ears. First Anton had invented the lie about the twig. Now suddenly he was telling the whole story, just as it had happened.

"I shot at him with a bow and arrow," he added. "I didn't mean to hit him in the eye. I was aiming for the apple on his head. But it's my fault anyway. I'm the one who did it." He looked straight at Doctor Kroman as he confessed.

A moment ago we'd forgotten all about him. Now we remembered him again, and we knew that no matter what happened, he'd always be our leader. There was only one Anton. And although he might not be the world's best shot, no one could beat him, not even the much bigger Kristian Stærk, three years his senior and sporting a pirate patch.

Doctor Kroman said nothing. We expected him to start scolding Anton, the way our teachers at school always did. We expected him to call him a rotten kid, a bad example, a thug, and a habitual criminal; to reproach him for his latest irresponsible breach of conduct; and to threaten him with the delinquents' home or even an adult prison. But the doctor was a practical man. He understood the body and its functions and he stuck to what he knew. He told us to get out so he could tend to Kristian's eye undisturbed. We headed for the door.

"Just a moment, William Tell," Doctor Kroman called after Anton. "I want you to come and see me tomorrow. There's something I want to take a closer look at."

"Perhaps it's my brain," Anton said afterward. "He wants to find out if I'm the dumbest guy in Marstal." He looked utterly devastated, and no wonder. This was all his fault. He'd wrecked Kristian Stærk's eye. Although we'd lied when he'd asked us to, we were well aware that he'd done something so terrible that it was beyond apology.

The next time we saw Anton, he was wearing glasses.

His face, which until now had looked so determined, hard even, appeared pale and defenseless behind the dark brown horn frames that seemed to drag him downward. He looked as if he wished he were someone else entirely, and if there was a message in the eyes behind the lenses, it was "Please pretend you haven't seen me."

Not only did the spectacles mean that he was finished as leader of the Albert Gang. They meant he was finished entirely. He'd wanted to go to sea one day. That had been the whole point of his life: what else would he do? But a sailor can't wear glasses. It's simply forbidden. He needs to have the eyesight of an eagle. He's allowed to become farsighted when he grows old, but if he's found to be nearsighted when he's young, it's all over. He won't even get his first job.

And over it was. Going to sea hadn't been Anton's plan so much as what nature intended for him, the culmination of his growth into manhood. He was getting taller, bigger, stronger, and older with every year that passed, and one day all these changes, which no earthly power could stop, would result in his stepping onto the deck of a ship and staying there to the end of his days. The spectacles were a farewell to all that: to Schipperstraat in Antwerp, Paradise Street in Liverpool, Tiger Bay in Cardiff, Vieux Carré in New Orleans, Barbary Coast in San Francisco, and Foretop Street in Valparaiso; they were a farewell to Amer Picon, Pernod, and absinthe. It was as if someone had come and trampled on his destiny and left it crushed.

Doctor Kroman might as well have told him he'd never be a man. Anton with spectacles was no longer Anton.

Now we knew why he was always narrowing his eyes, and why

he'd failed to hit the stork. It hadn't been Shooter's fault, but Anton's. He'd stopped being who we thought he was, and oddly enough, we felt sorrier for him than we did for Kristian Stærk. Perhaps that was because we'd all admired Anton and none of us had really liked Kristian, with his rocking ears and casual abuse of anyone younger and smaller. Besides, Kristian's life didn't change because he'd lost an eye. He kept his job as an apprentice ironmonger. But everything changed for Anton.

At first, our teachers interpreted the spectacles symbolically and thought that Anton had become bookish. Perhaps even a scholar. But they soon learned that he was as impossible as ever: the only difference was that they had to make him take off his glasses before they boxed his ears.

To us, Anton's lenses were like two locked doors. He hid behind them and he shut us out. He left the leadership of the Albert Gang to Kristian Stærk, but Kristian derived little benefit from his newly acquired power. The only advantage he had over us was his strength, and that was exclusively based on our age difference. Beyond that, there was nothing he could do that we couldn't do too; nor was there a single thing he could do that Anton couldn't do much better. He had no specific ideas about defending our position among the town's gangs and couldn't come up with a proper response when South, sensing our weakness following the loss of Anton, attacked us, and he was clueless about how to reestablish their respect for us. Kristian Stærk had run out of ideas. He lorded it over us and gave us horse bites and Chinese burns to cover up his anxiety, but his rocking ears told another story.

Not even the eye patch, which made him look quite formidable, changed matters. Especially because Anton refused to hand over Albert's boots and the dead man's skull. Without them, Kristian was unable to perform the initiation rites of the Albert Gang, and he didn't have the imagination to come up with new ones.

Without the boots and the skull, the Albert Gang seemed to lose its soul. In fact, Anton had been its soul, and Kristian Stærk had been nothing more than Anton's right arm. Now he was a right arm with no head, and that was the end of it.

The gang dissolved and new factions emerged. But things were never the same again. The truth is, Marstal became a more peaceful town once Anton got his spectacles. He sat alone in his attic bedroom in Møllevejen. When we learned about General Napoleon and his exile to St. Helena, we were reminded of him. But we judged Anton's fate to be sadder than Napoleon's, because Napoleon created his own misfortune. He'd lost his final, decisive battle, but Anton hadn't lost anything. He'd just become nearsighted.

Kristian withdrew from gang life altogether and no longer needed to beat up smaller kids to prove his worth. Instead, he concentrated on his apprenticeship with Samuelsen. He regarded himself as a grownup, and the ironmonger had come to share this opinion. He'd noticed that the chief effect of Kristian Stærk's conversion to adult-hood was that the stock of canes, which Kristian had considered part of his armory, stopped diminishing abruptly.

Initially, Kristian had felt that the score between him and Anton had been settled peacefully. Anton had said sorry and Kristian had said that he almost pitied him, the poor nearsighted devil, for having to wear those ugly glasses. But when Anton refused to hand over the skull, Kristian realized that he had plenty of reasons to bear him a grudge. First and foremost there was the business of his eye. Second, Anton had always tried to outmaneuver him and make him look a fool. It was his fault that Kristian had lost control of the Albert Gang, a position of power he secretly missed every time he held a cane in his hand. His newly acquired adulthood went no deeper than that. The sum total of all these reasons was the conclusion that he was en-titled to revenge. And, vindictive as he was, he chose the most devious and cruel payback he could imagine.

Anton had entrusted him with the name of the murdered man. And in this case, or so we'd heard, if you knew who the victim was, you'd automatically know who'd killed him. So Kristian decided to tell the murderer that Anton could prove his guilt.

One day Herman entered the ironmonger's shop to buy a fold-ing ruler. When the two of them were alone for a moment, Kristian blurted, "Anton Hansen Hay knows that you killed Holger Jepsen." He hadn't exactly thought through the wording in advance. His ears were rocking madly. "He has his skull as proof. And there's a big hole in it."

If Herman hadn't been as clever as he was, he'd probably have grabbed Kristian Stærk by the collar there and then, and given him a thorough shaking until he revealed where Anton kept the skull. Instead, he wisely played the part of the injured innocent—which entailed whacking Kristian across the head and sending him flying into the tool drawers.

"What the hell do you think you're accusing me of, boy?" he shouted.

Samuelsen came rushing in from the backroom.

"What's going on here?"

His voice sounded frightened. Like most people, he was afraid of Herman.

"I'm teaching your apprentice some manners," Herman said calmly.

Turning on his heel, he left the shop without buying the folding ruler. Kristian rubbed his sore cheek and tried to conceal a smile. His ears had returned to a state of peace. He'd seen Herman's hands shake. And he knew that he'd set something in motion.

ANTON HAD ONCE tried to make us believe that the murdered man stood in the potato bed every night, calling for his head, but we'd never believed him. Then one night a black, stooping figure really did appear in the dark garden below his window, and a voice halfway between a whisper and a hoarse cry called out to Anton for a head—not his own, but his victim's.

"Anton Hansen Hay!"

Anton, who was fast asleep, dreamt that he was being told off by a teacher or by his father, because they were the only ones who ever used his full name. It took a while for him to wake up and even longer to work out where the voice was coming from. He looked out the window and saw the figure, but couldn't make out who it was. He wasn't scared; it had been ages since he'd thought about the dead man's skull, and at first he had no idea what the man below was referring to. He'd never believed in his own story about the ghost haunting him at night, and besides, the black figure standing there now wasn't headless.

Then he woke up fully, and though the man beneath the window still hadn't identified himself, it didn't take Anton long to work out who he was. And then he was scared, more scared than he'd ever been of any ghost, more scared than he'd ever been in his entire life—though that wasn't really saying much. If Herman could kill his stepfather, he could kill Anton too. It would be no problem for him at all.

Having got this far in his reflections, Anton slammed the window shut and hurried downstairs to make sure that all the doors in the house were locked. They weren't, but fortunately the keys were in the locks, and he frantically secured them all, one after another, before running back to his room and hiding under the bed.

Eventually the voice outside the window stopped, but Anton was too exhausted to climb back into bed. His last thought before he fell asleep on the floor was that he was lucky there was no one around to see him.

Anton's father wasn't at home: he'd gone to sea nine months before and he wouldn't be back for at least another year. He knew nothing about Anton's spectacles and Anton was convinced that the day he came home and saw his son's face, his greeting would include the word "four-eyes." No: Anton would never confide in the Foreigner, nor would he ever dream of confiding in his mother or any other adult. Anton was of the opinion that a boy should solve his own problems without expecting help from anyone else, least of all from adults, who were the natural enemies of children. If they had to choose between believing a child and one of their own, they'd never choose the child. Least of all the Terror of Marstal, who'd shot Kristian Stærk in the eye and kept a murdered man's head in his room for months without saying a word, even though he knew who the victim was and could have helped bring the murderer to justice. Anton had always been completely indifferent to the legal significance of his find. As far as he was concerned, Herman was free to go about his business. Now he realized what a foolish attitude that was. But he saw no way out of the fix he was in.

The morning after he'd heard the voice in the garden, Anton found Tordenskjold dead in his cage; his neck had been wrung. His wings had been broken and nearly ripped from his body, as if by a person of unusual strength in an uncontrollable rage. Anton's hands started to shake at the sight and it was a long time before he was able to bury the dead seagull.

From then on, every night he locked all the doors of the house.

"What are you doing that for?" his mother said. "You've grown very strange recently." She was well aware that Anton had changed, but she didn't know whether or not it was cause to celebrate. She didn't ask him if something was wrong. Everything in Anton's life seemed so remote and alien to her that she sometimes caught herself wondering whether she really had given birth to the child known as the Terror of Marstal. Asking him if something was wrong was the same as asking him who he really was, and she knew from bitter experience that the only response he'd give her was a shrug.

"Do we have a chamber pot?" Anton asked.

"Are you ill?"

"Yes," Anton said.

"This isn't about trying to get out of going to school tomorrow, is it?"

"I'll go to school all right. Now get me that chamber pot."

With a puzzled look, his mother handed him the pot. In his room he emptied his bowels of their contents, which were impressive: he'd been holding out all day. When Herman returned that night and started calling out to him, Anton tipped the pot right over his head.

That worked. Herman didn't return, but Anton's victory didn't lift his mood. He started carrying a knife and he stopped eating. At night he slept with Albert's boots on. He didn't know why, but he felt safer with them than without. Perhaps he was preparing himself for death. His features grew stern and sunken, and his horn-rimmed spectacles, which had once made him look like a little boy, now turned him into an old man. Coal-black rings formed under his eyes. Once his head had been covered in bruises, cuts, bumps, and even cheerfully blazing black eyes that turned purple and later faded to yellow. In a boy these were all signs of good health. But black rings weren't: they seemed more a mark of death, like the chalk mark a forester puts on a tree he's going to fell. His mother started worrying about him in earnest, and for once she didn't threaten him with a punishment from his father when he returned home.

"Leave me alone," he said, every time she came near him.

He was always fidgeting with his knife. He wanted to kill Herman, but he couldn't work out how to do it. He could run much faster than Herman, but what good would that do? You can't kill a man by out-running him.

He went outside less and less, and when he did he was always looking over his shoulder. Before, he'd had a gang behind him. Now he was alone.

Not long after the incident with the chamber pot, he heard his name being called from the vegetable garden in broad daylight. He'd begun locking the doors of the house even in daytime, and now, as the rays of the afternoon sun came through the gable window and he heard a voice, he was pleased at his foresight. But it was calling him only by his first name, and the voice wasn't the usual hoarse whisper: it was a boy's voice, like his. Deciding to risk it, he went to the window to look down and saw Knud Erik standing below.

"Is it you?" Anton asked stupidly.

Knud Erik said something he'd wanted to say for a long time. No matter how many times he'd rehearsed it, it always sounded wrong and hopeless, even desperately girly. But it was something he felt driven to say by his useless urge to help and comfort, an urge that had no outlet now that his relationship with his mother had changed and his little sister Edith needed him less.

"I miss you," he said.

He'd known in advance how pathetic this would sound. He was the younger boy, Anton was the older, and, of course, the one always missed the other. But why would the older boy care? The older ones were fine as they were. They certainly didn't need the little guys. He hadn't dared to imagine Anton's response, and when it came it terrified him.

Anton started crying.

Anton wasn't like anyone else, and he didn't cry like anyone else. His tears were full of resistance. It sounded as though a ferret had crawled under his sweater and was ripping his stomach open, as though he suffered terrible physical pain rather than unhappiness. More than anything he looked as if he wanted to stop the sobs, but they escaped him anyway. He covered his mouth with both hands and wailed through his fingers. He cried away Herman, he cried away his fear and his loneliness: you might even think he was crying away his belief that he lived only for himself and had no need for anyone else. But he wasn't. When he eventually regained the power of speech, his voice was utterly matter-of-fact, even though the eyes behind the lenses were bloodshot.

"What the hell do you want?" he asked.

Knud Erik already felt defeated. He'd come out with it, and it had cost him, jeopardizing his still shakily formed manhood. "I miss you." Were those words so hard to understand? What else could he say? I want to help you, to be there for you, to hold out my hand to you? What good would it do, saying that. So Knud Erik said nothing. He'd run out of courage as well as words. He didn't know what else to say, and that's in fact what saved him, because in the pause that followed, Anton was able to compose himself and invite his friend up to his room.

There he blurted out the whole story. Knud Erik was too young to have heard about Jepsen's disappearance on that trip between Marstal and Rudkøbing, so he needed everything explained to him. The story was terrifying enough in itself, but it was more the way Anton told it that frightened Knud Erik. He heard a fresh sob hidden in every pause, which Anton managed to hold back only through considerable effort. The ferret was burying itself deeper and deeper in his intestines, and soon he'd start to scream again.

"He killed Tordenskjold," he said.

Knud Erik hadn't known Holger Jepsen, but he'd known Tordenskjold. He'd often joined in feeding the seagull fish and the sparrows that Anton could no longer sell to the farmer from Midtmarken because they were too far gone. The horror started to take hold of him as well.

"He's definitely going to kill me too." Anton closed his eyes as if he expected the killer blow at any moment.

"Why don't you just give him the skull?"

"I can't." For a moment it was still there, that old stubbornness. Then his despondency returned. "It's hopeless. He'll kill me anyway."

"Nonsense," Knud Erik said, summoning up more courage than he knew he had. "But it's definitely Kristian who told Herman about the head. He was the only one, apart from you, who knew who it belonged to."

Anton flared up in anger. "I'm going to kill Kristian," he hissed. "I can't get Herman, but I can get him."

"You've already shot his eye out. Don't you think that's enough?"

Knud Erik was increasingly astonished at himself. He'd never imagined himself talking to Anton like this. But Anton wasn't the boy he used to be. Which made Knud Erik free to change too.

"I've got an idea," he said.

AS HERMAN LEFT Weber's Café a few days later, he saw two boys hanging around on the other side of the road, staring at him. He walked up toward Kirkestræde, and they followed him on the opposite sidewalk. At first he thought it was a coincidence, but when he turned the corner to head south, they were still there. He didn't know either of them. He stopped and turned around: he wanted them to see that he was on to them. As he'd expected, they stopped too. But they kept staring. He stamped his foot on the cobbles. Startled, they retreated a step. But they continued to stare. When he reached the end of Kirkestræde, they disappeared. But then two more of them popped up in Snaregade, and when he started walking toward the seafront, they followed him, their eyes fixed on him in a persistent and mysterious manner.

"Do I look different from anybody else?" he roared at them. "What are you staring at?"

They didn't reply. He could see them freeze, out of fear, most likely. But they didn't run off. Nor did they taunt him. This baffled him more than anything. There was no point in chasing them. He was big and heavy, and they were better runners than he was. He just had to control himself and pretend they weren't there.

He was used to people in Marstal staring at him: he was a man who lived his life in full public view. He hadn't planned it that way, but he'd known how to exploit it when it happened. He had power, not over people's minds perhaps, but at least over the excursions their minds took. He was of the stuff that gossip and fear feed on, and in his case, both applied. They gloated when he fell, as he'd done when Henckel went to prison and the steel shipyard went bankrupt and he lost everything. But they only gloated because they feared him. They'd thought, back then, he was finished. But Herman was never finished. He'd always bounce back. He recognized the things he saw in them: hate, fear, glee, envy, and attraction. And he took nourishment from it all.

But he didn't comprehend the boys' staring. They were waiting for him outside the boardinghouse in Tværgade, where he stayed when he was in Marstal. He could enter a shop and leave it, or take a stroll along the harbor, or hang out in Weber's Café and always they'd be there, waiting for him. More and more he began to feel the need for shelter and for places to hide. A door to something unknown was opening up inside him. He'd done something once, something on board the *Two Sisters*. At times the memory made him feel stronger. At other times he avoided it. Now he felt dread at the thought of being found out and of the punishment that might ensue, and he understood instinctively that the boys' inscrutable stares held a power he couldn't fight. He'd believed he could scare off that damned Anton. But now every boy in Marstal was Anton's co-conspirator. And there were hundreds of them, with new faces all the time, an unpredictable people's court where he knew the charge but had no idea of the laws, or the nature of the verdict. Their eyes persecuted him everywhere, eventually following him all the way into the darkness around his bed and into his dreams, like a madness that threatened to overpower him. He couldn't kill the whole lot of them after all, though his fists began flexing as they used to in the old days, when something was gearing up inside him. He drank more than before and got into fights more frequently at Weber's Café. That kept the fists busy.

Dutch gin was no longer to his taste; Riga Balsam, famous for a century among the skippers of Marstal, lost its power to cure; whiskey, the greatest healer of them all, had no more effect on him than water. His hands started shaking when he raised his glass to his lips. Shunning the company of others, he drank alone.

Finally he gave in. One day he stomped down to the ferry with his sea bag slung over his shoulder. His intention was to go to Copenhagen and sign on at Jepsen's Shipping Office. The boys knew it. It was as if they could read his thoughts. He didn't bother counting them. But a farewell committee of at least twenty to thirty boys was waiting by the ferry to see him off.

In the usual inscrutable silence, their gaze followed him as he disappeared on board the ferry. He didn't go straight to the saloon to smoke a cigarette, which was his habit when saying goodbye to the town he hated but was linked to inextricably. Instead he stayed in the darkness of the enclosed deck, among the horse-drawn carts and trucks, breathing in engine oil and dung until he was certain he was no longer visible from land.

When he finally entered the saloon and lit the first cigarette of the crossing, he had trouble controlling the shake of his hands.

The idea had come to Knud Erik through a very straightforward process. He'd tried to come up with the most unpleasant thing he could think of, and then made the assumption that Herman would share the feeling. A good thrashing wouldn't work: it was beyond their abilities and besides, he wasn't sure Herman would have minded a fight even if he bore the brunt of it. But burned into his soul was the memory of a worse persecution: the look his mother had fixed on him after his father's death. He couldn't call the look reproachful. It was just a silent searching, and it had followed him everywhere with a question he couldn't answer. What did she want?

He'd collapsed under the weight of that look, which seemed to challenge everything he did without suggesting an alternative. That was the worst thing: when someone looked at you constantly, and you had to guess what they meant by it, while knowing that nothing you could say could ever lighten the burden. He imagined how one could put the same kind of burden on Herman. How the pressure of a silent stare might cause a hardened and unscrupulous murderer, who'd killed even as a boy, to crack.

And Herman would never guess what had hit him. That was the most satisfying part of all. Although he'd got the lads fired up about it, Knud Erik hadn't told them the real reason for their persecution of Herman. It was far too risky to tell them the secret of Holger Jepsen's murder. Who's Jepsen? they might well have asked, and been stupid enough to take their question to the adults, and then there'd have been trouble. No, he'd done something else. He'd taken them to Anton's home and dug up Tordenskjold, right in front of their eyes. He'd shown them the gull's limp neck, its dead eyes, its wide-open beak, the feathers that had lost their shine, and the broken, dislocated wings. The body was crawling with maggots. "Look," he'd said. "Herman did this."

After that, they'd itched to see the seagull killer lying at their feet, transformed into a mass of bloody pulp. His bones should be ground to meal, his skin should be flayed and hung from a tree, his guts should be dragged through the streets. But Knud Erik proposed something far better. They could make him shrink into something less than a man. They'd see his hands shake with fear.

The stares that had haunted and followed the terrifying killer everywhere he turned had been nothing but a boy's imitation of a mother's reproachful look.

No, Herman would never guess what had driven him out of town. We hadn't accused him of a man's murder.

We'd accused him of a seagull's.

HERMAN WAS GONE, but the horn-rimmed spectacles still sat smack-dab in the middle of Anton's face, and he still had no future. The Foreigner wasn't due home until the summer, and in the meantime the boys' confirmation was coming up. Without discussing it with his mother, Anton went up to his teacher, Miss Katballe, and informed her that after seven years he was now quitting school. It was the best day of her life, she replied. With unexpected politeness he bowed, thanked her, and said, likewise.

He was confirmed and publicly swore to denounce the devil and all his works. He didn't know if Hell meant the singe of fire or the gnawing of worms. All he knew was that he was already there, because for him, Hell was a life cut off from the sea and the world it offered. He'd never find out if French girls were the liveliest, or if Portuguese girls really did stink of garlic, or even what garlic was. During the service, he stood beneath the marine painter's altarpiece, which depicted Jesus saving his disciples from the raging storm. He wasn't seeking salvation from the sea, but access to it.

When Pastor Abildgaard placed his hand on Anton's head, he shut his eyes tightly behind his glasses. He was in Hell, and yet he didn't want to go to Heaven. He felt homeless.

Regnar came home and threw a glance at his son. "Why the hell are you still here?" he said. "Why haven't you gone to sea? I even bought you a sea bag."

Anton said nothing. He just waited for the mockery to start.

"Is it because of your spectacles?" his father said. "Runs in the family. I'm so nearsighted, I can't see farther than my own beer gut. Only no one's noticed." He chuckled noisily.

"You can't go to sea if you're wearing spectacles," Anton said patiently, as though talking to a child.

"No," his father answered, unperturbed. "Not if you want to waste your life on board some crock of a schooner. But you're going to be a proper sailor. You want to get yourself a job as a machine man on a steamer. Nobody cares about spectacles there."

So Anton was apprenticed to Hans Baldrian Ulriksen, the smith in Ommel. He learned to tell the difference between a sink hammer, a set hammer, a lock hammer, and a shoeing hammer. He knew when a horse needed a wedge shoe and when it needed a ring shoe. He handled hoof irons, hoof jacks, files, and rasps the way he used to handle the dead man's skull and Albert's boots. They started calling him the Horse Friend. He built his own bicycle so he could cycle the three kilometers to Marstal every evening to attend technical college. He found himself a girlfriend, a redhead just like him. Her name was Marie, and she cut her hair herself every week to stop it from getting too long. One day he'd watched her give a boy a bloody nose for making fun of her red hair, and afterward he'd chivalrously explained to her how to clench her fist when she hit, with her thumb on the outside, not the inside. Marie was a caring girl. When teasing Starry Jens, a filthy man who lived by Market Square, she'd throw a brick at his door like everyone else. But she'd wrap it in a rhubarb leaf beforehand, so as not to scratch the paintwork.

And Anton made a discovery. He found that the same strange rush he used to get when, as leader of the Albert Gang, he left the battlefield with the usual bruises and cuts from arrows, clubs, and spears, he could get again now, from shoeing a horse. He felt as if a great sail had filled with wind and unfurled with a snap inside the uncharted darkness of his head. When he first got his glasses, he thought he'd never again feel the triumph of having power over others. But now, power over people had been replaced by power over objects. When he saw the results of his handiwork, he felt a new kind of triumph. He felt like the upholder of the world.

"Precision is the soul of mechanics, and he who masters mechanics masters much more besides," the blacksmith said. He was a well-read man and fond of expressing himself in philosophical terms.

Anton had found a new course to steer.

Finally it was Knud Erik and Vilhjelm's turn to stand in the church and be confirmed. As they opened their mouths to sing, they stared at the black-hulled model ships hanging from the ceiling. That was their future up there. They sang, as generations had done before them, the old hymn dedicated to the sailing profession, which Pastor Abildgaard had loyally taught them: a hymn about their own fragility, and that of a ship's timbers, and the strength of God:

> The cruel sea shall be our grave
> Be Thou not by our side.
> Mid raging wind and crashing wave
> And lightning's flashing sword,
> Your word can calm the surging tide.
> Be with us now on board!

Knud Erik glanced furtively at Vilhjelm. He hadn't expected him to sing. He hadn't so much as opened his mouth during confirmation classes. But now he was singing, and his stammer had vanished, as if somehow the hymn carried him over even the hardest words. He didn't seem aware of it himself, but Knud Erik noticed it, and it changed his view of hymns.

But if God had worked a miracle, it wasn't a permanent one. On the way back from church Vilhjelm stammered just as badly as ever.

We didn't know it, but we were the last. Our children would never stand in the church and sing that hymn, or stand on the deck of a schooner, at the mercy of the elements. They'd travel to every corner of the world, but they'd barely see a sail. Everything was happening for the last time these days. The sails would be set for the last time. The harbor would be packed with ships for the last time. And then Frederik Isaksen's predictions would come true: for us, there would only be the worst voyages, the most inhospitable coasts, and the roughest seas.

But we were young. We didn't know that. For us, everything was happening for the first time.

THE SAILOR

THE FIRST MATE on board the *Active* didn't tolerate weakness, and when he beat you, he meant it. He'd use a clenched fist, and he'd hit you where it hurt most. But Anker Pinnerup wasn't a strong man. Ravaged by rheumatism and booze, he was a thug with no muscles. In his late forties, he was nearing the age when a sailor goes ashore.

Pinnerup was known as the Old Man, a nickname normally reserved for a ship's captain as a tribute to his skill and experience. In Pinnerup's case it wasn't a compliment, but a reference to his fast-approaching decrepitude. A sharp, clean-shaven chin protruded from his thick gray whiskers like the upended bow of a ship sinking in a sea of waste and dereliction, and this minimal shave was his only concession to personal hygiene. Beneath his filthy, greasy cap a few strands of colorless hair clung to his unwashed scalp. Clamped between his teeth, half-concealed by his beard, was a broken meerschaum pipe that he'd mended with a couple of wooden splints and a piece of twine. Behind his back the able seamen would joke that his patched jacket and trousers reminded them of a red Indian wedding night: Apache on Apache.

When, after serving him coffee for the first time, Knud Erik collected his cup and saucer to wash up, Pinnerup let out a roar and clocked him on the jaw. The cup and saucer were his personal possessions: no one else touched them. And to prove his attachment to his property, he spat in the cup and rubbed at it with his dirty thumb.

"Filthy swine," he cursed. "Monkey brain, snot rag, devil spawn!"

Every other morning, when he was on duty and came to rouse Knud Erik, he'd appear in the fo'c'sle with a thick rope and stand there, gathering his strength, before he began lashing out at the sleeping boy. He always went for his head, but the narrow berth hampered his swipe and diminished the force of his blows. Wakened by the first stroke, Knud Erik would scramble to the bulkhead, where the first mate couldn't reach him. He never uttered a sound: instinct told him that if he gave in to his fear, he'd have a hard job recovering.

One morning Olav, a crewman Knud Erik had known in the Albert Gang, arrived a few minutes before Pinnerup.

"Time to wake up," he whispered, tapping his friend on the shoulder. Knud Erik arranged his eiderdown and pillow so that in the dull light of dawn, they'd look like someone sleeping. The first mate lashed away as usual: when he realized the deception, he seemed to slump. His hand, still clutching the rope, fell limply to his side, and he shuddered as though in a high fever.

"Spawn of the devil," he hissed. "One day I'll get you with the belaying pin."

Then he stormed up the ladder and onto the deck.

When Pinnerup was at the wheel, Knud Erik would inevitably be wakened during the night watch to make coffee or to climb up and rope a sail in the pouring rain. Down below the sea raged, and in the darkness he could dimly make out the foam. Freezing raindrops fell, mingling with the salt on his cheeks. It wasn't impotence or self-pity that made him weep. It was rage and defiance.

At the beginning of his first voyage he'd cried, with his head buried in his bedclothes. He'd cried over his dead father and his rejecting mother, whose coldness he believed was his own fault, and he'd cried over his own nagging feeling of inadequacy. He wasn't sure he'd made the right choice in becoming a sailor. He was paying the price for it now. But he couldn't change his mind and go ashore. The loss of face would be unbearable.

Pinnerup used sleep deprivation as a form of torture. For whole days and nights Knud Erik might get no rest at all. He was called on incessantly, often in the deepest night, and there were times when he'd have to climb the rigging wearing only his underpants. He'd heard stories about what it was like to be the youngest on board. The inexperienced were sent to work in the topgallant sails, twenty-five meters up. Able seamen never ventured that high. You were sent up to the mainmast to take in the vane sail, wobbling on the footropes, with one hand clutching the hand ropes and the other grasping the canvas. You did it even if you'd never been taught how, or if you suffered from vertigo, or if you were just a clumsy idiot who was a danger to himself.

You just got yourself up there and hoped you'd get down again in one piece. Climbing around on the rigging of moored ships in the harbor, for fun, had been a kind of preparation for this, but out here the sea was high and the wind was screaming, for God's sake! Everyone took it for granted that you'd come back alive, but the way you saw it, you'd just become a survivor. Not that anybody noticed.

One time he'd hung up there with the narrow deck far, far below him, frightened out of his skin, every muscle so cramped from the strain that he thought his hands would let go by themselves, just to be free of it. He'd been so terrified that he'd screamed. But no one heard him. Yet it was that scream into nothingness that saved him. It forced the life back to his limbs, the strength to his hands, and the composure to his dizzy head, and brought him safely down.

For Knud Erik, the man who'd sent him up there personified the rule of law at sea. But Pinnerup was also the sea itself: rapacious and dangerous. Unless you toughened up, you'd go under. He stopped worrying about the injustices, the beatings, and the insults. Instead, he allowed himself to be filled with a new sensation: hatred. He hated the first mate. He hated the ship. He hated the sea. It was hatred that kept him on his feet when he staggered across the seesawing deck with the coffeepot in the pitch-dark and scalded his hands. It was hatred that helped him endure the saltwater blisters on his neck and wrists where his permanently wet woolen sweater chafed the unprotected skin, causing huge fluid-filled pustules. It was hatred that kept him silent and stoical when the first mate grabbed him by the neck and twisted his wrist, just where the worst boils were ready to burst.

Hatred was his apprenticeship, and in serving it, he grew up.

It was hard to become a man. But he wanted to. He dug in his heels and made himself stupid, pigheaded, and tough. He became a human battering ram. He'd gain access to life, he realized, only if he kicked its door in.

The skipper of the *Active* was Hans Boutrop, who came from Søndergade. He was a jolly, rotund man whose considerable girth was no thanks to the fare from the Marstal ships' cookbook, which, had it existed, would have had THRIFT stamped all over it in giant letters. As cabin boy, Knud Erik had to help out in the galley, where the captain taught him to make broth. His recipe, he said, was similar to pork broth but with a crucial difference: no pork was involved. Instead, you flavored it generously with brown sugar and vinegar, which you flung into the boiling water along with a handful of rusks.

On Sundays, if the ship was in port, the galley served pot roast. This festive dish was made in its own special pot, whose wooden lid was blackened with age, and the recipe followed the same principle as all other meat dishes: cook for a solid three hours. Period.

On rare occasions they had a pudding, which was left to set in coffee cups, then tipped out and served on plates in small individual wobbling domes that would fit in the palm of your hand. The crew called them nun's titties. The stringy tinned meat from Argentina they called cable yarn, while salt meat was known as red Indian's ass, and salami was never referred to as anything but Roskilde high road.

Often the smell of cooking and the enclosed atmosphere of the galley made him seasick, and he'd open the door and throw up on deck. In bad weather the waves usually washed the puke away, so no one knew about the half-digested meals he routinely sacrificed. When he wasn't seasick, his appetite for his own food was good, and he continued to be amazed that he could cook.

The fo'c'sle was so small that only two men could get dressed at the same time. Below the floor was the coal for the galley oven, and behind the ladder was the potato crate: when its contents began to rot, it exuded a penetrating stench like fermenting shit. A strange smell also emanated from the box where the anchor chain was stored: it was the odor of dried mud and old anchor weed that the broom couldn't dislodge. But from the rope berth came the good, strong smell of brown tar.

The crew relieved themselves into a beer barrel that had been cut in half. The seat was a rough iron ring that scratched the buttocks, and when the sea was bad and waves crashed onto the deck, you'd sometimes get knocked over as you sat on it. In fine weather Knud Erik would climb out on the bowsprit and shit directly into the bow splash. It reminded him of the flushing china bowl at home in Prinsegade.

Fresh water was for drinking only, so he never washed. The deck was cleaner than he was. Once a week, he and the crewmen would get down on their knees and scrub it with "Marstal soda," a brick rubbed against crunchy wet sand.

As a parting gift, Vilhjelm's father had presented Knud Erik with two leather patches, with straps attached. "They're for your hands," he'd said. Being a man of few words, he'd offered no further explanation—and it wasn't until the *Active* called at Egernsund to take on a cargo of bricks bound for Copenhagen that Knud Erik learned their purpose. Pinnerup showed him what they were for, strapping the leather patches to his hands and then giving him a slap across the face by way of encouragement.

So he did have some compassion in him after all, Knud Erik thought.

The bricks were brought from the wharf to the ship, then down a chain of men until they reached the first mate in the hull, who passed them into the stows. They came flying from man to man in packs of four, each bundle weighing somewhere between ten and fifteen kilos. The first one Knud Erik caught nearly knocked him over. If it hadn't been for the leather patches, his skin would have been flayed.

He stood panting for a moment, then took a couple of staggering steps toward the docker next to him in line.

"Listen, pal," the docker warned. "Don't break the chain. Your arms won't be able to stand it. If you don't keep the bricks moving, they get too heavy."

He showed Knud Erik how to twist his body and send the bricks on in a single movement. Knud Erik kept the chain going the next time, but whenever a pack passed through his hands, it felt as if his arms were being wrenched off. His limbs were lead weights, and he strained for breath. But he refused to give up. He found himself drawing on a violence he didn't even know he possessed, a force that came not from his paltry boyish muscles, but from some nameless inner place where it had lain dormant for years.

The docker glanced at him from time to time. "You're doing all right," he said, but the pity in his eyes belied his words. He was an older man who sweated profusely, but he knew the routine. He quickly forgot Knud Erik. There was a piecework rate to keep up.

Every time there was a hitch in the delivery, Pinnerup's hoarse voice would shout from the hull, "Is it that damn boy again?"

The crew of the *Active* had to help with the unloading in Copenhagen as well. They moored in Frederiksholms Kanal; its high granite wharves were a long way up, so it was hard work. The first mate kept well away, sitting on the hatch coaming and watching Knud Erik fall out of rhythm again and again. The difficulty wasn't just passing the heavy pack along, but throwing it upward too. Each time he pushed off, he had to squat deeper. "Lazy swine, Sunday sailor," Pinnerup snarled, and removed the broken meerschaum pipe from his mouth to spit on the deck.

Knud Erik was so used to this kind of thing that he hardly noticed. But one of the dockers put down his pack and went over to the first mate. "We won't put up with this," he said. He pointed to Knud Erik. "The work's too heavy for a boy. Swap places with him and give him a rest."

Pinnerup grinned and pulled his cap down. "So you think you're in charge here?"

"No," the docker said. "I'm the one doing the unloading. But perhaps you'd rather do it yourself?" He turned to his mates. "Feller here thinks he doesn't need us."

They swung themselves up on the wharf and sat down. One of them took out a cigarette, lit it, and passed it around. They didn't look in Pinnerup's direction, but started chatting among themselves, dangling their legs over the edge casually. Knud Erik stood there, confused. Something was happening that he didn't understand. These men didn't belong on the ship. They weren't familiar with its hierarchy or its unseen life-or-death struggles. They seemed to be a law unto themselves, with a strength of their own. They appeared to be their own masters.

"So when's break time over?" Pinnerup snorted sarcastically.

"When you take your hands out of your pockets," retorted one of the dockers.

The other laughed in approval.

Pinnerup shrank. Here he was no one.

Suddenly Knud Erik could see him: a ridiculous, filthy man in patched clothes with a broken pipe in his mouth and a clean-shaven chin sticking out of a beard that looked as if it belonged on a graying orangutan. He'd learned to suffer Pinnerup, yet the first mate had taken up his entire field of vision, like bad weather or a force of nature. Now he saw him as if from the top of the mast, a man the size of an ant on the deck. He saw him through the eyes of the dockers.

He climbed up on the wharf, sat down next to them, and dangled his legs just as they did.

That was Pinnerup's cue. He got up and went over to Knud Erik. The dockers sat up watchfully. One of them flicked his cigarette so that it landed at Pinnerup's feet, then jumped down onto the deck and looked him in the eye. Pinnerup's face tightened.

"Come on, what are you waiting for?" said Pinnerup, lifting up a pack from the deck. The dockers looked at one another and winked. One patted Knud Erik on the shoulder and offered him a cigarette. Then they took their places and the chain resumed.

Knud Erik stayed on the wharf, smoking the first cigarette of his life. He inhaled without coughing. He studied the hand that held it. Every single finger bore a long, painful welt where salt water and harsh ropes had split the tender skin open. Sea gashes, they called them.

"Piss on them," Boutrup had advised. "It rinses them. And then bind them with a bit of wool. That'll close them up."

The sun warmed Knud Erik's face and he felt good.

the sailor

WHEN HE SIGNED off from the *Active*, his mother asked him about the fountain pen. She'd given it to him as a confirmation present so he could write letters home.

"A lot of good that did," Klara commented.

He'd also received a pillow-and-eiderdown set and eighty-five kroner. He'd spent forty-five on a pair of new wooden clogs, which the shoemaker said would last him a lifetime. He bought his oilskins from Lohse's in Havnegade, where he also acquired a folding knife with a white bone handle. A seaweed mattress cost him two kroner, and he'd bought himself a green-painted sea chest with a flat lid as well. He needed work clothes: a sweater and a pair of moleskin trousers. When he was fully equipped, every last øre of the eighty-five kroner was gone.

He'd written to his mother twice during his fifteen months at sea. Both letters basically amounted to the same thing: "Dear Ma, I'm fine."

He couldn't exactly write to her about the time he doubted his decision to go to sea. It would have been the same as agreeing with her view that a sailor's life was brutal misery. Nor could he write about how he'd overcome that doubt, because that meant the die was cast, and he was committed to being a sailor. So he hid himself in his letters: between the "Dear" and the "Love" there was silence.

She could see that he'd developed. But she saw more than that. The gulf between them had widened with every inch he'd grown, almost as if his growth were rooted in spite and disobedience. He looked even more like his father. He had the same blond, curly hair and strong chin. But he had her brown eyes, and when she caught sight of him in an unguarded moment, she still felt she had a share in him. If he possessed an ounce of sense, he'd tire of life at sea in the end.

It was no use talking, or trying to pressure him. Instead, she served his favorite dishes in the months he spent at home, waiting for his next job. An unexpected warmth emerged between them, but then she realized that he'd misinterpreted it, thinking she'd finally accepted his choice. He showed her the scars on his hands and the saltwater blisters and told her about the loathsome Pinnerup, proud to show off his newly acquired status as an experienced sailor.

But she was outraged when she saw what the sea had done to him.

"I hope you've learned your lesson now!" The words escaped her before she could stop them. She heard their sharp desperation.

He looked at her and guardedly said nothing. But she could read the message in his eyes: *You don't understand.*

No, she didn't. She felt her own impotence. The warmth that had briefly flared between them evaporated. Again they withdrew from each other and ate their meals in silence. Her handsome son. Yes, he had her eyes. But nothing else.

That autumn Klara bought the five steamers, the *Unity,* the *Energy,* the *Future,* the *Goal,* and the *Dynamic,* from the widows.

We were pretty taken aback by this purchase, which would have required determination and willpower, not to mention the kind of capital we'd never have believed she had. We didn't know precisely how much she paid, but it had to be in the millions. For a long time we spoke of precious little else. She'd acquired a new, enigmatic quality. We'd finally caught on that she was up to something. But what it was, we didn't know.

The widows had never found a replacement for Isaksen. There'd been several applicants for the post of managing director, but none of them was found suitable, and the company's skippers had shaken their heads. The rumors about why Isaksen resigned had traveled far and wide, so the qualified candidates stayed away, and the company was almost at a standstill. But there was still a chance that a man with the clout to sway the widows and revive their halting business might one day appear and make the town flourish again. This was a risk Klara Friis wasn't prepared to run.

"But, my dear, there's really no need for you to do that," Ellen said when Klara put forward her proposal, after lengthy discussions with Markussen. Ellen seemed to believe that Klara was buying the ships only out of gratitude for the coffee and vanilla cookies they'd served her so frequently.

"It's the least I can do," Klara said, making it sound as if the enormous purchase was a display of good neighborliness, though she was fully aware of the craziness of this conversation. Perhaps the widows had an inkling too, for Ellen turned unusually pale, and Emma and Johanne's cheeks were scarlet. They glanced at one another, and Klara knew that despite their chronic indecisiveness, they'd cave in.

She hadn't exploited them. She'd offered them neither too much nor too little for the steamers, given the unfavorable state of the world market. Profit wasn't what drove her. What drove her was the damage to Knud Erik's hands.

It was the sea gashes that had made her buy the steamers. The saltwater blisters on her poor son's fingers, wrists, and neck had repelled her: they'd brought to mind the wounds of African slaves, chained and dragged across a continent before being stowed on ships and sold. They must have had scars like that, where raw iron had gnawed at bare skin.

This was Klara Friis's mission: to free the slaves. She wanted to release Knud Erik from the chains that his mad and misconceived manhood had shackled him to. Sailors who had barely returned home, bruised and battered by their constant battle with the sea, would set off again as soon as they could, as if begging for more, unable to get enough of the lashings that came at them from all sides: the storms, the waves, the cold, the poor food, the dreadful hygiene, the brutality, the violence. And the weakest always bore the brunt. It had to stop.

A few days later Knud Erik informed her that he'd signed on to a new ship. He would get his sea bag and sea chest ready himself.

THE *KRISTINA* WAS a topgallant 150-ton sail schooner. Her captain, Teodor Bager, was a lean man with an anxious, sunken face, which neither the sun nor the wind seemed to touch. He remained equally pale in summer and winter, in northern hemisphere and southern. People said he had a weak heart and he should have retired, but he was too miserly to do so. His only love was his eighteen-year-old daughter, Kristina. He'd named his ship after her.

There were five men in his crew, including Knud Erik, who was now fifteen. He'd graduated from the galley to the deck as an ordinary seaman and regarded himself as an experienced sailor. He knew his compass. He'd mastered eye splice and short splices, and he could whip a rope. He could heave in the stays, veer, and tack.

The boy in the galley, feeding the fire in the stove, was a pale little fellow, green-faced from seasickness. He was fourteen, as Knud Erik had been, an eternity ago. He recognized Helmer, who was scared of water and who'd once hung from the forestay of his grandfather's smack and made it capsize. And there was another Marstaller, an older man: Hermod Dreymann, the first mate on the *Kristina*.

The two able seamen, Rikard and Algot, were long-haul sailors from Copenhagen. They came from families with no seafaring tradition, as was clear from their kit. They had no sea chest or bedding. Apart from the seaman's classic canvas bag, with its cow horn of grease, sail needle, splicing fid, awl, and sail gloves, neither owned anything but a blanket and a cigar box with shaving gear. Their shore clothes looked just like the clothes they worked in: blue dungarees and sweaters.

Rikard had a tattoo on his right arm of a naked mermaid bearing the Danish flag. Both Rikard and Algot used Polish cigarette holders, fitted with a flat bottom so you could set them upright when there was no ashtray.

The atmosphere of the *Kristina* was much more convivial than that of the *Active*, but Knud Erik's old tormentor haunted him. Fighting exhaustion at night, alone at the wheel, with massive, ice-laden waves looming over the ship, he'd think of Pinnerup. He'd hear his curses in the wind's howl and see his face in the foam of a cresting wave. Yet even as he choked with weariness and felt the merciless torture of his saltwater boils, he knew, with a feeling of triumph, that he'd conquered Pinnerup. He could still hate the sea with a child's defiance, but now it held no fear for him.

He'd seen the first mate humbled. He'd sat on the wharf at Frederiksholms Kanal, dangling his legs with studied indifference, not really understanding what he was learning as he watched Pinnerup backing down in his clash with the dockers. Now he knew. Some things you had to pick up the hard way, but there was no need to humiliate someone just because they were new and green. The experienced man might even lend the inexperienced one a helping hand. And so when Helmer, exhausted and seasick, was ready to give up, Knud Erik helped him in the galley.

"Look," he said. "Your bread's too squishy and the crew keep complaining about it. The problem's in the rising. Shop-bought yeast doesn't work, see."

He found a couple of large potatoes and told Helmer to peel them and chop them up into small pieces. "Now get me a bottle," he said.

He stuffed it three-quarters full with potato pieces and topped it up with water. Then he corked it and secured the cork with twine.

"Leave it somewhere warm, and you'll have yeast in a couple of days. You strain it through a sieve into your dough. But be careful. Don't leave the bottle too long, or the cork will force the twine and explode. With an almighty bang."

Helmer looked at him as if he'd just revealed the secret behind a magic trick. This must be what it was like to be an adult, Knud Erik thought. When people looked at you like that.

The *Kristina* plied the Newfoundland route. It wasn't the voyage Knud Erik had dreamt of, but it was the only work available, and the trip across the cold North Atlantic was a new initiation. They sailed timber from Oskarshamn in Sweden to Ørebakke in Iceland. During the twenty-two-day journey, his seasickness returned and eroded his sense of being an experienced sailor. It took fourteen days to unload the ship.

Afterward they sailed on to Little Bay in Newfoundland with a ballast of volcanic sand from the Icelandic beaches. It was now November, and after a week at sea they hit dense fog. It lifted at noon and lay like a wall on the horizon while the sun shone brightly across the rest of the heavens. Then the fog returned, and the sails turned dark gray with moisture, which dripped heavily onto the deck. One minute they could see far ahead, and the next they couldn't even make out the yardarm of the flying jib boom.

On the third day of the fog, Knud Erik had just taken over at the wheel when the gray mass lifted once more. To one side he saw high, ice-covered mountains. To his surprise, they weren't white, but blue, purple, and a transparent sea green. One resembled a towering, massive cube; its right-angled corners and flat top made it look sculpted by human hands. It seemed so unnatural to him that he began to feel uneasy. He knew only Scandinavia's low, flat, scoured rocky coasts and had certainly never seen anything remotely resembling this savage, alien world of ice and snow.

"Greenland to leeward, Greenland to leeward!" he yelled, and could hear his own fright. The skipper and the first mate rushed up from the cabin. Bager stared briefly at the bizarre mountain landscape. "It's not Greenland," he said. "Those are icebergs."

He pointed to the horizon. More icebergs appeared to windward now, scattered so randomly that any illusion of a continuing coastline was shattered. Then the fog returned, and they were once more marooned on deck.

The skipper looked worried. His sunken face was paler than usual.

"We're in God's hands," he said.

The fog bank remained with them for a fortnight. There was little wind, and the moist sails hung limp most of the time. The great Atlantic swells moved in a slow rhythm that left no ripples under the *Kristina*'s vulnerable hull. The water, which was smooth as oil, seemed to be thickening in the humid cold as if it were turning to ice. They were surrounded by silence, and at first Knud Erik thought that fog must dampen sound, in the same way that it limited the view. It dawned on him that the crew had begun whispering, as if the icebergs crouched behind the wall of fog surrounding the *Kristina* were evil spirits whose attention it was vital not to attract. Their silence got to them, and yet they dared not break it. Knud Erik wondered if even God Himself could keep an eye on them inside this dense gray shroud, as the skipper hoped.

When the fog lifted at last and they saw the sea around them, free of ice, they started shouting. They could have cheered, but they didn't; they just yelled incoherently, wanting to hear the sound of their own voices. Each man had been isolated by the silence: now they were united again. No icebergs were stalking them. Shouting was permitted.

On the following day they spotted the coast of Newfoundland. They'd been at sea for twenty-four days since leaving Iceland.

They docked at Little Bay, and Knud Erik rowed the skipper ashore. He was going to speak to a broker and the port authorities, and he told Knud Erik to wait for him there. When he returned, his face looked strange. Knud Erik positioned the oars and started rowing toward the *Kristina*.

"Knud Erik," Bager said. His tone was confidential, and one that Knud Erik wasn't used to, for the skipper normally addressed him only to give orders. "The *Ane Marie* hasn't arrived." The *Ane Marie* was a Marstal schooner that had left Iceland eight days before the *Kristina*. The skipper sighed and looked across the water. "So she's probably gone. I imagine she hit an iceberg." The skipper kept looking across the water and said nothing else for the rest of the trip.

Vilhjelm. That was Knud Erik's first thought when the skipper told him. Vilhjelm was on board the *Ane Marie*. He looked down at his hands: they were gripping the oars so tightly that his knuckles had gone white. He took huge strokes, as though shaking himself from a trance, and nearly fell off the thwart.

"Mind how you row," Bager said. His voice sounded absent, almost gentle.

In the evening Knud Erik lay in his berth, grieving. Had Vilhjelm surfaced twice? Or had he gone straight to the bottom, pulled down by his clogs and heavy oilskins? What was the last thing he'd seen? The bubbles in the water? Or the frozen chaos of the icebergs? He remembered the unnaturally square iceberg he'd seen on the first day of the *Kristina*'s voyage through the ice and the sinister feeling it had given him. Had the *Ane Marie* collided with it? What had Vilhjelm felt in that moment? Had he cried out for help? But why would he? There was no one to come to the rescue out there in the open North Atlantic.

He recalled their confirmation classes, marking the end of their childhood, where they'd sat in church every Sunday beneath the model ships suspended from the ceiling: symbols of Christian salvation. He'd looked up at the altarpiece, at Jesus calming the storm on Galilee with just a gesture. He'd joined in the old sailor's hymns that they'd all had to learn by heart.

> Abide with us and turn away all evil,
> Send good winds and kind weather,
> To see us safely home!

That's what they'd sung. Had that hymn been on Vilhjelm's lips in the final minutes before the ship went down? Or had he, like Knud Erik in front of the marine artist's Jesus on the Sea of Galilee, begun to doubt?

Where had God been when the *Hydra* vanished without trace, with his father on board? Perhaps God was like Vilhjelm's father? Perhaps He was sitting with His back to us, and just when it really mattered, heard nothing?

It was pure luck who came home and who didn't. Knud Erik could find no meaning in any of it, and he thought this must be how Vilhjelm had felt when he sank for the third time: God was deaf and hadn't heard him.

They had to clean the hold to prepare for the cargo of salt cod. They hosed it down and scrubbed it for five days, covered the bottom with a layer of spruce branches, layered birch bark on top, and nailed more bark to the lining. The smell was pungent and fresh: it was the unfamiliar scent of mountains and woods. They were building a log cabin in the bottom of the ship. Salt cod was a demanding guest. Its lodgings must be ready and waiting.

Every day around midmorning a curious event broke the monotonous routine of loading. A boat approached diagonally across the harbor, passing close to the *Kristina*. At the oars sat a young girl with black hair, cut short so that her neck was bared. She was tanned, with full lips, Oriental eyes, and strong brows. She rowed like a man, with long dogged strokes, and her skiff moved quickly. As she passed the *Kristina* she always glanced up. The crew would stand along the rail and stare back at her, but she never turned away: she seemed to be searching for a particular face.

After a couple of days Knud Erik grew convinced that she was looking at him in particular. One day their eyes met, and he blushed and had to look away himself.

Rikard and Algot talked about her afterward. She always wore a baggy sweater and moleskin trousers, which made it difficult to comment on her body. She was slim, though, that much they could see, and this spurred their speculations. Judging by her dark eyes and generally Oriental appearance, they were sure she was a descendant of "the cunt ladder."

"That's the ladder the hookers in Bangkok use to get on board the ships," Rikard explained. Knud Erik said nothing. He pondered the look he'd exchanged with the girl and blushed every time he recalled the way her eyes had rested on him. Mostly, though, he thought about Vilhjelm. He couldn't sleep at night, and during the day his head buzzed.

The next time the girl came by, Dreymann waved at her. She waved back, and this took the tension out of the situation. She always rowed the same stretch, out to a certain rock, behind which she disappeared. She'd reappear a couple of hours later, but on her return she didn't come close to the ship, or look in its direction. Instead, she fixed her gaze straight ahead and rowed hard.

The question of where she was going and what she did when she got there was another topic of discussion. Rikard puffed on the cigarette in its Polish holder and stated his opinion that she was visiting a lover. Dreymann dismissed that as nonsense.

"Look at her," he protested. "She's not a day over sixteen—seventeen at most."

Rikard responded that the girls started early in Newfoundland, and looked around as if he wouldn't mind being interrogated on how he'd come by this special knowledge.

Dreymann said he thought that the girl was going to piano lessons.

"On a rock?" Rikard mocked him.

At least they knew who she was: the daughter of Mr. Smith, a tall, broad man who went about dressed in plus fours and tartan socks. He lived in a large green-painted wood villa set on a small hill behind the town. Mr. Smith shipped fish—which made him the most important man in Little Bay.

He'd come on board from time to time, and he talked to no one but Bager, though he glanced at Knud Erik occasionally.

Then one day, after Mr. Smith's usual visit to the skipper's cabin and his usual departure of the ship without a word to the crew, Bager came on deck and approached Knud Erik. Clasping his hands behind his back, he leaned forward and spoke quietly to him, as if afraid of being overheard. "Miss Smith would like a visit from you. Tomorrow at four. I'm granting you shore leave."

Knud Erik said nothing.

Bager leaned even closer. "Do you understand what I'm saying to you? A man from Mr. Smith's office will come for you." Knud Erik nodded. "Good," the skipper said, and turned to leave. Suddenly he stopped, as if he'd almost forgotten to deliver another message. "Watch that little madam." He gave Knud Erik a warning look. Then he spun on his heel and left quickly, like a man who'd just got an unpleasant duty out of the way.

The others hadn't noticed the exchange, so there were no comments. Knud Erik was completely dumbstruck. He wasn't generally afraid of girls. After all, he'd often taken care of his little sister. It wasn't until Marie caught Anton's eye that he realized that a girl could be something other than a friend. Still, he couldn't imagine what this girl wanted and was worried that her interest in him would somehow brand him as "girly." He'd stand out from the rest of the crew, and if there was one thing he didn't want, it was that.

Knud Erik was picked up the following day shortly before four o'clock. Rikard and Algot stared and called out after him. All the way up to the villa, his escort ignored him, as if he too found the whole business embarrassing and would prefer not to be involved with it at all. When they reached the house, he abandoned Knud Erik without a word.

Knud Erik stepped onto the veranda and knocked cautiously on the door. An elderly woman in a long, old-fashioned woolen dress opened the door and led him through a large hall into the drawing room. So far no one had spoken to him. She closed the door behind her and Knud Erik found himself alone. Tea was waiting on a small table set with a cloth by the window. Next to the cups and the silver teapot was a china plate of cookies. He remained right inside the door, not sure whether he should sit down on one of the upholstered chairs. Still nothing happened, and he started to wander around the room. He took a cookie from the plate, and at that very moment the door behind him sprang open. Flustered, he turned around and hid the cookie behind his back. It was the girl from the rowboat, but she was no longer wearing her sweater and men's trousers. Instead, she wore a dress. This instantly unsettled him. So did her face, which looked far more vivid than before. True, he'd only seen her from a distance, and now he was seeing her close up for the first time. But that didn't account for her eyes being so much darker and her wide mouth being so red, which made it look even bigger. He had to look down: the impression she made was almost too strong. As she came over to him he noticed that she was taller than he was. But then again, she was older.

She offered him her hand. "Miss Sophie," she said.

"Knud Erik Friis," he said, unsure if he should have added a mister or if that title was exclusively reserved for men like her father, the mighty Mr. Smith.

"Sit down, please," she said in English, and gestured.

Knud Erik obeyed. He was still hiding the cookie. Sitting down with one hand behind his back was awkward, so he furtively placed it on the chair as he lowered himself into it, and felt it crunch underneath him. He was so embarrassed that he couldn't concentrate on a word Miss Sophie was saying to him. Not that he understood it: it was all in English. He felt completely out of place, sitting on a crushed cookie and drinking tea with this girl, who was taller than he was and had strange colors on her face, while a flow of incomprehensible words poured from her mouth—words to which she apparently expected him to reply.

He stared at the amber-colored tea, which he didn't like, nodding earnestly from time to time. Well, that would have to suffice as his contribution to the conversation. It was the best he could do. Suddenly he heard her laugh out loud.

"You're just sitting there, nodding. But you don't understand a word I'm saying."

He gave her an amazed look.

"Yes, I can speak Danish." She kept laughing with her big mouth. "My mother was Danish. But she died a long time ago." She said this in a casual tone, as if she didn't attribute much importance to it. She leaned toward him.

"Are you shy?" she asked.

"Of course not."

He suddenly felt defiant, and without his being aware of it, this dissolved his bashfulness. He was angry now. She'd made him feel like a little boy. On the ship he felt like a man, and he wanted his newly acquired dignity acknowledged here too. Besides, she spoke Danish. He was back on familiar territory. Miss Sophie simply needed to be treated like Marie.

"You know we talk about you on the *Kristina*," he said. "We don't know what you're doing. Some of us think you go to piano lessons. But one fellow says you have a boyfriend you visit every day on the rock."

Miss Sophie gave him a teasing look. "A boyfriend. Well, I might have. And what do you think?" Knud Erik didn't reply. Miss Sophie went on. "No, I don't have a boyfriend out on the rock. I have a dream place. Do you know what a dream place is?"

He shook his head.

"It's a place where you dream. There's a narrow sandy beach just beyond the harbor. That's where I sit and look out across the water. And then I dream. About passenger steamers, airplanes, and zeppelins, about big cities and streets filled with cars and shop fronts along every sidewalk, about movie theaters and restaurants." She reeled off this list without taking a breath, as if she was releasing longings saved up over a long time. "Do you have a dream?"

"Yes," Knud Erik said. "I dream of sailing south around Cape Horn."

"Cape Horn," Miss Sophie said, surprised, and then laughed. "Of course, you're a sailor. But why Cape Horn? It's cold, it's always windy, and ships sink there."

"That may be," Knud Erik said. "But you're not a real sailor unless you've sailed south around Cape Horn."

"Says who?"

"Everyone."

"Are you scared of drowning?" Miss Sophie asked.

Knud Erik hesitated for a moment. Could this odd girl with the face that was at once so strange and so pretty really make him tell her everything?

"Yes," he replied honestly. "I'm very scared of drowning."

"Have you ever come close?" Miss Sophie stared intensely at him from her deep, dark eyes: two lights beaming out of a mineshaft.

"Yes, once."

"How was it?"

He didn't feel like replying to this. "My best friend's just drowned. He went down with the *Ane Marie*, which was headed for here," he said instead.

She looked down, as if she needed some time to compose herself. When she met his eyes again, she smiled encouragingly. "You'll probably drown one day too."

She said this in a completely ordinary tone, as if she was announcing that dinner would be served shortly. It was a ridiculous thing to say. What did she mean? Did she think she could foresee the future? Again he felt her gaze on him. She was scrutinizing him as if exploring the effect of her words.

Knud Erik looked away. The trust between them was broken. His grief at Vilhjelm's death overwhelmed him again and he flared up. "Are you putting a curse on me?"

"Have you ever visited a big city?" she asked, and he detected hesitation in her voice.

"I've been to Copenhagen."

"I don't believe that's exactly a big city. Don't you ever dream about London and Paris, about Shanghai and New York?"

Knud Erik shook his head. "I dream about Cape Horn," he said stubbornly.

"What a shame. In that case we can't elope together. I don't want to go to Cape Horn, it's cold and horrible. Ugh, how boring you are." She started laughing. Then she leaned forward and cradled his head in her hands. "Still, you'll get a kiss before you leave."

She looked into his eyes. For a moment he thought about freeing himself, but then he realized that it would be childish to resist. He had to take it like the man he'd turned into these past few months. He stared back, and something strange happened to him. A shiver went through him, not of fear, but of something else, something unfamiliar. A quiet trembling ran through his body in expectation of something big and joyful. He closed his eyes to receive the kiss and be transported to some place where he instinctively knew no ship could bring him.

He felt her lips against his, their soft fullness pressing against his, with a slightly sticky sensation that made him wish that they need never let go of each other again. His hands, which had been lying on the chair's armrests, slipped up her back, and as they did he felt a crackle of electricity. Then he got hold of her exposed neck beneath the short hair and gently caressed its soft curve. He opened his mouth slightly. He wished she would do the same so their breath could meet, and he could inhale her air into his lungs and breathe through the element that was her. It was like drowning while still being able to breathe. Now he opened himself to another element and let it fill him. He sensed how she followed him and let her lips part slightly. They breathed through each other's mouths and drew air from each other's lungs. Kissing Miss Sophie, he kissed the world. It kissed him back and he was filled with its sweet breath.

Then she pulled back from him, placed one hand on her chest, and laughed. "You really know how to kiss." She handed him a napkin from the table. "Here, you'd better wipe off the lipstick."

He held up his hand to stop her as if she was about to take something valuable from him. "No, come here."

She laughed again. She took hold of his shoulder and wiped his mouth with the napkin. "We can't have you leaving Mr. Smith's house with lipstick all over your face." She gave him a critical look. "Has anyone ever told you how handsome you are?" Her voice was teasing. She got up and took his hand. Then she led him to the door to the hall. "We'll say goodbye here."

"Will we see each other again?" he asked, and realized instantly how this question had exposed him.

She held out her hand and winked at him. "Have a good trip to Cape Horn."

She didn't appear the next day. Late in the afternoon he kept going to the rail to scout across the sea. Ever since he left Mr. Smith's house he'd been agitated. He didn't think that he could be in love. This was different, more like when the *Kristina* heeled unexpectedly and you had to grab hold of the nearest fixed point on the swaying deck.

He thought of her with irritation—no, with more than that: with anger and a fierce desire for vengeance. She'd humiliated him, wiping his mouth with a napkin as if he were a child. He barely dared recall their kiss. Words couldn't contain all the contradictory feelings the memory stirred in him. He'd felt both tiny and huge, as if endlessly transforming. The kiss had sown a longing, and the longing hurt; it bruised his self-esteem.

The others noticed his restless pacing by the rail. "Looking for something in particular?" Dreymann asked. The other seamen laughed, even Helmer, the little shit. They'd been bursting with questions when he returned from the villa, but he'd been dismissive and kept his answers to the minimum.

"What was she like?" Rikard asked, wriggling the naked mermaid on his arm.

"She was nice enough" was all he said. "We drank tea and ate cookies."

"Didn't you do anything else?" The crew studied his face.

"Look at those pretty brown eyes." Rikard sneered at him. "Do you know why your eyes are brown?"

Knud Erik shook his head defenselessly, sensing something crude coming.

"It's because you were kicked so hard up the behind when you were a kid that the shit went the wrong way."

They were making a fool of him, and it was her fault.

And then she didn't even show up!

One by one the days passed, all filled identically with the loading of the salt cod beneath a sky of unchanging gray cloud. Still she didn't appear. He hung around on the deck, unable to stop thinking about her.

The others kept teasing him, and he reddened every time. They referred to her as "Knud Erik's girlfriend."

"Have you had your kiss today?" Rikard would ask.

Or, worse: "Surely she's not bored with you already?"

By now the salt cod was piled almost as high as the hatch coaming: they'd nearly finished loading it, and soon they'd be off to Portugal and he'd never see Miss Sophie again. Out of sheer desperation he decided to do something rash. He'd return, alone, to the big green-painted villa. He'd stand outside the door on the veranda. And when she opened the door, he'd turn his back on her. Or perhaps even spit on the ground. Or something, anything, to show that she meant nothing to him. That he had his own world, and she couldn't rock it.

It was the day before their departure and they were getting the sails ready. With no idea of how he might escape to visit her, his agitation was turning to full-blown panic. If he didn't get to see her one last time, his whole world would come crashing down. Unable to stand it any longer, he leapt over the rail and onto the wharf, then started running toward the green villa. He heard Dreymann call out behind him, but he didn't turn.

Though the villa was visible from the *Kristina,* it was a long way to run and it was mostly uphill. He was out of breath when he got there, but he didn't stop until he reached the front door of the house. He knocked hard, then rested his hands on his thighs for support as he struggled to get his breath back.

He was still in that position when the door was opened.

He'd fantasized about this. With burning cheeks, he'd imagined their last meeting, the one that would set him free. But it wasn't Miss Sophie. It was the older woman who'd shown him into the house on his first visit.

She stared at him expectantly, as if she thought he must have an important message for the owner of the house, the mighty Mr. Smith.

"Miss Sophie," he gasped, still incapable of standing up and breathing normally after his long sprint.

Shaking her head, she said some words in English. He caught only the last two: "... not here."

But the shake of her head conveyed her meaning. If he hadn't been in this wretched state, he'd surely have attacked her, as if it was her fault that the object of his longing wasn't there.

"Where?" he panted, still breathless.

The woman gave him a disapproving look and seemed to consider whether she should even dignify the confused boy's question with an answer. "St. John's," she said finally, and gave him another look, in which he thought he detected both malice and pity, though he couldn't see how that worked.

His heart sank. St. John's was the biggest town in Newfoundland, a frequent port of call for Marstal schooners. That much he knew. He also knew that the *Kristina* wasn't going there.

Miss Sophie had left. That was why she hadn't appeared for her daily rowing trips. She was somewhere else on this endless earth, and they'd never see each other again. Something that had vaguely begun, heading in all directions, was already over.

Bager was waiting for him.

"What's the matter with you, boy?" he said and whacked Knud Erik across the back of his head.

"How far away is St. John's?" Knud Erik asked, ignoring the blow.

"What the hell's got into you?" the skipper exclaimed, and whacked him again. "One hundred and eighty miles, but we're not chasing skirt in St. John's. We're going to Setúbal with salt cod for the Catholics."

The whacks weren't hard. Taps, really. An amused tone had crept into Bager's voice. He looked as if he was enjoying himself. "Foolish boy," he said. "You think you're setting the course now? I told Mr. Smith. Keep that girl under control, I said. She drives people mad. Spoiled little missy."

The barometer had dropped the next morning when they left Little Bay and headed out through the Bay of Notre Dame. Showers of rain came and went, but the sea was calm. Late in the afternoon they came in sight of the lighthouse at Fogo. They'd follow the coast down toward St. John's until they could put out into the Atlantic.

That night a southeasterly storm rose, and they started drifting toward the rocky shore. During the day Knud Erik had observed the tall, dark cliffs through the downpour. Now they moved closer, invisibly, in the impenetrable darkness of the night, and only the distant thunder of the surf warned of their proximity. Everyone below was roused and ordered to put on their oilskins so they could get up on deck immediately if needed.

The searching beam of the Cape Bonavista lighthouse swung across the turbulence, briefly ghosting the sails before sweeping across the shifting veil of densely falling rain. They were close to the coast and the ship was reefed until they were left with only the fore staysail. With all her power lost, the *Kristina* was reduced to pitching in the storm-lashed waves as she fought the gale.

The flicker from the lighthouse came and went like a star that has come too close to the sea, swallowed by waves one minute and struggling free the next. Clouds appeared through the darkness, big-bellied sharks chasing across the sky. Dawn broke and supplanted the beam of the lighthouse. But the storm continued to rage.

The skipper looked at the barometer. "This is going to last awhile," he said darkly, and put a hand to his chest as if fearing his heart couldn't hold out that long.

Knud Erik never would have believed it, but mortal danger can bore a man stiff. The storm continued, day in and day out, ceaselessly battering the hull of the *Kristina*, howling in the rigging, tearing at the wheel, and putting them under constant strain. But paradoxically, the state of alarm anesthetized their nerves, leaving them with a sense of infinite emptiness.

The deck was constantly flooded by the onslaught of the waves, giving the impression that only the stern and the bow remained afloat, like two severed pieces of wreckage that stayed inexplicably equidistant amid the chaos of breaking waves and raging foam.

The low-riding clouds chasing one another across the sky; the ranks of waves rolling endlessly toward the shore; the black, menacing barrier of a coast that represented death rather than salvation if they came too near: all this emptied his head of thought.

The storm endured, but so did the *Kristina*. Even his fear of drowning took a back seat, ceding to the tedious grind and the constant pain from the saltwater blisters, which spread furiously up his arms and around his neck. The only reason the open wounds didn't become infected was that they were permanently wet.

They pitched up and down like that for thirty days. Sometimes the black coastline sank into the horizon until it was nothing but a pencil line between sky and sea; at other times it would rise up and tower over them, an anvil against which the sea could hammer their frail hull.

It didn't make any difference whether the coast was near or far: to him, the black cliffs represented neither destruction nor salvation. They weren't even land. They were just another aspect of the monotony, as real or unreal as the rain-laden clouds above their heads. Day and night came and went.

When he was off duty during the day he'd stagger, dazed, to the bow of the ship, clinging to the ropes the crew had suspended from the rigging for support as they crossed the flooded deck. He'd be waist-high in water already when a wave hit directly amidships and tugged at his legs, spume rampaging all around. He felt like a tightrope walker who has lost his footing and is hanging by his arms on a line suspended between two points in the sky. As if he wasn't aboard a ship at all, but swinging himself across the empty sea.

He'd tumble down the ladder into the dark, foul-smelling fo'c'sle, with its flooded floor and its stove, which remained unlit for fear of carbon monoxide poisoning. He'd climb into his berth fully clothed, because what was the point of undressing, and where would he dry his clothes? They were saturated with salt, which attracted moisture and spray. He'd curl up there like a baby and give way to unconsciousness until a hand shook him and he'd tumble out of his berth, barely awake. Splashing across the floor in his boots, he'd haul himself up the ladder again and meet either darkness or gray light. It was irrelevant which. He'd become a single-purpose being: a servant of the ship, its blind tool in the storm. He no longer considered the matter of his own survival. His only thoughts were of sails to be reefed or taken in, and ropes to be fastened.

Finally the wind died down. The sea still moved in heavy swells, but the rigging no longer shrieked, and the ominous froth disappeared from the waves. The sun broke through the clouds; the big-bellied sharks were gone. The black coastline became land again, a place one could reach, the fulfillment of an impossible dream: firm ground underfoot, an amazing notion that it took time to get used to after thirty days on a convulsing sea.

Two black mountains with almost vertical sides appeared ahead of them. Between them was an opening.

"The Black Hole," Bager said, paler than ever. "The entrance to St. John's."

He turned to Knud Erik, who was at the wheel.

"Seems you'll get your way after all," he grinned. "We'll call at St. John's to take in supplies."

IT WASN'T MISS SOPHIE so much as himself he'd forgotten: the monotony of the storm had swallowed everything. But the skipper's remark and the sight of the Black Hole brought her back. It was more important than ever to see her again. He'd been given a second chance, and it couldn't be a coincidence. Meaning returned to everything, and all the signs pointed in one direction: Miss Sophie.

He forgot about his blisters and his soaked clothes. The tension that had stiffened his body for thirty days and nights, making it ache more than any physical exertion could, disappeared. The storm had passed, only to make way for a new, internal one. The skipper's words had prompted more cursed blushing. An impatient wind whipped his blood and made his heart race.

Bager took the wheel and they passed through the Black Hole. Behind it the narrow entrance to St. John's opened, teeming with fishing boats, schooners, and small steamers. Wooden houses stood on the rocky slopes, and along the harbor front, dense rows of buildings faced the water, with warehouses and ship's chandlers packed cheek by jowl. The wharves were crowded with people and horse carts. The din from the street mingled with the screeching of seagulls, and the stench of fish and fish oil pervaded everything.

He could tell right away that St. John's wasn't a major city. Copenhagen was bigger, but compared to the life here, the wharves along Frederiksholms Kanal seemed deserted. Knud Erik had imagined St. John's as a slightly bigger version of Little Bay: somewhere behind the town Mr. Smith would have a house much like his other one. He could simply stroll up to it, knock on its door, and meet Miss Sophie again. Looking around now, his heart sank. He'd never find her here. There were sure to be hundreds of other Mr. Smiths. And—the thought almost paralyzed him—perhaps hundreds of other Miss Sophies too.

They lit a fire in the fo'c'sle stove to dry their clothes, they washed in buckets of warm water and put on clean clothes from their sea bags. For a while they sat around the table at the center of the fo'c'sle like something on display, before one by one they began to nod off.

"I feel like a damn chicken. Not a single bone left in my body," Rikard said.

The next morning the skipper announced shore leave that same evening, and they all headed into town together. Even Helmer was allowed to join them. The storm had been his baptism; the punctual coffee service he'd provided throughout its duration had earned him membership in the group. They made for Water Street, right behind the harbor front.

Dreymann winked at Knud Erik.

"You'll probably find Miss Sophie there."

They went into a pub and ordered beer. The place was full of women; one of them came over to their table. Her face was painted and she laughed at them with a big, red mouth.

Algot put his arm around her thick waist. "You're better off with this one," he said to Knud Erik. "You'll get more for your money than with that skinny Miss Sophie. Isn't that right, Sally, or whatever the hell your name is."

"Julia. My name's Julia," the woman said in English.

She was used to Scandinavian sailors and understood a little of what was being said. She leaned provocatively toward Knud Erik. She smelled of perfume and sweat: close up, he could see that the floury powder on her face had cracked, revealing wrinkles underneath. She made as if to kiss him: he instinctively turned away, but she grabbed hold of his neck and tried to shove his face deep into her cleavage.

"A pretty boy like you shouldn't sleep alone."

He squirmed free and turned his back on her while the others roared with laughter. He took a swig of beer to cover his embarrassment: its bitterness made him wince. He took another, hoping it would taste better on the second try. It didn't. Did he really have to drink this stuff?

He turned to the others. The woman was now sitting on Algot's lap, a bottle to her lips. The rest of the crew were deep in a discussion.

"Wait till we get to Setúbal; this is nothing," Rikard said.

"Setúbal!" Algot snorted. "Give me Martinique any day. The girls there dance on the tables naked."

"And give you syphilis," Rikard retorted. "We had this bosun once. Spends one night with one of them: three months later he's a goner. Priciest cunt in the world, that one. So no nigger bitches for me, mate."

"I suggest you enjoy it while it lasts, boys," Dreymann said indulgently. "When we get to England, we pick up the skipper's daughter. Once Miss Kristina's on board, you'll need to start watching your language."

Knud Erik looked across to Helmer, who sat clasping his bottle in silence. He hadn't drunk much of his beer, either.

"Don't you have something else to drink here?" Knud Erik said, trying to sound like a man of the world.

"You mean soda pop?" Rikard called out, laughing at his own wit.

"Gin," the woman said. "Give him some gin."

Dreymann sent Knud Erik a warning look. "Watch out," he said. "It's as strong as schnapps."

"Rubbish," Algot shouted. "Looks like water, tastes like water, even has the same damn kick as water." He pushed a glass of clear liquid toward Knud Erik. "Down the hatch."

Relieved to escape the bitter taste of beer, Knud Erik took a large gulp. The others looked at him expectantly. The taste was strong, but it wasn't sharp. Tentatively he took another swig. The gin filled his mouth with a pleasant softness, but rather than sliding down his throat, the sensation seemed to run the other way and creep into the walls of his skull. It felt like someone was stroking the inside of his head.

Algot nodded in approval. The woman grinned and presented her lips to him again, then turned to concentrate on Algot, who had one hand up her skirt.

Knud Erik looked at the others: pleasure was nudging at him. His gaiety needed an outlet. He laughed in the direction of Helmer, who returned his smile, glad of the attention. "You should try gin," he said knowledgeably. "It's much better than beer."

Helmer shook his head. "I'm not thirsty."

"It's not about being thirsty. It's about getting drunk!"

Helmer shook his head again, and Knud Erik decided to ignore him. "Well, what the hell. Cheers!" He raised his glass with a flourish and spotted his reflection in a large mirror with a gilded frame. A blond lock fell across his forehead. His eyes were brown. His mother's eyes. Perhaps he really was a *pretty boy.*

The world seemed to be in motion, but unlike the rolling of a ship, its movements were unpredictable. The floor kept finding new and surprising angles of tilt, and though he quickly learned that his chair was the safest place to be, he kept wanting to get up and stagger about on the floor. There was a playfulness in him that was too big for the company around the table: he wanted to watch the dancers, perhaps steady himself against a table and rock a bit to the music himself, or fling his arms out to embrace them. From time to time a woman's hand would glide tentatively across his chest or touch the seat of his trousers. But the look on his face soon told them that he wasn't heading in that direction tonight, and they'd push deeper into the crowd, their hips swaying.

He surrendered to the pushing and shoving: the sheer pressure of the bodies around him prevented him from falling flat on his face. Suddenly, through the blissful tickle of the gin, the thought struck him that Miss Sophie was out there waiting for him. All he had to do was walk out the door. He'd definitely find her. He contrived to get himself jostled toward the entrance, found the door, and disappeared into Water Street.

He had no idea how late it was, but the street was still teeming with people. Most of them were men swaggering heavily and unsteadily across the sidewalk or in the middle of the street, with whinnying horses and hooting cars navigating around them. But there were also a few women who sized him up with kohl-rimmed eyes.

At the end of Water Street the crowd thinned. He backtracked a few steps and turned off into a side street. Then, on the corner of Duckworth Street, he recognized her neck. She was walking ahead of him, dressed in a winter coat with her boots just visible beneath, and carrying a handbag. He could be wrong about anything else, but not her neck. That bare, exposed neck, suntanned against the winter fur collar: it was hers!

He ran after her, and then lost her. He got tangled in the crowds on the sidewalk, and when he and a hefty woman attempted a mutual sidestep, they bumped together instead. Stumbling again, he felt her sharp alcoholic breath on his face, and darted back onto the street, where a coachman cursed at him and lashed out with his whip. He started running along the gutter, and when he reached the crossing at

King's Road he spotted Miss Sophie, on the opposite side of the street. He soon lost sight of her, but now he was convinced that he was on the right track. He stopped running. It was part of the game. He didn't want to reach her too soon.

They'd kiss again. And afterward? Nothing. The kiss would be enough. Inhaling the air from her lungs into his just one more time.

He started jogging, to test the steadiness of his feet on the pavement. His body had a floating feeling of lightness. Never before had he had such faith in himself.

The street ahead was now completely empty. Signal Hill Road started its long, slow ascent, crowned by Cabot Tower, a black silhouette against the swirling belt of the Milky Way. The whole starry sky seemed to be moving in the same direction he was, like a shimmering flock of birds migrating south through the night.

He spotted her some distance up the slope, a black figure against a road white with frost. She seemed almost to glide, as if pulled by an invisible string.

He started running again but ran out of steam and had to stop to catch his breath. Then he sprinted on past a lake and some trees. Everything was silver, covered with crystals of ice that shone like the stars high in the frosted sky. Below he could see the black forest of masts in the harbor and the illuminated pubs along Water Street.

By the time he caught up with her, she'd reached Cabot Tower. Her back was turned to him, and she was staring out across the Atlantic, which stretched beyond the harbor in all directions, a matte black surface that sucked up all light. For a moment he stood too, completely lost in the sight of its vast expanse.

"Sophie," he called out, then suddenly felt a prick of doubt.

When she turned around, she showed no surprise. "Yes, Knud Erik" was all she said. Her lips were black in the faint starlight. "What do you want from me?" His drunkenness restored his courage. He flung out his arms and prepared to embrace her.

"Are you drunk? Have you been pub-crawling on Water Street?"

He was mortified. "I'm not drunk. I just want a kiss." A smile spread across his face. He'd already forgotten his resentment. He was in a place where the only thing that mattered was the joyful song in his head.

Grabbing her with unexpected force, he leaned forward and found her lips. She didn't move. He'd closed his eyes, but now he opened them again. She was staring straight ahead and didn't appear to see him. Carefully he pressed his lips against hers, hoping to rekindle the magic of their first kiss. But nothing happened.

Then she pushed him away. "Leave me alone," she said. "Do you hear me! Go away!"

Knud Erik stood open-mouthed and uncomprehending.

"Leave me alone!"

She was shouting now, and her eyes glittered. She stamped the frozen ground with her boot. "Stop chasing after me like some dog!"

He was overcome by a sudden anger as intense as his infatuation had been. "Don't you dare call me a dog!" he shouted.

He clasped her shoulders and started shaking her. She was taller than him, but he was stronger. Even with her head jolting, she kept up her defiant glare.

"Dog!" she said again.

All at once he let go of her. He was panting angrily.

"Bitch!" He spat on the ground between her boots, then turned on his heel and started running down Signal Hill.

"Knud Erik!" she called out after him.

He didn't stop. Sprinting wildly over the frozen ground, he nearly crashed several times, but his drunkenness made him strangely light-footed. The cold slapped his face.

At the foot of the hill he found a changed town. The pubs along the harbor front had closed, and the dense, heaving crowd that had filled Water Street had vanished. A fine layer of hoarfrost covered the street, and its cold sheen underscored the unnatural silence that replaced the din. The masts along the wharves were plated with silver and stood like a forest burned to white charcoal: ghost trees that at the slightest gust of wind might turn to dust.

He found the *Kristina* and stumbled down the ladder to the fo'c'sle, where his drunkenness finally overcame him. He collapsed dizzily onto his berth, and his eyes closed instantly.

The next morning Rikard's swearing woke him.

"Where the hell did you get to, boy? What makes you think you can run off like that?"

But the men's grins told him that they'd been too drunk themselves to be seriously worried. He remembered the maelstrom of people in the pub, but his hunt for Miss Sophie through the streets of St. John came back to him only in fragments. Their encounter on Signal Hill was equally blurred. If a door exists between dream and reality, that episode had occurred on the wrong side of it.

He was still stung by a sense of having been jilted. He vaguely recalled the vertiginous feeling that a void had suddenly opened, but he didn't know why. The memory kept churning away, but he remained none the wiser.

The frost had set in. It was ten below zero, and a thin crust of ice was already forming on the water in the harbor. In the afternoon the skipper came over to him. He was expecting a beating, but instead Bager asked him to join him on a visit to town the next day.

"Find a clean sack," he said. "We're going to the butcher's in Queen's Road tomorrow to get fresh meat."

As they walked through town the next day, they noticed clusters of people talking together in the street, where there was a strange, electric atmosphere, a kind of rippling unease. Strangers stopped to address one another, then peeled away toward the next agitated group. Bager, who spoke some English, asked the butcher what was going on. He was a giant of a man in a bloodstained rubber apron, busily chopping his way through heaps of red meat on a white scoured block. He took his time before answering. Finally, putting down his cleaver, he spoke, throwing his arms about and shaking his red-veined head sadly. Knud Erik didn't understand the words, but he recognized the name Mr. Smith.

Bager's face darkened, and he glanced sideways at Knud Erik. "I knew it," he muttered. "I told you so. That girl will come to a bad end. But it's a terrible thing all the same."

"What did he say?" Knud Erik asked after they'd left. Bager didn't reply but increased his pace until he was some distance ahead. They didn't speak all the way back to the harbor, where the skipper kept him at a distance.

The blood seeped through the sack of meat and left large dark stains on the gray sackcloth: Knud Erik felt people must be staring, and got it into his head that he looked like a murderer carrying the remains of his mutilated victim through the town in broad daylight.

When they were back on board, Bager asked Knud Erik to come to his cabin.

"Sit down," he said, seating himself opposite. Then he leaned forward, hands folded on the table. "Miss Sophie," he started, and then he stopped. He gazed down at the table and gave a deep sigh. "Miss Sophie," he repeated, "has gone missing." Then he slammed his hand down hard. "Damn it all!"

Knud Erik said nothing. The room didn't grow black in front of his eyes, but in his head, a kind of night began. He could see everything vividly, but he was incapable of thought.

"She's been gone two days now. No one knows where she is. An accident maybe. Or a crime. Personally I think she's eloped with some sailor. That girl's disturbed. I probably shouldn't be saying this, but she's not quite right in the head. Her mother died a long time ago—she probably told you that—and Mr. Smith was too busy to take care of her properly. She always got her own way. That's never healthy in a girl that age. All this nonsense about inviting crewmen to tea. Dressing up like a lady and turning their heads. You weren't the first, I'm afraid." Bager looked directly at Knud Erik. "And dear Lord, you fell for her too. And yes, I blame myself. I shouldn't have let you go. But Mr. Smith charters us, so it's no easy thing to say no. I didn't see the harm in it. But look what it's led to."

Knud Erik didn't speak. Now he knew what had happened to him in his drunkenness. Or did he? He saw Miss Sophie's slender coat-clad figure glide up Signal Hill where Cabot Tower stood, a dark silhouette against the Milky Way. He saw her face and her lips, black in the pale starlight. And he finally traced the source of the helpless, jilted feeling, which had haunted him these past days. He recalled his wild race down Signal Hill and the silent town shrouded in frost. He'd left Miss Sophie up there under the cold stars. Was whatever happened to her afterward his fault, because he'd run off? But she'd told him to go. She'd stamped her foot and called him a dog.

The whole thing seemed like a dream. Could he trust his own memories? What if something completely different had happened? Had he hit her? Suddenly he wasn't sure.

"I'm sorry," the skipper murmured, still looking at the table. It sounded as if he was talking to himself. "I'm sorry you met her. I know it's my fault." Then he looked up and noticed the vacancy in Knud Erik's eyes. "Are you even listening to me, boy?"

When Knud Erik came up on deck, he could tell right away that the others had heard the news too: it must already have made its way from town to deck, via the harbor. They eyed him gravely but said nothing. Only Rikard's mouth twitched, as if he had a stock of malicious remarks he was dying to use.

What was going through their minds? Did they suspect him of anything? What would they think if they knew the truth about his night on Signal Hill?

Well, what did *he* think?

Did you always know what you did when you got drunk?

The question stumped him. When it came to drunkenness, he had no experience whatsoever. He had no knowledge of himself either. He sensed that something fateful had happened that night on Signal Hill. It wasn't just his confusion that kept him silent: the whole event was too intimate. He couldn't speak about it without revealing his defeat. He desperately needed to confide in somebody, but an instinct for survival made him keep his mouth shut. If he didn't, he knew all too well that the others would fall on him instantly.

That night he climbed into his berth not having exchanged a word with a soul.

By now the temperature was between twelve and fourteen degrees below zero every day, and the next morning the deck was covered in snow. A snowball came flying through the air and turned to powder as it collided with the rigging; soon a full-scale snowball fight had erupted between the ships that lay close together in the narrow port of St. John's.

But Knud Erik didn't join in. He stood with his hands in the pockets of his fleecy moleskin trousers and shuddered in the cold.

THEY SAILED four days after the frost set in. A tugboat led them out through the Black Hole. A brisk wind was blowing from the north, and the Labrador Current was with them. They sailed through pancake ice but made good speed nonetheless. Around eleven in the morning the skipper ordered Knud Erik up the foremast to look for open water. He climbed the rigging until he reached the topgallant yard. Below him the sails were rigid with frost. To the south the ice extended as far as the horizon. The vast unbroken surface gleaming white in the sun gave him a mild feeling of nausea, which stayed with him back on deck.

There was pot roast for lunch, but Knud Erik thought of the butcher's chopping block and the dark patches on the sack where blood from the meat had seeped through. He had no appetite but didn't want to leave his plate untouched either. He put a piece of meat in his mouth and left it there. It seemed to swell. Then he rushed onto the deck and puked over the rail.

On the second day they spied open water. The wind was rising and the sea began to shift. With the temperature still low, the *Kristina* had started to freeze over. During the night and the following day the ship became encased in a thick armor of ice. The halyards froze together in lumps. The bulwark became a frigid wall, and on the main deck the ice stood a foot deep. The bowsprit was a single compact block that reached as far as the martingale.

The fully laden ship now lay even lower in the water, her weight increased by several tons. The bow was already dangerously sunken, and the deck was level with the sea on the other side of the frozen bulwark. The sails looked like heavy sheets of wood that for inscrutable reasons had been hoisted from the mast.

It was like being on board a giant block of ice that a sculptor was trying his best to carve into a ship. But he was hampered by the block's continual growth, which returned the shapes he carved to formlessness: the elegant rigging, the beautifully curved lines of bulwark and bowsprit—everything that gives a ship her definition and her advantage over the sea had become a jumble of lumps and cubes. No longer a ship, nor even a reasonable imitation of a ship, the *Kristina* became a death sentence signed by the frost, stripped of her last remnant of seaworthiness, transformed into a dead weight of ice and salt cod doomed to sink.

The crew knew their lives depended on a successful battle against the relentless freeze. Opening up the tool chest, each man grabbed a maul and attacked the glittering castle that was building itself around them. Ice chunks clattered brightly down from the rigging and the halyards before hitting the deck. But the deck itself resisted all their efforts. They hammered themselves sweaty and red-faced, producing a crack here and a crack there, but the heavy sheet of ice wouldn't shift, and the slope of the bulwark remained imprisoned inside. They couldn't even get close to the frozen lump that was the bowsprit. You risked your life venturing onto it.

At first the challenge excited them, and they yelled out to one another. But after a while they fell silent. In the end their hammer strokes stopped too. Bager was the first to give up. He put a hand to his chest and his eyes turned glassy as he gasped for breath. Then Dreymann called it a day. They slumped, exhausted, where they'd stopped, each wrapped in his own loneliness, as though absorbed by the growing masses of ice all around.

Icicles hung from Dreymann's mustache. He had hoarfrost in his eyebrows and under his nostrils. On Rikard's and Algot's cheeks, where day-old stubble grew, the frost was sprinkled like white powder, giving the men's faces a deathly pallor.

Would their lashes freeze their eyes shut too? Would that be the cold's last gesture, to close their lids so they didn't freeze to death staring up at the gray sky?

BUT IN THE END, the ice that threatened to kill them was their salvation. They'd reached new subzero waters: not pancake ice this time, but a compact layer that in the course of a few hours enclosed them, lifting the *Kristina*'s laden hull half out of the water. For the moment the danger of sinking had passed. The ship's heavy timbers groaned in the ice's powerful grip. If the *Kristina* had been steel, the hull would have cracked from the pressure and they'd have been doomed. Now, while the ice toyed with them, they were granted a stay of execution.

For days they'd been so caught up in struggling to survive that they'd barely glanced at the horizon. Now they spotted another ship far off, also stuck in the ice: a badly damaged schooner with a broken mainmast and sagging rigging.

Dreymann fetched his binoculars and directed them at the distressed ship, trying to read the name on her bow. "Damn it to hell. It's the *Ane Marie*."

"Anyone on board?" Bager sounded hopeful. Knud Erik's heart started pounding. He was thinking about Vilhjelm.

"Not that I can see."

"Let me take a look." Bager snatched the binoculars and began scanning the ice. "Am I seeing things or what?" he exclaimed. "Penguins live at the *South* Pole, don't they?"

"Yes," Dreymann said. "Penguins live at the South Pole. There aren't any around here."

"That's what I thought. Call me crazy or whatever you want. But there's an emperor penguin out there on the ice, right in front of the *Ane Marie*."

The binoculars were passed around. Sure enough, an emperor penguin was rocking back and forth on the vast icy plain in front of the battered schooner.

"It's coming this way," Knud Erik said.

They crowded together by the rail. The penguin approached them slowly, with that unique waddle, dragging and swaying as though pulling a heavy burden across the ice.

"Poor little bastard, you're going to be disappointed," Dreymann said. "What grub we've got left we'll be keeping for ourselves. You won't get a crumb."

Knud Erik stood completely silent, not listening to the others. He was squinting. "That's not a penguin," he said.

Dreymann raised the binoculars again. "Boy's right. If that's a penguin, it's grown old and gray." He scratched his head under his cap. "God only knows what it is then."

"Penguins have a white chest," Algot said. He'd once visited the Zoological Gardens in Copenhagen.

"It's a human being!" shouted Knud Erik. He leapt over the rail and landed with a thud on the ice below, then started racing in the direction of the strange creature, which continued its awkward waddle toward the ship without seeming to notice him. Bager shouted for him to come back, but he didn't hear. He ran like the wind. He could see that what they'd taken for a penguin was a man wearing a winter coat that reached all the way to his feet, completely concealing his legs. He must have been wearing several layers of clothing underneath because the buttons barely held. The sleeves stuck out on the sides like two flippers. A scarf was wrapped around his head, and an oversize flat cap was pulled deep down over his wool Elsinore hood so the brim almost hid his face. From a distance it had looked like a beak.

Knud Erik was closer now, and the man in the coat made an attempt to wave his arms up and down, just like a penguin. Then the two men stood in front of each other. Knud Erik couldn't make out the face; it was buried in clothing. The man had stopped moving and stood as if he had a key in his back and was waiting to be wound up. Knud Erik's hand shook as he removed the flat cap, whether from impatience or fear of what he might find, he barely knew. A small face with sunken cheeks and deep-set eyes appeared. The skin, red-veined from the cold, was marked by frostbite. On the chin grew a fine blanket of down—not a big manly brush, but enough to be called a beard. The hoarfrost hung from it just as it hung from everything else.

"Knud Erik," the face said.

"You've grown a beard."

Tears rushed to Knud Erik's eyes, and he began to sob at a volume that surprised him. Vilhjelm's smile was careful: his lips were badly cracked. Then he rolled his eyes, and his penguin-like shape collapsed on the ice. Behind him Knud Erik could hear Rikard and Algot approaching. They'd finally caught up.

They were sitting in Bager's cabin, staring at the small figure wrapped in blankets and eiderdown, and lying in the berth. Vilhjelm slept peacefully, his sunken face resting on the white pillowcase. They were waiting for him to wake up.

Rikard and Algot had gone on to the *Ane Marie*, where they'd discovered the skipper, Ejvind Hansen, and the first mate, Peter Eriksen, both from Marstal, lying dead in their separate cabins, both looking as if they'd died in their sleep. There was no sign of the crew, and they assumed the men must have been washed overboard in the storm before the ice trapped the ship. The waves had cleared the deck and taken both foremast and mainmast. The crew had tried to rig an emergency mast, lashing the ship's derrick to the stump of the foremast. Through the layer of clear ice that covered the deck of the *Ane Marie*, they could make out a tangle of rigging, spars, and sails. More wreckage was frozen to the side of the ship.

When Rikard and Algot had delivered this account, they both fell silent. They kept shivering as though they were cold, though the narrow cabin was well heated.

When they undressed the unconscious Vilhjelm they'd counted four layers of clothing. He'd probably been the smallest person on board the *Ane Marie*: he must have taken outfits of different sizes from the sea chests of the lost men and put one on top of the other.

"How did he manage to take a shit?" Algot asked.

"I don't think shitting was his biggest problem. It was more getting something down the other way." Dreymann lifted the covers gently and pointed to the boy's emaciated ribs. "Taking his clothes off was like opening a can of sardines and finding nothing but fish bones."

They'd rubbed his naked body with rum, then dressed him in clean clothes, wrapped a blanket around him, and settled him in the berth. Over the thirty-six hours he slept, they took turns watching over him. Knud Erik sat with him the whole time, and Bager let him. Rikard and Algot went to the front to turn in, and Bager and Dreymann swapped shifts sleeping in the first mate's cabin. All rules were ignored. The frost had brought them together, and the *Ane Marie*'s broken silhouette against the gray sky was a fixed reminder of the fate they'd all share unless luck was on their side.

It was in the middle of the second night that Vilhjelm opened his eyes. The only light in the cabin came from the petroleum lamp that was bolted to the bulkhead.

"I'm hungry" was all he said. He sounded like a small child.

Bager, who'd been snoozing next to Knud Erik, bolted up from his sofa. "Damn it," he said drowsily. "The sand digger's boy is awake."

He stumbled toward the berth with a bottle of rum in his hand. Supporting Vilhjelm's head with his other hand, he lifted the bottle to his lips. "That's it, boy, have a swig. It'll do you good." Vilhjelm drank but began to splutter when the acrid taste of undiluted rum filled his mouth.

Bager straightened up. "Dreymann!" he roared, so his voice could be heard across the whole of the rear of the ship. "The boy's awake. Let's have roast beef." The first mate came stumbling into the cabin.

"Aye, aye, Captain." He stood at attention and made a mock salute.

"Dreymann will cook you a Sunday roast you'll never forget." He winked at Vilhjelm, who gave him a pale smile in return.

"But I think the boy needs a few biscuits to start with, Captain."

Bager found the biscuit tin and handed a couple of biscuits to Vilhjelm. He munched them with stiff jaws, as though the movement of chewing had become unfamiliar. Bager, Dreymann, and Knud Erik all watched him as if they'd never seen anyone eat before. "What did you eat before we found you?" Knud Erik asked.

Vilhjelm had survived on sea biscuits, but they'd run out some days before. During the storm a freak wave had cleared the deck and the galley and taken the rest of the provisions with it. The galley boy was already dead: the lifeboat had torn itself loose and crushed him against the bulwark. He didn't know what had happened to the other seamen. He assumed they'd been washed overboard. He had no concept of time anymore and no idea how long the *Ane Marie* had been trapped in the ice.

He spoke in a very weak voice and there were long pauses between the sentences. He didn't sound like Vilhjelm at all.

"The sea biscuits were disgusting," he said. "They were frozen solid and I had to keep them in my mouth for ages to thaw them. I was really scared that the maggots would start wriggling in my mouth when they warmed up. But they'd died from the cold. So I ate them too."

"You probably owe your life to those maggots," Dreymann remarked dryly.

Knud Erik stared at Vilhjelm. He realized suddenly why the emaciated boy in the skipper's berth didn't sound like his friend from Marstal.

"You're not stammering anymore!" he exclaimed.

"Aren't I?"

Rikard and Algot had arrived. They all stared at Vilhjelm as if he were the most wondrous sight they'd ever clapped eyes on. Here lay a boy who couldn't just munch a biscuit: he could articulate properly too.

"Well, would you believe it," Dreymann said. "Seems that keeping your mouth shut can cure a stammer."

"I didn't keep it shut," Vilhjelm said with his new voice.

"So who did you talk to, if I may ask?"

"I read the *Merchant Navy's Book of Sermons* that the skipper had. Every day for hours. I walked up and down the deck and read it aloud. Everyone else was dead. And it was so quiet."

"Helmer!" Bager roared. "Where's that blasted boy? We need to get that roast in the oven."

They all looked toward the door and then back at Vilhjelm. He'd turned his head on the pillow and closed his eyes. He'd fallen asleep again.

Rikard and Algot retrieved the dead first mate and captain from the *Ane Marie,* carried them across the ice on laths, and laid them out on the deck of the *Kristina.* Dreymann wrapped the bodies in canvas and left them there, face-up, waiting for the ice to break so they could be buried at sea. Captain Hansen had once been a hefty man, and his body still looked big under the canvas. Cold and hunger alone couldn't have finished him off; age and the physical weakness it entailed must have played a part too. He'd been in his late fifties, far too old for the North Atlantic.

The first mate, twenty-seven-year-old Peter Eriksen, didn't take up much room next to his skipper. He had a wife and two little girls back in Marstal, and there they were, not knowing what had happened to him. Why had he succumbed and Vilhjelm survived? The first mate of the *Ane Marie* lay on the deck like a great unanswerable question. Knud Erik looked at the contours of his face, which you could faintly make out through the canvas, and thought of his father.

Bager also stood there, contemplating the dead. He'd known Captain Hansen well and was probably asking himself a similar question. Why him? Why not me? The two ships had left Iceland roughly a week apart. It could just as easily have been Bager brought to rest on Captain Hansen's deck. As he gazed at his friend he held the *Book of Sermons* in his hand, and from time to time he read it. Vilhjelm had given it to him, and he was presumably rehearsing the ceremony for burial at sea.

By now Vilhjelm had recovered enough to leave the berth and take a walk on the deck. He even asked if he could help out in the galley. For the time being there were sufficient provisions, and when Vilhjelm and Knud Erik wanted some time alone, they'd give Helmer a break and send him to the fo'c'sle. But he was reluctant to leave: apart from the skipper's cabin the galley was the warmest place on the ship. Besides, he was convinced that the two older boys would begin to share secrets the moment he was gone, and he had the young boy's appetite for tales of experience.

However, little was said about Vilhjelm's time alone on the *Ane Marie*. Whenever Knud Erik asked about it, Vilhjelm fell silent and looked down at the floor. Knud Erik feared he might even start stammering again.

Vilhjelm, who was keen to change the subject, noticed that something was troubling his friend and made Knud Erik tell him about his meeting with Miss Sophie. What bothered him, Knud Erik admitted, wasn't her rejection of him, or the stinging contempt in her voice that night on Signal Hill when she told him to stop chasing her like a dog, but the mystery of her fate and his own part in her disappearance. He was haunted by vague, nagging guilt.

When he'd finished telling the story, Vilhjelm looked at him directly.

"You think everything's about you," he said in his new, clear voice. "She was just crazy. That's all."

Knud Erik objected. "But—"

"I know what you're about to say. You can't remember what happened that night, so you think you might've done something bad. But that's rubbish. She's run off with someone, that's all."

Vilhjelm didn't have a mind superior to Knud Erik's, but in the matter of Miss Sophie, his was a more open one. He wasn't the one in love with her so he could see things objectively—which put him in a better position to judge what had happened.

Knud Erik was greatly relieved.

Having got this far, Vilhjelm started asking in detail about the kiss and its effect.

"I've never tried that." He pondered it, his curiosity finally satisfied.

"You will." Their roles had been reversed. Knud Erik suddenly felt like the wise, experienced one.

"Well, I nearly missed out on it altogether." It was the closest Vilhjelm ever came to admitting that his life had been in danger.

They kept waiting for the ice to break. Finally, the current turned south, the thaw arrived, and with it promise of the first open water. Soon they could say goodbye to their dead passengers. Water started raining down from the rigging: huge icicles came loose and crashed onto the deck. The sails, which had been too rigid to take in, dripped constantly, soaking everything on deck, as if the *Kristina* were an island with its own climate.

A sudden wind began to blow: a sure warning that the ice would soon break. Then a shower came, and they donned their oilskins. A huge crack split the ice close to the hull, followed by another. It was time to bury the dead.

Bager stayed in his cabin and refused to join them. He mumbled through the closed door that he was feeling ill and that they should leave him alone.

Dreymann went to fetch the *Book of Sermons*. They used boards to build a ramp against the rail and placed the bodies on top, so they could glide over the side and disappear into the sea. Soberly they lined up, clasping their sou'westers in their hands.

Dreymann turned to the final pages of the book. The lines were set in old gothic type and he had to squint to see them. The rain was pouring down his cheeks. "Damn it," he muttered. "I'm too old. I can't read those tiny letters. Could one of you young boys do it?" He held the book out toward Rikard and Algot.

"Let me, please," Vilhjelm said. "I know it by heart anyway."

Dreymann stared at him. "Are you telling me that you read aloud the rite for burial at sea on the *Ane Marie*?"

"Yes," Vilhjelm said. "I know the entire *Book of Sermons* by heart." Without waiting for Dreymann's reaction, he started reciting. "Our Lord Jesus Christ says: The hour shall come when everyone in their graves shall hear the voice of the Son of God and they shall go forth—those who have done well, to their resurrection, but those who have done ill, to their judgment."

Helmer stepped forward. In his hand he held a small shovel with ashes from the oven in the galley. This had to serve as the soil, to be scattered over the wrapped bodies before they were surrendered to the sea.

"Earth to earth," Vilhjelm said in his new voice, which Knud Erik still hadn't grown accustomed to. Helmer scattered ashes over the deceased. The rain was falling hard now, and the ashes dissolved and spread in a huge stain across the gray canvas.

"Ashes to ashes."

Another shovelful. The ashes landed in a new place; the canvas grew dirtier.

"Dust to dust."

Rikard and Algot stepped up to the boards and raised them, one after the other. The laced-up canvas bundle that contained the mortal remains of Skipper Hansen fell vertically into the water and disappeared with a splash, muted by the falling rain. Peter Eriksen followed.

The sea was black beneath the gathering storm clouds, and the surrounding ice had taken on a yellow glare. Then suddenly, as if the sea had finally lost patience with its forced burden and now shook its enormous back with irritation, the ice sheet shattered into an infinite number of pieces that shot out sideways and smashed against one another. In the distance, the *Ane Marie* slowly keeled over and sank down on her side: the ice had supported her damaged hull, but now the sea reclaimed her from its grip, to wreck her fully.

Dreymann ordered them on deck immediately. Overhead they saw a nimbus cloud like a huge granite fist, clenched and ready to strike. They were being freed from the ice, but now that very freedom posed a new threat to their survival. They took in the reefs until they were using only the forestay and a close-reefed gaff. A hailstorm hammered them, and the sea raged, with waves mounting on all sides and ice floes riding atop their foaming crests. When the ice broke across the deck, the huge shards collided with everything in their path, and the sound of their crashing fought against the devils' chorus that howled up in the rigging.

They watched the pattern of the waves as they swept the deck: three huge ones were usually followed by several smaller ones, and they chose those quieter moments to slosh their way across the flooded deck to the fo'c'sle.

Bager was still lying down in his cabin. Dreymann took the first shift, together with Knud Erik. Rikard and Algot were sent below to get some sleep. In the galley Helmer clung as tenaciously as a monkey on a falling tree: he'd already proved himself able to provide coffee even if the ship were on her head. Dreymann had ordered Vilhjelm down to his own cabin.

"How hard's it blowing?" Knud Erik shouted. He was clinging to the wheel next to Dreymann, who was practiced enough to keep his balance on the madly veering deck.

At intervals the stern would be lifted by a mountain of water while the bow dove into the foaming sea. Then the bow would rise until the entire ship aimed at some distant point high in the sky. Knud Erik's stomach lurched horribly each time. It was as if the sea, which had so often challenged and not yet conquered them, now demanded one final, decisive rematch.

He'd already learned that in a North Atlantic storm, expert seamanship went a long way, but not the whole way. No sailor could guard against the freak wave that cleared the deck and wiped off the masts. So much depended on luck. Some called it Providence, others God, but luck and God had one thing in common when it came to these waters: their intervention was always arbitrary. Peter Eriksen and Skipper Hansen, whose bodies they'd just given to the sea, were probably no better and no worse seamen than those who'd survived the worst storms. There was no point in trying to make sense of it. Nor were prayers of any use, except to calm and encourage the person praying. He didn't believe they had any influence over whether a ship reached her port safely or not. He understood very well what Vilhjelm had been doing when he'd read aloud from the *Book of Sermons*, all alone on the *Ane Marie*. It was his inner stammer he'd wanted to overcome: that stammer of the soul that sapped his will to survive. But Knud Erik didn't have Vilhjelm's ability to let the word of God work for him.

"How much is it blowing?" Knud Erik shouted again.

"Gale force twelve," Dreymann said.

They reached Newcastle ten days later. Bager reappeared from his cabin, sullen and withdrawn. There was a fear in his eyes that had nothing to do with the hurricane.

Together with Dreymann he surveyed the damage to the ship.

They'd lost the lifeboat, the cabin door had been smashed to pieces, the collar on the mizzenmast had snapped, two water barrels had gone overboard, a gaff had broken, the sails were torn, 190 feet of bulwark had been warped, the name board aft on the starboard side had been smashed, and so had the starboard lantern board.

The damage had to be repaired, but that wasn't the only reason they'd called at Newcastle. Bager's daughter, Kristina, was expected on board. She'd sail with them to Setúbal, in warm and sunny Portugal.

Knud Erik found his fountain pen and wrote a letter to his mother. He asked her to give his best to everyone before describing the fair weather that had followed them right across the Atlantic. There was no need to worry her unnecessarily. He also wrote that he was looking forward to the voyage to Portugal.

Later he admitted that if he'd known what lay ahead, he'd have signed off in Newcastle.

WHEN HERMAN HAD recounted the story before, it had always gone down well. But with Miss Kristina it had the completely opposite effect. Something about it frightened her. Well, that had been his intention, but it had frightened her too much and she'd got up, turned her back on him, and gone to the cabin. With a slight sway of her hips. Damn it, that woman confused him!

Women should never get what they ask for, he thought. Ideally they should be weeping and pleading in front of a locked door. Never be nice to them, even though you might be tempted. That's what made it all so damned difficult. You had to scare them a bit. Not too much and not too little. Too much and they'd panic, and you wouldn't get what you wanted. Too little and they'd wipe their dainty little feet all over you. It took experience to get the balance right. You had to feel your way.

Women liked a man who could make them laugh. But they loved a man who made them cry. They respected only what they didn't understand. Respect was what it was all about. He'd seen enough of the world to know that it wasn't a woman's love that made life bearable for a man. It was her respect, and respect always contains an element of fear.

Knud Erik and Vilhjelm had been there on the hatch, listening to him tell the story about Ravn, the car mechanic who'd sailed with a German U-boat during the war and sunk Danish ships, and who late one night in a doorway in Nyborg had got what was coming to him. Miss Kristina had listened with interest too, until he got to the part about the punishment in the doorway. Then she had left without saying a word.

Afterward Herman had sounded off to Knud Erik and Vilhjelm

about the awkward and fundamentally incomprehensible nature of women. They'd laughed at his remarks but remained guarded, as they always were when he was around. When he'd first come on board, he'd scrutinized them as though trying to retrieve something from his memory. They'd both looked away and he'd brushed it aside.

"There's the Seagull Killer," Vilhjelm had said, when he saw Herman board the *Kristina*.

Everything had gone wrong in Newcastle. Dreymann received a telegram from home, informing him that his wife was gravely ill and might not have long to live.

"I hate to leave my post before the job's done," he said. "I've got four children. Three of them were christened and I wasn't there. Two were confirmed, and one was married — and I wasn't there either. I can't bear the thought that Gertrud might kick the bucket when I'm not around to hold her hand."

Rikard and Algot signed off and made no effort to hide the reason why. They'd had their fill of ships from Marstal that did nothing but sail into one storm after another, and if they'd wanted to be undertakers, they'd have sought a different apprenticeship. The *Kristina* could get along without them, and good luck to her.

They grabbed their kits and half-empty sea bags, stuck their Polish cigarette holders in their mouths, and left.

Bager offered Knud Erik the job of ordinary seaman. He hadn't sailed for quite long enough to merit it, but he knew the job, broadly. And the sail mending that was part of a crewman's duties he could surely pick up. He couldn't increase his wages, though.

"What about me?" Vilhjelm asked.

He and Knud Erik had agreed that they wouldn't be parted.

Bager thought for a long time.

"You'll get your food," he said.

They still needed a first mate. There was none to be had, but Herman, who'd fallen out with the skipper of the *Uranus,* happened to be in Newcastle and was broke. He had the experience and plenty of sailing time, but not the exams: he'd never pulled himself together enough for Navigation College. Bager offered him the job.

When Herman demanded the same wages as a qualified first mate, Bager did the mental arithmetic. He'd already saved the wages of two seamen and had some money to spare. "Your papers aren't in order," he said. "So I'm actually doing you a favor. But I'll add twenty-five kroner to what you usually get as an able seaman."

"Forty kroner," Herman said.

They agreed on thirty-five.

In fact it was Bager, not Herman, whose papers weren't in order—something that Mr. Mattheson at the shipping office in Waterloo Street pointed out to him. All right, they were prepared to overlook the situation with Herman. After all, they'd failed to find him a first mate for the *Kristina* and they wouldn't want to stand in the way of a man trying to make his living. But he couldn't have two boys running around pretending to be seamen. He'd need to sign on at least one qualified man. If he didn't, they'd report him.

That was how Ivar came on board.

The *Kristina* had barely left Newcastle before the first clash occurred.

Knud Erik and Vilhjelm had instantly warmed to Ivar. He came on board wearing his shore clothes, a tailor-made, double-breasted cheviot suit, with French cuff links, a white collar, and a silk tie that he'd bought in Buenos Aires. Ivar was a man of the world. He didn't need to tell them all the places he'd been, from South America to Shanghai: they could tell just by looking at him. He'd gained his experience on steamers and had signed on to a sailing ship only out of curiosity. He was the son of a captain from Hellerup and had yet to decide if the sea life was for him. He was tall and well built, with a mass of raven hair, and he carried himself with the assurance of a man who's left more than one fight victorious.

Ivar had a talent for things mechanical. He brought along a radio that he'd built himself and could take apart and reassemble any way he wanted. He settled it on the hatch when they were in port and attached the antenna to the rigging.

"You'll never get that thing to work," Herman said, the first time Ivar set it up. Which made Herman look a fool because of course the radio had worked. They heard fragments of foreign languages, voices from different parts of the globe, and dance music, the kind you normally got to hear only in the French Channel ports.

Even Herman couldn't stay away when Ivar hooked up the radio. Ivar glanced over and smiled at him. "Right, the first mate's come to join us," he said.

Herman spun on his heel and left.

When they were sure he was out of earshot, they laughed at him.

Knud Erik and Vilhjelm always referred to Herman as the Seagull Killer, though Vilhjelm had learned the true extent of Herman's crimes long ago. One day Ivar, overhearing the odd nickname, asked about it, but they immediately deflected him. It was just a name. Anyway, didn't he look just like someone likely to strangle seagulls with his bare hands? Ivar shrugged. Their explanation didn't really make sense, but he didn't probe further.

Later they regretted not telling him the truth. They knew what Herman had done: they'd held the skull of his victim in their hands. They used the nickname like a counterspell, to dampen the terror they constantly felt in his presence.

They sought out Ivar's company because they knew they needed protection.

Ivar hadn't been on board long before he expressed indignation at the food. He found their evening meals, in particular, entirely inadequate. Twice a week, on Wednesdays and Saturdays, they were given a cheese, a salami sausage, a tin of liver pâté, and a tin of sardines: this was to be shared among four men. The upshot being that they'd always wolf down the cold meats, cheese, and sardines the first evening and survive on rye bread until the next handout.

"But it's not my fault," Helmer said, spreading his arms helplessly.

Ivar went to the captain and on behalf of the crew complained about the small portions. By the crew he meant the three boys he shared the fo'c'sle with.

Miss Kristina was in the cabin when Ivar arrived. She was tall and slim, with a mane of chestnut hair, and she had the frank, energetic nature typical of most girls from Marstal. It was in their upbringing; they knew that one day they'd have absolute rule of the home. She also had dimples and a beauty spot by her right nostril, which always made her look as if she'd just dressed up for a party.

At first Bager said nothing. He glanced furtively at his daughter, as if he wanted to ask her opinion. He was clearly caught between his own meanness and the desire to make a good impression on her.

"Just because you've worked on a steamer," Herman snarled. He was present as well and considered himself the captain's spokesman.

"I know maritime law," Ivar said calmly. "We're not getting the food we're entitled to. In the future I insist on seeing the food weighed out." He turned and smiled at Miss Kristina. "You might think it strange to attach such importance to a few grams of food, miss?"

She shook her head and returned his smile, unaffected by the tense atmosphere in the cabin. Herman looked from one to the other with a watchful eye. It was obvious what he thought. Ivar was trying to influence the captain through his daughter.

"Please don't think that we're afraid of hard work, miss," Ivar continued. "We work hard, but most of us have yet to turn twenty. Just take a look at the cook and the two crewmen: they're only fifteen, not even fully grown. And then we work in the fresh air all day. You've probably noticed yourself that the sea air gives you an appetite."

Herman cleared his throat menacingly. Ivar's eloquence had paralyzed him, and he needed to gain time. But Ivar wasn't even looking in his direction. He was still smiling at Miss Kristina, and she was returning his smile as though they had a secret bond.

Bager didn't seem to notice any of this. But now he spoke—and what he said was so striking that it should have been clear even then that something was bound to go wrong on board the *Kristina*.

"Five loaves and two fishes," he said. He seemed to be trying to make his voice sound firm, but it was strangely insubstantial, as though his thoughts were somewhere far away.

"Sorry?" Ivar made an effort to be polite. "I don't think I understood you."

Bager raised his voice. "I said five loaves and two fishes. That was all Our Lord Jesus Christ needed to feed five thousand people. Are one cheese, one salami, a tin of liver pâté, and a tin of sardines not enough for you, though you are only four?"

"We're not talking about Bible history. We're on board the *Kristina* of Marstal, and maritime law states—"

"Do you deny the Lord your God?" Bager said in a sharp tone, giving Ivar an accusing stare. "How is it possible, after God has borne you, clothed you, and kept you for so many days, for you to doubt that He can and will continue to do so?"

Even the articulate Ivar was left speechless by this outburst from the normally taciturn Captain Bager. He gave Kristina a questioning look. She spread her hands, at a loss. You could expect just about anything from a Marstal skipper. He could be unyielding and harsh, unreasonable in his demands, unfair at times. First and foremost he could be stingy. Thrift was essential for his survival. But no one had ever heard a captain back his actions with religious quotations, and certainly not in such foggy terms.

Herman suppressed a brutal laugh. This was promising to be truly entertaining.

"I'm talking about maritime law," Ivar said again, firmly.

Miss Kristina leaned toward Bager and placed her hand on his. "Be reasonable, Father. It's no skin off your nose if the crew gets a bit more to eat."

Bager clutched his chest, like a man suffering some deep inner turmoil. "As you wish," he said finally, in a weak voice.

"Father, are you feeling unwell?" Miss Kristina asked anxiously.

Back in the fo'c'sle Ivar told the story to the crew. Then he looked at Knud Erik.

"You've sailed with him the longest. Is he normally like this?"

"Stingy, yes," Knud Erik said. "But speaking like Pastor Abildgaard?" He shook his head.

"What did he say again?" Vilhjelm asked.

"It was that bit from the Bible about the five loaves and the two fishes." Ivar thought a moment. "Then he asked me how we could doubt the Lord who'd clothed and kept us."

"It's from the *Book of Sermons*," Vilhjelm said. "Seventh Sunday after Trinity. A sermon for the poor and for the rich. By Jonas Dahl, a seamen's priest in Bergen. Bager seems to have memorized it. He must be in a really bad way."

From time to time Miss Kristina invited the whole crew for pancakes or went around the deck with the coffeepot. In the galley Helmer was constantly beaming. She came in often to help with the cooking. It was so narrow there that they had to stand close to each other, and the rustling of her dress and her female presence intoxicated him. She praised his skills, and he made an extra effort. They all did. It was good to have a woman on board.

Miss Kristina would often sit down next to the helmsman and chat while he kept one eye on the rigging and the other on her.

One evening as they approached the coast of Portugal, she strolled the deck in the moonlight with Ivar. Herman stood by the rail, trying without success to eavesdrop on their muted conversation. She'd turned her back on him after he'd told the story about Ravn in Nyborg and kept him at a distance, though she wasn't generally reserved. Since the confrontation about the food, his stock had been lower than ever.

He felt Miss Kristina's presence like something poisonous and something infinitely sweet mixing together in his blood. Inside him, a lack of willpower and a colossal tension battled it out. He felt both weak and furious at the same time. He went around with his fists clenched, ready to fight, yet what he wanted most of all was to hold and be held.

The *Kristina* cut up against the south wind that always blew along the Portuguese coast. When Ivar was on duty, Miss Kristina would sit at the helm next to him. Herman went over to them, stiff and haughty, relishing his role as the first mate. "The helmsman is not to be distracted," he said curtly, and remained there, with his hands folded behind his back until she got up and left.

Yes, she had to yield to him there. However, he was uncertain whether her yielding had been a victory or a defeat. He got no closer to her and was beginning to think of her and Ivar as "the couple." After all, that was what they were becoming.

One afternoon a shoal of dolphins broke the monotony. "Springers!" the helmsman cried out, and the crew bustled to arm themselves. Ivar led the way. He jumped out on the bowsprit and hurled the harpoon into the water just as the ship dived, shortening the distance to the nearest leaping creature. The dolphin struggled powerfully as Ivar pulled in the line. Then Knud Erik came over and managed to get a hawser around its tail.

Herman disappeared down to his cabin and reappeared on deck with a revolver in his hand. The crew formed a circle around the dolphin, which arched its smooth, elegant body in dying spasms while its strong tail beat the deck rhythmically, its blood pouring out and flowing in a greasy stream across the planks. Miss Kristina watched from a distance, with her hands over her mouth. Someone had to deliver the deathblow to the convulsing animal.

"Move!" Herman shouted.

They turned to look at him. He waved the revolver at the circle of men as if he'd not yet decided on his target. They stepped back. He walked up close to the dolphin, aimed carefully, then fired twice. The dolphin's eye exploded in blood. Its tail slammed against the deck a final time, and then it lay still.

He looked up and saw Miss Kristina huddling against Ivar. Both were staring at him. He grinned at them. Then he stuck the revolver into his belt and returned to his cabin.

He sat on the edge of his berth. He was still smiling. This had been a perfect moment. No one had known he had a revolver. They were surprised when he came up holding it, and he'd seen the fear in their eyes. They'd turned from the dolphin to stare at him. He'd been in control. That was how he wanted it.

Early one morning the wind fell, and after that their progress was slow. Around noon they saw Setúbal ahead of them: large whitewashed villas sitting atop steep cliffs; lush, green vegetation hanging like a veil over the rocks. When the sails were down, Miss Kristina served each man on deck a glass of wine. It was an old custom.

Her eyes lingered on Ivar, but when she reached Herman, she turned her face half away, as if she couldn't wait to move on to the next man in line.

There was already one Marstal schooner in the port. Over the next few days, more arrived and soon there was a small flock: the *Eagle*, the *Galathea*, and the *Atlantic*, all veterans of the route, loading salt in Setúbal for Newfoundland, then sailing back across the Atlantic with salt cod for Setúbal.

Not that they were short of fish here. The port teemed with fishermen who caught sardines as big as herrings. The men were small and sinewy and their chests were bared to the sun, the muscles clearly defined beneath their tanned skin. Spotting Miss Kristina, they called out and waved, their white teeth gleaming beneath their black mustaches; she waved back to them and they raised their huge baskets of glittering fish as though offering a joyful tribute to her sex, so rarely sighted on the deck of a sailing ship.

Bager was rowed ashore to buy provisions, but he came back empty-handed. There were neither potatoes nor bread to be had. Setúbal was in the grip of a strike—or was it a lockout? At any rate, some sort of uprising or revolution. A nine o'clock curfew had been imposed, and anyone found in the street after dark would be shot.

"Why is there a revolution?" Miss Kristina asked, her eyes lighting up with excitement.

Her father shrugged. "I suppose people are starving," he said. "There's a lot of poverty here."

"But that's awful," Miss Kristina said. "Those poor, poor people."

"Don't fret about it," Herman interjected. "It's nothing unusual. There's always some fuss going on here. They create havoc and shoot at each other. They say they want change, but the next time you visit, everything's the same as it always was. It's the way they are. They can't control their tempers and they never get anything done."

The word *revolution* went around the deck. Everyone wanted to taste it, like an exotic fruit bursting with a strange, tantalizing flavor. Revolutions were a part of the south. Now they'd be able to return home and say that they'd witnessed one—though as far as they could see there was nothing to witness. The sardine fishermen seemed unperturbed by the revolution—if that's what it was—and heavily laden ships arrived every day. Then the uprising spread farther, and it was rumored that the sardine factories were striking too.

For the next few days the fishermen stayed in port, and the docks around the *Kristina* fell silent. The *Nauta* and the *Rosenhjem* showed up, and soon a tiny floating Marstal was established, with plenty of traffic between the ships. Visits were paid, coffee was drunk. Miss Kristina stopped strolling around with Ivar in order to meet the other skippers, who were all friends of her father and used to visit their home in Marstal. One day she went with them to see the town, which seemed peaceful enough despite its revolution. Like the proper skipper's daughter she was, she rowed the boat that ferried them all to shore.

She returned with a bunch of flowers that a park gardener had given her, and treated the crew to a lively description of the large café in the town square where a military band had been playing. "Lovely to hear a brass band again," she said.

Herman shrugged. A woman of the world probably spoke like that, but he couldn't recall a brass band ever playing in Marstal. She'd been to the cinema too, where the film had been accompanied by a string orchestra. Twenty men at least, she said, and her eyes sparkled.

Several of the crewmen on the Marstal ships had brought instruments with them: two accordions, three harmonicas, and a violin. Off duty, they made up an entire orchestra themselves. That night there was music and singing. Ivar had a very fine voice, but it was his radio, in particular, that made him popular among the other crews. They were proud of him on the *Kristina*. He was theirs; no other ship had a man like Ivar. He'd switch on the radio, and voices came zooming in from all over the world, and music too, including the Portuguese fado. Ivar was the only one who knew that word, and he explained the mournful music to them. But even stranger sounds came from the radio—such as Arabic music from a station in Casablanca. Ivar had to admit defeat there. He couldn't put a name to it or tell them anything about it.

When Ivar turned on his radio, even the skippers couldn't resist, and came out of the cabin, where they'd been enjoying their Dutch gin and Riga Balsam. Miss Kristina did her round with the coffeepot and asked if anyone fancied pancakes, and a chorus of "Aye, aye!" rose from the men.

the sailor

IN SETÚBAL Herman found himself among his peers again. They were sailors, and they were from Marstal. He'd beaten up a man in a doorway in Nyborg and claimed he'd done it for the sake of his town—but now he felt like an outsider. The trouble wasn't simply his jealousy. Perhaps it wasn't jealousy at all, but the fact that he didn't know where he belonged: he only really felt at home when he was in charge, treated with respect and fear.

The wind and the waves had a lawlessness and unpredictability that felt familiar to him. He sensed it the moment he embarked. On land, life became lilliputian again, and he stumbled around like an awkward, homeless giant, unable to squeeze through the doorways that bid others welcome.

There was a gentle feel to the evening, an intimacy that came from the warm air of the south—the way the stars were mirrored in the calm sea, the enigmatic quiet of the town, and the caress of music and voices. The skippers broke their habit and turned up together to mingle with the crew, amid the smell of pancakes that spread from the galley.

He was with his own, but he didn't belong among them. It stung him suddenly, a terrifying feeling of not being whole, but crippled. In one horrifying flash he observed himself from the outside and saw a monster. He wanted to hide, to flee this world he couldn't cope with, where he was on a lonely track that led nowhere.

He felt no urge to drink or fight. He just had to get away.

He went down to his cabin to get his revolver. Then he climbed over the rail and into the lifeboat that was moored to the side of the ship. He pushed off and began rowing.

Where was he going? He didn't know. He stopped and rested on the oars, at a loss. The port was deserted. No lights were lit, and the silence of the empty town seemed to fall from the night sky, as though Setúbal had been sucked into the vast vacuum of the universe the moment the curfew descended.

Suddenly he realized what he wanted. He wanted to walk the darkened streets. This was his territory: a forbidden zone where being spotted could cost you your life.

A moment ago a storm had raged within him. Now the tide in his veins turned, giving way to the dangerous silence of the ebb.

Making his strokes as noiseless as possible, he rowed slowly toward the nearest wharf. Only the faintest splashes were audible, and they were instantly swallowed by the dense darkness. The music and voices coming from the *Kristina* were now so far away that they seemed the echoes of another world, a world he'd left behind and could never return to.

He didn't know what awaited him in the abandoned streets, nor did he care. A magnet was pulling him: he abandoned his will and obeyed. It was there, in the magnet's powerful stillness, in its deadly metallic cold, that he belonged. He felt the weight of the revolver in his pocket and readied himself.

He moored the boat and climbed up onto the wharf. There was no moon, yet the town hadn't been completely absorbed by the dark. Here and there, light streamed from a window or slid through the slats of a shutter. He could hear voices, then the sound of a piano—a delicate music protesting against the silence, only to be engulfed by it.

He stood between two rows of houses and tilted his head back. He could see the Milky Way running parallel with the street, a celestial track of shining pebbles forging through the wasteland of the night. He recalled the first time he'd seen it. He had been a boy then, alone in the night. He'd stood on the beach and cocked his head the same way, bursting with impatient hope. But now, tonight, he turned his back on everything. He was alone with the Milky Way and a gun.

Did he want to survive this night? Was this a test he had designed for himself, or was it something else? He didn't know. He didn't understand the language of the stars well enough for that.

He stood in the middle of the street, looking upward. The white walls of the houses glowed blue as if reflecting the starlight. Gates and doorways pulsated black. Was it wise to be standing in the middle of the street?

His peculiar intoxication, which had been generated not by drink but by his loneliness beneath the night sky, evaporated. He ran across the sidewalk and pressed himself against a wall. Here he was likely to be just as visible: a dense black mass against its glowing blue.

He hadn't come here to hide. He returned to the middle of the sidewalk and started walking.

Suddenly he heard steps. He stopped. They sounded measured. Was it one or more men who were approaching? He listened again. It certainly wasn't a group, he decided. Perhaps there were only two of them? Soldiers on night patrol? Who else would be out and about after dark in a town with a curfew? He looked behind him, then ahead. It was a wide street, and palm trees blocked the starlight: he had to be on a boulevard. He ought to head for the narrow, winding lanes where it would be easier to escape. He wavered, but stayed put. Then he raised his gun and turned around slowly. Darkness: nothing but darkness. He could still hear the measured footsteps. Were they coming closer or moving away?

He walked on cautiously, gun in hand. If they were to meet, it would be them or him. He knew that.

The footsteps continued.

Yes, they were definitely approaching, but he couldn't decide which direction they were coming from. He might just as easily be walking toward them as away from them.

He'd been going for a while when he spotted them. They were standing still, just three or four meters in front of him, as if they'd been waiting. He stopped at once. One of them called out.

The cry was drowned out by a deafening explosion. Herman looked around to determine the origin of the blast and saw the revolver in his hand. He must have fired it.

He had no idea if he'd hit anyone. He started running. No shots or footsteps rang out behind him. At one point he was tempted to stop and look back, but the pulse of his blood gave his flight a momentum he couldn't fight. His head felt completely clear. But his legs pounded like pistons; they seemed to have a will of their own.

He rounded a corner and kept going until finally he regained control of his muscles: stopping, he pressed himself against a wall and listened to the night. At first he heard nothing. Then, far away, he made out the sound of running feet, coming first from one direction and then another. A shot was fired, then several more in quick succession, drowned out by the long stutter of a machine gun. He heard orders being shouted and the stomping of boots, as if a whole army had started marching. Somewhere a car engine revved.

Firing the gun had broken the silence, and now it sounded as if his shot had detonated a mine, and that mine, now exploding, was the entire town.

He was surrounded by darkness and the noise of salvos. One moment an intense fusillade, the next a loaded silence. Who was shooting whom? Was the army firing on the strikers, and were they responding? Was it just a chaos of feral predators lurking in the dark, hissing and lashing out with their claws before withdrawing again into the shadows? Was this what revolution meant? Guns rebelling and overpowering their owners under cover of darkness, wooing men's blood, and luring it out to flood the streets?

Were they shooting at each other to celebrate that there was no longer good or evil, order or disorder, only untamed life, a town of stones splashed red with life's essence?

He started running again. His breathing was laborious, but he didn't stop; his heavy body stampeded like a raging rhinoceros through the lanes. At some point he was fired at: he heard the bullet slam into the wall behind him. Later he surprised two men hiding in a gateway. He shot at them and resumed his manic race. Who were they? Had he hit them?

He didn't care.

He spotted a division of soldiers marching toward him and found a doorway to crouch in. They'd barely gone past when he emerged, turning in mid-run to fire a shot in their direction.

Someone had built a barricade across the street, and he saw shadows moving behind it. The dark was too intense to make out what was going on, but he knew instinctively that this was revolution: the clash of guns, here to drain blood. There was a brotherhood between rebels and soldiers. They were united by a common urge to kill.

They called to him, and he answered in a sailor's broken Spanish. They invited him to join them on the barricade, and when they saw his revolver, they slapped him on the shoulder and called him *compañero*, a word he well understood, a gesture based on an assumption as naive as they were. He didn't care about their cause. They needed an excuse to shoot their guns. He didn't.

Shots were fired at the barricade, and they fired back into the darkness. He saw the flames at the muzzles of the revolvers and felt something warm on his cheek. Had he been hit? The man next to him slumped against his shoulder, his head resting there for a moment as if he'd fallen asleep. Then he slid gradually to the ground, his shirt-sleeve soaked in blood.

The shooting intensified, the flames from the gun muzzles at the end of the street erupted into fireworks. The din was deafening. He felt a wild, dry heat burst through his skin as if his heart were on fire. He was alive!

The firing was coming closer: the soldiers had launched their attack. The men around him abandoned the barricade. As their footsteps retreated into darkness, he set off afresh, in a wild sprint. He heard a man's laugh, then realized it was his own. A prostrate body lay in front of him in the street. He leapt over it. Someone grabbed his arm and pulled him into a side street and under an archway. Together they scaled one wall, then another. Herman muttered *gracias*, though he felt indifferent. His whole body screamed with the ecstasy of immortality. He still had the gun in his hand.

It felt as if he'd been in this darkened town forever, as if all that had gone before had faded to insignificance. He felt it suddenly: tonight he was liberated. Here in the dark, where the only streetlights were flames from the mouths of guns and the gutters flowed red, he could exist without feeling incomplete. He was simply blood, body, instincts, and reflexes. He was his revolver, and through it, he belonged with all those like him, who moved through the night, armed. He was at one with all men, with life and death.

From the hills behind the town the huge red ball of the sun came rolling down the boulevard toward him, and all around the colors lit up, weak at first, then vivid. He met the dawn with a mixture of disappointment and relief. The sunlight seemed to tidy up the chaos of the night, and within the space of an instant, it put the houses and their inhabitants back in their rightful places.

He looked down and saw that his shirt was bloodstained. He ripped it off and hurled it into the street. He felt the heft of the revolver in his hand. He hesitated for a moment. Then he let it drop and walked on.

He reached a large square, where upturned chairs and tables lay scattered about and men in uniform were carrying bodies away. Soon the tiles would be washed clean of blood. Day had returned.

As he crossed the square, a soldier called out to him and came up, followed by two others. They looked him up and down. He stood there, bare-chested and smelling pungently of sweat, the face beneath his short blond hair reddened by wind, drink, and sun. What was he? A sailor who'd forgotten time, place, and curfew in the excitement of the moment?

He stank—but they assumed it was from bed linen and women: he could see it in their faces. He grinned at them, and they grinned back. The tallest of the soldiers pointed to his cheek. Herman touched it and felt a scab where a bullet had brushed him.

"*Mujer*," he said. Woman.

"*Mujer*." They laughed. One of them made a cat's paw of his hand, with its claws out.

He'd shot at them in the night and they'd shot back at him. Shadows firing at shadows. Now they were simply men in the first light of dawn. They let him go.

He went down to the harbor and found the boat. He loosened the mooring and began rowing slowly back to the *Kristina*.

THE NEXT DAY Herman was quiet. The crew shot him furtive glances. They'd noticed his absence, but no one said anything. From time to time he'd smile an odd smile that seemed to be directed at no one in particular. They exchanged warning looks. What would follow this calm? Ivar gazed thoughtfully at Herman's massive back. Only Bager seemed not to notice anything.

Herman was aware of their glances. What were they thinking about him? What did they think he'd been up to during the curfew in Setú-bal? If they thought all he'd been doing was whoring, why didn't they just say so? Were they afraid of the answer?

With the strike broken, the *Kristina* could dock. A couple of barges arrived and the dockers began unloading the salt cod. Bager had gone into town to buy provisions, taking Miss Kristina with him. She came back in a state of excitement and told them that the chandler had invited them to lunch: they'd eaten fish with fried olives.

"But imagine, all the windows in the restaurant had been smashed. I wonder if there was fighting last night?"

Herman smiled but said nothing. He watched the dockers working in the hull and on the wharf; he watched the fishermen rowing out to sea with empty vessels and returning with full nets; he watched the soldiers standing with their bayonets at the ready; he watched the people of Setúbal. His gaze took in the whole world. Time stood still, and in its silence he solved all the riddles of the earth.

Was that the moment he was struck by the fatal certainty that Miss Kristina would be his?

The *Kristina* was readied, and they left Setúbal. For the first two days a southerly wind was behind them. Then calm set in. They lay-to with the fore staysail and topsail; the helm looked after itself. The sea was still heaving with lingering swells, and the water rose all the way up to the bulwark. High overhead the midday sun leached the color from sea and sky until everything melted into a white mist of heat. The *Kristina* heaved and dipped with the slow breathing of the sea. Their world had fallen into a deep slumber. They wandered around the deck like sleepwalkers and breathed in the rhythm of the waves.

Miss Kristina sat on the deck, embroidering. No one spoke. Bager sat next to his daughter with the *Book of Sermons*. They didn't converse, and they looked as if their closeness didn't require it. He turned a page, then looked absent-mindedly across the sea before returning to his book. She concentrated on her embroidery. Her skin had tanned, and she let her hair hang loose. Helmer served the coffee.

These were the last warm days before they approached the Bay of Biscay.

The calm continued through the following afternoon. Then at around seven in the evening a brisk wind set up, and Ivar and Knud Erik climbed up to set the sails. During the night the wind freshened. When Miss Kristina appeared on deck the next morning, a wave hit her in the face. She wiped the salt water off and laughed at Ivar, who was at the helm, then threw an expert glance at the sails. The gaffs had been reefed during the night, and of the squares, only the foresail and the lower topsail were left. The flying jib was taut and would soon be taken in.

"The canvas is taking a beating," she said, still laughing and wiping her wet face.

She had put on her father's wooden clogs and an oilskin jacket that was far too big for her. She had tied a scarf around her hair, and now it was soaked. She wrung it out and stuffed it in her pocket, leaving her thick brown curls exposed to the gale.

We passed two small fishing boats heading south. Miss Kristina positioned herself next to Ivar and watched them as they dipped violently and vanished into the trough of one wave, only to reappear a moment later riding on the next. Her eyes followed them as if searching for a fixed point. Then a strained look came over her, and she suddenly clapped a hand over her mouth and ran to the rail. Ivar looked away discreetly.

She returned to him. "I think I'll go to the cabin," she said.

He nodded.

At noon the wind turned. Wind and current were now working in opposite directions, and the *Kristina* plunged hard in the waves, her bow repeatedly disappearing into the swell.

Herman was at the helm.

"We need to take in the flying jib," he said to Ivar.

Ivar stared at him. "Are you telling me to climb out on the bowsprit?"

"Are you thick in the head or something?"

"Are you seeing what I'm seeing?" Ivar was openly defying him now.

"I can see that the flying jib needs to be taken in."

"I can see that the bowsprit's underwater half the time."

"Scared of getting wet?" Herman made no effort to hide his contempt.

"Unless you run her into the wind and slow her down, I'm not going out there."

They glared at each other.

"Are you giving me orders?"

"You're the first mate, and I'm an able seaman. I'm simply urging you to do what anyone with the faintest knowledge of sailing would do. Or the flying jib can stay where it is."

Herman looked away. He knew that Ivar was right. It would be irresponsible to send a man out on the bowsprit with the bow plunging so deep. He eased his grip on the wheel, and the ship ran into the wind. At that moment Miss Kristina came up from the cabin. She was clasping her mouth again, as if preparing another sacrifice to the sea. But the two men facing off caught her attention. She looked from one to the other, her hand still covering her mouth.

Ivar crossed the deck. The ship had stopped plunging, and the flying jib was flapping in the wind. The dripping bowsprit pointed up at the slate-colored sky. Ivar climbed out on the bowsprit and started rolling up the sail.

Herman watched his tall straight figure, which held itself so confidently out there on the smooth bowsprit, poised over the raging deep below.

Time contracted and stood still.

It wasn't just a man's strength that made him strong. It was also his knowledge of others' weaknesses. Herman had despised Ivar from the moment he met him, but with a strange unfocused contempt that had had nothing firm to fix on. Did Ivar have an Achilles' heel? Could he perform under pressure?

Gripping the wheel, Herman felt the pull and strain of the eternal arm wrestle between helmsman and sea: he had to shift it continually to keep up the steering speed. He slackened, just for a moment—and with an explosive boom, the wind instantly refilled the sails. The bow shot skyward on the rolling crest of a wave, and the whole ship plunged and kept plunging, plummeting through the air before hitting the surface of the water and sending fountains of spray flying to both sides. The *Kristina* cut through the spume like a knife, and her entire stem dove down, as if heading for the seabed.

Time slowed, as though the sun had shifted to an invisible point in the galaxy. And yet the whole thing had happened so quickly that no one had time to react; Miss Kristina was still clasping her mouth, her eyes wide open. Then the ship rose slowly once again, and the water raced sternward across the deck. The bowsprit pointed triumphantly toward the sky. And there was Ivar, clinging like a baby monkey, white-faced.

Even in this brief instant, Herman could see that Ivar was frozen. He'd have to fling himself onto the fo'c'sle right away: if he didn't and the ship plunged again, he'd never make it. This was as decisive a moment for Ivar as the one Herman had in Setúbal.

But Ivar clung on, his brain and body paralyzed. His fingertips dug in, as though his terror had turned him into an animal that could sink its claws into the hard wood. On impulse, Herman cupped his hands to his mouth and shouted out to him. "Jump, sailor, jump, damn you!"

He didn't know himself whether he intended to snap Ivar out of his trance or just taunt him. Then the ship dipped again. When she came back up, Ivar was gone. The bare bowsprit pointed briefly at the clouds, as if that was where he'd disappeared to, rather than down into the foam around the bow. Herman turned the wheel and let the ship run into the wind, halting the upward movement of the stem.

At this point everything happened very quickly. Miss Kristina ran up to him. "You bastard," she choked. "I saw what you—" Suddenly overcome with nausea, she vomited in a stream that hit him in the middle of the chest. She buckled from stomach cramps; this time the stream hit the deck. When she straightened up, gasping, a half-digested yellow-white substance dripped from her chin. She stared wide-eyed, her face distorted. "You swine, you monster, you disgusting . . . you , you . . ." She collapsed in convulsive sobbing.

She'd seen what had happened, and as a skipper's daughter, Miss

Kristina understood what it meant. She'd seen Herman change course. And she knew what that entailed, when there was a crewman on the bowsprit.

And it was true. He couldn't deny what he'd done. Yet he'd always claim she was mistaken. It wasn't he who'd taken Ivar's life. It was the sea. The sea had claimed Ivar because he'd failed at the crucial moment. The sea took him because he didn't belong on it. Herman had just been its tool.

There was a second witness: Helmer. The galley boy had been ready and waiting by the downhauler while Ivar took in the flying jib. But he understood nothing of what he'd seen, and even if he'd formed the opinion that something was wrong, Herman had the means to shut him up. He couldn't be accused of anything, and for a very good reason. He hadn't done anything.

"Man overboard!" he yelled.

At once Miss Kristina stopped screaming and regained her senses. She tore the life buoy from its housing and flung it into the sea to mark the spot where Ivar had disappeared. Knud Erik and Vilhjelm appeared from the fo'c'sle.

"Who? Who?" they yelled anxiously.

"Ivar," Helmer screamed, with panic in his voice.

Herman ordered him up the rigging to be on the lookout for Ivar in case he resurfaced. Then he gave the order to brace aback. Miss Kristina was standing by the rail, vomiting again. From shock this time, he thought.

Bager came rushing up from his cabin and Herman gave him a brief report. He made his voice deliberately calm and matter-of-fact. "Ivar went overboard from the bowsprit. He'd gone out to take in the flying jib."

"How could that happen? Didn't you sail into the wind?"

"Of course. But suddenly he wasn't there." Herman shrugged, a gesture that suggested the accident was Ivar's own fault.

Knud Erik and Vilhjelm were busy lowering the lifeboat into the water. Bager ran over and took command, jumping in himself. Herman watched as Miss Kristina too climbed up on the rail, then pushed off and disappeared over the side.

A moment later the boat appeared. Miss Kristina was standing at the stem, her hair whipping madly. Strings of vomit were still visible on her chin, but she kept her balance with ease. Bager sat slumped on the thwart. Knud Erik and Vilhjelm rowed. Herman stayed at the *Kristina*'s helm. It gave him a soaring feeling to be in charge of the ship.

They rowed around in circles, not knowing what else to do. One moment they were on the crest of a wave, the next they'd disappeared behind one. The *Kristina* drifted in the wind, and so did the life buoy. Where exactly was it that Ivar had disappeared? There were no signposts on the sea. They drifted farther and farther away until the lifeboat was nothing but a white-painted nutshell in the middle of the changing landscape of turbulent waves, which eternally reared and ran themselves out, tired from chasing the distant horizon.

Then something seemed to be happening out there. The tiny figures stood up in the boat, waving their arms. They bent forward, as if they were struggling with something. Had they found him?

Herman called out to Helmer in the rigging. "Do you see anything?"

"I think they've got him!" Helmer began waving with one hand, as if welcoming Ivar back to the land of the living.

It was unclear what happened next. The figures bent forward even more, almost disappearing over the side, and the lifeboat rocked perilously from the sudden imbalance. Then they straightened up again. Only one of them remained crouched. Again Herman called out to Helmer. "What's happening now? Have they got him?"

While he waited for the reply, he felt neither fear nor its opposite. If Ivar made it, he made it. Life went on regardless of what happened out there on the water. Herman was calm and openly indifferent.

"I think . . ." Helmer hesitated and narrowed his eyes. "I think they've lost him again . . . at any rate, I can't see him." They were still lying against the wind. The sails flapped in the storm.

The lifeboat started circling again. It did so for a while, before heading back to the ship. Bager was the first to climb on board. He held his hand to his chest and he was pale. Miss Kristina followed him. She buried her face in her father's shoulder. She was shaking all over and sobbing loudly. Bager held her tight. He put his arm around her shoulder and led her down to his cabin, a clenched fist pressed to his chest, his mouth a thin line that cut across his anguished face.

Herman called Knud Erik over. "What happened?" he asked.

"We found him. He'd managed to stay afloat, but he was half-drowned and his eyes were strange."

"Strange?"

"Well, I don't know what to call it. As though it wasn't him. Like he'd gone mad. When we tried to pull him on board, he just thrashed about. We couldn't get a firm grip under his arms. So we started pulling at him—well, and then it just happened."

"What happened?"

"Well, his oilskins must have opened up. He slipped out of them. Suddenly all we were holding were the empty sleeves." Knud Erik's voice grew thick and he struggled to carry on. "He went right down. We never saw him again. But we'd just held him. We'd looked into his face. I was closer to him than I am to you now. He was saved. And then . . ." He stopped and gave Herman a peculiar look. "But that's what you wanted, wasn't it?" He shook his head and turned away.

Herman looked long and hard after him. Then his attention was caught by a loud slamming noise. It was the flying jib, still flapping in the storm. He called out across the deck. "We still have a flying jib that needs taking in. Any volunteers?"

Helmer was hanging in the rigging. Herman ordered him down and told him to get lunch going. There was a ship to be sailed and life had to go on.

Herman started thinking about what Knud Erik had said, and the peculiar look he'd given him. He had a feeling that the boy had looked straight through him. He remembered Kristian Stærk's warning about Anton Hansen Hay, who'd found the skull of his stepfather. The boy might know something. Those blasted kids had stared at him until he was driven half crazy and had to leave town. But nothing had ever come out. Surely that story was long forgotten?

He took his lunch with the three boys. The mood was edgy and they ate in silence. He made a mental note to put them back on their old rations, since Ivar was no longer around to speak up for them. "Does anyone here have something to say?" he asked.

Helmer cowered and concentrated on his food. Herman looked at Knud Erik and Vilhjelm. They both shook their heads.

"We lost a mate today," Herman said. "It's happened before and it'll happen again. That's life at sea. There are good sailors and then there are those who aren't so good . . ." He let the last sentence hang in the air.

"Ivar was a good sailor," Knud Erik said.

Herman felt like lashing out at the boy, but he controlled himself.

"It was the sea," he said soothingly. "When the sea's in that mood, there's nothing to be done." Even he could hear the hollowness of his words. "But you'd got hold of Ivar. What happened? Did he panic?" Knud Erik shook his head, unwilling to reply. Herman knew that he'd hit a weak spot. After all, they'd found Ivar. He could have been saved—but he'd sabotaged his own rescue. A good sailor, yes. Was this how a good sailor behaved when his life was at stake? Knud Erik might suspect a murderer in Herman, but the boy had also seen the coward in Ivar, and this made him less certain of his accusation. Herman repeated the question. "Did he panic?" The silence that followed the question was an answer in itself.

When Helmer got up to take coffee to Bager's cabin, Knud Erik looked up, his eyes dangerously defiant. "I'm going to tell the skipper everything," he said.

"Tell him what? You were asleep in the fo'c'sle." Herman's voice was calm.

"Vilhjelm knows it too. We'll tell Bager."

"That old story?" Herman laughed. "All of Marstal has spent the past fifteen years wondering if I killed Holger Jepsen." He flung out his arms and laughed again. "And look! I'm still here!"

Helmer returned with the plates from the skipper's cabin. Neither Bager nor Miss Kristina had touched their food. "Skipper wants a word with you," he said.

Herman stood up. Once on deck he breathed in deeply. He had to focus and direct his energy. He had no idea what he was going to say. The survival instinct that he depended on was about to be tested again. He saw Miss Kristina standing by the helm next to Vilhjelm. He'd be alone with Bager. That was probably for the best.

He opened the door to Bager's cabin and stepped over the high threshold. He'd been there before, but it felt as if he was seeing it for the first time. His eyes scanned the framed family photographs screwed to the bulkhead. Above the leather-covered couch was a bolted-on shelf filled with books. Finally his eyes rested on the skipper. Bager had undergone a dramatic change. He was still clutching his chest with one hand, and with the other he gripped the table as if to keep himself from sliding off the couch. He'd grown even paler, and his eyes had sunk deep into his head. His thin hair was damp, and tiny beads of sweat had formed on his hairline. He blinked nervously.

Herman remained standing right inside the door. Straightening his back, he made his voice as formal as possible. When it came to will-power, he was stronger than Bager. He had never doubted that, and at this moment it was clearer than ever. But the captain outranked him. He had to impress and intimidate, but he couldn't show disrespect for the hierarchy he was bound to uphold, no matter how much he despised its chief representative. He was no mutineer.

"You wanted to speak to me," he said.

Bager looked down at the table as though he'd forgotten what he'd wanted to say and was now looking for it in the grain of the lacquered wood. Then he loosened his grip on the edge of the table and let the palm of his hand glide across the surface. Suddenly he slammed the table hard, as if signaling to himself that now was the time to talk. He looked up and fixed his eyes on Herman, but the nervous blinking continued.

"A serious accusation has been made against you," he said, and stopped, as though awaiting a reaction from Herman. Herman simply looked at him. It would be funny if he suddenly started quoting from the *Book of Sermons,* he thought.

Bager looked away before focusing again on Herman, clearly over-coming his reluctance. "Someone . . ." He hesitated as he struggled to find the right word. "Someone . . . someone whose word I have no rea-son to doubt claims that you deliberately endangered Ivar's life when he went out on the bowsprit to take in the flying jib."

He stopped, exhausted, and waited for a reply. Herman didn't react but remained standing, as calm as before. Bager wiped his forehead with a handkerchief, sweeping a few strands of sweat-soaked hair so they stood upright. His lost face took on a comical resemblance to a big question mark.

Herman said nothing, and Bager had to break the silence again. "You were at the helm, and the moment Ivar was out on the bowsprit, you changed course so the ship fell off and the stem dove under."

Herman took a step forward. Bager jumped. "Who says so?"

"That's none of your concern. Besides, it's not for you to ask the questions. I'm holding this inquiry. Remember your place!" Again Bager wiped his forehead with the handkerchief. For a moment he seemed to be listening to something that was going on elsewhere, and Herman began to wonder if it was this situation that was scaring him or something else altogether. Then Bager spoke again.

"Not only have you acted irresponsibly and contrary to all good seamanship, but everything suggests that you changed course on purpose."

"What are you trying to imply?" Herman could no longer control himself. Positioning his hands on the table, he leaned menacingly toward his captain.

Bager pressed one hand against his chest. He was panting now, and had completely given up on mopping the sweat from his forehead. His hair was still standing up. But his voice was calm. "I'm not implying anything. No, I'm putting it to you directly that you killed Ivar." He stopped to catch his breath, which was coming in long, wheezing gasps. Herman stood frozen, still pressing his weight on the table.

Bager got his breath back. "There will be a maritime inquiry in Copenhagen. The truth will come out there, I can promise you that."

"It's Miss Kristina, isn't it? She's been telling you a pack of lies! Fucking bitch. He panicked. That's why he drowned. He was a weakling. There's no room for his sort at sea. That's all there is to it. That's all I've got to say on the matter." Herman's face was now dangerously close to the captain's. He had to suppress the urge to grab hold of him and throw the skinny old man's body against the bulkhead.

Bager was looking at him, but his eyes seemed distant. The sweat was streaming down his pallid forehead. Again he looked as if he was listening to something far, far away, barely aware of Herman's presence.

"Are you even listening to what I'm saying?" Herman roared. "It was that bitch. She'd got the hots for him!" He didn't care what he said. He'd lost his head but still kept control of his hands, though the effort made his whole body shake. Surely the old fool knew he was playing with fire? How much more would he have to put up with? "Are you saying I'm a murderer?" he thundered, and felt how liberating it was to say the words out loud. A feeling of righteous indignation welled up in him, and he regained his self-control.

The captain's face remained unchanged. His gaze was still intensively fixed on some distant point: it seemed to preoccupy him. Suddenly he inhaled deeply and something like a hiccup or the beginning of a belch escaped him. His facial muscles tensed, his eyes widened, and his lower lip grew slack. Then he slumped forward, and his head thumped onto the table right between Herman's hands.

Herman leapt back. He stared down at the captain's hair, which fell in thin strands across a scalp as gray as parched earth. He stuck out his hand and checked Bager's pulse. He felt it fade and stop. Then he ran up the ladder and out onto the deck.

Vilhjelm was at the helm, with Knud Erik standing next to him. There was no sign of Miss Kristina. She was probably in the galley with Helmer. He went over to the two boys. "Do you have a problem with dead bodies?"

They stared at him, baffled. He pointed to Knud Erik. "You're coming with me." He led him back to Bager's cabin. Knud Erik froze when he saw the figure slumped across the table.

"What happened?"

"What do you think?"

"Is he dead?"

"I've looked for his pulse. I couldn't find one, so I suppose he is." Knud Erik's shoulders started to shake. "We need to put him in his berth," Herman said. He took hold of Bager under the arms while Knud Erik slid an arm under his legs: together they pulled him sideways off the couch and carefully laid the skinny body in the berth. The eyes were still wide open. So was the mouth. Herman closed the dead man's eyes and pressed his jaw shut. "This was an accident." Aware that Knud Erik was staring at him, he shot him a challenging look. Knud Erik looked away. "Trouble always comes in twos," he added. He said it to placate him. He could speak only in platitudes now: meaningless phrases, tired expressions. Yet there was something soothing about uttering them, as if he wanted to console not just Knud Erik but himself. Bager's death had scared him: it was as if the captain had suddenly shouted "Boo!" in his face. Not that he'd miss him. He'd instantly realized that Bager's death was nothing but an advantage for him. He'd avoid a lot of unpleasant accusations. "I need to speak to Miss Kristina," he said, and went up the ladder.

Knud Erik followed. Herman opened the door to the galley. She was there, huddled on the little bench. Helmer was standing by the stove with his back to her. She looked up at them. Her face was pale, grimy, and red-eyed. The salt water had flattened her hair, and it stuck to her head in messy clumps.

"Miss Kristina," he said. "I need to speak to you. It's about your father."

"My father?" she asked, uncomprehending.

"Let's go outside." He stepped aside so she could pass through the galley door. She obeyed without asking further questions. There was a somnambular quality to her movements. He led her to the rail on the lee side. Facing each other, they gripped the rail while the ship heaved and dipped on the heavy sea. He didn't know what would happen next, but he was aware of his own tension. Would she break down? Or would she fly into a wild rage and hurl fresh accusations at him? The uncertainty he always felt in her presence was back, but magnified a thousandfold. Could he handle this?

With great effort he made his voice matter-of-fact. "Miss Kristina," he heard himself say. "I'm terribly sorry to be the one to deliver this sad message to you, but your father has just died. He had a heart attack."

He didn't look at her as he spoke but kept his eyes cast downward, hoping she'd interpret it as a sign of sympathy and respect for her grief. But he knew deep down it was uncertainty that stopped him from meeting her eye. He felt that he'd already lost the game and that something terrible was about to blow up in his face, a chain reaction of unstoppable events that would sweep him to his doom.

He'd spoken and then awaited her reaction. But nothing happened. Unable to bear the wait, he looked up. She was still facing him. Her expression remained unchanged, as if she hadn't heard a word he'd said.

What happened next came as a total surprise to him. She took a step forward and bowed her head. Then she rested her forehead on his shoulder and started to cry. For a few seconds he stood stock-still, his arms dangling at his sides. Then he embraced her, swaying steadily to the ship's roll, so they wouldn't lose their balance and fall onto the wet deck. Everything in him opened up all at once, and the uncertainty that had gripped him a minute earlier was transformed into a feeling of triumph that surged like an erupting geyser.

They stood like that for a while. He could have stayed there forever. He felt his own strength, and the light pressure of her forehead. He stroked her wet, tangled hair and muttered a stream of comforting, meaningless sounds. An unexpected bond had been created between them. He had no idea how. But it was there. He felt it so strongly that he responded with an upsurge of tenderness. It was like embracing a child.

"Come," he said. "It's time for you to see your father." He escorted her to the door of the cabin before opening it for her. "I think it's best if you have some time alone with him," he said gently.

Then he relieved Vilhjelm at the helm.

.   .   .

He ordered more sails to be set. He sailed hard. The ship tilted from the pressure of the wind till the rail was nearly level with the sea. He could see the boys' unease, but nobody said anything. He called them over. "Bager's dead. I'm the captain now."

Then he was alone at the helm again. He felt the power of the sea travel through the wheel into his hands. The tenderness he'd felt settled and became a certainty. She was his. It was irrevocable.

He thought about the dead man in the cabin. Most of all he wanted to wrap the body in canvas and ease it overboard without too much ceremony, but he knew he wouldn't get away with that. St.-Malo wasn't the nearest port, but if the wind lasted and he continued to sail hard, they could get there in two days. Obviously Bager couldn't stay in his cabin. And Miss Kristina couldn't sleep in the room with her dead father. The fo'c'sle was an option. After all, there was a spare berth there. He chortled. That would serve them right, the little brats. They could sleep with a corpse.

Herman stayed at the helm for the rest of the day. He had no desire to be anywhere else. The ship was his. He shot across the sea with a dead captain and a woman waiting in the cabin. He hummed the old chantey about the drunken sailor: "Put him in the bed with the cap'n's daughter." A dream. And now it was coming true.

That evening he took Miss Kristina a plate of soup. The cabin was dark: he struck a match and lit the petroleum lamp that was screwed onto the bulkhead.

"You need to eat," he said, handing her the bowl.

She raised the spoon to her lips obediently. He stayed there and waited silently for her to finish. Then he took the bowl back to the galley.

At midnight he was still at the helm. He'd done three shifts in a row. Now the middle watch started. He secured the wheel and crossed the deck to the fo'c'sle entrance, then climbed down the ladder and woke Vilhjelm. The boy tumbled out of his berth. He'd been sleeping with his clothes on. In his hand he held a jackknife that he'd probably been given as a confirmation present. Knud Erik leapt down from the other berth. He too was armed.

The *Kristina* was still sailing hard against the wind, and the fo'c'sle boomed every time the stem hit a wave. Herman glanced at the knives and shook his head. "That's some pretty impressive manicure equipment you've got there," he said jovially. "You'd better stick those in your belt. Or I might start thinking you're mutineers."

Every word he spoke made them flinch. They were so scared, they were on the verge of tears. He told Vilhjelm the course and climbed back up the ladder. He crossed the deck and tried the handle of the door to the captain's cabin. It was unlocked, and a moment later he was in the darkness on the tilting floor. He listened. He couldn't hear Miss Kristina breathing, but he knew he had to act now. The certainty of it had been growing in him up there in the stormy darkness.

He stuck his hand into the berth, fumbling in the eiderdown. He felt her hair: she must be lying with her back to him. He'd dreamt of her back. He stroked her hair, which was still stiff from the salt water. She didn't react: he was sure she was asleep. He allowed his hand to wander across her neck, which felt warm and soft. His grip enclosed it. Feeling her delicate spine, he was flooded with tenderness. Still she didn't react. He couldn't hear her breathing, and he had to suppress the urge to take her pulse. Was she still asleep? Was she holding her breath out of fear? No, he was certain of it: she'd been waiting for him. His whole body was telling him so. He flung her eiderdown aside, grabbed hold of her nightdress, and yanked it up to her shoulders.

He hesitated for a moment. I don't know her, he thought; perhaps she's stronger than I am. He was overcome by a sudden fear. Then he unbuttoned his trousers and clambered into the berth next to her. He didn't speak. He felt awkward with his clothes on; he should have taken them off first. Now it was too late. He put an arm around her and pressed her to him. His woolen pullover must be scratching her naked skin. At this point he felt he was exploiting her vulnerability rather than protecting it. The contact made him grow hard, but the heat of passion had deserted him, leaving him coolly detached. He observed himself from the outside, and his self-observation made him hesitate; but his erection was still there, like an animal's, responding to the heat of another body and blindly seeking release. He continued to watch himself from a distance. A big, clumsy man in sea boots and a pullover, fumbling with an immobile woman in a narrow berth.

Suddenly she stirred. She mumbled something as if half asleep, and tried to turn over. Instinctively he tightened his grip around her neck and shoved her face into the bed. She screamed, but the pillow muffled it. Her body arched in protest, and her arms flailed about.

As he entered her she let out a sigh, as though he'd dislodged the air inside her: a sigh without emotion, the noise of lungs emptying. After that she was silent, as if a spear had impaled her.

He paused, and strained to make out if she was still breathing; seconds later he ejaculated in an involuntary surrender that made him feel he'd stepped off the edge of an abyss and was falling in the dark. His hips kept shaking for a long time. She continued to lie there, completely passive. He hugged her motionless body tight. A swarm of words buzzed through his brain: he wanted to say something, but nothing came out. To him she was Miss Kristina. But he couldn't call her that in this moment, when he'd finally become one with her. Thinking about this, he fell asleep.

He woke up, perhaps only a few seconds later: she was shaking herself free. He managed to sit up, but before he'd had time to react, she'd kicked out at him. He was flung out of the narrow berth and landed heavily on the floor. He got to his feet and tried to button his trousers. His groin felt damp.

She screamed and screamed.

He felt nothing, apart from irritation at the endless screaming, which filled the narrow cabin and forced him to the door with an almost physical pressure.

He stumbled out onto the deck. It was blowing harder, and the sails were taut. For a moment he looked across the sea. The foaming crests glowed in the dark. The only sounds were the howling of the wind in the rigging and the thud of the waves as they crashed across the deck. He went over to relieve Vilhjelm at the helm. He decided not to take in any sails, though he knew the risks of driving the ship so hard. Heavy rain pelted his face.

He wasn't a man to weigh up the pros and cons of things. Totally emptied of thoughts, he welcomed his inner blankness just as he'd recently welcomed sleep.

When he asked the boys to relieve him at the next shift, they refused.

"Do you want a shipwreck?" he asked them.

They didn't reply. They just stood there, waving their ridiculous confirmation presents, which they considered deadly weapons. The wind had fallen, and the ship lay calmer on the sea. Having secured the wheel again, he strode toward the captain's cabin. But the boys ran ahead of him and blocked the door, still holding their knives. Miss

Kristina must have told them everything. Now they thought they were her protectors. He'd outraged their childish sense of justice. The worst thing about a sense of justice is that it makes people wild and crazy. In giving them courage, it robs them of their caution and their instinct to survive.

"If you come closer, we'll kill you," Knud Erik said, and his voice trembled.

Helmer was sobbing loudly, but he held on to his knife. They were blind with fear, and in their blindness they had only one point of reference, the jackknives in their hands. He didn't doubt in the least that they were capable of stabbing him. Perhaps it was the only way they could cope with the terror he'd provoked. They were unpredictable, and for this reason alone they suddenly presented a danger.

He realized that nothing would ever come of his plans, whatever they'd been, exactly. Miss Kristina was lost to him. He was alone with three boys who might do just about anything out of panic, and who didn't care whether they lived or died. He could snap their spines one by one, but what good would that do?

Disgust welled up in him. It was time to move on and do what he always did in these situations, when all other exits were closed: show the world that he didn't care and that he could leave it all behind. His life heaved and collapsed like the rise and fall of a wave.

He returned to the wheel. From now on it was an endurance test. He'd get no more sleep. The French Atlantic coast stretched to the east. In harsh weather like this, its surf could mean ruin for a schooner, especially one without skilled mates.

It was sometime later that day that he changed their course.

THE HOMECOMING

MONSIEUR CLUBIN WAS the first person to notice that the topgallant sail schooner pitching in the sea by Pointe de Grave was in distress. At first he wasn't sure there was anyone on board, but after watching the ship through his binoculars for a few minutes, he realized that some desperate will was fighting to keep the ship clear of the dangerous beach. No distress signals were being sent, but Monsieur Clubin's sense of duty, forged over thirty years as a ship's pilot in Royan, demanded that he investigate.

On board the *Kristina* he found three boys and a young woman, all of whom seemed bewildered. The captain lay dead in the fo'c'sle. There were no able seamen and no first mate, and the lifeboat was missing.

The boys' explanation, as presented to the port authorities and subsequently to the police in Royan, was that the first mate had murdered an able seaman and the captain, and then assaulted the captain's daughter. Precisely what they meant by assault, the boys either could not or would not specify, and the young lady herself refused to open her mouth: during her entire stay in Royan, the young woman uttered not a single word.

They further claimed that the first mate had committed a murder in his hometown, the same town they came from, though he'd never been punished for it. He'd jumped ship earlier that morning when Monsieur Clubin came on board, and used the lifeboat to make his escape.

After a thorough examination, the police found no cause to charge the missing first mate. The captain's body showed no signs of violence, and the subsequent autopsy established that he'd died of heart failure. The circumstances surrounding the drowning of the able seaman were not sufficiently well documented to bring charges, and his death was ascribed then, and later, in the maritime inquiry that followed in Copenhagen, to one of those unfortunate incidents that occur at sea, though it was acknowledged that the first mate's disappearance might justify any number of suspicions. However, none of them could be proven.

Ultimately what triggered the unfortunate chain of events that culminated in the *Kristina* of Marstal drifting around Pointe de Grave was her captain's lack of judgment in signing on as first mate a notorious character without proper papers. Nor did the alleged assault on the young woman lead to an indictment. The lack of evidence was due to her stubborn and persistent silence, along with the boys' unclear description of the nature of her assault.

The captain was buried in the town cemetery. Because the local newspaper, *La Dépêche de l'Ouest,* had written about the ill-fated ship—*"le navire maudit"*—a number of curious onlookers turned up for his funeral.

Monsieur Clubin's compact figure was also to be seen there, but it was duty, rather than curiosity, that made him attend. After all, he had come to the ship's rescue, led her to a safe port, and looked after the crew, who in his eyes were nothing but children. He'd welcomed them into his home, and Madame Clubin had provided the young lady with a room and lent her a black hat and veil so she could be suitably dressed for the funeral.

The young woman put up with it all and allowed the pilot's helpful wife to treat her like a doll. She didn't express any gratitude; nor was there any sign of grief on the pale, rigid mask she showed the world. Madame Clubin was experienced enough not to attach importance to outward appearances, and made no attempt to coax emotion out of her young, stricken guest. She was firm only when it came to meals. Madame Clubin was a French Basque, and in a voice that tolerated no contradiction she ordered her guest to finish the platefuls of *ttoro,* *gabure, camot,* and *couston* that she placed before her every day. The young lady obeyed without thanking her for the food or expressing any opinion about it. But she ate it, and Madame Clubin announced to her husband, as she was in the habit of doing, that the sum total of her life's experience amounted to the verdict that what an unhappy person needs most is maternal care and good food.

After receiving orders from the shipping company back in Denmark, one of the young men stayed on board the *Kristina* to await the arrival of a new crew. The other two left Royan with the young woman, who retained her silence to the last.

When she stepped onto the train, her two escorts carried her luggage with brotherly care. She carried only a sea bag, said to have belonged to the drowned seaman.

ONE DAY KLARA FRIIS returned home to find Kristina waiting in her drawing room. Klara was well aware of her story. We all were. Vilhjelm and Helmer reported only that Herman had assaulted her, but it was obvious to everyone that it had been a case of rape. Whenever the boys said the word *assault*, we nodded knowingly in a way that must have done more than simply irritate them. Of course they knew what had happened to her. Boys know that sort of thing. But they chose their words carefully because they wanted to protect her.

We referred to Kristina Bager as "the poor little thing," but Klara was the first to learn that she had a secret. When she came in, Kristina rose from the sofa and stared at her. She didn't speak: she hadn't uttered a word since her homecoming. Then she pointed to her belly with one hand and made an arc in the air in front of it with the other. Klara understood right away, and her eyes welled in compassion. She felt so helpless. Not only had the poor little thing been raped, but she was carrying her rapist's child. It couldn't have been any worse, and how money could help her now was beyond Klara—though she imagined that was why Kristina had come.

Immediately, she took the young girl's hand and said, "Come with me." Together they went to Teglgade, to Mrs. Rasmussen. Anna Egidia settled Kristina on the sofa. She served coffee and placed a bowl of home-baked cookies in front of her while making a range of comforting noises, which, like the cozy, everyday domesticities she performed around her distressed guest, were aimed at calming her down. It was a ritual Klara had observed many times before, and as always, it seemed to work. Anna Egidia placed her hand on the girl's belly and stroked it. And, as if her touch had activated some sort of inner mechanism, Kristina opened her mouth and spoke for the first time in several weeks.

"I want to go to America," she said.

The two women looked at each other.

"I don't want to have this baby in Marstal," she said. "And I don't want to be sent away to have him in secret and then give him up for adoption. I want to go to America and build a new life for me and my son."

"Your son?" Klara was stunned.

But Anna Egidia, who knew more about matters of the heart than Klara, didn't ask her what made her think that the child was a boy. Hearing the tenderness in Kristina's voice when she spoke about her unborn child, she'd known immediately that there was more to this story than rape.

"So Herman isn't the baby's father?" she asked.

Kristina shook her head. Her face was lit up by a sudden happiness that quickly turned to grief, the grief she'd hidden behind her silence and stiff features. She started crying hard, and the two women sat down on either side of her and held her.

The father, she told them, was Ivar, an able seaman to whom she'd given her heart and much more: the heart's natural companion, her virtue, which in a moment of such great and true love was not worth keeping, because he was the most wonderful man, the most handsome, the wisest she'd ever met, not like that animal, that heartless swine Herman, the monster who had murdered the best man in the world.

"My husband," she said. "He was my darling, darling husband. We would have been married. I'm sure of that. There was no one else in the world for me."

They understood then that when she spoke of Ivar as the baby's father, she wasn't talking about a fact so much as a hope.

"America isn't such a bad idea," said Klara. Anna Egidia nodded. One of her daughters had been there during the war.

Anna Egidia spoke to Kristina's mother, and Klara organized the ticket for the boat to America, making sure there would be someone to meet Kristina in New York. Now all they had to do was wait for the baby. Who would it look like when its head popped into the world? Would it be born with the signature of crime or love?

A jubilant new mother telephoned from New York.

"If it had been a boy, he was going to be called Ivar," Kristina said. "But it's a girl and her name will be Klara. Need I say more?"

A small face, too small even to smile but big enough to bear witness to its origins, had confirmed her faith in the conquering power of love. Nature had delivered her gift and the baby's true father had signed it. Ivar had sent his last greeting from the Hereafter in the form of a strong chin, a straight nose, a clear forehead, dark brows, and black hair.

Klara shared her joy. At least Kristina had cheated fate. And yet something inside Klara wept too, as if she'd been abandoned yet again. When we're wretched, we long for the company of others who also mourn, for the bittersweet confirmation that we aren't suffering because we've been unlucky or made the wrong choices, but because it's the law of life. When Kristina cheated her fate, Klara found hers all the harder to bear.

Her own child had been on that ill-fated ship, alone with a man no one in Marstal now doubted was a murderer. Knud Erik could have been killed, and she knew that she'd have experienced his death—as she'd experienced Henning's and Albert's—as a stinging rebuff. No one wanted her. They turned their backs on her and disappeared into the darkness. Or they went to sea. And that was the same as dying.

Helmer and Vilhjelm had returned with Kristina. Vilhjelm was still weak from his ordeal in the Atlantic. Helmer sobbed like a baby when he saw his parents. Now he was apprenticed to Minor Jørgensen, the grocer.

And Knud Erik? He'd stayed in France to look after the ship until a new crew could be found. Klara assumed this was something he'd been ordered to do. She went to visit the owner of the *Kristina*, the late Captain Bager's brother, Herluf Bager. She'd imagined it as a meeting between two shipowners. Man to man: that was how she described it to herself before entering the shipping company's office in Kongegade.

"Of course I realize that the boy has been through a great deal," Bager said, after getting up to welcome her and then sitting down again in his leather office chair, which seemed to absorb him until chair and man melded into a single mass of unperturbed and—she could not help thinking—manly authority. "But someone had to stay on to watch the ship."

"He's only fifteen," she exclaimed.

"He's a robust boy. I hear only good things about him. Of course he's welcome to sign off, though it would make things difficult for us. However, he hasn't expressed the wish to do so."

He looked her up and down, and in that moment she knew he was not going to order Knud Erik home as she'd asked. And she knew the reason, a reason that until now she'd failed to understand. This was not a meeting between two shipowners. This was a meeting between a woman and a man. And a worried mother knew nothing about the business of seafaring.

She stamped her heel on the floor and left without saying good-bye. He could tell the whole world about this if he wanted to. Her impotence made her burn with rage. Who did he think he was, the fat, smug little so-and-so? It would require no effort at all to ruin him, to crush him under the heel she'd just stamped his floor with.

Then she calmed down. Her agitation gave way to common sense. No wonder she couldn't get through to Knud Erik. The whole town was in the grip of this delusion that the future lay at sea, when in reality the sea promised nothing but brutalization and an ice-cold death by drowning.

THE DAY CAME when she thought Knud Erik was dead.

But when it turned out he was still alive, she decided she'd have to kill him herself. It was time. He was twenty when he told her, in his usual monosyllabic way, that he had signed on to the *Copenhagen*. A couple of months later, the big bark had disappeared en route from Buenos Aires to Melbourne. They looked for her everywhere: Tristan da Cunha, the Prince Edward Islands, the New Amsterdam Islands. But nothing turned up. No name board, no capsized lifeboats, not so much as a single life belt.

When the list of the sixty-four crewmen was published, Knud Erik's name wasn't there. It turned out he'd been sailing on one of Klara's own barks, the *Claudia*. He'd repeatedly asked her for permission to do this, and Klara had always refused. But she hadn't checked the crew register, and the captain had signed on Knud Erik behind her back.

During the dreadful days and nights when she believed that he'd gone down with the *Copenhagen*, she'd gone over their last conversation again and again. He'd asked her again if he could sign on to the *Claudia*. It was one of the few times he'd opened up to her, and she'd rejected him. Now he was gone. Her obstinacy had sent him to his death.

"Do you realize," he'd said to her, "that the barks you inherited from Albert are the last big sailing ships in the world?" They weren't just the last, they were also the most beautiful, and the final vestiges of an entire era. With their thin summer sails set, they'd ply the northeast trade wind right across the Atlantic to the West Indies to fetch dyer's broom. Every sailor, just once in his lifetime, had to experience what it was like to stand under those towering white sailcloths, with the trade wind behind him and the hot sun above, or to sit on the yardarm of the main sixty feet above the deck, king of the whole world. His eyes lit up as he spoke. He'd let her see inside him.

He was a man now. Long-limbed, but no longer gangly. Muscular and straight-backed. She could see Henning in him. She'd always been able to, but now she could see something more, something better and stronger.

"No" was all she'd said.

She couldn't even be sure that he *had* died, because his name was missing from the list of those lost when the *Copenhagen* went down. So where was he? She walked past the Collector's workshop. She was afraid to look in. What if he was carving her drowned boy right at this very moment?

There were nights when she paced the rooms restlessly, screaming out her loneliness and the loss she felt so cruelly responsible for, while Edith lay in her room with a pillow over her head. She too was weeping for the brother they both thought was lost, but her mother's uninhibited grief terrified her.

Those of us who passed by in the street didn't label Klara insane. We're all familiar with the line that separates grief from madness, and we know that sometimes the only way to stay on the right side of it is to scream.

Then a letter arrived from Knud Erik, postmarked from Haiti. Klara's hands trembled. She waited a long time before opening it. She thought it was a missive from the Hereafter: that the devil himself had written her a letter, mocking her hubris for thinking she could prevent the sea from taking her son.

But from the letter it was clear that Knud Erik knew nothing of the loss of the *Copenhagen*—and consequently nothing of what she'd gone through. He was simply writing to apologize for telling her he had signed on to the *Copenhagen* when he hadn't: for the past few months he'd been sailing on the *Claudia*. He closed his letter as he always did, with a line that always upset her because she knew how many unspoken things it must hide: "I am doing fine."

Her response was instant. She wiped her remorseful night vigils from her mind completely and sold the deck right out from under his feet. When the *Claudia* called at St.-Louis-du-Rhône, she offloaded the bark to Gustaf Erikson from Mariehamn on the Åland Islands. The remaining barks followed shortly after.

Having practically destroyed all seafaring in Marstal, she now decided to kill her son too. It would put an end to her constant fear of losing him.

For several tortured months she'd believed him dead and reproached herself for it. Then she'd found her agony was based on a lie. When Knud Erik returned to Marstal to pass his first mate's exam at the Navigation College in Tordenskjoldsgade, and she spotted him from the bay window coming to pay her a visit, she immediately ordered the maid to turn him away.

"Tell him he's dead," she said.

"I won't say that," the girl answered.

"Do it!" screamed Klara, losing control.

The girl went to open the door, but instead of remaining in the doorway and delivering Klara's message, she stepped out and closed the door behind her. "She doesn't want to see you," she told Knud Erik. "I don't know what's the matter with her. You'd best come back another day when she's in a better mood."

From her bay window Klara watched her dead son as he walked back to the harbor.

Was she a good person? Or a bad one? Was she someone who'd wanted to do good but ended up doing the opposite? These were questions she'd asked herself during her night vigils when she believed Knud Erik was dead and blamed herself. The doubts lingered, and her only way of suppressing them was to shut Knud Erik out of her life completely.

She'd founded her orphanage, and according to the school, its children were among the best in the class and always full of confidence. That had to be a good deed. She'd donated a library to the town and created a financial base for the Maritime Museum. She'd even done it anonymously. She'd given money to the Østersøhjemmet, the big old people's home that lay to the south, with a view over the meadow and the beach huts on the Tail. She'd donated funds to purchase equipment for the hospital in the neighboring town of Ærøskøbing.

Kristina wasn't the only young girl she'd helped get to America. Sometimes she thought she ought to send every young woman in Marstal across the Atlantic, so the men could learn their lesson. She kept in touch with the teachers at the school, and if a girl showed academic promise, she'd step in and pay for her education off the island. This was the future she'd planned for Edith. She wanted to make women independent. They had to help themselves and provide their own counterbalance to the tyranny of the sea.

In the old days, in the crisscross grid of Marstal, the main streets had always been those that led to the harbor and the sea. Then along came Kirkestræde, full of shops, with women bustling in and out. It was around their lives that she wanted to build a new town on the ruins of the old one. The orphanage, the old people's home, the library, the museum. Women would leave the island and return home stronger and wiser. And that was just the beginning.

It was a secret conspiracy and she was heading it.

"THIS IS YOUR big chance," Markussen said in his dry, detached manner. "War in Asia, civil war in Spain, crop failure in Europe. Things are looking up. Freight prices will rise again." He scrutinized her with that look of his, which she could never quite fathom and which made her feel both safe and uncertain. He took care of her. She never doubted that. Not once during all these years had he given bad advice. He'd trained her and she was an apt pupil, and every time she made the right decision, she received a look of approval that assured her that she'd not yet exhausted all her options. But there was also a cool curiosity in him, and she sensed that if she was to fail and go under, it wouldn't disturb him unduly. He'd regard her downfall as merely another chapter in the endless textbook of life; he might even feel enriched by the new knowledge that the study of her ruin might afford him.

It was like walking a tightrope. He was a father to her. She'd never known what it was to have one, and had always longed for one. But because she had never been able to satisfy her longing with a real person, she didn't know that a father had limitations. Now at last she was learning them. Yes, he was a rock she could cling to. But he was also a rock she could smash herself to pieces against. She learned to keep her distance and this distance lay at the heart of their relationship. Distance was his element.

Markussen was old now. Rheumatism had bent him so that it looked as if he was growing in the wrong direction. He walked beside her, hunched over his cane, taking tiny, cautious steps as if doubting the solidity of the ground beneath his feet. His helplessness filled her with maternal tenderness, an emotion she hadn't felt in a long time. But she knew she should keep those feelings to herself. Not because he'd be offended if she recognized his increasing decrepitude: indeed, he made a joke of it, laying bare his own weakness with the confidence of the powerful. That's the luxury of power, and power was what he was all about, she could see that clearly. He was surrounded by people who depended on him, and in their attentiveness and helpfulness he recognized nothing but rational self-interest. Of course they'd want to keep on the good side of him. It benefited them personally.

She took him for a stroll through Marstal; Markussen himself had insisted on it. His photograph was never in the newspapers, so no one recognized him. She was obviously entertaining a distinguished visitor, but people knew no more than that.

They walked past the vacant plots, and as he cast his glance across the nettles growing high behind the tarred fences, she was aware that the sight intrigued him. He eyed her sideways and smiled, acknowledging her willpower. Money could have been growing in there instead of weeds.

"What do they think of you?" he asked.

"That I'm a bit odd, maybe. But they don't think ill of me."

"They should." He laughed conspiratorially. He saw the destroyer in her. The avenger. The punishing fury who operated underground. This was what attracted him, and this was the pact they'd entered into: he'd make all his experience available to her, and then let her do the opposite of what he'd have done himself. He created; she demolished everything. What she wanted to do besides that, he didn't understand.

They turned toward the harbor. Moored to the black-tarred posts lay the true evidence of her efforts—a sight that made him point out, not for the first time, that her big chance was now.

There they lay, with their huge black hulls and their tall narrow funnels, towering as high as the smaller masts, which were there only because of the derricks. Two thirds of the town's tonnage was distributed among those five steamers, the *Unity*, the *Energy*, the *Future*, the *Goal*, and the *Dynamic*. The rest were smaller ships, including the last three or four Newfoundland schooners; the others had been converted to motor-powered vessels, which sailed only local routes. The hope of progress had foundered on a rock. And the rock was Klara.

"My steamers will stay where they are," she said. "I won't allow them to sail again."

Markussen nodded. Klara Friis was an apt pupil. She was strangling Marstal. The town needed to get back on its feet after the long depression that followed the 1929 crash, sentencing large parts of the merchant fleet to idleness.

Instead, she made sure that nothing happened.

The laid-up steamers represented an era that, thanks to Klara Friis, was gone forever.

People talked about it. She was well aware of that. But she hadn't been lying when she told Markussen they spoke no ill of her. They saw the steamers idling in the harbor as evidence of female indecisiveness and lack of skill in running the affairs of men. They forgave her for her impossible gender. They were tolerant, almost condescending. Women included. And although Klara Friis received no thanks for the things she *had* achieved, either, she enjoyed the secret satisfaction of having done the right thing. She saw herself as a breakwater, shielding the land from the ocean's destructive force.

It wasn't until that evening, when they were sitting down to the dinner her housekeeper had served, that Markussen aired an objection that made her temporarily doubt her own wisdom.

"What if," he said, smiling, as if merely testing her intelligence, "what if the men run off to sea anyway? There are no longer any significant shipping companies in Marstal, so they might just decide to sign on elsewhere. They won't find it hard to get work. They've proved their skill over the course of several centuries."

For a moment he reminded her of Frederik Isaksen. "They won't do that," she retorted sharply. "Every year the Navigation College admits fewer and fewer students from Marstal."

"Congratulations," he said, and raised his glass. "Then you've almost completed your mission." She couldn't avoid noting the sarcasm in his voice, but nodded to him all the same over the rim of her glass.

"You don't understand me," she said.

"You're right. I don't understand what your goal is. You pretend to do one thing while simultaneously doing the exact opposite. A library, an orphanage, a museum, a home for old people: you act like the town's benefactor, while pulling its means of living right out from under its feet."

"The sea was never a real way to make a living."

"I built up this country's greatest shipping firm. I'm a shipowner."

They both fell silent. They'd reached the point they always reached.

"Your son's a sailor," he said, out of nowhere.

She looked down. "And his father was lost at sea. You don't need to remind me of that. Can't you understand what I want?"

"Yes," he said. "You want the impossible. You want to whip the sea until it begs you for mercy."

That was the last time they saw each other. She'd known it would be. Their conversation had come to an end. She'd learned what she needed to learn, and he'd conveyed what he'd wanted to convey. He'd built a monument to Cheng Sumei, and even though that monument existed only inside Klara Friis's head, at least he'd shared the story. It was up to her to extract meaning from it. He'd never managed to fathom it himself.

Klara Friis had put herself in Cheng Sumei's place. Like her, she was a player who never revealed her hand, and they both had an excuse for their subterfuge. Cheng Sumei's was love. She'd wanted to make herself irreplaceable to a man who'd never previously needed one particular human being any more than another, and then she'd built an empire around him. True, he hadn't needed her heart, her sex, or her lips. But he couldn't do without her talent for business, and the cynical methods she'd learned in a lawless town. And these became her gift of love.

Klara too had a gift of love to offer. Not to a man, but to Marstal. She wanted to save it from the sea. She wanted to return its lost sons—boys to mothers, husbands to wives, fathers to children.

Oh, she knew well enough that the night of the flood would never really end. She'd still keep plunging her hand into the waves over and over again, trying to save Karla. Every time she sold a ship or laid it up, every time Marstal was ruled out as the possible home for yet another ship, every time the shipyard received one order fewer from one of the town's shipowners, every time a young man found a livelihood on land, every time the number of students from Marstal at the Navigation College declined—then her hand grasped Karla and pulled her upward through the dark water. The flood would abate, and for a while the pressure would ease. She dreamt of a globe on which the seas retreated and the landmasses merged, offering people a home where they could all live together. Fathers, mothers, and children united forever.

· · ·

"This is your big chance," Markussen had told her, when they said goodbye for the last time. He'd been referring to the wars in Spain and Asia. Thousands of people killing one another was good news. The freight market would go up, and his ships would be busier than ever.

Unlike her steamers. They lay still, their boilers cold.

Now was the time to act. Here was the moment to seize. But she wouldn't be sending them out to take part in orgies of profit while drowned men floated in their wake.

She went to her office and inquired about the prices of ships. And she heard what she expected to hear: it was time to sell. She'd bought the steamers from the widows ten years ago when the freight market was in a slump and everyone was suffering losses. Now that the freight prices had increased, she could resell at a huge profit. She knew what the town's businessmen would say.

"Damn it to hell," one would exclaim. The others would nod in agreement. They'd be reluctant to acknowledge her good move with anything more than a curse. But that at least would be a tribute to her skill. They'd thought her female brain was short-circuited when it came to profit, and that her ships were laid up simply because she couldn't make up her mind what to do with them. Now they'd realize that every step she'd taken, or failed to take, had a basis in cold calculation.

Others would take a different view. They'd think that she'd sold off not just the ships, but Marstal's livelihood. They'd be closer to the truth.

Was she taking more than she was giving?

What would be left of Marstal once she'd sold off her steamers? A tiny fleet of schooners with auxiliary engines, many of them rigged down to ketches and reduced to plying the local Baltic routes, with perhaps an occasional venture into the North Sea. The circle was complete. The town would end up where it had begun more than a hundred years before.

The sea would be the loser, because there'd be no more human sacrifices to His Merciless Majesty. And the winner? That would be the women.

Or would things go the way Markussen had hinted? Would the men sign on elsewhere and settle at the ends of the earth?

Would the flood never end?

IV

THE END OF THE WORLD

IT WAS THE END of the world.

He was on an alien planet or somewhere in the future. Whatever it was, it was heading for destruction. Convinced he was about to die, Knud Erik closed his eyes. Then suddenly he realized where he was.

He was in the middle of a dream. But it wasn't his own.

He was seven years old, sitting on the thwart of Albert Madsen's boat as they rowed through Marstal's harbor. The old man's voice came back to him, talking about a phantom ship painted gray all over, huge tubular buildings on fire, a night sky lit by a blinding phosphorescent white light, and air that quivered from the pressure of exploding bombs and collapsing houses.

Yes, that's where he was: in a dream that had visited the old man more than twenty years before. He opened his eyes and saw what Albert had seen, and for the first time he understood that the old man's dreams had been prophetic. What he'd presented to a child as tales of adventure had actually been his own visions of horror.

"That's the best story you've ever told me," Knud Erik had said back then. And now here he was, right in the middle of it. He'd never heard the ending. But it was on its way, and he sensed it would involve his own death.

Just then, a Stuka dived toward the ship and dropped a bomb. As he watched the missile falling, time stood still: he realized it would plummet right through the gray-painted funnel and detonate in the engine room, with devastating consequences. Preparing himself for death, he tensed his muscles.

Now!

The bomb disappeared with a splash into the water a few meters from the side of the ship. He'd mistaken its trajectory. His muscles were still locked rigid. He waited for the column of water and the sudden keeling of the ship, for the water pressure to burst her steel plates and come flooding in. But nothing happened. The bomb was a dud.

He waited for the next one.

The noise was deafening. Two oil tanks on the north side of the Thames had caught fire, and a frustrated roar sounded from the sea of flames, like the great mythic wolf of Ragnarök straining on its chain at the end of time, howling to be unleashed on the whole world. The black smoke was a clenched fist headed for the distant stars, extinguished one by one in the roil of darkness and toxic fumes. Beneath its black lid everything was ablaze, as though the sun itself had been shot down and was flaring for the last time in the midst of the ruined oil tanks.

The whole of Southend was on fire. The windows in the tenement blocks glowed in the blaze; flames leapt from the roofs like strange vegetation growing at explosive speed, determined to consume the very soil it grew in, and the docks shuddered in convulsions of destruction. Fire flashes spurted from the anti-aircraft batteries on the roofs that were still intact. The ships on the river were firing too. Knud Erik could hear the sputter of the old Lewis machine gun that had been mounted on board the *Dannevang* some months earlier: the British navy had trained four of the crew in the use of weapons. He was one of them. The machine gun, which dated from the First World War, they'd soon discovered to be useless when it came to defending the ship, but it had another more important function. It beat whiskey, and if anyone still remembered to pray these days, it beat praying too. Clutching and firing it gave you a blissful feeling of calm—though its services came at a price. Its overheated metal stock burned your palms, and its explosive coughing deafened you. But for a moment, the waiting stopped.

You were responding. You were taking action.

In a strange way the machine-gun position was the best place to be during an attack, even though you were clearly visible on deck, which made you the perfect target for a hail of enemy bullets and bombs. But at least out there, your helplessness didn't drive you insane.

When the air-raid warning sounded, the crew would instantly release the mooring and head for the buoys in the middle of the Thames. It was procedure for all ships to leave the wharf during air raids because it took weeks to clear the wreckage of a bombed ship and in the meantime it blocked the wharf to other vessels. So, resigned, they'd head for open water, where they couldn't just jump onto land if the ship took a hit. "We're off to the cemetery," they'd joke.

So it was good to have your hands on a Lewis.

Several of the ships around them were on fire now. One capsized slowly and began to sink. The crew in the lifeboats rowed haphazardly: the whole harbor was ablaze, and a crane had fallen halfway into the basin. High up above them one parachute after another unfurled and floated down toward the river, swaying calmly. As they drew nearer, Knud Erik was able to see that what was suspended from them wasn't human. The parachutes hit the water and their vast fabric canopies crumpled languorously before settling on the river. They looked like flowers scattered across a grave.

An hour later the air-raid alarm sounded the all clear. Fires were still blazing on the wharves, and the oil tanks were belching black fumes into the night sky. An acrid smell of oil, soot, and brick dust hung over the river, along with a faint trace of sulfur whose origin he couldn't identify. His eyes stung from exhaustion.

Knud Erik had been through the same scenario in Liverpool, Birkenhead, Cardiff, Swansea, and Bristol. Sometimes it seemed that they were sailing in an ocean of flames, and the sky was filled not with cumulus, stratus, and cirrus clouds, but a whole weather system made up of Junkers 87s and 88s, and Messerschmitt 110s. When their ship passed into the English Channel, they came within reach of the German batteries at Calais; in the North Sea U-boats awaited them. It was everywhere and it was constant. The whole world had contracted and turned as black as a cannon mouth. They didn't call it fear: it manifested itself as sleeplessness. At sea, they always worked double watches, and when they were attacked, nobody slept. While in port, the whole crew frequently had to move the ship to another mooring point, so their sleep was constantly interrupted. Did they sleep at all? Well, they closed their eyes and they were gone in a moment, free of memories, until death yelled "Boo!" again and they tumbled out of their berths, wide-eyed, as though dreaming of exit. But there was no escape, no hatch in the sky, no trapdoor in the deck, no horizon to escape behind. They lived surrounded by three elements—not sea, sky, and earth, but what they concealed—U-boats, bombers, and artillery. They were on a planet that was about to explode.

Albert Madsen had been right. He'd seen the end of the world. But the old man hadn't told Knud Erik he'd be trapped in the middle of it.

Tonight he'd manage two hours' sleep before rousing the crew. They were going farther up the Thames with the tide, and for him, it was a matter of honor to be ready before any of the other ships. He prayed for a dreamless sleep.

He didn't know that the next day he'd get to learn a new word. He'd expanded his vocabulary over the past few months, with technical expressions that bore witness to mankind's endless ingenuity. This ingenuity was so convoluted and contradictory that he found it impossible to follow, but he knew its mission well enough. A newer and even fancier way had been found to destroy him.

Yes, he got the sleep he'd asked for. Darkness descended and contained him—that rare, longed-for darkness in which, for a moment, he could renew his strength. This time it held him for so long that when it finally released him, he stumbled out of his berth with those wide, dazed eyes that are the normal reaction to an attack. He'd neglected his duty. He'd overslept.

He rushed out of his cabin. Many of the other ships already had smoke emerging from their funnels. Then, within the space of a second, more than just smoke was pouring out. A massive explosion that recalled last night's bombardment rolled across the river without warning. Another followed. Nearby, the bow of the *Svava* rose into the air, then snapped off. The ship started sinking immediately while smoke and flames devoured their way toward the wheelhouse. He saw several men jump into the river, one with his back in flames. Then the bow of the *Skagerrak* exploded. Two Norwegian steamers blew up next, and then a Dutch one.

His first thought was to get away. But what were they fleeing from? Where was the enemy? The sky was clear and it couldn't possibly be a U-boat.

A dinghy approached from one of the British escort ships. At its front a man with a megaphone hailed him with the day's new word: "*Vibration mines!*"

Knud Erik needed no further explanation. The mines were triggered when a ship's screw started turning. The objects he'd seen last night, falling gently through the air suspended from parachutes, were vibration mines.

A couple more ships exploded. Those that remained lay still, their boilers cold. Around them, flaming ships were reduced to sinking wrecks in seconds. A grim regatta of burned bodies floated between the wrecks.

Later, they were ordered to drift upriver with the tide, without using the engine. The only sound they heard was the lapping of waves against the side of the ship. It was as quiet as if they'd returned to the age of sail.

THEY WERE ON their way to England in a convoy from Bergen on the west coast of Norway when the radio announced Germany's occupation of Denmark. Their captain, Daniel Boye, immediately called a ship's counsel and presented the choice: to continue to an English port or reverse course and return to Denmark or Norway.

In a way, they felt the decision had already made itself. They were sailing in a convoy under the protection of British warships. Didn't that mean that they too were at war with Germany, like the ships escorting them?

The answer was clear. Thanks to a war that wasn't their own, freight rates were high. So were wages, which now came with a 300 percent war supplement. With overtime and various allowances, this meant a quadrupling, sometimes a quintupling, of a man's income. The reason they'd sailed was money. Now they were being asked to join this war and to be at its front line. Danish neutrality was no protection: seventy-nine Danish sailors had been killed last Easter and more than three hundred had lost their lives since the outbreak of war, despite having sailed on ships with the Danish flag painted on the side. The torpedoes on the U-boats couldn't tell the difference. A ship on her way to an enemy port was a ship on her way to an enemy port, regardless of the stripe of those on deck.

All of the seventeen crewmen on board the *Dannevang* agreed to continue on to England, out of sheer defiance more than anything else. They'd made the decision to go to sea. And now no one was going to frighten them off deck.

They sensed it was this same defiance that would pull them through and keep them alive, rather than patriotism, or love of the motherland, or ideology, or indeed any understanding of what the war was about. Doubtless these motives played some part, whether large or small, in each crewman's decision, but they weren't being asked to offer their opinion on the war. They were being asked to make a choice that would have unforeseen but crucial consequences for the rest of their lives. In what way they couldn't know, but their sailor's instinct told them it was a matter of life and death. They felt all of the sailor's stubbornness when faced by an overpowering force—a hurricane or a Messerschmitt 110—and they said yes, not to the war that raged this year, but to one that had raged for eons; not to England, but to the road to England: to the sea, and to a challenge that made them feel like men.

They arrived at Methil, in Scotland, on April 10 and were immediately ordered to sail to Tyne Dock in Newcastle, where their ship would be assigned to the British Admiralty. There was no ceremony to mark the transfer. An officer from the British navy stuck a note to the aft mast: a brief text stating that the ship had been requisitioned by the British in the name of King George VI. The Dannebrog was lowered, and the Red Duster, a scarlet cloth with a Union Jack in one corner, was raised in its place.

They'd never taken very good care of their Danish flag. It was frayed around the edges, and its white cross was blackened by soot from the funnel. But it was theirs. Among strangers, it was half of their identity. Now they'd lost the right to display it. Their country had surrendered to the Germans without a fight, and so their flag was taken away. From now on, they counted only if they no longer considered themselves Danes. They'd be fighting the war stark naked: their stripping had just begun.

The second engineer asked what wages they'd get under the British flag.

"Three pounds, eighteen shillings a week and one pound, ten shillings for victuals," the officer replied.

The second engineer did a quick mental calculation. He glanced around at the rest of the crew and shrugged. They could do the math too. The pay was a quarter of what they'd been getting. That said, they wouldn't be providing for their families anymore: they'd been severed from them indefinitely.

"Don't worry, you'll be home for Christmas," the officer said. He'd observed their faces closely.

They forgot to ask which Christmas.

· · ·

They were ordered to paint the *Dannevang* gray, as gray as a winter's day on the North Sea. Not even the varnished oak doors and window frames around the wheelhouse escaped. This was their ship. That winter they'd scraped off the rust and painted every square centimeter of her: the black hull, red below the waterline, the white superstructure, the red and white stripe that ran like a ribbon around the funnel. They'd lovingly traced the white letters on the bow, and they'd kept the *Dannevang* so clean you could walk about on her in shore clothes even after loading coal. They'd maintained the steamer in the old sailing ship style, as they called it, with a scrubbed deck and washed-down bulkheads. It was miserable and hard work, but it gave them pride. Now the *Dannevang* they'd cherished had slipped through their fingers, almost as if she'd sunk into the wintry sea from which she'd borrowed her new color.

The *Dannevang* had once been registered in Marstal. The steamer had been owned by Klara Friis and had been laid up for years before being sold to a shipowner in Nakskov. The captain and the first and second mates were from Marstal, the seafaring town that no longer had its own ships, but whose men had become the aristocracy of the Danish merchant fleet. Marstallers were everywhere, and most commonly on the bridge as first mates or captains: the only ones who sailed as seamen were those still too young to be anything else. Daniel Boye, a distant relative of Farmer Sofus, had been captain of the *Dannevang* when she still belonged to the family and sailed under her old name, the *Energy*.

He'd been among Frederik Isaksen's supporters and he'd stood near the wharf when Isaksen caught the ferry to Svendborg after his defeat.

"You won't remember Isaksen," he'd said to Knud Erik, "but he remembers your mother." Knud Erik had shuddered slightly. His mother was a sore point. He'd neither seen nor spoken to her in a decade. However, he knew Isaksen well. Isaksen had retained his affection for the people of Marstal and never closed his door to a Marstaller if a voyage brought him to New York. He'd even married a Marstal girl: Miss Kristina.

Always the gentleman, he'd been waiting for her on the pier in New York when she arrived. Klara Friis had written to him, "I know that you do not owe me anything. But I do believe that you are a man with a strong sense of responsibility."

Isaksen certainly was. He'd not only taken Kristina Bager under his wing but ended up marrying her. Knud Erik had visited them from time to time. Isaksen was a wonderful father to Ivar's child, but he and Kristina never had children of their own, and Knud Erik couldn't work out whether they were happy together: he had his doubts about Isaksen's relationship with women. He was fond of the vivacious Kristina and he had good reason to be, but as far as Knud Erik could see, he wasn't fond of her in quite the way a man should be of a woman. Although Knud Erik and Kristina Isaksen confided in each other, on this matter he never inquired.

"My little knight," she'd call him. She used a sisterly tone, though he'd outstripped her in size a long time ago.

Knud Erik had been in New York when Kristina's daughter was confirmed. It had been a strange experience to sit in a Protestant church in the Upper East Side, watching the fourteen-year-old Klara, a girl named after the mother he hadn't seen since the day she'd declared he might as well be dead. Her kindness to Kristina Bager was a side of his mother he'd never seen himself.

Whenever anyone tried to talk to him about why his mother had renounced him, Knud Erik always turned away in silence.

Captain Boye had received two telegrams on the morning of April 9. One was from the ship's owner, Severinsen in Nakskov, ordering the *Dannevang* to return to Denmark. The other was from Isaksen.

Boye read it aloud and looked at his first mate. "Isaksen suggests we go to a British port," he said. "It's actually none of his business, as he doesn't own the ship. But I happen to agree with him."

"Isaksen's a man of honor," Knud Erik said.

The majority of Danish shipowners had done what Severinsen had done. Møller, who appeared to be well informed, had stayed up with his son the night before the Germans invaded Denmark, telegraphing his ships with orders to seek a neutral port. The crew of the *Jessica Mærsk* had mutinied, tying up the first mate and locking him in the chart room: the ship had been bound for Ireland, which was staying out of the war. The crew had forced the captain to sail to Cardiff instead. Rumor had it that the *Jessica Mærsk* too had received a telegram from Isaksen. From his New York office he'd been just as busy as his former boss. As Boye remarked, Isaksen had stuck his nose into something that was none of his business. But this was how a man of honor sometimes behaved.

On the other hand, it was hard to feel honorable on board the *Dannevang*. You'd behaved honorably, all right, but you'd been stripped of dignity for your pains.

They might be in a pub in Liverpool, Cardiff, or Newcastle, downing as much Guinness as they could manage between two air-raid alarms. And always there'd be someone who noticed their accent and asked them, "Where are you from, sailor?" That was the killer moment.

They learned quickly. The one thing you never did in that situation was tell the truth. If you said you were from Denmark, the information was received with cold silence or open contempt. You'd be called a "half-German."

In the Sally Brown, a pub by Brewer's Wharf, a girl with a low-cut blouse and remarkably red lips had approached Knud Erik, and he'd bought her a drink. They'd raised their glasses and she'd looked deep into his eyes across the rim of her glass. He knew the routine and how the evening would end. That was all right with him. He needed it.

Then she'd asked. Back then he hadn't heard the question often enough to know the effect the word Denmark would have.

"Why aren't you in Berlin with your best mate Adolf?"

He was furious. Hell, because he was here, in a pub where half the windows were broken, in a bombed-out city, risking his life for measly wages, cut off from his family and friends! He could have been lying under his eiderdown back in Denmark. Instead, by way of payment for his willingness to face an abrupt end to his miserable life, he daily confronted every kind of explosive devilry ever invented. She wiggled her bottom as she walked off in her tight skirt, determined he should know what he was missing out on, for having the wrong nationality.

When news came of Denmark's fall, Danish shipowners and the government had encouraged Danish sailors to seek neutral ports right away. But the crew of the *Dannevang* had done the opposite, risking homes, families, safety, everything. It didn't help. There was no free Guinness from the barman, no sympathy pussy from women with low-cut blouses and red lips.

Instead, they were reduced to watching the good fortune of others from a distance. Down there, at the other end of the bar, for instance: the underage boy with blue eyes and a lock of blond hair falling across his forehead. For him there was no end to the backslapping, the flirtatious looks, the free beer, the invitations to an all-expenses-paid night in a room where a mattress with broken springs would squeak the night away. The kid didn't even speak English, apart from the crucial words "I'm from Norway."

They were fighting the Germans in Norway; the king and the government were in exile in London; thirty thousand Norwegians sailed in the service of the Allies, and they sailed under their own flag. The Norwegian merchant fleet had been assigned to the state, and the king was now its official owner.

Scandinavians were popular wherever they went. But to English ears, Scandinavian meant Norwegian. Denmark had dropped off the map, and if a sailor mentioned that was where he came from, it sounded as if he was offering a shameful reminder of the past. On April 9, 1940, the crew of the *Dannevang* had become stateless. They were in the line of fire, but they were buck-naked.

They downed their Guinness in silence.

The end came the following January, one day at around four o'clock in the morning. The *Dannevang* was on her way from Blyth to Rochester, with coal. Afterward they were unable to decide whether it had been a vibration mine, an acoustics mine, a magnetic mine, or just an old-fashioned horn mine—but her bow was ripped apart. The ship started to take in water immediately, but she didn't sink right away. They'd been blacked out during their voyage, and when they climbed into the lifeboats, Captain Boye ordered the lights turned on. They rested on their oars as they bid farewell to their ship, and a bottle of rum was passed around. They'd rarely drunk on board. On New Year's Eve, Boye had held long discussions with his officers before he decided to give each man a glass of cherry brandy. When the bottle of rum came back to him, it hadn't even been emptied. Seventeen men! He gave them a look of approval.

The *Dannevang* keeled over. The sound of explosions came from the engine room as the water reached the hot boilers, and lumps of coal flew out of the shattered skylight. The stern rose up in the water, and the screw gave a brief screech as it spun around for the last time. Then it stopped, and all over the ship the lights went out.

Knud Erik closed his eyes. Albert had dreamt this moment. He'd seen a sinking steamer and he'd described everything. Just as it was happening now.

When he opened them again, the sea had closed over the *Dannevang*.

The men sat in the lifeboat and watched, their wool-lined Elsinore caps in their hands. No one spoke. Knud Erik felt the captain ought to say a prayer. Or recite the funeral text from the *Book of Sermons*. How the hell were you supposed to send off a ship?

The steward was puffing on a cigarette; its tip glowed red in the night.

"A cigarette would be welcome right now."

It was Boye who broke the silence. He looked at the steward. "Hammerslev, did you remember the cigarette cartons?" The steward nudged the mess boy, who looked miserable. "The cigarettes, Niels."

The mess boy dived under the stern thwart and triumphantly pulled out a carton. They got a pack each. They'd been forced to leave their sea chests and sea bags on board—there wasn't room for them in the lifeboat. Now all they owned were the clothes they were wearing, their discharge books, and their passports, which proved that they belonged to a nation that no longer existed because the war had swallowed it up. And a pack of cigarettes.

It was all right. They would manage. They were alive, and soon their lungs would be filled with smoke.

"The matches," Boye said. "Where are the damn matches?" He looked sternly at the mess boy. "I'm throwing you overboard if you've forgotten them."

The mess boy flung out his hands in desperation. "It all happened so fast," he said. So the steward passed his lit cigarette around, and soon seventeen tiny red dots glowed in the winter darkness. Dawn was still a few hours away.

"Niels," the captain said to the mess boy. "It's your job to make sure that at least one cigarette is always lit, even if you have to smoke in your sleep. Is that clear?"

The mess boy nodded gravely and puffed away as if his life depended on the orange spark in front of his nose.

Knud Erik looked around. It had been a good crew. He'd been first mate on the *Dannevang* for three years. On board were seven men from Marstal and one from Ommel. The rest were from Lolland and Falster. Now they'd be scattered all over the place.

A couple of years later he would return to this moment and do the math. Of the seventeen survivors of the *Dannevang*, eight were dead: the captain, the second mate, the steward, an able seaman, two ordinary seamen, a junior ordinary seaman, and the chief engineer.

Five were Marstallers. Captain Boye was run down by an American convoy ship. The junior ordinary seaman was on board a munitions ship when she was torpedoed. There'd been only three survivors out of a crew of forty-nine, and he wasn't one of them.

But right now they were all together, waiting for dawn. They were close to the English coast and they knew they'd be spotted soon. Death was the last thing on their minds. Their only concern was keeping the red glow of the cigarettes going until they were picked up.

THE CREW OF the *Dannevang* remained unemployed for a few weeks in Newcastle, where they spent most of the time at the newly opened Danish Seamen's Club, honing their pool skills. It wasn't exactly that they missed the air raids, mines, and U-boats: any nostalgia for bombs could be easily satisfied by taking a stroll around the docks. It wasn't as bad as London, but almost. No, the fact was they'd made a choice, and it seemed ludicrous to spend a world war playing pool. Besides, the food ashore was disgusting. Powdered eggs, Spam, and gray bread smeared with a reeking, oily substance known as Bovril. Meat inevitably meant corned beef. The British diet wasn't dictated by stinginess but by the war, and it showed on the British. Their patched-up, prewar clothes were a fair measure of how much weight they'd lost. The food on the *Dannevang* had been better: from time to time they'd had real eggs or a piece of fresh beef. "The Brits eat the way we did on the old Newfoundland schooners," Knud Erik commented.

He hadn't sailed the Newfoundland route since the fatal voyage on the *Kristina,* and the *Claudia* had been his last sailing ship. Once he'd passed his navigation exam, he'd decided to crew on a motor ship. He'd applied to the *Birma* and the *Selandia,* vessels belonging to the Far East Asia Corporation, but they'd both turned him down. Knowing nothing of the connection between his mother and the owner of the company, old Markussen, he'd never understood why. So he'd taken jobs on steamers.

Helge Fabricius, the second engineer of the lost *Dannevang,* laughed at what Knud Erik said about the food. He was in his midtwenties and not old enough to have sailed the Newfoundland route. Knud Erik was thirty, less than ten years older, but they'd been born on either side of the great divide between the age of sail and the age of steam. They weren't even separated by a generation and yet they were children of two different worlds.

Behind the pool table hung a blackboard with VACANCIES written on it in chalk. Under this was scrawled NIMBUS OF SVENDBORG. Nothing else. What were they looking for, a first mate, a steward, a chief engineer? Knud Erik and Helge went to see the Danish consul, Frederik Nielsen, to find out. To their surprise, he offered them the whole vessel: its crew had jumped ship. The *Nimbus* was theirs if they wanted her. Knud Erik would be promoted to captain.

This was the other side of the war. It imposed restrictions, but it also offered opportunities. They went to inspect the ship. On the bow you could make out the letters that had once spelled *Nimbus* and more marks on her stern that had probably said *Svendborg*. But you had to apply your imagination.

As they walked up and down the wharf, inspecting the vessel, Helge Fabricius started counting. Knud Erik didn't need to ask him what he was up to. "There's no way that crew jumped ship," he said. "They're all dead."

"One hundred and fourteen . . . ," Helge intoned.

"The only cheese they ever got on that ship must have been Swiss."

"I'd like to see them make a cup of coffee," Helge said, abandoning his numerical litany.

They both laughed and walked up the gangway. They'd seen ships with half the bulwark ripped away, with the superstructure blown off, with craters in their sides, that had nevertheless managed to stay afloat. But they'd never seen anything like this. The *Nimbus* had received not one direct hit, but a thousand. The steamer was riddled with bullet holes. She was intact yet utterly destroyed. Waves and waves of Messerschmitts must have strafed her. Not one of the Germans' aircraft bombs or torpedoes had struck her; if they had, the *Nimbus* would be at the bottom of the sea. But their machine guns certainly hadn't missed. There was something awe-inspiring about the sight of the ship's perforated superstructure: it exuded a defiance that seemed almost human.

They entered the galley, where a blue enamel coffeepot still sat on the stove. As if to give the lie to Helge's joke, it was still in one piece.

"I'll be damned," said Helge.

They found some English coffee substitute, made from acorns, in a cupboard, and sat down at the table while they waited for the water to boil.

"We'll take this ship," Knud Erik said. Helge poured the boiling water and shot him a questioning look. "She's a lucky one."

"You mean her coffeepot was lucky. It's the only thing on board that doesn't have holes in all the wrong places."

Knud Erik shook his head. "No, the whole ship's lucky. Have you ever seen so many direct hits? But the *Nimbus* is still here. She's still afloat. And she'll share her luck with us."

They were both well aware that this was pure superstition. On the battlefield—and the sea was a battlefield—no rules govern who will be spared and who will fall. Whatever decides a soldier's or a sailor's fate is unfathomable and random, so they might as well call it luck and trust it as such. On the *Dannevang* they'd had a Lewis. On the *Nimbus*, they'd have the more effective Lady Luck.

They returned to Consul Nielsen and told him that they'd take over the ship. He looked relieved.

"These are our terms," Knud Erik said. "We won't be needing all that ventilation on the Atlantic, so we want the holes mended. We want some decent tackle on board so we can defend ourselves. And we'll be in charge of the hiring. We want to decide whom we sail with."

The *Nimbus* was taken to the shipyard to be repaired, and Knud Erik and Helge returned to the Danish Seamen's Club to find her a crew. On the chalkboard under VACANCIES they wrote a list of the crewmen they needed. Then they settled themselves in a corner near the pool table and waited.

Within a few days they'd hired a first mate, a mess boy, a donkeyman, and a couple of able seamen. They were still looking for a second mate, a steward, a chief engineer, and a few more able and ordinary seamen. It would be a crew of twenty-two.

Knud Erik hadn't expected to become a captain this early in his career. He didn't doubt his abilities, but he wasn't sure he had the necessary authority. Could he judge a man well enough to make the most of his strengths and help him forget his weaknesses? And what about twenty-two men all at once?

On the fourth day Vilhjelm stepped through the door and asked to sign on as second mate. It was two years since he and Knud Erik had last seen each other, and that had been in Marstal. Vilhjelm had a family now: a son and a daughter with a woman of his own age, who was the daughter of a fisherman from Brøndstræde. His stammer had never come back, and whenever he was in Marstal he went to church every Sunday. He kept the *Book of Sermons* from the *Ane Marie* at home. He didn't need it with him on board. He still knew it by heart.

"How's your father?" Knud Erik asked.

Vilhjelm's father had stopped his hard job as a sand digger a long time ago. Now he fished instead, though he was actually too old for that as well. But he persisted doggedly, trapped in his own deaf world.

"He was fishing over at Ristinge when the Germans came. He couldn't hear the sound from the aircraft, of course. He looked up because shadows were crossing the water, one after the other, too fast for clouds. Apart from that, he didn't give it a second thought. He was more interested in how many shrimp he'd caught. That's the war, as far as he's concerned."

The next man to turn up was also from Marstal: Anton. He was appointed chief engineer on the spot, and he wanted to know everything about the engine.

When he heard that the *Nimbus* had only eight hundred horsepower, he said, "I have my doubts," and fiddled with his black horn-rimmed glasses. "Don't think there's much top steam in that old tub." He wanted to know what type of coal they'd be using. "I'd like it to be Welsh coal," he said. "Coal from Newcastle gives off too much soot."

"You'll get all the coal you want," said Knud Erik.

It was a joke, of course: he didn't know the first thing about coal, and he had no idea what they'd be able to get hold of.

Anton sulked over this for a while, and Knud Erik suspected he'd get up and leave. They'd been friends once and they still were, though they were often on opposite sides of the globe. But Anton wasn't sentimental; he was a professional and wanted a decent vessel on which to exercise his talent for mechanical work. So his answer took Knud Erik completely by surprise. "Well, what the hell," he said. "We Marstallers should stick together. I'll take the job. I'll get this old tub to shift."

The third man to approach the corner table that day had applied for the job of able seaman. Under his open shirt he wore a white T-shirt that emphasized his gleaming black skin. They assumed he must be an American.

"Fritz says hello," he said in Danish.

Knud Erik's jaw dropped. Fritz! He didn't even notice that the man had addressed him in his own language. "I thought Fritz was in Dakar?"

"He is," said the man. "Or at least he was the last time I saw him." He stuck out his hand. "I'd better introduce myself. Absalon Andersen from Stubbekøbing. Yes, I've heard it all before. I'm a Negro. Black

Sambo and all that. But I grew up in Stubbekøbing and if you promise not to ask me where I learned Danish, then I promise not to ask you where you did."

He smiled at them as if pleased that introductions were now out of the way and they could get down to business. "I was in Dakar with Fritz," he went on. He pulled out a chair and made himself comfortable. Knud Erik offered him a cigarette. "Well, that bit of the story you're familiar with, I suppose?"

Knud Erik nodded. Dakar, in French West Africa, was every sailor's nightmare. There was nothing wrong with the town itself. But when France fell to Germany, the governor of Dakar proclaimed, initially, that he was on the side of the Allies. A few days later he changed his mind, and the many ships that had come to the port to enter Allied service were interned instead, dooming the sailors who had been willing to sacrifice themselves in battle to months of idleness on their own sun-baked decks. Vital engine parts were confiscated to prevent them from escaping. And when the British bombarded the port, they'd suddenly found themselves on the wrong side. It was one hell of a situation. One Norwegian ship managed to escape: the crew claimed that the ship's engines would rust unless they were run from time to time, so the idiot French handed over the missing engine parts and the crew gave them back replicas, then made their getaway in the middle of the night. The other ships—six Danish ones among them—were still rotting there. The war was calling out for them and they couldn't go. They must be feeling absolutely and utterly useless.

"But you're not Norwegian," Knud Erik said. "So how did you get out?"

"I'm something even better than Norwegian," Absalon Andersen said with a self-assured grin. "I'm black. I just walked out of Dakar. No one tried to stop me. I looked like all the other Negroes. After various detours I ended up in Casablanca. By the way, Captain Grønne says hello too. You boys from Marstal, you're just about everywhere."

"How did you manage to get here?"

"I have beer to thank for that."

"Beer," Helge said. "You're telling me you paddled from Casablanca to Gibraltar in a beer crate?"

"That's not the whole story," Absalon said. "But almost. Many try to escape, but only a few succeed. The French don't miss a trick. A few of us found this rotten old dinghy upriver. The French knew about it, but they never suspected a thing. It would have been sheer madness to try to go to sea in a tub like that. The problem was water for the crossing. We couldn't just stroll through town with a whole water cask. The French would have seen what we were up to right away. So Grønne gave us a couple of crates of beer. The French just grinned when they saw us carting them along. They thought we were off on a picnic. We rigged a mast and some sails and set off late at night. We had to bail out the whole voyage. That tub took in water like a herring crate. We reached Gibraltar after four days. The dinghy sank right under our feet as we sailed into the harbor."

"So you made it at the very last minute." Knud Erik said. He was impressed.

"Damn right we did," Absalon said, nodding gravely. "Damn right it was at the last minute. We'd just run out of beer."

When the next man appeared, Knud Erik gave him a curious look, and raised a hand before he could open his mouth.

"Let me guess your name. It's Svend, Knud, or Valdemar."

"Valdemar," the man said, without batting an eye.

"How can a Chinese end up being called Valdemar?" Helge asked, looking him up and down. He was young and slender, with the high cheekbones and narrow eyes of the East. A mocking smile played on his well-formed lips. He was handsome, in a surprisingly gentle, almost feminine way.

"I'm not Chinese," he said, in a patient tone of voice. "My mother's from Siam. And my father's surname is Jørgensen."

"You have a Danish passport, I hope?" Helge needled him. The young man's reply had unsettled him, and he wanted to recover his authority.

"Don't worry about that, as long as your discharge book is in order," Knud Erik said, to smooth it over.

A harsh glint appeared in Valdemar Jørgensen's dark eyes. "I was born in Siam," he said. "I have a Siamese passport and a Danish passport. The Danish one I cheated to get. I'm a member of the Seamen's Union of the Pacific. Is that good enough for you guys?" He gave them a combative look.

Knud Erik laughed. "The job's yours, if you want it."

"I want to know if we're going to America."

"Ask the British. If I were you, I'd prepare myself for the North Atlantic."

"I want to give you a piece of advice. Just the one. Don't marry an American girl."

"And what's wrong with American girls?"

"They're up for anything. Real hot chicks. But then they want to get married. I've been on ships where the guys were boasting of their conquests: wedding rings, wedding photos, true love, happily ever after—the whole shebang. And then two of them discover they've married the same girl. Know why? Those broads get ten thousand dollars in widow's pensions if a sailor's lost in Allied service. Pain in the ass. Get my drift?"

"Sure do." Knud Erik was finding it hard to keep a straight face. But the guy didn't appear to notice.

"You should, because you're not married, are you? You old guys are easy pickings for them. Take care, buddy!"

The kid really didn't miss a thing. He'd noticed Knud Erik wasn't wearing a wedding ring. Knud Erik leaned forward. "Listen to me," he said. "I'm not your buddy. I'm the captain of the *Nimbus,* and if you want to go to sea on my ship, you'll have to change your tone. Is that clear?"

"Aye, aye, Captain," he said. He was halfway across the room when he turned and addressed Helge. "Listen. If you've got a problem with Valdemar, then just call me Wally."

THEY SAILED IN convoy, first from Liverpool to Halifax, Nova Scotia, and back, and then to New York via Gibraltar. They sailed in ballast westward and returned with timber, steel, and iron ore. They had mounted four 20-millimeter machine cannons, one fore and one aft. The remaining two, placed on the bridge wings, pointed menacingly out to sea. These weren't manned by the crew but by four British gunners who sailed with them.

The *Nimbus* wasn't built for the North Atlantic. In fact it was hard to identify what she *was* built for. Anton did his best in the engine room, but he could never get her above nine knots. When they sailed in convoy and the U-boat alert sounded, they had orders to zigzag to avoid the torpedoes. The forty ships in the convoy left Liverpool in a straight line, then regrouped into a square, four by four. It was hard to maintain position, as the *Nimbus* wasn't sufficiently maneuverable; they inevitably fell astern.

Captain Boye had once told Knud Erik that in any situation that threatened the ship's destruction, the captain must forget rules, regulations, and ship's insurance, and follow a single unwritten law: treat people the way you'd like them to treat you.

Boye's words summarized Knud Erik's experience as a sailor. Later he heard that Boye drowned after giving his life jacket to a stoker who'd panicked and left his own behind. More than once he'd seen a captain risk his ship to come to the aid of another vessel. And he'd seen sailors in the navy do the same for one another.

Sailors were neither better nor worse than other people. It was the situation they found themselves in that encouraged loyalty. In the finite world of the ship, mutual dependency overrode individual survival instinct. Every man knew he'd never make it alone.

Back then he believed, naively, that the war had turned the whole world into a ship's deck and that the enemy they were united against resembled the sea in its brutal, uncontrolled power. He didn't know that war had different rules, or that those rules would break his loyalty and the strong sense of fellowship that the years at sea had rooted in his soul. He sailed ballast one way across the North Atlantic and timber and steel the other way, under armed escort, and he risked his life, and he did it because he'd learned on deck that no human being can turn his back on the fate of another. Yet the day would come when his commitment to the war would reduce him to a lesser human being, and he wouldn't realize it until it was too late. A time would come when he'd feel his existence was dictated by little red lights rather than the torpedoes that sought to end it. And the effect of the lights would be far worse.

There were rules for sailing in a convoy. A meeting was held ashore before departure, and each time the order from the convoy's commodore was the same: maintain speed and course. Every ship had her position, which she must stick to at all costs. And another order would come to balloon in their consciousness like a tumor: never go to the aid of a stricken ship; do not stop to pick up survivors. A ship that was stationary even for a moment would become a target for U-boats and bombers, and risk losing cargo essential to the war effort. They sailed to deliver that cargo, not to rescue drowning sailors.

This rule sprang from bitter necessity. Although Knud Erik recognized this, he still felt it was an assault on his whole identity. It wouldn't be a torpedo that destroyed him, he suspected, but an order that forced him to ignore drowning men crying out for help.

Escort vessels sailing at the rear of the convoy were tasked with picking up survivors, but they were often prevented from doing so by the wrath of the bombers or forced to divert their course to avoid torpedoes. Then the shipwrecked men would drift behind and disappear on the vast sea. The last trace of them would be the red distress lights on their life jackets.

They were the lucky ones. As their body temperature dropped, they'd drift into sleep, and then death. Or they'd give up, undo their life jackets, and let themselves slip into the darkness that was awaiting them. The red lights glowed on for a while longer. Then they too went out one by one.

When a ship was torpedoed, the destroyers would speed over to the attacking submarine and drop their depth charges. Any survivors in the water would implode from the enormous pressure, strong enough to rip away the U-boat's armored steel plates, or be propelled into the air on a powerful geyser of water, with their lungs forced out through their mouths: tattered human remains of which not even a scream was left.

He'd seen it happen on the voyage back to Halifax.

They had orders not to deviate from course because the danger of colliding with the other ships in the convoy was greatest when they sailed at top steam while attempting to flee the U-boats. He'd stood on the bridge, his hands on the wheel, and sailed right into a whole poppy field of red distress lights in front of the *Nimbus*'s bow. He'd heard the frantic pummeling against the ship when the life-jacketed survivors drifted alongside and desperately tried to push off, so as not to be caught by the screw propeller. The ship's wake foamed red with blood from the severed body parts being churned around, while he stood on the bridge wing, looking back.

Don't look back was the rule for moments like this. Having done it once, he never did it again. But something inside him still watched what a moment ago had been men, and it kept watching until it turned to stone. No one, *no one* willingly did this to another human being. And yet he'd done it. Treat other people the way you'd like them to treat you. If he couldn't believe in that, what was he left with?

Nothing. Absolutely nothing.

He counted the little red lights from his captain's cabin. Their glow stripped him bare. He'd lost his last point of reference. He'd got his cargo to its destination. Yet he was doing the wrong thing. He'd done damage to others and in doing so, did damage to himself. He felt that close to the men in the water, screaming out for help.

When the convoy was attacked, he appeared on the bridge with a face that was frozen and hard. He didn't think about the U-boats. Nor did he think that the ships taking a direct hit might just as easily be the *Nimbus*. He simply braced himself for the little red lights. If they came, he'd push the helmsman aside without a word and take the wheel himself. He had the bridge cleared. He wanted to be alone, not only when he tried to avoid the bobbing distress lights ahead, but also when he plowed straight into them because there was nothing else he could do. He was the captain. He set the course. It was his responsibility.

He shielded his crew from it, determined that their hands, at least, would stay clean. If they wanted to, they could point him out as the guilty one.

He didn't know what they thought. He never discussed it with them.

When it was over, he'd go to his cabin, open a bottle of whiskey, and drink himself unconscious. It was his substitute for penance; he knew no real penance was possible. He'd done something irreparable. There on the bridge he'd forfeited the right to his own happiness. Any thoughts about the purpose of his life faded away. He watched himself from the outside, but he could no longer make anything out. His soul had turned to dust, pulverized on the grindstone of war.

He isolated himself. He never went to the mess. Nor did he fraternize with the first or second mates. He didn't even speak to his boyhood friends from Marstal anymore. He took his meals alone and opened his mouth only to give orders.

No one tried to coax him out of his solitude. No one addressed him with jocular remarks or asked him a question that didn't relate directly to daily duties on board. And yet they helped him. They helped him maintain his solitude, as if they knew that the price he was paying was on their behalf too.

An outsider might have thought that the crew was behaving coldly—ungratefully, even—by keeping their distance. But the contrary was true. They knew that the smallest sign of sympathy—a pat on the shoulder, a kind word, a glance—would have made him break down. Instead, they kept him going. They shielded him so he could get on with the job of shielding them. They needed a captain and they gave him the chance to be that man.

Dear Knud Erik,

I am writing to tell you about a dream I had last night.

I was standing on the beach, staring across the sea, as I used to do when I was a child. I felt the same mixture of fear of the sea and longing to sail on it that I used to feel back then. Then suddenly the sea started to withdraw. The pebbles on the beach rattled as they were sucked out by the pull. The water lay flat as though a huge wind was passing across it. This went on for a long time, and finally there was nothing left but bare seabed all the way to the horizon.

If you knew how I have longed for a moment like that! You know how much I hate the sea. It has taken so much from us. But I felt no triumph, though I saw my most ardent wish come true at long last.

Instead, I was filled with a premonition of something terrible.

I heard a roaring. Far out, a wall of white foaming water had risen and it was approaching at speed. I made no attempt to escape, even though I knew that I would be swept away in a moment.

There was nowhere to escape to.

What have I done? What have I done?

This question screamed itself inside me when I woke up.

You might think this sounds insane, but I feel a terrible guilt when I wander the streets. I see boys and girls, I see people out shopping, I see the women—and there are many women—I see the old people. But I see so few men, and I feel that I am the one who chased them away when I deliberately ruined the seafaring business here.

Marstal is not in the habit of counting those who are missing. But I am. Somewhere between five and six hundred men are no longer among us—sons, fathers, brothers. You are on the other side of the wall that the war has built around Denmark. You sail in the service of the Allies, and the outcome of the war will determine whether you can ever return home. But even victory is no guarantee that you will survive.

The flood of my nightmare is upon us, and I was the one who provoked it.

I wanted to banish the sea from men's hearts, but I achieved the opposite. You looked for work elsewhere because there were hardly any ships registered in Marstal. You sailed farther away. The time you were home with us became even shorter than it used to be. Now you are all gone indefinitely. Some of you, many, I fear, forever. The only proof we have that you are still alive is the letters we receive. There are long intervals between them. When letters fail to arrive, we are left guessing why.

Dear Knud Erik, I once said that you were dead to me, and this is the most dreadful thing a mother can do to herself. I know so little about you, only what I hear from other people, and they fall silent in my presence. I feel they regard me as something unnatural. I do not know if they have forgiven me for what I have done to this town. Maybe they do not even realize that I was behind what has happened. But no one has forgiven me for disowning you, and I have grown even lonelier than I was to begin with.

You will not get to read this letter. I will not send it. When the war is over and you have returned, I will give it to you.

I ask for nothing more than that you read it then.

Your mother

KNUD ERIK DIDN'T go ashore in New York. The land scared him more than the sea did. He suspected that once his feet touched the pier, he'd never be able to walk up the gangway again. And that would be a failure of duty. He'd no longer be part of the war—but men who stayed in it were failing in their duty too. The red lights had taught him that. So the choice the war offered him was a choice between two failures. Alone on the bridge, he honored his duty to the Allies, to the war, to the victory to come, to the convoy, and to the cargo. But he didn't honor his duty to the men who screamed for his help. It felt as if every single one of them was calling out his name.

When Vilhjelm went to the Upper East Side to visit Isaksen and Kristina, Knud Erik was briefly tempted to go with him. The last time he'd seen them had been at Klara's confirmation, and he'd been invited to dinner afterward. Then he shook his head. He preferred the solitude in the cabin. He huddled inside it as though it were an air-raid shelter.

There were men who, when they feared they were losing their nerve, started counting women, as though recalling their conquests in foreign ports made them feel stronger: women on one side of the scale, death on the other. It gave them a sense of balance.

Knud Erik could have gone ashore and tipped his own balance. He was thirty-one and unmarried. It wasn't too late, but—as he often told himself—neither was it too early. He was restless, and he'd known many women. It wasn't immature lust that prevented him from making a final choice. His indecisiveness was caused by something he could neither pin down nor articulate. At times he still thought of Miss Sophie, the crazy girl who'd turned his head at the age of fifteen. Surely she couldn't be what was stopping him? He'd barely known her. And her behavior, which he'd found enigmatic and compelling at the time, had been nothing but youthful pretentiousness. And yet it was as if she'd laid a curse on him. By suddenly vanishing into thin air—a disappearance that might have been anything from an amorous adventure to death by foul play—she'd tied him to her. It wasn't her he was seeking in the harbor bars or in Marstal's down-to-earth girls. But he was missing something, and every time he reached out for it, it vanished.

He'd managed one engagement in Marstal, to Karin Weber, who'd later broken it off. "You're always so distant," she'd said, and she wasn't referring to the normal absences of a sailor. He was well aware of that.

Something inside him longed desperately for a family. He needed to have a human being to miss. He needed a counterbalance to the terrible things the war had done to him, and he couldn't find that in port bars. He was a ship with no moorings.

He sat in his captain's cabin like a monk in his cell, but there was nothing edifying about his solitude. He counted the red lights. He counted his soul into tiny pieces. His dreams about the life he could have had crumbled like a child's sandcastle.

IN LIVERPOOL he deserted. He was running away from his sense of duty. The same whiskey that had helped him maintain a balance could also make him lose it. And in Liverpool he lost it.

Even shaving every day had become an ordeal. How do you shave without looking in the mirror? Shaving was the last struggle before the final rot set in. He knew this was an unwritten law for prisoners of war in the German internment camps. And that was how he felt: like a prisoner of war. He'd fallen into enemy hands. Only the enemy was inside him.

On the last voyage they'd sailed with ammunition in the hold. A hit would have meant total annihilation: no men in the water with their pleading little red lights. Not even the captain's cap would have survived if the *Nimbus* had disappeared in a gigantic spurt of flame. He'd caught himself fantasizing about the relief that death would bring. But no torpedoes struck them. Nor did any bombs drop through the deck and hit the cargo.

Yes, the *Nimbus* was a lucky ship. She kept a steady course through the drowning men and he cursed it all.

The ship's radio could pick up the frequency of the Royal Air Force, and when they approached the English coast after crossing the Atlantic, they'd gather on the bridge to listen to the conversations between the flight command and the RAF pilots. They heard the words "Good luck and good hunting," which signaled the start of a radio transmission of a life-or-death battle. They cheered and shouted in support of their team. They cursed the enemy whom they could not hear but sometimes saw, because the fights took place in the sky right over their heads. They clenched their fists; the veins bulged in their foreheads. They rooted for the pilots, who shouted their warnings or triumphs out into the ether. And then sometimes suddenly slumped in their seat, shot to pieces. These men sacrificed themselves for the ships, and yet the sailors all wished they could swap their eternal waiting position on the deck for the pilot's exposed cockpit. There wasn't one of them who didn't long to deliver death, instead of waiting for it. They got so worked up during these transmissions that if someone had handed them revolvers, they'd have been hard-pressed not to gun one another down like dogs.

Knud Erik was the only one who didn't fantasize about firing a gun. He'd have preferred to be the target of one. They were welcome to pull the trigger on him. He'd be happy to oblige.

He stopped Wally as he made his way down the gangway, suitcase in hand. He'd heard Wally boasting about its contents, which he'd acquired in New York: nylon stockings, salmon-pink satin brassieres, and lace panties.

Knud Erik made an effort not to sway. "Take me with you," he said in a thick voice. "I want to see what your underwear buys you." It was a plea, but he made it sound like a command. Not that it was the kind of command a captain would give to a crew member if he wanted to maintain respect. Show me the way to the gutter, let us be companions in degradation!

He'd left his cell to commit weaponless suicide.

Anton and Vilhjelm weren't there. If they had been, they'd have stopped him. Wally didn't have the maturity or the experience for that. He saw the boy's eyes flicker, but he knew he wouldn't dare raise an objection.

"Aye, aye, Captain" was all he said.

Absalon came up next to him. "But Captain . . . ," he said.

Knud Erik could hear it was the start of a protest. After all, leaving the ship was tantamount to deserting it. The Liverpool docks were bombarded incessantly. They had to keep remooring. A captain couldn't just walk off in circumstances like that. It would be an unforgivable dereliction of duty. Never mind; he'd just have to add that one to the list. He made a deprecating gesture. "Vilhjelm will look after her."

Absalon looked away.

He and Wally kept their distance from Knud Erik on the road to the railway station, which ran between rows of bombed-out houses, where lean men and women were sifting through the bricks. There was no hostility in it. He was the captain, and they were just trying to uphold what remained of his dignity.

He'd once told Wally that he wasn't his buddy—but this was what he was trying to become now. He felt the poison of self-loathing spread. He hoped that it would kill him.

He fell asleep on the train to London, and Wally woke him when it stopped at the platform. Dazed, he looked around the compartment. Moving between New York and England always felt like time traveling: the Americans existed in a permanent prewar state, with well-nourished bodies and faces that exuded health, while the English, with their skin drained of color, looked like blurred, yellowing photographs of half-remembered people in an old album kept in a dusty attic, vegetating in a shadowland of ever-decreasing rations.

They'd just left the station building when the air-raid alarm sounded. It was night, and a dense darkness lay between the houses. They stopped short, not knowing what to do. Spotting some people running, they took off in the same direction. Somewhere a faint red light glowed, marking the entrance to an air-raid shelter. The irony wasn't lost on him. At sea, a red light meant yet another life on his conscience. Here it meant salvation. For a moment he had the urge to simply stand there and wait for the bombs to rain down on him. Seeing his hesitation, Absalon grabbed him by the arm.

"This way, Captain."

He let his legs take charge and followed the others.

There was no light in the air-raid shelter. They sat tightly packed together, surrounded by pitch-black darkness. He could hear whispers, a cough, a child crying. He'd lost track of Wally and Absalon, and it was a relief to be among strangers. There was a powerful smell of unwashed bodies and musty clothes. An anti-aircraft battery right above the bunker started firing, making the air tremble. Then the bombs started falling. Chalk and dirt dropped from the ceiling: it felt as though death had grown hands and was tentatively feeling their faces before it grabbed them. He heard gasping and whispering. Someone began sobbing uncontrollably and someone else murmured words of comfort, then broke into a panicked "Shut up for Christ's sake!"

"Leave her alone," another voice interrupted.

"Please, can we go home?" a child's voice begged.

A little girl screamed for her mother, and the voice of an old woman responded with the Lord's Prayer. A bomb exploded nearby, and the whole floor shook. For a moment Knud Erik expected the shelter to collapse on top of them. Everyone fell silent, as if death itself had hushed them.

Then he felt a hand on his. It was a woman's: small and delicate, but with a work-hardened palm. He stroked it reassuringly. He felt her head rest on his shoulder, and he held the unknown woman to him in the darkness. Another bomb fell, and the concrete walls of the shelter groaned from the pressure. Someone started screaming. More screams followed, and soon the darkness vibrated with panicked shrieking as the confined people surrendered to mass hysteria, while the bombs drummed outside in accompaniment.

The woman put her hands around his neck and started kissing his mouth greedily, then fumbled at his groin. He slid his hand inside her coat and felt the contour of her breast. Her burning hot sex welcomed him. The screaming surrounded them like a wall as they took each other in blind, brutal lust, with the bombs dictating the rhythm of their thrusts. Yet there was selfless tenderness in the soft, anonymous body that united with his own. She offered him the warmth of life itself, and he offered it back until their moans of pleasure mingled with the cacophony of terrified voices.

And for a moment he escaped the little red lights.

Some hours later the anti-aircraft battery above the air-raid shelter stopped rattling, and the sirens sounded the all clear. The door opened onto a dark street. It had to be the middle of the night.

He lost her in the crowd heading for the exit. Or perhaps he'd let her go deliberately. And perhaps she'd let him go too? Fires burned outside. He scanned the faces in the flickering light. Her? Or her? The young girl with the scarf around her head and her eyes fixed on the ground? Or the middle-aged woman with the hard face, trying to fix her smeared lipstick in the glow of burning houses? He didn't want to know. Both he and the unknown woman had found what they were looking for. Faces and names were irrelevant.

He stayed in London for three days.

He did it in back yards, in pub toilets, in hotel beds; he did it to the thunder of bombs and he did it without any accompaniment other than his own panting and that of his arbitrary partner; he did it until he reached a place where silence and darkness met and took him. He drank with men and he had sex with women who felt just the same way he did. When the bombs dropped, nobody knew who would shortly be joining the rapidly growing numbers of the dead, or whose workplace had been reduced to rubble or whose family was buried under a collapsed house. They all lived so steeped in fear that the losses they had yet to suffer had already consumed them. Every single second was a rebirth, every kiss a stay of execution, every shuddering breath in the arms of a stranger a declaration of love to life. Every drunken stupor—the permanent stupor he'd sought and found—was a gift, because just like a bullet to the brain, it eradicated all he was—his face, his name, his past—and unleashed all the hunger in his body. For three days he was his own ruthless appetite for life and nothing more.

On their last night they gathered up the remaining contents of their suitcases: underwear, nylon stockings, coffee, cigarettes, and dollars. Dollars especially. They behaved like Yanks and paid for a night in a hotel suite that took up an entire floor. They brought in the girls themselves and tipped the waiters generously. The porter kept an eye on their bar account to warn them when their money was running out. They ate, drank, danced, and whored through yet another night of bombing. Wally was in charge of the gramophone. They danced to Lena Horne and knocked back beer, whiskey, gin, and cognac.

The air-raid alarm went off at eleven o'clock. The waiters hammered on the door and called out to them to go to the basement.

"I suggest we stay here," Knud Erik said. He'd dropped the commando tone. He wasn't the captain now, but a mate among mates.

"Aye, aye, Captain." Wally saluted him and poured himself another cognac.

They switched off the light and opened the curtains. Outside, searchlights were strafing the night sky. The first bombs fell, far away to begin with, then closer. It sounded like a drummer testing his kit before his great solo. The building shook, and they dived under the beds. They knew that a mattress was no protection. But the intimacy of another body was. Their instincts took over: sex made them invincible.

The bombs came closer and closer. Outside a purple light flickered sporadically and a fiery glow dappled the ceiling. Every time common sense wormed its way into their muddled brains with the message that they should leave this minute and head for the safety of the basement, they grabbed their women tighter and thrust deeper, lust and fear driving them to ecstatic heights. Then they collapsed together, limp and exhausted, flung out their arms, and dozed briefly but blissfully, as if they'd already made it safely through the night.

But they hadn't. The bombs wouldn't let go of them. The fear returned, with its constant companion, ally, and friend: desire. From the darkness beneath a bed, someone would suggest, "Change? Who wants to swap?" And then a scramble would start, and they'd shuffle across the floor on their stomachs to a fresh, uncharted love nest, where new arms, a new greedy mouth, and new moist openings awaited, while the German bombers beat their kettledrums on the roofs of London.

At last all went quiet. They crawled out from under the beds, closed the curtains, and lay down next to one another on the untouched beds.

They'd won.

KNUD ERIK WAS there when the *Mary Luckenbach* was blown up.

The *Nimbus* was sailing in a convoy north of the Arctic Circle, on its way to Russia, with supplies for the Red Army. The weather was fine and visibility good. They were half a nautical mile behind the *Mary Luckenbach*.

The men on the bridge of the *Nimbus* watched in total silence. They'd seen tankers take a direct hit before; they'd seen two-hundred-meter flames. But they'd never seen anything like this. Neither had Knud Erik. It wasn't terror that silenced him. It was relief.

The German Junkers flew in so low over the water that it seemed to skim the waves. Just three hundred meters from the *Luckenbach*, it dropped its torpedoes, then roared across the ship's deck and got caught in the machine-cannon fire. Small flames darted from one of its engines.

Then the torpedoes reached their target.

One moment the *Mary Luckenbach* was there. The next, nothing but a stillness as terrifying as the explosion itself. There was no sign of fire, no wreckage floating on the sea: just a black cloud of smoke that rose with majestic slowness, as if it had the power to lift up thousands of tons of steel and carry them off.

The smoke rose unbroken to the clouds, several kilometers up, where it slowly spread out until it covered half the sky. Black soot fell silently as snow over the sea, as if the explosion had come from a volcano, rather than the war they were in the middle of.

There would be no little red lights: that was Knud Erik's only thought. Fifty people had just been wiped out, right in front of his eyes. A minute ago, through his binoculars, he'd seen gunners crouched behind the machine cannons and a black mess boy calmly crossing the deck with a tray. Now they were gone and all he felt was relief: he'd been spared. Not his miserable life, which he no longer valued, but his wrecked conscience.

They attacked in waves of thirty to forty aircraft, flying only six or seven meters above the water, swarming blackly over the gray sea. The sirens mounted on their wings let off a terrifying howl designed to drive the enemy mad and short-circuit his ability to react. Their twenty-millimeter machine cannons pounded the ships, and white and red tracer bullets sprayed the deck as the planes dropped their torpedoes one by one. The inexperienced gunners on the decks panicked and aimed wildly, their bullets hitting lifeboats and the wheelhouses of surrounding ships.

It made them shudder with reluctance, but they were forced to admire the German pilots' courage. With suicidal determination, they flew into a wall of fire intensified by the four-inch cannons aimed at them from the escorting destroyers.

The *Wacosta* and the *Empire Stevenson* were hit next, then the *Macbeth* and the *Oregonian*.

It was all over in five minutes. A Heinkel made an emergency landing on the water at the center of the convoy. The aircraft stayed afloat, and the crew crawled out onto one of the wings and held up their hands in surrender. They were no longer enemies. Without their machines they were just defenseless human beings. They kept looking around as if they wanted to catch the eye of every single one of the sailors crowding the rails of the surrounding ships. Then they meekly lowered their heads, awaiting sentence.

A shot rang out. One of the men clasped his shoulder and turned halfway around before sinking to his knees. A second shot finished him off. He slumped forward into the water, but his lower body stayed on the wing. The three remaining crew started running around him in a panic, looking for cover. One of them tried to crawl back into the cockpit. He was shot in the back. He fell and rolled into the water. The two survivors threw themselves to their knees and clasped their hands beseechingly.

They'd realized what was happening. They hadn't been transformed: they hadn't become human beings. They were still the enemy, and the proof hung over their heads in the shape of the black cloud that had been the *Mary Luckenbach*. The *Oregonian* was lying close by, capsized and sinking slowly after being hit by three torpedoes on her starboard side. Half her crew had, mercifully, drowned. The rest had been rescued by the *St. Kenan*, where they lay on the deck, vomiting oil, their limbs so frostbitten they'd probably have to be amputated.

Knud Erik remembered the nights on the *Nimbus* when they'd tuned in to the RAF frequency. Every one of them had longed to come face to face with a German he could empty his revolver into. At last the enemy was standing before them, not in the form of a war machine, but as a living, vulnerable human being they could hurt and take revenge on. Finally they had a chance to redress the massive imbalance of their lives. In those days, he'd desperately wanted to be on the receiving end of an enemy bullet. Now he felt the same blood lust as the others. It was urgent and strong. The imbalance in him was greater than in any of his crew.

He saw the two men kneeling on the wing of the aircraft that had been shot down, and the sailors in their hundreds, teeming along the rails of the surrounding ships, some with rifles in their hands, and the gunners in their positions behind the machine cannons. They fired lightheartedly, as if at the shooting gallery of a summer fairground. They probably felt that they were men again, because men aren't cut out to take a pounding and not fight back. They were fighting back.

The bullets whipped at the water around the aircraft. One of the two remaining airmen shot backward from the wing, as if a mighty hand had come to sweep him off and in doing so, prove just how pointless his life was, how futile his prayers to preserve it. The shot must have come from one of the heavy-caliber machine cannons. He landed in the water and vanished instantly.

The survivor slumped. He unclasped his hands and settled them on his thighs, leaning forward and baring his neck as if awaiting the mercy shot.

The rattle of bullets stopped: the men lowered their rifles, and the moment became a solemn one, as if they were all holding their breath before completing the execution. Slowly it began to dawn on them what they'd just done. Even before the enemy had been annihilated, their thirst for blood was quenched.

Knud Erik pushed the *Nimbus*'s gunner aside. He was an untrained shot. At first the machine cannon spat its bullets straight into the sea, drawing a long stripe of foam across the water, before starting to strike the aircraft wing. Then they hit their target.

Now he'd killed another human being, and everything inside him collapsed. He fell on the machine cannon, sobbing, oblivious to the hot metal burning the skin of his palms.

THEY'D SAILED NORTH around Bear Island, on the seventy-fourth parallel, when a new order came from the British Admiralty: spread out. From the briefing Knud Erik had received in Hvalfjörður on Iceland, where the convoy had set out, and from his experience of every other convoy he'd been with, he knew the order was a death sentence. Many rules applied to convoy sailing, but one overrode them all: Stick together. You'll only get through if you're united. On your own, you're lost, and an easy prey for the U-boats, with no protection and no one to pick you up if you're sunk.

How often had his crew heard that message over the megaphone from a passing destroyer, when, despite Anton's efforts in the engine room, the *Nimbus* lagged behind: "Stragglers will be sunk." This wasn't so much a warning as a sentence, a farewell unaccompanied by the usual encouraging assurance: we'll meet again.

They knew one thing for certain: the cargo had to arrive. The tanks, vehicles, and ammunition in their hull would continue via some complex route and end up on a distant front, where the fighting between the Germans and the Russians would determine the outcome of the war—and ultimately their own fate. They knew it because that's what they'd been told, but they'd never been sure about the actual mechanics of it. The only part they were familiar with was the sea, the Junkerses and the Heinkels attacking them, the wake of the torpedoes, the ships exploding and sinking, and the men fighting for their lives in the icy water.

Their contribution to the war effort was important. They needed to keep faith in that. But the moment they received the order to give up their place in the convoy and fight their way to Molotovsk on their own, they realized such faith had been pointless and supplanted it with speculation about the reason for the fatal order. And as always, in a shaky situation involving immense pressure, their guesses hardened to suspicion, and they recalled the rumor that had dogged every single convoy they'd ever sailed with to Russia, a rumor that clung with the persistence of smoke to a funnel, the wake to a propeller, and a torpedo to your precious cargo: they were bait.

In one of the Norwegian fjords a forty-five-thousand-ton German battleship, the *Tirpitz*, lay in ambush. She was the biggest battleship in the world, a threat to everything that moved in the North Atlantic and a symbol of the Nazi dream of world domination. Probably the battleship's greatest value lay in simply being that symbol: certainly she rarely ventured out of her hiding place in the fjord, with its protective mountainsides. Instead she lay chained there like the great wolf of myth, threatening a Ragnarök that never came. But now that Ragnarök was imminent: the wolf at the end of the world was going to snap its chain at last and grab the bait.

Hard experience convinced them of this, the same experience that had lined their faces and tortured their bodies with frostbite. When the thirty-six ships of the convoy abandoned sailing in formation and tried limping on their own to Murmansk, to Molotovsk, or to Archangel on the White Sea, the Germans wouldn't require the overwhelming firepower of the *Tirpitz*'s fifteen-inch guns to sink them: the U-boats could manage it with ease. Now that the British destroyers and the corvettes that had escorted them had been called off to go chasing after the *Tirpitz*, the convoy's thirty-six ships were left defenseless. No, they were doomed. Their own protectors had tricked them into an ambush.

They realized their insignificance with bitterness. They were expendable.

But what about their cargo? In Hvalfjörður they'd been told that in total they were carrying 297 aircraft, 594 tanks, 4,246 military vehicles, and 150,000 tons of ammunition and explosives to Russia. Were the British navy's officers prepared to sacrifice all that, simply to boast that they'd sent the *Tirpitz* to the bottom of the ocean?

They didn't get it. The only thing they understood about this whole business was that they couldn't trust anyone but themselves if they wanted to stay alive. If they didn't survive, they'd die without a soldier's sense of duty fulfilled or the comfort of knowing that their sacrifice made sense. If they were sunk, they'd disappear not just without honor, but without any acknowledgment that they'd so much as existed.

The defiance that flooded them wasn't directed solely at the enemy, but at friend and foe alike. As if they'd lost all notion of the difference.

The order came as a relief to Knud Erik. It meant that he could stop worrying about the drowning men. From now on, it was all about him and his crew. He could finally allow himself to surrender to the cynicism that comes when a crisis of conscience has exhausted itself. His sole priority was survival. They'd be alone in the middle of the ocean, and that was where he wanted to be. Alone, with no little red lights.

He changed course and headed north for Hope Island, sailing as close as he dared to the rim of the ice. Dense freezing fog covered the entire area. He ordered the crew to paint the whole ship white. They lay still for a couple of days, with the boilers switched off so the funnel smoke wouldn't give them away. The pack ice grated against the sides of the ship, and her steel plates protested in an ominous bass growl that from time to time shrilled to a treble scream. The message from the hull was clear: with a little more pressure from the pack ice, the *Nimbus*'s luck might just run out.

Knud Erik thought back to the time the *Kristina* had been trapped in ice. The heavy timber of the sailing ship had been pliable; it didn't need to prove its strength the way steel did, but instead let the ice push the vessel about until the weight that threatened to crush her ended up supporting her.

He ignored the *Nimbus*'s screaming hull. Better ice than U-boats. He dreamt about letting the *Nimbus* freeze and stay frozen until the whole world began to thaw and the weapons fell silent. He'd fought the sea his whole life. Now he embraced the dangerous ice as a friend.

He switched on the radio and invited the crew to gather around it as they'd done when they listened to the RAF frequencies. They heard nothing but distress signals: one SOS after another, and each cry for help a funeral service. There were only minutes between a ship's being attacked and its sinking. No one came to its rescue. Their crews went down alone in the icy cold sea. The *Carlton*, the *Daniel Morgan*, the *Honomu*, the *Washington*, the *Paulus Potter*. They counted twenty ships. There was nowhere to hide, not even here in the freezing fog at the end of the world.

They got going again and the *Nimbus* followed the ice edge north of the seventy-fifth parallel until she reached Novaja Zemlja, then headed south toward the White Sea. The ship encountered four lifeboats containing survivors from the *Washington* and the *Paulus Potter*. Both ships had been sunk by a formation of Junker 88s. The planes had flown over them as they climbed into their lifeboats, and the airmen had waved to them cheerfully while a cameraman filmed them for the German weekly newsreels. They hadn't waved back.

Captain Richter from the *Washington* came on board to consult a chart. After a while bent over it, he asked if they could spare a compass. His crew were still crouching in the lifeboats.

"Why d'you want a compass?" Knud Erik asked. "We'll take you."

Richter shook his head. "We'd prefer to sail on alone."

"In an open boat? The nearest coast is four hundred nautical miles away."

"We'd prefer to get there in one piece," Richter said, eyeing him calmly.

Wondering if the captain was suffering from shell shock, Knud Erik addressed him in the kind of tone he might use to persuade a wayward child.

"We can't offer you berths, but of course we'll find you a warm place to sleep. We've enough provisions, and in this weather we can manage nine knots. We'll be there in a couple of days."

"You do realize what's happened to the rest of the convoy?" Richter said, in the same calm tone. Knud Erik nodded. "A lifeboat's the safest place to be. The Germans won't waste their bullets on men in a boat. They're only interested in ships. They'll get you too. I'm grateful for the offer, but we'd prefer to go it alone."

He climbed down the ladder with the compass. In the boat, his men were slapping themselves to keep warm. If the wind rose, they'd get splashed and become encased in an armor of ice. But still they preferred their lifeboats.

The men pulled at the oars while Knud Erik ordered the ship full speed ahead. He stood on the bridge and watched the boats as they disappeared.

The next day a solitary Junkers appeared on the horizon and headed straight for them. You could hear its machine guns rasping from a great distance. The gunners on the bridge answered back. The wheelhouse took several direct hits, but no one on the bridge was wounded. Then the Junkers dropped its bomb. The plane was so close, it almost collided with the mast. The bomb exploded in the water near to starboard, not near enough to tear up the side of the ship, but enough for the detonation to lift the *Nimbus* half out of the water and land her again with a force that snapped a steam pipe in the engine room, which made the engine cut out. They were no longer maneuverable.

The Junkers turned around and came back with a howl. The machine cannons on the *Nimbus* were firing at maximum capacity. The wheelhouse was pierced again, and they threw themselves to the floor. Only the gunner on the bridge wing was left standing. They waited for the explosion that would signal the ship's deathblow. She was loaded with British Valentine tanks, trucks, and TNT. If they received a direct hit, there'd be no time to climb into the lifeboats. They all knew that.

"Do it then, goddammit!" Knud Erik cursed.

Outside the gunner kept firing as if his hands had frozen fast to the trigger. Then, through the rasping of the cannon, they heard the noise of the Junkers's engine die away. Had the pilot decided to spare them after all? They remained on the floor, unable to believe that the danger had passed. Surely any minute now, the plane's engine would roar over them again, and they'd be finished.

Total silence. The machine cannon on the bridge wing was quiet too.

"It's over," the gunner said.

They were still shaking as they scrambled to their feet. The Junkers was now a tiny dot on the horizon. The pilot must have been on his way home after an expedition when he spotted them. He must have had only one bomb left, and chanced it.

Once again, the *Nimbus* had proved herself to be a lucky ship.

Dear Knud Erik,

Grind a man into the dirt and observe him beneath your heel. Is he fighting to get up? Does he cry out against the injustice he has suffered? No, he stays there, proud of all the punishment he can take. His manhood lies in his foolish endurance.

What does such a man do when he is held underwater? Does he fight to get up?

No, his pride lies in his ability to hold his breath.

You let the waves wash over you, you saw the bulwark smashed in, you saw the masts go overboard, you saw the ship take her final plunge. You held your breath for ten years, twenty years, one hundred years. In the 1890s you had 340 ships, in 1925 you had 120, a decade later half that. Where did they go? The *Uranus,* the *Swallow,* the *Smart,* the *Star,* the *Crown,* the *Laura,* the *Forward,* the *Saturn,* the *Ami,* the *Denmark,* the *Eliezer,* the *Ane Marie,* the *Felix,* the *Gertrud,* the *Industry,* and the *Harriet:* vanished without a trace, crushed by the ice, rammed by trawlers and steamers, lost, smashed to pieces, stranded by Sandø, Bonavista, Waterville Bay, Sun's Rock.

Did you know that one in four ships that sailed the Newfoundland route never returned? What would it take to make you stop? Fewer cargoes? But freight rates kept falling: they halved in a decade. You simply lowered your wages, ate even worse food, gritted your teeth. You practiced holding your breath underwater.

You sailed where no one else dared or wanted to. You were the last.

You didn't have chronometers on board. You'd stopped being able to afford them. You could no longer work out the longitude, and when a steamer passed you, you would signal, "Where am I?"

Indeed, where were you?

In despair,
Your mother

WALLY WAS THE first to notice it. The others were on the bridge, supervising the unloading, when he turned to them and remarked enthusiastically, "Can't you see what a great place this is?"

They shrugged in their duffel coats and looked out over Molotovsk. Half-sunken, battered ships languished in the port, while along the pier stood vast piles of rubble, which were the remains of warehouses. Farther off in the low, rocky landscape loomed sooty barracks-like buildings roofed with tarpaulins. It was the height of summer, and although the sun was in the sky twenty-fours hours a day, it did little to warm the air. In the perpetual light they felt as if their eyelids had been cut off and they lived in a world where sleep had been abolished. The rocky gray landscape, the sunlight, and the knowledge that they were one hell of a way from civilized society filled them with a creeping, woolly-headed lethargy.

"Fetch the straitjacket," Anton snarled. "The boy's gone mad. He thinks he's in New York."

"This is better than New York. The chief engineer may have gone blind as a mole down in the machine room, but surely the rest of you can see what I mean."

And then they did. The workers unloading and placing tackles around the ammunition crates in their hull weren't men: they were women. Women with machine guns, patrolling the wharf where emaciated, thinly clad German prisoners of war stacked the crates onto the waiting transport trucks. And behind the wheel of each, a woman, preparing to drive the freight to the front line.

"Take a look at her behind," Helge said, pointing.

Not that you could see much: they wore felt boots and baggy boiler suits that concealed their curves. All they could do was guess at the bodies hidden under the shapeless clothing, speculating whether they were slim or thickset. Some of the women were young, though most seemed to be over thirty. It was hard to work out their ages. They had broad faces and gray, unhealthy complexions. Their hair was hidden under caps, though a few wore headscarves.

Not that any of that mattered. It had been three months since the men's last shore leave, and the sight of women in the hold or on deck was enough to stimulate the most important component of sexual desire: imagination. They started talking animatedly about their favorite parts of women's anatomy, while mentally stripping the dockers and guards in the insane hope that beneath the coarse, filthy uniforms every single one of them was a pin-up girl: a butterfly trapped in a grubby gray cocoon.

Knud Erik was wearing his captain's uniform. Normally he never put it on, but it was universally acknowledged that the Communists respected uniforms and nothing else, so when you negotiated with the Soviet authorities, it was smart diplomacy to look as official as possible if you wanted to get anything done. He noticed that one soldier kept staring at him, and he imagined it was his uniform that attracted her. He met her gaze and held it. As far as he could tell, she was slim and about the same age he was; she had ash-blond hair fixed in a tight bun at the nape of her neck. He didn't know why he looked back at her. It was a reflex he couldn't control, though he realized that it could be taken as a provocation. She didn't turn away but stared straight back, as if testing him. He couldn't interpret it any other way, though he had no idea what the point of it was.

His concentration was broken by a loud bang. A crate of ammunition had slipped out of its tackle and crashed onto the wharf, where it had sprung open. One of the German prisoners immediately began rummaging inside it, probably hoping to find something edible. Two female dockers grabbed hold of him and pulled him away. He struggled briefly, then gave up and let himself be dragged along the wharf. The unloading had stopped.

The soldier who'd been staring at Knud Erik the moment before shouted a brief command, and the dockers released the prisoner. The soldier stepped up to him, released the safety catch of the machine gun strapped across her shoulder, and fired from a short distance. She glanced briefly at the skinny figure lying prostrate before her, as if to make sure he was dead, then looked up at Knud Erik. This time he was in no doubt what she was up to. It was a challenge.

. . .

That evening, as he sat alone in his cabin, slowly numbing his brain with the bottle of whiskey that he never touched during the day, he had no doubt who the woman was. She was an angel of death, come to claim him. This crazy—even revolting—notion, which he didn't have the strength to resist, filled him with desire, and for the first time since the nights of bombardment in London he got an erection.

The town, which lay a couple of kilometers from the port, was nothing but a handful of wooden houses arranged around a square. The streets radiated from it like wheel spokes that led nowhere: a few hundred meters away, the wilderness began.

The town had an International Club, and that's where they headed that night. The first sight that greeted them was a badly stuffed, scrawny-looking bear standing on its hind legs, with its mouth open, baring a row of yellow teeth. The two fangs were broken, as if snapped off by someone afraid that the creature might spring to life and attack the customers.

Behind a table in a corner sat a bald man wearing a white shirt and red suspenders and guarding a money box, a crutch at his side. An accordionist sat on a chair on a makeshift stage made of roughly sawn timber. He too was unable to walk without the help of a crutch. Both men were around fifty, and each had a row of medals on his chest. They were the only other men the crew of the *Nimbus* ever saw in the club.

They'd got a general picture of the losses the convoy had suffered. Only twelve out of thirty-six ships had reached their destinations. Most had been bound for Murmansk or Archangel, and only the *Nimbus* had managed to reach Molotovsk, which meant that in this town of women, they had no rivals. They saw other men in the streets, but like the cashier and accordionist in the International Club, they were crippled or white-haired.

The few children begged the foreign sailors for cigarettes and chocolate. Their faces, which seemed wise beyond their years, would light up with an inviting smile as they approached.

"Fuck you, Jack," they said. It was British sailors who'd taught them this greeting.

"Fuck you, Jack," Wally answered, and passed out cigarettes.

The beer in the club tasted of onions, so they drank Russian vodka, which tasted like meths and most likely was. Every time they sat down on the red velvet sofas, the only furniture apart from the bare tables, they raised clouds of dust. The floor was filthy too. Anton's explanation was that once a woman had wielded a machine gun, a mop did nothing for her.

The crew from the *Nimbus* sat at one end of the club, and the Molotovsk women at the other. In the evening the women changed out of their work clothes and into dresses that looked like altered smocks. They put up their hair too, but their broad, heart-shaped faces were as colorless as before; they didn't own any makeup. Rumor had it that they were all spies who seduced foreign sailors in order to wangle secrets out of them, and this added to their fascination. Not that the crew of the *Nimbus* had any secrets.

"They're welcome to have a go," Wally said. "They can spy on me all they like." He crossed the dance floor and pulled a lipstick out of his pocket. The women looked at him with bright eyes and started giggling. He handed the lipstick to a hefty blonde in a faded blue dress, who immediately started painting the lips of the woman closest to her. The lipstick was passed around, and a bevy of red lips turned to him, united in a huge smile. He pursed his own lips at them, and another wave of giggling rolled through the room.

He walked up to the stage where the accordionist had yet to start the evening entertainment, and handed him some cigarettes: the musician stuck them behind his ear and began playing. A moan sounded from his instrument as he squeezed the air out of it in a heavy, stomping rhythm.

Wally went back to the women and bowed to one of them. She leapt up with surprising agility and led him to the center of the dance floor, where she placed her hand on his shoulder. He responded by putting his arm around her generous waist. She was older than he was and didn't hesitate to guide him through the unfamiliar steps. When the dance was over, she curtsied and returned to her seat.

"That didn't get you very far, did it?"

It was Anton. Wally turned to him.

"That was merely the preliminary discussion. I start by showing them a small selection of my wares. Then I give them time to think about it."

"You can't have much faith in yourself if you have to buy them."

Helge gave him a scornful look, and howls of protest erupted from the others.

"Quit that sanctimonious shit," Absalon said. "We all do it from time to time. You wouldn't stand a chance with that potato face of yours unless you left a few bank notes on the dresser." The others laughed.

"They're just like us," Wally said. There was an unaccustomed tenderness in his voice. "They're in need. So are we. Yes, we probably *could* get some Commie pussy for free. But where's the harm in spoiling them a bit? I mean, they don't look as if their life's all that much fun as it is."

Knud Erik didn't join in this conversation: he sat alone, scanning the women at the opposite end of the hall. Was his angel of death among them? He wasn't sure he'd recognize her out of uniform. He knew now that it was the unexpected sight of a machine gun in female hands that had attracted his attention. They'd stared into each other's eyes. And he felt oddly convinced that if she was here tonight, she'd try to catch his eye again. He didn't need to look for her. She'd find him.

Nevertheless, he continued studying the women's faces. Most were fleshy and worn, with a bottomless exhaustion that seemed close to resignation. It provoked tenderness in him, but it wasn't a human being he was searching for. It was the most extreme kind of self-obliteration.

They visited the club three nights in a row but not once did he feel the unease of that penetrating gaze on him, though women did look at him. He wore his captain's uniform to make it easier for her to recognize him, but the gold stripes on his sleeve and cap attracted women other than the one he sought. A young one in a green dress that matched her eyes kept staring at him, but he turned away and ignored her clear interest.

The dancing was well under way. Men and women settled down at one another's tables. The barrier between the Russian women and the foreign sailors had fallen. Wally, the experienced boy-man with the big appetite for women, was—as ever—at the center of it all. As for Knud Erik, he stayed on the red velvet sofa and avoided the dance floor.

That same evening Molotovsk was attacked from the air. The German Junkerses were aiming for the harbor. The midnight sun glowed on the horizon when the air-raid alarm sounded. The *Nimbus* was the only ship in the port and an obvious target. The half-drunk crew jumped from the deck onto the wharf and started running around in panic. There were no shelters in the area, and the first bombs were already falling. The anti-aircraft guns around the harbor were responding furiously. They too were operated by women.

A little distance away lay some huge cement pipes that could serve as shelters: the men ran inside them. They were big enough to stand upright in. One of the already destroyed warehouses took a direct hit. Farther away a transport truck exploded. Hard cracking noises resounded in the pipes, and they jumped. It was the heavy-caliber shells from the anti-aircraft guns; they hadn't made it to their target and were showering down from the sky like iron rain. Then they heard the shrill sound of a Junkers spinning, followed by the hollow boom of a bomb. A bomb, or a stricken aircraft colliding with the ground.

The anti-aircraft guns kept on firing. They saw an unfolded parachute float toward the ground, with the pilot dangling from the cords. The man hit the ground flat and the chute settled on top of him. He didn't reappear and nothing stirred under the thin material.

The alarm was called off shortly afterward. The *Nimbus* was still lying by the wharf where they'd left her. She didn't appear to have been hit, but a bomb crater on the wharf showed that it had been a close call.

A sudden impulse made Knud Erik head for the parachute. Anton came with him. He lifted the fabric and pulled it away to reveal the pilot's face. His blue eyes were wide open, and so was his mouth, as though his own death had surprised him. He lay in a dark red pool of guts. His lower body and legs were twisted at an odd angle; looking closely, they could see that he'd been torn almost in half. He couldn't have received the injury when his aircraft was hit: he'd never have been able to leave the cockpit. The women who operated the anti-aircraft guns must have used him for target practice as he drifted down. The heavy cartridges designed to bring down an aircraft had shredded his body, and dark stains soaked through the fabric of the parachute. He must have landed with the blood squirting from his exposed intestines. Something in them came to a standstill. "It's no use, Skipper," Anton said eventually.

Knud Erik looked up. Anton had never called him skipper. Yet he felt as if it were the first time in months that another human being had addressed him. "What do you mean?" he asked.

"I know what you're thinking. It's no use you trying to make any kind of sense of what you go through in this war. No use blaming yourself, either. The only thing that helps is forgetting. Forget what you've done, and forget what others have done. If you want to live, then forget."

"I can't."

"You'll have to. It's the same for all of us. Talking about it does nobody any good. It only makes it worse. One day the war will be over. Then you'll be back to who you were."

"I don't believe that."

"We have to believe it," Anton said. "Or I don't know what'll become of us." He placed his hand on Knud Erik's shoulder and shook him gently. "Come on, Skipper. Time for us to turn in."

The next day, he saw her. She was standing on the wharf in her uniform, with the machine gun hanging from the strap. Even before he looked up, he felt her gaze resting on him as if they had a secret connection, a kind of sensitivity to each other's presence that created a bond. He didn't understand its nature; her look never developed into a smile or a nod that might betray her real intentions. He held back too. Only their eyes connected. In her rigid face, unapproachable as any other soldier's, he saw no sign to suggest that this exchange was anything but a test of strength; its only possible outcome would be one of them finally falling on their knees in surrender.

A sudden thought filled him with terror: she'd execute another German prisoner working in the harbor. And she'd do it for him, as if a dead body might provide a new link in some secret connection that strengthened by the day. To his relief, nothing happened.

The unloading was proceeding slowly, and they guessed that it would be some months before they'd be able to leave. By now most of the crew had found themselves girlfriends, and all of the women appeared at the club with red lips. Several had eyes lined with kohl, and in the breaks between the dances, there was unashamed hand holding.

It was another seven days before she appeared in the club.

He was disappointed when he saw her. Had it not been for those eyes, which, as usual, stirred a tickling sensation at the nape of his neck, he wouldn't have recognized her. Her thick ash-blond hair was parted at the side and fell heavily across her forehead. She'd put on red lipstick like the others, and she stared continuously at him from the table where she sat alone. The other women seemed to keep their distance from her. He immediately stood up and went over to ask her to dance. The others, both men and women, were staring at him now. It was the first time the captain of the *Nimbus* had joined them on the dance floor.

She was wearing a white, freshly ironed shirt. She had lines around her mouth and was probably in her midthirties. Life had left its mark on her, but she wasn't unattractive.

It wasn't her appearance that disappointed him. But now that she'd taken off her uniform and laid down her machine gun, she was just a woman like the others. She was no longer his angel of death. He'd been mistaken about that. She'd simply looked at him the way any woman looks at a man and there'd been nothing else to it. He'd been so affected by all the destruction he saw, and participated in, that his normal sense had evaporated. All he sought was oblivion and he sought it with such intensity that it was indistinguishable from a desire for obliteration.

He put his arms around her and she pressed herself against him. She was a good dancer and they stayed on the dance floor for a long time. She never took her eyes off him, and he could see the longing in them. She wanted something that he felt he no longer was: a human being. She wanted his tenderness and his embrace. But he had nothing to give to anyone, only a brutal, urgent lust that sought its own relief.

How could she hope for anything, she who'd shot down a defenseless human being before his eyes and made herself a part of the horror that surrounded him? How could she feel tenderness, love, longings, or even infatuation? Did she see something in him that he couldn't see in himself? Did she think she could find salvation in him, that one night of love could give her back what she had lost forever when she killed another human being? Where did such optimism come from?

Or was she simply so callous that she could inhabit two separate worlds at once, that of killing and that of love? He couldn't. He knew it for certain, but his body reacted when she pressed herself against him, as though a part of him still possessed a hope that the rest of him had lost.

They left the club together some hours later. They hadn't spoken.

Unlike the others on board, he hadn't bothered learning the Russian for those few words that pave the way: *yes, no, thank you, hello, good night, goodbye, you beautiful, we make love, I never forget.* She'd tried exchanging a few words with him, but each time he'd shaken his head.

It was light outside, the smoldering, dying, yet powerful light that fills the summer nights north of the Arctic Circle. She rested her head on his shoulder. All he knew about her was her name, Irina, though he'd have preferred to go without even this basic information. He wondered if *Irina* was the equivalent of *Irene*. He'd never met a girl with that name, in Russian or Danish, but he'd always thought it embodied feminine refinement and fragility. Now he was walking beside one, and she was a cold-blooded murderess.

They walked in the direction of the sooty, tarpaulin-roofed huts. He supposed that they must be barracks, but there were no guards or blockades. He'd heard a story about a sailor smuggled into such a barracks by a girl. They'd lain down on a bed in a large dark dormitory, and he'd just got his trousers off and was ready for action when the lights came on. And there he lay with a proud erection and a circle of women standing around the bed, gawking.

These barracks turned out to be empty. They stopped in front of a cubbyhole with a padlocked door. She found a key and unlocked it. Then she rolled down the blackout blind and lit a petroleum lamp. A bed and a table were all she had. On the table stood a photograph of a woman he thought must be her. She stood in a clearing among some trees, with a man in uniform; they held the hands of a girl about five years old. The sunlight dappled the ground, and the man and woman were smiling at the photographer. The soldier had taken off his cap and put his free arm around Irina's shoulder. She was wearing a white shirt just like the one she was wearing tonight.

Where were they now? The man had to be at the front or dead. God only knew where the girl was. She certainly wasn't in Molotovsk. Perhaps she'd been evacuated to a safer place, deep in this vast country?

Irina looked away when she saw his eyes linger on the photograph. Her averted face gave him the feeling that both the man and the child had died. She lay down on the bed and waited for him. He slipped in and put his arm around her. He touched her breasts with his hands. How soft and warm her skin felt. He wanted nothing but this softness and warmth. It was need, more than desire, that welled up in him—bestial but without violence. All he wanted was to touch living, breathing skin, even if its warmth came from a woman who was used to killing and did so without so much as blinking.

What had she thought when she'd looked at him after firing her machine gun? Had she sought forgiveness, understanding? Had she asked herself, and perhaps him too, if he could still look at her and see a human being?

He felt the warmth of her skin under his palm, its infinitely pliable softness, and he placed his cheek against her naked breast like a shipwrecked man who has got himself out of icy waters and presses his face against the beach and feels solid ground. He wanted to lie like this forever, never stir again, merely exist on a continent of naked, warm female skin that stretched endlessly in every direction.

Then she started to cry. She hugged him tightly, her hands ran through his hair, she repeated his name in a pleading voice, nothing but his name, over and over. She was drowning, just like him. Everything in him contracted. Two drowning people can't save each other. All they can do is drag each other down.

He struggled to free himself from her embrace. He couldn't do this. He'd been alone all along, even when he lay with his cheek against her naked breast. And he was doomed to be alone. He'd sought an angel of death and found a human being, and he couldn't cope with that.

He sat up in bed with a jerk, leapt out, and ran through the empty barracks, where his footsteps echoed as if all the soldiers who'd once filled the building and were now dead had come back.

KNUD ERIK WAS sent for just after lunch. Sent for: that was how he thought of the summonses to meetings with the local Soviet authorities. A soldier and an English-speaking official turned up, both in uniform and both female. The official was young, and confident in a way that suggested she regarded herself as a representative of something great. The Soviet state spoke through her, in an English superior to his and in phrases that took the form of commands.

She wore a faint trace of eye shadow and he couldn't work out where it had come from. He'd never seen her in the club, and he was certain she didn't mix with any of the sailors who called at Molotovsk. If there was any truth in the men's rumor that some of the women were spies, then she was an obvious candidate.

These meetings generally concerned cargo. Endless discussions were sparked by small details that didn't add up, and he always attended them in the same resigned mood. He knew that he'd be wasting yet another day on bureaucratic squabbling and be forced to listen to insulting comments about the Allies' inadequate war effort.

On one occasion, however, he'd been pleasantly surprised: they'd handed him an envelope filled with checks for the crew. It was a war supplement. The Russians were paying one hundred U.S. dollars to each man; Joseph Stalin had personally signed the checks.

"You'd have to be stupid to walk into a bank with this and get your hundred dollars," Wally said, when he was handed his check.

"Anyway, they might be fake," Helge said. "And then we'd get arrested."

"One of my friends, a guy called Stan, got one of these checks and went to a bank on the Upper East Side to get his hundred dollars from Uncle Joe. The cashier kept turning it over. 'Do you have a moment?' he said, and took him up to the fourth floor to see the manager. He started staring at it too. Like Helge, my pal thought that something was wrong. 'I'll give you two hundred dollars for it,' the bank manager says. 'What?' my friend says, gasping. He doesn't understand. 'Okay, okay,' the bank manager says. 'Three hundred dollars.'"

"I don't get it?" Helge frowned.

"It was the signature. Stalin's personal signature. It's worth way more than the check."

But this time the meeting wasn't about checks or cargo. The official told him he was going to the hospital.

"I'm not ill," he snorted. It had to be some kind of mistake.

"It's not about you," the official said sharply. "It's about a patient we want you to take back to England."

"The *Nimbus* isn't a hospital ship."

"The patient is as well as he'll ever be. He can take care of himself. We can't continue to look after him."

"So can he work on board?"

"That depends on what you want him to do. By the way, he's Danish. Like you." He'd never told her he was Danish. She was well informed.

"Let's go," he said brusquely.

He'd expected the hospital in Molotovsk to be located near the harbor, but it turned out to be some distance outside town, along one of those roads that seemed to lose itself in the wilderness. The hospital was a long, low building, and no signs suggested that there might be hospital activity behind its crude wooden walls. A heavy woman in dirty overalls had turned the floor into a pool of mud and water, which she stirred with a mop in a doomed bid to give the impression of cleaning. Their footsteps splashed loudly as they turned down a long, murky corridor filled with beds of patients who, judging by the sounds that escaped them, were all dying.

In a ward where you could barely have squeezed in one more bed, a figure sat slumped in a high-backed wheelchair by the window. He appeared to have nodded off, but he woke when the official greeted him, and looked up drowsily. He was wrapped in a blanket that concealed most of his body, but Knud Erik could see that his left arm was missing. His face was swollen and flushed scarlet.

According to the information Knud Erik had received, the man had been in the hospital for four months, so the stark color of his face wasn't due to excessive sunbathing. This was Russia, where the vodka doubtless flowed freely even in the hospitals.

The man's red face broke into an ingratiating smirk when he spotted Knud Erik in his captain's uniform. He was keen to sell himself, and Knud Erik could see why. He was desperate to get away from this backwater and return to civilization, no matter how bombed-out civilization was at the moment.

"I understand you're Danish," the man said in a cracked voice, as though it had been a long time since he'd spoken.

Knud Erik nodded. He held out his hand and said his name. The other man clasped his hand enthusiastically, then appeared to hesitate, as if he couldn't remember his own, or was considering giving a false one. Then he came out with it.

Knud Erik turned to the official, who was standing behind them with her normally pursed lips relaxed in a friendly smile, as if congratulating two long-lost relatives on their reunion.

"You can do what you like with this creature," said Knud Erik. "You can take him to the basement and shoot him on the spot, for all I care. Or you can send him to Siberia or wherever the hell it is you send unwanted people here in Russia. But there's one place he most definitely won't be going, and that's my ship."

He marched out of the ward without looking back, splashing his way up the corridor, where the cleaner had resumed her efforts with the apparently inexhaustible bucket.

"Captain Friis," the official called out after him. Yet again he had to admire her pronunciation. Her English accent was perfect, and when she said his surname, so was her Danish one.

He left the hospital and started walking toward Molotovsk. He'd got a fair bit of the way and could already make out the low wooden houses of the town when a car pulled up in front of him. The official stepped out onto the road. It wasn't until then that he noticed that she had a black holster attached to her belt.

"I don't think you understand how serious this is, Captain Friis. I gave you an order. You don't have a choice."

"You're welcome to shoot me," he said calmly and nodded at the holster. "And make that freak an honorary citizen of the Soviet Union afterward. I really don't care. But he's not coming on board my ship."

"Watch your words, Captain."

She spun on her heel and got into the car, which turned around and drove back to the hospital.

He returned to the *Nimbus* and issued orders to sail immediately. The first mate gave him a startled look. "We can't do that, Captain. We need to light up the boiler first. And our papers aren't ready. They'll come after us and make us turn around."

"For Christ's sake!" He started pacing up and down the bridge, awaiting the inevitable. Sure enough, in just half an hour a truck pulled up on the wharf in front of the *Nimbus*. On the back of it sat the man in the high-backed wheelchair, with a sea bag on his lap. The official stepped out of the cab. The crew crowded around the rail to stare at the man, who raised his one arm and waved to them.

"Hello, boys!"

The official ordered two men to lift the man off the bed of the truck and carry him up the gangway. Once he was settled on the deck, she saluted Knud Erik with irony.

"Over to you, Captain."

"He's going over the side as soon as we leave the harbor."

"That's entirely up to you."

She turned around and got back into the cab of the truck. The engine revved and the truck drove off.

The man in the wheelchair waited. Knud Erik crossed the deck and placed himself next to him, then turned to face the crew, who were standing in a semicircle, eyeing the new arrival curiously.

"I'd like to introduce our guest," Knud Erik said. "His name is Herman Frandsen."

Vilhjelm and Anton looked shocked. In the eighteen years since they'd last seen him, Herman had changed into something so ravaged and burned-out that they hadn't recognized him until his name was uttered.

"He's known to several of us on board. But not for good reasons. He's a murderer and a rapist, and if any of you accidentally push him overboard, you'll be rewarded with a bottle of whiskey."

Herman stared into the distance, seemingly unaffected by the speech with which Knud Erik had honored him.

"In the meantime we'd better find you some work to do," Knud Erik said. "You've rested long enough. Get up."

"I can't."

With his remaining arm Herman calmly flipped the blanket aside. His trousers were empty from the knees down. It was more than an arm he'd lost. Both his legs had been amputated.

HERMAN WASN'T THROWN overboard when they left Molotovsk, and nobody tried to win the whiskey bottle on offer to whoever sent him to the resting place he deserved at the bottom of the sea.

"I've still got the most important thing," Herman said to the crowd that had gathered around him in the mess. "My right hand. A sailor's best friend in those long off-duty hours. And I can still raise a glass," he said. "What more can a man ask for?" His jerking-off hand, he called it. "Shake," he said, offering a big paw. "I've washed it." He wriggled the tattoo on his arm. "The old lion still roars."

They lined up to greet him.

Herman spent most of his days in the mess. He helped out at mealtimes, setting the table and clearing it afterward. He could just about manage that with one arm. It was degrading work, but that didn't seem to bother Herman. There was always someone ready to go for a stroll with him on deck when the weather permitted. Someone, Knud Erik didn't know who, had rigged up a pulley so they could lift him onto the bridge. One day he found him sitting on a high chair in front of the wheel, which he controlled with his one strong fist.

He'd given strict orders that Herman was not to be given alcohol, knowing full well that at the heart of it lay a secret desire to make Herman's life unbearable. Yet again and again, he came across him obviously under the influence. There was a secret cache of vodka somewhere on board, and the crew were supplying him with it. They treated him as if he was a mascot rather than a murderer.

There were three people on board who wouldn't have been alive if Herman had had his way: Vilhjelm, Anton, and Knud Erik himself. Miss Kristina's life would have taken a different and happier path without him. Ivar would still be among the living. And so would

Holger Jepsen. God only knew how many people around the world Herman had killed since then because they'd been in his way for one reason or another.

And yet here he was, calm, relaxed, jovial, and sociable, making himself popular with the crew, who seemed unaware that he was a monster who'd only been rendered harmless through amputation. The younger men, especially, seemed fascinated by him. When the mess boy brought coffee to the bridge, he described Herman as "an amazing guy who's had lots of adventures."

"He's got some incredible stories," Duncan said. He was seventeen and from Newcastle.

"Did he tell you the one about smashing his stepfather's skull till his brains spilled out? When he wasn't even as old as you are now?"

He glanced furtively at the boy to see if it had had any effect. It hadn't. Stubbornly, the boy looked straight ahead. He had his own view of Herman and there was no way the captain was going to change that.

Knud Erik knew perfectly well why. Before the war, everyone would have avoided Herman if they'd known the truth about him. They'd all have shunned his company, and whoever had the guts to would have treated him with open contempt. But the war had destroyed their moral defenses. They'd seen too much and perhaps done too much as well. Why should a mess boy take his captain's strictures seriously when only a few months ago he'd seen him shoot a pilot who was kneeling on the wing of a wrecked plane, pleading for his life? Where was the difference between Herman and Knud Erik?

The war had made equals of them, and Knud Erik could only hope that Herman would never find out what he himself had done. He could imagine his reaction. "I wouldn't have thought you had it in you," he'd say, bursting with malicious joy at knowing that Knud Erik too had succumbed to the worst in himself.

Herman was made for war. He was the type of man who felt naturally at home in it. He had that ability that Anton had said was essential to survival: he could forget. The big, brutal muscle man had been reduced to a helpless, barely human lump of meat, and yet he didn't give up. He didn't brood on the past but adapted to the present. Once he'd had four limbs. That was one kind of life. Now he had one. That was another kind of life, but it was still a life. He was like the worm you can cut in half without injury. A pioneer, in fact. In war, everyone had to become like him or go under.

"He took part in the battle for Guadalcanal in the Pacific, sir."

The mess boy was still standing there.

"Is that what he told you?"

"Yes, sir. His ship was sunk and he was in the water for an hour, fighting a shark. He says you have to punch them on the nose or in the eye. Those are their weakest points. But the shark kept coming back. Their skin's like sandpaper, it scrapes you."

"So he knocked out the shark in round three and got away with a scrape?" He couldn't control the sarcasm in his voice.

"No, sir," the mess boy said. The naïveté in the boy's voice made him feel ashamed. "The shark was shot by someone on the ship who came to his rescue. It took a chunk out of his legs and some of his lower arm."

"Has he shown you the scars, perhaps?"

"No, sir. He says they were on the parts that were amputated."

"So it wasn't the shark that took his arm and his legs?"

"No, sir. That wasn't until later. That was frostbite."

The core of the crew came from Marstal. There was Knud Erik himself, Anton, Vilhjelm, and Helge. Then there was Wally, who was half Siamese, and Absalon, who, though he'd grown up in Stubbekøbing, must have roots in the West Indies from the days when a few of its islands belonged to Denmark. They made up the Danes on board the *Nimbus*. The rest of the crew were from all over the place. There were two Norwegians, a Spaniard, and an Italian; the gunners were all British, as was the mess boy; there were two Indians, a Chinese, three Americans, and a Canadian. They were a floating Babel, at war with a god intent on ruining the Tower.

What united them?

The captain did. He was its fragile core. Though worn down by his own inner strife, he embodied the law of the ship and issued the commands they had to follow if they wanted to reach the next port alive.

Did they ever wonder why they sailed? Was it duty, conviction, or something deeper that kept propelling them into the danger zone?

At the start of the war, he'd believed that behind their willingness to risk their lives fighting was the same moral attitude that kept them united and determined to rescue fellow crewmen in a storm. He'd stopped believing that. But his old belief hadn't been supplanted by a new one.

At times he agreed with Anton: they were united by their silence. If they began articulating their thoughts, they'd feed one another's insanity and everything would fall apart. This was merely a ceasefire, and he knew it couldn't last.

"What's he been telling you now?"

Knud Erik never entered the mess, so whenever Duncan appeared on the bridge with coffee, he questioned him, with the excuse that as captain, he needed to know what was happening on board.

"He told us about the time they were torpedoed and climbed into the lifeboats. The water was as clear as gin. He could see the two red and white bands on the torpedoes before they hit. The cook had taken an ax with him and started chopping at the rail. 'What the hell do you think you're doing, chef?' the captain asked. 'I'm making a notch for every day we're on the lifeboat.' 'If you keep hacking away like that, there won't be many more.'"

Duncan stopped and looked at Knud Erik. He was clearly expecting the reaction that Herman had got in the mess for this tale: a roar of laughter.

Knud Erik didn't laugh. He took a sip of his hot coffee. "What else did he say?"

"Well, a few days after that they spotted a cork bobbing up and down. They couldn't see any land. But it cheered them up because the cork meant it couldn't be far off. Then a few hours later another cork floated by. Still no sign of land, and they started thinking it was strange, all these corks floating about in the middle of the sea. And that's when they discovered that some of the crew had a stash of whiskey in the bow and they were emptying one bottle after another on the sly. That's when Herman got his frostbite."

"And how did that happen?"

"Well, you see, sir. They started fighting about the whiskey. And he was pushed into the water. Herman said that it took them a hell of a long time to pull him back on board."

Herman turned every tragedy in this war, including his own, into a joke. Through the stories he told them, he came as close to conveying the unspeakable as you could get without saying the words out loud. That was why they listened to him.

When he heard that their nickname for him was Old Funny, Knud Erik realized that it was no longer silence that united the crew.

It was Herman.

The latest tale to come from the mess was that Herman could drink scientifically. During surgery, the doctors had removed some of Old Funny's surplus guts, which meant he had plenty of extra space inside. There was skill involved, he explained—like packing a hull with the maximum cargo. You had to have a method based on scientific fact, and he'd found it. To be perfectly frank, they couldn't see that his drinking was so special. He just knocked it back in the same way they did—the only difference being that he could keep at it longer. But this, he argued, was surely proof that he was drinking scientifically. He never needed to stop. As far as that went, they had to agree with him. They'd retire one by one to their cabins, and he'd stay on in the mess, downing more.

The only time Old Funny had met his match was when a young Salvation Army officer had come on board in Bristol to convert the crew to the Lord Jesus Christ. Old Funny had proposed a bet. If the evangelist could drink him under the table, he'd become a believer. But if Old Funny was the winner, the youngster would have to leave the Salvation Army for good.

"It was more than just a question of who could drink the most," Old Funny said. "It was a battle between faith and science. He had his Jesus, and I had my method. But he won, the bastard. I went under the table at four o'clock in the morning. To this day I still don't know how he did it."

"So you're a believer now?"

"I'm a man of my word," Old Funny said. "I believe in the Lord Jesus Christ, and I renounce the devil and all his works. The good Lord looks after me. It's thanks to Him I've still got my jerking-off hand."

He put down his glass and made the sign of the cross, while his stump waggled as if wanting to join in the fun too.

"But you're still drinking," Wally protested.

"Only when I take communion, and I'm a frequent churchgoer. Besides, I think I owe it to old Jesus. You see"—he looked around, and they could tell that the story hadn't yet reached its climax—"when he'd drunk me under the table, and he realized he'd won, he got up, threw his coat on the floor, and shouted, 'I'm through with the Salvation Army!' No one got what the hell he was talking about until he explained it. 'I realized it as soon as I emptied my first glass,' he said. 'I like drinking. I didn't win because the Lord was on my side. I won because I couldn't get enough!'"

They howled with laughter around the mess table. Old Funny enjoyed this applause for a while as he studied the transparent liquid in his glass. Then he raised the vodka to his lips and drained the glass in one gulp.

"Here's to Jesus," he belched.

FREIGHT SHIPS FROM Archangel and Murmansk joined them along the route back to Iceland, making them a pack of eight in total. A destroyer and two refitted trawlers, both equipped with depth charges, escorted them. It wasn't much protection, but apart from the ballast, they were sailing empty, and the British Admiralty probably assumed that the Germans would think it a waste of ammunition to attack ships with no war matériel on board. They'd soon discover that the Germans took a different view.

It was now October and the ice rim had shifted farther south. They sailed as close to it as they dared, but for the German bombers based in northern Norway, it was still no distance. The autumn gales provided some unexpected help. The weather was severe most of the time, and in heavy winds the aircraft never left the ground. But a storm in the Barents Sea made no difference to the U-boats.

Wally was on the lookout at the bow, and he managed to sound three false torpedo alarms in the course of a single hour. "It's the stripes of foam on the waves," he explained apologetically.

"He's anxious," said Anton, who'd appeared on the bridge from the engine room to moan about all the times he'd been ordered to reverse or stop for no reason.

Knud Erik thought it over. "I'd better find someone else," he said.

"Being up there all on my own with no one to talk to drives me round the bend," Wally said, with a look of gratitude.

Knud Erik went down to the mess. As usual Herman was sitting by the table, holding court. Only Duncan and Helge, who were busy getting dinner ready, were there. Helge had grown used to Herman and called him Old Funny along with the rest of the crew. Sometimes they'd talk about Marstal.

Knud Erik hadn't spoken to Herman since he'd come on board.

Now he went up to him and announced, without a greeting, "It's about time you made yourself useful." He ordered him dressed in an Icelandic sweater, duffel coat, and oilskins, and his head wrapped in a cap and woolen scarves. A mitten was put on his hand. His lower body was covered by blankets and a tarpaulin. Then he had him tied to the wheelchair.

Herman was undisturbed. "I feel like a baby being taken for a stroll" was all he said. Not once had he asked the captain what he was supposed to do.

"May you freeze to death," said Knud Erik.

Two of the crew carried Herman up onto the stem, where they secured his wheelchair so the heavy rolling of the ship wouldn't send him flying. The *Nimbus* didn't plunge deep enough for the bow to be submerged, but an icy spray washed over it. Knud Erik stood on the bridge and looked down on the bundled-up figure, who seemed to occupy the whole bow. The circle was complete. Once, Herman had sent Ivar out on the bowsprit. Now Herman was similarly exposed.

Knud Erik saw him bend his arm and raise something to his lips. Someone had managed to slip him a bottle of vodka. Oh yes, Old Funny was one of theirs, all right.

Two hours later Herman raised his hand: a torpedo was heading toward them.

Knud Erik ordered the ship to reverse, and Anton responded instantly down in the engine room. Knud Erik had time to note the strangeness of their putting unconditional faith in a man who'd once threatened their lives. Then he spotted the stripe of foam just ahead of the bow. Herman's warning had come at the last minute.

The torpedo sped onward, now aiming for another of the convoy ships, the tanker *Hopemount*. Another foam stripe appeared, parallel to the first. The torpedoes hit the *Hopemount* amidships just ten seconds apart. The ship broke in two, and the halves drifted in opposite directions in the raging sea; the front half began sinking immediately. The water around the stricken ship was filled with men, with and without life jackets, fighting to stay afloat in the freezing water.

The *Nimbus* was still reversing at full speed. They were now the last ship in the convoy. A trawler approached; Knud Erik hoped she was there to pick up survivors. If she dropped a depth charge, it would mean certain death for the men in the water.

On the deck of the *Hopemount*'s rear end, still afloat, a half-naked figure appeared. The sailor had managed to fasten his life jacket around his heavy belly, but his legs were naked. He climbed up on the rail and let himself fall into the water. Knud Erik saw him surface and make brisk strokes to escape the suction from the half-upright stern, which was rapidly taking in water and would soon plunge to the bottom of the sea. The distress light on the life jacket glowed red against the gray waves.

He'd seen it so many times before and he already knew what it meant: yet another betrayal, yet another piece of his already wrecked humanity sinking to the ocean floor along with the *Hopemount*.

Then he snapped.

Shoving the helmsman aside, he ordered full speed ahead and simultaneously pulled the wheel hard to port. They quickly approached the sinking stern. Knud Erik kept his eyes fixed on the struggling man in the water.

The swimmer threw back his head toward the overcast sky as if fighting for breath. A heavy wave lifted him up and hid him from sight. When he resurfaced, he seemed to be screaming, though the racket from the engines prevented Knud Erik from hearing anything. Then the water around him turned red.

For a moment Knud Erik thought the trawler had released its depth charge, and he expected to see the drowning sailor shoot out of the sea with his chest exploding, but nothing happened. Had he been attacked by a shark? It was unlikely. Perhaps he'd been injured before he jumped into the water?

By now a couple of minutes had passed, and the sailor was very close. But his time was nearly up. No one survived that long in the icy water.

Knud Erik ordered full stop and ran out of the bridge. He climbed the rail and stood on it for a moment, swaying as though hesitating.

Then he jumped.

Later, when he tried to explain it to himself, he'd say, I did it to restore the balance in my life. But when he jumped, he didn't have a single thought in his head. He jumped the way you rub your eye with your finger when something irritates it. A red distress light was on, and it was bothering the hell out of him.

He'd broken the most basic rule of convoy sailing: a ship must never stop to pick up survivors. The rule wasn't there just to prevent them from becoming an easier target for the U-boats, but also to stop the ships behind from colliding with them. In plenty of cases a single deviation from course had set off a chain of collisions, often with fatal consequences for the ships involved.

But the *Nimbus* was at the rear of the convoy, so no one would run into them from behind. When Knud Erik leapt into the sea from the bridge wing, it was only the lives of his own crew he was risking. Like every other act committed during a war, it confirmed one rule only to break another. It was simultaneously right and hideously wrong.

The icy water hit him like a kick to the head. He instantly felt the cold soak through his clothes. He got his head out of the water, gasped, and looked around wildly, already half panicking. He couldn't see the drowning sailor. Then a wave lifted him up and he spotted him. He swam toward him with furious strokes that made his blood pump faster. The drowning man's mouth was still open, and now he heard his scream, full of pain and ecstasy. Then, as the distress light threw its red glow across his face, Knud Erik saw that the sailor wasn't a man at all, but a woman with short black hair and narrow, Oriental-looking eyes, of which only the whites were visible. If it hadn't been for her scream, he'd have assumed she was dead.

Then he reached her. Her eyes returned to normal, but her gaze was oddly elsewhere, as if she was concentrating on something happening inside her. He thought she must be in shock. He started dragging her back to the ship. He had to hurry now. The cold spreading through his body was beginning to paralyze him. He'd have to give up soon, and he had no life jacket to keep him buoyant.

Most of the men at the rail were cheering him on as if he was a runner approaching the finish line. They'd hung a ladder over the side. Absalon was waiting on the bottom step, holding on with one hand and stretching out the other. The raging sea had soaked him through. Someone threw a line; Knud Erik grabbed hold of it and let himself be pulled over to the ladder. Then Absalon grasped his hand and pulled him up. His other hand supported the woman by her arm; she still seemed unaware of what was happening. She'd stopped screaming and a gentle smile had spread across her lips. As he yanked her out of the water, her naked abdomen revealed the guts spilling out of her. It was death that had made her gaze so distant and quelled her screams.

He tried to throw her over his shoulder, but a soft object blocked him. He looked down a second time. There was something coming out of her, but it wasn't her intestines. It was an umbilical cord. And in her arms she was cradling a baby. A small, creased, puce-colored human bundle, born underwater.

Her childbirth must have started even before the *Hopemount* was torpedoed. In the icy water, with only a few minutes' grace before she froze, the mother had fought not only for her own life but also for the baby's.

Gripping the woman beneath the thighs, Knud Erik lifted her up to Absalon, and from the rail countless hands reached out for them.

Just then he heard the dull undersea roar of depth charges, followed by the sound of heavily falling water. He closed his eyes and knew that the woman in his arms was now the sole survivor of the *Hopemount*.

Dear Knud Erik,

Last night they bombed Hamburg, and the whole sky was lit up by the glow of the flames. They say that the fire reached several kilometers into the air and that the asphalt in the streets melted. It thundered all night as loudly as if the bombs were falling on Ærø. The cliffs at Voderup started collapsing. The last time that happened was in 1849, when the *Christian the Eighth* blew up in Eckernförde Fjord, and Hamburg is so much farther away.

An American pilot was found drowned in his parachute out at the Tail. The Germans ordered him buried at six o'clock in the morning. I think this was to avoid a scene, but we all turned up at the cemetery with a rake and a watering can and told them it was a Marstal custom to tidy family graves early in the morning. I don't think the Germans fell for it.

Apart from that the Germans here on the island are calm and sensible.

Everything in Marstal is peaceful. As always, death comes from the sea.

The fishermen are afraid of catching corpses in their nets, so no one is eating the eels this summer, though they are much fatter than usual.

Many people are keeping pigs in their back gardens even though there is a ban. Marstal must have looked like this a hundred years ago, when there were still pens in the center of the town. However, it burns to the south, and we hear the bombers day and night.

Few sailors attend the Navigation College, but those who do get a lot of attention from the many women in this town who have not seen their husbands for more than two years. I don't judge them. There is a shortage of everything, including love. Personally I broke the habit of needing love, but not everyone is like me, and the older I get, the more understanding I grow. I missed out on so much. Some of it is my own fault, some of it not. I had a great mission. I wanted to make it possible for women to love. Today I think I failed. I did achieve a few things, but not for me. On the contrary: I pushed you away, and Edith, who now lives in Aarhus, I see only rarely.

I used to think that when a woman met a man, she would lose not only her virtue but also her dreams. When she has a son, she is rewarded for losing her virtue, but she loses her dreams all over again.

There was so much I wanted for you. You wanted something else. I was disappointed and I withdrew my love. I have never learned to love without conditions. I did not think that life had given me anything, so I decided to take what I wanted for myself, but life was not prepared to bargain with me. Perhaps the greatest thing you can achieve is to love without demanding anything in return. I don't know. I don't think I can make the distinction. So much of what is called love seems to me merely bitter constraint and self-sacrifice.

I think about you every day.

Your mother

EVERY COMMUNITY HAS its own myths, including the community of ships that sailed the convoy routes to Russia. Their myths were improbable, verging on the completely unnatural. They made you listen and gawk at the same time. And yet unlike most popular legends, they were true. Take the one about Moses Huntington.

Moses Huntington was black, from Alabama: as well as a sailor, he was a tap dancer. He had a deep, melodious voice, and he tapped his feet to his music. But it wasn't these talents that gave him his mythic status and made men who met him ask for his autograph.

It was the *Mary Luckenbach*.

Moses was the mess boy Knud Erik had seen through his binoculars, carrying a pot of coffee across the deck of the *Mary Luckenbach* in the last moment of her existence. A second later the torpedo had hit, and instead of a ship there was a column of black smoke rising several kilometers into the sky, where it began to spread and rain black soot.

The *Mary Luckenbach* was gone. But Moses Huntington was still there.

He reappeared half a nautical mile down the convoy, where the British destroyer *HMS Onslaught* picked him up. No one could explain his survival, least of all Moses himself. It defied nature. Yet it had happened, and here he was to prove it, alive and tap dancing. And all the men who heard his story straightened their backs and renewed their faith that there'd be life beyond the war.

Then there was Captain Stein and his Chinese crew, on board the *Empire Starlight*. The *Starlight* was the most-bombed ship in history. From the April 4, 1942, up to and including June 16, 1942, the ship was attacked almost daily by German bombers: Messerschmitts, Focke-Wulfs, Junkers 88s, you name it, sometimes up to seven times a day. The *Empire Starlight* took one direct hit after another. She was anchored off the coast of Murmansk, and the crew could have gone ashore if they had wanted to. But they didn't. The *Empire Starlight* was their ship and there was no way they'd abandon her. Every time she was attacked, they'd fix whatever could be fixed. They took in survivors from other ships. They shot down four enemy bombers. "Come and have a go" was their attitude. They were nothing but a bunch of Chinamen with a Yankee skipper, but they never gave in.

During the ship's final days they camped on land because by then the *Empire Starlight* was so wrecked, it was impossible to stay on board. But they kept rowing out to carry on repairing her, so that she grew to be their ship, literally, more and more as each day passed.

They wouldn't give in.

Like the story of Moses Huntington, it sounded impossible. It defied nature. But it had happened. Which meant it *could* happen. And those who heard the story gritted their teeth and held their heads high.

And then there was Harald Bluetooth, the boy born in a sea filled with U-boats, torpedoes, depth charges, and drowned sailors—a sea where lives usually ended rather than began.

Everyone believed he was dead when he arrived on deck, and they gathered around him and his mother in respectful silence. But he wasn't dead, and Knud Erik cut the umbilical cord and they wrapped him in woolen blankets, though they all thought that within a few days he'd be heading back into the freezing waters he'd just emerged from. But he didn't.

The Danes on the *Nimbus* christened him Harald Blåtand. The ship already had a Knud, a Valdemar, and an Absalon on board, so why not a Harald Blåtand, another early Danish hero? However, the Danes were a minority on board, so of course his name got Anglicized, and he ended up as Bluetooth.

It was under this name that he became a myth. Like Moses Huntington and the *Empire Starlight*, he should have died, but he'd gone on living, contrary to all expectations. In his case, the borrowed time was counted from his very first breath.

His mother had no objection to the name and said so once she'd recovered, which she did very quickly. New mothers are hardy creatures. She turned out to be Danish as well, though she didn't look it. Her grandmother and her mother were from Greenland, and even the Eskimos there are a kind of Dane. Her grandmother had been a *k'ivitok*, an oddball who ran around the icecap on her own and refused to mix with other people. However, she'd done so eventually—and rather thoroughly too. The man she chose was a middle-aged Danish artist who never even saw the daughter he fathered. The daughter had married a Canadian called Smith.

They were sitting in a semicircle around her as she told her story. She was lying in the berth in the captain's cabin—nothing less would do. But it was Bluetooth who was the guest of honor. He was snuggled at his mother's breast, sound asleep, as if nothing more astounding had happened to him recently than a perfectly ordinary birth.

It was when she mentioned her Canadian father that Knud Erik leaned forward and studied Bluetooth's mother.

"Miss Sophie," he said, hesitantly.

"No one's called me that for a long time. Neither Missus nor Miss, though I happen to be unmarried. Not that it's relevant. I still go by my maiden name, Sophie Smith. Yes, that's me."

"Little Bay?" Knud Erik said. He wasn't checking that he was right. He just didn't know what else to say.

"Yes, Knud Erik, I recognize you. You don't need to introduce yourself. You called me a bitch when we said goodbye. You're still the same handsome boy. You've grown taller. But then you hadn't quite grown up then. And your eyes—they're not quite the same."

"When you disappeared, I thought you'd died."

"Yes, I guess I owe you an explanation. I was wild in those days. I wanted to see the world, so I ran off with a sailor. He soon got tired of me and I got tired of him. So I became a sailor myself. I was the steward on board the *Hopemount*." She looked around at them. "Where are the others?"

"You're the only survivor."

She looked down at Bluetooth and caressed his face with a finger. A tear rolled down her cheek.

"It was Knud Erik who . . . ," Anton said.

She looked at Knud Erik. "I once said that you'd drown. But I was just trying to make myself interesting. Instead, you saved me from the water."

"I still have time," he said. "To drown, I mean."

Sophie didn't say who Bluetooth's father was, nor did she seem to attach much importance to it. He hadn't been one of the lost men of the

Hopemount, as they'd originally believed, and they got the impression that Bluetooth was the fruit of one of the many casual encounters that wartime so lavishly offers. She assured them that she hadn't planned to give birth on the open sea in the middle of a convoy on the most dangerous route the war could offer. She'd intended to be back in England before her due date, but the *Hopemount* had been stuck in Murmansk for five months, and given the choice between a Russian hospital and the sea, she'd definitely preferred the latter.

She helped out in the mess with Duncan and Helge. A stoker cobbled together a cradle for Bluetooth. Herman sat in the mess, as usual, except when he was sent to the bow to keep a lookout, and when he wasn't washing down his vodka according to his scientific method, he used his jerking-off hand to gently rock the baby. Together, Old Funny and Bluetooth, the ugly idol of war and the small growing seed of defiant, promising life, formed the core of the ship.

The *Nimbus* sailed to Iceland and from there to Halifax, Nova Scotia. From Halifax they returned to Liverpool. They celebrated Christmas on the Atlantic.

Old Funny told his stories. For the time being, all the crew demanded of Bluetooth was his existence. And exist he did. He wet and soiled his diapers, which were improvised from dishtowels and dishcloths; he burped and gurgled, sucked and cried; he got diaper rash and then colic. But most significant were the happy times when his eyes, like telescopes, would examine the mess as though it were the universe, whose secrets he was trying to discover. Twenty sailors stared back at him as if they were at the movies. They all wanted to hold and tickle him, they all wanted him to chew at their fingers and tug on their ears. They volunteered for diaper changing and babysitting and gave advice on care and diet. Together they possessed a wealth of knowledge about babies that Sophie had to admit exceeded hers. She'd given birth to Bluetooth, but he was her first, so she was no expert, and if anyone offered good advice, she was happy to take it.

"He's a degausser," Anton said.

The degausser was the electrical cable that circled the waterline. It reversed the ship's magnetic charge, to prevent her attracting magnetic mines. That was Bluetooth's function too: not only to unite the crew but also to protect them, mostly from themselves. He helped them take some kind of root in the middle of the heaving sea.

Your roots aren't to be found in your childhood so much as in your child. It's he who provides your link to the world, and home is wherever he is. It suddenly dawned on Knud Erik that it was Bluetooth he felt connected to, not Sophie.

They'd met twice, both times by coincidence, but two coincidences don't make a pattern. The first time had been nothing but an immature infatuation, and on Sophie's side not even that, but just a frivolous game with an impressionable boy. She admitted so herself when they happened to talk about it. He'd barely got to know her. The only thing that had tied him to her was the unresolved way they'd parted, and her sudden disappearance.

Knud Erik was no longer attracted to her. But then, he wasn't attracted to any women. That was the problem. He was attracted to a moment's ecstasy in the thunder of an air raid, and nothing else. He preferred to make love in the dark and he only wanted to see a face in a flash of phosphor from a bomb detonating close by. He suspected that, deep down, Sophie was a kindred spirit and that Bluetooth had been conceived during a blitz.

Something united them, but it was no longer budding desire. It was those icy minutes they'd spent together in the water, close to death, when he'd leapt into the sea to save her. Really, it was he himself he'd been trying to save, he supposed. She'd just been the random pretext.

They spoke a lot, and that was what made the greatest change in his life. She'd moved out of the captain's cabin into Helge's; Helge now bunked with the second mate. Though she'd stopped sleeping there, the captain's cabin was no longer a solitary den. She was a few years older than Knud Erik, and both were experienced and disillusioned. She'd lived the dream of her youth to excess, but in the meantime she'd outgrown it and hadn't found a replacement. She'd seen the world too: he could reel off one port after another, and she could match his list, as one sailor to another. That was the note they struck together.

It was a stage he never got beyond, nor did he try to. He never sought out the feminine in her, and perhaps that was why she accepted him. Once she'd hidden behind the stilted, literary language of a bookish and dreamy young girl. Since then she'd acquired the manner of a hardened sailor. It was a world he knew and felt safe in and he had no need to explore what lay behind it. He had neither the energy nor the courage. Anton's advice was still valid: it was better to forget.

He didn't want to get to know another human being too well. He was afraid that what he discovered might destroy him.

He put the whiskey bottle in the cupboard and didn't take it out again. He overcame his contempt for Herman and started turning up in the mess. Bluetooth was the attraction. Though Knud Erik wasn't his father, the boy wouldn't be in this world if it hadn't been for him. He'd stood on the threshold between life and death and pulled a newborn into life. No, he didn't know whether he'd saved himself. But he'd saved Bluetooth, and that mattered more. Suddenly he felt his own lack of children as the greatest absence in his life. Bluetooth wasn't his, but his death-defying leap into two-degree water had won him a parental right.

It was pure coincidence that he'd run into Miss Sophie again. But it was no coincidence that he'd saved Bluetooth. Life had singled him out and found a use for him.

AROUND THE MESS TABLE, Anton told them about a man called Laurids Madsen, who nearly a hundred years previously had fought in a battle on Eckernförde Fjord and had been standing on the deck of a ship when it blew up. Like Moses Huntington, he'd come back down alive. He also told them about a schoolteacher called Isager whose students had tried to kill him by setting fire to his house, and about Albert Madsen, who'd searched for his missing father across the entire Pacific and returned home bearing the shrunken head of James Cook.

Knud Erik, who'd heard the same stories—indeed, he was Anton's source for most of them—interrupted. There were some things he had better knowledge of. He told them about the First World War and about Albert's visions. Then Anton cut in, saying that he wasn't telling it quite right, and Knud Erik realized that when his friend had got hold of Albert's famous boots, he'd also purloined his notebooks and read them.

Anton told the story of how he'd found Albert dead, and together he and Knud Erik told everyone about the gang named after the old captain. Vilhjelm brought up their discovery of the skull of the murdered Jepsen. Knud Erik looked over at the man the crew called Old Funny to see what effect this story had on him. He'll change the subject, he'll deny everything, he thought.

Herman looked distant for a moment, then said pensively, "Vilhjelm is talking about me," as if this was the first he'd heard about his stepfather's murder. "Yes, I killed my stepfather. He was in my way. I was young. I was impatient."

He started telling how, at the age of fifteen, he'd sailed a topgallant yard schooner back to Marstal single-handed, as though his first murder was merely the beginning of the story and the best part was yet to come.

The crew stared at him. They were gripped by the tension of his tale. Old Funny was a born storyteller. All right, so he was a dangerous killer as well. All right, so the captain had been right about him after all. But take a look at him now. He'd certainly been punished.

Knud Erik understood that Herman's pathetic state, legless and one-armed, was a ticket to a free pardon, already granted. There was no need for him to ask for his audience's pity: they gave it to him voluntarily. Old Funny had once been a man. A man capable of killing other men. But what was he now?

Anton, Knud Erik, and Vilhjelm exchanged a glance. They hadn't been expecting a confession and they wanted to investigate further. But Herman's Marstal Adventures were now in full flood and the audience wanted more. "Then what happened?" they asked, and Anton had to tell them about Kristian Stærk and the killing of Tordenskjold. "Did you really kill his seagull?" Wally asked Old Funny accusingly.

Knud Erik couldn't suppress the triumph in his voice when he told them how they'd driven Old Funny out of town simply by staring at him, and how most of the gang members didn't even know that he was a murderer but thought the whole thing was about the death of a bird.

Old Funny looked irritated, as if he regretted his departure all those years ago. Then he winked at Knud Erik and laughed. "You really got me there," he said. Then he started talking about the Copenhagen stock exchange and Henckel, and how he'd lost the inheritance he'd waited to get his hands on for so many years. His life had had its ups and downs.

Vilhjelm talked about the loss of the *Ane Marie* and about the *Book of Sermons*, which he still knew by heart. They were welcome to test him if they wanted.

"So you've been in the ice before; you know what it's like," one of the British gunners said. "You practically had a dress rehearsal for convoy sailing."

"Bloody Marstal sailors," a Canadian said. "You poke your noses into everything and you've been everywhere."

Miss Kristina and Ivar entered the story, and Knud Erik recounted their chapter in a tone that grew increasingly condemning.

Old Funny defended himself. "I confess to nothing," he said. "Ivar's death wasn't murder. Some men can take it, others can't. I was just testing him and that's all there is to it." He looked around the company, and several men nodded.

"And Miss Kristina?" Knud Erik persisted.

Yes, that had been stupid. He was happy to admit it. He flung out his jerking-off hand as if to say, all things considered, it was a trifle.

"You've ruined lives!" Knud Erik was angry now.

Well, he supposed he had, Herman admitted. He didn't add: Look at me now. But his body did, and that was enough. It was all in the past. No more evil would come from him.

Knud Erik got up and left, but the story continued. Nothing could stop it now.

Old Funny told them about the night he broke the curfew in Setúbal. Was he boasting or telling the truth? It was hard to tell. He'd certainly been one hell of a guy once. Anyone could tell that his audience thought so, just from their faces.

The story spread in every direction and contracted again until it formed a protective ring around the *Nimbus*.

Bluetooth lay awake in his cradle and his telescope eyes wandered from face to face. He was exploring the universe as usual, and he looked as if he understood it all.

The crew had found true fellowship around the table in the mess, however reluctantly and unwillingly at first. Old Funny had helped them become the "us" that every ship needs. Even Knud Erik conceded it.

WHEN THEY ARRIVED at Liverpool, Herman asked to see the captain. Their meeting took place on the deck where Knud Erik had introduced him to the crew and Herman had first revealed that his trouser legs were empty. He hadn't come to say goodbye and thank you. Instead, he requested permission to stay on board the *Nimbus*. After all, they were fellow Danes, from the same town. He believed he could be useful around the mess and as a lookout. And he'd like to remind the captain that on one occasion he'd saved the ship from a torpedo.

Knud Erik shook his head. At this, for the first and only time, Herman seemed to crack.

"Look at me," he said. "They'll shove me into some home."

"They can lock you up and throw away the key, for all I care."

"What's going to become of me?" Herman looked down. He was pathetic now, and his misery only heightened Knud Erik's rage.

"As far as I know, nothing stands in the way of hanging a man with no legs and only one arm."

The crew was standing some distance away, whispering. They could tell, from Old Funny's slumped figure, the way the negotiations were going. Absalon came up to them.

"Captain," he said, "we've drawn up a petition." He handed Knud Erik a piece of paper. Knud Erik cast his eyes over the list. Practically the entire crew was demanding to keep Old Funny on board; the only ones who hadn't signed were Anton and Vilhjelm. Sophie's signature was missing too; he assumed she didn't want to get involved. Besides, she didn't count as a crew member.

"I'll think about it."

He asked Anton and Vilhjelm to come to his cabin.

"Will you sign off if I keep him?"

They both shook their heads. "We'll stay," Anton said. "The *Nimbus* is a good ship, and though I hate to admit it, I think Herman has a share in that. We knew you'd say no. We just wanted to show you that we're on your side. I hate the bastard, but sometimes you have to rise above your own feelings."

Knud Erik pondered this for a while. "All right, I'll let him stay," he said. "For the sake of the ship."

The crew celebrated his decision by taking Old Funny on a trip into town. The next morning he was back in his usual place in the mess, with bloodshot eyes and an even redder complexion than usual. When he spoke, it was with biblical solemnity.

"There shall come a day when all the women in the world will lie in the gutter screaming for cock," he intoned. "But not an inch shall they be given!"

"Am I to understand," Knud Erik asked, "that nobody wanted to screw you?"

It was Knud Erik who invited Sophie to stay.

"I'm pleased that you're asking," she said. "I was going to ask if I could."

"You can carry on in the mess. I've spoken to Helge about it."

They were silent for a while. He felt relieved, but he had no idea how to express his joy at her decision. "The crew will be pleased to hear that," he said instead. "They all love Bluetooth."

"I don't know if it's irresponsible to sail with a baby during a war. But if I stayed ashore, I'd be working all day in a munitions factory and I'd never see him. He's only two months old. I wouldn't be able to stand that."

"There are bombs everywhere," he said. He realized that they were discussing Bluetooth the way a married couple would discuss their child.

"I don't know what I'd do with myself if I couldn't sail," she said. "It's my whole life. I can't live in any other way."

He knew what she meant. He'd chosen to be a sailor himself, but at some point the sea had chosen him too. It was something that could no longer be undone. He and Sophie had seemed so very different the first time they met, but since then, they'd lived parallel lives. That said, something seemed to be holding him back and he sensed the same in her too. He wasn't physically impotent. So the impotence must lie in his soul. Finding oblivion in a moment's ecstasy was all he could manage. He couldn't look into someone's eyes while making love.

"I'm like my grandmother," she said. "She was one of those crazy people who can't be with anyone. She couldn't fit in. She needed her independence too much. She had the ice and I have the sea. But it comes down to the same thing."

"You've got a child now. You have to fit in. You're all Bluetooth's got."

"He has us," she said.

He was uncertain if by "us" she was referring to him or the crew of the ship, which she was now a part of. He wanted to ask but feared the question might spoil something. It was she who broke the increasingly tense silence.

"I do know who Bluetooth's father is," she said. "He's not, as most of you probably think, some sailor I happened to meet on shore leave. I know his name, I know his address, I've met his parents and his friends. We were engaged to be married."

"So what went wrong?"

"What was wrong was that he looked like Jimmy Stewart. You know, the American actor. Six foot something, with the face of a boy."

"But Jimmy Stewart's handsome!"

"Yes. And he was so damn nice, I didn't know whether to cry or throw up. He was sweet and decent and reliable and he loved me. He had a flourishing law practice in New York. Plenty of money, plenty of everything. We'd have lived in Vermont and our children would've grown up in the country and the war would've been so far away, we wouldn't have heard it even if they dropped the biggest bomb in the world."

"And you couldn't stand that?"

"I wanted it more than anything. But I was promised to another. What was his name again, the ugly little manikin, Rumpelstiltskin? No prince can save me. I briefly believed Jimmy Stewart could. But the reality is that I prefer life with Rumpelstiltskin. Do you know what I ended up hating about him, my Jimmy Stewart boyfriend? It was his damned innocence. I ended up seeing it as dishonesty. He took me out to dinner. We raised our glasses and looked into each other's eyes. We planned our future. The war might just as well never have happened. We just sat there enjoying ourselves in our nice, quiet way, and afterward we went home and slept in our soft bed, and I knew we'd carry on doing that until the day we died. I couldn't bear it. So one evening, instead of clinking glasses, I threw my drink in his face. It wasn't his fault. He can't help it that he hasn't seen a ship blow up and a hundred men drown in front of his eyes. At bottom, I guess I'm the one with the problem. But his innocence came across as an insult." She flung out her hand. "It's not that I love all of this. I can't even explain why I'm here. I don't fit in anywhere. Unless it's here. Or, rather"—she smiled from sudden relief, as if all that talking had finally led her to the right word—"it's the *k'ivitok* in me."

The trust between them grew, but the distance was still there too, and it didn't decrease. She was right, he thought. It was the war. It was inside them both. Nothing could happen between them until the war was over. But when would the war end? Would they be there when it finally happened? He wanted to have a child with her. It was a blind urge in him, but how long could they wait? She was a couple of years older than he was, thirty-four or thirty-five. When was a woman too old to have a baby?

He gave up. There was Bluetooth. Bluetooth was his child—and the whole crew's.

They celebrated Christmas somewhere north of Ireland. In Halifax, Wally had gone ashore and come back with a fir tree slung over his shoulder: he'd lashed it to the bow, so it didn't start to lose its needles until they put it up in the mess. Helge had managed to obtain a bag of hazelnuts from somewhere, and the crew got four each. He'd wrapped them in pink tissue paper and handed them out as gifts. Meanwhile other presents were piling up under the Christmas tree. They were all for Bluetooth, though he was still far too young to appreciate them. Sophie unwrapped the packages on his behalf. Inside them was a world he'd not get to know until the war was over: cows and horses, pigs and sheep, an elephant and two giraffes. Most were hand-carved in wood and then carefully painted with any available paint—though the colors tended to be those of the world of war they were trapped in: black, gray, and white.

Bluetooth took the cows, the horses, and the elephant, put them in his mouth one by one, and gnawed at them tentatively.

BLUETOOTH WAS ABOUT a year old when Sophie went ashore with the crew in Liverpool one night. She left him asleep in the seamen's fo'c'sle with Wally, his special pal, who'd volunteered to babysit. Knud Erik didn't know what she was looking for. Was it something they couldn't give each other, something they could find only with strangers?

He went ashore alone. He'd put the whiskey bottle back in the cupboard and never taken it out again. But he couldn't give up his shore nights. They ran into each other in a pub in Court Street. She was wearing a dark red dress and her lips were painted. He was reminded of the first time he met her, in her father's house in Little Bay. They both looked away as if by mutual agreement and pretended they hadn't seen each other.

He went straight back to the ship and turned in immediately. Half an hour later the door to his cabin opened, and an unfamiliar scent of perfume filled the narrow room. Had he deliberately forgotten to lock his door?

"We can't go on like this," she said, and began to undress in the dark.

"I've killed a man," he said. "He was kneeling down, pleading for mercy, and I shot him."

She snuggled up to him in the berth. She cradled his head in her hands. He could barely make out her features in the dim light from the skylight. "My Knud Erik," she said, and her voice was thick with a tenderness he'd never heard before.

He freed himself from her embrace and stepped out onto the floor. "I need light," he said. He switched it on and went back to her. "The red distress lights."

He didn't know why he'd said that. Those words were taboo: they conjured forbidden memories he must keep at bay if he wanted to survive. But deep down, he understood that if he wanted to be able to love, he must speak them aloud.

"There isn't one of us who doesn't think about them," she said.

"I sailed over them."

"We," she said. "We all sailed over them."

He let his hand glide down her face and he noticed that her cheek was wet. He pulled her to him and looked into her eyes.

All was completely quiet around them. No air-raid warnings shrilled, no bombs thudded, no waves splashed across the deck, no thunder roared from exploding ammunition ships. There was only the sound of the generator working away deep in the bowels of the *Nimbus*.

He kept holding her tight.

"My Sophie," he said.

IN AUGUST 1943 the Danes rose up and built barricades in Copenhagen and other towns. The government ceased working with the German occupying forces and resigned. Naval officers scuttled their own ships and sent them to the bottom of Copenhagen's harbor.

The Dannebrog once again became a flag that could fly from a ship in the service of the Allies. By now, however, the crew had grown used to their Red Duster, so they kept it. Besides, there were almost as many nations on board as there were crew members, and the Danes on it were a mixed bunch. Bluetooth had been born in the Atlantic Ocean and was an honorary citizen of the sea. The *Nimbus* was a sailing Babel, at war with the Lord.

"We could fly one of Bluetooth's diapers from the mast," Anton suggested.

"Clean or dirty?" Wally asked. He was the *Nimbus*'s champion diaper changer.

They all scrubbed the deck and soaped down the bulkhead. It was cleanliness, sailor-style, just as it had been on board the old *Dannevang,* may she rest in peace. And it was all in honor of Bluetooth.

Now they could go ashore and visit a pub as Danes, with no one calling them "half-Germans" or "Adolf's best mates" anymore. When other seamen heard they were from the *Nimbus,* the next question would inevitably be "And how's Bluetooth?"

He's very well, thank you. He lost his hair, but it grew back again, as black as his mother's. His first tooth probably bothered him a bit. He took his first steps a while back, and now he's got his sea legs. He must think the whole world's made of hills—up, down, up, down: in any case, he seems disappointed when the ground's solid. Sometimes he falls over. Then he wants his ma. Or one of his umpteen dads. Seventeen languages is a lot when you're learning to say *Daddy.* Seasick?

Bluetooth? Never! No one in the entire Allied merchant navy has a better stomach for the sea.

Oh yes, indeed, the *Nimbus* was a lucky ship. Until one spring day in 1945.

They were bound for Southend, and for the first time in four years they were sailing through the North Sea again. There were still U-boats, but they were fewer and farther between, and reports of losses continued to fall. It was approximately ten o'clock at night when the war decided to blow them a parting kiss, just to remind them never to trust it, even when its end seemed imminent. The sea was calm. There was still a faint light to the northwest; summer wasn't far off. That's when the torpedo—the one they'd expected all the years they'd sailed in Allied service—finally tracked them down. It struck them by hatch number three, and the *Nimbus* began to take in water at once. The starboard and stern lifeboats were undamaged and ready in their davits. The stokers appeared in nothing but their sweaty undershirts, and any crewman who'd been off duty was also in just his underwear. Knud Erik scolded them. He'd ordered them to sleep fully dressed in case they were torpedoed, but it was an order no one took seriously anymore. There'd been a time when they'd even slept in life jackets. Now they could barely remember when they'd last heard the sound of a nose-diving Stuka. As for the U-boats—were there actually any left?

Three minutes later they were in the lifeboats and pushing off. The *Nimbus* had been running at top steam in calm weather when the torpedo hit her: now she continued at the same pace, with her bow sinking ever deeper, so she looked as if she were on tracks that led directly to the sea bottom. When the water rose over the deck, a bang sounded from inside the engine room, and a column of smoke and steam soared into the cloudless spring sky, where the first stars had begun to appear. The *Nimbus* continued on her downward course. The last they saw of her was the stern, stamped with her name and town of registration, SVENDBORG. Then she was gone, with barely a ripple disturbing the tranquil surface of the sea.

"All gone," Bluetooth said. He was sitting on his mother's lap wrapped in a blanket, with just his head sticking out. He sniffed, as though the cold night air had given him a cold. Then he started to cry.

"You go ahead and have a good cry, my boy. You've got plenty of reasons to."

It was Old Funny, parked in state in his wheelchair in the center of the lifeboat. He looked around as though he'd become Bluetooth's mouthpiece. "That was the boy's childhood home we just lost."

They sat in silence and let his words sink in. You had to admit he had a point. At two years and seven months, Bluetooth had never known any world but the *Nimbus,* and now it was gone. The ship had become a kind of home for them too. Only a few of them had ever believed in the *Nimbus's* inherent luck. What had taken over instead, gradually, was the notion that it was only their own steely determination, the care they took in maintaining the ship, and—above all—their love for Bluetooth that kept the torpedoes and the bombs away.

Suddenly they felt that determination slacken. The war had ended for them now—not because it had been won, but because without their ship they could no longer fight. There was no joy in the realization. They barely knew whether they were winners or losers. They were survivors, and now they wanted out. They were balanced on a knife-edge between disappointment and relief, and when the captain spoke, he spoke for all of them.

"I think we should go home," Knud Erik said.

Go home: that was easier said than done. The crew had more homes than there were corners of the world. "As far as I can see," he went on, "we're roughly halfway between England and Germany. Anyone who feels at home in England rows that way." He pointed westward. "And the rest—"

He was interrupted by Old Funny: "What are you saying? There were no Germans on board the last time I looked."

"We're not going to Germany. We're going home."

"To Denmark?" Sophie asked.

"To Marstal."

The crew split up again, this time according to destination. Old Funny remained in Knud Erik's lifeboat: it seemed he'd given up on vanishing from Marstal and was now ready to go home. Anton, Vilhjelm, and Helge wanted to head back too. Knud Erik looked at Sophie for a moment. Then she nodded. Wally and Absalon too were curious to see the tiny town that had been presented to them as the center of the universe. So why not?

They divided the provisions between the two lifeboats. There were three wool pullovers and three sets of oilskins in each. These were given to the freezing stokers. The boats rocked alongside each other as the crew shook hands across the rails. Bluetooth was passed around and got a hug from every man. He'd just said goodbye to his child-hood home. Now he had to say goodbye to half its occupants. He didn't understand and cried for his mother as if she was the only fixed point that remained in the world.

They started rowing, and Old Funny insisted on being lifted out of his wheelchair and settled on the thwart so he could do his bit. He pulled hard at the oar with his one arm but struggled to maintain his balance on the thwart, so Absalon moved closer and supported him with his shoulder.

The other boat soon vanished from sight in the growing darkness.

Dear Knud Erik,

When I believed you had been drowned, I did something I have never liked to think about since.

I became so visible to myself, and that is never comfortable.

It happened one afternoon. I was wandering about aimlessly in the cemetery and suddenly found myself in front of a grave in the northwestern corner. It was Albert's. I had never tended his grave, though he was my benefactor.

Old Thiesen, the gravedigger, was busy painting the cast-iron fence around it. He had already weeded it, and it was clear that he would soon turn the neglected grave into a fitting memorial to one of the town's great shipowners.

Suddenly everything inside me—my fears, my grief and uncertainty, my eternally hidden and lonely life, my self-reproach, and the heavy burden of the almost impossible task I had set myself—all of it came out in a huge eruption of rage. It was not caused by any particular offense, but sprang from that feeling of helplessness that has dogged me all my life. I grabbed the paint bucket and flung it at the cracked gray-and-white marble column where the dates of Albert's birth and death were engraved. And I screamed the same three words over and over. I suppose I wanted them to sound like a doomsday curse. But I cannot imagine they would have stirred any feeling but profound pity in anyone who might have heard my shouting, because my madness was so obvious.

"Everything must go! Everything must go!"

I had given away my plan—but fortunately Thiesen was

the only one who heard me. He understood the words, but not their meaning.

The gravedigger knew my story well. He knew that I had spent many days in the most agonizing uncertainty about your fate. He seized my hands, as if he was trying to protect me, rather than prevent me from causing further damage.

"Calm down, Mrs. Friis. Everything will be all right. I don't think you're quite yourself," he said.

He meant it reassuringly, but the terrible truth was that, in that moment, I had been precisely that: myself. I was being myself more than I ever had been before or would be again. The words came straight from my heart: everything must go. I had revealed the entire purpose of my life. Everything must go. Finally I had said it.

I collapsed, exhausted, on the grass at Thiesen's feet. "I apologize," I said, as he helped me back up. "I'm not myself."

So I encouraged him in his error. I agreed with him. I had to, if I was to go on living among people. "No, I don't think I'm quite myself," I repeated.

Everything must go. Everything has gone, and now I know that this was never what I truly wanted. I walk the streets of this town, which seems to have been hit by a curse, empty of the men who made up half of its inhabitants. And I see more and more women with an expression in their eyes that tells me that it has been so long since they last received a letter that they have finally given up hoping.

We are not in the habit of keeping accounts of the dead in this town. But I do know that far more have not returned from this war than Marstal ever lost in the last war or on the Newfoundland route. And it goes the way it always goes for those who drown. No earth for them to rest in.

I visit the cemetery every day and place flowers and wreaths on the few graves that we do have. Now I am the one who tends Albert's.

I ask you again to forgive me for having once exiled you to the dead.

Your mother

IT TOOK THEM three days to reach the German coast, an endless sandy beach with white dunes behind it. They arrived in the early dawn. The sky was overcast, and a pink rim across the landscape announced the sunrise. The weather had been calm all the way. They maneuvered through the surf, and Absalon and Wally jumped into the water to push the lifeboat ashore. Then they eased Old Funny out of the boat and into his wheelchair. He was heavy to push in the sand. Bluetooth ran alongside. He needed to move his legs after the long period of inactivity. He was clutching his stuffed toy dog, Skipper Woof, who'd also been born at sea, according to the boy. A new life awaited both of them. The up-down, up-down of the waves was a thing of the past. Now they were on boring land, and here they'd stay, for the time being at least.

"Where are the houses?" he asked. He'd never seen a beach before. The only world he knew consisted of the sea and bombed harbors. But some things hadn't changed. He looked around. There was Daddy Absalon, there was Daddy Wally (his special pal), there was Daddy Knud Erik, Daddy Anton, and Daddy Vilhjelm. There was Old Funny in his wheelchair, and there was his mother.

They found a road that led away from the beach. There was no traffic on it. Knud Erik walked with a battered leather suitcase in his hand.

"What's inside it?" Wally asked.

"Money."

"You have German marks?" Wally gave him a look of surprise.

"Something better. Cigarettes."

"You're a man with foresight," Sophie said.

"Only sometimes," he said.

. . .

They hardly knew where the front line was: whether they were ahead of it or behind it, or whether the Germans were still holding out or had already been overrun. The Russians were far away, but the Americans were pushing forward. They'd landed somewhere in the German Bight and would still have to cross northern Germany to get to the Baltic. It was only the last leg of their journey to Marstal that they'd be able to complete by sea.

During the first few hours, they saw no signs of war. The road ran through flat marshland sparsely dotted with farms. The main road ahead of them was still empty. Bluetooth grew tired of running about and climbed onto the lap of Old Funny, who'd miraculously conjured a bottle of rum from beneath his blanket. Wally always maintained that Herman's wheelchair had a false bottom that concealed a stash of booze.

Later that morning they reached a village. Seeing smoke emerging from the chimney of a house, Knud Erik walked up the garden path and knocked on the door. No one came to open it, but he saw a face staring at him from behind a curtain. They continued: the first bomb craters appeared in the road, filled with water and reflecting the blue spring sky. Soon they found themselves skirting craters and burned-out transport trucks. They were nearing a town, and people began to appear on the road, while unshaven soldiers in filthy uniforms trudged along indifferently. It was hard to decide whether they were on the run or had merely been sent on a mission they no longer believed in. Horse-drawn carts rumbled past, piled with towers of tightly packed furniture and mattresses, followed by dead-faced people moving with the mechanical steps of prisoners in a chain gang. Others struggled along with wheelbarrows and pushcarts. No one spoke: they kept their eyes on the ground and seemed lost in mute introspection.

"Look, a horsie!" Bluetooth cried out in his baby English, pointing a finger.

They hushed him—not for fear of standing out in the growing crowd, but from a worry that in the midst of this silent, funereal traffic, any exclamation of joy was out of place. Soon, though, they realized that they were no different from anyone else. A man in a wheelchair with a child on his lap, a woman, and a group of men trudging along: just another motley crew of refugees. The main roads of Europe were teeming with people like them, who'd lost a home and were on the lookout for another that hadn't been wrecked by war. But they had two things that most of the others didn't: they had hope, and a fixed goal. They must keep a low profile: if they showed any curiosity or raised their voices, they'd attract attention. Knud Erik had feared that Absalon's black skin might give them away as foreigners, but in the end no one paid them any heed. The Germans were too busy with their own wrecked lives and dreams, oblivious to anything but the blind onward trudge from one blasted city to the next.

They arrived at a town. Most of it had been destroyed by bombs, but they'd seen ruins before, in Liverpool, London, Bristol, and Hull. In some places the house fronts were still standing, four to five stories high, their sooty walls punctured by empty windows. In others, even the façades had crumbled, exposing the gaps between the floors. They looked into rooms, guessing at which had been bedrooms and which kitchens. They kept expecting the people they saw in the streets to return to the half-houses that had boards nailed across the doors and start a new shadow life that matched their dead faces and downcast eyes.

Bluetooth was used to ruins. He thought houses were meant to be burned out. So for him, it wasn't the somber, ravaged landscape that stood out, but the big white bird sitting high up on the spire of a shelled church.

"Look," he said. "That's Frede."

He said it in Danish. He switched freely between that and English. They'd told him about the stork on Goldstein's roof, but they never mentioned Anton's attempt to kill it. Now he thought he was seeing Frede.

"No, it's not Frede. It is a stork just like him."

Knud Erik couldn't help laughing. A passerby stared at him as if his laughter was a kind of high treason, and he'd cursed Hitler in a loud voice.

The stork took off and flapped heavily above the street. They followed it. When it reached the railway station, it landed on its damaged roof as if showing them the way.

The puddles on the stone floor inside the station suggested that it had rained recently, and there were people all over the place, lying and sitting on piles of rubble as though they were benches and chairs supplied by provident authorities. The majority had to be homeless. They didn't look as if they were going anywhere. Where would they travel to anyway? To the next bombed-out railway station?

In a corner someone was handing out coffee and bread; a notice announced that later that day soup would be served. Though they were hungry, the former crew of the *Nimbus* avoided the bread line, afraid of giving themselves away. Knud Erik went off alone with a pack of cigarettes and returned shortly with a loaf of bread, a sausage, and a bottle of water. Bluetooth bolted his share eagerly, but the others chewed theirs for a long time. They didn't know when their next meal would be.

They spent the night in the railway station and took a train to Bremen the next morning. In Bremen they'd change for Hamburg. They had no tickets, but Knud Erik's cigarettes solved that problem. The platform was overcrowded, so they used Old Funny as a battering ram. People moved out of his way, doubtless presuming him to be a tragic war invalid. All that was missing was an Iron Cross pinned to his chest.

A woman in an oversize winter coat was standing in the middle of the platform: she didn't seem to be headed anywhere, but just stood there. Her pale, emaciated face, half-covered by the scarf tied under her chin, wore the most lost expression Knud Erik had ever seen. She wasn't withdrawn so much as absent: her eyes were completely blank. She was pushed and shoved from all sides by the blind throng, and the suitcase that she carried in her hand suddenly sprang open and an infant fell out. Knud Erik saw it clearly. It was the burned body of a little child, withered and practically unrecognizable, a mummy shrunk by the heat of the same fire that had clearly devoured its mother's mind too. A man, focused on the train, pushed her away, and without even noticing where he put his feet, trod right on the tiny corpse that lay in front of him. Knud Erik turned away.

"Look," Bluetooth said, "the lady dropped her Negro doll."

As they approached Hamburg, for almost thirty minutes they traveled through nothing but ruins. They thought they knew what bombs could do to a town, but they'd never seen anything to compare with this. No ghostly scorched façades rose from the piles of rubble: there was no guessing what streets might have once existed there. The devastation was so complete that you could barely believe it was caused by man. But it didn't look like a natural disaster either: that would have left something standing, however randomly. This destruction was so systematic that it looked like the work of a force that knew neither earth, water, nor air, but only fire.

For the first time in almost six years of war, they felt they'd existed only at its periphery. Like the other passengers in the overcrowded train, they averted their gaze: they couldn't bear the sight. The scale of the city's destruction was so unfathomable that they gave up trying to understand what neither their minds nor their eyes could take in. They knew that if they stayed here any longer, they'd end up like the people around them, and lose the hope that drove them on. Even Bluetooth looked away and started fiddling with a button on his coat. He didn't ask any questions, and Knud Erik wondered if it was because he was wise enough to fear the answers.

AT FOUR-THIRTY in the morning on May 3, 1945, they stole a tugboat from Neustadt Harbor.

They'd planned to go to Kiel but had to accept the transport options that presented themselves. Knud Erik's last carton of cigarettes secured them places in the covered bed of a truck that was going to Neustadt. The harbor was deserted; they walked the length of the wharf and looked for a boat that would fit their purpose. Bluetooth was sleeping, curled like a puppy on Old Funny's lap. Anton decided on a tugboat named *Odysseus*. When they'd quietly lowered Herman's chair down from the wharf, Bluetooth woke and demanded to be put down on the deck, where he stretched and yawned, and his telescope eyes began their eternal search for news in the universe.

"Look," he said, pointing at the sky.

They glanced up. High above them a large bird was flying northwest, with huge, slow wing beats.

"It's the stork," Bluetooth said cheerfully. "It's Frede."

"Do you know, I'm beginning to believe it is," Anton muttered. "Looks like he's heading for Marstal."

On their way out of the Bay of Lübeck they passed three passenger ships lying at anchor, the *Deutschland,* the *Cap Arcona,* and the *Thielka*. Though there was no sign of any crew on the bridges or decks, they were nervous that their theft would be discovered and someone would chase them, so once they were some distance away, they sailed at full speed. They'd planned to head north around the island of Fehmarn. Of course this would mean going far into the Baltic, almost as far as Gedser, before they could turn west and then south around Langeland. It was quite a detour, but they didn't dare sail any closer to the German coast.

It was early afternoon when a hollow roar rolled across the sea. Several more followed, and for a moment they felt the firmament vibrate above them. Tracks of smoke etched themselves across the bay and they guessed that Neustadt was under attack or the three anchored ships had been hit. As the day progressed they realized they might as well have followed the coast. No one would have pursued them. The Germans seemed to have lost control of the Baltic altogether; it was now patrolled by British Hawker Typhoon bombers. Again and again they heard the faint echoes of bombs exploding far across the sea.

There was heavy traffic on the water, but most of it came from the eastern part of the Bay of Lübeck, where the Russians were advancing. There were all kinds of vessels: fishing boats, freighters, smaller motor ships, yachts, smacks, and rowboats with makeshift masts and sails. Columns of smoke drifted up along the horizon. They constantly came across pieces of wreckage and once nearly sailed into a huddle of charred bodies bobbing face-down in the water. From a distance they'd looked like a raft of seaweed; the crew saw their mistake just in time to change course. The drowned—women and children as well as men—were everywhere. None of them had life jackets; clearly they too had been refugees like themselves.

Will it never end? thought Knud Erik.

The euphoria of having escaped was gone. They understood that if they were to get across the Baltic alive, their luck had to hold. They were sailing a German ship, and there was nothing to stop the next Hawker Typhoon from dropping its lethal load on them as it passed overhead. They hadn't flown a Danish flag in five years: now they wished they had one. But maybe not even that was enough. It was as if the sea had turned itself inside out and was disgorging all the thousands of people it had swallowed across the centuries. Crossing it, they felt a fellowship with them.

Knud Erik was at the helm. He ordered everyone to put on a life jacket, but there weren't enough to go around. He glanced briefly at Herman in his wheelchair. Then he shrugged. Captain Boye had drowned because he'd given his life jacket to a stoker who had left his own behind in the engine room. He handed his life jacket to Wally and ordered him to help Herman put it on. If they sank, he'd have given up his life for a man he despised, but he had no choice. The war had taught him one thing: the Allies might be fighting for justice, but life itself was unjust. He was the captain and he was responsible for his crew. Duty was the only thing he had left. He must cleave to it or else surrender to pure meaninglessness.

"Aren't you going to put on your life jacket?" Sophie asked. She hadn't noticed him glancing at Herman.

He brushed her question aside with a smile. "The captain's always the last to leave the ship. And the last to put on his life jacket."

"A true Odysseus you are," she said, returning his smile. "And a lucky one too, having Penelope on board."

"We aren't like Odysseus," he said. "We're more like his men."

"What do you mean?"

"Have you read the story?"

She shrugged. "Not properly."

"It's depressing reading, actually. Odysseus is the captain, right? He has fantastic adventures. But he doesn't bring back a single one of his crew alive. That's the part we sailors play in this war. We're Odysseus' crew."

"Well, you'd better get moving, Captain Odysseus," she said, looking at him. "Because this particular crew member happens to be pregnant."

THEY SAILED AT half speed and switched off the boat's lights at night. The closer they came to their destination, the more they feared they'd never reach it. Until now they'd existed only in the present, as all who put their trust in the vagaries of luck are obliged to. Now that they dared to believe in the future, they were terrified of losing their lives. The old daily dread from the time of the convoys returned. Again, the sky above and the sea beneath seemed packed with hidden menaces.

The sea was like dark blue silk, and the bright spring night was cloudless. There was a warmth in the air that heralded summer, and had it not been for the tugboat's pervasive smell of coal and tarred hemp rope, they'd have caught the scent of apple blossom coming from the shore. But the water was cold. Winter clung to its depths, and all they could think about was that chill: it felt as if they were still sailing the Arctic, still on the lookout for the foam stripes that signaled torpedoes and the red distress lights that had once bankrupted their souls and could do so again. Again, they listened for the sound of oars or cries for help. Again, they enacted an eternal dress rehearsal of death by exposure. Spring welcomed them, but the memory of the five-year winter they'd endured still held them in its grip.

In the bay they'd left behind that morning, eight thousand Allied prisoners of war were incinerated when their transport ships were bombed. Earlier, another ten thousand refugees had drowned in the same sea the *Odysseus* was now crossing. But her crew knew nothing of this either. They'd seen ships go down before, but they'd never seen a refugee ship sinking with ten thousand passengers trapped on board, or heard the collective scream as the water gushed in from all sides and sent the ship down to the bottom, or the wail that followed the final plea for help, when those still living realized that *rescue* is just a word. No, they'd never heard that vast cry, and yet it entered them that night.

They spent the night on deck; they dared not go below. They wrapped themselves in blankets they'd found on board and sat awake, watching the sea with restless eyes, and listening.

Bluetooth didn't sleep either. He lay silently, watching the fading stars. As dawn broke, he was the first to hear the deep whoosh of wings. "The stork" was all he said.

They looked up. There it was, flying low above them, still heading northwest. Far away they could see Kjeldsnor Lighthouse in the early morning light. They were approaching the southern point of Langeland.

Ærø appeared in the late afternoon after they'd sailed along the Langeland coast for most of the day. Trying to save coal, Anton kept the tug at half speed: they were running out. They saw Ristinge Hill rise to the north. Open water followed. Farther out to the west lay Drejet and the hills at Vejsnæs. In the midst of it all rose the red roofs of Marstal, with the copper church spire, now green with verdigris, towering high above. There were still a few masts in the harbor, looking like the remains of a stockade that had been overrun by some unknown force. From here they couldn't see the Tail and the breakwater that embraced the town like a useless arm.

Some distance outside the harbor, they saw black masses of smoke pouring into the calm air. Coming closer, they saw flames. Two steamers in Klørdybet were ablaze. The war had beaten them to it. Knud Erik had been so sure that it would all end the moment he set eyes on the Marstal skyline. Fatigue overwhelmed him, and he felt close to giving up. If he was an exhausted swimmer trying to reach the shore, this was the moment he'd simply let the water take him.

They were just level with the steamers when they heard the howl of a dive-bomber. They looked up: a Hawker Typhoon was coming straight for them. One of its wings gave a flash, and a rocket sped toward them, trailing white smoke.

There was a bang, and the whole boat shook.

IT WASN'T A good time to be a child. Corpses floated onto the beach and the little islands around the town on a daily basis, and it was the children who found them. They'd always fetch an adult, but by then the damage had been done. They'd seen the decomposing faces of the drowned, and afterward they were full of questions that we found hard to answer.

Early in the morning of May 4, a ferry docked at the harbor. It came from Germany and it was packed with refugees. Only a few on board were men: soldiers with blood-soaked bandages around their arms and legs. The rest were women and children. The children said nothing, but simply stared pale-faced into the distance with their scrawny necks sticking out from winter coats that seemed far too big for them, as though nature had gone into reverse and they'd grown too small for their clothes. They hadn't eaten a proper meal in a long time. But it was their eyes that made the deepest impression on us. They seemed to see nothing at all. We reckoned it was because they'd seen too much. Children's heads are quickly overloaded by ugly things. The eyes simply go on strike.

We offered them bread and tea. They looked like they could do with something warm. We behaved decently toward them, though we wouldn't exactly claim they were welcome.

At eleven o'clock that morning two German steamers ran aground, attempting to navigate the south channel. British bombers had flown over the island several times during the past few days, and we'd often see them flying over the sea. Two of them appeared now. They fired their rockets and both steamers caught fire. They had machine cannons mounted both fore and aft and they returned fire. The British planes kept coming back, and one of the steamers took several direct hits and was soon engulfed in flames.

We didn't dare approach the ships to rescue the survivors until the shooting was over. The water was filled with people, many of them burned or wounded by shrapnel. They screamed and wailed when we hauled them on board, but we couldn't just let them lie there in the cold water. It was a dreadful sight. Their hair had been singed off. They were black from soot, and you could see bloodied flesh where the skin had been burned away. Many were naked. We'd brought blankets, but wrapping them around the poor shivering creatures would be of no help: the wool would just stick to the exposed flesh. Helping them ashore on the wharf, we handled them as gently as possible. There were many dead too. We left them in the water. Survivors had priority.

The wounded were taken to the hospital in Ærøskøbing, and the others billeted in the house we called the Lodge, in Vestergade. Then we started recovering the bodies. There were quite a few—twenty in all. We brought them to the wharf by Dampskibsbroen, right by the entrance to the harbor, where we laid them out in a row and covered them with blankets. One of the bodies was missing its head, but somehow that one was the least horrific: no face, and no mouth gaping in a rigid scream that it would take to the grave.

Several hundred people had gathered in the harbor to watch the steamers burn. One of them was almost extinguished, but she was still giving off plenty of smoke, while the other one burned amidships. Some drunken German soldiers were on board, manhandling a group of half-naked women on the foredeck. Fear of death combined with booze had made them lose all inhibition.

Late in the afternoon the British resumed bombing the two steamers. The crowd was swelling. We'd all come to watch the sad scene unfolding on our waters. Many of us had lost husbands, brothers, and sons in this war, and it would have been easy for us to think that these Germans had got what was coming to them. We didn't, though. How many times had we, our fathers, or our grandfathers been on a ship that was sinking or on fire? We knew what it was like. A sinking ship was a sinking ship. It didn't matter whose.

Suddenly a tugboat appeared in the south channel. We'd been so preoccupied by the burning steamers that we didn't even notice it at first. Marstal harbor's south channel is tricky to navigate if you're not familiar with the waters, but the captain seemed to be managing well until one of the British bombers flew low over the boat and fired its rockets. The explosion that followed could be heard all the way to the shore. The boat took a direct hit and went up in flames.

• • •

Gunnar Jakobsen, who'd been out there with his dinghy, would always say afterward that he'd never seen a more jumbled-up crew. One fellow was a Negro, another was a Chinaman, and another one was in a wheelchair: the others shoved him overboard before they jumped themselves. He had no legs and only one arm, but his life jacket kept him afloat. A woman with a child popped up in the water too. Half the world seemed to be floating around down there. Gunnar's surprise doubled when he pulled them all on board, and not only did both the Negro and Chinaman speak Danish, but the rest spoke like Marstallers. "Aren't you Gunnar Jakobsen?" one of them said.

Gunnar Jakobsen narrowed his eyes—not because he couldn't see the man properly, but because he needed time to think.

"Goddammit," he exclaimed. "You're Knud Erik Friis!" Then he recognized Helge and Vilhjelm. The man with no legs and one arm said nothing, nor did any of the others introduce him.

"Anton," Knud Erik Friis said suddenly, looking around desperately. "Where's Anton?"

"You mean Anton Hay? The Terror of Marstal?" Gunnar Jakobsen asked.

They looked around. "He's not here," Vilhjelm said.

He wasn't visible in the water either. The *Odysseus* was about to keel, and the flames soared high. No one could be on that ship and still be alive. They circled about the water for a while, calling out for Anton.

The bombers kept attacking the steamers as if they'd been ordered to use up their entire supply of bombs and rockets before the war ended. Just when the men in Gunnar Jakobsen's dinghy were about to give up and head for the harbor, the *Odysseus* took another direct hit. This time she must have been struck below the waterline, because she keeled instantly and began to sink. Gunnar Jakobsen switched off his motor, as if he felt he owed the tugboat a minute's silence as it died. A moment later the ship was gone. In the place where she'd been, they could see something floating on the water. Gunnar Jakobsen started the engine and headed for the spot. At first they couldn't make out what it was, but then they recognized the horribly charred remains of what had once been a human being. They saw its back and its head. Anton was naked and his hair had been burned off. His life jacket was gone, or if it was still on him, there was no telling it from the flesh of his back, which was as black and porous as charcoal.

Sophie covered Bluetooth's eyes with her hand. Knud Erik reached into the water to get the charred body into the dinghy. He didn't think about what he was doing; he simply couldn't leave it there. But when he hauled up the corpse the whole arm came off. Startled, he let go, and when the body hit the water again, what had once been Anton's flesh fell off his bones, which began sinking at once.

The engine was throbbing violently.

Gunnar Jakobsen wanted to get back ashore as quickly as possible. None of the survivors from the *Odysseus* objected. They sat in total silence, with the same blank expression he'd seen in the German children, which he hoped he'd never see on the faces of his own kids. He didn't know much more about the war than what he'd read in the newspapers. He'd heard the pounding in the south when the British dropped their bombs, and he'd seen flames on the horizon when Hamburg and Kiel were razed. Now he was learning more in a single day than he had over the past five years, and he'd have the same experience in the months that followed every time he met someone who had spent the war outside Denmark's borders. Something was wrong with them, and he just couldn't explain what it was. It wasn't anything they said, because they said nothing; it was almost as if they were all brooding over a huge secret that they kept to themselves only because it wouldn't help to tell anyone. They were part of a dreadful community that no one else could penetrate and that they couldn't escape.

The boy was crying. He'd seen nothing, but he sensed that something had happened.

"Will we never see Anton again?" he asked.

"No," said the woman, whom Gunnar Jakobsen thought must be the child's mother. "Anton's dead. He's not coming back."

It was a brutal thing to say, Gunnar Jakobsen thought, and he'd probably never have been so frank with his own children. Yet something inside him acknowledged the honesty of the woman's reply. To the children of war, you told the truth.

High above them a stork flew past. It came close to one of the burning steamers and seemed to vanish briefly in the clouds of smoke before emerging on the other side, unharmed. It continued across the town, and when it reached the other end of Markgade, it folded its wings and prepared to land in the nest on the roof of Goldstein's house.

Gunnar Jakobsen put in at Dampskibsbroen. This was where most of us were standing, and though he'd been shaken by the sight of

Anton's body, he nevertheless felt that he was returning with a great story that deserved a big audience. He was bringing home the first people to return to Marstal from the war after an absence of more than five years.

Gunnar Jakobsen hadn't noticed that the dead were still lying on the wharf when the big legless man was helped out and settled among their covered bodies. We stared at him with curiosity and suddenly Kristian Stærk said loudly, "That's Herman."

A wave of unease went through us as the news spread, and those who didn't know who Herman was had it explained to them in terms that were far from flattering. Herman hadn't shown his face in Marstal for twenty years, but the mere mention of his name was still enough to fill those of us who'd heard the story of the *Kristina* with disgust. He sat strangely lost among the dead. His arm and leg stumps made him look like a stranded walrus waving its flippers, but his vulnerability didn't lessen our contempt.

"Help me up," he said.

We did nothing; we just kept staring at him. None of us wanted to go near him, so he just sat there in the puddle of his wet clothes, and his big body started shaking from cold.

A man in Kongensgade was running toward us, waving his arms and shouting, but we couldn't make out what he was saying: he was too far off.

At the same moment the church bells started to peal in a wild and breathless rhythm we'd never heard before, as if someone was improvising a melody fit for an occasion unique to the history of the town—neither funeral nor wedding service, sunrise nor sunset.

In a way that we couldn't explain, we knew that something momentous had happened, something much bigger than the burning steamers out on the water or Herman's sudden reappearance.

Finally the running man came within earshot.

"The Germans have surrendered! The Germans have surrendered!"

We looked at Herman and Knud Erik and Helge and Vilhjelm and the other men whose names we didn't yet know, and we looked at the woman and the child, and we understood that they were just the first. The sea was about to return our dead.

We lifted them up and bore them high through the streets. We even hauled Herman out of his pool of water and found a cart to pull him around on. Cheering, we marched through Kongensgade, along Kirkestræde, down Møllegade, along Havnegade, up Buegade, through Tværgade, and down Prinsensgade, where Klara Friis, as always, sat in her bay window, her pale face staring out to sea.

We went back along Havnegade and as we marched, more people joined us. An accordion appeared, and then a trumpet, a double bass, a tuba, a harmonica, a drum, and a violin. We mixed "King Christian" with "Whiskey, Johnny" and "What Shall We Do with a Drunken Sailor?" There was whiskey and beer, there was rum and more beer, there was Riga Balsam and Dutch gin; it had all been saved up for this moment, the moment we'd always known would come. Lights were lit in the windows, and blackout curtains were burned in the street, crackling as they blazed.

We ended up on Dampskibsbroen, where the dead lay waiting for us in their rows. And we drank and danced and stumbled about among the corpses, and that was as it should be. The dead had been piling up throughout our entire lives: the drowned and the missing, all those who'd remained unburied across the centuries, lost even to the cemetery, those who'd ruined our lives with longing. Now they rose up and took our hands. We danced and danced in a huge churning circle and in the midst of it all sat Herman, no longer shivering from the cold but flushed with intoxication, brandishing an already half-empty whiskey bottle. He sang in a voice that was hoarse with toil and drunkenness and evil, with impatience and greed and battered lust for life:

> Shave him and bash him,
> Duck him and splash him,
> Torture him and smash him,
> And don't let him go!

There was a black man, a Chinese man, an Eskimo woman, and a child we didn't know; there was Kristian Stærk and Henry Levinsen with the crooked nose; there was Doctor Kroman, there was Helmer, and there was Marie, who'd finally learned how to clench her fist but didn't yet know that she'd been widowed this very day—Vilhjelm would tell her later. There were Vilhjelm's parents, deaf but smiling; there were the Boye widows, Johanne, Ellen, and Emma, and tonight they didn't hesitate to join hands with us and dance; there was their distant relative, Captain Daniel Boye; and there was Klara Friis, running down Havnegade, breaking through the circle until she found Knud Erik and he nodded at her, and the little boy whose name we didn't know went up to her and said a word we guess Knud Erik must have taught him: "Granny." And the child took her hand and pulled her into the dance, and our dance was like a tree that grew and grew, adding rings for every year.

There was Teodor Bager, still clutching his chest; there was Henning Friis, once the most handsome man on the *Hydra*, with the blond forelock Knud Erik had inherited; there was the indefatigable Anna Egidia Rasmussen, and there were her seven dead children, and they too joined the dance alongside the one living daughter; there was the cassocked Pastor Abildgaard, who before he died had finally found himself a rural parish that suited him better than Marstal, looking at us through his steel-rimmed glasses and taking a hesitant step forward. Albert followed, with hoarfrost in his beard and the head of James Cook under his arm, and then came Lorentz; he was panting and struggling, but nothing was going to stop him from joining the dance; there was Hans Jørgen, who went down with the *Incomparable*, and Niels Peter. Even Isager took his place with us, and so did his fat wife, with the resurrected Karo in her arms, and their sons, Johan and Josef, with the Negro hand; behind them came Farmer Sofus and Little Clausen and Ejnar and Kresten, the poor creature with the constantly weeping hole in his cheek. Laurids Madsen towered above us in his heavy sea boots; others appeared behind him; and finally there was Anton, whose charred face broke open in a smile that revealed his tobacco-stained teeth. Then came whole crews: the men of the *Astræa* and the *Hydra*, the *Peace*, the *H. B. Linnemann*, the *Uranus*, the *Swallow*, the *Smart*, the *Star*, the *Crown*, the *Laura*, the *Forward*, the *Saturn*, the *Ami*, the *Denmark*, the *Eliezer*, the *Felix*, the *Gertrud*, the *Industry*, the *Harriet*, the *Memory*: all the drowned. And there, in the outer circle, with their faces half hidden by fog, danced everyone who'd been away at sea for these five years of war.

So many of them had died. We didn't know how many.

We'd count them tomorrow. And in the years to come we'd mourn them as we'd always done.

But tonight we danced with the drowned. And they were us.

ACKNOWLEDGMENTS

We, the Drowned is fiction. The novel is inspired by and largely adheres to the history of the town of Marstal in the years 1848 to 1945. I have made use of the town's traditional family names, but I have shuffled the deck so that any resemblances to people living or dead are purely coincidental.

The historical parts of the novel are based on my research in the archives of the Maritime Museum in Marstal and on its many publications. I also found valuable material in the newspapers *Ærø Folkeblad* and *Ærø Tidende* as well as the quarterly publication *Ærøboen*.

I have found inspiration and gained essential knowledge from—among others—the following writers and publications: Henning Henningsen (*Crossing the Equator, Sømanden og kvinden, Sømandens våde grav, Sømandens tøj*), Ole Lange (*Den hvide elefant, Jorden er ikke større*), H. C. Røder (*Dansk skibsfarts renæssance*, vols. 1, 2, and 4), Joseph Conrad (*The Shadow-Line*), H. Tusch Jensen (*Skandinaver i Congo*), Adam Hochschild (*Kong Leopolds arv*), *Søndagstanker—kristelige Betragtninger på Søn—og Helligdage af ærøske Præster, Sømandspostillen*, Knud Ivar Schmidt (*Fra mastetop til havneknejpe*), Harriet Sergeant (*Shanghai*), E. Kroman (*Marstals søfart indtil 1925, Dagligliv i Marstal og på Ærø omkring år 1900*), Hans Christian Svindings ("Dagbog vedrørende Eckernførdetogtet og Fangenskabet i Rendsborg og Glückstadt," *Danske Magazin*, series 8, vol. 3), *Marstalsøfolkenes visebog*, J. R. Hübertz (*Beskrivelse af Ærø 1834*), C. T. Høy (*Træk af Marstals Historie*), Victor Hansen (*Vore Søhelte: Historiske Fortællinger*), "Salmebog til Kirke—og Husandagt 1888," Anne Salmond (*The Trial of the Cannibal Dog: Captain Cook in the South Seas*), Homer (*The Odyssey*), Nordahl Grieg (*Skibet går videre*), W. Somerset Maugham (*The Trembling of a Leaf*), Herman Melville (*White Jacket*), Robert Louis Stevenson (*Tales of the South Seas, A Footnote to History*), Mark Twain (*Roughing It in the Sandwich Islands*), Victor Hugo (*Les travailleurs de la mer*), F. Holm Petersen (*Langfarere fra Marstal*), Knud Gudnitz (*En Newfoundlandfarers erindringer*), Rauer Bergstrøm (*Kølvand*), Per Hansson (*Hver tiende man måtte dø*), Martin Bantz (*Mellem bomber og torpedoer*), Andrew Williams (*Slaget om Atlanten*), Richard Woodman (*Arctic Convoys*), Claes-Göran Wetterholm (*Dødens Hav:*

Østersøen 1945), Edward E. Leslie (*Desperate Journeys, Abandoned Souls*), Anders Monrad Møller, Henrik Detlefsen, Hans Chr. Johansen (*Dansk søfarts historie, vol. 5, Sejl og Damp*), Mikkel Kühl (*Marstallerne solgte væk*), "Marstals handelsflåde 1914–1918" in *Maritim Kontakt* 26, Karsten Hermansen (*Søens købmænd*), Karsten Hermansen, Erik Kroman a.o. (*Marstals søfart 1925–2000*), H. Meesenburg, Erik Kroman ("Marstal—et globalt lokalsamfund," in *Bygd, vol. 17, no. 4*), Tove Kjærboe (*Krampebånd og Klevesnak*), Finn Askgaard (ed., *Fregatten Jylland*), "Samling af søforklaringer over forliste danske Skibe i Årene 1914–1918," Christian Tortsen (*Søfolk og skibe 1939–1945*), Ole Mortensøn (*Sejlskibssøfolk fra Det Sydfynske Øhav*), and Poul Erik Harritz (*Rundt om Selma fra Birkholm*).

APPRECIATION

I wish to thank the people of Marstal who turned up at my evening readings at the Navigation College and at the public library in Skolegade, as well as the following individuals, each of whom in their own way provided invaluable assistance: Lis Andersen, Iben Ørum, Henning Therkildsen, Jens and Hanne Lindholm, Henry Lovdall Kromann, Knud Erik Madsen, Connie and Martin Bro Mikkelsen, Lars Klitgaard-Lund, Nathalia Mortensen, Annelise and Poul Erik Hansen, Astrid Raahauge, Pulle Teglbjerg, Leif Stærke Kristensen and Berit Kristensen, Regitze and Ole Pihl, Hjørdis and Kaj Hald, Erik and Lillian Albertsen, Hans Krull, Karla Krull, Erna Larsen, Adam and Anne Grydehøj, Søren Buhl and Marjun Heinesen, Gunnar Rasmussen, Pastor Emeritus Finn Poulsen, Lars Kroman, Lone Søndergaard, Frans Albertsen, and Kristian Bager. A special thank-you goes to Erik Kroman, director of the Maritime Museum in Marstal, for making the museum archives available to me. And to Karsten Hermansen, who shared his home-baked currant buns as well as his inexhaustible knowledge.

I owe Christopher Morgenstierne my thanks for helping me with maritime terminology and expressions. Any errors in sailing techniques and wind force lie entirely with the author.

Huge thanks to my dearest Laura. It has taken me half your life to write this book, and you have voiced your strong views about it with unswerving enthusiasm the whole way through.

And to my beloved Liz I owe a debt of gratitude it would take more than a lifetime to repay. You have supported me with your unique blend of professionalism and love, and it is thanks to you that I finally made it safely to port.